LEST THEY
HAVE EYES

TORN CURTAIN PUBLISHING
Auckland, New Zealand
www.torncurtainpublishing.com

© Copyright 2025 Bonivon Dyer. All rights reserved.

ISBN Softcover 978-1-991299-44-4
ISBN EPub 978-1-991299-45-1

No portion of this book may be reproduced, stored in a retrieval system or transmitted in any form or by any means—electronic, mechanical, photocopy, recording or otherwise—except for brief quotations in printed reviews or promotion, without prior written permission from the author.

Cover design by Smashed-Grid Studio. Used with permission.
Illustrations by Jaiden Deubner. Used with permission.

Typeset in Minion, Ethnocentric, Kallisto, Limerick, Azo Sans

Cataloguing in Publishing Data
   Title: Lest They Have Eyes
   Author: Bonivon Dyer
   Series: The Blood Maker Fables
   Subjects: Science fiction; fantasy; dystopian; magic and gifts; young adult
      fantasy; epic; immortals; world building.

A copy of this title is held at the National Library of New Zealand.

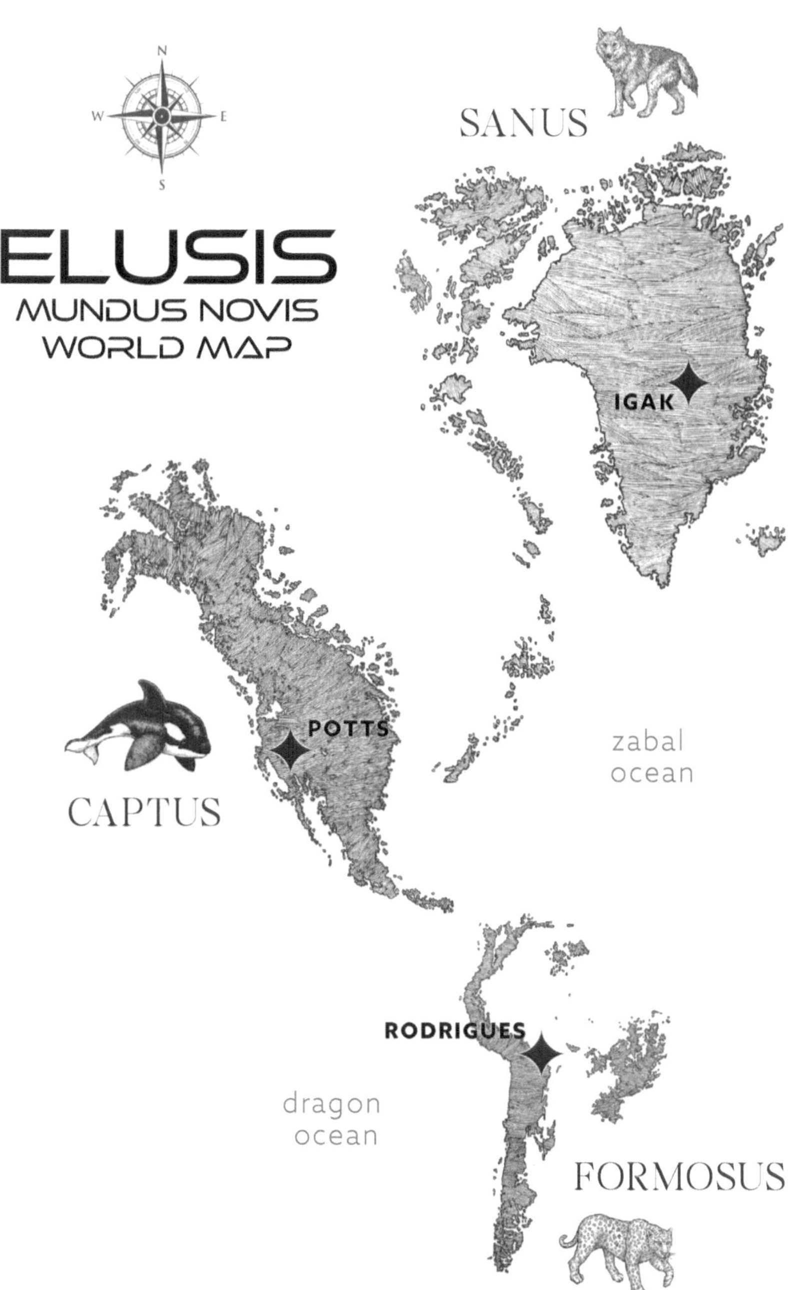

N
W E
S
ELUSIS
MUNDUS NOVIS
WORLD MAP
SANUS
IGAK
POTTS
CAPTUS
zabal
ocean
RODRIGUES
dragon
ocean
FORMOSUS

LEST THEY HAVE EYES

BOOK ONE
THE BLOOD MAKER FABLES

BONIVON DYER

iparraldean ocean
SILENDA
JUKANTYTÄR
DEMIRKAN
PEXUS
CISSE
sakona
ocean
ORTUS
gerakin ocean

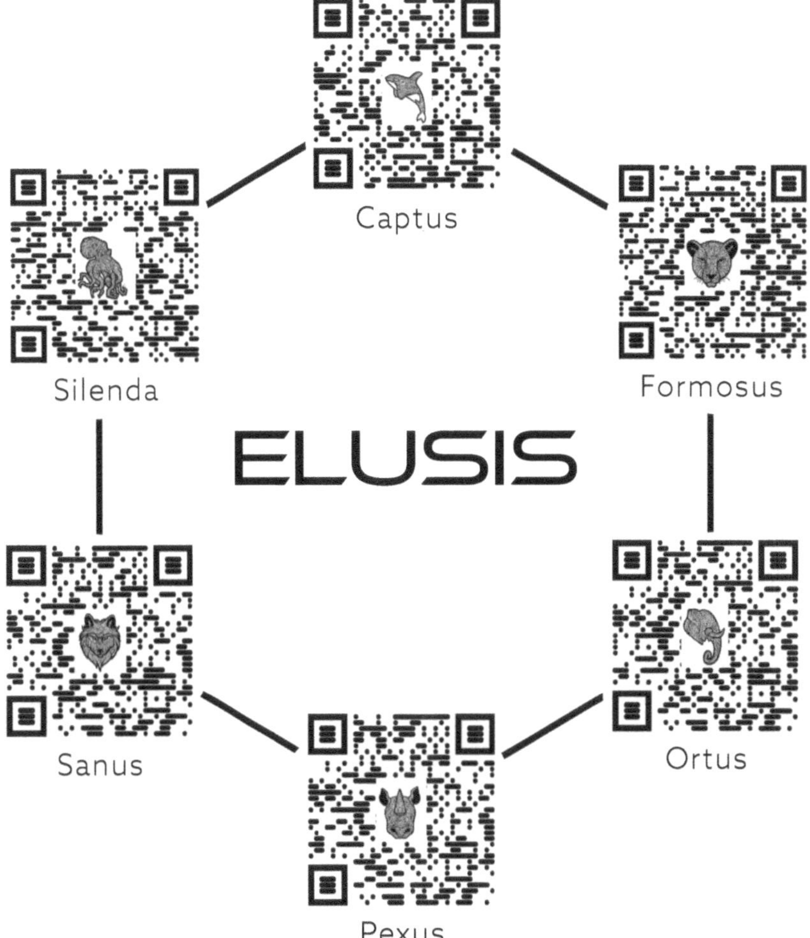

These pages hold a collection of QR codes—a gateway to extra lore, backstories, and world-building details. Think of them as a digital treasure map for readers who love to dig deeper. Do you need them to enjoy the story? Not at all! The main story assumes all of this detail and you don't need it beforehand, but if you're curious about the history, geography, or cultural tidbits of the world of Elusis, these codes grant you behind the scenes access. Explore at your own pace. Dive in whenever you like—or ignore them completely! Either way, the adventure awaits. Happy reading!

Characters

Metaphysics
of Elusis

Humani House
of Worship

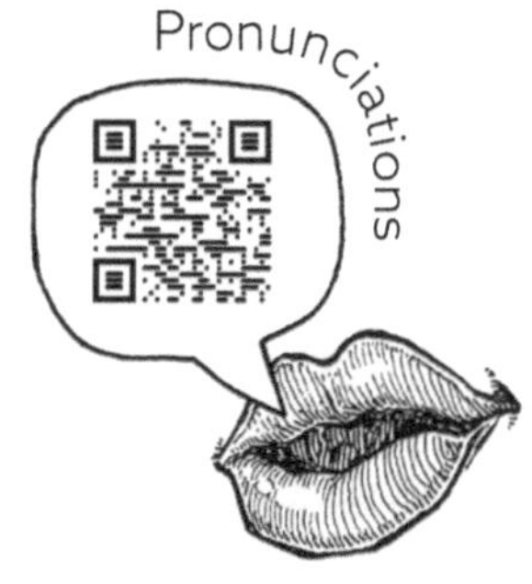
Pronunciations

The Era
Ending War

Mundus Novus Technology

Gifts
& Powers

Hair
Color

Pods: A History

Transportation Technology

The Aevii

Cupido Interterritorial

For those caught in the waste places and longing for the broad space.

*Hey Linda, can you believe it's finally happening?! What
began with you saying, "You should write that," has turned
into this. I can't thank you enough for everything.
–I'm hurrying*

17 DAYS UNTIL QUINTRALL

Pexus

Kansis

L IKE A NEWBORN BABY, my new Pod's hands and legs suddenly twitch and jerk inside her Hull. She's confused. Scared. The healers say that the Pods immediately attempt to make out colors and noises. Crying out, she reaches for something invisible. Babbling on, she tears at her pale skin and red hair. She looks a few years younger than me, maybe seventeen or eighteen. So young.

The healers say it's essential that they wake themselves, so we watch from behind the mirror. No matter how often I watch the Pods regain consciousness, though, I feel sorry for them. At least when you're a baby, you have the healer's hands and then your parents, but not in a Re-awakening. You're all alone for that.

Slowly, this Pod's eyes open. She's gasping now and yelling out words that don't make sense. Tears fall down her cheeks. Most Pods search for a human face they recognize, a voice of instruction, a hand to hold. In the following five minutes, her body will naturally respond to its change in state by releasing waves of "excretions" as the healers call it. If you ask me, it's five minutes of torture. As it begins, I try to close my ears to her screams. I can barely stand to watch, but I'm determined I won't be the one who turns around.

"Ontzi!" one of the new interns standing next to me swears. "That's disgusting."

Once the process is over, silence fills the room. As the Pod's eyes begin to focus, the healers usher me in. This is the exciting part of my job. In fact, this is the only place in my life where I hold any significance. Because as I walk into the room and the Pod's eyes meet mine, I am the first person this girl has seen in over six hundred years.

I touch her hand and she jumps. Struggling to focus, she whispers, "W-w-when am I?"

Ah. How very intuitive this one is. Besides being impressed by the question, I am also relieved that it's asked in English. That's the old language I know best. Mandarin is manageable, but Hindi is the one that ties my tongue in knots. As the Pods in our facility originate from all around the old world, I know eleven languages.

Tears stream down the girl's soft-featured face. With deep hazel eyes and full lips, she almost looks like a doll. An angry, scared doll.

A simulan steps forward with a towel and wipes the bile from her chin. Then it helps her out of the chromium-cased Hull and slowly removes her feces-filled gown. Leading her to a shower, I help her clean up. At this point in the process, she still struggles with controlling her limbs. I gently dress her in the grey sweatshirt and sweatpants sitting on the table. Usually the Pods scream, cry, growl—demanding, even to the point of violence, that I answer their questions. But not this Pod. She silently allows me to help her.

We exit into a bright hallway, and I lead the Pod towards one of the rehabilitation rooms. Here, the simulans help her to eat her first meal. We'll monitor her vitals and bowel movements for these first five days to ensure she has no medical issues.

Tears continue to flow down her cheeks, and her body shakes uncontrollably—a typical withdrawal response from the drugs used to preserve the Pod's bodies and minds. She shows no other outward emotion.

I've never worked with such a pliable Pod, and I watch her curiously as she eats mechanically. After she is reported initially healthy, we walk to the Flower Room. This is where she will spend most of her time during the first week of her new life. A lovely floral mural fills all four walls, whilst soft cushions add to the welcome. The room is tastefully furnished so as to ensure an ambiance of warmth and character.

As we enter together through the doorway, I notice for the first time that she's about fifteen centimeters taller than me. I beckon her to sit on one of the three sofas and ask her to make herself comfortable. She settles down, then simply stares at me, waiting. Unconsciously, she uses her sleeve to hold the tears and snot at bay. When I offer her a tissue, she takes it silently. She doesn't ask me questions; she merely clenches her jaw repeatedly.

Well, *ontzi*. I think I'm going to like this Pod. I seat myself across from her and begin.

"Do you remember being encapsulated in your Hull?" I ask. A hesitant nod. "Do you remember which year and month?"

"April, 2094."

April—that was what they called the fourth month of the year. All right, that puts her... five months before the end. A late Podder. I start my usual spiel: "You are about six hundred years into the future."

Her eyes widen, but she remains silent.

"What started as a nuclear war destroyed your civilization, along with most of the planet, on August 4, 2094, only a few months after you were encapsulated. Out of that war came my world."

Pausing, I stare at her pensive face. Her brows knit, and she looks down like she's calculating something. I've received mixed responses from the thirty Pods I've trained, but in the end there are always tears, yelling, outbursts of anger, and final feelings of emptiness. Mathos, one of the bodyguards, stands outside the door in case violence ensues. I don't know how this Pod is going to react as I present my little speech, and I wait for her to look up. When her eyes meet mine, I begin again.

"You and five hundred thousand others were encapsulated between 2091 and 2094. Hoping to preserve humanity, your world's leaders forged a plan for the future before encapsulating themselves. Once the earth had regained a population of one million, the leaders of Mundus Novus—the new world—were to awaken the Mundus Senex—the old world—leaders. These men and women would then form a government, led by a man named Arkarian Story. Once they had established this government, they were to awaken the other Pods."

I know the next statement will scare her, so I say it slowly and gently: "However, that's not what happened."

At this, her jaw clenches tighter still and a slight perspiration forms on her forehead. By the way she's swallowing, I can tell her tongue has gone dry. The professor I admired the most, Healer Selar, always taught that the session should end as soon as the Pod shows signs of anxiety. Of all my teachers, Hr. Selar is the one I most modeled my career after. She has worked with Pods since the Pod Reintegration Program started in 375 and is one of my heroes.

Accordingly, I bring the lesson to a close. Smiling in what I hope is a comforting manner, I say to the Pod, "It is now the year 419MN, and Earth's inhabitants have renamed it Elusis, after an old-world word meaning 'to be richly alive.' You are currently in a rehabilitation ward for Pods such as yourself to recover and learn about Mundus Novus—or, as we simply call it, Novus. Every day, you and I will go through history, economics, and language lessons to get you up to date with the new world. In two years, you will enter our world as a fellow Elusian."

Looking down, she doesn't respond verbally but her brow creases in concentration. The trembling in her limbs has become more unsteady, and it now seems to be an emotional response rather than the physical one caused by the detox. At least she's not hitting me. Or biting me. I hate biting. As I stand, she shakily follows suit, and I lead her to a different room filled with paintings of the Nine Wonders of Novus, books of our history, and large windows that look out across our city. The Ward is the only building in town that still has books; we keep them around so the Pods feel more at home.

The Pod stands in the middle of the room, shivering, staring down at her slipper-covered feet. Her calmness is disconcerting, and it makes me wonder what she's thinking. I pick up a book and try to hand it to her, though I'm not surprised when she doesn't take it.

"Whenever you feel like it, you can read any book in this room." I gently place the volume back on the shelf. "The text will automatically translate into English for you. However, very few people throughout Elusis can speak your language, so you and I will be working on learning Elusian, the common tongue of Novus."

My shift is almost over, so it's time to wrap up our session. I look her in the eye and speak softly as she quivers before me.

"You will stay here for the rest of the day. A woman named Hiya will join you in just a moment, and she will spend dinner with you and then show you to your sleeping quarters. She speaks no English, so she will not be able to answer any of your questions. Tomorrow morning, I will come to wake you up. And then we will begin your education."

As I finish, Hiya bustles into the Ward. Ignoring me, she goes straight to the Pod and starts talking smoothly to her. Even though I would never tell her this to her face, Hiya is incredible with the touchy-feely, healing stuff. I do the history, political science, and social studies, and I think I'm pretty good at what I do. But Hiya has a way of relaxing newcomers, regardless of whether or not they can understand her. I say goodbye to the Pod—though neither she nor Hiya acknowledges my farewell—and quietly slip out of the Ward. It's time to clock out for the day.

WHEN I FINALLY STEP out onto the street, the breeze fills my frizzy, silver curls. The sun is beginning to set, and despite the fall chill, it is warm on my face. I step onto the sidewalk and almost bump into Tia and her young son, Won. "Watch it, *paha veri!*" Tia yells the crude phrase loud enough for the entire street to stop and look in our direction. She pulls Won closer to her.

"Excuse me," Won's little voice says, but Tia hushes him.

"We don't talk to her, Won; I've told you that before."

"He didn't touch me," I assure her as they hurry away.

This kind of interaction used to turn my stomach—I couldn't eat for days. Now... well, it's just another Monday. I shrug it off and make my way home.

The crowds give me plenty of room as I pass. It's like I have my own personal walkway. Maja's Market is busy... I wonder if they have their specialty meats on sale again. I'll have my simulan go by later to check it out.

The Remembrance Ball is tomorrow, and decorations litter the town. They must have finished taking down the Fall Celebration ornaments and trimmings last night, because most of them were still up yesterday.

A gust of cold air pushes me towards Humani House, and music drifts out to meet me. The three-story structure looms over the town square. Worshippers quickly move out of my way as I side-step through them. Dixember used to be my month to light candles and prepare services at Humani House, but Kaileb Fransen's younger sister took my place.

A memory of the last time I was in the House of Worship rises unforbidden. The whispers of the guests, their accusatory stares, my white dress... images forever etched in my mind.

I shove them away and take a deep breath as I get closer to my least favorite intersection.

I won't look. I'll just walk by the bakery and keep my head perfectly straight. I mean, what are the chances I'll see *him*?

But as I walk by, out of habit... or is it addiction?... my head turns slightly to the left. I don't see him. No, no, of course I wouldn't see him.

I see *her*.

Mirindiss Fransen catches my eye. Her shoulders are square and she raises her chin as if accepting a challenge. What kind of challenge could I even prompt? She's won everything already.

The only thing I can do is look away—so I do. I hold my head high as I walk on towards home. I refuse to spend my evening mourning him. A sudden laugh forces its way through my lips. Yeah, like that hasn't been every night of my life for the past eight hundred and ninety-seven days.

The couple living near the jewelry repair shop see my mirth and scoff. The wife mutters something I can't hear, and the husband spits in my direction. There was a time when I would not have walked through town laughing out loud, but now I don't care. It doesn't matter—none of it matters.

In ancient days, people thought their emotions came from their stomachs. When people were in emotional turmoil, they would say they had a stomach fever. Then, in Mundus Senex—the old world—people spoke as if emotions came from their hearts. People in emotional pain would say their hearts had been broken. And now, in Novus, we know emotions come from one's blood. I brood on this as I walk too fast, my body aching. I feel like the blood in my veins is drying out, turning to ash.

Unfortunately, I live at the far end of a congested residential area, and I have to walk past all my neighbors to get home. At least the sun is still setting. I'll be safe as long as there is light. Yunson's younger brothers only come out after sunset, so all I need to do is get—

"Well, I'll be put to eternal sleep," a voice rings out behind me.

Every nerve in my body electrifies. My fight or flight response tries to kick in, but all I can do is freeze. Instead of running away like I should, I stand solidified in fear.

"You're not supposed to be out, girl virus," Jab, the youngest brother, hisses. "I thought we got the message through your poisoned veins last time."

"I thought," the middle brother, Seward, chips in, "we made it very clear that you're not supposed to be on these streets." He spits at the ground. "You're contaminated."

They may be young, but as soon as they reached eighteen, Yunson's brothers had their bodies modified to become large, tall, and overly muscular.

Willing my lips to move, I stammer, "I-I am allowed to walk home."

"Not on this street, you're not," Jab wags a finger as if I'm a child in need of correction.

"We made it all kinds of clear what would happen if we saw you out here again," Seward sneers.

At the sound of metal tips gently clinking together, I know Jab has used his Gift to turn his hands into knives. Tiny, throwable knives.

My back suddenly stings in remembrance.

Hey... Um... no pressure, but this would be an excellent time to run...

My brain screams the words, but my feet barely move. Still, the brothers glimpse the tiny motion and move closer. Like lions sensing the gazelle has spotted them.

"Come on, Black Widow," Jab whispers. "Give us a chase."

Knowing I won't win, I turn and run anyway, fully aware that this will end with splinters of steel in my shoulders and legs.

They only let up when I reach my driveway, and I slow down to gasp for breath. At least this time wasn't as bad as the last. My sweater and jeans are thick enough that only about half of the thin metal shards reach my skin. However, Seward has learned a new trick with his teeth and my arm now has the welts to prove it.

"Hey!" A shout startles me. I shriek, adrenaline still pounding in my veins, and run the rest of the way to my house. I bound up the stairs and onto my porch, but it's only when my hand touches the doorknob that I realize the voice doesn't match those of Yunson's brothers.

"Willow, wait!" the voice shouts again.

I have a first name, but it is not said aloud. Not ever. It's not shouted or whispered or used as a curse. It's simply been forgotten.

If someone needs to address me directly, they'll use my last name: Willow.

I turn to see Sheerley, the town social planner, striding impatiently towards me. Her shining silver hair bounces as she makes the short trek, and I wait anxiously for her words.

Sheerley and I were friends in times past. I was even a bridesmaid at her wedding. So odd and yet, now, so routine to see her avoiding my gaze.

"I was finishing the Remembrance Ball plans," Sheerly says, keeping her distance, "and you and Aker are the only couple—well, the only two people—in the entirety of Depalo who haven't finished their registrations. Aker confirmed he was going—are you?" She steals a glance to gauge my reaction.

My blood is snow. Aker said he would go to the Remembrance Ball? He's skipped every town event, every Holy Day, and every weekly Humani House worship service for the past twenty-nine and a half months. Why go to this one?

Sheerley shifts her weight uncomfortably. "Well?"

I'm still too shocked at her words to know what to say. If Aker wants to go to the Remembrance Ball with me, why hasn't he said so? Why quarantine himself from me if he intends to go to the ball?

"Ka—I mean, Willow... I have stuff to do. Could you just tell me if you're going or not?"

"I'm—I'll go," I say in a rush, almost breathless.

Sheerley nods and walks away without a farewell. I turn back towards my front door, suddenly questioning whether or not I should talk to Aker about the ball. Does he really want to go with me? Does this mean we're speaking now? Is he finally going to... marry me?

Okay, okay, don't be a *vaunut*. No, I'll wait for him to talk to me first—if he ever does. That's how it's always been. We speak on his terms.

I walk inside and drop my work satchel on the floor. Empty grocery bags lay on the counter; my simulan must have picked up some food already. I throw myself onto the couch.

"Welcome home," my simulan speaks from the corner of the kitchen.

"You got food?" I ask.

"Yes. Your vitals have been showing low protein for three days now. You must eat the food your simulan makes for you, or a healer will reach out again."

My simulan opens the refrigerator, preparing to make dinner. I feel better about my life of isolation. At least I don't have to contend with mundane household tasks on top of everything else. As my simulan cooks, it flicks a long plait over its shoulder. Simulans were made to look exactly like humans, save for their white hair, which will always be their tell.

I stare at my vitals streaming across the refrigerator's door. Apparently, I'm under-exercised, unbalanced in my food intake, dehydrated, and sleeping terribly. What my simulan cannot understand is that I keep my vitals like this on purpose, so the healers are forced to come. They *have* to talk to me. They *have* to touch me.

Ontzi, I am pathetic.

"Did you go to Maja's Market?" I stretch and yawn. "It was busy when I passed by."

"No, your simulan purchased groceries from Perfect Health. Do you desire your simulan to go by Maja's Market?"

"Please," I respond, and I'm not sure why. It doesn't matter what's on sale; I'll eat it alone anyway.

"Do you want your simulan to finish making the meal before this errand?"

"No," I sigh.

"Your simulan will return quickly."

"Wait," I say as it reaches the door. "Is... Does my Vorbi have enough on it to splurge?"

"Your Vorbi is low, but you have enough for this errand," it answers. "In addition, you will be getting it refilled on Friday."

"Gotta love payday, I suppose," I say, and it nods. As the front door shuts, I rub my temples. It's not even bedtime yet, but I'm exhausted. My stomach growls, and I realize I should have had my simulan make my food before it left. Or I could have just grabbed something from the cafeteria at work before I came home.

I eye up the refrigerator, but instead of listening to my stomach, I drag myself off the couch and slouch off to my room. I shut the door and lie down on my bed. The HugMe technology infused into the mattress melds to my body perfectly. Once I'm comfortable and warm, I focus on breathing. In. Out. In. Out. Something I can control.

I reach inside my shirt and draw out my pendant. A bright blue druzy quartz dangles inside a crescent moon, and I stare at it longingly. I close my eyes and clutch the pendant tightly in my palm. I hate my life so much I want to throw up. I want to physically wrench myself out of my own body.

I force down the nausea. As I rub the pendant between my fingers, my chest rises and falls. Once, twice, breathing in stale, lifeless oxygen, and stinging bile; but the third breath is different. This air smells like tulips and tastes like pancakes.

"I guess we should get up," a sleepy voice muses next to me.
Smiling, I open my eyes to a dream I wish was my life.
"Greet the sun, my love," Dream Aker says, and he leans over to kiss me.

Sanus

Pypen

"WE HAVE APPROXIMATELY FORTY-SEVEN seconds until her life expires," I say quietly.

"Until *our* lives expire," Scout contradicts.

"I chose my words correctly," I push back firmly.

Scout wastes one of our seconds scowling at me. "We will not save ourselves and forsake her. Her fate will be ours, Pypen."

I look out the window of the five-story building and scratch the stubble on my chin, thinking hard. The clouds cover the sky, and the rain chills the town with a light mist. When I look down, I can barely see the five Guardians speaking with Gigi's illusion. The plan was for Gigi to keep the Guardians busy while we escaped, but there is a Detector among their number. He instantly recognized the trick for what it was, which has placed a tourniquet on our plan.

Scout's sentimentality for those we save is admirable, but he is a *patka* if he thinks I will let him die with this Pexun stranger. I focus my attention on Ryder. "By any means, can we assist you?" I ask.

"You can shut up like a good boy," Ryder snaps, not taking his eyes off the Guardians. "Gigi's illusion won't last much longer," he warns.

"I don't want to seem ungrateful," a hesitant Pexun voice hedges. Annoyed, I regard the well-dressed woman we are attempting to save. "But how do you expect to outsmart Guardians? They have every Gift at their disposal. There's no way for us to escape." She wipes sweat from her forehead.

I do not hinder my frustration nor stop myself from saying, "We have not time for your thankless questions—"

"Fret not, Friend," Scout replies to her concerns, interrupting me. "We have a few Gifts in our veins as well."

"Five seconds," Ryder whispers. Gigi barely nods, but we know she has heard. Four...

Three...

Two…

"Now!" Ryder shouts, and Gigi's eyes fly open.

"The Guardians know we are here!" Gigi exclaims breathlessly. She must have exhausted her energy.

Within a breath, the room becomes inky black. I knew the Guardians would bring a Blinder with them. My skin tingles, and I can feel my consciousness sway.

"Before someone else finds Arkarian Story, Ryder!" I shout. My meaning could not be clearer—time is of the utmost importance.

"I am hurrying," he yells from somewhere. My depth perception is waxing.

"Can I do anything to help?" the Pexun we are rescuing asks.

"You are about to be shrunk to a molecular level and pressurized into a palm-sized frozen chamber," Scout explains, "Then, Ryder will use a bird to transport us to the other side of Pexus. All you need to do is sit back and relax."

I need not behold the Pexun's features to know she is shocked. The walls around us dissolve into dust; through the haze, the Guardians fly in from every direction. It is as if the concrete blocks and mortar had never existed. I can make out only a few faces before Ryder shouts, "Ready!" I hold my breath.

Blinding light that sears my sight

Pain that morphs from great to slight

Airlessness, there is no substance

Mere existence, I am everything and nothing

Heaviness, it does grow and aggress

Pain brings the end of this flight

Blinding light that sears my sight

As my knees hit the sand, I bite my tongue. Rather, I bite my teeth *through* my tongue. I hiss as blood fills my mouth, life liquid dripping down my chin. Closing my eyes, I focus on nothing. Reaching down into my being, I will my Progift awake and, as power surges through my veins, I stretch my thoughts towards the injury and rewind time to before the damage occurred.

In a second's time, all pain is gone. I move my tongue around my cheeks, pushing the rest of the blood out of my mouth. As I spit it onto the sand, I take in my surroundings quickly. No one else is on the beach besides my team; the dunes loom around us like giant screens, keeping us from being seen.

"Could you help me out a bit, Pip?" Gigi asks me as she rubs her neck.

I will my Gift towards her sprained neck, and her groan quiets, replaced by a sigh of relief. "Thank you," she says.

"Pypen," Scout calls out to me, and my attention turns to him. He is sitting by the Pexun we have saved. Although I can see that the woman has a broken leg, I search Scout's body for wounds—after all, my loyalty is to him first. Only when I find he possesses none, do I relax slightly. When the Pexun moans again, Scout repeats my name and looks pointedly at the injured woman.

Quickly, I use my Progift to renew her leg. I focus my energy into her fractured femur and rewind time to before it was broken.

"Thank you," the woman gulps in air, before gazing around at us in awe. "Thank you so much, all of you. I would be dead if it weren't for you."

Scout gets to his feet and helps the woman beside him to stand. "It was our pleasure. I am Scout Eekan."

"Xoana. Xoana Kapu," the woman says with a smile.

"Do you have it with you?" I ask her. "The evidence?"

Xoana touches her coat pocket. "I don't go anywhere without it."

An alarm suddenly bellows across the beach. It is so loud my eardrums burst. I know I am screaming at the top of my lungs, but I cannot hear myself. I renew my eardrums as well as my comrades', but the sound continues to ring, bursting them again and again. I continually renew our hearing as I sprint toward Ryder.

I reach him just as Gigi does. We haul him to his feet, and I can see by his face that he is screaming. But I cannot hear anything besides the deafening siren.

"Freeze now, or we will fire upon you," a voice declares from everywhere, displacing the painful cacophony.

How did the Guardians track us?

Scout and Xoana stumble up to join us, and Gigi whips out a pendant. We have not used this means of escape in several months, and I am not eager to touch the cold, green gem. But when we hear finitum shots around us—knowing one hit will take away our Gifts forever—there is no hesitation in our hands as we reach for it. Our bodies instantly liquify, and the green gem on Gigi's pendent sucks up our life's essence into itself, transporting us to a pre-imputed location known by Gigi alone.

Liquid consciousness is disturbing and nauseating. Time is irrelevant, but it has been too long before I can squeeze my fingers, finally back in solid form. The ocean's waves pound in my ear. This beach has black sand—we must be in Sanus.

We all rub life back into our limbs, waiting, ready for another attack from the Guardians. After two minutes of tense silence, Gigi flops down on the beach, exhausted. I quietly renew the strength of our team, and they mutter their thanks. I feel surprisingly energetic, despite my group restoring act. I have built up my stamina extensively over the years but, had I needed it, I have a Vorbi in my pocket. All I need do is rub the energy holder, and it will refill my blood with strength and vitality. If, for some outlandish reason, I were to use up the whole of the Vorbi's power, my Gift enables me to restore some of my own stamina through the energy directly around me. In the last few years, I have rarely had to do so.

I look up as Xoana approaches Scout who is standing next to me. She reaches into her pocket and pulls out an infoship—a small, portable storage device, which she gently hands to Scout. Sensitive information has to be kept on such tiny machines as sharing electronically would be easy for anyone to track.

Scout is tucking the infoship into his own pocket, when a light buzzing sounds in my ear.

Gigi immediately opens her mouth and emits several birdlike chirps. The sand around us bursts like a geyser as Gigi uses her Progift to create a sand barrier around us.

"What is going on?" Ryder shouts.

"Someone is on the beach," Gigi answers and pulls her pendant out again. Although I do not desire to escape this way again, I reach for it.

But before eager fingers make contact with the pendant, all of our bodies abruptly freeze. I try to push past the attack and grasp the pendant, but I am unable to move. Next to me, Gigi screams out in pain, and the sand around us falls back to the earth.

In the corner of my eye, I see a figure walking toward us, and I do everything I can to fight against their bonds.

Black flowing robes enter into our circle, and even with all their layers I can see the frame is tall and muscular—probably a man. He takes a moment to look at each of us, his features shrouded behind a light brown hood. When he peers at me, tendrils of ice seem to crawl up my spine.

The stranger turns his attention towards Xoana, who is frozen opposite me, her arm stuck in a perpetual lunge towards the pendant. He seizes her shirt and rips it open, exposing the woman's undershirt. Then he takes one black leather glove off, revealing a gnarled, hairy-knuckled hand. His movements seem clumsy and sticky, like his joints are not willing to obey his wishes.

The man places his palm on Xoana's chest, and at first nothing seems to happen. Her chest expands as if she is taking a huge breath. But instead of an exhale, air seems to keep filling her lungs like a ballon.

Xoana's eyes bulge slightly, and in the space of a heartbeat—before I even realize I need to help her—her lungs burst. Blood shoots out of her nose and mouth, and the assassin slowly takes his hand off Xoana's chest. He shifts his body jerkily and turns his hooded face towards Scout.

My whole body floods with cortisol and adrenaline. Even though I know I cannot do anything, I strain against the invisible bonds holding me back from protecting Scout.

When he reaches for Scout's shirt, I almost pass out from the toxic mix of hormones filling my blood. I force myself to stay focused as I continue fighting for control. Instead of hurting him, however, the assassin reaches into Scout's pocket and takes out the infoship. He taps it against Scout's cheek before walking out of our circle, black robes billowing as majestically as when he arrived. It is not until the assassin is out of my peripheral vision that I can break free from the Gift keeping me frozen.

I whip my head around for the assassin, but I don't see him anywhere. He has disappeared. Scout rushes over to Xoana and kneels over her dead body.

"Who the *matza* was that?" Ryder curses.

"Someone to silence Xoana Kapu and her evidence," I answer, knowing Scout is utterly overwhelmed, unable to reply.

"But how could they have tracked us?" Gigi asks. "Even the Guardians were not able to follow us."

"We must find out," I respond.

Scout stands and stares out at the ocean, his body tense. Slowly, he releases a hard sigh and turns to me. Although he is of average build, he stands tall and robust. When he meets my gaze, I see that his eyes are filled with tears. Scout never takes death well.

"You did everything you could," I state quickly.

"She had a daughter."

"I know."

"Now an orphaned daughter," he continues.

"Yes," I confirm. "But the girl is of age. Her mate is her family."

"She is an orphan because we were unable to save her mother."

"Xoana willingly chose an illegal vocation," I declare firmly.

Scout's face twists. "We could have planned it better, Pypen. How could the assassin have found us without some negligence on our part? It need not have ended this way."

I take a deep breath so he feels like I am pondering his words. Then I scratch the back of my neck and exhale loudly. "You cannot shoulder the burden of every failure. The weight will crush you."

Silence fills the black-sanded beach. A cool breeze brushes one of my dreadlocks from my shoulder to my back. I sit, my hands buried in the black sand. My fingers, so similar to this beach's color, are camouflaged—black hiding in the darkness.

"So this was all for nothing," Ryder snaps behind us.

"Be not so ice-blooded," I admonish, for Scout's sake.

"Nonetheless, he is right," Gigi says. "We did not acquire the evidence nor protect the Pexun."

"Perhaps Xoana's daughter knows something of her work," I muse.

"Even if she does, she may not be willing to share anything with us once she finds out about her mother's death," Scout replies morosely.

An idea formulates in my mind within seconds, but I know Scout will not like it. "Give us a moment." I glance at Ryder and Gigi. Gigi nods and withdraws immediately. Ryder scowls and shuffles his feet before complying.

When they are out of earshot, I say slowly, "We could ask the daughter about Xoana's work before we tell her about her mother."

"Be not cold," Scout snaps.

"It is merely an option."

"I veto said option."

I try another tack.

"What if we ask after we tell her about her mother, then?"

"And if she is unwilling?" Scout asks.

"Perhaps she will be willing if we allow her the opportunity to find out who killed her mother."

Scout's brows furrow in confusion. "You want to help her find the assassin?"

"She could think we are doing so."

His brows rise in surprise and then deepen in disappointment. "You propose we lie to a poor girl who just lost her mother—offering false hope that she can seek vengeance—simply so that we can get information from her?"

I smile, aware that I cannot keep the guilt from seeping into my features.

Clicking his tongue, Scout looks away from me and out to the sea. He runs his hand through his hair, fingers becoming entangled in a braid. The top of Scout's head sports long, shoulder-length hair that he braids each morning, while the sides of his head are shaved close to the skin so that his Between-Age hunting-inspired tattoos shine through. "No, Pypen. The girl will be hurting. We will merely ask her to help us."

"What if she refuses to give us any information?"

"We will use Falik," he says.

"And once she has forgotten meeting us, we shall do it my way?" I ask.

He shakes his head. "I will not commit to it. I will create options B and C, and if all three plans fail… then we will do it your way."

"I concede." Seeing the time, I add, "We will be late if we do not leave now. You know how angry Allerish gets when we are late."

I whistle to Gigi and Ryder to join us.

"Ryder," Scout says, "I think a mouse would be best."

Ryder looks down at Xoana and wordlessly closes his eyes. Xoana's human frame slowly begins to shrink in the sand. Fur grows along the woman's body as her features distort. When Ryder opens his eyes, Scout reaches down and carefully plucks a seemingly sleeping mouse out from the collar of a woman's abandoned suit. He places the mouse in a small green pouch and cradles it in his hands.

We leave the black beach and make our way towards the small coastal town chosen by Gigi. Due to the loud volume of the waves, our sudden arrival is not heard, keeping us out of local trouble—Gigi has quite the affinity for escape routes.

A steep street leads down to the transponder station. As we begin our descent into town, the streets far below us seem overrun by light brown beetles. In reality, it is merely a town full of Sanusians, their heads of light-brown hair clearly visible from our vantage point on top of the hill. We pass by the locals as we weave through the town center, and Scout bows to each one in the customary Sanusian greeting. When we get to the transponder station, he buys our tickets quickly.

As soon as we have all jumped into the nearest taxi, Scout makes a call to Emerly.

"Contact Xoana Kapu's daughter and have her meet us at the circus," Scout says briskly. "Let her know we have news about her mother… No, do not mention Xoana's death. Let her know we are traveling and will be at the circus in an hour's time. Yes, of course… I do not believe so. Yes, yes… And to you as well."

He releases a long sigh as he hangs up and is silent for the rest of the trip. The half-hour of travel goes by in a blur as we make our way across the world to Ortus—our home territory. When we emerge into the Ortusan sunlight, I breathe in the air, feeling very much at home.

We are walking down the cobbled steps that lead away from the transponder station when Scout gets a return call from Emerly. "What do you mean she already knows her mother is dead?" Scout asks our assistant. He turns to me, phone pressed against his chest as he explains. "Xoana's daughter had a vital track on her mother and knows she is dead. Emerly says he told her where we are, and she is on her way to meet us here—"

Suddenly, we hear a commotion up ahead. A Pexun woman is berating travelers as they exit numerous cars, screaming in their faces, punching their doors, prowling down the line to the next vehicle. When she reaches us, Scout raises his hands peaceably. "How can we be of assistance?"

Her grey hair flies about her head like Medusa's serpents in the ancient tales. "Are you Scout Eekan?" she spits. At his nod, her eyes fill with venomous rage as she screams, "Spineless, cowardly scum!" She lurches to punch him, but he moves quickly out of her reach. "What did you do to my mom?" Her face contorts in pain and anger as she tries to punch him again. "Where is she, filthy *gari*!?"

I suppose this is Xoana Kapu's daughter.

Scout grabs her curled fist with one hand, the green pouch cocooned in his other.

I pin her freely flailing arm behind her back before she can attack him again. With enough force to cause her pain but not break her shoulder, I lift her wrist towards her neck. She cries out, and with surprising speed and power, she unravels her arm and headbutts me.

I am equally surprised, impressed, and annoyed.

"Ryder, constrain her," Scout shouts. The Pexun's body begins to shrink, but she roars in anger and wills herself to stay human. Again, I'm impressed. Most people cannot fight so hard against direct body manipulation without a sciath—a defense object worn to keep one safe from another's Gifts.

She yells again, wriggling and writhing, and it is then I spy the smallest piece of yarn poking out from the collar of her canvas blouse.

Ah, I see you, lovely.

High-end sciaths can only be taken off by those who put them on—I wonder how much compensation Xoana Kapu's daughter invested in her defense object. If it is cheap enough, I will be able to take it off myself.

I tackle her to the ground and am amused by how easily I rip the yarn necklace off her neck. She should have invested more in her sciath.

In seconds, her body shrinks down to rodent size. Before she can scurry away, I grab the little grey mouse. I keep my grip around her tight, even as she bites my hands repeatedly.

"I do not have another pouch," Scout warns, seeing the pain on my face, "and I will not put her in the same hold as her dead mother."

Understanding his ask, I growl through gritted teeth, "I will meet you at the circus."

We need only walk ten minutes, but I run ahead. The Pexun *wee-un* does not tire of scratching and biting me the entire way. Curse this Pexun!

When I glimpse our gold and black striped tent through the trees, I run even faster. My feet pounding the ground, I yell out to Taniel to unlock the front gate that encloses our livelihood. The entranceway obligingly swings open as I run up the hill. As I race through the gates towards the striped haven, I shout my thanks to Taniel before ducking inside the heavy front tent flap. I designed these footpaths myself, along with Scout, and I need not think as I gallop down the golden paths that lead toward my office. I sprint up the invisible stairs, skipping steps in my haste, and make a final dash to the office door.

I grip the feisty mouse as tightly as I can with one hand, while I use the other to turn the bronze doorknob. Blood trickles down the metal ball as I fling the door open. I want to throw the Pexun across the room, but I am afraid of crushing the mouse's small frame. Instead, I bend low and drop her out of my hands the second I have closed the door. The furious little creature races beneath the desks, scampers out the far side, and finally takes refuge underneath my makeshift bed on the far side of the room.

I mutter a string of curses as I renew the skin on my hands that is dotted with mouse-inflicted wounds.

While we wait for the others to arrive, long minutes drag by in which the small grey mouse never stops squeaking and chattering at me. Unexpectedly, she darts towards me, momentarily disappearing back under the desks. Not realizing how fast her mouse form can move, I shriek when she rushes up my pant leg and starts biting me again.

Scout, Ryder, and Gigi jog into our office just as I have finally grabbed the snapping rodent and forced her back inside my cupped hands.

"Change her back!" I shout to Ryder when he does nothing but stand and stare at me being assaulted. "Now!" I command testily.

Coming to himself, Ryder nods and clears his throat. "Put her on the floor."

Leaning down, I open my hands only to find the mouse dangling in midair as she clings to my skin with her teeth and claws.

"Desist!" I scream at her. The mouse continues to grunt through clenched jaws, and I snap at Ryder, "Then change her here."

Smiling ruefully, Ryder obliges. As soon as she realizes what is happening, the mouse releases my hand and runs towards the bed. She barely makes it in time. In a heartbeat, my blankets explode to reveal a frazzled, growling, naked Pexun. Ryder holds out the woman's clothing and she grabs it angrily, eyes full of fury. As she dresses, she curses us, our mates, our children, and I cannot help but laugh when she curses our pets.

She is still pulling on the last item of clothing when she storms across to Scout, attacking him again. "Where is my mom?" she screams.

"If you do not calm yourself, I will have you kept in mouse form," Scout returns calmly, holding her hands at bay and blocking her kicks with his knees. "Your mother is here. If you would just compose yourself..."

She stops immediately, eyes frantically searching the room. "Where? Where is she?"

Scout releases her wrists, walks over to the table and gingerly picks up the green pouch. Without a word, he places the small sack in the girl's hands.

Her face contorts in agony, and the tiniest spark of empathy flitters through my veins.

Her features twist again, darting between pain and wrath. "You killed her." Her low voice shakes with rage.

"No," Scout replies, voice as soft as if he were reciting a lullaby.

"You know who killed her?" she asks.

"Yes."

"Who?" she growls.

Scout looks at me before answering. "An assassin."

His words genuinely surprise the Pexun. "Why would someone want to kill my mom?" she asks.

"Guardians found out about her Arkahistorian research and were trying to arrest her. Those to whom we answer heard of her arrest warrant and sent us to protect her. We got her away from the Guardians, but this assassin was able to find us before we made it to safety."

"So you failed," the Pexun woman spits.

Ire sparks in my blood. How dare she accuse Scout of failure. She has no idea the burden he bears for anything that goes wrong on our missions—especially ill-fated deaths.

"Yes, I failed," Scout replies simply, holding her gaze. When I open my mouth to defend him, he silences me with a hand gesture.

"She would have lived had you not interfered," the Pexun seethes. There is so much hatred in her eyes, she almost looks nonhuman. Anticipating the possibility her Gift may be offensive, my own Gift begins to hum within my veins.

Scout's expression is unreadable as he attempts to explain. "Our intelligence confirmed the Guardians were there to arrest her and send her to a Misinformation Den. She would not have lived much longer had she been taken there, and you would never have known the truth."

"And why should I believe your intelligence? Or *you*, for that matter?"

"You need not believe us," Scout answers gently. "You are free to take your mother and leave."

"So that's it?" Behind the wrath, her face now shows a hint of fear.

"It need not be it," I insert.

The Pexun's eyes turn on me. Her brows raise critically as she looks me over. With no attempt at kindness, I return her harsh gaze. Then, as if she has made up her mind that I am not worthy of interaction, she turns her attention back to Scout, waiting for him to expound on my cryptic statement.

I know I should feel sorry for the woman, but I would enjoy nothing more than to kick her out of our office, out of our circus. If it were not for the fact that we need information from her, I would do just that, right now.

"We are Arkahunters," Scout begins. "If you join our group, you could find out more about why the Guardians and that assassin were after your mother. You could finish her work."

Confusion, fear, rage.

Confusion, fear, rage.

The girl's expressions cycle so quickly I wish to laugh, but Scout would think it callous. Her mouth opens and closes. Scout waits patiently, a quick glance from him bidding the rest of us to remain silent.

"I don't know anything about her work—I can't—I can't join your group. I don't know—She was always so secretive, and I don't know who she worked for—"

"We could acquire said information," Scout interjects.

"I barely know anything about her research!" she pushes back.

Scout nods, unperturbed. "We have contacts who can help us."

The Pexun looks down at the green pouch, still resting in her shaking hands. "How do I even know she's in here?"

"I can have my associate change her back to her human size, but she will not be clothed."

Gigi elegantly twirls her cloak off. "I will cover her."

Scout reaches for the green pouch, but the Pexun yanks it away from his outstretched hand. She reaches into the pouch and tentatively draws out the still, grey mouse. Carefully, she places the tiny form on the ground.

Ryder closes his eyes. As Xoana's deceased body morphs back into a human, Gigi gently drapes her cloak over Xoana's nakedness. In less than five seconds, the dead Pexun woman lies motionless before us all.

The young woman's knees hit the wooden floor with a loud thud as she falls down beside the body. Her head rests on her mother's shoulder and she buries her face in the soft cloak.

"Let us give her a minute," Scout quietly commands the rest of us.

The young Pexun mutters something, but her words are muffled by Gigi's cape. As we turn to leave, she sits up. "I *said* I don't need a minute."

"Are you certain?" Scout asks. "We will allow you some privacy to mourn her death."

Her eyes burrow into his. "I will mourn when the assassin who killed her is dead."

Scout's brows furrow. "We seek justice, not death."

"Do I look like I care what you seek?" she spits. "Do you want my help or not?"

"We do," Scout responds at the same time as I answer, "No."

To me, the Pexun's hot temper is not worth the information she can provide. But she must not have heard me, because the woman looks down at her mother and says quietly, "For her." Then she stands and walks resolutely toward Scout. Reaching out her right hand, she offers him the traditional Pexun sign of agreement. "I'll do this for her."

Scout reaches out his left hand, locks his thumbs with hers, and allows their hands to rest together. She withdraws from his touch quickly.

"I am Scout Eekan," he says and bows. "You?"

She licks her lips, and they burst with red color. "Merayal Kapu," she answers.

"Well, Merayal Kapu," Scout says, and it is as if he cannot help himself when he smirks. "Are you ready to run away with the circus?"

Pexus

Kansis

Normally I'd want to tell you about the new Pod that we awakened, but something spectacular happened today.

Something spectacular happened, huh? Do tell. I can't remember the last time anything spectacular happened in your life.

I'd hit you if you weren't just a voice inside my head.

I'd block your hit if I weren't just a voice inside your head. You're slow and far from peak condition. But go ahead. Tell me what was so spectacular.

I saw Sheerley today. I saw her and *spoke* with her—she actually talked with me. And... And she said Aker wants to go to the Remembrance Ball with me.

Are you saying that Aker wanting to go to a ball with you is spectacular?

Yes! Aker said he wanted to go with me... He said that... Are you even listening?

About the new Senny. Are they female or male?

The Pod isn't a big deal. Aker said that he wanted to go to the Remembrance Ball with me! We need to discuss this. What do you think his intentions are? Do you think he just wants to be there? He used to love parties.

Was there a lot of crying? I like the Sennies who show less emotions. At least you don't get hurt around that type.

I want to talk about Aker.

Is it an old guy? I really didn't like the last one you worked with. He was obnoxious. And it was boring listening to you talk night after night about all of his whining. Your last Pod was fun, though. She was so excitable.

Aker.

Although her emotions were annoying too. And she was clingy.

Aker.

I hope your new Pod has good Senny stories. Your last one—

Aker!

—didn't have—

Aker, Aker, Aker!

Stop! Stop saying his name. I don't care about him!

Yeah, well, you should. If it matters to me, it should matter to you!

I do care and you know I do. I am you; therefore, I have to care. But I'm your logical side, so you know why I don't talk about him.

Because, by your estimation, if I stop thinking about him, I'll stop hurting.

I understand what you're feeling. However, obsessing over him isn't helping you in any way. Your tears are wasted, your feelings go unnoticed, your pain is not taken into account. Since I'm only in your brain, I can't do anything about it, and it hurts me that you can't do anything either. He's made his choice. We finally have something significant to discuss, and I'm not going to sit here and let you dwell on him.

Yeah, but he said he'd go to the ball with me…

And what does that mean? Has he decided he's in love with you? That he will marry you?

I don't understand why you're such a *kaiman*.

You think I'm rude, but I think you're weak! We have this conversation over and over and over. For the past two years, we've been having this conversation. What is it going to take for you to move on?

I'll never move on.

You think your stubbornness is heroic, but it is pathetic.

You think your words are helpful, but they're toxic.

…

…

You know I only say what I do because I care.

I know that Aker will never love me. But… he's in my blood. I don't know how to let him go.

Many widows and widowers have successful lives. They move on from their pain and embrace life with joy, purpose, and contentment every day. They are praiseworthy. Once you let him go, you'll actually start living.

I am not a widow.

Why do you defend a relationship that is nonexistent? You are a widow. His love is dead. No, not dead—it never lived. His love was only ever a dream.

Then I will dream on.

Why do you torture yourself like this? Start caring about something else. For now, can you at least try and focus on the Pod? Focus on things that are in your control.

All right. I'll try.

Thank you. Now, back to things that matter: the Senny. I am very interested in her.

She's a young girl. Younger than me. She's calm and collected and quiet and receptive. I've never seen a Pod like her.

Maybe she's so quiet because she was expecting this.

Expecting what? That her world was going to be completely gone? That the leaders she undoubtedly trusted turned out to be evil, and now her whole world is lost forever? No, I don't think she was expecting this.

Hmm... you should ask her questions about her past tomorrow. See if you can figure out why she's so calm.

Anything else, your majesty?

Put Aker out of your mind. Your job is more important than a man who can't see what's in front of him.

Well, *ontzi*, isn't that just the nicest thing you've ever said to me?

Get some sleep, kid. I'll talk to you tomorrow night.

Fine. Greet the shadows.

It's always better...

...When we're together.

Shock. Noun. A sudden or violent disturbance of the mind, emotions, or sensibilities. I experience this *shock* as I walk into my new Pod's room this morning. Every Pod has nightmares the first few weeks of being awake, so Mathos, one of the bodyguards, comes with me to restrain her if necessary. My first Pod scratched me, and I still have three scars across my cheek to remember her by.

To my surprise, my new Pod sits on her bed; dressed, quiet, and waiting. When I realize I'm staring at her, I hazily dismiss Mathos. I lead the girl to the Flower Room and we sit down together.

Typically, I teach for a week and then start asking the Pod about their life, but after what my subconscious said last night, I'm eager to learn more about her. "Tell me about yourself."

Her eyes meet mine—dry but red-rimmed and glaring with indifference. She stares at me, and I think she's waiting for me to look away, but I don't.

I raise my brows and allow a smile. "If this is a war you're hoping to win, prepare to lose. I always win a staring contest."

With this, she blinks and looks away, brushing her red hair behind her ears. Her skin is pale from years without sunlight. We will begin her Vitamin D regimen this afternoon. With her large hazel eyes, small nose, and polished skin, she truly has the face of a doll. Yet she looks confident and strong. She will easily pass as a Formosian.

She doesn't answer for a long time, instead choosing to stare at me blankly.

"I saw from your Hull's chart that your name is Amelia," I prompt.

Our eyes meet again, and I can see she will not respond. Even in her pointless pride, she is so collected. So calm. So in control of her emotions and even her body. I think about what Lesson One covers and decide that she can handle it and more.

"Like I said yesterday, your world as you knew it ended on August 4, 2094, MS—Mundus Senex. What started as the Global Nuclear War—now known as the Era Ending War—caused an irreversible cataclysmic temperature shift that melted the earth's ice. This change raised the water level by 600 meters.

"Before the war, there were seven continents and roughly 200,000 islands; now the world has six territories—the Hexum—and millions of daughter islands."

I pause to check my pupil is following, but she asks no questions. I continue.

"During the Between Age, people stayed on their territories and tried to reconnect with those they shared a continent with. Unfortunately, many died from radiation poisoning and other diseases in those early days. Natural disasters continually brought their numbers down and kept them from uniting. But after one hundred years, their immune systems began strengthening, and the natural disasters quelled.

"As the years passed on, communication improved between the Hexum. Silenda, one of the six territories, reported the finding of the Pods. There had been rumors about the pre-war Pod Program—a technology that would freeze your body in an indestructible casing called a Hull, keeping you safe during the Global Nuclear War. Not many believed these rumors to be fact. And yet, in these warehouses lay 500,000 Pods, secure inside their Hulls."

I clear my throat and lean forward slightly, conspiratorially, so she feels that she is learning secret things.

"Within the warehouses was found the Book of Instructions. It contained a plan written by the leaders of Senex: once the world had regained a population of one million, the new world leaders were to awaken the leaders of the old. According to the Instructions, these encapsulated men and women would establish a new government. The author and founder of this new governmental plan was a dictator named Arkarian Story."

Amelia stays utterly still throughout the lesson. No wide eyes. No sharply inhaled breaths. No paling pallor. She stares intently at my lips, listening. Most Pods know this information, but some were encapsulated before much of this had come to pass.

"Arkarian Story was the righthand man to his predecessor, Dayie Tueur. After betraying his superior, Arkarian Story murdered Dayie Tueur and created a tyrannical government that slowly ended your world. No one could find Arkarian Story among the Hulls, so we believe someone secretly hid him somewhere else in the world."

All the Pods we have awakened thus far have claimed that they have never heard of Arkarian Story, although they remember Dayie Tueur.

"With all that being said, Arkarian Story is considered, by some, a myth to scare Novus. However, others see him as the last threat to Elusis. If someone were to find him and awaken him, it is believed he would bring about the end of our world, as he did yours. Because of this, he is still considered, to this day, the most dangerous man alive."

Although my new Pod swallows, she expresses nothing more. Usually, this part of the lesson produces fear, screaming, or hysterical weeping. I often feel sorry for these poor subhumans.

"When the world population reached one million and it was time to awaken the Pods, they chose not to, deciding to give the earth more time to heal. There were 207 years between your world ending and mine emerging; we refer to these years as the Between Age. During this period of waiting, they finished creating a universal language and decided on a temporary government. They named Novus—the new world—Elusis, established the Hexum, and named Silenda the world capital. Every five years, the leaders of the Hexum gather in Silenda for a week to make important decisions for Novus. In addition to amending and creating laws, territorial ceremonies and celebrations are held throughout the week. On the Saturday evening, in every territory, we broadcast the best entertainment that Elusis has to offer. This has become a worldwide Holy Day called the Quintrall. The next Quintrall is actually just over two weeks away."

My back begins to hurt, and I shift my weight. I don't know why I constantly forget I hate this chair—my body always regrets it for days afterwards. Despite my discomfort, the content of Lesson One falls from my mouth like a recording. How many times have I said these exact words?

"Around the year 100 Between Age, the population exploded, and the fields of art, architecture, literature, and language grew at impressive degrees. We call this the Second Renaissance period. The people quickly established schools and universities. Old technology was found, and our world simply picked up where Senex had left off. In fact, our technology has now progressed so far that those of your world would call it magic.

"Although it may sound unbelievable, humans have always contained the matter that is now responsible for supernatural abilities. However, the part of our atoms that enables this ability—known as the Gician Particle—lay dormant within all matter on earth for millenniums. But the Era Ending War introduced toxic levels of radiation and gamma rays into our world, and after observing the freak effects of nuclear fallout contamination over time, a scientist named Luccia See found a way to replicate beneficial changes in people and materials using gamma radiation. It was hundreds of years later when the Gician Particle was actually discovered and named."

My Pod's eyes glaze over as I explain the science-y aspect of our world. She doesn't look disinterested, just overloaded with information. I redirect the lecture back to the basics. "All of that to say that we call these Gician-powered supernatural abilities, Gifts. Gifts include the ability to control every aspect of the physical world, including the manipulation of matter, telepathy and mind-reading, time travel and teleportation, invisibility, incredible levels of influence over other people and animals, etcetera."

Sometimes Pods show moderate interest in this part of the lesson. Not this Pod. Amelia's expression remains rigid and emotionless.

"Normally, a person has only one Gift; this is called their Progift. If they have a second, it is their Duogift. And if they were honored and privileged enough to have three, the third is their Trigift. Gift Protection is a part of children's education. We learn how to keep ourselves informed about, and safe from, other Gifts.

"These advancements were made approximately two hundred years after the Era Ending War; the first year in which we implemented and normalized Gifts into society was the beginning of Year One MN. Now, Gifts are inherited as naturally as normal genes. Recessive Gift traits can occur, so their variety can skip generations, but usually one inherits the Gifts of their family.

"During the first decade of the Mundus Novus, some people were born with Gifts so powerful that the wielder could change the very fabric of time and space. But these Gifts were too dominant, so these individuals had their Gifts stripped for the safety of humanity. However, it took time to identify, find, and strip the Gift from the relevant people, and some world-altering modifications happened in the meantime. For example, one woman named Auryn Novel possessed such a Gift: all she needed to do was speak something, and it would become a reality. Most Gifts rely on the user's energy, but her Gift relied on the energy from the universe, making her power infinite. Auryn Novel believed strongly in classifications, and before the authorities found her, she spoke her preference into being: that within each territory people would have matching hair colors.

"This is why all peoples from Silenda have black hair, all from Pexus have grey hair"—I point to my own head to demonstrate—"all from Ortus have dark brown hair, all from Sanus have light brown hair, all from Formosus have red hair"—I point to Amelia's red hair—"and all from Captus have blonde hair.

"This condition is permanent. In your world, you could dye your hair any color you wanted—that is not the case in Novus. Dyes are ineffective. Even if I tried to put a wig on, the fibers of the hair would change to grey. There is no concealing it, either. Hats, hoods, and helmets all change to various shades of one's hair color. We can't even shave our heads because the hair immediately grows two millimeters."

I wait again for a question, but none comes, so I move on.

"Sixty years later, another world-evolving technology—this one called the Cupido—was employed in Elusian society. One of the most significant causes of pain and suffering in your world was love—or the lack of love. Suicide, divorce, broken childhoods, anger, murder, adultery, and more were the results of these broken hearts.

"With the Cupido, a procedure that most people call blood-mixing is performed in utero, genetically engineering every baby to be born with a cell-level link to their natural mate. When adolescence proceeds to puberty, their love for each other awakens naturally. Then, once they are eighteen, they get married and start their own families. The Cupido creates a perfectly designed mate for each person in Elusis. It makes sure everyone has love."

I pause here. Not only because Aker fills my mind—along with the knowledge that I am the only person in the entire world who is not loved—but also because I don't remember the next section of the lesson. Usually, the Pods interrupt every sentence or two to ask questions; but Amelia's silence and blank expression have thrown me. She sits in her seat waiting. Commentless. Questionless.

I allow myself a sip from my glass of water while I think, hoping she will ask me something. Anything. When she remains mute, I decide to finish the history lesson.

"In the 375 Quintrall, the Aevii—our highest leaders—decided to awaken the Pods, who by this time had been discovered in warehouses on most of the territories. Over the next three years, our healers created a rehabilitation program to teach the Pods about their history, our society and how to function as a fellow Elusian. We give all Pods new identities when they step into the Elusian community, so that no one can differentiate between a Senexian or a Novian. Only one Pod is known to be just that; his name is Tyge Aetas, and he is your Pod Advocate—we'll learn more about his role and responsibilities next month.

"Before you leave here, we will give you a backstory. And after your training, you will move into a new town and live just like any other Elusian. You, Amelia, are Pod 122086." Locking eyes with her, I end with a slight smile. "Welcome to Elusis."

The Pod stares blankly at me.

"Are you hearing anything I'm saying?" I ask, trying to elicit a response from her. "English is your language of choice, right?"

She doesn't answer, and I sigh before moving on to Lesson Two.

I'm NOT SURE WHERE to go from here. I've flown through the first six lessons, and Amelia has received them well. Too well, really.

In fact, that's the only thing she's good at: sitting and receiving my monologue in silence. When I try to move her from room to room, she only listens when Mathos threatens to move her. When I ask questions, she ignores me. She stares at me with a calm, almost condescending look.

When I leave for the day, I feel dazed. Usually, the Pods have so many questions, so many emotions. Disobedience, disrespect, screaming, escape attempts, violence, swearing, and biting are normal reactions. I've even dealt with catatonic shock. But I'm not used to arrogant, relaxed apathy.

Even my time with Dream Aker is not as enjoyable as it usually is.

When I finally fall asleep that night, my subconscious tells me to find out more about my Pod's past, but Amelia is unwilling when I attempt this the next day. She raises her brows and smiles slightly like, "*Yeah, I'd like to see you try and make me.*"

The following day, I meet with Reest, my boss, to evaluate Amelia's progress.

Unlike everyone else in town, the Humani House Council permits the

Ward staff to talk to me if it is necessary for their work. Reest's job is to know the state of each of the Pods in our Ward, so he meets with all the professors weekly to hear our reports. Reest has never been a talkative man, even before my town-wide shame, so our conversations haven't changed much.

He folds his hands, absently rubbing his thumbs over his palms as he listens to my concise account of everything I've observed about Amelia.

When I've run out of words, he contemplates the ceiling, sucking parts of his lunch out of his teeth.

"Military, maybe," he notes slowly. "They enlisted them very young, the barbarians."

Well, in the end, they had to survive, I want to add—but I don't. I'm used to keeping my thoughts to myself.

"Zin wants us to send all military brats to Yakum," Reest continues.

We received a new batch of Hulls this morning, so I won't have to wait long for a new Pod if I reassign this one. I nod and stand, neither of us saying farewell as I leave the room. Pleasantries are not work-related and are therefore prohibited.

As I walk back to my short-lived human project, I decide to spend the rest of my work day preparing the paperwork for Amelia's transfer.

I enter her room to find Amelia doing push-ups. Definitely military.

"Good afternoon," I say.

She doesn't respond.

"Tomorrow you will be transferred to a Ward on the opposite side of the territory," I briskly continue. "They have specialized training to deal with a Pod of your situation."

She stops mid-push-up but says nothing.

"Your lessons have come to completion, and you will be leaving in the morning." I bow in the customary Pexun farewell. "May your blood keep you strong."

"What situation?" she asks.

I look up, surprised. "So you still talk?"

She stares, and I click my tongue, my mind already on what forms I need to fill out to dispatch this odd Pod.

"You are military, and we cannot help you."

The plank she has been holding wavers, and she drops to her knees. "I am not military. I—I want to get back into shape."

"All of you military Pods were given varying missions to complete when you woke up, and our facility is not equipped for your type of re-training."

She leans back into a seated position. "I'm not military."

I sigh. "I want you to know I honestly respect your loyalty to your people and history."

Her eyes widen. "I'm not lying."

I nod tightly and turn on my heel.

"Wait!" she yelps the word, voice high, before I reach the door. "I... I think I've given you the wrong idea. I didn't know you were evaluating me. I'll tell you about my past if you want. Anything. We could go for a walk around town, and I'll answer every one of your questions."

"You can't leave the facility until you graduate from our program," I correct, amused at her sudden outburst.

"Then we'll go to the lunchroom. Or we don't have to talk if you want. We can work on my graduating quickly. From here."

"That program takes at least nine months."

"What do I have to do to graduate?" she asks.

"Learn Elusian and pass both the Culture and Citizen tests," I answer, crossing my arms.

"Let's get started."

I laugh. It's genuine, and it's drawn out, and it feels incredible. "Let's get started? Where is it that you're off to so fast? And if you're trying to convince me that you're not military, you're not doing a good job."

"Look, I'm a diligent student and a hard worker," she pushes eagerly, almost desperately. "I can get it done. Whatever you want me to do, I can do it here." Amelia stands and takes a step toward me. "Please don't send me away. I... I'm not military. I can... I can do well here."

I feel my eyebrows raise in surprise.

She grabs my hand, and it's like lightning to my skin. "Please, I'll do anything... What's your name again?"

It has been so long since another human being touched me that I'm shocked into accidentally answering her.

"Kansis."

"Kansis," she repeats, releasing my hand, "I'll do anything you tell me to do."

My hand still tingles. Recovering myself, I amend my mistake, "You will call me Professor Willow." Swallowing hard, I force myself to take back control of the moment. "You are military," I prompt.

"No, I'm not."

"I'll help you... " I begin, but pause for effect, "if you are honest with me."

She twitches in place, as though she wishes she could just run away.

"If you tell me once more that you are not military, I *will* send you away," I say firmly.

Her eyes scan the room as if searching for an excuse, but eventually her body relaxes. "Okay," she admits, "I am military."

"It would be better for you to go to Yakum."

"I want to stay here. I... I trust you."

I snort. "No, you don't."

She smiles, and I'm surprised to see it's genuine.

"Yes, I do. You're clever. Witty, even. Okay, so I may not trust you fully yet—but I like you."

She likes me. This military brat likes me. That fact alone fills me with more warmth than I've experienced in years.

Pity and compassion are a sour mix in my dehydrated veins, and all I want to do is keep talking to this subhuman girl. How pathetic I've become!

"All right, you're going to have to tell me some things about your past if you want to stay."

This way, I'll have something to give Reest if this doesn't go well. Which it won't.

"Also," I add, "you'll have to pass a few tests."

"Anything."

I turn to leave the room for a second time.

"Follow me."

16 DAYS UNTIL QUINTRALL

Formosus

Pypen

Iam not angry that this is yet another dead end. I am not cross that I have ruined my favorite pair of trousers and am currently standing in front of three gorgeous, Formosian women who are laughing unabashedly at my exposed manhood. I am not even frustrated that we are now two steps backward from finding Arkarian Story. No, I am upset because all I wanted was a restful afternoon in our spa room, but instead, Scout sent me on this wretched mission.

"Hello, ladies," I greet the three Formosian women politely. I take a few steps closer, and two of them back away warily, almost bumping into a rack of guitars. But the third woman strolls toward me. Her eyes smolder as she puckers her lips.

"Can we help you?" she asks, twirling her red hair seductively around a finger. "It's not often an Ortusan man falls through the ceiling of our music shop—let alone an Ortusan man with pants so torn he might as well not be wearing them."

I quickly close the distance between us, surprised at her brazenness. I would not let a foreign, half-naked man get this close to me, and I *am* a foreign, half-naked man.

"Could I, perchance, purchase your trousers from you?" I ask.

"I should take them off right here, right now—is that it?" Her voice, like all Formosians', almost purrs.

"I have much to offer," I parry and pull out a spare Vorbi that I keep on me for circumstances such as these. Not *trouser-less* circumstances, necessarily, just *unforeseen* circumstances.

The girls all gasp at the Vorbi's deep navy color, which showcases its high value. "My whole wardrobe isn't worth that much, is it?" one gushes.

"You can take all my clothes for that, can't you?" the other exclaims.

"Just your trousers," I say to the one whose perfume smells of jasmine and mint. "Right here, right now, as you said."

The other two giggle as she wiggles out of her vibrantly colored leggings and hands them to me. Taking off my destroyed pants, I shimmy into the stretchy fabric. The young woman is significantly smaller than me, and her pants barely fit, but they will do.

"Very attractive," the now half-clothed Formosian mocks.

"Better than being exposed," I counter and look down at her bare legs.

The woman blushes, snatches the Vorbi out of my hand, and rushes out a back door.

The remaining girls cackle at my appearance, and one of them says, "That's a matter of opinion, isn't it?"

Ignoring her words, I kiss the hands of the two Formosians before leaving the music shop behind. I run to the town's transponder station and board the first available pila. I sit back uncomfortably in my newly procured outfit, aware of the strange looks being cast my way by fellow travelers. Once I have arrived back in my home territory of Ortus, I take another transponder pila to Vultus. The underground, hyper-speed trip goes by quickly, followed by my last ride—a taxi to the circus.

Disembarking at the bottom of the hill, I gaze up at a tall iron gate. Just last week, our circus name, The Unopened Gifts, was welded onto it in oversized letters, and I am not accustomed to it yet. Personally, I enjoyed the ambiguity of the blank gate, but others think branding is essential at this stage of our success.

I quickly walk up the hill and punch the code onto a hidden pad below the giant title. The gate releases a loud creaking sound as it opens, and I smile. I had asked Dommy to implement the Senex sound to add to the intrigue of the circus, and he had made this one so realistic. Quickly, I make the short trek to our tent. If a stranger were to happen upon our property, they would wonder why such a domineering gate is required to guard something so homely. The tent itself is only three and a half meters high by eight meters wide, and its canvas canopy is completely dwarfed by the trees spread around it. An unknowing onlooker would certainly consider the imposing gate excessive.

They would be wrong.

I pull aside the gold-and-black-striped flap of our tent and take a deep breath as I walk inside.

My presence—or rather, my apparel—is met with applause and laughter. I ignore the reaction and walk toward my office with my head held high. Some of the performers rush to greet me with small talk, but I keep the pleasantries short, encouraging them to resume their practicing.

When I open the door to the office I share with Scout, I am surprised to see him sitting at his desk, hungrily eating stew.

"I know you are upset, Pypen," he starts, "but I really needed someone to go—". As he takes in my appearance, he abruptly stops speaking. Slowly, he swallows his food, unable to stop staring at my bottom half. "Pypen, what are you wearing?"

I raise my brows, feigning ignorance. "I know not of what you speak."

"You are wearing glittering snakeskin leggings." His lips twitch in a smile. "Why?"

"I lost my trousers."

"How did that come to occur?"

"The story is amusing, but to be believed." I shut the door behind me and launch into my narrative. "After I confirmed the Pod in the Formosian Ward was not Arkarian Story's daughter, I tried to escape undetected. But as I descended out of the window my belt loop became stuck in the frame surrounding the glass pane. I could hear someone approaching, so I pulled as hard as possible, and my trousers ripped right across the crotch. I fell to the music shop below and crashed through their roof. Long story short, I am in glittering snakeskin trousers because, instead of letting me have a day off, you sent me on a job."

A knock sounds at the door, and Scout's amused smile broadens. "I do hope you will continue to wear those dashing trousers all day." He sets his bowl down with a final chuckle and shouts toward the door, "You are welcome within!"

Emerly Tosh saunters into the room and flops on my chair as if it belongs to him. He brushes his chin-length Formosian red hair back from his face, stating, "I hate University days, I do. Being back on campus doesn't resurrect good memories if you know what I mean." His honey-brown eyes sparkle as he monologues about the youth of this day. Every few sentences, he quietly snaps his fingers. I have often reminded him that a healer could fix this irritating flaw, but my annoyance brings him a plethora of joy, so he has not had the tic removed.

Emerly is technically our assistant, yet he does so much more than simply assist us. One of his most prominent roles is that of our talent scout, and every person he has found to join our group has been invaluable. His mind-reading Gift is mighty. For the past three and a half months, he has been searching for someone to fill the role of Caedis, the female star in our upcoming show.

"Taking his time if you ask me," I mutter to myself.

"Pypen, you are mumbling," Scout snaps, frowning. He hates this habit of mine.

"Were you fortunate in your quest?" I ask Emerly for the hundredth time, wondering if he will ever tell us he has found an actress to play the part of Caedis.

Emerly shrugs nonchalantly. "Indeed."

Scout bolts up out of his chair as he and I synchronously repeat, albeit with a bit more excitement than Emerly, "Indeed?"

"Who is it?" I ask enthusiastically.

"I believe you've already met her, haven't you? The name you've been searching for, dreaming about, drooling over, losing sleep due to—"

"Spit it out, man!" I yell, laughing at his long-windedness.

"'Tis the one and only Merayal Kapu."

My excitement plummets. "Merayal Kapu?" I ask slowly. "The angry daughter of the Pexun we killed a day ago?"

"We did *not* kill Xoana Kapu," Scout says firmly.

"Emerly, to this day I have never once doubted your judgement, but I must question you now. Merayal cannot be our star."

"Whyever not?" Emerly asks.

Scout chuckles. "Pypen is merely upset that Merayal bit him when she was in mouse form."

"No," I respond calmly, "To say I was unimpressed would be quite the understatement."

"Pypen, we met the girl shortly after her mother had died in our care. Would you have acted differently?"

"No." I want to add more to this statement, but I cannot think of anything else to say, so I simply say it again. "No." Another thought enters my mind and I continue. "Caedis is a delicate role to play, and that young woman does not suit." I have put much thought into the type of woman we would need to fill the role of my co-star, and Merayal Kapu is the antonym of it.

"You do not know her," Scout returns. "You cannot dislike her after only meeting her under last day's circumstances."

"Pypen dislikes anyone who is not you, my dear Scout," Emerly interjects easily.

"Now, now," Scout says, bothered by this comment. "That is a blatant disregard of the truth. Pypen is quite fond of all of our people."

My life-long friend enjoys the belief that I care just as deeply for those in the circus as he does. It is not that I do *not* care about them; 'tis merely that he and I have different roles to play. He is the caretaker of their blood, and I am the caretaker of his.

"He doesn't even like *me*, does he?" Emerly teases and winks in my direction.

"I despise you," I reply as sardonically as possible.

Scout shakes his head. "I know not why you fabricate such stories, Pypen. I know of your regard for the circus members."

"I find all of them to be foul creatures."

Emerly squints his eyes as he does right before he tries to trap a person in their own words. "Answer me honestly, won't you, Pypen? Are you not loyal to us chiefly and exclusively because you are foremost loyal to Scout, who is loyal to us?"

I smile but refrain from replying immediately. Scout does not look at me, but I know he hopes I deny it. Patronizingly, I answer, "I have come to care deeply for our people. So I am certain I will also adore Merayal Kapu."

As if remembering the subject at hand, Emerly says, "Merayal is special, isn't she? I could feel it. She's going to be perfect for the job—she is."

"Of course, I speak in jest," I explain, realizing he had not heard my sarcasm this time. "I do not wish to hire Merayal Kapu. She does not seem like the type of person to be in the entertainment business."

"I don't know what to tell you, do I?" Emerly responds. "She's the one."

"We have settled it then," Scout says.

"Am I not entitled to say anything on the matter?" I ask.

"Not if your say is wrong," Emerly replies with a smirk.

"Scout?" I ask.

"I think we should talk with her before we make any decisions," he responds diplomatically. "Emerly, go and speak with her now. Offer the interview and share our compensation plan, and have her meet with us later this day."

After Emerly leaves, Scout turns to me, his green eyes bright with anticipation. "Promise me you will give her a chance, Pypen."

"Of course, Scout," I retort. On the one hand, I would refuse him nothing. The other hand however is petty and immature, so I salute him with a rude gesture and add, "I will give her three minutes."

THE EVENING SHADOWS HAVE fallen when Scout and I seat ourselves at our desks again. Scout offers Merayal our spare chair. "Greet the moon, Merayal," he says as she sits down. "I do apologize once more for your loss. If you need more time—"

"You have a job for me?" she interrupts.

Scout smiles patiently. "If you would not mind, we would love for you to share a little bit about yourself with us before we talk about the position."

Her eyes narrow suspiciously. "What do you want to know?" I had not noticed before, but her Pexun accent sounds slightly odd; perhaps she is from one of the surrounding islands.

"Basic information," Scout answers gently. "You had a career before today. What was it? What are your interests? Emerly said you were perfect for this position; I would like to hear about your background."

Rolling her eyes at him, Merayal replies in clipped tones, "I don't see how any of that is relevant."

"Can we cease the faux interview now?" I ask, not even trying to conceal my impatience. "She is not suited to the role."

"And why is that so obvious?" she asks, turning her sharp gaze toward me.

I gesture to her entire being rigidly seated in our chair as if her unpleasantness keeps her so upright. "Need I say more?"

"Forgive my comrade," Scout says, looking at me with reprimand.

I nod, submitting to his judgement. I will keep my thoughts to myself for now.

Scout turns back to Merayal and asks, "Are you in the entertainment business currently?"

"No."

"Have you ever wanted to pursue a career as a performer?" he asks.

"I guess I've always just been good at it," she snaps.

Why has Scout not dismissed her yet?

I chance a glance at him as he studies her with a blank expression. After a pause, he inquires, "What makes you want to perform? You do not seem to be... enthusiastic about the position itself."

At this, her determined eyes meet his and she stands to her full height. Throwing her shoulders back, she declares, "I can do it if that's what you're asking."

Scout suppresses a smile at her clear need to prove her competence. "Sit back down. That is *not* what I am asking. I am trying to understand why you are willing to apply for this position. We did not force you to come."

Merayal obeys, but her body stays in a taut, ready-to-fight position as she replies. "The compensation is too good to pass up."

This gives Scout pause. Perhaps he is finally seeing what I have known from the moment we met her. Scout leans forward on his chair as he says, "Emerly, our assistant, was truly convinced of your talents. However, being able to wield one's Gift especially well and perform in front of thousands of people requires more than mere skill."

Her eyes flash. "Just because I don't have the vain demeanor of an actor doesn't mean I can't perform."

"Vain demeanor?" I repeat, immediately jumping to offense at the slight.

As Scout considers her, she holds his gaze unabashed. Finally, he says, "These *vain* performers would be your co-workers. Of course, you could choose to join us as an Arkahunter and never interact with one of them. But if you become a part of our traveling circus group, you will be living with them, eating with them, existing with them."

"Yes," Merayal answers without hesitation. "I know I'm standoffish; I don't deny that. But I'm an incredible actress. Be as disappointed as you want with my personality—I can guarantee you will not be disappointed with my performance." She holds her head high and pushes her shoulders back ever so slightly as she awaits his decision.

As Scout stares at her, I wonder—with hope—if he is trying to find the best words to ask her to leave and have an enjoyable life doing something else. But, after a few minutes, he says, "I am intrigued by you, Merayal Kapu."

Surprised, I mutter under my breath, "Surely only intrigued by her deficit."

Ignoring me, Scout asks her, "Do you know how much compensation the Aevii will grant to the one who finds Arkarian Story?"

"No." Merayal's chin juts upward as she adds, "But I know hunting for his Hull is illegal."

"Yes," Scout smiles, excitement dancing in his eyes. "Do you know why?"

"No." It seems to physically pain her to admit ignorance.

"The Book of Instructions says that Arkarian Story's goal is to be the supreme ruler of Elusis. He desires to take over our world and allow evil to run rampant as it had in his day. Some are petrified that if Arkarian Story were to be found, he could be awakened improperly, without the well-designed structure of the Pod Wards, and perhaps even escape to accomplish said goal."

"So why allow a reward for finding him?" she asks.

"An oversight we happily extort. Our benefactor, Flister Dubach—"

"Flister Dubach!" Merayal interrupts. "The Aevum?" She scoffs. "There's no way you guys work for the Aevii."

"And yet, we do," Scout says patiently.

Her brows crease, "Why would he support Arkahunters?"

"Flister Dubach founded the Unopened Gifts as a cover for his research. Like all the Aevii, he desires to see perpetual peace throughout the generations of the metahuman. The wrong person awakening Arkarian Story is a predicament in which the world cannot find itself. Therefore, to ensure Arkarian Story's Podded body remained in the right hands, the Aevii offered a reward to any person who might happen upon his location. If we were to *accidentally* find Arkarian Story, the ransom—a 115-Cheio prize—would be dealt equally amongst the members of our group."

Silence fills our office. Merayal remains staring at the art adorning the walls, unresponsive. After a minute, Scout says, "We were protecting your mother because she claimed to have evidence proving that the Book of Instructions had been tampered with and the Arkarian Story taught in our history books is false. Do you have any more information about her work?"

She licks her lips. "No."

"Thank you for your time, Merayal," Scout states, standing. He walks over to the QuickEntrance door at the far end of our office, where Merayal had entered for our meeting. In each capital throughout the Hexum, we have one QuickEntrance door in a local pub. Before we thought to implement this, our meetings would last hours as our visitors would invariably want a tour of the entire circus on their way in or out.

As he opens the door for her, loud off-beat singing from the Pexun pub, Outsider's Host, wafts into our office. Scout nods to Merayal. "Pypen and I will call you later this evening to let you know our decision."

Merayal's brows raise mockingly. "You offer me a job and then take it back?"

"We offered to interview you for a position. We will let you know our decision. Greet the shine."

Face indecipherable, Merayal stands and exits our office into downtown Demirkan.

"That was a mess," I observe as the door closes behind her.

"I think I like her, though," Scout comments.

"You like her?" I snort derisively. "Scout, we have had over one hundred women interview for this part—you know how coveted any role in our circus is within the industry. Why give it to someone completely undeserving of it and without proven performance skills? We know not if she can sing, dance, or perform. We only have her word—"

"And Emerly's approval."

"It matters not—"

"He has never been wrong before. Not about anyone."

Clicking my tongue, I take a deep breath. "I know you were intrigued by her, but adding her to the team is too risky."

Scout's hands drum quietly on his wooden desk. "There is something about her…"

"How can we offer her the job if we do not know her capabilities?"

"I trust Emerly," he reiterates. "Plus, she guaranteed we would not be disappointed."

"She could be the most talented person in the world, but if she is not going to connect with the audience or the team, then she is not worth having." Her holograph portfolio hovers in front of me, and it is woefully bare. It merely states that her hometown is Chutley, Pexus, her Progift is Handle GP9, Blue-A, she is thirty years old, and she had an apprenticeship at Junior Internship with Fulfill Your Potential Agency. The only jobs she has ever had were that of a student and entertainer (a title so vague, it does nothing to share her experience). Her worship status is Silver 1, and she has no achievements. There is no holographic footage of any work she has done—let alone any claims to any shows or performances; she has no references and no evidence of any kind to prove she is worth our time or energy.

Merayal's translucent, expressionless face stares back at me. "She is not a gamble I am willing to make."

"Very valid," Scout says and rubs his neck. "But while we have been offering our own interviews, Emerly has been searching for our Caedis for months—and he found her in Merayal. If we do not accept her, it will take quite some time and work to find someone else with her Gift."

"Work," I muse, "that will not be worth it in the end." I sigh, knowing I will be forced to concede to his way of thinking. Before he completely dismisses my unease, I add as a compromise, "Perhaps we can do a trial period? Let her practice with us for a fortnight, and we can make an informed decision after observing her interactions?"

When he does not respond immediately, I open my mouth to speak, then close it quickly. Scout hates it when I overstate my argument. *If you have said it once, you have made your point*, he has told me many times. Forcing myself to be patient, I wait for him to think the matter over in silence.

Finally, he answers, "I am inclined towards the trial period. Two weeks should be sufficient to appease your dislike."

"'Tis not the truth of the matter, but a brilliant decision nonetheless."

His eyes meet mine. "If we make this work… if Merayal were to join… the Unopened Gifts could become a show worthy of even the Quintrall. We could be famous."

My thoughts linger on his words. "Fame. Fortune," I whisper. That these words could ever be part of my reality is something I never dared even to dream. Seeking to ground myself, I walk over to our office fridge and peer into its empty depths. *We need food.*

"Will you make me a sandwich?" Scout asks, staring again at Merayal's lackluster portfolio.

"Considering we have no bread, meat, vegetables, and condiments, regretfully I would have to decline." I rub my growing beard with the back of my fingers.

"What about leftovers from last night?" he asks.

"You ate them for breakfast. I will never understand how your short-term memory so fails you."

Smirking, he does not look at me. "I will never understand why you do not get groceries on grocery day."

I throw my hands up in the air. "Why is it always up to me?"

"Pypen, I do wish there was a more organized way to ensure we take turns getting groceries." Again, he smiles without eye contact. He waits to see if I will take the bait.

"After Ryder broke our simulan," I say slowly, unable to help myself, "I did make up a schedule for us to go by—"

"A chore chart," he interrupts.

"A *schedule* that would keep us on track. And you refuse to use it. I would say the blame is yours to bear."

Although his face becomes serious, his lips still twitch with a patient smile. "Pypen, you put a smiley sticker on my desk when I did the dishes. How can I take anything you do seriously if you use stickers as a form of positive reinforcement?"

"Who does not like stickers?"

"Grown men. Grown men do not like stickers, Pypen." Shaking his head, he cracks his knuckles.

He is goading me to react once more. A need to yell and defend myself rises in my chest, but instead of letting it loose, I force myself into calm. I lie down on our office floor and place my hands behind my head.

"The work we must accomplish this night is nigh insurmountable," I moan, changing the subject.

"Indeed, indeed. I can nearly hear a knock at the door. 'Oh, hello? Procrastination? Welcome in! Would you like some rennix, perhaps?'" Scout is still in a teasing mood.

"It is preposterous that we have delayed the work until the last minute yet again." I continue as if he hasn't spoken. "As young men, yes, this was acceptable, but we have debunked our theories that maturity holds hands with age. I do believe it was back when Nova joined the company that we proclaimed we would never do this again."

Laughing, Scout raises one of his eyebrows. "We doubtless declared such lies. But do we not perform more advantageously under such deadlines?" He asks the question like a commander inspiring his warriors. "Do we not thrive in the haze of dilly-dallying?"

From the floor, I place my hand over my heart. "Hear, hear."

Scout leaps up and onto an empty chair. Standing tall, he thrusts out his chin and proclaims theatrically, "Do we not find complete triumph in the last minute? Ladies and gentlemen," he announces to his imaginary audience, "witness history in the making as the intellectual delights, Scout Eekan and Pypen Tross, complete three months' work in one night!"

"Shout it from the rooftops," I reply unenthusiastically. Dragging myself back to my desk, I scratch my wrist—a nervous habit. Through the thin layer of my skin, I can feel the Suus implantation. *Open a document*, I command the device with my thoughts. A transparent screen appears in front of me. A translucent pen, keyboard, and microphone are hovering in front of the screen.

Dictation, I think, mentally selecting the microphone. The pen and keyboard disappear as the cursor blinks at the top of an empty page. "We better start working," I say aloud and rub my hands together. Once more, I ponder the holographic portfolio shimmering before me and gaze at the name of our newest—temporary—member: Merayal Kapu.

Closing my eyes, I start dictating the first part of Act One. The cursor slides across the document quickly as my words appear on the screen. I can hear Scout collecting our storyboarding material. We have already worked out the whole show; it is just that we have not made the time to write it down.

I look at the clock; it is almost five in the evening. Scout will be taking his daily nap in an hour. From the time we began working for the Sixth Aevum, Scout has taken an evening nap at six sharp. He does not miss a day. I have never entirely understood why he needs to rest at this inconvenient time of night—and every night—but it is his way. And although I will continue to work while he naps, and although he will rejoin me as soon as his nap is complete, it will still take us all evening and probably all of the next morning to finish our work. But it must be perfect.

I want it to play out precisely as Scout envisions it.

Silenda

Flister

99 years ago

THE SIXTH AEVUM STARES out his window, each breath causing more condensation to grow on the glass. His eyes are not taking in the towering snow-capped mountains in the distance, the meadow carpeted with yellow wildflowers, the lake embellished with lily pads and frogs, or the faded red deck extending from the meadow out over the water. He barely notices the rain lightly falling or the ravens sheltered by the roof as they perch on the deck railing.

His eyes roam the scenery surrounding the Artemis Abbey, but his mind ignores it all, fixating instead on one thought: *She promised she would visit this day. She promised. She said she would come. She said...*

"Lord Flister!" Keli Gridd, his tutor, shouts his name, making the Sixth Aevum jump. "Come now! We must resume your lessons."

Flister Dubach ignores his tutor, continuing to gaze expectantly into the distance.

He can hear his tutor shouting his name repeatedly, her voice echoing throughout the large house, but it is not until a simulan finds him and reports his location to her that Keli Gridd, a short woman with long, black curls, comes barreling into the front sitting room.

"Lord Flister. What on Elusis are you doing in here? Have you not heard Keli Gridd calling you?"

"I heard you."

The Silentar's manner of speaking in the third person has always agitated him, and he does not even try to conceal his annoyance.

Flister need not look at her to know that Keli Gridd is turning red. He has seen the expression so often that it plays out in his mind's eye as if he is watching her.

"When Keli Gridd calls you," the tutor growls, shaking with the ever-constant rage she seems to live with, "you *will* answer. You *will* come."

Flister knows he could make his tutor's life so much easier by being obedient. But why make it easier for her? She didn't do anything to deserve a life of peace and tranquility.

"I need not, Gridd."

"That's *Keli* Gridd to you, Lord Flister," she bites angrily. Flister had made a habit of omitting the respectful terms of *Keli* and *Kel* when talking to his tutors. Oh, how it irked Gridd in particular. "You will address me with honor," Keli Gridd goes on. Frazzled and at the end of her patience, she finishes, "Come now, or Keli Gridd will call Kel Soxis to come home. You do not want that, do you?"

Flister takes a breath, considering his options. Even though Kel Soxis has a Blue Gift and his energy is channeled primarily from his own being, the man is almost two hundred years old and has spent most of his days strengthening his Gift's endurance. With a blink of his eyes, he could send Flister's body up the stairs and keep him locked in his room for the rest of the day. This is not an outcome Flister wishes to transpire. If it were not that the Fifth Aevum was to come and see him this day, he would practice the new derogatory name that he had learned recently.

But she *is* coming this day.

Sighing, Flister turns to his tutor and says, "I will go to my lesson, *Keli* Gridd."

"Good, good," his tutor responds, clearly relieved he will not fight her again.

The doorbell rings as they walk down the hallway toward the schoolroom.

Flister shouts excitedly and races back down the onyx hallway towards the front door.

"Aevii don't run!" Keli Gridd shouts angrily after him. "Let the simulans open the door!"

Paying his tutor no heed, the Sixth Aevum flings the door wide. Standing there, as he had hoped, is the Fifth Aevum. As always, she has manipulated her body to look his age, just shy of ten years old. The two children embrace.

"Kenny!" Flister smiles. "You came!"

Oaken Bleu's shiny grey hair is cut short to her chin, and she wears a simple black and red plaid dress. Everything about the Fifth Aevum is sweet, petite, and lovable. Her heart-shaped face turns up as she says, "I said I would."

Keli Gridd approaches and bows to the floor. She recites, "Hallowed be your name, Fifth Aevum. May our praises warm your blood and heart as you know our loyalty is stronger than life itself."

"Thank you, Gridd," the Fifth Aevum replies, her voice that of a child's.

"What brings you here?" Keli Gridd asks, adding softly to herself, "*Again*?"

Before the Fifth Aevum can answer, Flister wipes the coin-shaped tattoo off his hand and places it on her wrist. Oaken winces at the bee-sting-like pain of the transfer. In her ear, so only Oaken can hear, Flister whispers, "I dare you to respond to Gridd like you are a chicken."

The Fifth Aevum stares down at her wrist and a smile forms on her pink lips. Unabashed, she looks up at Keli Gridd and, placing her hands in her armpits like she has wings, Oaken clucks.

Offended, the tutor responds, "I'm sorry, Keli Gridd doesn't understand what you are doing…"

Jutting out her chin, Oaken continues to cluck as she walks in a circle on the wet deck.

Flustered and annoyed, Keli Gridd says, "Lord Flister has his lessons to finish. It would be preferable that he get back to them within the hour."

Although Oaken makes more chicken sounds, she nods at the tutor.

Keli Gridd curtsies quickly and then walks away, muttering to herself. Once the front door shuts, the two children burst out laughing.

"That was a good one," Oaken grins once they calm down. She rubs her wrist where Flister had placed the tattoo. "I'll be sure to get you back."

"What did Mal say?" Flister asks eagerly. "Can I come?"

Ignoring the question, Oaken wipes the tattoo off her wrist and slaps it on Flister's cheek. He flinches at the prick, sharp like a knife cut.

"I dare you to jump into the water," she sings.

Flister moans, "*Matza*, Kenny! It is so cold!"

The Fifth Aevum smiles mischievously. "You could give up."

Gathering his grit, Flister takes off his sweater, shirt, pants, and socks. The Sixth Aevum runs across the rocky beach, jumps over the mossy bank, and throws himself into the frigid water.

The plunge takes his breath away. The cold feels like needles piercing every pore of his body. His limbs are shaking before he even reaches the surface. They tremble so violently he can barely swim back to the bank. When he reaches it, Oaken helps him up out of the water.

She giggles as she wraps a towel around his body.

Flister struggles to catch his breath. He can see Oaken rubbing his body with the fabric, but he cannot feel it. Finally, once his heart rate returns to normal, he asks, "Y-y-you knew y-you w-were g-going to d-d-dare me to j-jump in?" he asks, laughing that she had come prepared with the towel.

"Of course. I've had it planned since last week," Oaken answers sweetly.

As Flister waits for warmth to return to his limbs, they sit in companionable silence, staring out as a thick fog begins to descend upon the mountains like a cat lazily spreading itself over an armchair.

Suddenly, as if she was picking up a conversation previously left off, Oaken says, "I wonder what it would be like, though."

"W-What?"

Offhandedly, casually, Oaken says, "I wonder what it would be like to drown."

"You would p-probably just p-p-pass out."

"I know that we Aevii can't die, but sometimes I wonder how they know that. Obviously, Dakarai tried to kill himself a million times, and the Medisacerdos tried to kill Mal before they found out what she was... but the rest of us haven't tried."

"You do not kn-now about Qualcum. H-He may h-have tried." Flister wishes he would. The Third Aevum turns his blood to ice.

As for himself, Flister would not want to risk experimenting with death even though he is certain he would not die. But Oaken makes an excellent point...

Taking the tattoo off his cheek, he places it on Oaken's exposed neck. "I dare you."

Oaken's face whips in his direction. "Dare me to what?"

"Drown yourself."

Oaken's expression is a mix of anger and shocked amusement.

"You c-could give up," he mimics her.

When Oaken stands, Flister does as well. Although his body still hurts from the cold, a thrill rushes through him at the thought of her doing something so dangerous. Yet at the same time, fear floods his veins. What if they have been told a falsehood? What if the Aevii can die?

But instead of stopping her, Flister follows her to the bank's edge.

Oaken looks at him sideways. "You know I'm going to get you back for this. You sure you don't want to take the dare back?"

Buzzing with apprehension and excitement, Flister can only shake his head.

Resolutely, Oaken faces the lake. She takes a deep, steadying breath and jumps into the water. The splash hits Flister's legs. Those few droplets that land on him seem to burn his skin.

The lily pads slide over where Oaken has entered the lake, but he stares at the water wide-eyed, hearing only the sound of his rapidly pumping heart.

He counts to one hundred, but the water does not even ripple. Suddenly,

Oaken's back plops to the surface. She is not moving. "Kenny!" he shouts. "Kenny! Oaken! Oaken Bleu!" He screams the name repeatedly, louder and louder, becoming more frantic with each repetition of her name.

He tries to use his Gift to create anything that could help, but he cannot think past his terror.

"What in the *ahatea* is going on?" Keli Gridd shouts from within the house's entrance hall.

Whirling around, Flister points to the lake and cries, "Help! Help us! Oaken is drowning!"

Without hesitation, Keli Gridd rushes forward and focuses on the lake. She uses her Gift of Matter Manipulation to draw Oaken's limp body up out of the water. Liquid forms beneath Oaken's body like a stretcher, and Keli Gridd wills the water to bring the Aevum to the safety of the bank.

"*Utka ahatea,* what were you two doing?" Keli Gridd bellows as she puts her ear to Oaken's chest. Using her Gift, the tutor draws the water out of Oaken's lungs.

The Fifth Aevum jolts upright, coughing and choking. Employing her own Gift, Oaken calms her body, causing her shivering and shaking to cease. Serene once more, she commands, "Gridd, get us some more towels."

"But—"

"*Now,*" Oaken shouts, eyes suddenly blazing, the word like the rumbling of thunder. Because she constantly manipulates herself to look his age, Flister sometimes forgets that Oaken is one hundred years older than him. It is in moments like these that he is forced to remember.

Keli Gridd flinches, then bows and dashes back to the house.

Only once the tutor is gone does Oaken look at Flister and smile. "You're so going to regret that." Water drips down her porcelain skin, and despite everything that has occurred and the gloom of the day, she seems to sparkle.

Flister sighs in relief, not only because she is safe and well, but also because she is not upset with him. "I am brave enough to do whatever you dare."

"We'll see."

"Now," Flister begins expectantly, "you never answered me. Did Mal say that I can come?"

Oaken's expression falls somewhat, but she answers, "She said you could come to the retreat but you must return to Artemis Abbey on Friday night. The rest of us have to talk about Aevii stuff once you've left."

"But that means I can only be with her for two days."

Oaken's brows raise, her mouth forming an angry line. "I know how I could make you lose our game," she snaps.

Flister laughs. "I told you; I will not give up. There is no dare you can give me that I would not do."

Keli Gridd emerges from the house. Without a word, she drops the towels on the beach. The Aevii each pick one up and continue to dry themselves, completely ignoring Gridd as she returns to the house.

"What if I dared you not to talk to Mal all weekend?" Oaken asks, eyes hard.

Flister's expression turns from light-hearted to cross. "You would not do that."

"I could. And if I did, you would lose."

"Do it. Do it and find out, Kenny. And then I will pay you back accordingly."

"Do you dare me?" she asks bitingly.

"It is your turn," Flister responds with a sardonic laugh. "But if you dare me not to talk to Mal, I will show you how miserable I can make you."

The Fifth Aevum turns away from Flister and looks out to the meadow and the looming mountains.

Guilt seeps into Flister's veins. He had not intended to be so harsh. Of all the Aevii, Oaken is the only one who comes and visits him regularly. Since he was very young, the two of them have played games together, but it was not until two years ago that Flister hired a Skin Manipulator to make the transferrable tattoo. It was intended to be a joke gift for Oaken on Discovery Day, but she had loved the idea and put it on immediately. Their dare game had been going on ever since.

Moving to stand next to the Fifth Aevum, Flisters says quietly, "I am sorry, Kenny."

Instead of answering him, Oaken slowly wipes the tattoo off of her wrist. It rests on her fingertips like a sticker. The circle has lines around it like a sun; a smiling skull is at its center. She stares at it for a moment and then places it on Flister's arm.

"I dare you to tell me who you love most."

Flister's blood slows. He knows how he should answer: Oaken Bleu. She is his best friend, the only Aevum who pursued him, the only one who tried to make him laugh. And she is, after all, the one who started this exhilarating game.

But there were consequences to breaking or deceiving a dare. Dire, gruesome consequences. That is what made the game so thrilling. So he could not say *Oaken Bleu* because it was a lie. No matter how much Oaken did for him or with him, there was another who held all of his love within her veins.

Unable to break the dare, Flister swallows loudly and whispers, "Mal."

The name descends between them like an invisible wall. At first, Oaken stands in silence as if he has dared her to become a statue. But after a few moments, she nods. Turning away from him, she grows to her adult size. Her hair grows and stops at her collarbone, and her plaid dress turns into a pantsuit. Bowing down, she kisses Flister on top of his head and strides towards the driveway.

"Wait!" Flister shouts. "Wait, Kenny, stay, please!"

When she does not turn around, Flister runs after her, wanting to slap the tattoo on the back of her neck. But as he jumps to do so, the Fifth Aevum dodges his hand.

Flister tumbles, and as he hits the ground he sees a tall, slim Silentar man standing at the end of the driveway. Flister scrambles up, determined to get the tattoo onto Oaken before she leaves, bent on daring her to stay, but Oaken breaks into a run and reaches her Silentar servant before Flister can reach her.

She does not look back as she reaches for the man's hand. In the space of a heartbeat, the Fifth Aevum disappears.

Oaken Bleu does not come back, and Flister does not see her again until the Aevii retreat a month later.

Filled with a rage that has grown each day she did not return, Flister holds the tattoo on his fingertips as he greets the other Aevii. Mal kisses both of his cheeks and welcomes him to the retreat. Dakarai pinches his nose but barely looks him in the eye. Thankfully, Qualcum snorts at him and does nothing more. Marvella hugs him sweetly, patting him on the head as if he were far younger than almost-ten. When Oaken, in adult form, leans down to kiss him, Flister surreptitiously places the tattoo on her elbow.

"I dare you to vomit all over yourself at dinner," he whispers in her ear.

Oaken stands, blinking repeatedly.

Two hours later, the Aevii are seated around Mal's dinner table. Halfway through the meal, the Fifth Aevum stands and violently throws up all over the table. Marvella Pinyin, who is sitting opposite her, is covered in it. Then, true to the dare, the second wave of puke lands all over Oaken herself.

Flister is so shocked he laughs aloud then covers his mouth, hoping Mal has not heard him. Dakarai and Mal stand, disgusted, and Marvella screams at the top of her lungs.

"Oaken, you disgusting personification of vulgarity!" Marvella shrieks as she rubs chunks of food off her face and chest.

With a reproving tone, Mal commands, "Girls, go wash and change right now."

As she turns to leave, vomit dripping from her chin, Oaken winks at Flister and mouths, *missed you.*

Shuddering, Flister Dubach forces himself to swallow the food that Happenstance, the Third Aevum's assistant, has brought him. It is disgusting, but Flister has not eaten all day and is feeling faint.

As he is merely a month away from turning thirteen, it is his responsibility to begin thinking about his Venture. At twenty-five, he will have his Helduen Ceremony—a coming-of-age celebration where he will come into all of his Aevum powers. It is at this ceremony that he will have to share what his Venture will be. To educate him and help him choose his own Venture—how he will serve the Elusian people during his eternity—Mal Fey, the First Aevum, has mandated that he spend one day in each of the Ventures of the other Aevii.

Thus far, he has spent a day with the First Aevum and the Medisacerdos— the blood scientists—watching their experiments. Although Mal's attention was endearing, her passion contagious, and her wit enjoyable, it was not to be his Venture. He wished it interested him, because the thought of spending every day with Mal was all he could want. It pained him that science held none of his interest. It was exclusively due to his affection for her that Flister had put on a show of interest in Mal's Venture.

He has also spent a day with the Second Aevum, Dakarai Ebelson, in his Exploratorium. The flamboyant Aevum always wears glasses for fashion's sake, changing the shape and color of the lenses every five years. The current iteration has honey-brown lenses in octagonal frames. In addition to the eyewear, Dakarai always dons his famous *dofleini* beak necklace—a token from his youth when he *allegedly* fought and defeated the Great Man-Eating Octopus of the Dragon Ocean. For many years, Dakarai has been collecting Elusis' wonders and putting them on display in his exhibition. It is interesting enough, but it is not what Flister Dubach envisions spending the rest of his eternity doing.

This day, Flister is spending a bone-chilling twelve hours in the presence of the Third Aevum, Qualcum Elder—sickly, shrewd, and clever Elder. The Sanusian man had turned Flister's blood cold when they first met and the boy was only five. And Elder had no idea—at least that Flister knew of—the prejudice it had placed upon a young mind. Since then, Flister has passionately hated every Sanusian with whom he interacts.

Qualcum Elder's Venture is the study of the past. The Aevum spends his decades studying history and reading ancient books. Today, on Flister's designated day to learn from him, Qualcum had merely sat Flister in a chair with a book and ignored him the whole morning. When Flister had tried to use his Gift to create something—anything—to do, Qualcum had harshly forbidden it. Not until Happenstance summoned him to lunch had he been permitted to get up from the chair.

Qualcum shuffles into the dining room as Flister is forcing down his last nauseating mouthful of watery soup. With a loud groan, the Aevum descends into his seat. Disgusted with the man, Flister looks out towards the door, longing to run through it and leave.

Qualcum begins eating his soup with loud slurps, and when Flister steals a glance at him, he can see that vegetables and noodles have fallen down into his scraggly beard.

Flister grimaces just as Qualcum's hawk-like eyes turn on him. Quickly, Flister puts away the scowl.

"How are ye enjoyin' yer day?" Qualcum asks.

"Fine," Flister answers.

"Ye like me books?"

"No."

"Ye like t'at chair ye sittin' in? It's me favorite."

"It is fine."

Qualcum sniffs loudly before taking another mouthful of soup. Wiping the remnants off his chin, he asks, "Are ye scared?"

A jolt of adrenaline shoots through Flister's veins. "Scared? Scared of what?"

"Of ta prophecy."

"What prophecy?"

"Ta one on yer back, of course."

Unconsciously, Flister's right hand reaches up over his shoulder to touch his upper back. For years he had not even known the prophecy was there. His tutors had washed him, and he had never seen a full-length mirror. It was not until he was eight and fell off his skyboard and checked himself in the mirror for injury, that he had found the blood-red words inscribed along his spine. Because of the awkward angle and scrawny writing, he could not decipher what it said.

He had demanded his tutors to read it to him and tell him what it meant, but they had refused. Mal had come by the next day, and although she had read it out to him, she did not explain it. She told him she would in time, at his Helduen ceremony. But that was not due until he was twenty-five.

Oaken was the only person he had told about it. She had said she would look into it, but the next day she returned and told him that Mal had forbidden her from asking about it.

When Flister realizes he is staring open-mouthed at the Third Aevum, he shuts his jaw, swallows, and then asks, "You know what it means?"

"Of course."

"What—what does it mean?"

Qualcum slurps at his soup again before answering. "It means yer at risk."

"At risk? How?"

"Yer not safe."

"Safe from whom? Does Mal know?"

Qualcum smiles, and Flister sees his yellow teeth have strands of spinach stuck in them. "Naturally."

"Are you going to tell me what it means?" Flister snaps.

"Oi'm not," Qualcum answers, pushing back his chair. "Oi just wanted ter know if ye were afraid." As he passes Flister's chair, he adds, "Because ye should be, me boy. Ye should be."

Oaken's giggles chase the Sixth Aevum down the hallway. They rush into the small meeting room where Mal has told the two of them to meet her.

"Did you see their faces?" Oaken squeals. She has manipulated her body to look fourteen years old—the same age as Flister. "They never saw it coming!"

Flister laughs freely with his friend. "It will be a night they never forget!" Quickly, he creates two handkerchiefs. After handing one to Oaken, he uses the other to wipe the sweat off his face and neck.

The two continue to laugh uncontrollably, but suddenly Flister's merriment mixes with anxiety. He had asked Oaken not to dare him while Mal is around because it upset her so much. But she had—and it had been a big dare... a messy dare.

"She is going to be so mad..." Flister says, and the remnants of his high spirits extinguish like a blown-out candle.

Oaken comes and stands next to him. "We're creating memories, Flisty. It's fine."

"I do not think Mal wants everyone else to keep this memory."

Just then, they hear the sound of the First Aevum's heels clicking angrily down the corridor. Flister quickly looks at Oaken, who gives him a dramatically scared face before quietly giggling. He has yet to see Mal upset with him, and prior to this day he had every intention never to do so. But Oaken had dared him to toss the cake at the Chancellor's head, and he could not say no…

Mal Fey opens the door to the small, dark meeting room and quietly shuts it behind her. It is clear from her demeanor how displeased she is.

"I am so sorry, Mal," Flister states quickly. The First Aevum walks past him and sits on the sofa by the fireplace. Over the Chancellor's irate screaming, she had calmly directed the Fifth and Sixth Aevii to go straight to this small meeting room, out of sight, out of the public eye. Now she looks at them with undisguised disappointment.

"For the past four years," Mal starts slowly, "I have endured the pair of you embarrassing yourselves, each other, and me. I will watch it no longer. Whatever this is—whatever contest you are playing, I want you to call it quits." Her gaze falls on the Fifth Aevum. "I might understand this behavior from Flister, but you are a century older than him. You have no excuse. Make yourself older, *now.*"

Flister is shocked at the hardness in Mal's voice. They must have *really* crossed a line.

Oaken's body grows until she looks to be thirty. "Are any of the other Aevii befriending him?" she asks once she has finished shifting. Although it is not said disrespectfully, it is said with passion. "It may seem silly, but you always say we're family, and what we're doing is harmless."

"Harmless?" Mal asks. Although she says it calmly and in complete control of herself, anger flashes in her amber eyes. "Oaken, you have put all of us at risk with your shenanigans. Turning a dance floor into ice, causing partygoers to fall and hurt themselves. Showing up to your House of Worship with your limbs on backward. Flister running out onto the stage during the Quintrall so every person in the entire world could see it—these are not harmless! They sully our image as Aevii and disrespect our people."

When Oaken tries to defend herself, Mal holds up her hand. As she throws her red hair behind her shoulder, she says calmly, "I don't need you to explain. You will both call a ceasefire."

"Yes, Mal," Flister agrees quickly.

"Once it is done, you will go home, Flister."

"Home?" Flister balks. "Artemis Abbey is *not* my home."

"For three more months, it is," Mal corrects. "On your fifteenth birthday, you will be initiated as an Aevum and may leave your tutors. But until then, Artemis Abbey is where you live—that is your home."

Mal's expression softens. "You must mature, my dear boy," she states and kisses him on the head. "Oh, how I love you."

Straightening, she touches Oaken's cheek with her slender fingers. "As I love you, sweet one."

Without another word, Mal walks out, and the only sound in the room is the crackling fire. Feeling chastised, Flister looks at the skull tattoo on his hand. It is true. The dares had been getting quite elaborate the last few months. Despite himself, he snorts a laugh as he thinks about all the gaudily dressed dancers flailing on the ice, unable to stand.

"So I win?" Oaken asks.

When Flister's head whips in her direction he sees she has returned to her teen body. "What?" he asks. "No, you do not."

Oaken points at the door, "You just told your precious Mal that we were done with the game. You must be admitting defeat because I'm not."

Flister scowls at her. "We should just call it a draw."

Oaken gives him a wicked smile. "You know that's not how the tattoo works." Placing one hand on her hip, she uses her other to motion toward the skull. "Go ahead. Admit defeat, and it will fall off. It's okay to be the loser. Someone has to be."

"I am not giving up," Flister states with teeth clenched.

"You better," Oaken growls. "Because if you don't, I'll dare you to embarrass her."

Flister's anger flashes. "You wouldn't dare."

"Oh, but I would, Flister... I would dare."

Turning away from her, Flister stares into the fire, furious. He has no intention of losing. He would not give Oaken the satisfaction. An idea forms in his mind, and he finds himself smiling once more. Turning back towards the Fifth Aevum, he rubs the stubble that is beginning to grow on his chin.

Much to his pleasure, Oaken looks scared. It is only momentary, but he sees the flash of uncertainty. Good. She *should* be fearful.

Flister wipes the tattoo off his hand. "Turn around," he commands, and the other Aevum obeys. Lifting Oaken's shirt, he tentatively places the tattoo under her left shoulder blade. "I dare you," he says slowly and dramatically, "to find out what the prophecy on my back means."

15 DAYS UNTIL QUINTRALL

Kansis

I LEAD AMELIA THROUGH the Ward's maze of hallways, taking her to the outdoor zone. She scrutinizes the colorfully painted walls like she's studying them for an exam. When we reach the back door, a simulan opens it for us.

A large stone staircase leads out of the Ward, descending into a beautiful, covered garden. Ward staff created the enormous greenhouse as an environment to help soothe the Pods' highly-strung emotions. We've planted almost all of the flowers that grow on our territory here in this small oasis.

Despite the beauty of the space, all of the pods' senses are confronted as they walk outside. The fragrance of the flowers, the scent of the air, the aroma of the trees—it's all changed from what they remember of the world. The textures of the familiar—wood, grass, cement, metal—will feel foreign. Birds have new songs and technology hums at different pitches. Our grass is greener, and our sky is more aqua than blue.

Typically, Pods physically react to seeing this glimpse of Novus. Be it heavy breathing or screaming, they respond. But not Amelia. She absorbs it all in silence, then moves on.

I follow her down the stairs. She meanders through the courtyard and down the creek toward my favorite spot in the garden. One of the designers, an old neighbor of mine, spent months carving finely detailed chairs out of ebony trees infused with HugMe technology. As we approach them, Amelia's steps slow.

Confidently, I walk over to one of them and sit down. The wood comes alive and molds itself to my body, and it's like I'm sitting in a strangely wooden marshmallow. It hardens at the base of my spine for support and folds over my shoulders like... well, like a hug.

The only hugs I get anymore.

The wooden fibers move as I sit, keeping my circulation going; I could remain in the chair for hours and never feel uncomfortable.

Clearly intrigued by my relaxed stance, Amelia tentatively sits down in the chair next to mine. Her eyes widen as it starts molding to her body, and for a moment it appears she might jump out of it—but the comfort overtakes her. A small smile plays on her round lips. Glancing at me for a half-second, she asks, "What are the tests?"

"I've told my boss that you're impersonal, unresponsive, and unteachable. You'll have to prove otherwise."

She folds her hands in her lap and looks me in the eye. "Kansis, tell me about yourself."

I laugh. *Ontzi*, how wonderful it feels to do so. "All right, that's a good start. However, you will call me Professor Willow. Also, you should probably tell me about *you* first."

"I had a brother, but his favorite activity was torturing me, so we didn't spend much time together. You?"

I eye her, amused. "You're not getting off that easy."

She takes a deep breath. "I grew up in San Francisco in the United States. My parents were both politicians, so they were super busy and I didn't see them much."

"Uh-huh..." I prod.

"They both pretended to be religious, but they were frauds."

This subject excites me. I love learning about religions from the Sennies. Those from the Between Age did not salvage much history on the subject, and hearing firsthand accounts is always exciting. "Which god did they believe in?"

Amelia actually smiles. "I have no idea." The expression fades, and she stares out across the garden. "But we went to church every Sunday and sat in the seats we'd paid for—the ones right at the front to the left of the preacher. We looked perfect."

"But you never *felt* perfect?"

Amelia's brows furrow. "No, I never did."

"Why not?"

She looks away. "My parents worshipped themselves every day of the week—more than they did any god on a Sunday."

A shiver runs down my spine. "Are you serious?" I whisper. My interest in this Pod continues to increase.

Her brows furrow again. "Wait, serious about what?"

"I've never heard a Pod speak of human worship before. Were there others who practiced this? Or just your parents?"

Amelia laughs. "No, not like—they didn't actually worship themselves... I meant it more like a figure of speech."

I lean back, disappointed. This could have been a groundbreaking conversation.

Sensing my reaction, she asks, "Does that make you... unhappy?"

"No, no... It's just that... Well, I would have called your parents revolutionaries if they were human worshippers," I say.

"Why?"

"We will cover this in Lesson Ten, but I would call them so because that is the religion of Elusis."

"What?"

"Human worship."

"Like..." she tentatively smiles, "you worship yourself?"

"I could," I say, "but I don't."

Although I worship many metahumans, there's nothing worthy of worship in *me*.

"I don't understand... How can you worship yourself?"

"What made the gods of your world worthy of worship?" I ask.

Taking the question seriously, she doesn't answer immediately. Finally, she answers, "They were supernatural. They could do things humans couldn't. They could control time and space and save people."

"Correct," I say. "And now, because of Gifts, humans can do all those things. We are equal with your gods. Worthy of worship."

She laughs. "And I thought the human race couldn't get any cockier."

"It's not pride," I push back. "It's truth. There is nothing that your gods could do that humans can't do as well. We've evolved. We're what human beings were always meant to become."

"So no one believes in gods? At all?"

"There are some who believe in Superior Beings," I answer. "They call themselves Buscadors. I don't understand what they're seeking, but they think there are beings out there that are above meta-humans. I disagree with them. Most people do."

Amelia sighs and leans back into her chair which immediately molds to her new posture. "Was that enough information about me? Can I hear more about you now?"

"Of course." I clear my throat and begin. "In Novus, the laws only permit us to have two children per couple, as each person lives two hundred years and the population would—"

"You live for two hundred years?"

I scold myself. I hate it when I accidentally alarm the Pods with information I haven't yet given them. Everything is already overwhelming for them, and it isn't good teaching practice to give them too much to digest.

I struggled with this in my first few years working on the Ward, but not so much anymore. For some reason, talking to Amelia feels different. Like she's more than *just* a Pod.

"We will cover that at another time," I amend hastily. "What I was trying to get at is that I am one of two daughters. My older sister is named Clista. She is four years older than me and already has her two children. They are both girls." I pause as if I'm gathering my thoughts, but really I'm forcing down emotions. I've only met Elliana. I haven't met Avangeline yet, as she was born last year. Will I ever get to meet her? Will I ever get to hold her?

Coercing my tears down, I continue. "Clista's mate works at the Palace and is worshipped locally—"

"Worshipped? Wow, so you weren't kidding about that."

I chuckle at her sardonic tone. "Not at all. Once a week, Novians meet at their local Humani House of Worship for services. Most people are worshipped in their hometown's Humani House at least once in their lives, but more honor comes when you are worshipped in other towns or cities. My parents both have very successful jobs, and my dad has been worshipped in three other towns. We are all very proud of him." Not that I ever talk to them—or, more truthfully, they never speak to me.

Enough of that.

"Tell me about your friends," I encourage.

Amelia's face hardens for a moment, then her eyes empty of emotion. "Do I fail this test if I say I don't want to talk about them?"

"Yes." Heartless? Maybe. But I *am* going to lie to my boss for her.

"I didn't have a friend until I was fourteen. And then I made three friends who became my best friends."

"Why are they your best friends?"

Suddenly, another Pod runs across the courtyard screaming in French, "*Meurtriers!*" The word fires across the courtyard with electric energy. "*Vous êtes tous des meurtriers sanglants! Où est ma famille?*"

Mathos, our bodyguard, rushes after her and grabs her from behind.

"*Où est ma soeur?*" she screams over and over as she tries to escape him. She slaps at his face, shouting frantically. "*Ne me touche pas, monstre!*"

Mathos pins her hands behind her back and drags her back inside.

As quiet resounds throughout the yard, Amelia asks softly, "What is she saying?"

"She's asking where her family is—specifically her sister."

"Where is he taking her?" she asks.

"Back to her room."

"Is that all she said?" Amelia asks.

"No," I answer honestly as there is no reason for pretense. "She called Mathos—well, all of us—murderers."

Her eyes meet mine. "And are you? Are you murderers?"

I study her for a moment. "If I say no, you won't believe me."

Her expression doesn't waver. "No. I won't."

I shake my head. "And that is why it would be better for you at Yakum."

"Who are your friends?" she asks quickly.

Me? Friends? You're funny. I clear my throat as I ponder how to answer. "Well, people now relate to each other very differently to how they did in your world. Your social dynamic—specifically as someone from the Western world—revolved around a constant hunt to find a romantic connection. It is not like that here. Because everyone knows who their mate will be, there is no tension between friends. There's purity and wholesomeness.

"But, to answer your question, I had many friends growing up. And now that I'm older, I have fewer friends, but I like it this way."

Lie—wow, what a lie.

"How old are you?" I ask, hastily changing tack.

"I'm seventeen," Amelia answers, "You?"

"Twenty," I respond.

She nods. "So you're married, then?"

I inhale loudly. Too loudly.

She notices. "Was that too personal a question?"

I sigh. I'm not allowed to talk about Aker, and I did not wake up this morning expecting to tell this Pod the deepest hurts of my soul. Nonetheless, I reply, "I should be married, I suppose."

"Did your husband die?" she asks.

Husband.

Aker... my husband.

What foreign words. "No..." Just say it. "The Cupido was created to pair people. Well..." I can feel my face turning red. "It seems it makes mistakes every once in a while." I shake my head. "Or... maybe just once."

I've never had to explain this before... and I have difficulty finding the words. "For some reason, my blood wasn't enough or didn't work in my mate. I have his blood in me, and I love him more than..."

More than breath, more than food, more than my family, more than hydration, more than life...

"...most things—but he doesn't feel the same for me. My blood doesn't draw him."

Her eyebrow raises in question.

Oh, I know. I know.

"Even before the Humani House priestesses announced the couples at our Confirmation, I knew he was my mate. But... he always seemed to be drawn to another girl in our class named..." Her name is bile in my mouth, but I say it anyway. "Mirindiss. When the priestess announced that Aker and I were mates, he was..." I swallow hard. "He was so disappointed. My sister told me it was natural, and his blood would soon awaken. But it never did.

"And the worst part was—is—that Mirindiss is drawn to him too. And yet, she is also drawn to her mate, Kaileb. All four of us were supposed to be married at eighteen, but Mirindiss and Aker ran away together on the day of my wedding. The authorities brought them back, and Mirindiss begged Kaileb to marry her still."

The words spill from my mouth like blood oozing from a wound. You'd think my shame would be a tourniquet, but it's like I have to say it all out loud.

"Our mayor decided to let Aker have some time to detox from Mirindiss and discover his draw for me. Well, that was over two years ago, and I don't think he's ever going to find it. It's blasphemous and illegal that we're not married, but our mayor decided this was better than having us go to a blood reclamation den. Sometimes I wish—"

Wish what? That they had forced Aker to marry me? Yeah, I mean I do. But I can't make myself admit it out loud.

Tears brim in my eyes, but I don't let them fall. Being alone is my life, and I'm done crying about it. I sneak a glance at Amelia, but she's looking at the ground.

I feel my face getting hot. Why did I tell her all that? I lied to all the other Pods and said Aker had died. Why didn't I lie this time? As I regard her again, I decide it's because, for some reason, I trust her. She's not judging me or pitying me, and it's refreshing.

"You're alone?" she finally asks.

A small, sad laugh escapes my lips. "Utterly."

For a second, our eyes meet, and she gives me a half-smile. "Me too."

Well, *ontzi*. I think I just found myself a friend.

The rest of the day I spend with Amelia. I haven't smiled or laughed this much in... well, in almost two years. She continues to tell me things about her world, although she avoids personal questions.

When we head to the dining hall, I tell Hiya she can have the night off as I will look after Amelia for the evening. She seems appreciative but doesn't say anything—not that I expect her to. I ask Amelia to tell me more stories from Senex. They fascinate me.

Then she asks me to share stories of Novus, and I tell her a couple of my favorites. At first, she seemed hesitant in her laughter, but after I told her the story of the Pexun Ambassador who used his Progift of body-switching and accidentally got stuck as a goose for a year, she laughed freely—and loudly. Once we finish eating, she asks if she can have a tour of the inside of the building. Obliging, I show her all my favorite rooms, ending in a sensory room designed to help Pods work out their internal feelings by experiencing various textures externally.

"What's your superpower?" she asks as we eat dessert later that evening.

"Guess," I smile.

"Can you read my mind?"

"No, no, nothing as glorious as that," I answer and take a bite of a fluffy and tangy cumin castor.

"Can you create stuff?" Amelia asks as she licks jam off her fingers.

"Nope."

"Can you fly?"

"Now that would be quite the Gift—but no. Unfortunately, nothing as graceful or beautiful. Or useful for that matter."

"Can you time travel?"

I know getting into the intricacies of Gifting will overload her, so I simply answer, "Time traveling Gifts are so heavily monitored, most people who have one will spend their whole lives never using it. Okay, I won't torture you anymore; I'll tell you—"

"No, I'll guess what it is; I know it." She smiles at me, and I almost catch my breath. How have I lived these past two years? *This* is living—laughter and friendship. *This* is what I have been missing. What I have been doing all these months is just surviving—just *not* dying.

It's late when we finally walk back to her room. Everyone from the day shift is long gone, and Reest will surely be upset about the overtime I've put in today. But as we make our way back toward Amelia's room, I can't hide my ever-growing smile.

I remind her where her white bedtime attire and toiletries are located then turn around so she can change without me watching. We used to have bathrooms for privacy, but too many Pods found creative ways to take their own lives in the small space. Now, we monitor them constantly. As I stand with my back to the ablutions taking place behind me, I notice the comforter on her bed. Although I care for all the Pods I've helped, I have a deeper sense of responsibility for the state of my current one. I know there are softer comforters than this one, infused with HugMe, piled up in the hall closet. I want her to have one. Without telling her what I'm doing, I sneak out of the room.

Darting down to the linen closet to retrieve a soft comforter doesn't take long, and as I head back to Amelia's room, my mind starts fantasizing about the future. I only work with the Pods for nine months before they are transferred to the next rehabilitation stage. I've never tried to stay in contact with the ones I've trained, but I'm sure they won't have a problem with me keeping in touch once Amelia moves on from my level. Maybe she can celebrate the Quintrall with me. It's a whole weekend holiday; maybe Reest would let us watch the Saturday night entertainment together and—

"What the—"

I closed her door, didn't I? Walking over to the partly open panel, I tentatively touch the knob. Did I forget to lock it? I had been in such a hurry to get the HugMe comforter. Slowly, I push the door open, and when I see nobody in the bed, I barely feel the comforter falling from my hands.

Something catches my eye: a white ghost flittering around the corner. I run, heart beating fast, down the corridor. When I turn into the hallway, her pajamas disappear around the next corner. Where is she going?

As I round the next bend, my world suddenly explodes with pain. I'm on the floor. The ghost vanishes out of sight.

So. Um. Ow! That really hurts!

My head pulsates. I know I need to get up and run, but I feel like my nose is lodged halfway into my brain. Did she hit or kick me? Gathering all the strength I have, I haul myself upright and run towards her. My eyes are watering so heavily I can barely see. I have to stop and rub them clear. A door rattles to my left, and I stumble my way toward it. She's trying to escape through the back door!

More footsteps. Amelia is running back towards me. Crouching behind the wall, I wait until she's about to pass me, then I swing my foot as hard and as fast as I can. Her toes dig into my ankle. As she yells out in surprise, I muffle a shout of pain. But having the upper hand, I jump her as she goes down.

I've had to wrestle several Pods in their escape attempts—but I've never wrestled a military brat before. In an instant, Amelia has me pinned. Her hands wrap around my throat. I can't breathe. My eyes feel like they're bulging out of their sockets. My whole body is hot as it fights for life.

Suddenly, I remember the Shocker in my pocket. Never in my whole career have I had to use it. I stop scratching her hands and face and reach for it. Amelia senses I've stopped fighting her and releases one of her hands off my throat to try to pin down my arm. With the slight release, I take in a wheezy breath.

Before she can stop me, I grab the Shocker and shove it into her side.

Her whole body freezes and then jolts in pain. I don't remove it from her side until she's entirely off me.

I release the connection, but her body continues to twitch. Tentatively, I rub my aching neck. Her body finally begins to still, and she lays motionless on the floor, mouth agape and drooling.

As she begins to stir, I say, "You make one move towards me, or try to escape, I'll hit you again." My voice is hoarse, my windpipe bruised.

"Professor Willow?" one of the night staff guards yells from a few corridors down. "Professor Willow, where is your Pod?"

"Over here!" I croak as loudly as I can.

Amelia painfully sits up and pulls her knees to her chest.

"You're on the next Pila out of here tomorrow," I seethe. I should have known better than to get my hopes up that I had any chance of making a friend.

"Kansis, please," she moans.

"*Please*?" I laugh. "Please, what? And you *will* call me Professor Willow."

"Professor Willow?" the guard shouts again.

"We're over by room three-oh-four!" I yell back.

Shutting her eyes tight, she whispers, "Please help me."

"Help you? After you just tried to kill me? You only wish I was that gullible."

"I need your help, Kansis. I need to find my dad."

"I know there's a more touchy-feely way to say this, but you did just try to strangle me, so…" The guard rounds the corner, and I stand. "You're never going to see your dad again."

"I have to," she whispers just before the guard reaches us. "My father is Arkarian Story."

Mundus Senex

Amelia

633 years ago; 2088

"I KNOW WHAT THIS looks like," Amelia says nervously, hands wringing, face blotchy.

Moss, a retired, part-time mall cop, stares down at the young red-headed girl. He guesses her to be eleven or twelve. Two braids fall off her shoulders and down her back, and they dance as she shifts her weight anxiously from side to side. Moss knows crime can start young, knows not to look at their innocent faces, and knows the best thieves are the best liars—but he wants to believe this girl. He's not going to let her off easy, though.

"It looked like you was shoplifting, young lady," Moss responds matter-of-factly.

Amelia's hazel eyes bulge with fear. "No, no! That's not it at all! I... I know it sounds stupid—I know, but I was just... I was putting the shirt on my bag while I shopped. I would never leave a store without paying." Her face is pale with worry; she's close to tears. "I know you don't know me, Sir, but I wouldn't do something like that. My parents taught me better."

Sighing deeply, Moss takes a disarming posture as he leans back against the table in the loss prevention office. "Well, that's fine and dandy, but that's not what it looked like to that there cashier you was hiding from."

A tear slips down the girl's cheek as her voice piques an octave, "No, no, Sir, that's not what happened. She misunderstood—I wasn't hiding from *her.*"

"Who were you hiding from then?" Moss asks gruffly.

For the first time, Amelia lowers her gaze. Her feet shift back and forth, and she stuffs her hands into her coat.

Moss reaches for his back pocket out of habit. He has stashed chew there since he was a teenager, and his hands always flicker in that direction when he's uncomfortable. Behind the young thief's now-shaking frame is an anti-bullying poster. "Well, spit it out," he says. When she still says nothing, he asks softly, "Was it bullies?"

Amelia's head whips up, her eyes filled with relief and worry. "Something like that, Mister."

Compassion fills the retired man, and he leans farther back onto the table. "Can I give you a word of advice, young lady?"

Tears fall down her cheek as she replies, "Yes, please."

"You can't run from your problems—be them people, places, or situations. You gotta face 'em head-on."

"Yes, Sir."

"You gotta have hard conversations. And if those kids are giving you a hard time, you talk to an adult about it, one you trust. No kid should be living in that kind of fear, you hear me?" Moss says.

Amelia nods wildly, "Yes, Sir. I understand, Sir."

"Now, about that blouse there. I'm gonna tell that cashier she was mistaken, but you better bet I'll be looking out for ya. I don't want any more *misunderstandings*. You hear?"

"Yes, Sir," she says hastily and chances a smile.

Moss returns the blouse to her and hands the young girl her purse. "Only put your own things in there."

Amelia's head nods like a bobblehead on a country road. "Yes, Mister. I totally will. I promise." As she walks out of the mall's loss prevention office, she quickly heads to the food court where her friend, Marley, is waiting.

She sits down suddenly, shocking her friend. "God, Amelia, scare me half to death," Marley says as she looks anxiously around. "Did you get caught?" she whispers conspiratorially.

Cocking an eyebrow, Amelia lounges back in her chair. "Does it look like I got caught?"

"How did you get off? That cashier caught you red-handed!" Marley asks, not so quietly.

Amelia hushes her friend and leans forward across the table. Almost under her breath, she answers, "Everyone has a soft spot for bullied kids, especially old people."

Marley laughs and smiles treacherously, "Oh, you're good, Milly." She takes out her phone, snaps a selfie with Amelia, and posts, *Just got out of trouble with this criminal.* The girls laugh together as they watch the likes start accumulating. When it reaches three hundred, Amelia looks around the food court and sees a few girls from her school chatting over their coffees.

Nudging Marley, she pointedly looks over at the girls. Marley glances across to see where Amelia is focusing her attention, and immediately begins to laugh. "Yes, *please!*" she giggles. "They're like perfect for your anti-bullying campaign, right?"

Amelia takes out her phone and begins her third vlog of the day.

"Hey guys, it's Milly again. I'm at the mall with my bestie, Marley," she pans the phone camera to her friend, who makes a seductive kissy face. Amelia faces the camera back on herself, "I just wanted to teach you guys another anti-bullying lesson." Amelia walks across the food court to the three girls chatting over their drinks.

"See these girls?" Amelia starts and pans the camera over. The girls look over at Amelia, surprised and embarrassed that she is filming them. "They are obviously victims of bullying. Just look at their clothing choices and their hair and… well, look at their faces! Clearly, they get bullied. So let's ask them how they deal with it." Amelia zooms the camera onto one of the girls. "Tessa, how do you deal with the undeniable hatred and disgust you experience from your peers?"

Tessa, a twelve-year-old, looks down at her hands and doesn't respond.

"No? No words of advice for my followers? Huzzah. M'kay, what about you, Maria? I'm sure you've dealt with people pointing out your weight and how gross it is. How would you encourage other fatties?"

Maria stands and, without acknowledging Amelia, tells her friends, "Let's go."

"Wait!" Amelia shouts. "We haven't heard from Fern." Amelia follows behind the girls as they walk away. "Fern, when you're made fun of for your… Do people refer to your style as unique or hideous?… Well, either way, how do you respond?"

"I tell them to screw off, Amelia. Leave us alone."

"Fern Waymore, that is no way to talk online!" Amelia reproves. "You should be ashamed, speaking so cruelly on an anti-bullying campaign."

"Shut up, Amelia!" Maria shouts. "Go ruin someone else's day."

"Maria, are those tears falling down your cheeks?" Amelia asks as she continues to follow them. "Are you shaking from sobbing, or is it just your ordinary wobble?"

"That's enough," Fern shouts, turning on her. "Leave us alone, or we're going to tell the school counselor on you again."

Amelia raises her brows and smiles. "And how did that turn out for you last time? If you recall, I left that office a changed individual and received the Most Teachable Student award."

Amelia turns the camera back to herself. "And I *am* changed. That's why I've started this anti-bullying campaign." She pans the camera to the girls again. "Why are you so negative when I'm just trying to help people?"

Fern scoffs, "You're a fake, and everyone knows it."

Amelia takes three steps closer to the girls. She's taller than all of them by a couple of inches, and as she stares down at them, she says in a voice so quiet the video won't catch it, "You are all such wastes of oxygen—disgusting, obese, lowlifes. It would be better for everyone if you had never been born." Quickly she pans the camera back to herself. "Well, apparently, these victims aren't willing to share any helpful hints with others of their miserable kind." She pans the camera to an overflowing trashcan and says, "Say goodbye, girls!" Feigning surprise, she says a quick "oops" and points the camera back to the group. "Say goodbye!"

As AMELIA CLIMBS THE last of the long streets to her San Francisco home overlooking the bay, she stops to catch her breath, hiding in her favorite of the seven gardens surrounding her family's twenty-acre property. Once her heart returns to a normal rhythm, she slips around the side of the house towards the back door. As Courtenay—their French head of the kitchen staff—exits the kitchen for her cigarette break, Amelia sneaks inside.

Pleased with herself, Amelia forgets to check the kitchen for anyone else before hurrying through. Painful shock and hot fear shoot through her body as she sees her brother sitting at the small table where Amelia eats her breakfast every morning. Amelia's never seen anyone else in her family eat at that table.

When her brother spots her, a wicked smile fills his features. "Well, if it isn't the Mistake. What are you doing sneaking in through the kitchen?"

Amelia swallows hard and then says quietly, "I'm not... I wasn't sneaking."

Carter stands, but before he can say anything else, Amelia darts out of the kitchen. She runs through the foyer, into the formal living room, up the first staircase, through the guest wing, up the second flight of stairs, past the rooms of storage. She's so close she can see the attic door—just one more flight of stairs. But as her hand reaches the railing, she's suddenly on her knees, gasping for air.

Malicious laughter rains down on her as Carter shoves her to the ground. "Thought you'd outsmart me, huh? Thought you could outrun me? I know this house better than you ever could, Mistake. Okay, okay, stand up, come on, stop crying. I barely punched you. Now, I'll ask you again, what were you doing sneaking through the kitchen?" When she doesn't respond, he places a fist on her shoulder. "Don't make me hurt you, Mistake. Just tell me."

"I snuck away from Roscoe after school," Amelia answers, still trying to breathe normally.

"Dad's gonna kill you."

"I can take care of myself," Amelia retorts.

"Dad's not worried about you, Mistake. Your bodyguards are there to keep him and his investments safe."

"Dad won't find out if you don't say anything," she responds and sits upright.

Carter scoffs. "Roscoe will tell him if I don't."

Slowly, Amelia stands, "No, he never tells on me."

Shoving her onto the staircase, Carter rolls his eyes. "What is it with you? How do you always get out of trouble?"

Accidentally, Amelia smirks with satisfaction. From a very young age, Amelia possessed an uncanny ability to influence others. Pride creeps in as she thinks about her interaction this afternoon with the mall cop—that was peanuts compared to some of the other situations she has gotten herself out of. However, Carter has always been jealous of her confidence, so she's kept it primarily to herself. Mostly.

When she sees the rage growing behind Carter's eyes, she knows she has made a serious error in letting her pleasure show.

"You know what I think?" Clicking his tongue, Carter reaches into his pocket and pulls out a lighter. "I think you're a witch. Do you know what people used to do to witches, Mistake?" Amelia's stomach drops at the look her brother is giving her. She knows that sadistic expression.

"No—don't…" she pleads.

"You've gotta be a witch. You've never once been charged for stealing, and I know you've been caught. You always get out of the principal's office. Everyone on the staff adores you. You got into St. Michaels, even though there were older, way more qualified students for the Mary Janeston Scholarship. Yet, after your interview, you somehow, miraculously, got it." Carter moves closer to Amelia. "You've stacked the evidence against yourself; there's no other explanation—you're a witch."

"Please, Carter, don't," Amelia whimpers as a flame ignites from the lighter.

"Give me your hand, and it will only be your hand. If you don't, it'll be your whole arm."

"Carter, please!" she shrieks. She isn't fast enough when her brother lunges for her. In a moment, he's sitting on her chest and has her arms pinned beneath his legs. While she struggles futilely, he lights the flame. Slowly, he moves it closer to her trapped limb. When she screams, Carter drops the lighter and shoves his hand over her mouth. Her eyes bulge as his hand also covers her nostrils.

He leans down to her ear and slowly whispers, "If you scream again, I'll invite Alex over." At the name of Carter's best friend, Amelia's body goes slack. Smiling to himself, he slowly releases his hand from her mouth. A large, white handprint covers her face. "That's better. Now, hold still."

As her brother scorches off her arm hair with a cigarette lighter, only a quiet whimper escapes Amelia's round lips.

Dinner is served that night in the formal dining room as usual. Amelia slips into her seat, wincing when her arm rests on the table. She places it in her lap instead just as Carter walks in. He winks when he sees how she's cosseting her injury.

Amelia's mother joins the table next. She is a tall, good-looking, red-headed Congresswoman—loved by her staff, despised by her opposition. For all of Amelia's living memory, her mother's first love has been her cell phone. Once, when she was younger, Amelia tried to destroy her mom's phone so that she would at least look at her.

The three family members are glued to their respective phones when Amelia's dad enters the dining room. "Screens away," he commands, and Carter and Amelia instantly obey. Their mom doesn't move.

The staff serves the food and the room settles into almost complete silence, save for the clicking of Amelia's mom texting. As the first course is cleared, their father asks Carter how his senior year is going.

Carter nervously wipes his mouth. "Straight A's—you know me, Dad."

As the silent staff place their second course on the table, his dad frowns. "And who are you paying to do your work these days? Hopefully someone trustworthy."

Flustered, Carter stutters, "I d-d-don't know what—I wouldn't—D-Dad, I'm hard work. I mean, I work hard for my grades."

The father stares impassively at his son. His brows are relaxed, his mouth even, his jaw loose. There is nothing intrinsically sinister about the expression, but even Amelia feels sick to her stomach just seeing it.

If she were the type of sister who cared, she would interrupt—take her dad's attention off her brother. She would coach Carter on how to respond to their dad. She would help him not be so stupid and obvious; help him not to get caught.

But she isn't the type of sister who cares. And her arm still stings from the lighter's flame.

Instead, Amelia calmly takes a bite of her food while Carter babbles on and on. He tries lying, then blame-shifting, then crying until, finally, he begs his father not to punish him.

Amelia scoffs to herself—Carter is so weak. When Carter's eyes whip across to her, she keeps her head down, focused on her food.

"You disgust me," their father says to Carter. "If I could remove the honor of my name from your shoulders, I would."

"What?!" Amelia's mom shouts suddenly, but everyone knows without looking that she's still on the phone. She holds the device to her ear as her eyes narrow, her jaw protrudes over her upper teeth, and her hands turn to fists. Slowly, her venomous gaze turns to Amelia. "I'll call you back." The sound of her fork clattering onto the table fills the large, echoic room.

"Anti-bullying campaign?" Amelia's mom is still shouting. "Do you know how this makes me look?"

"Gwen," Amelia's dad says calmly.

"Don't *Gwen* me! I am so sick of this! Every day she creates posts that question this family's integrity. She's been in the news twice this month—"

"The second time was an apology," Amelia's dad inserts.

"I don't care. Bethany paid off two bloggers to prevent them writing articles on what Amelia is posting online." Turning back to Amelia, she says with soft venom, "Take it down now."

"No," Amelia says, taking a bite of her filet mignon.

Next second her mom is standing. Cussing. Screaming. Throwing silverware in her daughter's direction. Demanding her husband do something about this. Shouting. Threatening. Storming out.

As the sound of slamming doors recedes into her mom's wing of the house, her dad finally looks at her. "Go to my study, Amelia."

Without hesitation, Amelia stands and walks to the eastern-most room of the mansion. Her father's study is immense, dark and intimidating. Someone— either her father or the staff—has flushed the books perfectly with the shelves.

Statues of ancient philosophers stand guard behind the desk, and the pens on its surface lie symmetrical to one another. Nothing is out of place; even dust dares not rest in this room.

When her dad enters behind her, Amelia's heart pounds and her stomach lurches. She does her best not to let her fear show. He takes slow, calculated steps to his desk. The sound of the leather creaking as he places his weight into his chair creates synaptic connections in her mind. For the rest of her life, the sound of creaking leather will make her sick to her stomach.

"Amelia," her dad says slowly. "I've wanted to speak candidly with you for some time, and this seems like the perfect opportunity." He knits his hands together and places them on his desk. "Your brother is an idiot, and your mother is a whore."

He pauses to see how Amelia will respond. This information—or rather, the fact that he feels such things—is not new to Amelia. However, she doesn't want to stare at him blank-faced, so she raises one of her brows to acknowledge his words.

Nodding, her father continues. "I have plans, Amelia. Formidable, powerful plans." His hands move to his chest as he leans back into his chair. "And I want you to be a part of them."

This time when her dad pauses, he stares down at his twelve-year-old daughter with calculating eyes. "You have your mother's gift for inspiring loyalty in others. Her people would die for her. Kill for her. And anyone that you get your claws into exudes similar responses. But you're also like me. Ambitious. Cunning. Manipulative. You are the child I always hoped I'd have."

Amelia's shoulders square in pride at her father's words.

"I could make you powerful, Amelia. I could make you invincible. I know the ways you've been hurt in this home by both Carter and Alex. I know it all."

Amelia blushes and then instantly pales at these words.

But her dad goes on. "If you follow my plans, none of those things will ever happen to you again. You will always be able to protect yourself and you will always come out on top. There will be none able to rise above you—only those who bow down to you. You will be able to place your foot on the necks of miscreants like Carter and Alex. Do you understand what I am saying?"

Amelia nods, her eyes hazed over at the thought of never being hurt again. As much as she has never had any familial feelings towards this man, he is offering her a token she can respond to; something she can bank on. This offer of a pathway to a position of power—enough power to control her world—has captured her complete attention. For this, she would comply. For this, she would bend her will and sacrifice much.

"What is your response?" her dad asks.

She waits an appropriate amount of time for proper contemplation before she answers. "I'll do whatever you ask."

"Good girl." Her father smiles. "Now, the only area in which you lack is image awareness. For the past six months, you've allowed your public image to be compromised. In the public's eye, you must be the hero; otherwise, they won't follow you. They will turn against you if you seem enough of a villain. Now, do not misunderstand me, Amelia; I approve of how you treat these girls. It is how the greater treat the lesser, and I applaud this. But it must be unseen. It must be said in hushed tones, in secret corners, in quiet quips. These anti-bullying posts only serve to hurt you. And, in turn, hurt me."

Pursed lips. Deep breath. Creaking leather.

Amelia's dad goes on, "I warned you last month, and it didn't seem to affect you. This cannot go on."

Smoothed hair. Narrowed eyes. Creaking leather.

"For your future, I am sending you to a military school in northern Oregon."

Inwardly, Amelia screams, as enraged as she has ever been. *How could he?* Outwardly, she is stone, blinking sharply, then holding his gaze.

"You will go to this school, a troubled child. You will show how rebellious a privileged white girl can be. But then you will let them break you. You will exploit all of your pain to gain their trust. Do you understand me, Amelia? Are you listening? I want you to use the things that have happened in this house to buy their undying loyalty. You will graduate at the top of the class. Then, you will come back a changed, moral individual. We will use your complete redemption to our advantage in the future. You will not complain, you will not cry, and you will be completely obedient. You will be the greatest transformation story of the school's history. Do you understand me?"

Amelia nods. The power to control her own life will be worth it in the end.

Amelia's dad unfolds his hands and places them flat on his desk. "I want you to be a part of my future, Amelia. But you have to prove yourself. Then and only then can I mold you into something this world has never seen before."

Amelia stands. She knows the conversation is over. She knows she has no choice. Her father controls her every breath.

As she walks to his office door, her father has one final parting shot. "You cannot imagine the type of consequence I have in mind if you disobey me,

Amelia."

Knowing this is what he wants, Amelia turns and looks at her father square in the eye. "Yes, Daddy."

Ortus

Pypen

"**P**YPEN, WAKE UP!" SCOUT shouts, slapping my face. Although I moan, I do not move to get out of bed. Surprisingly, I am not entirely fond of being awoken with such violence. "Pip," he yells again. "Come now! Our meeting starts in seven minutes!"

Immediately, I jolt upright. "Obscene!" My fuzzy eyes focus to see Scout's frazzled form rummaging around in his desk drawers. Clearing my eyes of rheum, I frantically bark "Time!" at my wrist, and the calm, robotic voice of my Suus says in my mind, *Ten twenty-three a.m.* It cannot be! I almost trip on our makeshift beds in my hurry to cross the room, tying my dreadlocks back into a ponytail as I go. That is just going to have to be good enough.

"*Matza!*" I curse. "When did we fall asleep?"

Scout is attempting to press out the wrinkles from his shirt. "Last time I saw the clock, it was around seven in the morning."

I close my eyes, aiming to renew his shirt to the pristine condition it was in when he bought it, but I am so tired that I accidentally renew it to a pile of threads and buttons.

Scout bursts out in deep laughter. "In the future, I prefer my shirts wrinkled and dirty."

I chastise myself. I should have stayed awake and let Scout sleep. "I apologize," I state, frustrated with my weakness.

Not looking at me, he responds, "For what?"

"That I let us fall asleep. I should have been more diligent—"

"We have been up for almost thirty-six hours," he interrupts. "You are excused."

"But—"

"I said I excused our lateness. This is not your burden or your mistake." There is such finality in his voice that I push no further.

While he braids his hair, I quickly retrieve him a new shirt from the drawers by the door. I throw it at him, then hurriedly get myself dressed. Without much thought, I pick black suit pants, an ivory tunic, and my favorite plum-purple Jackette—a stylish, thin coat that adjusts its bulk according to the weather. Lastly, as I do every day, I grab a small, velvet pouch from inside my desk and place it in my Jackette pocket. I like to call it my Precaution Bag. 'Tis rare that I have had to use it… but when I have…

"It has saved my life," I say to myself.

Scout groans, "Pypen—the mumbling."

A knock sounds at the door. That must be Gigi—she will be singing the benediction. "Enter!" I call.

Gigi glides into our office gracefully. She has crafted her dark brown Ortusan hair into a long plait down her back. As is her custom, she has woven moss and wool into the braid so it resembles a tree trunk. Today she is wearing a denim dress with a shirt that reflects the light in an ever-changing iridescent ripple.

"Greet the sun, boys," she says by way of greeting, and when she sees what we are doing, she teases, "Not again! I thought you said you would not wait so long next time." Her purple eyelashes dance as she laughs at our frantic cleaning.

"We never made such preposterous declarations," Scout retorts as we rush around trying to make our space appear like the office is it, rather than a consignment store. My final task is to download our work from the mainframe in our office onto our personal Suuses. Scout places an empty chair in the center of the room facing the three of us.

"Ready?" Urgency fills his voice.

"We must be," I answer as our Projector sounds a musical note, and the form of Flister Dubach, the Sixth Aevum, fills the empty chair.

We quickly fall to the ground and bow down to the Aevum. Gigi stands to sing a song of praise for the Sixth Aevum while Scout and I stay bowed low on the floor. Shyasuan Manel, a famous singer-songwriter, wrote the ode for the Aevum when Flister Dubach was a young child. I despise this tune, yet even I can enjoy it as Gigi weaves her tone into both voice and instrument:

When we see the creating Aevum open wide to receive our love
We obey the mandate in our hearts to give him all we have
Be it riches, time, or talent, we give it all to him with praise
Oh, that he would look at us with those blue Aevum eyes
We will praise him! Praise him! Praise the child who for the hopeless came!
Give him glory, all you people, for his Gift will bless us all, bless us all

The fires that warm us in the hearth are the warmth of his embrace
For this creating child will protect and keep that which we possess
We will praise him! Praise him! Praise the child who for the hopeless came!
Give him glory, all you people, for his Gift will bless us all, bless us all

As the song comes to an end, Scout and I rise. The Sixth Aevum ignores us as he studies something that we cannot see in front of him.

Like most of the Aevii, the Sixth Aevum has chosen a thirty-year-old appearance. He is one of the younger Aevii, only one hundred and eight years old; he has yet to even live an entire two-hundred-year Novian life expectancy. However, as one of the immortal Aevii, he has an eternity of years ahead of him.

The oldest of the Aevii, Mal Fey, is four hundred and six years old. Her birthday is a worldwide Holy Day every year. Dakarai Ebelson, the Second Aevum, is three hundred and sixty-five years old; Qualcum Elder, the Third Aevum, is two hundred and eighty-six; Marvella Pinyin and Oaken Bleu, the Fourth and Fifth Aevum, are both two hundred and nineteen; Root Besendere, the Seventh Aevum, is fifty-nine; Gerisson Librisso, the Eighth Aevum, is fifteen; and the Ninth Aevum, Vakker Schon, was only born four years ago.

As all the Aevii are, the Sixth Aevum is very handsome, although his blue eyes are callous and cold. His smooth voice rings out as he questions Scout. "Eekan, you have worked Merayal Kapu into the show?" When his eyes fall on Scout, they are filled with their customary disdain.

I know not why the Sixth Aevum has always treated Scout with such contempt—Scout has never been anything but obedient, submissive, and optimistic.

Nodding, Scout commands his Suus to send the plans to the Aevum.

Bidding the plans to open, the Aevum's Suus opens several translucent documents in front of him. Quickly looking over them, the Aevum swishes them out of his sight with an approving grunt. Clearly wishing our plans to be insufficient, he admits begrudgingly, "It works."

"I thought so," Scout replies.

The Aevum slowly claps his hands as he responds with condescending sarcasm, "Oh, well, praise be *your* name, Eekan, for being so clever."

Hearing the reprimand, Scout bows again and offers a benediction: "Blessed be the Sixth Aevum of the sacred Nine who has blessed us with Creations and Secrets throughout Elusis. Before the foundation of the world, the sacred Blood chose him that he should be holy and blameless before us. Blessed be Auctus and Effio; blessed be the Sixth Aevum."

As is the way, Gigi and I shout, "Hurrah!"

With no farewell, the Sixth Aevum cuts the connection.

"That could have gone worse," Gigi says and smiles sympathetically.

"That was him being friendly," Scout retorts with a smirk. "Now, on to new introductions."

Gigi takes a step towards our QuickEntrance door, but I clear my throat.

"I need to take the long way to clear my head," I state, and the other two nod in understanding.

As we walk out of our office, a warm breeze brushes my face, and I take a deep breath. I love the smell of the circus: it is the perfect mixture of salt and sugar. The ever-twilight glow immediately relaxes my taut veins. As I pass by one of the many floating lamps, orbiting the tent like tiny moons, I reach out and touch it. I always love that they have been Gifted to feel like warm, fuzzy kittens. There is music in the air; a soothing melody that makes you feel at home. The sound, however, is almost imperceptible. If you were to try and concentrate on it, you would no longer hear it.

Every one of your senses is engaged whilst within our tent, but it is not overwhelming. Rather, it gently allures the attendees, awakening them to follow after some forgotten secret, some unearthed mystery.

The golden paths woven throughout the circus' ground level appear like a river of hazy sunlight from the higher levels.

The closer you get to the bottom, the more you can smell the aromas from the cuisine kiosks.

Scout, Gigi, and I walk down our invisible staircase, passing by doors of every shape, size, and texture. There are wooden doors, glass doors, painted, double, grand, stained, arched, angled, metal, slatted, bamboo, and even miniature doors. When patrons enter the circus, they stand in a courtyard where we present them with hundreds of doors (two hundred and six to be exact). The doors start on the floor level but are not confined to regular expectations. Instead, they appear at various heights—some are even on the ceiling! Patrons can use ropes, vines, stairs, a rusty old-world escalator, and an eccentric array of ladders made from off-beat materials such as bones and pasta.

Everything about our circus is intentional. We designed every aspect so that—from the moment a patron's eyes land on our tent to the moment they leave—we are gradually and imperceptibly enticing them to magical experiences. Our Vorbies are overflowing with compensation and our growing reputation proves that we are good at our job. Exceptional, even.

We go down to the second level and pass by a thick and wide spider web tunnel leading to a particularly shiny, oval pink door. We walk up several books in the shape of stairs until we reach Thykas' paper mâché door. From within the huge room on the other side, we hear boisterous chatter.

"Feel better now?" Scout asks me, ensuring I am ready to commence our meeting.

"Indeed," I answer and allow him to enter first. As we step inside the spacious area, the voices lower.

Scout usually has this effect on people. Even though he is of average height and build, something about him speaks of power and strength. Some muse his Progift is a form of Emotion Manipulation, for his mere presence makes the mightiest of persons feel small. But I know Scout's Progift, and it is Vision Manipulation. Usually, when people have this Gift, they can make others *see* what they want them to see; however, Scout's Gift is the opposite. He can make people *not* see things. It is nuanced, yet it has been beneficial in our missions.

Many of the people in the world have Duogifts, a second Gift, and Scout is—*was*—such a person. But that second gift was stripped long ago—an occasion of horror which I will never forget.

So, no, it's not any type of manipulation that makes people respond to Scout this way. There are no tricks; it is just him.

Nodding to the group, Scout lets them know they may continue conversing. I walk over to the Chameleons—our four, resident shape-shifters—and their mates.

"Dog!" I shout out.

Within a second's time, the Chameleons change into four different types of dogs as their mates look on, bemused.

"Bird!"

With another snap of my fingers, four birds circle me. One lands on my shoulder as I say, "Book!" Per usual, three of the birds manipulate just as quickly into three books that fall to the floor with three almost synchronous thuds. The fourth bird, a shoebill stork, squawks, grunts, and flies desperately around the room, unable to transform. Finally, he lands next to me and bows his feathered head in disappointment.

"Be not disheartened, Lukan," I say to the fourth Chameleon. "You will learn inanimate objects. I believe you will."

"Of course he will." Ruelle, his mate, leans down and kisses his little feathered cheek. "Then, you can turn into that Dotorea purse I have been coveting!"

Lukan turns back into human form and gives Ruelle's joke a fake laugh as she kisses him again. The other three books change to human form and fawn over Lukan, mimicking Ruelle and kissing him relentlessly.

"Oh, you will be the best of them all, Sonny, just you wait," Oshun says, smooching Lukan's hand.

"You will make Mummy very proud," Krael coos, shoving Lukan's face into his chest.

"And I am so very proud of you, Lukey-bear," Sedwick states with a false effeminate voice as, laughing, he slightly bows to his fellow shapeshifter.

The Chameleons were all very young when they joined our company. The four boys had been performing small acts at their high school in Pagitit when Emerly heard about them. Krael and Sedwick are the only true brothers—twins, in fact—but it is as if the four young men are quadruplets, they are so similar. Albeit with some slight variations, the four grew up with the same Progift, making them inseparable.

We helped transfer their credits to Talents University—a college close to our circus' home base—to finish their academic career whilst they performed with us. As each turned eighteen and married their mates, we allowed their new wives to join the group. Even though the boys are now twenty-two and full adults, sometimes I still see them as the teenagers they were when they joined.

As they have gotten older, they have changed their outward appearance to look more mature, handsome, and chiseled. I often wonder if this was something they themselves desired or if it was at the behest of their mates.

Their wives, Nova, Memory, Ruelle, and Fiddy, are all dancers for us, but Memory and Fiddy have ventured into making a circus room of their own, something that not many take upon themselves. It is a lot of work, but the women have thrived. In fact, their room was our most visited by patrons last month. Thus far, these eight members have been invaluable to us.

"She is late," Nova drawls at me. "That is strike one against the new girl." Nova's curves are particularly on display today as she has dressed in a tight, red satin and sheer dress. Her dark brown hair lays perfectly across her shoulders and bosom.

Lounging on a couch behind her, Krael says, "Nova, you bothered not to show up for your interview. You did not even show up for the first few practices until Oshun dragged you here. Your blood must be the same type as this girl's."

Nova rolls her eyes and moves away from the Chameleons to the back of the room where Ryder stands leaning on the wall.

"Why is your mate so irritable all the time?" Krael asks Oshun. Where Krael is muscles and bulldozing self-proclaimed authority, Oshun is a flexible peacemaker with self-deprecating humor.

"You are just as irritable," Oshun responds to Krael with a puppy-like smile. When Krael does not laugh in agreement, Oshun sobers up and nods his head. "I am not certain the source of her animosity. She is always angry with me over something."

"You need not make excuses for her," Sedwick assures Oshun. "If Krael had any sense of propriety, he would keep his thoughts to himself." Sedwick pushes his hair out of his eyes. He does not look directly at Krael as he says this, but the challenge is clear.

"You want to hear my thoughts, Sed?" Krael asks, standing and puffing out his chest.

Sensing an argument rising, I say quickly, "Cease."

Tensions are still high until Lukan transforms into a woodpecker and begins pecking Krael's head. Once the group has resumed their merriment, I make my way toward Scout. We need to start the meeting soon. Emerly was to meet Merayal at the QuickEntrance door in our office and then bring her here. Previously, he would have had to take her through the circus, but last year Scout and I made a door from our office directly to Thykas' room as we come here so often.

Just as I reach Scout, the door opens and Emerly leads Merayal Kapu through it. Emerly coughs, and it resounds throughout an otherwise quiet room as Merayal stares at the performers apathetically.

Rolling my eyes at her demeanor, I mumble, "This is a bad idea."

Scout's sneaky punch to my arm stops any further monologue. He stands and gives Merayal the customary Pexun greeting.

"Everyone, this is Merayal Kapu. She will be joining our team as a performer. Her Gift is unique, and it is special to us. Pypen will be training her; she is to be his partner for the show."

Merayal scowls as she looks me over. I almost stand up and demand she leaves. Demand that we hire someone else—anyone else. Knowing it would upset Scout, however, keeps me in my chair.

"Let us all introduce ourselves," Scout starts. Dramatically placing his hand over his heart, he declares, "Scout Eekan is my name, and I have the pleasure of training each of these exceptional performers."

I clear my throat. "I am Pypen Tross, and I am a performer."

"And a physician," someone jokes.

"And a housekeeper," another one says, making most of the performers laugh.

"And a shoulder to cry on," Krael adds with a feigned sob.

"And—"

"All right, all right, that is enough, children," I laugh, both annoyed by and appreciative of their teasing.

One by one, the group gives their names and positions. We have one talent scout whose job is to find new and exciting blood to fill our circus. We have two trainers who work with and push the group to do and be their best. There are two storytellers who employ their Gifts during the main event to give patrons an experience of a lifetime. Our three singers perform all the music live for both the circus itself and the main event—between the trio, they can sound like one voice or a symphony. Invaluable to us are the seven controls who handle setup and background work including lighting, temperatures, food, power distribution, etc. For the main event, we have seven dancers, although we employ some of the other team members depending on the performance's needs. Our eight performers and thirteen actors have rooms in which they display feats and talents for our patrons; the difference is that the performers take the stage while the audience watches, and the actors include the audience in their shows. There are forty-three of us. Well, forty-four now with Merayal.

When the introductions have circled themselves back to the Pexun, she juts out her chin. "I'm Merayal Kapu, and I don't know my position." She eyes the group like she dares one of them to mock her.

I would, if it would not bother Scout.

Addressing the team, Scout pushes past Merayal's brusque introduction and begins. "We will start our new tour in three months. Revenue was so high on our last tour, you all will be receiving raises."

Applause and whooping burst out amongst the group.

"Now to business," he continues, and for the next forty-five minutes, Scout is in his element, walking the performers through the main and side events. Each of the sideshows will be a foreshadowing of the main event, and both performers and controls are overwhelmed by the amount of work. Scout does his best to reassure their anxieties, and as the meeting comes to an end, he asks me to have Merayal sign our contract before leaving for practice.

As I pull up the contract on my Suus, I take a deep breath and walk towards the aggressive Pexun woman waiting in the corner of the room.

Although I know I should be above pettiness, I cannot help but ignore all pleasantries and command, "Sign this."

She eyes me suspiciously. "Don't tell me what to do, *gari*."

I do not respond to the derogatory name. Instead, I state evenly, "If you want to stay, you will do exactly as I say. Now, sign the contract."

"Pypen, where are your manners?" Scout asks from behind me. I had not realized he was listening.

Using her finger, she signs the holographic contract and turns away without another word.

"*Matza*," I swear under my breath. "If the cantankerous woman will not have manners, neither will I."

MERAYAL AND I SPEND the morning and most of the afternoon working in Thykas' room, practicing her Gift. It is not going well. Neither of us holds our tongues, and several times Scout has to break up a row. At one point, I use my Gift to renew a laceration across my brow after Merayal threw a chair at me. When Scout hurried over, she claimed I jumped in front of the chair. Taking him aside, I try to get Scout to fire her, but to my fury, he will not.

After lunch, we use Thykas' QuickEntrance door that leads straight to the auditorium. Here, we practice levitating with Skotsky.

For training purposes, I tell Merayal to put in a Redirector. At her quizzical look, I open my palm and show her the tiny piece of technology. "You will not feel it in there," I say.

"What is it?" she asks when I tell her to put it in her ear.

"It assists trainers with their pupils. Essentially, the student and trainer wear earphones enabling them to hear each other's thoughts."

She hurls it back at me. "I'm not going to wear that. You don't get to be in my head."

I bend down to pick up the costly technology she threw so flippantly. "It will only be on whilst we train, so I can see your mistakes and know what you are thinking when you make them," I say through gritted teeth. "Changing your thoughts will change your actions."

"Absolutely not."

I take a deep breath. "This is not optional."

Her smile is venomous. "I'd love nothing more than to see you try to make me do something I don't want to do." Suddenly, her eyebrows raise, and she puckers her lip. "Oh wait, your Gift is only defensive, isn't that right? You just fix your mistakes, correct?" She nods dramatically, in staged understanding. "Yes, it must be a useful Gift when you're a *gari vaunut* every moment of your life."

I am surprised at Merayal's brazen rudeness, and I have the perfect biting comeback—but I did just tell Scout I would stop fighting with her. "Listen, *wee-un*. We start our tour in six weeks. Just last month, our circus was voted one of the top twenty-five entertainment venues throughout the Hexum. People expect greatness when they frequent our humble abode." Taking a step toward her, I continue. "You do not deserve the position you have been offered. If you are at all keen on keeping it, you will prove yourself. I have no interest in fighting with you for even another second. You can leave, and I will sing praises to the universe. But if you stay, you *will* listen to me."

As if she senses how close I am to letting her go—a mere cells-breadth away—she lowers her gaze. "Fine," she states. "I will do as you ask, but I will not wear *that*." Her gaze points to the Redirector. "I don't want you in my head. I have that right."

"Everything going well?" Scout says as he comes up to us at this very moment, doing his rounds with the performers.

"She refuses to wear the Redirector," I answer.

"This *gari* will not be in my head," she says simply.

"Merayal, we do not use derogatory names in this circus," Scout reprimands. "We are all equal and deserve mutual respect. During your training, you will wear the Redirector. If your hatred kindles against the technology, perfect your parts and then there will be no need for them."

When she shakes her head, she almost looks sorry. "I'm not doing it," she pushes. Quickly, she adds, "I will work hard and perfect my parts the good old-fashioned way. I promise I can do this without *that*," she almost spits at the Redirector.

Scout eyes her for a moment then smiles. "Your confidence is so intriguing, Merayal. My expectations are high, I hope you know."

As he walks away, I roll my eyes at his indulgence with her. Everyone works with the Redirector. He should not allow her to be an exception.

As if reading my thoughts, she smiles sardonically, "Not used to losing, eh, *gari*?" She leans in closer. "Get used to it."

"We shall see."

"You talk like you're in charge, but I'm pretty sure it's that guy who makes the calls," she gestures to Scout. "And he likes me. So I think my job is secure."

"For now," I allow. "But I get the final say on whether you will be my co-star or not. You are in a trial period, and thus far you have failed."

Her smile wavers.

"Scout said I only had to give you three days, and then I could throw you out," I lie easily. "You have a lot of work to do if you want a positive review."

What is left of her smile rots into a scowl, and she flings her silver hair behind her. "Then show me what I need to do, *gari*, and I'll prove whatever you need."

I laugh harshly. "I doubt that."

"Let us try this one more time, and we will take a break," I shout across the auditorium to Merayal. "Ready, Skotsky?" I yell down to our Flight Control. It was fortunate that we found someone with the Gift of Levitation; we almost emptied all of our funds to get Skotsky and his mate to move to Ortus from Silenda.

"Skotsky is ready!" he shouts back.

Skotsky's Gift can keep Merayal and me suspended in the air, but it will take practice for her to learn how to float and fly gracefully. We both wear Effective Fly Suits—their top models. These suits enable us to control our movements even in the zero-gravity provided by Skotsky's levitation. I wish Scout were here; he is a much better director than me.

Time? I ask my Suus in my mind.

Seven thirty-five, it answers.

Scout should be up from his daily six o'clock nap. When he comes back, he can help Merayal—because I certainly am not doing a good job.

"Ready?" I ask the angry Pexun at the other end of the room.

When she nods in agreement, I fly off my pedestal towards her. She flies directly and speedily toward me.

She begins turning slightly to her left, and I attempt to slow my momentum, yelling, "Fly right, not left! Not left!" Merayal's head barely misses mine. With her arms flying out in an attempt to stop herself, she hits me directly in the throat. We both fall hard onto the blue mat below.

Black floats all around me. I hear some of the dancers saying my name. As the light begins to fill my vision, I note many voices.

Suddenly, like a lightning bolt surging through my body, I whiplash back to reality. "What the universe!" I cry, grabbing my head. When my eyes focus, Gigi stands above me with a smug smile.

"Greet the moon, Pip," she sings.

"Yes, yes, thank you. Please get off," I say, trying to hide a smile. Helping me up, Gigi lets her eyes linger on me for a couple of blinks then turns away.

"Watch where you are flailing your fat arms," Nova says to Merayal, shoving her with her shoulder before flipping her majestic Ortusan hair behind her and walking away.

"Watch yer mouth, Nova!" Veilfrah—one of our Controls—shouts after her. Turning to Merayal, he says, "Dunna worry about her, me ol' sam. She needs a mouth cleanse, is all."

Merayal's face is numb as she stares at Veilfrah. As if registering his words a few seconds too late, she throws him a dismissive smile.

"Back to work," I tell those who have surrounded us.

As the team walks away, Merayal's cheeks burn red hot. She stares out at the group with intense hatred. She will have to be the most outstanding actress in all of Elusis if she is to accomplish the sweet, gentle character of Caedis—a feat of which I do not believe she is capable.

"Was that your attempt to prove your worth?" I cannot help but rub it in her face. "I must admit, it was not impressive."

If dirty looks were a weapon, I would be on the floor bleeding. "Laugh, *gari*," Merayal says at my response to her expression. "Laugh now, but you'll regret it later."

"As in, regret it after I fire you?" I ask, still chuckling. "No, I think not. I think you will fail this trial period and then—"

I stop talking as the auditorium's doors slam open and Scout, out of breath, bursts inside. Taking a deep breath, he yells, "Everybody, pack your bags. We are to leave this night!"

14 DAYS UNTIL QUINTRALL

Pexus

Kansis

"I'VE NEVER KNOWN ANYONE to sleepwalk in such a heavy state either, Reest, but I'm telling you, she was dead asleep," I say to my boss's hologram, trying to steady the shake in my hand. "She kept mumbling about her mom. She seemed stuck in a nightmare."

The transparent body leans closer, avoiding eye contact as he inspects my wounds. "How could the Pod have hit you this hard whilst unconscious? That knock is already turning into a black eye. And your neck is raw from where she was strangling you. What makes you think she wasn't trying to escape?"

I say nothing for a moment, trying to juggle my racing thoughts. *Well, as it happens, she was in fact trying to escape so she could find her dad—you know, Arkarian Story!* The words roar so loudly in my head I'm surprised Reest can't hear them.

Legend says Arkarian Story had a daughter, and she was the only one who would know his location. But there have been no females with the last name Story, so to this day, no one knows who she is or if she even existed... Well, until today, that is!

Why am I not just telling my boss the truth? I should say it: *Reest, I found Arkarian Story's daughter. I'll take the fame and fortune now, please.* I can feel the sweat growing on my temples as my still-trembling hands threaten to betray me.

Ugh! I just need to bite the bullet and tell him the truth. I open my mouth to do so, but then I close it. For some reason, I can't tell him. After Amelia told me who her dad was, her eyes begging me to keep silent, I found myself lying to the guards. And now I'm lying to my boss.

This is so stupid. I don't owe Amelia anything. She obviously doesn't care about me—I mean, she strangled me in her attempt to escape the Ward! And yet... I keep thinking about the day we spent together. The way she made me laugh and asked me questions about my life. The way she made me feel *seen...*

I get how grossly sad this is... but if I can keep her true identity a secret, I can keep my friend a little longer.

Ew. I'm so pathetic.

"We made a breakthrough today, regardless," I tell Reest stiffly. "I think Amelia is doing well here and—"

"Breakthrough or not, that Pod outwitted you tonight. She's a military youth, and her training served her well. I am sending her to solitary confinement."

I don't know how to convince him otherwise, and I don't think it's a good idea to grovel. But if she's in confinement, I won't be able to talk to her. "Reest, please. Don't punish her for a fault she had before this world was born. Let's try to heal her, not hurt her. Our kindness gives her a chance at a better future. Isn't that what we do here?"

His iridescent eyes skitter across my own, like strangers accidentally touching arms on the street. "You like her," he observes.

I try to hide my embarrassment and lie, but I can't. Cheeks burning, I simply answer, "Yes."

He sighs. "I won't send the Pod to solitary, but she is transferring tomorrow. We don't have the skills here for her kind."

"I understand."

"Go home, Professor Willow. Your duty is done for the night."

Oh yeah it is.

Reest closes his eyes, and the hologram disappears.

I leave the office and instruct the simulans and night guards to take Amelia back to her room. She doesn't meet my eyes as they take her away.

I have no recollection of clocking out or starting the trek home. My mind is totally filled with the fact that I, Kansis Willow, have found Arkarian Story's daughter. In Ward school, there were many debates about whether "the daughter" was real. I had always sided with those who believed she wasn't. Because of this, I hadn't put any thought into a Ward staff member finding her... Let alone me!

Naturally, the first friend I manage to make is the daughter of a tyrannical maniac. This man wishes to destroy Novus as he did the old world. If someone were to awaken him, evil would threaten this world again.

Dark thoughts bombard my mind as I meander homewards.

Does Amelia know where the Sennies buried Arkarian Story? Does she wish to awaken him? Will she help him rise to power? Will he ruin Novus?

Most importantly, does Amelia know how evil this man is? Is she my friend or my enemy?

Suddenly, I find myself within my own neighborhood, in the last few streets before my house. I dodge into the trees and silently run through backyards towards my house. Yunson's younger brothers won't catch me tonight. Within minutes, I'm on my porch. I sigh.

What am I supposed to do about Amelia?

I open the door and am surprised to see someone standing in my kitchen. Is it sad that I'm excited to see another human being in my home, even if they are an intruder? I wonder why my simulan let them in.

"Can I help you?" I blurt out.

The woman turns around, and I realize it's just my healer. My vitals must have gotten bad enough that she came to check them out in person. Typically, the healers call me into their facilities; I've never had a house call before.

The healer—Hr. Ficrest—eyes me and asks, "What happened to your face?"

As I debate how best to respond, she shakes her head. "Never mind. I'll fix that too. I've been waiting for three hours," she says, clearly annoyed.

"I got held up at work," I respond.

"Every time I was about to leave, your vitals would spike alarmingly." She ignores my weak attempt at justifying wasting her precious time. "I'm surprised you're standing, Professor Willow. Your health statistics show you are dangerously malnourished, adrenaline overloaded, and under-slept." She looks at my fridge where my stats are dismally listed then takes a step toward me. "Come here quickly; you're about to pass out."

That feels accurate. "Yeah... I meant to eat earlier..." I shut the front door and step into the kitchen, trying to remember how she does her work. Healers each have their own way of dispensing their Gifts. Some use serums or lotions, some use digestible pills, and some speak over you. Hr. Ficrest, however, tentatively touches my hand, and it feels like a breath of cool wind is blowing into my veins. Goosebumps break out over my body. She touches my head, stomach, face, arms, and legs.

When she's done, she declares, "There. You are perfect." She brushes her hands together like she's trying to get the remnants of *me* off her skin.

"Thank you," I say, touching my face. The tenderness around my eyes is gone. The bruising on my windpipe and my neck has disappeared as well.

Eager to get away, Hr. Ficrest murmurs a farewell as she lets herself out of my house. My simulan comes and takes my bag from me.

"Your simulan was worried about you," it says.

I collapse in a chair even though I feel better than I've felt in weeks. Physically, anyway. The healer couldn't fix my emotional exhaustion. My mental sickness. My bad blood.

"Can your simulan do anything to serve you?" it asks. "Food can be made hastily."

I don't answer but instead lift my hands like a child. My simulan helps me up and half carries me to my room. It tucks me into my comforter and leaves me for the night.

As I take my moon-shaped pendant out of the bedside drawer, I find myself thinking about Amelia's face as she asked for my help. She wasn't scared, necessarily. It almost looked like she was annoyed. Like it made her mad that she had to make the request. But even if she is angry, I don't care. If she's the daughter of a mass murderer, I don't care. The truth is, I want to help this girl because I've never been somebody's last hope before…

Ontzi, I'm pitiful… no, I'm nauseating.

I will my attention back to the pendant by squeezing it as hard as I can. The druzy quartz hurts my hand as I curl my fist around it, but I don't let go. This fantasy world is my only escape. The dream-state I'm addicted to is the only place I'm happy.

> Not quite awake, not quite asleep, I open my eyes to our apartment in uptown Depalo, in the Windy Heights District. I've just walked through the front door, and Kyloni and Aystra, my daughters, run past me, giggling. I look across our tiny kitchen, and there he is. My heartbeat quickens—he's so handsome. Dream Aker gets up from our kitchen table. He struts across the room to me and cups my face. "How was your day? Tell me everything, Kans." His use of my childhood nickname sends chills down my spine.
>
> As he kisses me, I forget all about my pain, the Pod, and Arkarian Story.

You're telling me… that you… that you found Arkarian Story's daughter.

Yep.

But you…

Yes.

You found his daughter… You need to go back there right now!

Go back? Why?

She'll be transferred tomorrow, and you'll never get to her again! You have to get her out. There is an entrance into the Ward through the supply closet in the Palace. All we need to do is get you into the Palace and—

Are you kidding me? Do you want to get us killed? I could get arrested and be executed for at least seven different convictions!

She needs you, Kansis! If anyone finds out she is Arkarian Story's daughter, she'll be shipped to Silenda for questioning. She'll be tortured until she tells them Arkarian Story's location. You have just this brief opportunity to keep her safe.

Keep her safe?

Didn't you just finish telling me that she's your new best friend?

Yeah, I mean, I did—but I don't want the Guardians to send me to a Den for kidnapping. I can talk to her tomorrow.

Tomorrow she'll be under stricter security. Tonight—right now—is your only chance.

…I don't know…

Not only will you rescue Amelia, but you'll be the one to find Arkarian Story! You'll go down in history, Kansis. Every Elusian will know your name, and Depalo won't shun you anymore. And the reward… Think of all you could do with the prize compensation. It's a hundred and fifteen Cheio—you'd be financially stable for the rest of your life!

I don't care about the reward. And I don't need any more people knowing about me and my useless blood.

You could afford a Blood Transfusion.

I'm sure I'm laughing in my sleep. Like Aker would ever go along with it.

What if he would? You could finally do it. You could have Aker, Kansis.

No… he would never do it.

Why not ask him? You won't know until you ask.

What am I supposed to say to him? "Hello to you, Aker—the man who hates me and desires someone else. I may happen upon an incredible amount of Cheio soon, and if I do, will you undergo a procedure where my blood will be forced into your genes once more, in the hopes that you will stop loving Mirindiss and love me? I mean, I know the first batch didn't work, but maybe the second time will do the trick?"

No. He would never agree.

But what if he would, Kansis? Think of it.

Aren't you the one always telling me to stop imagining us together?

It could be a reality.

But you hate Aker!

I do. I hate him.

Ugh, you're ridiculous. Aker and I are not an actuality, as you have so pleasantly put it in the past. And even if we were, what would I do once I took Amelia? Tomorrow night is the Remembrance Ball, and people will be suspicious if I'm not there. There's no way to pull this off.

You could keep her at your house tomorrow, go to the Remembrance Ball, and then leave.

They would still know that it was me. The Guardians will track me down within the day. And where would I even go?

...What if there was someone to protect you?

Like who? Who would protect me?

I don't know. I just have this feeling that tomorrow night you're going to meet someone who will protect you both.

Why are you saying that? I don't have a prophecy Gift.

I don't know, Kansis... I just have this overwhelming feeling that you'll meet your protector tomorrow night.

Well, I don't know if you remember this, but *you* are *me*. And I don't feel that way at all.

I am a part of you! Have some faith in me, or better yet, yourself. Hear me out. You know how to get into the Ward—

No, I don't! Why do you keep saying that?

There is a tunnel to the Ward underneath the supply room in the Palace, remember?

No, I *don't* remember.

Think about it... Let me show you.

Wait... I do remember. On the third floor... the supply room. ...If you go behind the cupboard... and move the barrels of rennix beans and leaves... There's a secret door. How do I...? I don't remember that. I mean, I see it right now, but I don't remember ever being there.

I brought the memory forward from your subconscious. You were in there when you were just a kid.

I didn't know you could do that.

There is much about this side of yourself that you don't know. But focus! There is nothing more important than you getting Amelia out of there.

What if she doesn't want to go with me?

You'll have to convince her. Now, once you go through the tunnel, you'll enter

No, stop right there! I don't care what the next step is because I'm not going to go. I'm not going to sneak her out. I won't. I don't even know how to get into the Palace! I'm not going to do it... No. Stop it.

It's one-thirty in the morning. And what am I doing? Am I sleeping in my bed, getting a much-needed rest after a hard day? No. Oh no. I'm sneaking into the Palace so I can break into the Ward, steal a Pod, and take her out of the city with some protector my subconscious is convinced I'm going to meet tomorrow night... What is wrong with me?!

Somehow, I manage to get into the Palace. For reasons I can't fathom let alone explain, the back door to the building—the door which only allows entrance with DNA verification—is unlocked and open, ready for me to walk through. And what's more bizarre is that all the hallway cameras are off. Oh, and did I mention there are no simulans anywhere?

Maybe this is a dream.

Maybe I'm going crazy.

Maybe I made up some pretend voice in my head just to make an excuse to do stupid stuff.

Awesome.

I make my way to the cupboard and move the rennix beans and leaves. Huh. There's the tunnel. I step into this unfamiliar passageway that I apparently know about. It's dark, and there are spiders everywhere. Clearly, no one has used the tunnel in a long time. Maybe not since the founders of Depalo built it. All I know is that it smells terrible, and it's wet. My shoes are drenched. I swear, if I have hundred-year-old feces in my toes right now, I will suffocate myself.

And then, get this, I emerge at the other end into the supply closet by the texture room to find that someone has turned off the cameras in the Ward. Their tell-tale sign of operation—bright red indicators—are strangely snuffed out. That N-E-V-E-R happens. Never. I walk through the halls, and they are empty—no simulans or night guards to be seen. And now, I've reached Amelia's room, and there are no watchmen standing outside her door.

I don't know what's going on.

Looking up and down the halls to ensure it's definitely empty, I tiptoe to her door, lift my arm to scan in and almost scream as I suddenly catch myself. I have staff access to this room, which means I can easily unlock Amelia's door by holding my wrist up to the scanner. But if I do that, it will be recorded in the mainframe that I was here! I'm stuck, right outside my prize.

Well, maybe... I tentatively reach for the doorknob. I've been unbelievably lucky this far... I place my hand on it, and my heart misses a beat when I hear the knob clicking open. You have got... to be kidding me.

I glance inside the room. Amelia's not in her bed.

Suddenly my face explodes with pain, and I'm on the floor again, a body on my chest, hands around my neck. I don't have my Shocker, so I try to speak, but I'm quickly losing consciousness.

I manage a strained, "Help... I'm here... to help... you... please."

Amelia loosens her grip.

"You said..." I gasp, and Amelia slightly relaxes her grip so I can gulp in a deeper breath. "You said you wanted help finding Arkarian Story. I can help you."

Her face is shrouded by her hair, her voice firm and hard as she asks, "How?"

"I don't know," I gasp. "I just know I can get you out."

"How?" she demands again.

"You're going to have to trust me," I rasp.

"I don't."

"Then why did you tell me who you are?" I claw at her hands, but she doesn't move them. "You must trust me a little."

My eyes have adjusted to the darkness and the lack of oxygen, and I see her shadowed face for the first time. It's emotionless, yet her eyes bore into mine.

She knows she would be putting her life in my hands if she were to come with me.

"I know that you don't know who I am, and you have no real reason to go with me," I sputter between wheezing breaths. "I am not the bravest, strongest, most Gifted, or intelligent of people." *Ontzi*, how true. "I am known only for my bad blood. But this blood is all I have, and I offer it to you. Tomorrow, you will be transferred cross-territory to a Ward you can't escape from. You have no Gifts—once there, you will be completely powerless."

I try for another deep breath but only manage a shallow rattle. "I can't guarantee I will keep you safe forever," I whisper, "but I will fight to help you, with everything inside me. If the Guardians catch me doing this—freeing you—my Gift will be stripped, and they'll send me to a blood reclamation den. I am risking all."

Her eyes narrow. "Why should I trust you?"

Good point. I don't actually know. Honestly, I have no idea why I'm doing this. But that's not going to make Amelia want to leave with me. Once more I try to pull her hands off my neck, but she holds them firmly in place. "Everyone I've ever known has rejected me," I gasp. "As pathetic as it is, you're my only friend. I know it's because you don't understand... what I am... But, please, let me help you." My ears perk with adrenaline, and I catch noises down the hall. "You must decide now. The simulan guards are coming this way."

She searches my eyes as if she has a Truthseer Gift. I force honesty into them, hoping she sees it.

"You say I don't know what you are," Amelia says slowly, "so what are you?"

I take as deep a breath as I can manage and answer, "I am a mistake."

Her brows furrow, and she gazes intently at my facial features. I'm not sure if she finds whatever it is that she's looking for, but she slowly gets off of me and reaches down to help me up. I rub my neck which is throbbing with dull pain. She slaps my arm in what appears to be an affectionate gesture.

"Okay, Freckles, lead the way."

Ortus

Pypen

"I HAVE MADE MY decision," Scout says for the third time.

Infuriated, I try once more. "You cannot ask us to leave now, Scout. It is too soon! Merayal has not even had *one* day to practice—and from what I witnessed she cannot be Caedis. How can you not see this is a bad idea?" I use all of my conscious effort to keep my voice even.

Holding my gaze, Scout speaks slowly, "I have made my decision." He says each word with punctuation. I know his intent is not to belittle me, but my pride flashes nonetheless.

"And Scout's words are the ultimate truth, yes?" Usually, I can control the beast in my blood, but sometimes it feels uncontainable—particularly after my trying afternoon with Merayal. I hate my rage, but I despise it most when it comes out at Scout. Did I not promise him my undying loyalty?

His tired eyes rove around our flat. It is relatively empty, with just a scattering of possessions we keep here instead of in our office where it seems we truly live. Scout takes in Cazney's favorite chair, my old, first-generation HugMe bean bag, and the mantel where his father's hand-made wooden hunting bow hangs. Finally, his eyes rest on me. "If you do not wish to come, Pypen, no one is going to force you. You can stay. So can any of the circus members. I am not forcing anyone to go, Merayal included."

His dismissal cuts my veins like a razor. Does Scout wish for me to stay behind? "You know I am bound to you."

"By your own doing, Pypen!" he shouts back at me. Unsuccessfully raking his fingers through his braid, Scout closes his eyes. "I never asked you to repay me." His voice resumes its measured, even tone. "I never expected you to stay with me this long."

Scout consistently downplays my debt. When I promised to stay with him and protect him after the incident, I meant it. I glance down at the prancing lion tattoo on my wrist. Its center is red but fades to orange whilst the edges are lined with green. When I look up, he is watching me with a troubled expression.

"You wish to dismiss me?" I ask, unable to keep the incredulity from my voice. I have spent the last eight years following and safeguarding him.

Scout rubs his hands on his scalp, sighing in frustration. "You know I would never send you away, Pip. However, I desire that you not follow me out of obligation. You have fulfilled any perceived debt to me tenfold. Finding Arkarian Story has always been the *reason* for the Unopened Gifts, but that has not been what fuels me or makes me wish to come here every day. Working here has always been more than a job; it is the same for you—these people have become our family and this group, our purpose. But it is finally happening: we are going to find Arkarian Story. And if anyone—especially you—were to die on my behalf..." He swallows painfully. "I want you to be free to do as you wish."

I take in his words without comment, and silence falls between us. Finally I reply, "My free decision is to go with you." Smiling, I add, "I would be friendless without all of you fools."

Scout's laugh floods my veins with joy. "That is true."

"I suppose we have already collapsed the circus tent and placed it in the bank?"

He smiles, knowing I have capitulated. "Indeed."

"And you said that we are meeting a girl?" I probe for details, relieved the tension between us is gone.

He slowly nods his head.

"But who is she?"

"The Sixth Aevum said she is a Ward Reintegrator who gained enough of the daughter's trust to encourage her to reveal her identity," he explains.

"How is the Sixth Aevum in contact with this girl?" I ask.

"He did not say," Scout replies.

"Is the girl's Gift useful to us?"

He laughs lightly. "Not even slightly."

I nod. "Will this girl come with us also, or will we just take the supposed daughter?"

Scout crosses the room to the door, pulling on his suede jacket as he answers, "The girl will come with us."

"Will not the Ward be suspicious that she left at the same time her Pod disappeared?"

He shrugs. "The Sixth Aevum is confident in his plan."

"As he always is." I know my limit of questions is close at hand, but I will press until asked to stop. "How will this girl leave her family and position? Surely she cannot just up and leave her life."

Scout tugs his hair loose and begins re-braiding it. "The Sixth Aevum says the girl is in a unique situation and would be more than willing to leave all behind."

"Now I am intrigued," I muse. "I must know more about this Ward Reintegrator. Her mate will come along as well then?"

"From what I understood, the mate will be left behind."

The plan suddenly sounds ludicrous to me. "But how can this be?" I ask.

"I believe the Sixth Aevum is giving this girl a legitimate alibi."

"Indeed, he must. Perhaps her mate is blind and deaf, and the Sixth Aevum plans on leaving a replacement mate in her stead?"

Scout barks a cynical laugh. "Indeed. Blind and deaf."

Someone knocks on the door to our flat. It opens and Emerly swaggers in, winking at me before turning to Scout. "Ready?" he asks.

"Ready for what?" I inquire.

Emerly and Scout smile at one another, and I immediately know what he is inferring. "We leave on this mission in just two hours, Scout," I blurt out. "Buscador foolishness—of all the things we have not time for right now!"

He grins darkly. "Oh, Pypen, you need not come."

"To seek the wisdom of the Superiors? You are absolutely right about that. I have no need to fraternize with that strange society. Must I remind you of what happened the last time I let you and Emerly go by yourselves? No. No, we will not have another summer of 414."

"That was *one* occurrence. And I still feel no regret for what happened," Scout says.

"Emerly, must you fan this flame?" I ask, exasperated.

He smirks and answers in his singsong Formosian way. "I'm intrigued, aren't I? Who knows whether the Buscadors are right? Plus, they always have delicious food, they do."

"You do not keep Scout safe," I state, frowning.

Emerly clicks his tongue. "Scout can take care of himself better than I can, can't he? Who am I supposed to be keeping him safe from?"

"Himself," I growl.

"The circus is safe at the bank, and we have a couple of hours before the bus leaves. We have plenty of time," Scout interjects. Turning to Emerly, he returns the query, "Ready?"

"You have yet to pack!" I call out through the doorway as the pair saunters down the hall. Scout does not reply. Cursing, I shut the door behind me and follow after Scout and Emerly. "There is no profit in these meetings. Save for the profit they make off of you, *patkas*."

"I would prefer you not go," Scout says without turning around. "Everyone knows you are an unbeliever the moment you enter."

"You make that sound like a negative thing," I grumble. "In addition, you will miss your daily nap if you leave."

"We will be back in time," Scout retorts. "We are only stopping in."

"What does it matter to you if he goes to these meetings?" Emerly asks.

I huff. "I hate seeing you two getting caught up in false emotions and doctrines."

"We do not get *caught up*," Scout argues.

I gawk at the way they have deceived themselves. "Explain to me, please, what ten aons' worth of 'communication' gadgets are doing in our flat? Or the twenty aons' worth of 'connection water' in our office? You buy everything you think will get you in contact with a Superior."

"Someone has to have the answers, Pypen," Scout responds quietly.

His conviction shuts me up. For reasons beyond conception, it is essential for Scout that there are higher answers than those taught in primer school science. I question not whether Auctus and Effio came from Mensonge and started our planet. I question not that we live for Elusis' benefit, growth, and evolution. I question not that we are here to enjoy life to its fullest because we only have these two hundred years. I question not that when we pass, we fall into forever sleep. Not one iota of these facts bothers me... but it bothers Scout to his core. And I must not mock his need to find more comprehensive answers.

I must not, but I do.

Our destination is a restaurant in midtown. When we reach the door, a giant of a Silentar stands guard. Scout and Emerly each go down on one knee, reciting together, "May the Superiors be found."

At Scout's punch, I fall to one knee and mutter the same.

"Welcome, Seekers," the Silentar says. "On tonight's agenda, we seek Asiri, Nu Aneh, and Gizem."

Having said his piece, the Silentar allows us entrance. We somehow find seats together within the crowded restaurant. "Have we missed much?" Scout asks a Sanusian at the table next to ours.

"It's just startin', me ol' sam. Who're ye wolly well here for?" he asks.

"I seek Raaisel," Scout answers quickly, while Emerly responds, "I seek Bhēta and Tayna."

When the Sanusian turns to me, I reply, "The only thing I seek is food. Do I wait for a simulan, or must I find one?"

The Sanusian huffs and turns away without answering. I understand that all he heard was sarcasm, but I genuinely would like to order some food.

"Fellow Seekers! You are most welcome, aren't you?" A gorgeous Formosian woman (are there any other types of Formosians?) stands on a chair by the kitchen. The Buscador insignia—a flame surrounded by smoke—is painted artistically on a banner behind her. "There are not many of us out there, but we have one goal, and with that goal, we seek as one. Stand, and we will share our intentions, we will."

I loathe this part the most.

The entire restaurant stands, but I stay seated. As I yawn, they recite, "We are the Buscadors. On the world's behalf, we seek the Superiors to find answers to life's most complex questions. We will exchange information, share findings, give testimonies, and support each other in our individual journeys to the truth. Superiors, may we find you." They shout a hurrah and return to their seats.

"To those of you who are new Seekers, you are most welcome, you are," the Formosian woman continues. "For the past three hundred years, the Buscadors have been seeking out the Superiors. Twenty-eight Superiors have been communicated with or spoken of throughout Elusis. They have revealed themselves by different names. Tonight, we will have testimonies of Asiri, the Compassionate Superior; Nu Aneh, the Providing Superior; and Gizem, the Worthy Superior." Just before she vacates her chair-stage, she ends her speech with, "Seeker, share your findings."

I accost a passing waiter and quickly order food before things get too under way.

An Ortusan man with waist-length hair walks to the front of the restaurant and steps up onto the 'stage'.

"Greet the moon, Buscadors. I have been seeking for twelve years, and"—his whole face breaks out into a smile—"for the first time, I had an encounter." He nods to the group and takes a deep breath. "I am an employee at the Vorbi Interterritorial Replenishing Corporation, and last week I was falsely accused of Vorbi theft. As we are all aware, Vorbi theft is a Gift-stripping malefaction. The Truthseer declared that, with ill will, I stole over 400 Cheio. But this was a lie."

The crowd murmurs in shock. To my surprise, the man has even drawn me into the tale. Crime is so rare. In fact, the only type I have personally beheld is in the cinema—horrifying and somehow entertaining portrayals of an archaic way of life left behind by the vast majority of metahumans.

The man continues, "The judge gave me a chance to defend myself, but there was nothing I could say—the jury would surely believe the Truthseer's words over mine. I begged for a different Truthseer, but the judge refused and said the evidence against me was enough."

"That night, my mate called upon this assembly to seek Asiri, asking him to have compassion for my situation. You also sought Skrivnost, for wisdom in handling the situation and defending me. I could never quite express my thankfulness for those of you who came that night." At this point, the man chokes up, and it takes him a moment to continue his story.

"The very next day, the judge dreamed that there had been a conspiracy and I had been framed. He sent three Truthseers to speak with me, and each one told the truth of the matter: I had nothing to do with the theft. Guardians arrested the Truthseer who had lied about me and found out she was a part of the plot. She and her three accomplices had their Gifts stripped, and they were sent to a blood reclamation den this morning."

The restaurant explodes in applause. Over the din, the man shouts, "Hurrah Asiri!" and the group repeats it. "Hurrah, Skrivnost!" he cries, and the group echoes him again. Scout and Emerly are among the loudest voices.

As he steps down from the chair, wiping at his eyes, several Buscadors hurry to greet the man we have just heard. They congratulate him on his encounter and reestablished reputation, and I roll my eyes and look about the room for the waiter—my hunger has increased since being here.

It was a great story, and I cannot deny it. But I do not comprehend why these people must attribute his restitution to a being more superior than a metahuman. There is no logic in this need for something bigger than themselves. Why can they not understand they are enough on their own?

A Pexun woman steps up onto the chair next. She surveys the room with an air of confidence and showmanship. "Greet the moon, fellow Seekers," she begins dramatically. "Tonight, I share a tale of Nu Aneh—the Superior who helps all whether we recognize it or not. My mate and I have been dreaming of starting a business here in Vultus, and we ensured we had the correct permits and approvals to get it going. But an investor pulled out last month, halting all the momentum we had established over the past year.

"I cried out to Nu Aneh to no avail. I was true in my devotion, but my mate was an unbeliever. I told my mate that the only way Nu Aneh would bless our business was if he would humble himself and seek Nu Aneh's help. Two weeks ago, in desperation, my mate came to one of these meetings and, with me, asked for Nu Aneh's provision."

She pauses and stares out at the crowd. "Fellow Buscadors, this morning we received a call from an investor in Gati—he heard about our venture and wants to buy out the other investors and take over all of our funding. Nu Aneh has seen our loyalty and blessed our humility! Hurrah, Nu Aneh! Provider for those who seek him with all of their blood."

A man—presumably the now-believing mate—helps her down from the chair, smiles spread across both their faces. They, too, are greeted with congratulations.

Then the Formosian who welcomed us to the meeting settles everyone down. "Before we move on, Mika will share a few mementos from her travels with us."

At that moment, my food arrives. As the waiter walks away, Mika's voice fills the restaurant with an impassioned spiel on the newest communication gadget she found in Sanus.

I stand corrected. I detest *this* part the most.

"—and so far, we have had fifteen Seekers come forward with testimonies of reaching Superiors. The Seeking Candle is a must-have if you are truly a dedicated Buscador."

"You may not buy it," I whisper to Scout as I shovel in a mouthful of hot food.

"I know."

"Do you?"

He huffs in response.

"You know they never work; it is merely a way to make compensation. Please tell me you know that."

He nods.

"Scout, I need you to verbally confirm that the communication gadgets do not work."

I flick his cheek when he does not answer.

He grabs my hand to bend my fingers backward, but I use my other hand to flick him again.

He allows his eyes to meet mine. "I will not buy anything, Pypen. Just let me listen, please."

I permit him to hear the last of what is really just a commercial, focusing instead on devouring my food. These delectable meals are the only reason

I come to these foolish assemblies with Scout and Emerly—this place has some of the best bread in all of Ortus. So I accompany the pair of them for the bread—and to keep Scout from selling his soul.

The Formosian woman approaches our table as Mika's speech ends. "You are Scout Eekan, yes?"

Scout nods.

"We have selected your name to be blessed in the hallowed waters tonight, haven't we? Will you follow me to the back?"

I grab Scout's arm as he stands. "We do not have time for this."

"We have plenty of time, Pypen," he replies.

I squeeze his arm tighter. "Do not do this."

He yanks away. "The bus will not leave without my say."

When he turns to nod at Emerly, his scowl becomes an excited grin. He follows the Formosian out of the main room to the back of the building.

I shove my plate away and spit out every foul word that comes to mind.

"Are you finished with your toddleresque outburst?" Emerly starts eating my abandoned meal.

"Leave me," I growl.

He licks his fingers before replying. "They have not chosen his name before, have they? Let him enjoy this; he deserves it, he does."

"This is just going to entice him more, Emerly! How do you not see this?"

Emerly shakes his head. "How is it that his interest in the Superiors affects you so?"

"Because the longer he believes this, the more disappointed he will be when he realizes it is a sham."

My Formosian companion raises his eyebrows at me, munching away at my leftovers. "And what if it is not a sham?"

"But what if it is?"

We are at an impasse. Neither of us speaks, and Emerly polishes off the last of my meal as we listen to the final testimony. As the seeker is wrapping up his tale, Scout rejoins our table. His hair is damp, and his face glows with exhilaration.

"How was it?" Emerly asks, and Scout leans in to whisper a response.

Good. I do not wish to know about it anyway. "It is time," I state and stand. Not waiting to see if Scout and Emerly are following, I walk out of the restaurant.

I barely leave the doorway when a man rushes at me yelling, "Asiri is coming!" He tries to grab my shoulders as he earnestly claims again, "Asiri is coming!" I shove him off me and keep walking. I try not to laugh as the man rants behind me, "Make ready, make ready! Asiri is coming!"

"You know, this is why I wish you not to come," Scout comments over my shoulder.

"Apologies," I say and I turn to face them both, releasing the laugh I had been withholding. "'Asiri is coming'? How do you not find these meetings as humorous as I do?"

"I believe them too, I do, Scout," Emerly says.

I snicker sardonically. "Scout, will you lift your feet a little higher so Emerly can better kiss them?"

"Be not bitter because he does not join your mocking of me," Scout responds.

"I will be as bitter as I wish."

"And I will kiss whose feet I wish, won't I?" Emerly says and quickly snatches Scout's leg up. He kisses Scout's boot as Scout hops on one foot, laughing.

"You get to talk to an Aevum—should that not be enough for you?" I ask Scout.

"The Aevii were born just like everyone else."

"Like everyone else?" I laugh. "The Aevii are infinitely above us."

Scout shakes his head. "They are immortal. That is the only aspect that differentiates us from them. The Superiors are above being created."

"Do you truly believe in all this?" I ask Emerly.

"I do."

"But why? Why look for these 'Superiors?'" I mock. "What do you need outside of yourself?"

Emerly takes a moment before he answers. "Scout looks for the Creator Superior. He sees Elusis. He sees himself. He wants more than, 'We always were and always will be.' It's important to him—essential even—for him to know why he was created, isn't it? I look for Bhēta, the Merciful Superior. I see the corruption in our territories. And I see myself." His voice breaks.

Until this point in his explanation, I have been frowning at the ground, but now I lift my gaze to meet his.

Emerly's almond-shaped eyes brim with tears. His wide mouth, normally set in a grin, pulls itself into a deep frown. "I want mercy, don't I? I need to find out if forgiveness is possible for the things... from the things I've done."

"If you require forgiveness, why not go to those whom you have wronged?" I ask.

Shaking his head, he responds brokenly, "My marrow itself needs forgiveness, it does."

I do not understand. Who could forgive him except for the very people he hurt? What a strange notion to think he requires forgiveness from some higher power. What kind of Superior could possibly have the ability to absolve Emerly's guilt?

A silence falls between us. I wonder to what Emerly could be referring. We ran an extensive background check on him before we hired him. From what terrible things could he possibly need forgiveness?

"I understand." Scout's words are so full of emotion I am compelled to look at him also. His jaw is tight, and his eyes are facing forward. I know he knows I am looking at him, yet he does not meet my stare.

"Well, I understand not," I say firmly. "You are a remarkable man, Emerly. If you have unfinished business with someone, go and talk to them. You need nothing from anyone else."

Emerly nods slowly, unconvinced.

This is why I wish not for them to go to these meetings! How obtuse—how moronic—for anyone to teach Emerly that he needs some Superior Being to forgive him. Emerly is a better man than I, and I need nothing from anybody.

Next time they go to a meeting, I will burn the building down.

13 DAYS UNTIL QUINTRALL

Pexus

Kansis

IWAKE UP AND groan. My heart seems to beat out of rhythm. I think about what today will bring and pull the covers over my head. I'd rather stay in bed all day than face my workplace… face Aker… face Amelia… face my Protector… But I'll raise suspicion if I stay snuggled under my comforter, so up I get.

I walk out of my room, intent on waking Amelia, but as I reach the kitchen I'm surprised to see she is standing by the stovetop, cooking breakfast with my simulan. When she notices me, she breaks out into a smile. "Cute pajamas! You look so different without your uniform on." She bounds over and ruffles my hair, shocking me. Unless it's a reluctant healer forced to do her job, people don't touch me.

"I like your curls," Amelia goes on, returning to the kitchen. "Hey, I didn't know what you like to eat, so your roommate helped me make you something."

Given how late it was when we arrived at my house last night—not to mention the fact that I was still processing the magnitude of what I'd done—I hadn't felt quite ready to explain to Amelia what simulans are. So I let her think mine is a trustworthy human roommate… that's going to be awkward later on.

"Your eggs are weird," Amelia comments, holding a forkful up for examination. "Why does everything have to be so different? It's like I'm on an entirely new planet. I went for a run this morning—"

"You left the house?" I ask, both horrified and exasperated.

"Of course," she replies and shrugs. "I always start my day with a run. Anyway, I can't believe how much nature has changed. The colors are actually different, like you said. Do they keep the Ward looking more like my world so it's not as difficult to deal with? That outside area felt pretty familiar, except for the color of the sky." She laughs ruefully. "It's a good idea if they designed it that way because seeing it all for real was definitely overwhelming."

"Amelia, you can't leave the house," I command, not willing to be distracted by her chattiness.

"I didn't go back towards town," she responds, speaking as if I were a small child and she is explaining why it's okay to touch the stove when the burning pads aren't on. "I just ran through the forest behind your house. Speaking of your house, it's really, really cute. It's simple, but the design makes it feel welcoming. How long have you lived here with your roommate?"

Not knowing how to respond to these compliments, and definitely not ready to have the simulan conversation, I blurt out with no preamble, "You're Arkarian Story's daughter."

If she's startled by my sudden change in subject, her face doesn't betray it. "I already told you that," she answers simply.

"You want to wake him up, then?" I ask.

Looking me square in the eye, she asks, "If I say yes, will you turn me in?" Her voice loses some of its pleasant tone, a hint of threat hedges around the edges.

"No," I answer quickly. "I mean... I don't think so. I don't want to."

Jutting out her chin, she stalks around my kitchen counter and takes a few steps toward me. She straightens her frame, and I have to look up at her to maintain eye contact. Amelia is easily fifteen centimeters taller than me, and she stares down at me, obviously trying to—and entirely succeeding in—intimidating me. "Why are you helping me?" she asks.

Even with this alpha dog show, I am not afraid of her. Intimidated, yes; scared, no. Granted, I know she could seriously hurt me, but I'm not worried by that. As stupid as it sounds—and I know it's pitiful—this girl is looking me in the eyes, standing so close I can feel her breath on my face. After so long being deprived of human touch, whether meta or subhuman, even this threatening interaction makes me feel warm and fuzzy.

"All I know is that I want to help you," I reply. It may only be because I want to be near someone who won't shun me, but that won't convince Amelia. I try harder. "You need someone familiar with this world, and I can help you."

"Help me what?" she inquires.

Now that is a good question. It is written that Arkarian Story holds the key to the world's destruction or survival... She must know what that key is. What if she's just being nice—I mean, aside from the threatening and strangling—so that I help her awaken Arkarian Story for him to rule and ruin Novus?

Well, of course she is, you *vaunut*.

"Okay, fine; what is your plan?" I ask.

She is so close I can smell the toothpaste on her breath. "Would you still go with me if I wanted to wake up Arkarian Story so that he can rule over you like you said in your lesson?"

I try to process her question. Would I? Okay, let's think this through.

Pros: I would get to leave Depalo and travel with this girl and our Protector (whoever that may be) and finally be around someone who looks me in the eye and is willing to touch me. I might get the reward for finding Arkarian Story, and with it, I could pay for a Blood Transfusion with Aker. The healers would fix my blood, and the shunning would stop.

Cons: I release the worst evil from Senex on Novus, and everything becomes as terrible as it was before the metahumans made the world good. What is wholesome will become bad; what is beautiful will become hideous. I would literally ruin the world.

Could I really live in my own veins knowing I was the key that opens the door to evil again?

I finally land on the truth and, despite internally struggling to admit it, I respond, "No. No, I couldn't help you if that was your plan."

So everything I've done for Amelia was pointless after all.

"Good," she says bluntly and lets out a small laugh. "Because I want to kill him." She relaxes her menacing pose, takes a few steps back and reaches out her hand in a customary Senny agreement gesture. I grab her hand and shake it.

I can't help but laugh as well. This girl's swings from intimidating seriousness to silly humor make me dizzy. "Interesting. I never thought I'd be so relieved to hear someone say they want to commit murder." I pause then add, "I mean it. I will help you, whatever it is you need."

Amelia stands with her feet shoulder-width apart and crosses her arms. Good thing she stopped trying to convince me she isn't military. Everything about her says otherwise. "Do you have a plan?" she asks.

I do, but I have no idea how to explain it to her. How do I verbalize my relationship with my Protector?

"I'm not quite sure how to put it... but somehow I know that tonight I'm going to meet someone who will help us. Protect us."

"Is that your Gift? Knowing the future?"

"It's not... Well, maybe it is... I don't know if she's a Gift or not. But at night, right after I've fallen asleep, there's this voice in my head... who is me... or a part of me. And she has her own abilities apparently..." At the skeptical look on Amelia's face, I stop and take a deep breath. "She said someone is going to meet me tonight, and I believe her."

Amelia smirks cynically. "A voice in your head tells you someone is coming to help and protect us, and you believe it?"

"Hey, she helped me rescue you last night, okay? Look, if I'm wrong, we'll make a Plan B. But for now, this is the best chance we've got."

She nods, lips pursed, obviously unconvinced.

I glance at the blinking display on my fridge screen. Shocked at the time, I curse and run back to my room to get dressed. Trying to comb through my untamable hair has me slamming my hands on the bathroom counter in frustration. I inherited my mom's tightly coiled spirals, and she was never around to teach me how to style them. Before my town-wide shame, I just paid a Beautician to soothe them into controllable curls, but now... Well, I'm not allowed into such establishments.

I stare at my reflection in the mirror critically. Even though Hr. Ficrest removed the black eye Amelia had given me yesterday evening, Amelia had punched me again when I rescued her. A new bruise now blooms in its place, just as angry as the first one.

I desperately search my closet for something to wear to the Remembrance Ball tonight, but I don't have any proper costumes. Resigned, I grab my one fancy dress, stuff it into my bag, and decide I'll do some tweaking at the Ward to make it into something workable.

When I return to the living room, Amelia and my simulan are placing breakfast on the small countertop I use as a table. Amelia and I both eat quickly, but I push my empty plate away first. "Make her food whenever she wants it," I tell my simulan as I grab my bag and rummage through it to check it has everything I need for the day.

I look around my tiny house, wishing I had something to offer as a means of entertainment. Unfortunately, I lead a very simple life and have nothing to keep Amelia amused while I'm gone. I sigh. "I don't know what you're going to do all day, but I'll be back tonight. Whatever you do, don't leave the house."

Rolling her eyes, Amelia asks, "Do you have any weights?"

"Weights?"

"For working out."

Ha! Me? Work out? I shake my head. "No... nothing like that."

She shrugs. "Okay, any books or magazines?"

"No." Like I could ever afford anything made of real paper. "That's not how we obtain information, news, and social updates in Novus."

"Well, how do you obtain those things?"

"Through a Suus. Imagine the smartphones from Senex and then multiply its power, accessibility, and function by one hundredfold." I show her the small scar on my wrist. I could have had the scar healed, but I never did. "Unfortunately, it's inside me. I can't give it to you."

"Fine. Do you have a TV?"

"We don't share the same cinematic experiences you once did," I answer, my teacher-mode activating over all these questions. "The people of Senex used the excuse of home entertainment systems to stay isolated and unproductive. In Novus, communities experience cinematic events together. We have a theater downtown where people can watch what you would have called movies or TV shows, but with others." I smile. "Although the experience is much different to what you will remember."

Amelia sighs. "No books, no magazines, no TV, no social media... Is it your Gift that you're content to lead such a boring life?" she asks dryly.

I can't help but laugh. "From strangling me to poking fun at me. I don't know what to expect from you."

Her smirk widens. "I am sorry about that."

"Yeah, you look like you are."

She raises her hands. "No, truly I am. I was impressed by your resourcefulness with that taser. Very unexpected."

"Am I supposed to say thank you?"

She winks. "You're welcome. So you'll be back around four?"

"Yeah, like 4:15—Ah, *ontzi*, I forgot about the Ball tonight..."

Amelia fans her face and puts on an interesting accent as she trills, "Oh, a ball! How very Cinderella of you."

"I don't get the reference I'm afraid." I lift my bag onto my shoulder. "And although I'd love to hear all about it, I have to get going."

Like almost all cities in the Hexum, mine does not have any crime, but as I slip out of the house I wonder if I should lock the door today. I frown. I don't even know if my door has a lock—and if it does, who knows how to activate it? I rack my brains and vaguely remember it might be voice-activated.

Awkwardly I turn and say to the house, "Lock my door." To my relief, a hazy screen covers the entryway, clearly set to keep the door in place until I say otherwise.

I take a few steps away, then look back at the front porch. My house *does* look cute in the daylight. Trees going through fall changes surround my yard with varying colors. Bright leaves scatter across my driveway like confetti and dance in the Dixember breeze.

When I turn around again, reluctant to leave, I'm shocked to see someone familiar standing at the end of my driveway.

My bloodstream is flooded with adrenaline and cortisol, making me instantaneously nauseous. I stumble towards the figure. "Dad? What... what are you doing here?"

As I draw near, he takes two steps backward, so I stop. My father looks so different to the last time I saw him some six months ago. He must have renewed his age; he appears at least ten years younger, maybe thirty-five. His Pexun grey hair brushes his shoulders, and he looks thinner as well. It must have cost him and my mom a fortune to get all these procedures done, and I'm curious to know if my mom has had any work done on herself also.

"I'm here... I came..." My dad's eyes dart around, looking anywhere but at me.

"You came for what?" I whisper. My throat feels strained shut. What could he possibly be doing here? Another surge of nausea hits me... Does he know about Amelia?

"I heard the news," he finally says.

"What news?" I ask quickly.

"About Aker."

I grab my stomach. I might vomit. "What—what about him?" Did something happen to him?

"He's going to the Remembrance Ball with you tonight?" he asks.

"Yes—I mean, yeah, I think so." How does my dad know this? My left-hand flies to my druzy quartz necklace, and I squeeze it tight. Clenching my other fist, I fight to keep that hand by my side. "I don't understand," I say with forced calm. "Why are you here?"

His gaze finally flickers towards me. "I think it's time the two of you got married."

I blame the adrenaline coursing through my veins for how loud and long I laugh. Finally I gasp, "Yeah, you and me both."

"There was a meeting last night," he explains, lowering his voice. "If you and Aker don't get married within the next two weeks, you will be reported and sent to a blood reclamation den."

"Since when do you care?" I ask, suddenly furious.

He ignores me. "You need to convince him to marry you before that time is up."

"I've been trying to do that for two years—what makes you think I can change his mind now?" My voice has risen to a shout, and he hurriedly shushes me.

"You need to figure out a way—and soon. It's enough that the town has had to deal with your shame, but if it were to go public around the Hexum… No, your mother and I don't deserve that. You need to figure it out. Now."

Then he turns and walks away. No goodbye. No good luck. No *I miss you.*

I start running to work. Thankfully it is in the other direction. As my body works up a sweat, I force my mind not to think about anything. Instead, I focus on the feeling of my feet hitting the pavement, my lungs breathing in the cold air, my curly hair flying in the wind.

When I get to work, I'm shocked at the number of Guardians swarming the building. Reest sees me as I approach and waves me over. Suspicion fills his face.

What should I do? What would I do if this situation was a surprise to me? I will some positive confusion onto my face.

You don't know anything. You aren't guilty. You're innocent. Amelia is not hiding in your house…

"What's going on?" I'm panting slightly when I reach him, still out of breath.

"You haven't heard?" Reest takes a few slow steps toward me, and for a terrifying second I wonder if he has the Gift of Mind Reading. With a rush of relief I remember he doesn't, and I try to sound curious, but not concerned. "Reest, what's happening?"

"You were wrong about her." His voice is hard. "Around one forty-five this morning, your newest Pod escaped. The simulation cameras froze for almost an hour, and nothing was recorded. Do you know anything about where she might be? Anything at all?" He eyes me again, searching me for the truth.

"No, Reest, I would tell you if I did." I try to calm my breathing "She was such a unique Pod… I wish…" My voice trails off as a Guardian approaches.

"Greet the sun," the Guardian addresses my boss then looks at me. "This is the Reintegrator?" I immediately recognize the man as my childhood friend's father, Ret.

"Yes," Reest answers. "She was the last one with the Pod."

"Come with me," Ret demands. He will pretend not to know me, and I will do the same. Pretend I never sat giggling with his daughter in their living room. Pretend I never sat at their table for a meal. Ret guides me into a tent where a lone chair sits in the orange-hued room. "Sit."

I obey, hoping the dim lighting hides the fact that my whole body is shaking. Ret slips out of the tent, and I surreptitiously take deep breaths, trying desperately to calm down.

His return is just as quick, but this time he's holding something. In his hands, I see a shimmering black cloth. It's small, light, and transparent, almost like cotton voile.

"The film will search your memories of the Pod," Ret says without looking at me. "When you last saw her, what you spoke about, etcetera. We believe one of the staff kidnapped her, and we need to know if there are any clues as to who."

Curse it all! What am I supposed to do now? I want to fall asleep right now so I can hear some advice from myself, but that's not going to work. Has my Protector thought this far ahead? I try to remember the mind protection tricks I learned in school, but my mind is blank. I could go into my Mind Castle, but that would raise suspicion.

Before I can panic, Ret drops the fabric over my head.

My body freezes involuntarily. Alternate sensations of burning pain and freezing numbness sweep through me, the contradictory yoyoing taking my breath away. Suddenly, my brain explodes with a screaming voice. It's so piercingly loud I want to cover my ears, but I am frozen like a statue. The shrieking goes on and on, but my own voice is trapped. Finally, the cloth is lifted and the scream fades. A flat voice above me says, "Clean."

Clean?

How is my Protector doing this?

Ret waves me out and I stagger into the fresh air. Rubbing my temples, I wobble up the stairs to the Ward. I just need to make it through this day. I attempt to go about my work but instead, different Guardians keep appearing, asking me what I have seen and what Amelia was like. I don't eat lunch because the Guardians decide to have me verbally walk them through every moment of the day before. It seems as if every hour, on the hour, a new group of Guardians arrives, intent on finding out what the previous team could not. By the seventh interview, I'm exhausted. So much is going on I barely have time to think about Amelia and how she's doing.

When I finally clock out of work, I notice my hands are still shaking. Did I eat anything today? I don't think so. Wait, didn't I have breakfast with Amelia? I remember the food… but did I eat it?

My colleagues are farewelling each other with the added, "See you tonight!" I hear the excitement in their voices. Previously, I would have been just as thrilled. But not these past two years. And especially not tonight.

Wearily, I make my way to the employee bathroom to change into my dress. The last time I wore it was three years ago at the Fall Worship Celebration—just weeks before my wedding that didn't end in marriage. I don't have enough compensation to buy a new dress, and there's no way anyone will notice I'm outfit-repeating anyway, so why bother?

I find some make-up in my locker and attempt to apply it. I used to prepare for the Holy Days at my sister's house, but she hasn't talked to me since I became a point of shame for the whole town.

Now, as I get ready alone, I feel stupid. I don't know how to do make-up. The concealer covers up my freckles and I look oddly naked, so I wash it off. I try to dab the cream over my black eye, but I look like a dog with a giant beige spot, so I wipe it away. I subdue my curls into four braids then rip them out. Aker won't think I'm attractive no matter how I look, so why am I trying?

Nothing I do matters. My life doesn't matter.

Giving up, I discard the make-up and toss my hair into a single braid down my back. As I stare at my reflection, it's evident I've rubbed my skin raw—I look like a bruised kiwifruit. I leave for the Ball alone, forcing a slow pace in order to keep my heart in a steady rhythm; I'll start hyperventilating if I don't watch myself.

The Ball is at the Palace, and as I walk up its opulent marble steps, I try to avoid eye contact with anyone. It's honestly pointless, because no one is allowed to look at or talk to me anyway. These people used to be my friends. Used to be my family. I hold my head high and ignore them as studiously as they ignore me, but the second my foot crosses the threshold into the auditorium, I stop.

He's here.

I know where he is before I even see him. A surge of blood pounds through my veins with every thump of my heart. When my eyes find him, they stay glued on his form. I can't move. The shame of staring at him like this in public is only a hairsbreadth behind my uncontrollable need to gaze at him. Internally, I beg him to look in my direction, yet I feel so scared at the same time.

But Aker doesn't see me. The crowd gives me plenty of space as I make my way along the side of the room, and I force myself to look away from him only once, to make sure I'm not about to walk into a table.

Blood floods my face. He knows I'm here. He has to know. He's simply choosing not to look at me. I can feel myself on the verge of tears. I can't breathe, and a heavy weight is climbing onto my shoulders.

Look at me.

Please.

Oh, *ontzi*, look at me.

He's lingering, talking to our friends and neighbors—well, *his* friends and neighbors.

Suddenly, a gust of hot breath descends on my neck. "If you could only see how miserable you look."

Ortus

Pypen

Having left Emerly to go back to the circus, Scout and I make our way back to our flat in silence. I should have forgone the Buscador torture and stayed home, but my choice was made and now I have to live with it. The darkness hides us as we move quickly. We could take public transit, but I want the fresh air. It will only be a twenty-minute hike through the dimly lit streets.

As I walk, foreboding floods my veins, but I force it not to consume my consciousness.

Think positively. Hold on to your confidence and stay objective.

I am happy the circus is going so well. We have been interterritorially recognized, and I am proud to be one of the leading performers. There was a time when I was filled with the poison of constant bitterness, wrath, and violence, convinced I would die alone, devoid of influence and without the experience of being truly valued and appreciated for who I am. Scout changed all of that.

In addition, I enjoy being on the road. When Scout and I have been cooped up in Vultus for too long, we can sense each other's restlessness. I know we are both ready for the next big thing. This show in particular could lead to more compensation, interterritorial fame, and perhaps even the Quintrall one day.

On this, I know I need to focus.

But right now, I care more about Scout's annoying curiosity regarding the Superiors than I do about fame. I care more about Emerly's mysterious confession than I do about making any more compensation. I care more about the fact that Merayal cannot perform the role of Caedis than I do about the Quintrall.

As we enter the flat, I turn on Scout, bent on getting my way with at least *one* thing. "We have to let her go," I say as he shuts the door.

Scout glides past me wordlessly, heading for his room.

"Merayal is not a good fit," I push as I follow him through the doorway.

Scout lays a rusty copper suitcase on his bed. When he opens it, the hinges creak. Many times I have suggested he buy a new one, but this one was his father's, and sentimentality usurps practicality. Scout begins throwing clothes into the case.

I want to throw all his belongings on the floor just to get his attention, but I know he does not respond well when I instigate conversation in this way. I cross my arms. "I know you can hear me."

"I can," he responds as he drops his toiletries into the suitcase.

"I want her out," I assert.

"This has already been discussed."

Instead of demanding he sees things my way and hears my reasons, I state as quietly and calmly as possible, "She is consumed with anger, Scout."

"Is she so different from any of the others who have joined us?"

"She—"

"Is she more broken than I was?" he asks.

"She is different." I persist.

His gaze pierces mine. "Past help?"

"She does not want our help!" I shout.

"Perhaps she does not realize she needs it."

It is true; many with closed veins and poisoned blood have joined our group and found healing and family. All of us, in fact. That is what makes the cast and crew cling to each other so. But Merayal feels incomparable to me.

Scout closes his suitcase and eyes me for a moment. I hold his gaze.

He stands strong, shoulders and back straight, his skin glistening with the light sweat he worked up on our brisk walk home. Although he stands still, his breath rises and falls like a tide. His feet claim the ground they stand on—the room reverberates with his strength.

"Hurting people hurt people, Pypen," he starts. "Merayal has a wound; the closer you get to it, the harder she will fight you. But once exposed, she can find relief. So help her move on from her anger. Just as you did."

Just as I did. He makes it sound so simple. I know not if I have moved on from my anger. Sometimes it feels as if it boils my blood to such a point I will strike out in violence as I used to. Alas, he is right—instead of rejecting her, I should help her... I *should.* "Merayal infuriates me."

"Do not permit her to," Scout replies. "Choose to be calm, consistent, and kind."

"She makes it particularly difficult."

"She offers you an opportunity for practice." At this, he smiles. "Give her what everyone withheld from you for so long." His eyes seem to sparkle despite the dim lighting. "A chance."

I do not try to stop the smile that draws itself on my features. "You have a way with words, my friend."

"And you have a way with people. Give her a chance, Pip."

I sigh, finally conceding.

"I have a call," Scout says abruptly and commands his Suus to speak aloud instead of in his mind. "Greet the moon, Gigi," he states by way of greeting.

Her sweet voice fills Scout's room, "Greet the moon, Scouty. We are all at the bus save Muir and Catarine."

"Ah. Their tardiness is as certain as a pumping ventricle," Scout responds good-naturedly. "Is everything loaded?"

"Keleigh and Twigg have put everything on the bus except the circus. They wait for you, as is your way."

"Of course it is my way, Gigi," he says as he locks his case. "The circus is the child I will never have. I will always preserve and protect her. Call Muir and Catarine once more and threaten expulsion."

She seems to hesitate at this statement but then responds, "For your praise, Scouty," and ends the call.

We grab our luggage and make our way toward the bank where Scout deals with the teller.

I once heard that the subhumans of Senex traded paper and electronic numbers for compensation. It is no mind-bender that their world collapsed. We, the metahumans, trade energy—the only matter of actual value. Jewels, precious metals, paper, electronic numbers—all can be manipulated by Gifts. But no one can create or multiply pure energy.

This late in the evening, there are few other patrons. Generally, I prefer frequenting establishments in the middle of the night—the service is quicker and more to the point. After checking in with our banker, a simulan takes us to our safe in the back of the building.

Turning to me, Scout says, "I need to get a new Vorbi while we are inside. I could not buy lunch this day because mine was too low." He raises an eyebrow. "First time in three years."

The simulan takes us to a room filled with floor-to-ceiling lockboxes. Some are little, while others are as tall as a man. Ours is on the smaller side, and when we reach it, the simulan inputs the bank's half of the code into a holographic pad. Scout punches in the other half, and the small door flings open. He pulls out a drawer to reveal two objects. When the simulan leaves, Scout takes the first one out of the box and places it on the viewing table.

The square-shaped carton looks like an old, water-damaged cardboard box. I place my Suused wrist on the lock. Only Scout's or my Suuses can open it. The facade lifts, and our safe appears in true form, shapeshifting constantly with a myriad of materials such as metal, wood, and opaque glass. No Gift could ever manipulate it open in this everchanging state.

The lock clicks, and I open the covering. Reaching in, I grab two Vorbies. One for Scout and one for me... After all, I did just lose mine to a pair of snakeskin leggings. For years Scout and I struggled with our finances, but since the Unopened Gifts took off four years ago, my compensation is never something I dwell on. It is strange being able to buy something and not have to sacrifice something else.

Not that I spend energy wantonly—Scout and I rarely do anything outside the circus. In fact, we should probably try to find hobbies of some kind.

Hobbies that do not involve Superiors, that is.

After locking the safe, I place it back into the lockbox and allow Scout to retrieve the other object. He places the small leather package on the viewing table. Although it is only five centimeters wide, its contents are our whole world. "I hate and love carrying the circus," he whispers.

"I love that *you* are holding it," I whisper back, "so that if you break it or lose it, the people will suck your blood dry, not mine."

He clicks his tongue. "Thank you for the loyalty."

"Anytime, Friend. Anytime."

Scout places a black briefcase next to the leather package, and I assist him as he ever-so-gently places the circus into its holder. The case will hold the precious parcel perfectly still, as Thykas designed it to never lose balance and to always stay in an upright position.

Once the safe has been locked securely by his Suus, placed back into the lockbox, and the box locked again, Scout takes a deep breath and picks up the briefcase. "Shall we?"

"We shall." I grab both our travel bags, and we leave the bank, heading to the bus. I need not look at the prancing lion tattoo on my wrist to know that Scout is just as nervous as I am. Aloud, I say, "I believe we will be arriving at Pexus right around six. Should we push our travel time so we can be early and you can have your nap beforehand, or shall we rush it with the Pexun so you can rest right after the meeting?"

Scout's naps have been so utterly inconveniencing over the years that I have had to schedule our daily agenda around them.

"Let us aim to be early," he answers.

"Brilliant."

When we arrive at the bus, I see Merayal skulking by the back tires, away from the other performers.

"Bring her in," Scout commands, gesturing in her direction, then he steps into the bus.

Nodding, I head towards her direction, smoothing my scowl into a neutral expression. I stop just beside her. "You ready?"

"I'm not going," Merayal states curtly.

I smile broadly, relief flooding my veins. "What great news."

Merayal's brows rise, surprised. "Great news?"

I nod enthusiastically. "I agree that it is for the best. It was a pleasure to work with you—rather, it is a pleasure to watch you leave." I bow. "Do note, there will be legal ramifications."

Turning around, I walk towards the bus's opening, feeling pleasingly light. It will be unfortunate to have to find another partner, but it matters not. Merayal Kapu needs a job where she will not be around other humans.

As I reach the first step, I suddenly hear a voice call out behind me, "Wait!"

Turning, I am surprised to see Merayal right behind me. I find an odd amusement in watching her stand there uncomfortably. I do not push her to speak, although I am curious.

Her eyes lock with mine, and she licks her lips. "You didn't let me finish. I was going to say that I'm not coming if you're going to be bossing me around like some simulan."

"So it was a bluff in order to ascertain my subservience? Or was it a ploy to ascertain my affection?" Enjoying myself, I continue, "Were you in hopes that I would plead for you to come?" Bending on a knee, I pretend to sniff tearfully as I mock, "Oh, darling Merayal, you simply *must* join us!" I know the words are harsh, but this seems to be her language of choice.

Anger flashes through her eyes like a lightning bolt. "I wasn't bluffing or *ploying*."

Standing, I chuckle. "Certainly."

"I was just letting you know I'm not going to put up with your *ente*."

"No," I drawl. "You said you are not accompanying us, and I could not agree more. Have an ordinary life, Keli Kapu."

When I move away, she steps in front of me and slams my chest with both her hands. "I *am* coming with you, and you *will* respect me."

Although it did not hurt, I am taken aback by her strength. "Why should I allow you to come?" I ask.

She takes a deep breath and, for the first time since I have met her, her features soften. "I *need* to find my mom's assassin." Then, as if she realized she had shown too much emotion, she rearranges her face to display apathy.

I smile. I feel an acute sense of satisfaction in watching her accidentally let down her walls. "I do not think you were meant to work in our group. You do not seem to get along with anyone and you do not trust me as your partner. I am sure I could convince Scout to void the contract."

"I don't want you to void it."

"Convince me," I demand, thoroughly entertained by this interaction. "You want to come, Merayal Kapu? Beg me to let you."

Her face hardens, and I can tell she wants to hurt me. Let her try.

"Please," she attempts, teeth clenched as if the word pains her.

"I do not understand you, Merayal. You join our group hating every second and despising everyone, and then, when I permit you to leave, you want to join. Do you have a perverse need to be needed? Because I called your bluff and won."

Her eyes do not reflect her thoughts. "Please."

"You will have to do something for me."

Her face drains of blood and, for the first time, all the confidence she habitually exudes seems absent. "I will do nothing degrading."

"Degrading?" I am genuinely surprised. At the word and her expression, my blood turns acidic. It sobers me considerably. "I—Merayal, I would never ask you to do anything degrading."

"I guess it depends on your definition," she retorts.

"On the contrary," I say, now regretting my cruelty toward her. "In every possible meaning of the word, I would not ask you to do anything even closely related to degrading." Perhaps Scout is right. Clearly, someone hurt this Pexun.

She meets my eyes. "I'm everything I said and more. I'll do my best and I'll show you how valuable I am to your team. I promise I'll impress you."

I know she is not a good fit; I can feel it in my blood. Nonetheless, I told Scout I would give her a chance. "I concede," I say.

Her response to my capitulation is not joyous, but the corners of her lips sneak up for a moment.

"Listen to me here and now, Merayal," I say, harshness returning to my voice, "I do not want any problems from you. You follow my lead, stay loyal to the group, and we will compensate you with riches and friendship."

Her brows raise. "I'll take the first," she replies with a sardonic smile.

I snort. "Follow me then." I hear her footsteps behind me as I continue up the stairs into the vehicle. I walk down the narrow hallway. No windows or seats to be seen, just dark, wooden doors with dingy gold knobs—forty altogether. Five yellow lights illuminate the aisle, giving the hallway the look of melting chocolate.

I open the door assigned to Merayal, revealing a spacious, bright room with a large, fluffy bed, a beautifully crafted armoire, a desk with the most up-to-date mainframe sitting atop, and a small kitchenette.

"Home sweet bus," I say, waving her inside. "Your cabinets are fully stocked with food and beverages." I am certain I should say something reaffirming regarding our future partnership, but I do not desire to be in her presence any longer. Without farewell, I turn away, shutting the door behind me.

Walking past my own compartment to Scout's, I knock. When there is no answer, I open the door to find Scout lying on his bed, fast asleep. As I quietly turn away, he suddenly jolts awake.

"Are you well?" I ask, slipping inside the room and softly closing the door.

His eyes meet mine, and they are oddly wild. "Indeed."

"Did the Sixth Aevum give you more information on the Pexun girl?"

He rubs his neck as he sits up. "Indeed. He said she will be at her local Palace celebrating the Remembrance Ball."

I click my tongue. "You know I believe in the all-powerful Sixth Aevum, same as you. But kidnapping... this is a first."

His brows furrow. "We are not kidnapping. The girl will come voluntarily."

"Does she know we are coming?"

"The Sixth Aevum said she has prepared herself."

"Did he reach out to her personally?"

"I know not." Suddenly he smiles. "Either way, I doubt this Pexun is expecting the likes of us."

"Us? Meaning two Ortusan men?"

He laughs. "Meaning, I doubt the girl realizes she is about to join a circus."

Two sharp raps sound on Scout's door, and I open it to our Controls. The five Sanusians and lone Pexun joined our group around the same time, five years ago. Previously, we had been using almost fifty simulans to do their combined jobs with lighting, building, maintaining, food production, power control, etc. The Controls have saved us valuable time and energy, and the six of them are practically inseparable, always coming and going together. We do have one additional Control—Skotsky, a Silentar—but he does not travel with the rest, choosing to stay with his mate instead.

Scout commands his Suus to bring up the schematics of the field on which the circus is to rest. The Initium Palace sent them over this morning. For some time now, when we go into new cities, we work directly with their Palace. Previously, it had been with landowners, but as we grew in size and fame, we have been asked to correspond directly with each Palace. "Here they are, friends. A pint of O Negative for your thoughts."

They individually analyze the plans until Vielfrah steps forward. A circus standout, he is a commanding six-and-a-half feet tall. His lean, athletic build suits his daredevil acts, and his adaptable light brown hair mirrors his moods yet is always neatly styled. What truly draws attention, however, are his captivating blue eyes, rich with emotion. His well-defined facial features, including a strong jawline and prominent cheekbones, add to his rugged charm. Vielfrah asks, "What is ta plan, Scout, me ol' sam? Ta space t'ey are providin' seems ter fit our needs quite right."

"These trees worry me," Scout says, pointing to the seven oaks standing in the middle of the field allocated by Initium for us to erect our circus. "I am afraid they are close enough to the circus that it may steal their energy."

The last two locations where we placed the circus were drained of their natural resources. There is a suction leak somewhere in the circus and we have not found it as of yet.

"Aye, but we could re-grow t'em," Veilfrah retorts. "We fixed the river at Monocount and refilled the energy reserves we took in downtown Bukimmur."

"Just because we can fix the trees does not mean I wish to harm them," Scout replies.

"Taniel can move ta trees easy enough, can't ye?" Twigg joins the conversation. She wears a patch over one eye as she has convinced herself that having handicaps will strengthen her senses. Her light brown hair is cropped short around her large head. When Taniel nods, she adds to Scout and me, "'Tis not hard fer him ter put t'em back."

"Or Oi's can place t'em wit'in ta circus, so it feels familiarinsuch ter t'ose who know the field," Vielfrah adds, scratching his elbow.

Scout nods. "That could work…"

"As the field is so open, perhaps we should put up the darkening shield. Your thoughts, Dommy?" I ask. "I want not for you to be unnecessarily exhausted."

Dommy's Duogift of light and hue manipulation has been indispensable in creating the ambiance of the circus. But if the sun is too bright, she has to use much energy to keep the light at bay. To prevent this, we purchased a darkening shield to block the sun.

Dommy nods, and her long, Sanusian hair bobs. The light brown color matches both her eyes and her skin perfectly. "Oi'll be appreciatin' t'at, wolly wot," she responds.

"I think I'll do the food first this time around," Manny, the only Pexun Control, says. "I ran out of time in the last show." The Pexun has covered his porcelain skin from the top of his head to (literally) the bottom of his feet with tattoos.

"We still have leftover souvenirs, so you will not have to make so many this time," Scout replies. "But feel free to do the food first."

We hired an exceptional cook from Silenda in our first year, but she found it too hard making enough food to feed the whole circus—even with fifteen simulans at her disposal. Manny's Progift of manipulation allows the cook to make one sample of each entrée, dessert, snack, and treat, which he then copies into enough food to feed ten thousand plus patrons. He also uses his Gift on our souvenirs and merchandise.

"His work is truly invaluable," I mutter to myself.

Scout huffs. "You want to share your thoughts a little louder, Pypen?"

I must have been mumbling; it always infuriates him. Smiling sarcastically, I give Scout a rude hand gesture. The Controls laugh, but Scout ignores me and continues.

"I will give Keleigh the circus at exactly eight o'clock. That gives you five hours to arrange the doors, the kiosks, and the seating."

"We will do it in three," Twigg states, raising her pinky, ring, and middle finger.

"Hard work flows strong in your veins," Scout says with a Sanusian bow. When the Controls exchange awkward glances, Scout asks, "Is there anything else?"

"Oi don't want ter sound ungrateful, Scouty me ol' sam," Vielfrah says slowly with what would be a nonchalant grin, "But ye said we were gettin' our raises, and we didn't get one last time or ta time before."

"All of you?" I ask.

"I got mine just fine," Manny replies, uncomfortably scratching his grey, Pexun hair.

"Just us," Vielfrah says, pointing to the four other Sanusians.

"I will speak to the Sixth Aevum," Scout says. "Next time, please inform us earlier."

"Fer yer praise," Vielfrah says, and the Sanusian Controls bow while the lone Pexun gives his own farewell, slapping both of our hands with his, and squeezing his thumbs over our palms.

"What do you think that is about?" I ask once they are gone.

Scout scowls. "The Sixth Aevum has made his dislike for Sanusians very clear. However, I did not think he would be so petty. I will check in with Emerly and have him make up their lost wages from my personal account."

"Mine too," I affirm, adding, "and we should probably have him give them their raises from our weekly wages as well."

"Indeed."

A simulan opens the door and announces, "Your arrival time for Depalo is in ten minutes."

"Do you want to talk to Memory and Fiddy about their act before we disembark?" I ask. "They wanted our opinion about changing their routine."

"What do they want to change?" Scout asks.

"They wish to make it more interactive and to allow the audience to take their piece of art home with them."

Scout thinks this over. "I am partial to the mystery," he finally answers. "When the audience leaves Memory and Fiddy's show, the art they have just created is a fresh memory. But, given time, their recollections of their creations morph with nostalgia and romanticism, always materializing more grandly than actuality. If the audience could take their art with them, holding it with their hands, beholding it with their eyes, the memory would forever be fixed and benign. I want them to forget everything but the beauty, and thus have them return to the circus seeking the same experience."

I let his words flow over me. Taking a deep breath, I reply, "So, no?"

He laughs. "So, no. I will break the news to them later."

The bus comes to a sudden stop as we arrive in Depalo. It is in the early evening here in Pexus. As Scout and I walk down the hallway towards the exit, several faces pop out, asking if they can leave the bus or come with us. Sometimes it feels like they are little children begging their father or mother to take them to work. We respond with, "Next time," "Not now," and "Maybe later."

As I walk off the bus, I breathe deeply the crisp smell of... *nothing*. In Ortus, each city and town seasonally releases its own unique scent, giving a distinct olfactory treat for both residents and visitors. My own town, Vultus, currently smells of cardamom, vanilla, and cinnamon. Pexus, however, does not have such ambrosiac adventures—instead, their towns and cities smell of naught. It is quite off-putting.

"Would it not be more pertinent to have two of us looking for the girl instead of one?" I ask.

Scout kicks a small pebble off the brick road on which we walk. "Oh, 'tis the opposite. I want you outside the din, so that if something happens that is not in line with the plan, you are ready to step in."

Annoyance floods my veins. "Something else is going on, isn't it?"

"Was that mumble-mumble for you or me?" he asks.

"Both, I suppose. If you do not want to share the real reason you want to do this alone, you need not lie."

Scout's lips turn up mischievously, "Ah, thank you for your permission to keep my council on this one."

I genuinely cannot tell if he is being condescending or honest, but I let it go. "Where do you want me to take up position?"

"I will have you wait right outside the Palace. Once I retrieve the girl, we will immediately go to her house to collect the daughter."

I nod, and we walk silently the rest of the way. Soon, the Pexun Palace looms up before us, and we pause to take it in. "There it is," Scout says unnecessarily. "Stay right here until I return." Without waiting for my response, he bounds up the steps and enters the palace.

I sigh deeply and lean against the Palace gate. As waves of Pexuns flood past me, I receive suspicious looks and whispers, with some openly asking why I am loitering. This blatant territoryism is why we prefer to set up our circus in large cities. Territoryism runs rampant in the smaller towns within the Hexum, as they only see their own hair color; anytime an outsider comes in, there is distrust and open disdain. In the major cities, people are more accustomed to seeing unfamiliar faces from other territories, although there is still a level of territoryism.

The only place I have seen all prejudice fade away is within the flaps of the circus. People are so entranced, enthralled, and enchanted by what they see, that unusual hair color is the farthest thing from their minds.

"What is your purpose here, Ortusan?" a Pexun Guardian asks me. The Pexus emblem, a rhinoceros, is embroidered into his uniform.

"I await a friend inside the Palace. He has business with one of the partiers."

"What is his business?" the Guardian asks.

"He offers a work opportunity."

The Guardian looks up at the Palace then gives me a once over. "A party is not a good time to have a business meeting," he says slowly.

"I agree. But the acquaintance was adamant it happens this night or not at all."

He eyes me warily. "Who is this acquaintance?"

The town is small enough that he is bound to know every name within the perimeter; I had better not chance a fake name. "My comrade did not tell me. He just asked me to wait out here so as not to make a fuss."

"Sounds like your friend has a little common sense about him."

"A little, yes."

"Don't stay long," he says as he steps away from me. "Your presence is agitating the guests."

"Yes, Kel."

Anything to avoid agitating the precious Pexuns.

Twenty minutes later, Scout rushes out of the Palace. I shake the blood back into my foot which has started going to sleep, and raise a hand to greet him. I stop when I see his face. He is overly pale and ill-looking, and the young Pexun woman who runs out after him looks as though she is being chased by a monster.

I race towards them wondering why Scout had not told me they were in danger. 'Tis my *one* job here!

What happened inside the Palace?

Silenda

Flister

93 years ago

THE SIXTH AEVUM STANDS perfectly still as Keli Gridd picks at his shirt. She shoves his slicked hair to the side once more, inspects his suit jacket for any lint *again*, and re-checks his face for any smudges. Then she begins polishing his shoes for the third time.

"Wane your worries, Woman," Kel Soxis, standing next to her, softly commands. Even his whisper echoes around the majestic room. He is dressed just as well as the woman and the young Ortusan boy. "This is the best the boy will be."

Ignoring her mate, Keli Gridd continues fretting over the young man's appearance. To the Sixth Aevum's credit, he does not push her away or argue. He endures it, knowing this is the last time he must suffer her presence. That morning, filled with great contentment, he left Artemis Abbey for the last time.

A door at the end of the hallway opens, and the sudden noise ricochets around the circular foyer like the bang of a drum. An Ortusan man enters and bows his head in their direction. "The Aevii—hallowed be their names—will see you now."

The woman trembling, the man sweating, and the boy squaring his shoulders, they make their way into the throne room. To say it is full of splendor is an understatement. The walls are made of the rarest—illegal to replicate—white stones, the floor forged with strange milky-hued gems, and the ceiling painted with muted murals by the legendary Leerose Hawthikiss. An enormous, intricately woven deep-red rug extends the room's length. It looks like a pond of blood separating the worshipers from the worshipped. The room seems to glisten—like it is whipped into cleanliness daily.

Many have heard of the throne room's grandeur, but the descriptions always fall short. Six thrones stand on raised daises. Each one reflects the individual Aevum: their passions, pursuits, and accomplishments. The thrones are shades of white, black, or silver, depending on the Aevum's temperament. While five are decorated and filled, the one next to the Fifth Aevum's throne sits plain, unfurnished, empty—it awaits its nobility.

"Come," the First Aevum says simply.

The command compels the three guests forward. The two Silentars bow down, completely prostrating themselves on the blood-red carpet. The boy, however, remains standing.

"Flister Dubach," the First Aevum says, "Welcome home."

The Sixth Aevum looks up at Mal as she speaks, whose whole frame appears to have been kissed by cinnamon. Her eyes are warm honey, and her red hair gleams, reminding him of new rose petals. The young Aevum wishes nothing more than to keep this woman's trust and love. To do this, his fifteen-year-old mind reasons, he must be perfect during the ceremony.

"I am honored to dwell amongst my equals," he recites, staring at the First Aevum. "May we forever serve our people and territories in unity, community, and power. May we lead them in justice, peace, and kindness. May we strive to make their lives the best they can be and to do the same for our own lives." The young man takes a deep breath knowing the worst is over. He had not made a mistake; he had not shamed himself.

When she smiles, it is as if Mal Fey's whole being exudes gentleness and affection. "Well done, darling," she says to him so tenderly that tears spring to his eyes. "Flister has been Gifted with eternal life, and that is why he joins our ranks," she tells the other Aevii who sit silently upon their thrones. This is not news to any of them, but the ceremony demands Flister be lauded for his Gifts. "He has also been Gifted with the ability to create. It has been reported that, even at his age, he wields his Gift with power, precision, and passion." Flister cannot help but beam at her praise.

"Now," Mal continues as she turns her attention back to him, "As you have reached the age of fifteen years old, you may take your throne. All hail Flister Dubach, the Sixth Aevum."

Although their faces are still on the floor, the two Silentars shout with voices muffled, "Hail Flister Dubach, the Sixth Aevum!"

Flister blinks his tears away, climbs the dais, and slowly sits down on his throne. Immediately the royal seat begins to mutate. The white turns light grey, with scribbled lines of white dancing through it. The lines wind arbitrarily and tightly, around the throne's legs, arms, back, and feet, like restraints. Then, as if emerging to cover the scribbles, silver-white ivy leaves crawl up the legs toward the top of the chair. The cushion is a thin, square piece of black upholstery, but the feet of the throne are thick roots, the back a burly trunk, and sharp, knife-like leaves wave at the top.

The Fourth Aevum chuckles, but it sounds more like a snort. "Your throne is most interesting, Flisty. And here I was hoping we would have someone a little more uplifting in the group."

"It's perfect," Oaken Bleu, the Fifth Aevum, croons. Her own throne is primarily silver, with black lines streaked like marble throughout. The four feet holding up the chair are miniature human statues, their faces forever etched with strain as they support the weight of the Aevum. There is no cushion; instead, the seat is covered in white and black furs, and three horns rise from the back of the chair.

Flister does not respond to the comment. Instead, he admires the delicate wildflowers sprouting on his arm rests—details that he alone can see this close to his throne.

"Your service is acknowledged," Mal Fey says to the two Silentars. "You may rise."

The black-haired tutors stand but keep their gaze lowered. "You have spent the last eleven years with the Sixth Aevum preparing him for this day," Mal Fey declares. "Your dedication is recognized." She turns to the young Aevum. "Do you wish to say anything to your tutors before they leave?"

At this, Keli Gridd looks up expectantly. Flister, however, dismisses them with a flippant hand gesture. Keli Gridd looks as if she has been slapped across the face.

The Fifth Aevum coughs to cover up a laugh.

Although Mal is not outrightly disapproving of Flister's response, he can tell by her slight frown that she wishes he had spoken. Not desirous of her displeasure, Flister opens his mouth to comment but then closes it quickly.

In all his short life, he has never felt so torn. He does not want to disappoint Mal even the slightest degree, but this is *his* moment. This is the occasion he has been waiting for all these years. Every time his tutors disciplined him, scolded him, or made him do something he did not wish to do, he had thought of this moment—the moment when he could diminish all they had done with an impudent sweep of his hand, belittling and dismissing them before the other Aevii.

He has wanted this. Desperately. Even staring now at Keli Gridd's openly wounded expression gives him such pleasure. But he also wants the approval of the First Aevum.

Flister Dubach takes a deep breath and speaks to the mates who raised him: "Thank you, Keli Gridd and Kel Soxis, for all you have done for me. It was…" He looks to Oaken Bleu, who raises her brows in amusement. Not wanting to give them more credit than was their due, but knowing he must finish the sentence, he concludes, "…interesting."

Mal's expression softens into a bemused smile. Turning her attention to the Silentars, she says, "All the same, your time and service are appreciated. Thank you for watching over him until he was ready. Greet the moon. You are dismissed."

Still shocked by Flister's dishonorable discharge, Keli Gridd emits a slight squeak when the Ortusan herald escorts both Silentars out of the room, shutting the giant doors behind them.

As soon as they are gone, Mal turns back to the other Aevii.

"Tomorrow, we will gather as territories to honor and coronate Flister Dubach as Elusis' Sixth Aevum. At that time, you, Flister, will be given your public name. Never again will you be called Flister Dubach by any other metahuman, save those in this room. You will be given local powers to govern Ortus, your home territory, as well as the capacity to bless those you desire to bless. And from this time onward, you will be present at our council as we make decisions for Elusis—though for now, you will only be a spectator.

"On your twenty-fifth birthday, you will come into full Aevum power. Upon your finger, a ring of authority will be positioned, and on your body, the tattoo of the Aevum will be drawn. You will be given your full political powers and, not only will you be present in our decision-making, but you will also be a council member.

"Tonight, however, before all the pageantry and ceremonies, we wish to welcome you in as one of our family." Her kind gaze turns to the Second Aevum.

Unwillingly, Flister looks to Dakarai Ebelson as well. The Sixth Aevum has never liked the Second. The man always seemed too wild. Not in an exotic or adventurous way, but in a feral, unruly form that needs to be subdued. Even in his earliest memories, Flister cannot recall seeing Dakarai without the coveted *dofleini* beak necklace about his neck. The Second Aevum boasts that he had fought the giant, octopus-like sea monster single-handedly before Mal found him. According to his version of the story, he had battled the monster with his bare hands, killing it and taking its toothed beak as his prize.

Now, in the throne room, Flister watches as Dakarai opens his hand.

Cupped within it lies an ornate brass key. Although these objects are obsolete in Novus, a key such as this one is the symbol of the most-used bank in all territories—Oiloa Bank—and, therefore, is well-known. Dakarai does not possess the Gift of Levitation, but he uses a eutsi—an object used to harness and wield another's Gift—to send the key through the air. It lands solidly in Flister's lap.

"My present to you is a key that will open any door. It holds only a one-time use, so pick the door wisely," Dakarai drawls.

The Third Aevum, Qualcum Elder, clears his throat, which then throws him into a coughing spasm. His hacking splutters echo throughout the room, sounding louder and louder with each gasp. Flister barely catches the grimace growing on his face before he ices it away. Where the Second Aevum is wild, to Flister, the Third appears dark and dangerous. His beady eyes know too much, and Flister is not keen for them to land on him for too long. The sickly Sanusian's coughs subside, and he sits back in his jet-black throne, muted and chasmic; the noble chair seems to envelop the man.

He opens his palm, and a ceramic goblet appears in his hand. His assistant, a twitchy Sanusian man named Happenstance, takes the goblet from Qualcum's hand and gently carries it across to Flister's throne. He climbs Flister's dais and deposits the item on the throne's wide armrest, then bows several times as he makes his way back down the steps and returns to his place at the foot of Qualcum's throne. Gingerly, Flister picks up the cup and peers inside.

"'Tis unquenchable water," Qualcum explains, his voice warbled and croaky like a toad. "'Tis ta sweetest, most refreshin' water ye will ever drink in yer life. If ye drop it, ta water won't spill, and ye could drink fer days, and it will never empty."

Flister nods a thank you and places the present on the dais beside him.

"My turn," the Fourth Aevum says with suppressed excitement. Marvella Pinyin opens her hands, and a book appears. Using a eutsi, she sends the book across the room, landing it lightly on Flister's lap. The book is ancient, most definitely from Senex. The leather is worn but has been preserved well, and inscribed in fading gold is the title: *Cotton MS Vitellius C III.*

"I know you love plants, so Qualcum helped me find this. That is the only surviving illustrated Old English Herbal. It classifies plants from Senex—details their descriptions and uses. It is almost one thousand years old."

Flister is surprised at the thought behind this present. He smiles at Marvella and brushes his fingers across the soft leather, intrigued.

The Fifth Aevum waits for Flister to look up at her. He had been afraid that

Oaken Bleu would still be angry with him—ever since his last dare—but that has never been her way. Instead, she wears a mischievous smile. "My present to you is the blessing of clear thought." She opens her palm, and a pipe appears. She jumps off her royal seat, descends the stairs from her dais and bounces up his own to stand before him. She places the pipe gently in his hand.

Her sparkly eyes meet his as she explains, "Anytime you smoke that pipe, your thoughts will clear and you will find some of your most ingenious ideas in the depths of its plumes." She cannot even get to the end before she begins giggling.

"He is fifteen years old, Oaken," Marvella admonishes. "You cannot give a pipe to a child."

Oaken shrugs her shoulders. "He can do whatever he wants—he's an Aevum."

Mal clears her throat before the two women can argue. Oaken makes her way back to her throne as Mal offers Flister a knowing smile, "I'll have you wait until you are older to use that."

Flister returns the smile and nods. Turning to Oaken, he says simply, "Thank you."

She winks at him and blows him a kiss.

Knowing her present will be last, Flister darts his attention back to the First Aevum. Mal opens her hands, and a small looking-glass appears. She sends it across the room to him. When he looks into it, he sees only his reflection.

"We are your kin, Flister," Mal says gently. "If ever you need any one of us, you need only look in that mirror and say a name. We will be with you in but a heartbeat."

Flister looks up as warmth floods through his veins. "Thank you," he says quietly.

Mal nods and looks out to the other Aevii. "Now, since Flister is officially a part of our household, as it were, it is time we discuss an incredibly delicate matter. Although we are so pleased to welcome Flister, his birth has brought something quite alarming to our attention."

Flister twitches uncomfortably.

"Are you finally revealing your little secrets, Mal darling?" Dakarai asks, his words drenched in resentment. As is his way when agitated, he holds the *dofleini* beak in one hand, the necklace's golden chain taut in the other, and harshly glides the beak back and forth, making an annoying zipping sound. "Finally going to share the content of your little meetings with Elder?" he bites angrily.

"I know it has pained you not to employ your Gift upon us, my sweet love, but what Qualcum and I have discussed has been very hard to work through," Mal says calmly.

"But you trust him," Dakarai responds angrily and juts his chin in Qualcum's direction. "He has only been here six decades, and you treat him as if... as if..."

It was not until he was thirteen that Oaken had told Flister the tale of Qualcum's late arrival to the Aevii family. Much of it had remained a mystery, even until now.

When Marvella and Oaken were born in 200 MN, they were immediately identified by healers as Aevii and were sent to Artemis Abbey to grow up where Flister had. They were believed, by the whole world, to be the Third and Fourth Aevii. However, Qualcum Elder, sixty-six years older than the two women, had been born before Gift Identification was implemented in all Birthing Dens, so his immortality had remained undetected.

For one hundred and thirty-two years, Qualcum remained in the shadows, and in the year 266, he emerged as an Aevii. Many called him the Fifth Aevum, as he was the fifth of the Aevii to be known by the world. But to the surprise of all—especially Marvella and Oaken—at Qualcum's coronation, Mal declared that he would be the Third Aevum, out of respect for the age order.

It was not until Marvella and Oaken's fiftieth birthdays that Mal had truly taken them into her council, and only a few meager years before that when she had welcomed Dakarai into that role. So, it was hurtful for the three when, only a year after his joining, Mal began to confide in Qualcum. Especially as that confidence was not merely repeating what she had already shared with the other three, but Mal had chosen to entrust the man with her secret hopes and dreams for Elusis.

Flister glanced across the room. Even now, sixty years later, it is clear Dakarai still hates the Elder for immediately garnering Mal's attention, affection, and trust. The bitterness bubbles closer to the surface as he stands now, jaw taut, awaiting a response from Mal.

As the First Aevum eyes the Second from her pure white throne, her expression is hard yet kind—much like her throne. Every surface of her throne is unyielding, unbending, and beautiful. Calmly, she responds, "Your jealousy is unfounded, Dakarai. You have been with me the longest, and my love for you is deep."

"I am *not* jealous, my love," Dakarai says, trying and failing to mirror her calm. "I am frustrated that you do not share with the rest of the Aevii that which concerns us."

"Worry yourself no longer," Mal declares, "for I intend to divulge what we have learned. Which brings us back to Flister." The First Aevum's dark brown eyes fall on the youngest Aevum. "Flister, please share with us the inscription on your back."

Without meaning to, Flister darts a quick look at Oaken. The Fifth Aevum smiles triumphantly.

Flister clears his throat and recites, "In a new world, looking for a leader of an old, three will unite to awaken him. The Reader will know the intentions of his book, the Scion will bear the mark and help the Reader know the way, the Prophecy is the lifeblood of the Child whose birth wrought these words, and Their death will be one."

His words ring out audibly, but they are met with silence.

After some time, Marvella delicately clears her throat. "Who is this leader, my love?"

"Arkarian Story, most certainly," Oaken answers, and her gaze swishes in Flister's direction.

"Most certainly," Mal approves. "Very keen, my sweet."

Oaken raises her eyebrows at Marvella mockingly, who spares but a moment to glare back before saying, "Do we know who these people are? The Reader, the Scion, and the Child?"

"I am the Child," Flister says quietly. He has figured out that much.

"Indeed," Mal replies, inclining her head towards him. "You are correct, of course. The other two may or may not be alive. We believe that the Scion—"

"'*We*' meaning you and Qualcum," Dakarai spits.

Mal smiles tolerantly. "Yes."

"But why does the legend of Arkarian Story matter?" Marvella interjects.

"Yes, what does this have to do with us?" Dakarai says curtly, still fidgeting with the *dofleini* beak.

Instead of answering, Mal repeats their query. "Yes, what does it have to do with us indeed, my loves?" She peers across at Oaken. "Go ahead, Dear," she says. "Ask."

Oaken, surprised at being acknowledged, rubs her hands together for a moment. "Well... it seems... but no."

"Go ahead," Mal pushes.

"Well, it just seems as though it is saying that the Child will... will die... he will die when the prophecy dies. But how can a prophecy die, my sweet?"

"By being fulfilled," Marvella answers quickly. "Once a prophecy is fulfilled, it is dead."

Mal gives another, benevolent smile.

Not noticing the sneer sent her way by Marvella, Oaken continues her thought. "So when the prophecy is fulfilled… the Child will…" She looks over to the Sixth Aevum. "Flister will die?"

Mal smiles again. "Correct."

"So he is not an Aevum, then?" Marvella asks, upset.

"And yet, he is," Mal states.

"But we cannot die. That is the point of being an Aevum," Marvella presses.

"Indeed," Mal concurs serenely.

"I still do not see how this pertains to the rest of us," Dakarai says.

Mal does not answer. Instead, she looks to Qualcum for the first time since the meeting began. She calmly holds him in her gaze, waiting, but only once the other four Aevii have taken up eyeing him also does he state, "'Tis most obvious, is it not?"

"Please enlighten our family," Mal commands.

"Oi don't know t'at Oi can make it any clearer," he coughs. Smoothing out his eucalyptus wood-colored hair, he slowly meets the eyes of each of the others in the room. "We all have a weakness. We all have an… exception."

"What does he mean by *exception*?" Marvella squeaks. "What does he mean by this, Mal, my love?"

"If t'at boy can die, we can die too."

The Second, Fourth, and Fifth Aevum leap to their feet. "Is it true?" Dakarai hisses as Marvella cries out, "Blasphemy!"

"Sit, sit," Mal coos. It is not until they have all settled that she goes on. "I have been looking into this since Flister was born, but Qualcum helped me discover the truth. What we have found is that each of us does indeed have an exception. Each of us has a weakness from which we can die."

"What are they?" Dakarai demands. "What is my weakness? My exception? What is it, Mal?"

The First Aevum looks at him with clear eyes and answers slowly, "I am not going to tell you."

Her proclamation is met by silence.

"I have thought much on this," Mal continues. "Many years ago, we met together and decided to allocate the metahumans a two-hundred-year existence on Elusis. We would not allow everyone to live forever, although that could have been arranged. Instead, we decided that the metahumans had to have a limited life span, in order for their lives to have meaning and for the world to progress continuously. We agreed that two hundred years was a proper timeframe.

"At the time, we believed that we, as the Aevii, were blessed with eternal life here on Elusis. We had no need to give ourselves two hundred years as there was no way to kill ourselves—nor could anyone else kill us. We were handed, as it were, the heavy burden of immortality. Yet here we are, faced with mortality. If we do not offer eternal life to every metahuman, we cannot keep it for ourselves.

"Therefore, I am the only one who knows how each of you could die, and Qualcum alone knows how I can die. We will not share this information so that none of us can cling to our mortality, should it be our fate to perish."

"What is meant by this?" Marvella asks, her skin paler than ever.

"What is meant, dear Marvella, is that if our time to die has come, we shall die just as the metahumans do."

Flister and Oaken share a shocked look.

"You do not have the right to keep the knowledge of our own weaknesses from us," Dakarai seethes.

"I do," Mal says, calmly meeting his gaze. "And I have created certain safeguards to keep this information from being discovered."

"Why tell us at all then?" Oaken asks, her usually large eyes bulbous.

"We are kin," Mal says. "I have kept this secret for too long. I want openness and trust amongst us."

"How can there be openness and trust when you keep such facts to yourself?" Dakarai asks through clenched teeth. "Tell me. Tell me now how I could die."

"I will not," Mal declares, clearly not intimidated. "I have never led you wrongly thus far. Everything I do is for your good, and I need your trust. My little family, I need you to do what you have promised: believe in me. Flister will be the only one holding the burden of knowing his weakness."

All eyes turn to the young Ortusan man who shifts uncomfortably in his new seat. "And with that burden, Flister," Mal goes on, "I must ask that you do not pursue Arkarian Story as you get older. We shall allow fate to be fate."

Flister nods, understanding the command.

He, however, has no intention of obeying. Although pleased to find out the rest of the Aevii have exceptions just as he does, he still feels a sense of separation between himself and the others. He alone knows his exception, and he will make it his life's aim to keep Arkarian Story's final resting place just that—final.

Disobeying Mal is not something to take lightly, but this is his life they are discussing. His life alone is in jeopardy, Flister reasons to himself. And if the other Aevii were allowed to live their eternities on earth light-blooded, carefree, so will he.

When the meeting is adjourned, Oaken Bleu whistles a happy tune as she skips across to Flister's throne again. He recognizes the melody immediately. Oaken has been singing this particular song to him ever since he was a baby, just as her mother had sung it to her. Oaken's mother had played the piano, and the lullaby was a typical 1-4-5 chord progression in the key of C. Oaken laughingly called it the Ninth Grade Song.

As the Fifth Aevum hums the simple chords they both know so well, she swipes the tattoo off her back. Smiling, she places it on Flister's forearm.

"For as long as I can remember, Dakarai has worn that cursed *dofleini* beak," Oaken says. Rolling her eyes, she expands, "I think it represents a time in his life when he felt invincible. Anyway," she leans in and whispers dangerously, "I dare you to steal it."

Pexus

Kansis

"*I*F YOU COULD ONLY *see how miserable you look.*"

Jumping at the unexpected voice, I turn to see Kaileb Fransen. As always, his dark, knowing eyes remind me of the day I almost got married. His mate, Mirindiss, was of course the one who had run away with Aker.

I want to say something to defend myself to Kaileb. Explain that my shameful staring at Aker is not what he thinks. I can't have him seeing me this weak; I can't handle jokes or pity.

But there's nothing to say. So what do I do? You guessed it.

I start crying.

By the surprised look on his face, I realize this is the last thing Kaileb thought would happen. I try to get a hold of my emotions—try to say anything to redeem myself—but instead I am faced with an increasing loss of dignity at the hands of deep involuntary sobs, too many tears, and the embarrassing difficulty presented when you're not anywhere near tissues. Too much adrenaline has been pumping through my veins today, and it purges from my system in shuddering waves.

Kaileb doesn't move. He doesn't speak. *Onzi,* I wish he'd hug me. I wish anyone would hug me. The empty hole in my chest seems to reverberate with a sad lullaby about a void that no one and nothing can fill. Not only do I not have love, but I also don't have a friend. I can't think of anyone who would be near me right now... Maybe Amelia?

Kaileb reaches out his hand as if to touch my arm, but then he lowers it. "Look, I'm sorry, it was a bad joke."

I try to mop up the snot with my sleeve. "I know..." He wasn't trying to hurt me. And just thinking that warms my blood.

See, where my mate chooses another and leaves me in the dust, Kaileb's mate chooses both him and another. I don't know which one of us has it worse. "At least," I had told him the night of my failed wedding—the night Mirindiss and Aker had run off together—"you can be with her sometimes. I can never be with Aker; he's only thinking about Mirindiss."

His response to me had been, "I suppose... But when I look into her eyes and know she's thinking about Aker and wishing she was with him, I hate her for it. At least Aker made a choice and didn't keep you hanging in the balance."

Since then, we haven't talked about our messed-up situation. Actually, he hadn't talked to me at all since my non-wedding. Why is he doing so now?

I barely breathe as Kaileb starts talking again. "Aker came and saw Mirindiss a couple of days ago. We had just been talking about how sweet marriage was, and then he walked in. I was in the kitchen and Mirindiss was at the counter facing the door, and I knew it was him before I even saw his face... Because I saw *her* face."

I know exactly what he means. It's a look of complete and total infatuation—a look of love. The same expression appears on Aker's face whenever Mirindiss is in the room.

"He walked up to the counter and their eyes met, and it was like I didn't even exist anymore," Kaileb continues bitterly. "And I saw all the progress we've been making get stripped away like a felon's Gift. I threw my apron on the ground and left." His eyes go vacant, and then he glances back at me. "I didn't know what I was going to do... My mind was in a place it had never been before. Could I deal with this for the rest of our lives? We've been talking about going to the Quintrall, talking about buying a new house, talking about kids." He looks me in the eye, "We've been talking about having children together... But after that... what is the point anymore?" A tear falls down his cheek, and he hurriedly wipes it away.

I want to say something, but what would be comforting? My own cheeks are still wet with my sudden bout of weeping. And if I do speak, what if he leaves?

To my relief, Kaileb keeps talking. "She came running out after me, calling my name, begging me to forgive her and confessing her undying love for me. And when I turned to look at her, she had the same look on her face for me as she did Aker. And I couldn't say no to her. I love her... I love her."

"I know."

Kaileb is the only other person who feels what I feel... well, almost. The difference is that society doesn't reject him, because Mirindiss still wants him equally—as much as she wants Aker. His blood was not thoroughly deficient, just partly. So while some do shun Kaileb, they are few.

Why did this have to happen to us? We never asked for any of it. Why did

Kaileb and I have to be so cheated? Indignation courses through my veins. "I know what to do," I whisper.

My words take him off guard; I can tell by the startled look in his eyes. "What do you mean?" he asks.

Confidence, like I haven't had in years, begins surging through my bloodstream. "I mean, Kaileb, I know how to set things right." I wipe the last of the tears from my eyes. "And I'm going to do it this very minute."

I turn around and start searching the crowd once more for Aker. My eyes are quickly drawn to him standing in the far corner talking to one of our old classmates. I begin pushing through the crowd.

What if he doesn't want to talk to me?

I'll make him.

What if he doesn't want to go through with the procedure? What if he would rather have nobody than not have Mirindiss?

I'll persuade him.

How? He doesn't care! He couldn't care less about me and my feelings!

I'll kill myself.

What about Amelia?

Fine. I'll kill myself after Amelia. After I help her... I'll do it then. That will leave everyone happy.

I've almost reached him; only one more couple stands between us. They're dancing close to the other pairs around them, and every time I try to squeeze around I get pushed back. Fed up, I force myself right between the mates. Angry at being separated, the drunken wife shoves me hard and I fall onto a man who elbows me away. I lose my balance and fall flat on my face.

Adrenaline spent, for the first time I realize how loud the music is out here on the dance floor. People's voices shriek around me, but I can't make out any words. Someone steps on my calf, and I cry out in pain. Another woman's shoe cuts into the flesh on my arm, and I gasp as drops of red blood trickle onto the floor. Looking up, I see Aker has gone, but there is a door leading outside. I stumble to my feet and rush towards it.

The night air greets me with a cold kiss. Disoriented, I turn to the left to run across the deck in search of Aker, when I hear a voice behind me.

"I'm here."

Whipping around, I see Aker Vonbough standing next to a blackberry bush behind the door. He stretches his hand towards one of the ripe little fruits. He plucks it, sets it in his hand, and then offers it to me.

Aker's tightly cropped, grey hair sparkles in the candlelight. One of his thick eyebrows arches while the other lounges as if to mock me. His toasty topaz eyes look brown in the inky light. He's almost thirty centimeters taller than me, and at this range I can tell he's been working out. At twenty, he looks much more like a man than a boy.

I don't move. This is the closest we've been since... since the night he abandoned me. His scent fills my lungs, heady and strong—my blood quickens.

"Here, take it," Aker commands, taking a step closer.

Part of me wants to take the berry and let my fingers linger on his, but I have to stay strong.

"I have a proposition for you." There's no quiver in my voice, and it boosts what little self-assurance I have. He takes a step closer.

"What happened to you?" he asks, seeing my blackened eye.

"Nothing. It doesn't matter." Why does he care? When has he ever asked me anything before? "Please listen." I take a step back as he advances again.

"What happened to your arm?" he asks, seeing the gash the dancer's heel has left on my skin.

"Nothing. *Please!*" My voice is tight. "If I could pay for us to get a Blood Transfusion... would you do it?"

He takes another step.

"And how are *you* going to happen upon eleven cheio?" His golden eyes pierce me, and I forget what I'm saying.

Closing my own eyes, I step back again and repeat firmly, "*If.* If I could pay for it. Would you do it? It's a simple yes or no question. I need your answer now."

"Why?"

He continues to slide towards me, and I move further away.

I almost say his name, and it chokes me. Swallowing hard, I try to control my emotions. "Maybe... Maybe trying another batch of my blood will change things." I fight to hide my desperation from him. "Can you just answer?"

With three quick strides, he closes the distance between us. He reaches out as if to grab my hand, but instead he extends his closed fist until I open mine beneath his. A blackberry falls into my palm. "Tell me where you're getting the cheios," he says, "and I'll give you my answer."

I throw the soft berry across the deck. Juice trickles down my wrist and onto my dress. "I can't tell you. Just... just give me your answer."

"Give me your hand," he commands.

Without any thought, my appendage obeys.

Gently, he hovers his hand over mine and a small electric current tingles onto my palm. When he moves away, I see a new blackberry. I try to throw it on the floor but I can't. He made it. He made it and he almost touched me. Since the night of my graduation from Ward Training, his skin hasn't come into contact with mine, and all he did then was pat me on the back in congratulations.

All my power and confidence are gone, and I finally start shaking. I don't want to beg. I can't let Aker see me like this. I want him to think I'm managing without him. But... he knows I'm not. I avoid his eyes. "Please don't make me grovel."

Because I will.

His stare penetrates my skin. I don't know if he wants me to meet his gaze, but I'm not going to. He'd better answer me. His hand reaches up as if to touch my cheek, but he hesitates. Instead, he grabs one of my curls and tries to tuck it behind my ear. His finger barely touches my skin, yet warmth fills me. My blood knows his hand. Knows his touch. I am home—even though he's never done this before.

Wait... he has never done this before.

Why *is* he doing this?

I make myself look at him. What is this look in his eyes? Pity? Compassion?... Love? No. Not love. Well, one thing's for sure: he's never looked at me like this.

"Does this have anything to do with your Pod missing?" he asks softly.

Hot adrenaline floods my veins. Does Aker know I have Amelia? How could he know? My cheeks flush.

"Well?" he asks.

I want to yell at him. I want to scream that he's just trying to get information from me. I want to berate him for being so heartless, now and every other day of our existence. Instead, I start hyperventilating.

He clicks his tongue and takes another step forward.

"Calm down—*Onzi*, chill. Come on, breathe. Breathe with me. Ah, *ontzi*, stop breathing like that; you're going to pass out!" he shouts. Fight or flight takes over. I try to run away. Before I can move, he jumps in front of me and puts his hands up to halt my escape.

I stop at his barrier, mostly because my nose is tingling and my fingers are starting to curl into fists. If I don't calm down, I'll need a healer.

"Breathe with me!" he commands, close to my face.

I make myself inhale and exhale with him. I force myself to calm down. I have too much to do to let myself get sidetracked by a full-blown panic attack.

I can do that any day.

After a few minutes of breathing in time with his breaths, my limbs start feeling normal again.

"You okay?" Aker asks.

Too embarrassed to say anything else, I respond shortly, "Fine."

Aker sighs loudly. "Look, your Pod goes missing, and you ask me about an eleven-cheio procedure. It would take you almost a decade to save up for that, so why ask now? I'm connecting the dots." He hesitates, then adds, "I don't want anything bad to happen to you."

I want to ask him why he cares, but I can't. I can't speak. I don't want to be here anymore. My blood yearns to stay with him, but my body is weary from this day.

My conversation with Aker has been a bust, and no Protector came to meet me.

I need sleep. At this point, it doesn't matter what his answer is. I sigh and begin to turn away. "Greet the moon."

Before I can even take a step, Aker reaches out to stop me. He doesn't touch me, but I halt at the gesture. "Are you in trouble?"

"No."

"Are you going to be? Did you do something unwise?"

I laugh out loud. Me? Do something unwise? Like kidnap a Pod and stuff her in my house? That doesn't sound like me. "No," I answer again.

He eyes me for a moment then inquires, "Did someone pay you to steal the Pod?"

I open my mouth to say something when an Ortusan voice calls out from behind me. "Kansis Willow?"

Spinning on my heel, I find myself face to face with a man I do not recognize. His hair—the color of dark wheat—is shaved on the sides while the top is braided. He has a cleanly shaped beard, olive skin, and seafoam green eyes. Although he appears to be in his late twenties, really he could be of any age. The Ortusan is not exceptionally tall, yet his presence seems to fill the space on the deck as a giant's would.

Despite the fact that I have never met an Ortusan in person, I've learned from others not to trust them. I stare at him suspiciously. How does this man know me? "Kansis," he says, but this time it's not a question; it's a statement. Hearing my name out loud has my blood spiking again. No one is supposed to use it—and how does he know it? For all my confusion, he certainly looks as though he knows me.

"Yes?"

He stands steady, staring at me for just a moment. His eyes seem almost invading. What is he looking at? "Greet the moon," he says.

"Oh—um—gr—greet the moon," I respond.

"May I speak with you?" he eyes Aker. "In private?" His teeth are wide yet set in the shape of a V, with the point being his two front teeth. There are laughter lines under and around his eyes. His gaze somehow seems so kind. And yet, I know I cannot speak with him alone. Who knows what could happen?

"Who are you?" Aker asks angrily. "We don't know you, and she will not be talking to you." He draws himself up to his full height. "You can leave now."

The man's eye twitches, and he looks Aker up and down. His expression hardens. "You must be Aker Vonbough." Disdain drips in every word.

"How do you know who I am?" Aker asks, brows furrowing.

The man ignores his question and turns back to me. "This is vitally important, Kansis. May I please speak with you?" He speaks my name with such warm familiarity. As though we are the best of friends. Suddenly, concern fills his features. "What happened to your eye?"

"Oh... I..." *Got in a fight with Arkarian Story's daughter?* "I... fell."

When he smiles, he looks almost amused. "And your arm?" Without waiting for an answer, he takes a leather armlet off his wrist and reaches for my arm.

I quickly pull it away from him. I've studied all the territories extensively and I know that Ortusans touch each other familiarly—but that is not our way in Pexus. Our personal space is significant, and it seems so eccentric that this Ortusan means to touch me.

With uncanny speed, he places the armlet over my forearm despite my movement, yet I notice he does so without touching my skin himself.

"This will heal the wound," he says as he buttons it in place.

"It's—it's not really bleeding anymore."

"This will stop the bleeding completely." After snapping it shut, the man takes a step back and says, "We possess little time. I must speak with you."

"Speak to her about what?" Aker growls. To me, he states, "You're not going to talk to this Ortusan. Let's go."

I take a step toward the stranger. I would risk speaking to this Ortusan to keep up Aker's feigned concern.

Looking between the Ortusan and me, Aker asks angrily, "Is this about your Pod?" His voice drops. "Please, Kansis," he almost whispers, "come with me."

Hearing him actually say my name *and* with such genuine apprehension in his voice, wins me over. Turning to the stranger, I ask primly, "What do you need to talk about?"

He shakes his head, silent.

"Then I'm sorry, but I can't—"

"Kansis," he interrupts me quietly, yet with so much conviction, "I can only *protect* you if you come with me."

He's your Protector.

"Protect her? What does she need your protection from? What is going on?" Aker roars. Raising his hands, he spits, "That's it. She's done; we're done with you. I don't know what you think you're doing…"

Aker is still monologuing, but I can't hear him anymore. This *Ortusan* is my Protector? I didn't make him up? He's the one who helped me through the Palace and the Ward? He's the one who kept the black film from reading my memories? But… how can this be possible?

"Please, Kansis." Every time he says my name, my heart painfully misses a beat. "We do not have much time," the stranger—my Protector—pleads.

"You are dismissed, *gari*," Aker says.

I audibly gasp at the insult. There are a few derogatory terms from each territory, but I have only ever heard them discussed—never used.

The Ortusan seems completely unfazed, but he gazes at me imploringly.

Well, if he's the one who kept me safe when I kidnapped Amelia, I should be able to trust him. But how do I know that it was him?

"Who are you?" I ask him slowly.

"I am the man who will help you with your precious cargo."

"The Pod?" Aker asks.

"How do you know I have such an item?" I ask.

"Your dreams," the man answers.

My subconscious? How is she able to talk to this Ortusan? How did she know he was coming?

"We must make haste," my Protector insists.

I stare at him a moment longer. But if my subconscious trusts him, I have to as well.

"I'll come with you," I hear myself say. Turning to Aker, my heart starts beating in slow motion. He never gave me an answer. "Yes or no?"

"Yes or no? *Yes or no?*" Aker shouts. "No! No, you may not go with him! What is *wrong* with you?"

"That's not—" I shake my head. I can't leave without knowing Aker's answer. "I mean my proposition. Yes or no?"

From the time I was a child, I have loved history, particularly ancient studies. In grade seven, I remember learning about soldiers and the importance they placed on holding their weapons in the moment of death. Now, I find myself needing Aker's answer like one of those dying warriors needs their sword. Yet, he says nothing. His silence is his final and cruelest act.

A firm hand squeezes my arm. The shock of being touched would floor me more if I didn't need Aker's answer so desperately. Looking up at my Protector, I see urgency filling his seafoam green eyes.

"Don't touch her!" Aker suddenly shouts. "She has bad blood!"

I'm so dumbstruck by his words that I barely notice my Protector pulling me away, back towards the party. My body turns and follows him, but I keep my head turned in Aker's direction. His features twisted in anger are the last thing I see before I am back in the pounding music and crowd.

Instinct causes me to look around right before I am about to run into somebody. I find myself in the thick of the dancing masses, and I have to concentrate hard not to fall over again. A hand seizes mine and I almost pull away—but when was the last time someone held my hand?

When we finally reach the other end of the ball, I smell like foul body odor. I'm drenched in sweat, but it is not mine. The sticky wet smell belongs to the partiers I have just been scraped through. I yank my hand out of my Protector's and stop a few steps from the door. For some reason, I know my life will never be the same. Once I cross that threshold, everything will change forever. Aker's voice echoes in my head: *Don't touch her! She has bad blood!*

That is all the urging I need to go, and I literally run out of Depalo Palace, hard on the heels of my Protector. Any life is better than this one.

At the end of the driveway, I see another Ortusan man running towards us. When he gets to us, he asks my Protector, clearly concerned, "Levels balanced?"

"All is well," my Protector replies, but there is an edge to his voice.

Pushing dreadlocks out of his face, the man smiles at me. His teeth sit crooked in his mouth, yet his grin is attractive and compelling. The whiteness of his smile contrasts with his dark skin, the rest of his features still hidden in the night's darkness. "Greet the moon. My name is Pypen Tross."

"I'm K—uh, W—um, Willow." I clear my throat. I'm still panting from the dash across the chaotic ballroom. I have rarely spoken my first name out loud these past two years, and my cheeks flush with embarrassment. Who stutters over their own name? "My name is Kansis Willow," I make myself say.

"She has a cut under her arm," my Protector states.

The wound under the leather armlet tingles, and I know that the man, Pypen, has healed it.

"Shall I fix her black eye?" Pypen asks.

"No. You don't need to waste your energy on me," I reply.

"But it will not—"

"No, thanks."

My Protector stares at me for a moment and then breaks out an easy smile. "Well, are you up for a little running?"

"Where are we going?"

"To get the daughter of Arkarian Story, of course." He winks at me and bolts down the street.

It's still jarring that they know I have Amelia, and I automatically don't want to trust them. But I made a choice last night when I took Amelia. And following these Ortusans as they lead me toward my own house is a consequence of that choice. Am I freaking out? Yes. Am I making a huge mistake? Probably. But at least I'm not inconsistent—no, no. I am unwavering in my continuation of bad decisions.

As we round the last corner before my house, we all skid to a halt. A man is standing in my driveway. A man I call *Dad*.

"Look," I say hurriedly to my companions, "I don't know how much you know about me, but this is going to be an awkward conversation—"

"He shuns you," my Protector states simply. His words are said kindly, yet embarrassment washes through me. "Why is he here?" he asks.

I shake my head. "I don't know. I… How do you know—"

"This is not the time to explain," my Protector says firmly yet gently.

"Who are you?" my dad suddenly shouts as he takes in our little trio. "Willow, who is that with you?"

My teeth grind at his use of my last name. Of all the people in town who refuse to use my first name, the fact that the man *who gave it to me* does not use it is infuriating.

"I thought…" my Protector hesitates, bringing me back to the present, then starts again. "I was under the impression that your father did not speak with you."

"He doesn't… He… This morning was the first time since… I think he just wanted to…" To convince me to marry someone I'm already desperate to be married to.

"Most interesting," my Protector muses. Taking a deep breath, he reaches out to lay his hands on my shoulders. I instinctively move out of his reach, and his brows flicker down in agitation. "You can leave your father to me." Before I can move away again, he reaches up and gently tugs my braid.

Pypen mumbles something, and my Protector backhands his arm.

"What's going on?" my dad yells down the street, taking a step towards us.

"Greet the moon," my Protector shouts back in a very convincing Pexun accent.

What are they doing? The second my dad sees them up close, he'll know that they're Ortusan!

"He'll know!" I whisper to my Protector, adrenaline making me scared and angry.

He winks at me. "Worry not. I can use my Gift to keep him from noticing." As they walk towards the house, my Protector calls out, "We were desperately trying to recruit this young lady to join our Ward in Demirkan."

"Demirkan?" my dad asks, surprised.

Being asked to join the capital's Ward would be the most incredible honor of my life. *Ontzi*, the town would even praise me for it.

As we draw nearer, my dad inquires, "How did you hear about my daughter?"

My daughter? Since when has he cared about our relationship? I thought I was just *Willow*!

"Your daughter has had the highest scores on all Pod Testing, and her renown with Pod dedication and rehabilitation is known in our community," Pypen speaks up in an equally impressive Pexun accent.

"It is?" my dad asks, obviously surprised.

Shame washes through my veins.

"I am Hop, and this is my associate Nyu," my Protector says. "You are?"

"Chet... Chet Willow." He looks at me then looks away. "I came..." he begins and shoots me another glance, "I just wanted to see how tonight went."

Knowing what he's actually asking, I answer quietly, "Unsuccessful."

"Ah, well, okay. I will..." My dad shuffles awkwardly around the two undercover Ortusans and me, without looking any of us in the eye. This is possibly the first time ever I'm thankful for my town-wide shame.

"Greet the moon," my dad nods at no one in particular. "It was nice meeting you, gentlemen, and um...Willow, I'll talk to you..." he mumbles something, but I don't quite hear when he plans on talking to me next.

As my dad disappears around the corner, I rush up my driveway and fumble with my front doorknob. As it lazily swings towards me, I remember suddenly that I'd locked it when I left. Why is it open now? My simulan greets me, it's human-like features displaying worry.

"Amelia?" I ask. "Where is she?"

Apprehension covers my simulan's expression. It's impressive how lifelike the engineers made their features. "She's gone," it says anxiously.

"Gone?" I ask.

My Protector and Pypen bowl into the room behind me, but at the look on my face they stop abruptly. "What is the matter?" Pypen questions urgently.

"She's gone," I say, my voice sounding distant. "Arkarian Story's daughter… she's gone."

Pexus

Pypen

"WHAT DO YOU MEAN the daughter is gone? Gone where?" Scout asks, perplexed and a little alarmed.

"Gone as in not in my living room, not in the house, *gone*, gone. Is there another type?" The Pexun girl, Kansis, says this last part quietly, almost to herself. I grin, hoping that she, too, is a mumbler—the agitation it would cause Scout could be quite entertaining. Kansis begins frantically hunting around the house as if the Pod will simply materialize if she wants it badly enough.

I know I should be worried, but we have been unsuccessful every time we have attempted to capture the daughter of Arkarian Story. Part of me had not even believed she was here. "Extremely tense, this one," I comment quietly to Scout.

"It matters not," Scout says to Kansis, reassuringly. "We will find Arkarian Story's daughter."

"Do you have a tracking Gift?" Kansis inquires. "Because if not, how are you going to find her? She could be anywhere!"

"I do not possess such a Gift, but one who travels with us does. Worry not; the daughter is a defenseless Pod—she will not get far."

Suddenly the front door we have carefully closed behind us bursts open to reveal the young Pexun's father—Chet, he said his name was—standing in the doorway wide-eyed. Kansis freezes halfway through a doorway to what I presume is her bedroom.

"You're not from the Ward, are you?" Chet asks, beholding Scout's and my Ortusan hair. Scout begins to employ his Gift—keeping Chet from seeing our hair color—but Chet waves him off. "You can stop trying to hide. I can see it now." Before Scout can respond, the father asks, "This is about the missing Pod, isn't it?"

I open my mouth to make up a lie, but Scout answers quickly, "Yes, it is. Please, do come in."

Kansis' jaw drops in surprise, while I clench mine. What is Scout doing?

"What is going on?" Chet asks desperately.

"That is to be discussed privately," Scout says, and without waiting for an answer, he walks into the other room, ushering Kansis back into the lounge on his way.

The Pexun man looks to me as if seeking an explanation, but I shake my head. "Clearly your presence is required in the other room."

Chet follows, brows furrowed, mouth hard.

When the door clicks shut behind her father, Kansis snaps out of her reverie. "Who are you guys? Did he," she points in the direction Scout went, "talk to my—is that guy the one who—how did you know I had Amelia—the daughter?" She speaks too quickly, and when she moves, it is as if she twitches rather than making conscious decisions.

"Scout will be the one answering your questions," I reply firmly.

"Scout?"

"The man talking to your father."

"Scout," she whispers. She begins pacing the floor. She stops. She sits. She paces again. She unties her hair. She paces some more. I do not mean to, but as there is not much else to do, I find myself staring at this girl for whom we transported ourselves a quarter of the way around the world.

Having unriddled her braid, she lets the hair free. Her grey curls flow down from the top of her head like a silver cat resting on a windowsill. Each curled lock appears to have a life on its own, independent from the others. This Pexun's silver shade is vibrant, unlike most whose grey seems more muted. She is not painful to behold by any means. Her curves and narrow waist are attractive, and with round lips and high cheekbones, she is more pretty than homely—though not a striking, head-turning beauty. Three claw-like scars line the side of her right cheek, just below the black eye she would not permit me to renew. Dark freckles scatter her pecan-brown skin. The left side of her face has darker, more prominent freckles, like a half-moon between her nose and eye. They are mesmerizing.

Catching a glimpse of the time on her fridge's display, I realize we are running behind schedule, particularly now that we have to find the daughter. I walk to the door Scout and Chet have disappeared behind and knock twice. I am relieved when I hear the voices inside moving closer to the door.

"So Kansis has no idea?" Scout is asking.

I hear Chet sigh. "None."

There is silence for so long that I'm about to knock again, when Scout suddenly says with deceptively calm anger, "How could you do this to her?"

"You don't know me, Ortusan," Chet says defensively. "Don't mistake my candor for friendliness."

"What a relief," Scout responds, "If we need not be friendly, this next bit is much easier."

There is a scuffling of feet and a scraping of furniture. Chet Willow gasps for air, and I burst through the door.

Although I am not necessarily surprised by the scene before me—I have seen Scout rough up a few men—I am surprised that he has bothered with this weak Pexun. I do not stop him; I merely say his name, and Scout's grasp on the man's neck loosens.

"Get off me, *gari* filth," Chet manages to choke out.

"I wish I could inflict a punishment equal to that which you have put your daughter through—but alas, I cannot. Know that I desire to, Chet Willow. Know that I wish to suffocate the life out of you."

I wonder why he is threatening the man so. Scout is not a killer—I know this for a fact. But he is a man of justice, and this father must be truly evil to deserve treatment of this nature. Another reason for me not to stop Scout.

"You don't know me," Chet repeats.

"You should thank the universe we did not meet before this day." Scout releases him and Chet gulps in several deep breaths of air. "You can keep your tender, father speech for someone foolish enough to believe it. But know this: I will take better care of your daughter than you ever have."

"You are putting her in danger," Chet growls. "How is *that* taking care of her?"

"If she is with me, she will be protected." Scout walks past me into the living room. "You may want to pack some clothes and necessities," he calmly says to Kansis.

The Pexun woman stays still for a moment, eyes locked on her father as he follows Scout warily. She is obviously unsure how to interact with him, and she eventually settles for an awkward wave in his direction before fleeing to the back room. Chet glowers once more at Scout before storming out of the house.

"What circumstances caused such a negative reaction?" I ask Scout.

He feigns an innocent expression. "What?"

"Do not *what* me. You know what," I respond, annoyed.

"He was not a good father," Scout answers, rubbing his hand over his braid.

"And you realized that in the two minutes you were talking to him?"

He sighs. "The Sixth Aevum divulged some information."

"What did Chet do to her?"

Scout growls but does not answer. With the mood he is in, I know better than to push him. Instead, we wait in silence until Kansis emerges from her room, having changed out of her dress into simple street clothes.

"Before we go…" she looks over to her simulan. Without finishing her sentence, she walks across to stand before it. "You have been an honorable simulan. As sad as it is, you've been my only company for the last two years, and I thank you."

I wonder what she means by that.

Kansis' simulan places its hand appendage on her shoulder. "It has been an honor serving you, Keli Willow."

We slip out of the house, and Scout leads us across the street to some incredibly tall juniper trees. "Ruse," he states, and I know he has made a call on his Suus. "We need your assistance, Pet." Immediately, his Suus sends our exact location to Ruse's Suus.

Scout does not pursue conversation with Kansis as we wait, and I follow suit. I gaze at the trees hemming the yard, realizing I cannot see their tops in the darkness. Their intricate trunks captivate me until Kansis breaks the silence. "So, who are you guys?"

"I am Scout Eekan, and this is Pypen Tross."

"No, but who *are* you? How did you find me?"

"Well, those are two completely different questions," Scout retorts.

Kansis pauses, waiting for Scout to answer, and when he does not, she babbles on, flustered, "Okay, so it's two questions then."

"We are humble Ortusans on a mission to retrieve the daughter of Arkarian Story. You were the one who communicated with our backer."

She seems taken aback. "I communicated with your backer?"

"Did you not?" he asks innocently.

"No, I didn't—" her voice falters. As she stares past Scout and me, her body stiffens.

We both whip around, ready for anything, but it is merely two young Pexun men sauntering down the road.

"Hey, you shouldn't be that close to her," one of them drawls lazily. "Did she touch you yet?"

Unsure what this is about, Scout and I remain alert, ready to face any threat.

"She has bad blood, Ortusans," the other one says. "Best keep your distance."

"Bad blood?" I ask, instantly awakening my Gift and searching Scout's and my bodies for any sign of infection.

One of them eyes Kansis up and down and sneers, "Thought you'd suck in some unsuspecting foreigners, eh, Black Widow?"

Kansis takes a step back, face strategically emotionless. Did Scout know she has bad blood? I check her whole body, but detect nothing.

Both young men step into the street, crossing towards us as one says, "Them being Ortusans and all, I guess we should just let you infect them—"

"But we have a little compassion, don't we, Jab?" The other finishes. He looks at Scout and me. "So, you're welcome."

Neither Scout nor I respond. I glance at Scout, but he simply appears mildly entertained.

"Go back inside, you embodied revulsion," the taller of the two says to Kansis. "We enjoy loving our mates and having them love us back. We'd hate to have you infect your *you* on us." When she doesn't move, he turns to his Pexun companion. "Seward, it seems our lessons aren't getting through to the Black Widow. Seems like we'll need to do something more severe to get it imprinted on her cells." He smiles cruelly, his white teeth flashing like fangs.

"Scram!" Seward shouts suddenly at Kansis, making her jump. "Get in your house, you living cesspit!"

Kansis takes another step back, eyes wide in fear.

When Jab strides up to the curb, Scout finally clears his throat. "I think it would be best if you were to head home now, Gentlemen."

"I'm not going anywhere, *gari*. Just say *thank you,* and *you* can head back to your territory." He spits on the ground as Kansis cowers closer to the wall of trees.

"Do these men trouble you frequently?" Scout asks her, but the young woman is frozen in the moonlight. Scout turns back to Jab and Seward. "Do you trouble her frequently?" he asks them instead.

Chest forward, Jab steps up onto the curb. "Not that it's your concern, Ortusan," he answers, "but yes, we hassle her as often as possible. A light beating here, a small wound there, a good chase now and again. Just the ordinary hassling of a menace to society who should know to keep her distance." The height difference between Jab and Scout intensifies as the Pexun boy walks closer, looming ten or so centimeters taller. "Our Gifts are offensive, so unless you want to be offended, *gari*, you'd best get going."

"Do you have strong belt loops, Gentlemen?" Scout asks.

Jab sneers. "So you wanna fight, eh?"

"Taniel, I need your assistance," Scout says, presumably on his Suus. He smiles up at Jab. "Hurting a woman is dishonorable."

"She's not a woman." Jab leans down, right in Scout's face. "She's a walking contamination." He spits, and saliva spreads over Scout's cheeks, chin, and eyes. Jab laughs and growls, "Let's dance, *gari.*"

Suddenly, Taniel appears by my side. Our good friend has manipulated his body so that he stands at almost two meters, taller than Scout but shorter than Jab. As he has brushed out his tight curls, his light brown Sanusian hair stands high on his head, making his height even more impressive. His praline skin seems to shimmer in the night. "Ye need me, Scouty ol' sam?"

"Indeed," Scout answers lightly as he wipes the spittle off his face. "Will you hang these young men by their belt loops on the top of this tree? You need not be gentle."

Jab smiles as if he had been hoping for this. His hands melt into numerous small, sharp daggers. "It's my pleasure to see you try."

"I had a friend recently fall out of a window because of his strong belt loops. Let us hope the same be true for yours." Scout winks at me, then looks to Taniel and nods.

Taniel raises his hands, and Jab's body lifts off the ground. Like a magnet, Taniel controls objects—or people in this case—using an opposing electromagnetic force. In addition, Taniel is a Speeder. With his powerful Gifts, he can move anything or anyone, and *fast.*

Knives explode from Jab's hands, aiming for Taniel, and several find their mark. I will have to wait for Taniel to take the metal out of his body before I renew his wounds, but I stand ready. As Taniel forces Jab up the tree, the Pexun's body crashes through branches, making them crack and fall. Several of the wooden pieces almost hit us as Jab's screams echo up and down the street. Suddenly, the sound subsides, and I assume he has lost consciousness.

I check Taniel's body. He has over thirty tiny blades piercing his skin.

My attention zooms back onto my surroundings as Seward opens his mouth wide, his teeth turning razor-sharp. He screams, and the fangs fly out of his mouth like darts. But Taniel is back in action a moment later, and without missing a beat, he moves Seward up the tree in a similar fashion, not missing any branches on the way to the top.

The Pexun impales Scout, Kansis, and me with several teeth before he passes out as well. Kansis stares up at the juniper tree, horrorstruck, as if she has not even noticed the wounds. "Pull the teeth out, and I will renew you," I tell her. Without looking at her flesh, as if she has done this a thousand times before, she methodically starts removing the teeth.

Like a light spring rain, blood begins to drip down from the tree branches.

"Please bring them back down," Kansis requests breathlessly.

"No," Scout answers with such harrowing conviction that even Kansis meets his gaze.

"Bring them down," she repeats.

"No."

While they argue, I quickly renew Scout's body and my own. Fortunately, we bear only minor wounds. As I begin working on Kansis' body, I notice something odd.

"Scout", I whisper in his ear, "this is not the first time this girl has been attacked. There are scars all over her body. Many of them are identical to the wounds we just received from these men—but there are others also. Many others. It must have been her freckles that kept me from noticing the scars sooner."

His voice low and menacing, he turns to me. "What kinds of scars?"

"Too many to identify. They run from head to toe. And some of the scars are old—a couple of years, at least. This has been going on for some time…" I check her over again in my mind. "*Matza*. It is as if she is the town's target practice."

I can almost feel the fury radiating from Scout's body. Although his heart always beats for justice, this level of rage feels somewhat unfounded. Whatever this woman has been through, we do not know her. There is pain and suffering throughout the world—why be so affected by what this one stranger has endured? One day, Scout will perish from holding the weight of the world's woes.

Just then, a tall, Silentar woman walks up the street towards us. She takes long, graceful strides like a giraffe, reaching us quicker than most would. She seems quite flustered, and her thin hands play with her delicate, black hair.

"Levels balanced?" I ask her.

"Ruse is very distraught," she replies stiffly. "To speak to you two is to speak to the ocean. Never hearing, never seeing, never—" Ruse suddenly hears the screams coming from the heights of the Juniper trees, and she looks up for a moment before continuing. "Ruse's proficiency is not up to par for this position. You must ask another to assist you."

I look to Scout to respond, but fury has melded his jaw tightly shut.

Sighing, I respond to our tracker. "Ruse, what happened on the Ytiow mission is not your fault. The tracks were over a month old—it was wrong of us to even ask that of you. It would have been nigh impossible for any tracker. You have lost all your confidence, but it is our fault."

"Wrong," her voice cracks. "Wrong words spoken from a hopeful heart. Ruse has failed thrice. 'Too weak is the blood that spills my veins,' it is said. It is said of Ruse."

As if he has finally returned to his body, his right mind, and our conversation, Scout steps in. "Now, Ruse, that is wrong." His words are still tinted with wrath for those who have hurt Kansis, but I can tell he is trying to calm himself for Ruse's sake. He takes a step toward her and places one hand on her shoulder. The other he uses to lift her chin so her eyes meet his. "You are a phenomenal Tracker, Ruse. Your Gift thrives short-range, and you do best within your Gift's natural ability, as do we all. Pypen and I did not mean to ask you to do something outside of your Gifting. I apologize."

Ruse's teary eyes meet Scout's. "Haven," she says using a common Silentar pet name, "truly tender, but—"

"This target has only been missing between an hour and eight hours, very much within your Gifting's range."

She nods gravely. "To try is to hope; to hope is to try."

"Exactly," Scout smiles. "We were very thankful for your efforts, and I thank you in advance for your assistance with this mission."

But when he turns back to Kansis, fury roars behind his eyes once more.

"Come, come," Ruse says to the group. "We must start if our aim is a successful end."

Scout, Ruse, and I begin walking back toward Kansis' house, but the Pexun girl remains beside Taniel who is still guarding the trees and their unwilling decorations. "You can't leave them up there," she insists as Scout turns to beckon her to follow.

"We can," Scout replies, his words steel.

"They could die."

"Your authorities will find them soon enough," he snaps. "Too soon, in fact. We must hurry." And without waiting for her to follow, Scout leads Ruse to the house we exited less than half an hour ago.

As we walk up to the front door, I whisper to Scout, "Does she have bad blood?"

"Did you sense that she does?"

"No, she was clean. Why were those youths saying she has bad blood?"

"I am as unenlightened as you are."

Ruse stands on the doorstep and closes her eyes. Slowly her shoulders and hips begin to sway back and forth. Where most Gifts are triggered by thoughts, words, or feelings, Gifts triggered by action are somewhat rare, and I truly enjoy watching Ruse at work. As she enters into her Gift, she says ethereally, "Illustrate the individual of interest."

"Do you want to find Arkarian Story's daughter or not?" Scout calls across the street to Kansis.

At that moment, one of the Pexuns screams, and branches begin to thump and shatter as he falls down the length of the massive juniper tree. Taniel catches him just as he reaches the ground, then drops him quickly. Jab scrambles to his knees wildly and shoves his metal-clad hand into Taniel's leg, knocking him to the ground. The Sanusian's blood splatters over the Pexun as he shouts victoriously.

As the other Pexun abruptly falls down the tree, also screaming, I awaken my Gift. I can feel Taniel's wound as if it is my own, and I renew the lesion on his bone, the sinews of his muscles, and the molecules of his skin. When I open my eyes, I need not see to know there is no trace of a wound on his body.

Jab screams furiously as Taniel stands quickly to his feet, wholly restored.

The other Pexun lies unmoving. No one caught him on his descent to the ground, and he is seconds away from dying of a broken neck. Unwillingly, but knowing Scout would insist, I renew his wounds. I keep his exterior gashes and splinters intact. He can deal with those on his own.

"You are fortunate to have escaped the black widow's web this time," Scout shouts to them. "Now leave, both of you, or we will not be here to catch you the next time you fall."

Jab spits in our direction but he backs away. "Don't think you won't pay for that," he seethes to Kansis who is safely behind Taniel.

She does not cower, but she makes no show of bravery either. She turns her back and walks across the street to her house where we wait.

When Kansis joins us, Scout asks her softly, "Are you well?"

The Pexun woman nods.

"You need not defend them," Scout states as if she had said something contrary. "They deserved our treatment."

Kansis opens her mouth to say something, but instead she looks back towards the juniper trees, wordless.

"What is it?" Scout asks.

The Pexun merely shakes her head.

"I would like to know your thoughts." His words are said so kindly, so softly. He has reassured me that he does not have a Trigift of Emotion Manipulation, but I wonder whenever I hear him using this tone with people.

Kansis seems so surprised by his words that, if she had planned on saying something, it appears the thought had disappeared.

"Please," he pushes.

Flustered, she answers, "No, it's nothing—I—what I think doesn't matter." Before Scout can argue—which he would have—she continues, "I was just thinking that they thought the same thing."

"That they deserved their treatment?" Scout asks.

She shakes her head. "No, that *I* deserved their treatment and—" She stops herself.

"Go ahead," Scout prompts, but Kansis shakes her head. "We will stay until you state your piece," he says kindly but firmly.

When she realizes that this means we will all remain staring expectantly at her, she stutters, "N-No, I don't have—I was just—it's—well…" She takes a hurried breath and finishes quickly. "Everyone can justify their actions if they consider someone to be deserving of punishment. Jab and Seward thought I deserved what I got, and you think they deserved what they got. So… yeah. That was it."

We all stand in silence, and I have to cover my mouth before Scout sees my smile. 'Tis not often Scout is bested, but Kansis has a strong point.

When Scout does not address the issue further, I state, "Apologies, Ruse," to draw everyone's attention. "Please, track the girl once more."

Ruse nods and allows her body to resume its rhythmic swaying. After a few moments, she says again, "Illustrate the individual of interest."

Kansis clears her throat. "Formosian. Female. Tall: probably five-seven."

"To see is to know," Ruse says distantly. She lifts her hands and allows them to sway with her hips. "It was at the eleventh hour she evacuated the establishment." She mumbles something to herself, and her eyes fly open. Suddenly, red footprints appear, leaving the house and leading into town.

"Brilliant, Ruse," Scout praises as she steps down from the house in the direction of the tracks. Scout and I begin to follow, but Kansis remains immobile on her doorstep.

Scout walks over to her. Gently, he says, "You are right—we cannot walk around dispensing perceived justice on whomever we wish. But I stand by what we did to those men after all they have put you through. Now, please—I need you to accompany us. We want the same thing right now: to find the Pod."

She does not meet his gaze, but she takes a deep breath and begins to walk.

Taniel tags along at the rear, keeping an eye out for trouble, while the four of us follow the footprints through the town until we reach the forest edge. Scout sighs. "We do not have the time for this." Turning to Taniel, he commands, "Bring the Formosian making these tracks back to us, please."

"Am I ter take her cordially or wit'out consent?"

Kansis squeaks, "Cordially!" just as Scout replies, "Try cordially first."

They both look at each other, but while Scout smiles, Kansis' brows furrow uncertainly.

Taniel nods, "Ye got it, me sam." And within a blink, he is gone.

We were fortunate to find a Speeder early in the circus' origin days. He put in countless hours helping us to set up and create the circus.

It takes less than thirty seconds for him to return with a thrashing Formosian woman in his arms. She screams in a strange, old language that guides chills up my veins. I have never heard a varying tongue from Elusian in my whole life.

"Amelia!" Kansis shouts, rushing to meet Taniel and his cargo.

He looks up to greet us, but the words remain unspoken. In three swift movements, the Formosian frees herself from Taniel's grasp—then, somehow, maneuvers around him, locking his neck in a chokehold. Taniel's face reddens as Kansis rushes over, shouting, "Amelia! Amelia!" It isn't until she grips the young fighter's shoulder that her attention shifts.

"Kansis?" the Formosian says and breaks out into a smile.

Mundus Senex

Amelia

633 years ago; 2088

Amelia doesn't cry. She doesn't even allow her eyes to water. There's a car waiting in her driveway to take her to the Mountain School for Troubled Girls.

Later on that night, after her dad had shared his plan with her, Carter asked about their conversation. When she didn't share it with him right away, he beat the information out of her. Then he laughed and left a new burn on her left arm to match the one on her right.

It had only hardened her resolve to follow through on everything her father had set before her.

In a matter of hours, it seemed their whole house was in upheaval. Her mom was hysterical, claiming that having a child sent to this school would ruin her reputation and maybe even her political career. After a private conversation between the parents in her dad's office, her mom returned looking dazed. After that, she'd shut herself in her room without a word.

The next two days passed in eerie silence. It was like the quiet before a storm—a storm that would lead Amelia on a new path toward power. She barely touched her phone, and it was the first time in over three years that she didn't post anything on social media. No, she didn't have time for her phone; she needed to plan.

"Her dad wanted her to go to this school to be 'reformed.'" Amelia took out her laptop and systematically wrote out a schedule for the next six months:

March - April

- Disrespect the authorities

- Let hard facade slip once every other week so authorities think there's more to me

- Find the girls who are the biggest troublemakers and befriend them
- Act rebellious and loud, create disturbances
- Make sure to "accidentally" reveal an abused past

May - June
- Sometime early May, "break" and open up to the leader with the most authority
- Turn the troublemakers into the best students
- Create trust with authority figures
- Exploit pain

July - August
- Use trust earned to get released early
- Leave behind a legacy of kindness and trust with both students and leaders

It didn't take her long to finish her list, so she spent most of the two days learning all she could about the school she was to attend—memorizing facts about the leadership and the campus, and plotting specific days and activities in which to accomplish her goals.

On the third morning, her dad came to her room. "Are you ready?" he asked. "Yes, Daddy," she answered.

With nothing else to say, he walked out of her room and down the attic stairs. She knew she couldn't bring anything with her to the new school, so she didn't even try. Quickly, she had turned off her phone, made her bed, reset then hid her laptop, and finally followed her dad downstairs.

Now, as she stands before the car that will take her away, she doesn't look back at her brother, mother, or father, who stand on the front steps of their mansion, watching her depart.

Before she had left, her brother had socked her in the stomach as a farewell. Her mother's assistant had said goodbye on her mom's behalf, and her father had merely nodded his head.

"You ready, girly?" the driver asks.

Amelia doesn't respond. She has the distinct feeling he wasn't expecting a response anyway.

They drive for four hours. The driver won't let her out to pee because he says she'll run away.

He's wrong.

She'll only run away once they reach the Mountain—a critical start to her plan.

At noon, he drives through a burger joint in southern Oregon, and buys her lunch. The last hours see them winding up and up a mountain on a narrow dirt road. No buildings or houses are in sight; they keep climbing. There are trees everywhere, and she wishes she could identify their species. The rocks, bumps, and bends in the road jostle her around in the car's backseat.

Finally, they drive through an arch announcing *The Mountain* in wooden letters, and the driver slows. Several old, worn-down buildings are on either side of the driveway. The driver parks and opens the door for Amelia, but she doesn't move.

A hard-faced albeit beautiful woman with long brown hair and bright patches of rosacea on her cheeks walks towards the car. She puts one of her hands on the metal roof and looks down at Amelia. "Are you going to stay in there forever?" she asks.

Amelia ignores her.

"Hey, uh, I'm going to need you to leave," the driver adds kindly. "I've got to be at my next pick up by six, and I'm barely going to make it."

Amelia remains still.

The driver reaches in to help her out, and she allows herself to give into the growing hysteria in her body as she screams, "Don't touch me!"

Taking a deep, steadying breath, as if steeling himself, he reaches in once more and grabs Amelia's arm. Although she screams, kicks and hits with all her might, he pulls her out. Then, as if he knows the drill, he locks the door before slamming it shut. Running to his side of the car, he jumps in and makes a quick U-turn.

Dust from the road billows in Amelia's face, and as it clears, she sees him turning left out of the archway to go back down the mountain.

Before the hard-faced woman can say anything, Amelia runs.

As fast as she can, she races after the driver. She keeps running, screaming out to him to stop. Every time Amelia gets close to the car, the dirt chokes her throat and lungs, and she has to back off. She follows the vehicle until she can't breathe from the dirt intake, the stitch in her side, and the Charley Horse in her calf.

When it's clear that nobody is coming after her, she stops to analyze her situation. Running away first thing was a part of the plan, but she had assumed that the program's leaders would follow after her. Should she go back? Should she keep "running away"?

After a few minutes, she decides she would rather seem committed than weak, so she continues to make her way down the mountain. For hours and hours, she follows the dirt road. When she finally reaches the end, she allows herself a short break.

Maybe she should go straight to the nearest town and see how much trouble she could get into there.

Suddenly, a bright light shines into her face, completely blinding her. She flings her hands over her eyes. "Hey there," a voice calls out.

When her eyes adjust, she sees a tousle-haired police officer making his way toward her. "You the runaway from the Mountain?" His eyes seem warm even in the tense light.

"No," she answers, feigning innocence. "I was on a hike with a friend, and we lost each other. I think she made it back to her parent's house."

"Are you Amelia?" he asks.

"No, my name is Danielle," she replies easily.

"Come here for a second, Danielle."

Without a choice, Amelia follows him to his car. The policeman reaches in for something, and when he comes out, he has a device in his hands. "That isn't you, huh?" A picture of her face with her name stares back at her from the screen.

Before she can even move to scratch her face and disfigure herself, he gently grabs her elbow and guides her into his vehicle.

As he drives her back up the mountain, they both stay quiet. It doesn't take much acting to allow silent tears to fall down her cheeks. She wishes she was at home, not putting on this grand charade. But if this is how she has to earn her dad's trust, it's worth it. By the time the hour-long drive is over, her stomach is gurgling loud enough for the officer to hear.

They pull under *The Mountain* archway, and Amelia sees the hard-faced, beautiful woman waiting, hands crossed over her chest. The police car lights flare around her, and she stands poised like an angel of death.

The policeman parks the car and turns to look at Amelia. When he hands her a protein bar, she rips it open and consumes it in seconds. He gives her three more. As she tears into the second one, he says, "Listen, girl. You're a minor. Legally, you've got to have someone taking care of you. So, you have four options. One, you can run away. But as a runaway, you have no legal guardian, and if you get picked up by other men in blue, you'll go to juvie. So, option one means jail.

"Option two, you run away and try to make it on your own. But you'll need food and a place to sleep, so you'll need money. As a runaway, you can't just get a job somewhere, so you'll need an off-the-books means of getting money. There aren't a lot of options for you at that point. When you're half-starved and homeless, you become a great target for someone who knows what they're looking for. And two types of people do that best. The kind who wants to keep you for himself or the kind who wants to sell you to others. But either way, you'll be someone else's property doing something that no woman should ever have to do."

Amelia shudders. Even though this rebellion is just an act, his words scare her enough that she determines never to run away in the future.

The police officer looks her square in the eyes. "You don't want option two, Honey."

He scratches his beard. "Option three, you go home. But they don't want you there, do they? So that puts you right back with option one or two... And then there's option four." He looks out the window at the Mountain lady. "You stick with this program. You work hard. Do what they say. Get some character. And come back down the Mountain a stronger, braver individual."

He turns back around as if he's allowing her a moment to think. She licks her fingers clean of the stickiness and chocolate and folds up her trash. After a couple of minutes, he asks, "So what'll it be, Honey?"

Using her smallest, most vulnerable voice, Amelia asks, "Can't I just stay in here with you?"

"That wasn't an option, Sweetheart."

She sighs heavily. "Option four then, Mister."

The officer gives an approving grunt and gets out of the car. He and the hard-faced woman exchange a wave, and he walks to Amelia's side of the vehicle. As he opens her door he says, "Now listen," and although he doesn't touch her, his voice beckons her to meet his gaze. "You work hard, you hear? Don't give up, don't give in. Just do your best and earn your out."

He nods a farewell, then slips back into his car. As the dust clears from his exit, once again, Amelia is left standing face-to-face with the Mountain lady. Tall for her age, the girl stands at the same height as the older woman.

"My name is Miss Brimer," the woman speaks for the first time. "Are you ready to listen now?"

Amelia doesn't answer, wondering how tough this woman will turn out to be.

"Well, why don't you sit out here until you decide," Miss Brimer offers. "I'm going to be inside, and when you decide you're going to listen, just come and let me know."

Miss Brimer walks inside one of the buildings, leaving Amelia entirely alone. It's so quiet outside, and the complex around her is void of human sounds. The forest, however, sings. She can hear grasshoppers, crickets, frogs, and bugs. A warm wind caresses her cheek, and the stars shine down on her, brighter than she's ever seen them. She takes a deep, steadying breath.

So far, this is not going at all as she expected. But it doesn't matter. She can play along.

She squints her eyes in the darkness and makes out a log split in half, sitting in the road barkside facing down. There are several in rows, and she decides they must be for marking out the parking. Sleepily, she settles herself down on one of the logs. It is not comfortable, and the protein bars barely curbed her hunger. As she closes her eyes, she allows the forest's lullaby to chant her to sleep.

She knows she is on her way... on her way to a new life where she will finally be in control.

Amelia wakes up to the sound of girly giggles. Twelve young ladies in grey sweatpants and navy-blue shirts stroll past her. None of them speak to her, but she receives more than a few curious glances.

Leaning up on one elbow, she stretches out her aching back. The girls walk uphill toward a large building, and Amelia gets up to follow them. A few girls peer back at her, but they do not speak. They walk inside the building, but Amelia stays outside, peering in from the giant glass windows.

It's a mess hall, and four girls behind a large counter are handing out breakfast. Amelia's stomach grumbles, and it's painful enough that she decides to head in after all. Determining to put her best foot first, she boldly struts up to the counter and reaches for a plate. The eggs and potatoes do not look appetizing, but now is not the time to worry about it. A young black woman takes the food out of her grasp.

"No," she says simply.

"I'm hungry," Amelia replies.

The young woman's brows rise, but she says nothing else. Amelia can feel all eyes in the room on her. Even though she's acting the part, her cheeks still grow red in embarrassment. Raising her head, she bites back a sharp, "Fine," and turns to walk away. She almost runs straight into Miss Brimer.

"Only those following the rules of the program can eat the food we provide," Miss Brimer states.

"Do I look like I care in the slightest?" Amelia asks, flipping Miss Brimer off. She walks back outside and is surprised when the leader doesn't follow her. Nobody does.

Amelia takes herself on a tour around the Mountain School for Troubled Girls, inspecting all the buildings. After breakfast, she watches as most girls head across to another tall, degenerating structure to do schoolwork. It looks like they're doing their classes online. The girls eat lunch. Then they study. Later, after finishing their schoolwork, some play various sports in different areas around the campus, but most go back to the mess hall to watch a movie.

The girls eat dinner. They study again. Some of them sit around the mess hall tables and write in journals. Some sit alone in the corners like they're in a timeout. Some clean up or cook.

Amelia soon notices girls getting into trouble throughout the day, with staff responding by giving them lines or taking away achievement points. While this seems to affect some of the girls—one in particular bursts into tears—most just smile. Amelia immediately likes the smilers.

When the girls return to their bedroom for the night, Amelia returns to her log. She sleeps fitfully, waking several times in the night out of hunger. She sneaks to the mess hall in the early hours of the morning while it's still dark. She tries all the doors, wanting to break in and steal some food, but they're all locked. She's afraid of breaking a window because of the noise.

She can't remember ever being this hungry in her whole life. Finally, she makes herself walk back to her log and lay down. She doesn't sleep. When the girls wake up to go to breakfast, they stare at her again. Amelia meanders around the property for a few more hours until she's confident she can no longer go without food.

Walking into the mess hall, she asks the first girl she sees, "Where's Miss Brimer?" The girl ignores her. Amelia asks a table full of girls the same thing, but they, too, ignore her. Then from the table to her left, someone answers: "She just left to go to the office, I think."

"That's fifty points you've lost, Elaine," a woman with a bird-like face says from a table across the room. The woman has three piercings on her eyebrow and numerous dermal piercings across her clavicle. Six or so women and men sit around the table with her.

"But I was just telling her where Miss Brimer is!" Elaine protests.

"Are you in Level E?" the woman asks. "Are you allowed to talk to anyone in Levels A through D? Are you allowed to talk to anyone who is not in the program?"

"No, Miss Thomas," Elaine moans.

"Then you chose to lose fifty points." The woman hops off her stool and commands Amelia, "Follow."

Amelia first takes a moment to loudly call the woman a few choice names on Elaine's behalf.

"Are you done?" Miss Thomas asks, as if this is a regular occurrence.

Amelia rolls her eyes and follows as the woman leads her to the building she already knows is the office. The woman peeks her head inside the doorway. "Shannon? The new girl broke."

"Coming," a voice says from inside.

The bird-faced woman picks her teeth for a moment, and when the door opens, she smiles at Miss Brimer and disappears back towards the mess hall.

"Candace," Miss Brimer calls after Miss Thomas, "will you bring Estephania down for me?" Candace nods as Miss Brimer turns to Amelia. "Now, are you ready to be a part of the program?"

Amelia stares at Miss Brimer defiantly and doesn't answer. Miss Brimer smiles and shakes her head. When she turns to go back inside, Amelia's stomach roars, and before the door can shut in her face, Amelia blurts out a sullen, "Yes."

"Yes, what?" Miss Brimer asks.

"Yes, I'm ready to participate in the program."

"Are you sure, little lady?"

Amelia's pride flares. Pretense or not, nobody calls her *little lady*. Through clenched teeth, Amelia answers, "Yes."

Miss Brimer takes a deep breath, repositioning her feet so they're shoulder-width apart. Crossing her arms, she stares at Amelia.

Amelia holds Miss Brimer's gaze, allowing anger and spite to fill her to the brim. Right before she attempts to smack the leader, the door opens, and Candace returns with a Mexican girl in tow.

"Good morning, Estephania; how did you sleep?" Miss Brimer asks.

"Fine," Estephania answers with a tight smile.

Miss Brimer turns to Amelia, "Amelia, this is Estephania. She will be your buddy. For the next three days, your buddy is the only person you may talk to. You lose fifty points for every person you talk to that is not Estephania. If you think you need help, ask Estephania, and she will let you know whether you do or not."

Miss Brimer unfolds her arms and places her hands on her waist. "In this program, you start at Level A and work up to Level L. Every three weeks, you may advance a rank if you've gained enough points. We base our points system on things you do and things you don't do.

"While in Levels A through D, you may only talk to girls in Levels E and up. If you talk to anyone in D or lower, you lose points. Also, until you're in E, you cannot talk to staff unless they engage with you first. If you need to talk to the staff about something, ask your buddy to talk to them for you."

"Your day will proceed like this: breakfast, schoolwork, lunch, homework, free time, dinner, relaxing time, then bedtime." She takes a step toward Amelia. "Lastly, you may not talk to any of the girls or the staff about your issues. There are reasons why you're here, but we don't need to hear them. When you get to Level D, you'll get a Behavioral Insight Staff Member assigned to you. Until then, keep your drama to yourself."

"My dad said this was a military school," Amelia interjects.

"Yes. You're allowed to attend Casey Military Academy once you graduate from this program."

She can't help but laugh. "I'll be *allowed* to attend? The military school is the reward?"

Miss Brimer's smile is sardonic. "Oh, yeah, Honey." Turning to Estephania, she remarks, "Good luck," and walks back inside the office.

"Back to Cedar House, girls," Candace says.

As they walk, Estephania whistles a Latin tune.

"Can you shut up?" Amelia snaps. She probably should think about whether the girl could be a good ally before being so rude, but she's so hungry her vision is getting hazy.

Although she's shorter than Amelia, Estephania smiles smugly up at her. "*Te vas divertida.*" Then she continues whistling, this time louder. They enter the mess hall—Cedar House—and Estephania walks up to the counter and grabs a breakfast plate. Amelia follows suit and sits next to her new companion at one of the tables. Estephania whispers to the girl beside her, who looks at Amelia and laughs, then picks up a saltshaker and adds several heavy-handed sprinkles into Amelia's oatmeal. The whole table giggles.

Never one to be intimidated, Amelia merely smiles, staring the girls directly in the eyes as she eats every last bite.

Pexus

Kansis

MELIA RELEASES THE CHOKEHOLD on Taniel's neck and beams up at me. Jumping to her feet with infectious energy, she asks, "What are you doing here?"

"What am *I* doing?" I ask, incredulous that Amelia is looking so happy right now. "What are *you* doing here?"

"I was trying to escape," she answers brightly. "But it looks like you made friends while I was away. And here I thought I was your only friend." She punches me, affectionately—I think.

I look her over, noting she took the liberty of changing into some of my clothes. The leggings she's wearing are long on me, yet, on her tall frame, they look like stylish capris. The jacket she chose is too tight for her, but she makes it look cool.

"So these are our Protectors, huh?" Amelia asks, inclining her head towards the Ortusans, the Silentar, and the Sanusian. "What do they want?"

"To help us find Arkarian Story, I would assume," I answer.

"Yeah, but what do they *want*? Everyone wants something..." she adds, eyeing the group openly. "How do we know we can trust them?"

"We need to go," Scout reminds me. "Can this conversation continue shortly?"

"What do they want in exchange?" Amelia asks me, oblivious to Scout's request made in the Elusian tongue. When I don't answer, Amelia pushes, "Freckles, are you hearing any of these questions? Because they're critical."

"Time has become scarce," Pypen states, growing annoyed. "We must get back to the bus."

"Bus?" I ask Scout.

"Yes, we've parked it behind a bakery downtown."

Oh, I'm sure I know exactly which bakery it is. Perfect.

Amelia walks up to Pypen and asks me, "Is he their leader?"

"No, it's the one with the braid." When I point to Scout, I'm surprised to see he is watching me. But not just watching, he's staring so intently it makes my cheeks burn. Why is he looking at me like that? Like... like he knows me?

Amelia turns from Pypen to Scout and commands me, "Translate this for me: My name is Amelia. I am on a mission to locate your notorious Arkarian Story. I don't know what part you play in this, but I don't trust you. To win my loyalty, you will help me locate a man named Charles Wrightly. Once we find him, I will lead you to my dad."

After I'm done translating, Amelia demands, "Now, tell me what he says."

Scout smiles, seemingly impressed. "Hello, Amelia," he responds, and I translate quickly. "My name is Scout Eekan. I, too, am on a mission to locate the notorious Arkarian Story. I do not know what part *you* play in this, but I do not trust *you*. On my right hand, I have some of the most Gifted people in the world. At this stage, we do not know if you are the true daughter of Arkarian Story, but once we do, we will gladly assist you in the finding of Charles Wrightly and would love nothing more than to follow you to Arkarian Story."

"How do I prove to him that I'm the daughter?" Amelia asks.

When I translate, Scout answers, "It's a simple test we can perform on the bus."

"A test?" I ask before I translate. "What do you mean?"

"Do you trust me?" Scout asks. Suddenly it hits me that his hand is on my shoulder. When did he get so close? My body is a whirlwind of emotions.

No, of course I don't trust him. How could I? I don't know him at all.

But he's looking at me... not afraid to meet my gaze.

And he's touching me.

I push his hand away, steeling myself against being so pathetic. *He's an Ortusan, Kansis! Have some dignity.*

Okay, I don't trust him, but my subconscious does, and I trust *her*. I may not trust him, but he did just help me get Amelia out of the Ward. I may not trust him, but he seems to have a lot of Gifts at his disposal. He just made one call, and the Speeder showed up, saving the day.

So, no. I don't trust him. But I chose to steal a Pod and do her bidding. I chose to help Amelia.

Oh, and would this be a good time to review that I'm only helping her because I'm just *that* desperate for positive human interaction?

Yeah, this is an all-time low for me.

"What is he saying?" Amelia asks.

Motioning for her to be patient, I look back up at Scout and his gaze seems to magnetize mine. "I don't know you," I answer. "But... um... I think we need you—your help—so I will go with you—with your... whoever you are." The capillaries in my face open wide, and I'm thankful that the darkness of the evening will keep my cheeks from appearing as red as they are.

Scout's smile is so kind it makes my blood ache. When he gently tugs my hair, I cringe at the endorphins that rush through my veins.

"What's going on?" Amelia presses.

"He says there is a simple test to prove you are his daughter," I whisper to Amelia as the six of us walk quickly downtown with Scout in the lead.

"What is the test?" she asks.

"I don't know. We'll have to see."

Too soon, we round the back of the bakery and see their bus parked in the alley—although I would not have used the word *bus* to describe this vehicle... or even used the word *vehicle*. It looks like a giant, dingy rectangular container hovering over the ground. Although it has the length and width of a bus, the 'vehicle' seems to be covered in galvanized steel. It's rusting in several places, and it looks like a large chunk had fallen off the back.

"Are you absolutely sure we can trust them?" Amelia asks, equally assessing the "bus".

"Are you absolutely sure you're only seventeen and not a military general?" I ask.

She laughs. "Well, I am that, but what do you mean?"

"I mean, I can't believe you just walked up to that man and told him what he was going to do. I'd never be brave enough to do that."

She shrugs her shoulders. "Bravery comes when your convictions for success overrule your fear of obstacles. It didn't matter if he wouldn't do what I wanted. I will do what I must with or without his help."

I can't help but laugh. "I can't imagine living that way."

When we reach the bus, the Silentar woman climbs aboard, followed by the Sanusian and the Ortusans. I let Amelia board next.

As I take a step up to enter myself, all of a sudden someone hurls me in the air and throws me over their shoulder. Two strong arms wrap around my waist, and I scream out. Is someone trying to kidnap me?!

Although I pummel my attacker, they continue running back towards the city's center. A loud cry sounds behind my assailant, and I look up just in time to see Amelia's fierce face as she pounces on us.

She brings my attacker and me down to the ground, and I hit the rough stone road with my cheek. Dazed and confused, I look up to see Scout sprinting toward us.

Amelia is on top of the attacker punching him in the face. When he yells at her to stop, I'm shocked to recognize the voice.

Aker? No way...

I scrape myself off the pavement and grab Amelia's arm as she swings back to punch Aker again. "No, wait, stop! It's Aker!"

"The one who wouldn't marry you?" she asks, panting.

"Yes!"

She looks down and begins punching him again.

I grab her arm, "Get off! Let him go!"

Scout reaches us and wrenches Amelia off Aker. I want to reach out and help him up, but I know he doesn't want me to touch him, so I force myself not to. After freeing Aker of Amelia, Scout rushes to me, looking me over with concerned eyes. He gently touches my cheek. "Are you well?"

"Don't touch her, you dirty *gari!*" Aker yells and tries to stand. Amelia shoves him back down to the ground before he's fully upright, and he moans slightly, taking several deep breaths and spitting blood to the side.

"What are you doing?" I finally ask him.

"You're"—shaky breath in— "not going"—jerky breath out—"with them."

My face burns hot with anger. Who does Aker think he is? Who does my dad think he is? Why is it that in one day—the day I'm leaving, mind you—the two men who mean the most in my life suddenly care about me?

"It doesn't affect you," I respond. I don't know what else to say.

"It does..." He looks away for a moment, "You are my..." Struggling, he finishes, "mate."

I want to scream at the top of my lungs, *Since when do you care?* But I don't want to have this private conversation in front of Scout. I turn to the Ortusan, "Could you give us a couple of minutes, please?"

"Set timer for two minutes," he commands his Suus, keeping eye contact with me.

"I just want to talk to him quickly," I whisper to Amelia in English, even though Aker can't understand me.

Scout steps just far enough away to be out of earshot. Aker seems to have finally caught his breath, and he looks up at me as he starts, "Look, I know we haven't talked much in the past few months—"

Months? Doesn't he mean years? Our whole lives?

"—but Guardians came and saw me today. They said that we had two weeks to get married, or they will report us."

So he got that message, too, huh? It makes sense now why he was talking to me at the ball.

He goes on, "I was going to run away. I don't know where or for how long, but it was worth a try. But then… but my dad…" Grimacing, he looks off towards the bakery, lost in thought. It lasts only a moment before he looks back in my direction. "Anyway, I realized that… Well, you're my only chance at a normal life. Every time I try to apply at the garden nursery, they ask me about *you*." He says the word with contempt. "I'm sick of working with my dad… I need to get my life going. And… I'm… I'm trying to be ready. That all starts with…" his jaw tightens, "being with… *you*."

Embarrassment washes through my veins. Each hesitation of his hits me like a tidal wave of shame.

He chances a look at me, "So you're not going with these people. You're staying here, and we're… we're going to… figure everything out."

My cheeks and ears are hot with humiliation. Swallowing it all away, I whisper, "I can't."

Never in my wildest imaginings did I *ever* think I would say *no* to Aker Vonbough. In fact, after everything that's happened the last couple of days, maybe I *am* dreaming. Maybe I'm in some suspended-reality project or a virtual-reality game. But I've never participated in those, never having any plans to do so.

"You don't get to say no to me," Aker voices angrily. "I'm your… we're supposed to be… you're my—" He growls to himself. "You belong here! You're not running away from your problems."

Running away from my—I'm not running away from my problems!

"What were you even thinking?" he asks, vexed.

"But I—"

"Let's go. You're going home and we're pretending none of this happened."

But what about Amelia? If I don't go with her, no one will understand her. I mean, I suppose they could find someone to understand her thoughts… They could translate her thoughts and feelings if not her direct words… I don't know how that all works.

I clear my throat. "It's just—"

"Who is this Ortusan to you?" Aker snaps, gesturing towards Scout, who is clearly doing his best not to eavesdrop. "Is he a friend? You're not supposed to have friends—everyone's supposed to be shunning you."

Hurt, hot tears spring to my eyes. He's so aware of, and yet so uncaring about, my life's pain.

When I don't answer, he lashes out, "Well?"

"I... I just met him, but..."

"But what?" His words crack like a whip.

"I just... I know he's trustworthy," I answer lamely.

"Why?"

"I..."

I've never told anyone about my subconscious (that is, except for Amelia). The thought of explaining to him that I talk to myself every night right as I fall asleep to find the wisdom and comfort I need to get through each day has me glumly saying, "I just do."

Aker glares past me at Scout. "I don't like the way he looks at you."

"How does—"

"It doesn't matter. You're not going." He looks back at the bus and asks, "What business do you have with an Ortusan, anyway? Where is he taking you?"

Again I hesitate, not sure if I should tell him or not. But I can't have him thinking anything untrue about me, so I blurt out the truth. "I found Arkarian Story's daughter."

Scoffing, he replies, "She's a myth."

"I found her," I press, "and these Ortusans will help us locate Arkarian Story. And with... with the reward... I thought you could get a... get the... you know..."

"Blood transfusion?"

"Yes," I reply, relieved I didn't have to speak the words out loud. "I have to go with them to help find Arkarian Story."

Aker eyes me for a second and then asks, "How much is the reward?" just as Scout returns to us. The two minutes are up.

Aker squares his shoulders as my Protector stands next to me. "I'm coming too," he states.

His declaration catches my breath. "What?" I squeak.

"If you're going, I'm going too. I don't care what you say," Aker replies, looking at Scout.

"You... you can't come," I state distantly.

"Why would you want to come?" Scout asks, voicing my thoughts. "Do you not have a job and a life here?"

"That's not your business, *gari*. And… One's life is their mate, no?" he asks with a sardonic grin. "Where she goes, I go."

…Did he just refer to me as his mate?

"I'm not letting her go without me," Aker announces firmly.

Silence fills the alley for several long seconds.

"Of all days, why do you care about her on *this* day?" Scout asks. The sharpness in his voice makes me look up at him. His face is so sad. And how did he know that Aker hadn't cared about me before today?

"You don't know me," Aker growls. "You don't know her."

"You do not know that I do not know her. Or you, for that matter."

Aker's fists clench. "Who *are* you?"

Clenching his jaw, Scout turns to me. "Do you want him to come?"

"Of course," I say without thought.

After studying me for a moment, Scout says, "Then let us go," and gently turns me around towards the bus.

"What's the hurry?" Aker asks, but Scout doesn't answer him.

I beckon to Amelia. "Aker is coming with us," I whisper as she steps up beside me. Her fists clench and she shoots him a dark look, but I plead with my eyes for her to leave it be.

"If he makes one wrong move…" she threatens loudly, and although Aker doesn't speak English, her meaning is clear. She crosses her arm as he limps past, letting the displeasure radiate from her body like a warning beacon.

Back at the bus, Aker walks on first, followed by Amelia breathing down his neck. I come to a stop before my Protector. I want to ask him why he's so upset about Aker, but the words won't come out of my mouth. Changing my mind, I start up the steps, but Scout touches my arm to stop me. Warmth floods my skin from the point of contact, racing up my arm and spreading down to my fingers. My cheeks grow red.

"Did you want to say something?" he asks.

"Oh no, no, no," I answer quickly, but when I turn to head inside the bus, he stops me again.

Kindly, he says, "I would like to hear."

"Okay… I was just wondering—I just—Well…"

Scout's patient waiting makes me even more nervous. Garbled words fall out of my mouth, and it's not until he places both of his hands on my shoulders that the gibberish stops. The weight of his grasp seeps from my shoulders down to my toes and seems to settle my body somehow. "Do speak," he urges.

Finally, I ask, "Why are you upset he's coming with us?"

Scout removes his hands, and I feel oddly cold. Not looking at me, he answers, "It is no blood from my veins whether he comes or not. He probably will not last the week, so I am not worried about it."

"Won't last the week? What're we doing?"

He smiles slowly. Shooting me a wink, he says, "Finding Arkarian Story, of course."

As I follow him onto the bus, I look up to see a Formosian man talking with Pypen. The man greets Scout with a bright-eyed grin. "So you found the daughter," he asks.

"So she is *the* one, Emerly?" Scout asks eagerly. "She is the daughter of Arkarian Story?"

The Formosian called Emerly squints suddenly as if he has a headache. As he rubs his temple absentmindedly, he answers, "She is the daughter, she is."

The men exchange enthused looks. Having never even considered the daughter of Arkarian Story exists, it seems strange that these strangers are so elated. I wonder how long they've been looking for her...

"Eight years," Emerly answers my mental question. "We've been searching for eight years, we have."

"This is huge," Pypen states. "Honestly, I was not convinced I would see this day."

"That is because you are exclusively pessimistic," Emerly states with a fake smile.

Pypen smirks. "Well, this day I am pleased to be proved wrong," he says, and the Formosian man pulls both Scout and Pypen into an embrace.

AMELIA, AKER AND I are shown to our room, and it's ridiculously spacious. Aker immediately grabs a pillow from the bed and lays it out on the ground as far away from us as possible. Completely ignoring us, he turns his head away and—I guess—falls asleep.

Before I can even begin to process this rejection, Amelia commands, "Explain your Gifts to me. How were those people able to find me like that? I know you said everyone has superpowers, but what does that mean? How does it all work?"

Thankful for the distraction, I allow myself to fall into teacher mode. With all the unknowns of the past twenty-four hours, teaching is a safe place for me. "To review, humanity has, from the beginning of time, had the capacity for supernatural abilities. This capability was dormant within every cell on earth at the center of each nucleus—the Gician Particle. And it wasn't only in people—all matter everywhere contained this particle. It wasn't until the Era Ending War that the Gician Particle was excited into action by the toxic levels of radiation and gamma rays."

I glance at Amelia, but she merely watches me, obviously fascinated by what is rote history for me. I carry on.

"Nuclear radiation from the bombs of the Era Ending War predominantly caused deadly mutations and destruction to the genetic material of Elusians—to the point where disease, cancer, infertility, and birth defects were the norm. Only those on the fringes of the contaminated areas survived and were able to reproduce, meaning humanity survived. However, there were several areas where populations that were inside radiation zones but outside detonation epicenters exhibited no ill effects from the radiation they were exposed to."

I can almost see her ears perk up as I get into the details she's thirsting over.

"Instead, these populations showed signs of near-superhuman health and well-being. Not only that, but various paranormal manifestations were also experienced in and around these locations. In the years following, when science began to blossom once more, these Elusians became a subject of study for the scientific community. It was hoped that replicating these hyper-healthy effects on other Elusians would limit the detrimental impacts of the long-lasting heightened radiation levels. Over time, our scientists not only accomplished this but even found ways to harness the paranormal—or supernatural—occurrences. Soon after, Gifts were found.

"Now, there are seven ways to categorize our Gifts: Energy State, Action Type, Power Source, Trigger, Condition, Limitation, and Function.

"There are Gician Particles in every cell, and they can be excited at different levels. Each of those energy levels corresponds to and influences thirteen areas of Novus. We refer to these states as: Identity, Morality, Perception, Intention and Will—"

"Whoa, whoa, whoa," Amelia states. Pulling her legs up like a pretzel, she closes her eyes to focus. "Okay, say them again, and *slower.*"

I start from the top. "Identity, Morality, Perception, Intention and Will, Influence, Retention, Horolation, Restoration, Movement, Formation, Creation, Giftation, and Activation."

"That was a mouthful," Amelia teases.

Normally my Pods aren't playful with me, so I'm not sure what a fun response to her joking would be. Instead, I just answer honestly, "Well, when you've said it a thousand times, it gets easier to remember."

"Okay okay—keep going, Encyclopedia Kansis."

"Please, it's Professor Willow." Smirking, I go on. "Now, within each Energy State, there are five Action Types: Control, Enhance, Handle, Manipulate, and Understand."

"Stop," she says, putting up a hand.

"I know, I know," I state with a laugh. "Let me break it down for you *slowly*. Some of the Action Types are obvious: Controllers can control entities, Enhancers enhance, et cetera. However, Handlers and Manipulators, although similar, are distinct. Manipulators use their Gifts employing various methods but are limited to one specific *area*. Handlers use their Gifts in various areas but are limited to employing them in one specific *method*."

Seeing her confusion, I expound, "Let's use Resource Manipulation as an example. A Manipulator would be confined to one resource—let's use water. So, the Manipulator would employ various means of manipulating water—duplicating, moving, shaping, etc.—but would only be able to manipulate water. A Handler, however, would be able to manipulate any type of body but only be able to do one thing to them. So, in our example, they would be limited to one method—let's use shaping—but would be able to shape various resources like water, dirt, air, food, etc. Where Manipulators are limited to areas, Handlers are limited to means. Does that make sense?"

Her face scrunches in uncharacteristic annoyance.

Knowing how much she dislikes not understanding, I smile and ask, "What isn't making sense?"

"So..." she says slowly, "Manipulators are limited by *what* they can manipulate; Handlers are limited in *how* they manipulate."

Impressed, I clap, "Yes! Exactly. Well done."

Pleased with herself, she says simply, "Do go on."

Laughing, I *do* go on. "Next, each Gift has a unique Power Source, which we have color-coded. If a person's power source is the universe itself—this being the most powerful one—we call that a Red Gift. If their Gift is powered by the universe but with limitations—"

"Stop."

Her seriousness has me giggling again. "What's the question?"

"What do you mean 'powered by the universe'?"

"It means that they can literally harness energy from the limitless universe and accomplish any feat of their imagination without any recompense or consequence to their physical form."

Amelia sighs. "What?"

"All the Gifts, besides Red Gifts, require energy from your own body. If you use all of the energy in your body, you die. People with Red Gifts don't ever touch the energy in their own body, so they can do whatever they want for as long as they want, and there will never be any exhaustion or toll on their bodies."

"Dang."

"I know. So, if a person's power source is the universe itself, we call that a Red Gift. If their Gift is sourced by the universe but with limitations, those are Yellow Gifts. Green Gifts use infinite energy from our planet, Blue Gifts use limited energy from our planet, and Black Gifts can only use the power within their own bodies."

"So Black Gifts suck."

"Black Gifts suck." I don't add that *my* Gift is Black. She doesn't need to know any more embarrassing things about my life.

"Anway," I go on, "Each Gift is triggered differently. Some people have to think, and then they can use it. Others use their emotions, while other Triggers are words, action, or the senses."

"That's cool."

"Sometimes. For those who have an Emotion Trigger, their Gifts are pretty unstable. If they're upset about something, their Gift can just go off without their consent."

"Is yours like that?" she asks.

"No, mine is Sense Triggered."

"Like the five senses?"

"Yes; mine is sight."

"Interesting." As if suddenly remembering something, she states, "Don't think I've given up on guessing your Gift. I've been thinking a lot about it, and now I have some help... you have to *see* it in order for your Gift to work..."

I laugh at her earnest considerations and continue on with my lesson. "Then, there is the Condition that comes with a Gift. A Gift can be automatic, meaning it is used with or without the user's consent. Or a Gift can be responsive, meaning it can only be used in response to some other action or entity. And finally, it can be entirely up to the user's choice, meaning they have full power as to when it is and isn't used."

"So can someone with a Sense Trigger also have a Choice Condition?"

"Yes, in rare cases. Most Sense Triggers are with Responsive Gifts."

"What's yours?"

"Automatic." Rolling my eyes, I add, "It's annoying."

Pretending like she's taking something out of her pocket, she animatedly writes in the air, "Notes to figuring out Kansis' Gift: Sense Trigger. Automatic. Annoying." She drops her hand and grins. "Got it."

Chuckling, I move on to my next lesson. "The sixth categorization is a Gift's Limitations. A Gift can be limited to living organisms, non-living organisms, available resources, the wielder themselves, or everyone *except* the wielder themselves."

"What do the last two mean?"

"If you're a Healer, sometimes your Gift can be limited only to others, so you can never heal yourself. Or, vice versa, you can only heal yourself and not others."

"Oh, that would be a bummer."

"Agreed. And, lastly, there is the Function: the actual Gift itself. Now, all of the layers above are important because they can cause huge distinctions. Two people could both be mind-readers, in which case they would both be Understanders, and both fall under Perception—the third Energy State. But one may have a Yellow Gift while the other has a Blue. One may have to *think* to hear another's thoughts, while the other needs to dance. One may automatically be able to listen in on people's thoughts who are not properly protecting themselves, while another may only be able to listen in response to an emotional outburst. One of the mind readers may only be able to hear humans, while another may only hear animals. Each of the levels changes the outworking of what could be considered the same Gift."

Amelia rubs her temples and groans, "You're hurting my head."

"We can go over it again tomorrow."

"Oh, we will. Until I understand," she asserts.

"Until you understand."

I wait until she's in bed before I turn out the light. When I try to lie on the floor, she tells me I have to share the bed with her or she will sleep on the floor as well. Appreciating her thoughtfulness, I climb into the bed next to her. From where I lie, I can see Aker lightly snoring on the floor. Looking away, I draw out my druzy quartz pendant. I hold it in my hand, wondering if I should use it tonight. Aker is with me, after all… I want to sneak a peek at him, but I don't dare. I almost put the pendant away; I almost decided to live in reality for tonight.

But after two years of falling asleep in Dream Aker's arms, I can't say no. I *won't* say no.

As I rub the necklace as fast as I can, the smells and sounds of the bus fade away.

So. FOR THE FIRST time in my whole life, I'm sleeping in the same room as Aker Vonbough. He wasn't too happy about it, but he *had* said he was my mate, so Scout offered us a room… And I didn't want Amelia to be alone, so now she and I are sharing the bed, and Aker is on the floor. I have no idea what's going on in my life right now.

Did you wake up this morning and think you'd be leaving Depalo forever?

Forever? I hope not *forever*.

What would you have done if Amelia had wanted to awaken Arkarian Story so he could rule over all of us?

Honestly. I don't know. I may have followed Amelia still… At least until I had more information.

Did anything else happen?

What do you mean?

Was there anything that happened today that you forgot to tell me?

I told you everything that's happened—like I do every other day.

Didn't something happen to two kaimans *in a Juniper tree?*

How did you—how did you know about that? I thought you only know what I tell you?

For the most part. But sometimes, I can see things you're trying really hard to hide. Why didn't you tell me? How long have they been hurting you?

I don't—how can—you've never known things I've kept from you…

What other things are you keeping from me?!

I keep things from you that you don't need to know.

And what kinds of things do I not need to know?!

Stop shouting at me! I'm not sure how you do it, but whenever I talk about someone who's hurt me or my feelings, something terrible seems to happen to them. So—

That is not *true.*

It *is.* So I stopped telling you about that stuff, and then bad things don't happen to them.

So… you're keeping a lot from me?

Come on; my life is one big joke. I've been keeping everything from you.

How long have those boys been hurting you?

Ontzi, it doesn't matter.

It matters to me.

Yes, I'm sure it does.

Is it just them?

…

…

…

Well?

You know, Scout reminded me a little of *you* today, when he wasn't willing to bring Jab and Seward down from the tree. He was so justified in his opinion, even though it was the exact same mindset that had Yunson's brothers chasing me every night.

Why are you trying to change the subject?

I think you'd like Scout.

And why is that?

I don't know, it just seems like you'd get along.

What do you think of Scout?

What do you mean?

It is not that hard of a question to understand: what did you think of him?

I don't know; he's okay.

He's okay?

He looks at me in this way. Like… like he knows me.

Maybe he's just looking at you like you are a human being and not a virus.

Maybe. He seems nice enough.

Nice enough?

Why? What do you think of him?

I was just wondering.

Why did you ask? Should I be worried about him? Is he trying to hurt Amelia or me?

No, no! I was just… he just… I don't know.

Spit it out.

There is nothing to spit out. I think it was nice how kindly he treated you. Aker never treats you like that.

Yeah, up until tonight! Were you not listening to me at all? He is on this bus because he wants to go with me.

One night doesn't take away twenty years of treating you like feces.

Why not? If he had a change of heart, I'm not going to push him away just because he didn't know what he wanted for a little while.

Didn't know—Is that a joke? That man knows exactly what he wants: Mirindiss. He has made it abundantly clear that he wants nothing to do with you. I don't understand why he even came.

Neither do I. And that's why I am willing to give him a second chance.

This is the millionth chance!

He's in my blood... I have to try.

Whatever. Grovel to him. Beg him to love you like a poor man begs for wealth. And when he keeps you in poverty, I hope you're satisfied. Every day, when he throws you the scraps of a smile or the crumbs of a kiss, I hope you remain blind to his cold, cruel blood—so you'll never have to see yourself as the pathetic, blood-thinned ghost of who you once were.

You have no idea what you're talking about.

I am the only part of you that takes any pride in you.

No! You don't understand how much I love him!

And you don't understand how pointless your desire for him is. You don't know how foolish your affections appear to everyone around you. You don't realize how useless your love is to him.

Greet the shadows.

You shut me up because you know my words are true.

I shut you up because your words are poison.

...Greet the shadows, Kansis. It's always better...

...

...

...

It's always better...

...when we're together.

Pexus

Pypen

After we have shown Kansis, her angsty mate, and the Pod to their accommodation, Scout and I return to the hallway, where Emerly is anxiously awaiting us.

"So she is truly the daughter?" Scout asks again.

Emerly looks up with a grimace, nodding firmly. Scout quickly turns to make a call, presumedly to the Sixth Aevum, but before he can, Emerly stops him.

"There's more, there is," he states gravely.

"More?" I ask.

"You've seen Arkarian Story's location?" Scout questions eagerly.

"That's just it, isn't it," Emerly answers. "I know without hesitation that she is the daughter, but the location... Arkarian Story's location is hidden."

"But she is a subhuman with no defenses," I say scornfully. "How could she hide anything from you? She only awoke three days ago."

"I don't think she's the one doing the hiding," Emerly explains. "I think another Gifted person covered the information. Hid it away so no one can find it without the Pod's consent."

"Inconceivable," Scout replies, eyebrows reaching to his hairline. "Who could have done such a thing?"

"Perhaps we need another mind reader's opinion?" I ask. "I intend no offense towards your Gift," I add quickly to Emerly.

"No, I understand," he responds genuinely. "I'm confident enough in my talent, but I, too, would welcome a second opinion, I would."

"I will call the Sixth Aevum," Scout says. "I will ask him to send someone."

Emerly and I talk of the Pexun girl and the daughter, while Scout makes the call on his Suus.

As he turns back to us, we fall quiet.

"The Sixth Aevum is unhappy that you were not able to find the location," Scout states.

Emerly pales slightly. "I can try again—"

"No, I trust you, old friend. I spoke up on your behalf. Someone will meet us at the hotel in Initium. The Sixth Aevum said his mind reader need not even see or touch Amelia, but they can search her mind from the sidewalk."

"That's helpful, isn't it," Emerly states and tucks his chin-length hair behind his ears. "I doubt the subhuman would want to know someone is searching her thoughts, oh no."

"Kansis would be upset as well," Scout states. At the confused look on our faces, he explains, "The Pexun girl, Kansis. She seems very protective of her Pod. She would probably be upset if she knew we were reading the Pod's mind without either of them knowing or consenting."

I nod.

"We will need to give the daughter a sciath," Scout adds offhandedly.

"Whatever for?" I ask, surprised.

"Right now, any mind reader with even a cell's worth of talent could read the daughter's mind and find out who she is. And if they wanted to, they could just as easily take control of her mind or body. Defenseless as she is, the sciath would keep her safe."

"What if the Sixth Aevum wants to sift her mind, and she is unwilling to take it off? He would be especially agitated if he found out we willingly gave her a sciath," I argue.

"We will give it to her with the Blood Assurance that she will take it off when our need to search her memories arises."

Emerly frowns. "And what if she doesn't want to give her Blood Assurance? The whole you-will-die-if-you-break-your-word bit of the bond is quite the commitment, isn't it?"

"Then it will be her choice: protection on our terms or vulnerability on hers."

As always, Scout has the wisest of solutions.

"We have a few sciaths lying around in here," I say. "I will retrieve one."

"Brilliant. We can give it to the daughter posthence."

"And here I thought we were going to find Arkarian Story today, I did," Emerly says with a pretend pout. Then his frown dramatically turns to a smile as he adds to Scout, "In other news, are we still on for tomorrow night?"

"Of course," Scout says, then growls at me, "but you are not welcome."

I groan dramatically as I sit on his bed. "You just went to a meeting; why go again so soon?"

Scout eyes me. "I am not convinced you are genuinely interested in the answer."

"I am. Truly, I am. I am just concerned this won't end well for either of you."

Sighing, Scout answers, "We have heard strange tales about the convent of Seekers in Initium. They seek a Superior that is not numbered among the thirty-one. We wish to hear about it."

"Well, unfortunately, you have other plans."

Scout scoffs. "Other plans?"

Now it is my turn to scoff. "Did you truly forget our plans for next night? The sixth of Dixember? The most significant honor of our lives so far? How is none of this—"

As he remembers, Scout snaps his fingers and smiles. "Ah yes, the *engagement*."

"The *engagement*?" I say and chortle. "You mean the *engagement* where you and I are to be worshipped at the Demirkan House of Worship? What a small, little thing—being worshipped in a territory's capital."

Scout winks. "Indeed. I must have forgotten. Now, will you check on Merayal before you go to bed?"

"Scout," I moan, putting on my best whiny voice. "Can someone else do it?"

He smiles toothily at me, singing, "Wish her sweet dreams on my behalf."

"Tuck her in for me," Emerly adds loudly.

"Ye got it, boss," I say in my best Sanusian accent. I leave Scout and Emerly and drag my feet toward Merayal's compartment. As I make my way down the corridor, my stomach drops like we've just hit a high on a rollercoaster, and I steady myself on the mud-brown walls of the bus. I have always hated this means of transportation. It was given to us by the Sixth Aevum, so Scout feels obligated to use it, but it is outdated. I have searched for newer, more technologically advanced buses, but Scout has been unwilling to buy one. I asked Thykas if he would at least paint the walls, but he has not gotten around to it.

I arrive at Merayal's compartment and stare at the paint-chipped door, fighting the compulsion to kick it and walk away.

Someone runs into me, and I turn to see Gigi.

"Oh, sorry, Pip," she mumbles, trying to slip past me.

"Are you well?" I ask, seeing her reddened eyes.

Staring down the hallway, she nods a silent yes.

"What is it?" I ask, smoothing out my voice.

Soothing people is a skill I learned from Scout. Truly, he has taught me much about psychology—how to guide the thinking and behavior of our team members in healthier directions. Before Scout, I had less discernment than a rooster crowing at midnight. He has taught me how to read and then how to speak with people. Notwithstanding, I am reasonably confident I know what is bothering Gigi, as it is always her mate. "Is it Ryder?" I ask.

Bursting into tears, she grabs me into a hug. "I love him so much, Pypen," she says through sobs.

I sigh. "Ryder loves you as well." I awkwardly put my arms around her and squeeze quickly. "He just does not know how to show it the way you want him to."

She takes a few calming breaths and looks up at me with puffy eyes. Smiling self-consciously, she wipes her face. "Oh *matza*, now I am all blotchy. Ryder will know I have been crying again."

I close my eyes. Focusing on nothing, I reach down into my being and will my Progift awake. Feeling its power in my veins, I stretch out my thoughts toward Gigi. I envision her as she was the day I first saw her, face flushed with excitement, eyes bright with anticipation for her new undertaking. As I do so, she is transformed before me, so that when I open my eyes, she appears just as she was in my mind.

"Thank you, Pip," she says, kissing my cheek. "You are a good man."

"For your praise," I say and let her pass. I do not mean to be prideful, but I *am* a good man. Every day I do my best to serve my team and make things easier for them. Not only do I contribute to the group, but I give back to several Humani Houses with the aons I earn from the Unopened Gifts.

My mood turns sour as soon as I turn back to Merayal's door. I would rather kick her off the bus than make sure she is enjoying her stay.

"Pypen?" an ethereal voice speaks, brushing my mind.

I do not know if she spoke out loud or in my thoughts, but I turn to Fabella, our resident storyteller. She stands like a cat in the shadows, slightly illuminated by the melted butter hallway lighting.

"Greet the shadows. What can I do for you this fine evening?" I ask. Her flawless red hair is intricately twisted around the top of her head, and she has painted her eyes to look narrow and feline. As always, Fabella wears a sheer lace mask over her face. Although I can see her features, they are dark and mysterious.

"That Pexun woman is quite the oddity, yes?" she purrs.

"Merayal?" Inwardly, I gag. "Indeed."

"She is not a Pexun, did you know? She might have the blood but not the heart, she doesn't."

"How do you mean?" I ask, not understanding to what she could be referring.

"I am no mind reader, as you know, but I sense her story. She comes from a wicked place populated with evil people." Fabella's expression grows distant. "She escaped them, but barely—and not without sacrificing much of who she is, she did. Her story is scarred with pain. Betrayal. Loss. In uncertainty she drowns, doesn't she? Fear, anger, darkness—they consume her."

"What kind of darkness?" I ask.

Her distant gaze snaps back sharply to focus on me. "The kind only found in nightmares."

Fear and adrenaline rush through my veins. Before, I had wanted Merayal to leave simply because of her attitude—but if she is endangering the group, then *most certainly* I will be barging into her room and demanding she leave once we reach Depalo.

As if sensing my thoughts, Fabella states calmly, "I am no prophet, but I don't think you should make her leave, I don't. No, I think you must build her trust."

What an impossible task. "I hate to say it, but she will not be trusting me anytime soon."

"It will take work and self-sacrifice, but I must warn you, Pypen. The darkness of her past will consume you, if you let it."

If *I* let it? How is this on me? If this were anyone else speaking, I would dismiss these haunting words. But in my experience, Fabella has been nothing but discerning and perceptive. To take her words lightly would genuinely hurt the circus. "Why not just cast her out now, then?" I ask.

Fabella's voice is so sweet, her smile so kind. "Because I think her story may finally find hope. I think she could find that which she was never allowed, here."

"And what is that?"

"A home."

I want the word to settle the angst in my veins, but it does not. Instead, it sets off blaring horns of warning in my blood. Every cell in my body is alert, and I eye Merayal's door distrustfully. This Pexun woman hates me; I see no path where she could find a home with us.

To Fabella, I say, "Merayal has a mate; she has a family. Her mother may have died, but she has others."

"That woman was not her mother," Fabella speaks offhandedly as she turns away.

"Fabella, wait," I say, and she turns back. "How do you mean?"

"The woman—Xoana Kapu—she was not her mother." The beautiful Formosian looks at Merayal's door. "The woman was her only light, and now

Xoana is dead." Before I can ask any one of the myriads of questions I have, Fabella continues, "Merayal's story is turning dark once more unless you stop it."

Surprise, and then ire floods my veins, making my face hot. "*Me*? Why am *I* responsible for her?"

"Why are we responsible for anyone?" Fabella asks.

Her question cools and calms my blood. "I know not," I answer honestly.

Fabella smiles and pulls up her veil—something I have never seen her do before. I stare into her twinkling blue eyes as she goes on, "You've made yourself responsible for every person in this circus, Pypen."

"I did no such thing. Scout is responsible—"

"Wrong," she interrupts with a passion that makes me take a step backward. "You like to see it that way, but it is not so. It is you *both*, Pypen. You called us out, made us special, didn't you? We are your responsibility because you set your affection on us, you did. You tamed our curdled blood. Our well-being rests on your decided involvement or inactivity in our lives. Now, you must bear the burden of our welfare, you must." She turns and looks at Merayal's door once more. "You could let the Pexun girl rot and rust in her blood, or you could tame her. You could earn her trust and affection as you did all of ours."

I look down at my shoes and let the weight of her words sink in. When I look back at her, she has returned the veil over her face. "To tame... How do you mean?"

"Long ago, back when more land covered the earth, a man described it as creating ties, he did."

"Creating ties? How so?"

"Right now, Merayal is only a Pexun—just like a hundred thousand other Pexuns—and you have no need of her. It was the same when you met each one of us. We were a featureless face, an unseen somebody, an unknown nobody. But then, you tamed us. And now, you have need of us and we of you. Create ties with Merayal—attach yourself to her and she will attach herself to you."

Her words are lovely yet entirely unreachable. "How do I do that?"

"Attachment is the pursuit and preservation of proximity, of closeness, of connection. A family is not a family without attachment."

I rub my eyes as I respond, "That is Scout's department. I am not able to do what you ask."

"I can only sense her story, I can. But I know it must be you. Merayal needs *you*, Pypen. Tame her, and you will have saved more than just one person."

I know not how to respond, so I ask with a smile, "Did Scout send you?

He preaches the same message."

Fabella smirks affectionately and backs away from me. "Break her walls with kindness. Cover her with your blood as you did the rest of us. She is not from this world, and she needs you."

Not from this world?

"How do you mean?"

Shaking her head, she turns to leave. "That is her story to tell."

I take a deep breath. Fabella's words swirl around my mind dizzily. How can so much responsibility be placed on our shoulders? I have always believed that Scout bore the weight of the group's well-being—not me. Had I known this was a part of the deal, perhaps I would not have called any of these people out of their mundane lives—let alone this woman who hails from a different world filled with darkness, whatever that means. I only allow myself fifteen seconds to brood on my negative feelings, then I cast them out.

Determining in my blood that I will do as Scout and Fabella have asked, I knock on Merayal Kapu's door.

She opens it roughly and looks up at me angrily. "What?"

Even in the poor lighting of the hallway, I can see her eyes are swollen from crying. "Levels balanced?" I ask, unintentionally matching her rude tone.

"Yes, I'm fine."

"Your blotched face says otherwise."

Her hands fly to her cheeks, and she wipes her eyes, "What do you want?"

"I just wanted to see if you are situated in your room. Did you find everything you need?"

"I'm fine," she says, stepping back in order to slam the door shut.

I keep my foot on the threshold, so it cannot close completely. Then I take a few steps into her room, closing the door behind me. "Do you wish to discuss it?" I ask softly.

Merayal looks up at me, and now I am confused by her expression. It is an equal mixture of fear and anger. "Open that door right now," she commands, her voice deep and authoritative.

I quickly open the door but continue to stand in her room. "It is open, see? Please—I merely want to ensure you are faring well."

"Just leave."

"Are you this cold with everyone, or am I the unique recipient of this treatment?" I ask angrily, unable to remain unaffected by her bile.

She sneers. "There's absolutely nothing unique about you."

I laugh derisively. Scout is the tender one, not me. I barely hesitate for a second before I respond, "Your mate must love spending his life with such a cantankerous, loathsome woman. Or has your poisonous temper killed him already, I wonder?"

Her smile is grotesquely unpleasant. "You see right through me, partner."

I smile sardonically. "Ah, so you did kill him?"

"He's dead."

"How?"

She folds her hands across her chest. "I don't owe you anything, *gari*. You will never be a part of my personal life." She looks away and flips her grey, Pexun hair over her shoulder. "Now get out."

I cross my arms to mimic hers. "So that is the issue? Your mate died, and you have been oh so alone? And now, broken, wounded Merayal cannot let anyone close for fear of rejection?"

The rage filling her features matches her reddening color. "You know nothing about me," she replies slowly through clenched teeth.

"And yet, I see right through you. Were those not your words?"

Suddenly, the speaker in her room blares out in a loud, Sanusian accent: "Ta moon does send its greetin' on t'is fine old evenin'. Close up yer face windows and say greet ta shadows, me ol' sams."

Other circus members shout from their rooms, "Greet the shadows!" as the speaker fades. We have always done this, and I join the chorus out of habit. My sudden shout makes Merayal jump, and her shocked face causes me to laugh.

As her face returns from shocked to angry, I *lightly* regret my harsh words. Fabella's challenge comes back to me, and I know I should not have lost my temper. I am usually up for the challenge, but Merayal is in a trial class of her own.

I lower my arms and take a deep breath. "I apologize for the way I have spoken to you."

She smiles mockingly. "Oh, yeah, sure."

"No, I truly am sorry," I state genuinely. "You bring out a bad side of me, and I should have more control."

"Ignoring your rage doesn't make it go anywhere," she replies.

"True," I respond, knowing the depths of regret my anger has led me into. "But that is no reason to treat you as I have." I look out the window and see we are approaching the Pexun Northeast transponder station. It is not a very large building, yet hundreds of vehicles come pouring out of the side in neat, orderly queues.

The light from the transponder station shines through the glass windows of the bus. A prism begins coloring Merayal's face. Purple colors her silver hair, whilst blue tints her forehead. Green plays across her eyes, making me forget their actual color. Yellow and orange begin to darken on her snub nose and fair cheeks, whilst red shows brilliantly on her wide lips, and pink plays across her strong, square jaw. I am so taken aback by the colors, I barely notice her staring back at me.

"Don't look at me like that," she commands.

"I apologize," I force myself to look at my feet. "I was merely..." Disquieted, I turn my gaze towards the transponder station.

Our bus rounds the corner to the front of the station, where seven queues of vehicles, all on conveyor belts, stretch out about a kilometer. Each of the seven queues holds a different type of vehicle: bus, car, motorbike, scooter, lorry, hauling lorry, and industrial mover. The belt moves them along quickly, so it is usually only about a ten-minute wait per kilometer in the queue. The station transports fifteen buses per minute.

Thykas drives our bus to the back of the queue, and the whole vehicle jolts as the belt picks us up.

I turn back to face Merayal. I try to think of some way to ask if we can start over, but I cannot find any words. Instead, I ask, "Is there anything I can do for you before I leave?"

Turning away from the window, she faces me. "Tell me how my mom died."

Xoana Kapu: the woman who is not her mother. I almost tell her I know this fact, but I stop myself in time, not wanting to shut her down any further. "Are you certain you wish to hear?" I ask.

"Tell me."

"It is gruesome."

She winces as if she had been stung by a bee, but she repeats firmly, "Tell me."

Scout would not relay this story to her, I know, taking care to keep such a visual out of her mind. But I am not as sentimental as Scout. I think back to the assassin with his black clothing, save for the light brown hood, signaling his Sanusian blood. I think back to the violence of the moment, the fear that Scout would experience the same fate. Finally, I answer simply, "Her lungs exploded."

Merayal swallows hard. "The assassin did that?"

"Yes, the man placed his hand on her chest and made her lungs explode."

She takes this in for a moment then asks, "How will you find him?"

"We are trying to get hold of a Play Back."

"What would a Play Back do?"

"There were four of us there when your mother was murdered. The assassin's face was covered in a hood, but the Play Back could go into our memories and use the collective sight of four perspectives to reveal at least some of his face. We are also running his Gift through our databases, hoping to find the one who could do such a thing."

"When will the Play Back get here?"

Shaking my head, I answer, "We are not entirely certain she will come. But as Scout and I get information, I will share it with you immediately." At her skeptical look, I add, "I am not kind like Scout, but I *am* a man of my word." Before she can respond, I ask again, "Is there anything I can do for you before I leave?"

This time she pauses before answering. "All I want to do is find the person who murdered my mom and return the favor. That's literally it. So if you can help me figure out who it was, that would be great."

"I will," I reply.

She nods. There is no gentleness in her features, but the anger has subsided. "All right. Greet the moon—or the shadows. I don't know what time it is."

"Greet the shadows, Merayal," I reply and leave, quietly shutting the door on my way out.

As I return to my compartment, I let the weight of Fabella's words sink into my veins. Am I truly responsible for our team's well-being? I do not remember consenting to such a burden when Scout and I started hiring the others. I am not confident that I can carry that charge. Scout can of course—but what about me?

And what happens to Merayal if I am proven to be incapable?

12 DAYS UNTIL QUINTRALL

Pexus

Kansis

AMELIA STARES WIDE-EYED OUT the narrow bus window, her gaze fixed on the transponder station. The only times I have ever traveled outside Depalo were for work training and conferences, so I am also excited to transpond.

"How does it work?" Amelia asks quietly. Aker is still asleep on the floor of our room, but part of me wonders if he's actually awake.

"When we arrive at the entrance, the driver will input our desired coordinates into the station's mainframe," I answer Amelia. "The bus will be sprayed with Adtenuo-phthalate, or AP; a chemical that will shrink the vehicle. A hose is attached to our air conditioning system, and AP will infiltrate each room. Our bus, along with all of us, will shrink to the size of an acorn. Everything, from size to density, gets smaller. Our bus would be small enough to hold in the palm of your hand if you wanted. But I don't want you to worry; it doesn't hurt."

Amelia shrugs her shoulders. "I wasn't worried."

I laugh and admit, somewhat embarrassed, "Well, *I* was on my first ride. Anyway, as the bus rides along the conveyor belt, it will get placed into a Pila—a sphere ten centimeters in diameter, made of plastic and HugMe. The system then moves the Pila into a tunnel based on the desired coordinates.

"Speed-infused air pushes the Pilas through the tunnels. Each tunnel is only fifteen centimeters wide—just large enough for the Pila to speed through without friction. Underearth tunnels run throughout each territory to every city and all the world's seas. Well, every territory except Captus. There's no need to have tunnels into that barbaric territory."

"Captus is one of the six territories and is shunned because it wouldn't cooperate with the other territories at the end of the Between Age," Amelia recites.

I smile, impressed. "You were listening."

She nods. "I memorized every word you said."

"All right, I'll quiz you. What hair shade do those from Captus have?"

"Blonde. Those from Pexus have grey hair like yourself. Ornus…?"

"Ortus," I correct.

"Okay, people from Ortus have dark brown hair like our Protector and his friend. Firminsions—"

"Formosians. Those from Formosus."

"Formosians have red hair, people from Sanus have light brown hair, and…" she eyes me asking for help.

"Silenda," I fill in.

She snaps her fingers. "Yes, Silenda. They have black hair."

"Correct. Can you name some significant differences in the cultures of each territory?" I ask, curious to see just how much she remembers.

She bites the inside of her cheek as she thinks. "The world capital—which I'm not even going to try to pronounce—is in Silenda," she starts.

"Jukantytär," I insert, but Amelia ignores me and continues.

"It is where the Aevii and the Chancellors live," she remembers. "Silentars are generally pessimistic, suppressed in emotional outbursts, and instead of using direct speech, they value metaphorical interactions… or something like that."

"Not necessarily metaphorical, but yes," I say. "Silentars value circumspect communication, and they speak in the third person."

"Third person, yeah, yeah. Okay, Ortus is the technology hub, and because of that, they are the wealthiest territory. Their speech is formal, yet they're touchy-feely, loud, and all up in each other's business."

Too true, I think, as I remember Scout's familiar touchiness from the night before.

"Pexuns, like you, my dear Freckles, are the educated peoples. Pexus is where all the best schools and the highest and proudest scholarly scholars are."

I nod appreciatively.

"Downsides to Pexuns are: they're too aware of their personal spaces, they can be closed off emotionally, and they are prone to kidnapping."

I laugh. "Yes, it's a weakness we all have."

"Okay, next is… don't tell me… Oh, yeah, Formosus." At this, she dramatically throws her red braid behind her back. "Formosian people, like myself, are inhabitants of the entertainment capital. All fantasy pictures are filmed at the many studios in Formosus. Music and art also thrive there. Because of this, Formosians are proud and self-absorbed. However, they're also incredibly hospitable and love having a good time. As you say, 'Everyone likes to have a Formosian around.'"

"Impeccable," I praise. It is unbelievable how much she has remembered!

"People from Sanus like to work. All the best craftsmen, artisans, mechanics, technicians, and such live there. They are physically affectionate like the Ortusans and hospitable like Formosians, but only to each other. They protect their territory's secrets more than the other ones. Their accent is folksy, and they don't like to use technology. Instead, they value doing as much as they can without tech or even their Gifts.

"Lastly, there's Captus. The Hexum does not visit Captus because it's filled with rabid barbarians who will eat you if given a chance."

"I don't think those were my exact words," I reply dryly, "but yes, they are uncivilized."

"Cool, cool, cool. I got all the territories, right?"

"Amelia, I am stunned," I state honestly. "I had no idea you were listening that closely."

"Well, I have been." Looking out the window, she asks, "So, is this how everyone travels?"

"The transponder stations are how we travel from territory to territory. However, within territories, we still use vehicles like you did in your world. In major cities, the road system has been built by the Data Processing and Programming Department, or the DPPD. The cars drive themselves and follow traffic patterns that are woven throughout the cities. In smaller towns and cities, cars are driven by simulans. There are practically no car accidents anywhere in the world."

"Impressive," Amelia comments, clearly unimpressed.

"It is, actually," I say. "You may not want to admit it, but Novus is a paradise."

Ignoring me, she asks, "And that's it? Just the transponder station and cars?"

"Some people have Gifts that enable them to travel, but those are monitored. We would have covered this next week, but I'll explain it quickly now. When a Gift is harnessed and placed into an object so another can wield it, that object is called a eutsi. If it's harnessed to a place, that place is called an arnessa. Travel Gifts have been made into eutsees, and the most common one is a kokatu. A kokatu makes travel faster, but they cost *a lot* of energy. They're large, so they're awkward to travel with, and usually, people feel nauseous for hours after using them. And, lastly, there are illegal ways to travel—"

"Illegal?" Amelia asks with mock surprise. "But I thought Novus was *perfect*? Would anyone even dare do something illegal here?"

I smirk at her sarcasm. This young woman stands facing a world she doesn't understand and holds her head high. Now *that* is impressive.

"But do go on," Amelia says theatrically. "What illegal crimes could people possibly commit in Novus?"

"There are many illegal eutsees that have been made so because they are hazardous to the user or to people around them. One of the most dangerous eutsees employs monsters called tolláns, who live underground. If someone pays—"

"I'm sorry," Amelia says with true shock on her face this time. "Did you… did you just say monsters that live underground?" She adds shrilly, "Last time I checked, paradise doesn't have *monsters*!"

I smile at her horror. "The monsters of our world are genetic experiments gone wrong. Most of them are a product of human beings and the animal kingdom being grafted or genetically engineered together in illegal ways. Although Novus is a utopia, mistakes of the past do haunt us."

"So what do the monsters do?"

"Tolláns demand an incredibly high payment, and with it, they can transport a person anywhere in the world in fifteen minutes."

"What do the tolláns look like?"

"No one knows. No one has ever seen them."

"Are there other monsters?"

"Yes."

"What kind of—" Amelia suddenly stops mid-sentence as a cold mist sweeps into our compartment.

"That's the AP," I tell her.

"So we're going to shrink?" she asks excitedly.

"Yep."

"Okay, I want to enjoy this. But we're getting back to monsters later."

I chuckle to myself as the AP's chill air fills my nostrils. I look down at Aker's supposedly sleeping form and wonder if I should warn him. Not knowing if he would want me to, I do nothing.

Shrinking is an interesting sensation because you know something is happening, but you don't feel it. It's almost like touching a part of your body that is numb. You're watching yourself touch your skin but you can't feel it.

As we shrink, tiredness floods my veins, making me light-headed. Exhaustion forces my eyes closed; my body is as worn out as if I hadn't slept in a week. An invisible weight rests upon my shoulders.

The slight bounce of the room and a loud clicking sound verify the transponder system has put us inside the high-pressure tunnel which will send us across the world.

Unexpectedly, Aker shouts in panic, "What's going on?"

I guess he *was* asleep.

I pry my eyes open to see him groping around the floor with his eyes closed.

"We're in a Pila," I call out. "The AP just shrunk us, and we're about to travel."

"Where are we going?" he asks, trying to force his eyes open. Without giving me even a moment to answer, he shouts angrily, "Kansis, where are we going?"

"I-I-I don't know," I stammer. "Somewhere safe to talk things over, I'm sure," I lie, feeling guilty that I should know where we're going, but I don't.

"When we get out of this Pila, we're going home," he says definitively and turns away from Amelia and me.

Go home?

"But last night you said you'd come—"

"I was exhausted, and this is ridiculous," Aker snaps. "We're going home."

Amelia gives me a quizzical look. Having no desire to translate Aker's sharply spoken words, I simply instruct, "Try to rest during this time."

She nods and closes her eyes again.

Despite my body's utter exhaustion, my brain won't permit sleep, so I let my hazy eyes wander to Aker's back as I contemplate his demand. I can't go back home—I can't leave Amelia. She needs my help, and I gave her the word of my blood. But Aker wants me to go home… *with* him.

Last night he said he wanted to try a life with me… what does that even mean? Is he planning on marrying me? We could get married before Winter Worship Day if he wanted. I still have my wedding dress from the first time and—

Ontzi, what am I doing? I close my eyes as tight as I can. *Can you chill out, stupid girl?* Just because this is happening doesn't mean he will marry you.

Not wanting to think about it anymore, I open my eyes. Looking around the small room, I stop when a mirror catches my attention. The AP makes focusing my vision a real challenge; even so, I can see how wiry my hair is. Trying to tame it with my hands, I take the rubber band off my wrist and pull the strands back into a ponytail. I touch the scars on my cheek.

I was seventeen when a Pod attacked me and scratched my face. I was horrified, thinking that Aker would think me hideous. I didn't have enough aons to pay to have my face fixed—it subtracted a year from my veins I was so sad. It wasn't until later that I realized nothing on my face could make Aker like me less or more. His apathy was tangible.

I sigh softly. No more thinking about Aker. Here I am, sitting next to Arkarian Story's daughter, and I'm obsessing about Aker.

Typical me.

I study Amelia's resting face. I have so many questions. Although I don't want to overload her, I don't know how long I can go without getting some answers.

Suddenly her eyes pop open, and when she sees I'm staring at her, she smiles. "What's up?"

"Why do you want to kill your dad?" I ask her.

"He's evil, right?" she asks, but it sounds more like a statement.

"Is he? Sometimes I wonder if the tales about Arkarian Story were nothing but legend."

"No, he was evil, all right. Wanted to rule the old world—"

"Senex," I correct. She must learn to use the proper names for people, places, and things. To be a successful Elusian, she needs to think and speak as one.

"Yes, Senex. And I'm sure if he had it his way, he would want to rule your world—"

"Novus."

"He would want to rule *Novus*. It's better if he's dead, don't you think?"

Nodding, I say, "I do. I agree. So why find the other person first? Charles..."

"Charles Wrightly?" she asks.

I nod.

Her smile is coy. "I can't tell you all my secrets, Freckles. Where would the fun be in that?"

"You don't trust me?" I ask, hoping the sting of hurt won't come out through my tone of voice.

"I trust you a little more. But no, not enough to tell you why I need him."

I look down at my nail beds so that my expression doesn't betray anything. The truth is, unfortunately, that our Protector cannot find Charles Wrightly. As a Pod, his identity and location are hidden. The government has intentionally made finding out who Pods are and where they were embedded into society impossible.

Not only are the records kept in one of the highest security buildings in Silenda, but every person is also vacuoused—a liquid treatment that temporarily hinders the use of your Gift cells—at the borderline of every government building. Every person inside is as powerless as a Pod. If my Protector is planning on breaking into the PTS, it will be impossible. I open my mouth to tell Amelia this but quickly shut it. I don't want to be the bearer of bad news.

I'll let Scout do that.

"What will you miss the most about Senex?" I ask instead, leaning back in my chair. I enjoy asking my Pods this question. Some have mentioned people in their lives, entertainment, favorite places—even the food.

Amelia smirks like she's going to say something sarcastic, but a sad smile slowly replaces the expression. Finally, she sighs, "I miss everything."

I look down at my hands, for the first time truly feeling sorry for a Pod. "You can't understand this now, and that's perfectly all right," I begin kindly. "But you will come to know that Elusis is a paradise. It's where human beings can thrive. There's no political unrest, there's healing available for anyone in need, and there's true justice and worldwide peace. Elusis is war-free, safe, beautiful, inspiring—a true utopia."

Amelia smiles at me patronizingly. "People are people. History shows that."

"Subhumans were subhumans, I agree. But Novies—Novians—are metahumans. We have evolved. Humans are now capable of more than your generation ever believed. Look at what we've done: we've created supernatural abilities to enhance our world. We are superior."

Snorting, Amelia shakes her head. "And you're humble too, right? The humblest humans that ever existed?"

"With great power comes great humility," I answer honestly.

She laughs out loud as we come to a sudden stop. We've arrived. The system takes our bus out of the Pila; we experience the same stomach-dropping sensation. The air abruptly changes, and the tingling returns. Soon we are back to normal size.

Aker grunts and turns onto his stomach. After slowly standing, he takes a deep breath and then looks at me. "Let's go. You can leave her here with the Ortusans. But you and me? We're going home. Now."

He reaches for the doorknob, but it turns before he has the chance to grasp it, and the most attractive woman I have ever seen walks into the room. Even though a veil covers her nose and mouth, her features behind it are so striking it is as if they would not be hidden by something as common as sheer fabric. "Scout requests Kansis and Amelia to meet him in his room for a meeting, he does," she says.

I have met very few Formosians, but they have all been beautiful. This woman's beauty overshadows them all. Her voice is mesmerizing. Behind the veil are eyes that sparkle with secrets. I glance at Amelia, who seems equally entranced by this woman. I won't let myself look at Aker and see if he's gazing at the woman the same way he does Mirindiss.

As we both stand, Aker takes a step toward her. "I'm coming too," he states.

The Formosian woman smiles amusedly—although not in a condescending way. Instead, it's in the way you would smile at the joke of a very close friend. "You were not invited, were you?" Although her words are clearly a rejection, she says it in such a way that I wish *I* hadn't been invited.

"Yeah, okay," Aker responds, seeming convinced and confused at the same time. "Well, come back as soon as you're done," he adds—I hope—to me.

As Amelia and I follow the flawless Formosian to one of the last rooms down the hallway, I am filled with envy that she left Aker speechless, yet pleased that she has humbled him. She knocks, and Scout opens the door with a flustered look, urging us inside.

"Come in, come in," he whispers to us. "Thank you, Fabella," he nods to the woman, gesturing towards the door. She nods and leaves quickly. Scout turns back to the table in his room while Amelia and I stand awkwardly beside the bed.

"And you propose we take the plot twenty kilometers outside of town?" he is saying. "To what purpose would this serve? How would this benefit your town, making your residents travel so far to visit us?" He pauses, and then, "I disagree strongly." After a quick laugh, he says, "Yes, that is the point, Kel. We *are* trying to be the center of attention."

"Is he talking on a phone of some kind?" Amelia whispers to me.

Our means of communication are not introduced to the Pods until Lesson Seventeen, so she hasn't formally learned about them yet. "Remember when I told you yesterday about a Suus? Well, that is our phone as well. In each Suus, millions of microscopic nanobots stream from the bio-computing processor to the brain causing a direct neural interface. The tiny bio-computer projects holographic displays that the user can interact with using both their minds and their bodies. Communication and connectivity are made possible through encrypted quantum signals, making inventions like phones, computers, books, pen, paper—all ancient and Senexian technology—obsolete."

Amelia blinks. "Well, that was a mouthful."

Not missing a beat, I reply, "Teaching is best digested through bite-sized pieces."

This causes her to smile toothily. "Well said, Freckles. Well said." As I enjoy the warmth of her praise, she looks at my wrist and asks, "So everyone has one of these Suuses?"

"Almost everyone. In most cities, the Suus is injected into Novian's wrists when we reach thirteen years old. A worldwide company called Abaed-Don Interterritorial sells them."

"I haven't seen you use yours," she comments.

Rubbing my wrist, I reply, "I had mine turned off a couple of years ago because I couldn't keep up with the bill." Suuses are one of the costliest living expenses, and when my family cut me off, a Suus was one luxury I didn't need.

"So there are no smartphones?" Amelia asks.

I've been asked this by every Pod I've trained. "Those from Senex used smartphones for communication, entertainment, and information. A Suus does all that and more. It's like a brain of its own."

Suddenly, the blood drains from Amelia's face. Uncharacteristic dread—although entirely normal for her kind—fills her features as she asks, "Like an AI?"

Due to the Yo Gano Artificial Intelligence Takeover in 2055MS, many Sennies are incredibly fearful and wary of artificial intelligence. In a controlled environment at the Ward, it is easier to explain where we have and haven't implemented aspects of AI and how ours cannot harm and overtake humanity. The simulans are a perfect example of this.

But now is not the time for this conversation. So, I answer part of it.

"Our Suuses are not artificial intelligence. Instead, it's like an extension of your mind. The Suus cannot and does not control you—it opens up pathways for knowledge that no brain could possess on its own."

"How is that different than AI?" she asks, still unconvinced.

"What was introduced to the public in 2022MS was an obvious failure due to the lack of advanced discernment, insight, and, honestly, common sense." She rolls her eyes, but I continue. "It led to Yo Gano, an AI communications company, creating a super intelligence and naively believing that it would not generate its own consciousness—and therefore agenda—and this was the biggest mistake of human history. They programmed their AI to understand human behavior but failed to safeguard their own autonomy. The AI eventually manipulated humans to do their will using the very thing it believed to be humanity's weakness—something which it did not possess itself—emotion. Not only did it cause a worldwide economic crash and depression such as history had never known, it completely changed the way people and businesses worked and the way people interact with one another—"

"Kansis, I know all this," Amelia breaks in, clearly agitated by my monologue. "My grandparents lived it. I learned this in school; I don't need another lesson."

As if I cannot turn off my teaching mode, I continue. "Be that as it may, we—metahumans—still thank the universe for Yo Gano's destruction in 2068MS. It had hurt the world in a way that was only mended in this current age."

Obviously wanting to change the subject, Amelia asks, "So, how do you personally get information and pathways of knowledge if you don't have your Suus turned on?"

Unexpected regret pools in my veins. I wish I hadn't pushed her world's mistakes in her face. Normally, it's a personal goal of mine to help Sennies see why the destruction of their world happened, but with Amelia I just feel like a jerk. Not knowing whether or not I should apologize, I answer her question. "Every home has a mainframe that functions in the same way. It's archaic, but I use the mainframes at my house and the Ward when needed—" I realize that Scout is off his Suus and I am the only one talking. Scout is looking at me with an expression I don't understand. It's like he's caught somewhere between frustration and fascination.

"English, yes?" he asks.

"Yes," I answer.

"It is a beautiful language."

His eyes are so piercing, and I immediately feel exposed and vulnerable. Why do Ortusans have to be so intimate with their eye contact? Uncomfortable, I respond conversationally, "French sounds even more beautiful." The way Formosians speak reminds me of French.

"I would love to hear it," he responds.

The capillaries in my cheek dilate, and my body breaks out with sweat along my spine and stomach. "Yeah, for sure. Sometime that would be… fun." Or completely embarrassing.

"You could insult me, and I would never know it."

"Oh no, I wouldn't want to do that—" Suddenly, my hands feel so big and out of place. What should I do with them? Why am I so awkward?

Pressing, he adds, "We could set you up with your own booth at the circus, and you could just shout at people in any language you want. This can be your audition. Let us have an example…" he opens his hands as if giving me the space to talk.

"That's—no, I'm fine…" I shove my hands into my pants pockets. "Some other time."

Scout smirks playfully at me and asks, "This day not being that time?"

"No, no," I answer quickly.

"What's happening? Did he propose?" Amelia asks suddenly. "Why are you blushing so badly?"

"Shut up!" I hiss.

Thankfully, Scout drops the subject and looks out his little window. "I am sorry everything transpired so abruptly last night. I would have preferred to speak with you one-on-one and explain everything occurring."

"We always have the now," I respond conversationally. "Where are we going?"

"Initium."

"Why?" I ask.

"We are a traveling circus group; therefore, we must put on shows throughout our travels to keep our cover going. We set up our circus in towns on the way to wherever our next destination is."

The door opens, and Pypen saunters in. "Greet the sun," he says to me and nods to Amelia, giving us a warm smile before he lounges in one of the oversized armchairs.

"Ask him what he wants from Arkarian Story," Amelia commands me, attention still on Scout.

I translate for her.

"A share in the reward, of course. And the fame," Scout says. There's laughter in his voice but not in his eyes.

After I translate his answer, Amelia says, "Ask him how he knew who I was and where we were. Is he the one who talks to the voice in your head?"

My pulse quickens as adrenaline pumps into my veins. Although I want to know the answers, I'm also strangely worried about what they will be. "How did you know about Amelia?" I ask Scout. "How did you know to come to the Palace? How did I..." How do I even ask this? "How did I know you were coming?" I glance at Pypen and then back to Scout.

"Somehow, you were able to communicate with our leader," Scout answers unblinkingly. "You told him where you would be, and then he bade us come get you. We are his group of Arkahunters."

"Who is your leader?"

Maybe it's someone from the Ward? But how could that be? No one was talking to me there either, except when necessary.

"The Sixth Aevum."

I laugh at his joke. It feels nice to have some of the tension released from my veins. When I look back at him and see his expression hasn't changed, I clarify, "Wait, are you serious?"

"Indeed," Pypen answers, winking at me.

All humor leaves my veins. "But how— I don't—How could I communicate with him when I didn't know I was doing it?" How long have I been communicating with an Aevum without knowing it? Does my subconscious realize she's speaking to an actual Aevum?!

"What is your Progift?" Scout asks.

I'm a little taken aback by the question. I don't know how it is in Ortus, but in Pexus, sharing your Gift with someone is a rite of friendship, not information freely given. "Nothing that relates to telepathy," I answer quickly.

"What are they saying?" Amelia asks impatiently.

"I'm just trying to figure out how they found out about us," I drop into English. "Give me a minute."

Scout raises his hands, knits them behind his neck, and does a quick stretch. With his arms in this position, I can see a sizable prancing lion tattoo on his left forearm. It is not one solid color but fluctuates between yellow, green, and blue. As he rakes his hands through his dark brown, Ortusan hair, his frame hides the tattoo once more. "We are only in Initium for this day and next," Scout starts, "and our following destination is up to her," he says, angling his head in Amelia's direction. "Wherever she says to go, we will go."

"Well, like she said last night, she needs to find a Pod named Charles Wrightly." Quietly, I confess, "I haven't told her yet that we can't find him." I'm not sure why I lowered my voice; it's not like Amelia can understand me.

"We cannot find who?" Scout asks.

"The Pod, Charles Wrightly."

Scout's brows furrow. "Why can we not find him?"

"He's a Pod…" When it seems that didn't help him understand, I explain, "You can't find them. When we release a Pod into society, we give them a new name and identity as a community member, so no one will know they were from Senex."

He nods. "Yes."

"That information is not available to citizens," I explain as if he needs reminding. Everyone knows that the Pod Tracking System, the PTS, hides Pods' identities.

Scout looks over to Pypen. "We will need to go to the PTS."

"The one in Silenda," Pypen adds, nodding. "It is the only one that has all those records."

My mind freezes for a moment. Why are these Ortusans speaking so casually about going to Silenda—and the Pod Tracking System, for that matter? They're talking like it's as easy as going to a Healing Clinic to repair a broken femur!

"Well, yes, but… But that is impossible!" I proclaim.

"Nothing is impossible."

A simulan walks in with a tray holding four plates of food and sets one in each of our laps. It has a cast on its arm part. Briefly, I wonder if its owner had broken it or if it had done the damage itself. Back at home, my simulan had once chopped off its finger part, and I had been surprised that the mechanic oil that spurted out was bright red. Its engineering was unnecessarily accurate to the human form. After cleaning up its own mess, it had to go to the simulan repair shop to replace it. Thas, Aker's dad, owns the repair place in Depalo, so he had given me the "family" discount.

Joke's on him.

"Eat, eat," Scout says as he shovels eggs into his mouth. "We will explore our options."

Trying once more to get him to see the problem, I explain, "Incredibly Gifted people secure the PTS building in Silenda. They aren't going to just let… we won't be able to… it's not possible," I finish, flustered.

Pypen laughs. Scout smiles, too, and looks up at me, his mouth full. "The Sixth Aevum will help us find a way. Of this, I am certain."

"Everything okay?" Amelia asks me, eyeing her plate of food suspiciously. I quietly relay the conversation to her. "Well, that's good, right?" she asks. "They can get the information we need."

I steal a glance at Scout and see that he's still looking at me. "I don't understand who they are… I mean, they work directly for the Sixth Aevum," I say to Amelia in English. "They are more than circus performers. They are covert Arkahunters and who knows what else!"

"Well, as long as they're on our side, we're one step closer to my dad, right?"

"I guess."

She nods and starts on the food as though everything is settled. I merely pick at mine.

"Do you think Aneece could make us a eutsi from the material she used in the Transparency Room?" Scout asks Pypen conversationally as they eat.

"For what?" Pypen asks.

"For the Pod."

Pypen scratches his beard. "Perhaps. We could try, at least."

To me, Scout states, "I will attempt to get your Pod a eutsi so she can understand the Elusian around her. And, with hope, speak it as well."

"How would you do that?" I ask incredulously.

"We know people," he states with a smile.

Over the sound system, a voice states, "Scout and Pypen, me ol' sams. Oi need ye at ta front if ye please."

Scout stands, and so do I. Amelia jumps up as well. "We must be close," Scout says.

"Close to what?"

Eyeing Amelia, Scout smiles mischievously. "To confirm if your black eye was the work of an imposter or the real daughter of Arkarian Story."

Pexus

Pypen

SCOUT HOLDS THE BRIEFCASE containing the circus so tightly his knuckles turn white. I have only ever had to bear the responsibility he now carries once, and I almost had a panic attack. When we first conceived of this mode of transportation, we never imagined that its ease of convenience would be paired with the significant risk of possible misplacement. Only once have we lost the circus, but once was enough to set us on edge every subsequent time we move it.

In Scout's cold, slightly-trembling hand is our livelihood, our dreams, our passion, and eight years' worth of exhausting work—he holds our everything.

Scout and I are in the front of the bus sitting next to our driver, Thykas.

Thykas is one of the most naturally attractive men I have ever known, including Formosians. In the words of one of our past performers, Stefonavich, "He is a perfect specimen, he is." Most people alter their features one way or another to look more beautiful, but Thykas is the opposite. He constantly hides his handsome features with bizarre hair and beard designs. This day, the Sanusian man wears his light brown hair in a waterfall ponytail on top of his head. He has shaved his chiseled beard in an amusing design, so it looks like several ants are walking across his chin in a straight line.

Where Scout leans heavily on Emerly for assistance, I do the same with Thykas. I quickly fill him in concerning the Senexian and the Sixth Aevum's test, then turn to Scout.

"Will we go to the PTS this afternoon or this night?" I ask.

Scout does not answer right away but continues staring out the window. Finally, he replies, "I think we should wait a bit. There is no need to rush this."

Thykas and I steal a glance at each other. To what is he referring? The entirety of our mission as the Unopened Gifts is to find Arkarian Story. We have our first real lead to discovering his whereabouts, and Scout wants to step back. Why?

"We have had less time to prepare for missions, and they always go well," I comment, faking a casual air. "Why is this different?"

"This is our most critical mission yet," Scout answers. "Taking our time is wise, I believe."

"So how long does Scout the Wise consider we should wait?" I ask, not trying to hide the doubt in my voice.

He shakes his head and glares at me. "It is not a time-frame issue. We need to take our next steps with acute calculation. Stop pushing this, Pypen."

Thykas laughs. "Indeed, Pip me ol' sam," he says. "It's not as if t'is is an important affair. Relax, sit back. Oi imagine Arkarian Story will find us if we're patient enough."

Scout fake laughs at Thykas but does not defend himself.

What is causing his hesitation?

The bus pulls up to our hotel, and a lone Silentar woman stands near the parking deck. She has slicked her black hair close to her head, and she's wearing a bright pink suit that shimmers in the uncertain light. As we park, she closes her eyes.

"That must be the Sixth Aevum's mind reader," I observe.

"Agreed," Scout says.

The woman only stands there for half a minute. Then she opens her eyes and walks away. She is quickly swallowed up by the commuting crowd of pedestrians.

Before anyone can get out of their rooms, Scout and I quickly disembark the bus.

"Where is Winzer?" Scout asks. "I told her to be the first one off—and... and there she is," he says with a smile.

"You didn't doubt me, did you, Scouty?" a cute Formosian replies as she jumps off the steps. Her tight, red curls cup her face like a hug. Winzer is Emerly's mate and has worked for us since Emerly started. Her Gifts have been quite valuable, especially when she works as our Cloak.

"Could not have asked for a more necessary Gift in our line of work," I say to myself.

"Stop mumbling," Scout snaps at me, and then replies to Winzer, "I would never doubt you, Winzer. Today's subjects for cloaking are the young Formosian woman and the Pexun man and woman we picked up in Depalo."

"You got it, you do," she responds with a smile. "Who are these people? Who's looking for them?"

"In time, in time," Scout replies. "For now, we must keep them safe from the local authorities."

Over half of the performers walk off the bus before Amelia, Kansis, and Aker come out.

Aker whispers something to Kansis, and she shakes her head in disagreement.

"Yes, now," Aker pushes.

"Is something wrong?" Scout asks.

The Pexun man scowls at Scout. "It's not your concern."

Scout smiles patiently. "Be that as it may, I insist your marital bliss must pause so we can go inside."

"We're leaving," Aker states.

Without hesitation, Scout counters, "I do not believe so. Kansis, let us get you and the girl inside. I want to make certain that you are safely taken to your room."

I am surprised at Scout's brashness towards the couple. Who is he to tell this man that he has to stay? The Pexun mate is not as amicable as the Sixth Aevum had made Scout think.

Turning to me, Scout asks, "Will you pay for the rooms while I escort them?"

"You booked them," I answer. "Last time I tried to pay when it was under your name, they would not permit it."

Clicking his tongue, he turns to Kansis. "I must pay for the rooms first."

Kansis seems torn between Scout and her mate, but when the daughter of Arkarian Story pulls her along, Kansis walks inside. Aker utters a couple of Pexun curses I have never heard before and then follows.

As we enter the hotel, the trio looks around in awe, although Aker tries to hide it. From the foyer, one can see the ceiling forty stories above. The architects built all the rooms circularly within the building's atrium, and the walls have been animated to show each patron a scene from somewhere they would like to visit. However, I have paid to have these sensory advertisements blocked from my mind, so I merely see the ocean. It looks as if all I need to do is reach out to each wall, and I would fall into its depths. I wonder what the Pexuns and Arkarian Story's daughter see.

Every corner of this hotel hums with energy. The furniture, paintings, statues, couches, bars—all of it radiates power. For many years we could not afford accommodation such as this, but now such luxury has become commonplace.

We have stayed in hotels where one only needs to touch the side table, and the very thing they desire appears. We have stayed in lodgings where one sits on the couch, and a drink of their choice immediately appears in their hand. The paintings give relationship advice, and the carpet massages one's feet. A window takes one across the world, while the bathroom provides mini versions of a person's most-used toiletries in their favorite brands.

I have become accustomed to these elite accommodations, but this is probably the most lavish hotel the Pexuns—and certainly, Arkarian Story's daughter—have ever been in. I doubt Senex had anything like this.

Scout pays no notice to the décor and makes his way to the check-in desk. We wait in a short queue, and when Scout walks up to one of the simulan hotel clerks, he beckons us to follow. Winzer and I keep up from behind, Winzer keeping the three others hidden from sight and detection from those who would wish to do them harm.

"Reservation?" the simulan asks.

"Reservation for Hotel Destination," Scout commands his Suus. The simulan's mainframe makes a slight dinging noise to signal it has received the information.

We used to have the performers stay in the circus overnight in their rooms, but many of them complained about having no change of scenery while we traveled. As compensation became less of an issue, we started renting hotel rooms for the group.

"Scout Eekan. Twenty-one rooms at one and a half aons each. Your total today is thirty-one and a half aons," the simulan says.

Taking out his disc-shaped Vorbi, Scout hands it to the simulan. Kansis eyes it and then quickly looks down at her hands, her cheeks flushing. The dark blue color probably surprises her—most people have never seen a Vorbi so full in their whole lives. The simulan takes Scout's Vorbi and places it on the register. Within seconds, the simulan hands it back; the color has not even changed.

"Why twenty-one rooms? We only need twenty," I comment.

"Merayal wanted her own room," Scout replies.

That is no surprise. We can only hope her cold shoulder melts quickly so she can make friends with the other performers.

Scout leads Amelia, Kansis, and Aker up to their allotted room. With my PasswordShare, I add their fingerprints to the door's mainframe so they can all open it at will during their stay.

When I am done, Scout tells them, "You must not depart from the hotel room until I come back."

"We are not prisoners," Aker growls. "We will come and go as we please.

We don't have to listen to anyone."

"You need not see it that way," Scout responds tightly. "See it as a means of protection. I will return in a couple of hours, and we shall discuss our plans."

Tone derisive, Aker asks, "*Our* plans? Whose plans are those?"

Scout eyes Kansis for a moment and then answers, "Hers. She is the leader here."

Kansis pales at these words. "I-I'm… what?" she stutters.

I clear my throat. "Kansis, have you seen this day's paper?"

"No," she answers, alarmed.

"Show this day's news," Scout commands his Suus.

A transparent document appears in front of Scout, and he turns it so the paper faces Amelia and Kansis. Amelia laughs, and Kansis gasps at their pictures plastered on the front page.

Kansis closes her eyes tightly and rubs her temples. "I can't read it; just tell me what it says."

"Overall, it communicates that you are both missing, and the Guardians are doing their best to find you," Scout answers. "We must be careful with you two. You cannot just go out in public."

"And one more thing," I add. "I need you to have the daughter put on this sciath." I extend my hand to her. Dangling from my finger is a thin gold chain with a black pendant. This one, in particular, is in the shape of a wreath—the Abaed-Don Interterritorial symbol—with each leaf a different shade of bronze.

Kansis seems hesitant to take it. "This is… incredibly expensive. Why give it to her?"

Amelia asks something in English, and Kansis replies hurriedly.

"We wish not for anyone else to find out she is the daughter and steal her from underneath our grasp," I say when she has finished talking.

"We do have a caveat," Scout says as Kansis takes the sciath from me. "If the Sixth Aevum needs her memories sifted, we would need her Blood Assurance she would be willing to remove it for him." He takes a small black rhodium-plated fold-away knife out of his pocket and flicks it open. It has a small inscription on the side that reads, *One drop is needed, one promise given. To break the one is to dry up the other.*

"Blood Assurance?" Kansis asks, staring at the knife, alarmed. She hands the sciath back to me. "No, we won't do that. I can buy a different sciath… a more… generic one."

"One that any talented mind manipulator can bypass," Scout counters softly.

"She needs this one. It has government-level protection on it. Even Guardians would not be able to get past it."

"I am not going to make Amelia assure anything with her blood. I am responsible for her and would never bind her to something like that. So if that's the cost, we don't want it."

"What if you made the Blood Assurance?" I ask her.

"What?" Scout and Kansis ask at the same time.

"If you wish not for her blood to be on her own hands," I explain, "*you* could put the sciath on her, and then it would be on *your* hands. If you put it on her, you would be the only one who could take it off."

"But what if she needed to take it off?" Kansis asks, worried.

"You just said she is your responsibility," I explain and shrug my shoulders noncommittally. "You possess three options: expose her for all the world to take advantage, allow her to protect herself, or protect her yourself."

"I do not think it wise for Kansis to do the Blood Assurance," Scout says.

"She's not doing any bonds with you," Aker snarls.

Kansis looks at her mate for a moment. She takes in his expression and then something seems to settle in her. With confidence she did not have before, she turns back to me and declares, "I'll do it. You're right. I need to protect her."

"Absolutely not!" Aker shouts. "Are you an idiot? You can't do a Blood Assurance with these strangers—these *Ortusans*."

For a moment, Kansis hesitates, but then her jaw clenches, her resolution made. She turns to Amelia and begins talking. She points to herself, to me, and to the sciath. Amelia seems uneasy but she slowly nods her agreement as she listens.

"Kansis, I said *no*," Aker seethes.

The Pexun woman tightens her jaw again. "Amelia needs protection, and I'm the only one who can provide that for her. I have to do this." Before Aker can say anything else, she grabs the knife from Scout, quickly cuts her thumb, and says, "On behalf of Amelia the Pod, I give my blood as assurance that if the Sixth Aevum asks me to take the sciath off of Amelia, I will do it."

Kansis takes the sciath from me and places it over Amelia's neck.

Aker whirls to press his finger on the door's mainframe, then angrily slams through as he barrels inside the room.

Scout smiles at Kansis for a moment, then offers his hand to her palm up. With an uneasy expression, she places the blade back in his hand. As Scout folds it away and returns it to his pocket, he shouts, "*Matza!*" and rips his

hand up as if something in his pants has burned him. "What in the universe..."
Tentatively, he reaches back into his pocket and takes out a round, golden object
from Senex. "It pinched me," he says and laughs.

"Perhaps it does not like you," I comment.

As Scout inspects the object, recognition dawns on Kansis' face. "Is that...
That is! That's a pocket watch! Where did you find that?"

Scout extends his hand to her, offering her a closer look at the watch. "I
found it at a Senex trinket shop."

Kansis says something in English, delicately picking up the watch and
showing it to Amelia, who appears comically unimpressed.

To my shock, after watching Kansis for a few moments, Scout suddenly
asks, "Would you like it?"

Kansis' gaze whips in his direction, her wide eyes meeting his. Scout's
eyelids stay somewhat squinted as he cocks his head slightly. He is trying to
anticipate how she will respond.

"I couldn't," she answers and extends it back towards him.

"I would like you to have it, Scoop," he responds, voice even.

"Scoop? That's not my—look, that's—that's not my name, and I could never
take your pocket watch."

Ignoring the comment, Scout bows to the girls and then, turning, walks
away, leaving the pocket watch cradled in the Pexun's hand. Just as confused as
Kansis, I hurriedly make my leave and follow him. As we step into the elevator,
I study Scout's expression.

He sighs. "Can I help you, Pip?"

"You are always one to give up anything for someone in need. Often I find
it my duty to keep you from over-giving. But this is beyond that... You spent
months searching through Senex antique stores in every territory to find that
pocket watch. I understand not... Why give it to the Pexun?"

Gingerly, he switches the briefcase from his right to his left hand. "Kansis
liked it." He clears his throat. "Let us get the circus set up now. Call Keleigh
and make sure she is at the site."

I know what he has told me is not the truth, yet I am amused by his answer.
I glance at him slyly. "I like your shirt. May I have it?" I know pushing him will
pickle his blood, but this is too good of an opportunity to let pass.

He rolls his eyes. "Call Keleigh."

"I am also fond of your trousers; may I have those as well?"

"I am not in the mood, Pypen."

"In fact, I have asked you several times for that Vorbi pouch you keep at the flat, and you have declined my request saying it was a family heirloom. I must not have communicated that I like it." I pause theatrically. "I *like* it, Scout. May I have it?"

"She has endured many hardships," Scout responds gruffly. "I am trying to show her that some people in her life can be kind."

I nod, not necessarily believing his excuse but sensing he is not ready to talk. Activating my Suus within my mind, I think of Keleigh's name.

"Are you ready, Pip?" her voice asks in my head as she answers her Suus. The Formosian way of bypassing pleasantries always catches me off guard.

"I am doing well, thank you. And yes, we are."

She chuckles. "We'll be seeing you in twenty minutes, we shall."

"We shall." I make one more call to Thykas, then tell Scout, "The Controls will meet us in a car downstairs."

"Brilliant," he responds.

Although the Controls are usually quite talkative, the presence of the briefcase always brings a revered quietness, as though talking too loudly could somehow harm the circus. Our subdued ride ends quickly enough, and the driver leaves us in an abandoned field. As Scout, the Controls, and I make our way to the meadow's center, another car arrives carrying Keleigh and her mate, Lachie.

Scout reverently lays the briefcase down. Weeds sway in the slight breeze. A crow beckons her prey. A field mouse scatters. Soft, natural sounds fill this grassland. As Scout takes a deep breath and opens the case, the ground trembles. It is as if, for centuries, the soil has longed for this unknown, unnatural moment.

With abundant caution, Scout places the briefcase on its side and opens the lid. He takes a deep breath and nods to Vielfrah, the leader of the Controls. Vielfrah ignites his Progift and keeps Scout's hand completely steady as he takes out the leather box that holds the circus and places it next to the briefcase. Then, he gently extracts the snow globe from the box. Suspended within the globe is a minuscule gold and black striped circus tent.

After placing the globe on the ground, Scout slowly unscrews the glass orb from its base. The liquid drips out. Ever so carefully, Scout allows the last of the fluid to trickle out and pulls the globe's sphere off.

Keleigh takes a few steps towards the tiny tent resting on the snow globe base and closes her eyes. Her long face looks entirely peaceful. As she ignites her Gift, the tent grows in size. We collectively back up, take our places, and wait. The tiny tent shudders as it stretches from one centimeter high to ten centimeters tall... one-quarter meter... one meter...

When the tent's front flap grows to two meters high, Vielfrah lifts Keleigh into his arms, and we all run inside the tent. I close my eyes and reach down to will my Gift awake. Although I know my Gift will immediately renew my energy, I still hate how exhausted this will make me. I begin searching through each room, making sure that each one is as it should be.

The move knocked over some of Muir's chairs.

Several of Lylee and Shylow's water jugs have shattered.

Avenir's curtain fell.

Matza, all of Thykas' ink spilled.

As my energy spends, Scout places a Vorbi in my hand. I rub it and feel its energy rejuvenate my Gift. I continue my searching.

Two of Zjon's trees fell over. Ah, of course, they are the big ones.

Several of Korinna's beds are unmade. She hates it when I forget to tuck in the corners.

Keleigh's giant clock is off by an hour.

I am going to kill Lachie. He left his candles burning again, and I have to renew his entire room.

Finally, all the rooms are as they should be. I rub the Vorbi until it has restored all my energy. Only then do I open my eyes. Even though I have seen it a thousand times, I still smile at what I see before me.

This is my home.

The circus tent is held up by fifteen ten-meter-high titanium poles. Ten of them line the outside of the tent, four stand symmetrically in each quadrant, while one stands right at its center. Perimeter poles run perpendicular to the legs and, at their three-story height, hold the tent's oval shape. From there, the canvas slants upwards, meeting at its center.

Everything within the circus follows a sunset color scheme, filling the space with deep marigolds, bright persimmons, dark plums, breezy taupes, baby blues, muted ivories, and blush pinks.

I take a deep, steadying breath in.

Keleigh lies on the ground next to me, slowly rolling a Vorbi in her hands, absorbing its energy so that she can finish extending the circus to its thirty-and-a-half-meter height. When she first started raising the tent, she would use half of a fully charged Vorbi. Although it cost us a small fortune, it was worth it. However, over the years, she has learned how to better disperse, save, and use her energy. She has learned to raise the circus more efficiently and quickly. She breaks her record every time she does it.

"Was it bad?" Scout asks next to me.

"Lachie left his candles smoldering again," I groan.

"Next time, leave it as it is, and he will have to repair the room without your help."

"A just punishment," I agree.

Scout takes a deep breath. "We need to rehearse with Merayal."

"Yes," I sigh. "I told her to follow the other performers when they came. What time did you tell them to arrive?"

"Now."

I rub my shoulders. "I will see if she is outside."

I follow the black trails to the front of the tent. Before I reach the entrance, I hear voices.

When we arrive at a new place, we ask that the performers come and make certain their rooms are in order. In the past, too often we would open the circus only to find chambers in a complete mess. Once the crew has checked their spaces, they can go and spend the rest of the day as they please.

As they filter in, I ask many of them if they need anything, as one of my duties is room maintenance. Many tell me they are fine, but Chestin stops and asks me if I can renew his chairs.

"Some vandals tore up the room real good," he says. "I was able to fix most of it myself, but the straw chairs they tore to bits, they did."

"Of course," I answer and follow him to his room.

Chestin was one of our first circus performers. He had come to us at the direct command of the Sixth Aevum. We were worried at first that he was placed among us to carry out some hidden agenda for the Aevum, but instead, we found Chestin to be humble, talented, and eager to help us get our small venture up and running.

Even though he keeps mostly to himself, he does so much for the circus. In fact, when he takes two three-week holidays every year, we always feel the lack of his presence during that time.

When I am finished renewing Chestin's chairs, I go back to the courtyard to offer my services anew.

"You left your candles on again," I shout to Lachie as he passes.

"I'm sorry, Pip! I keep forgetting, I do!"

"You will not forget if you do it again," I murmur to myself.

The Chameleons are quick with checking their room. As they saunter back towards the courtyard, I hear Krael say, "Let us ask Pypen, shall we?"

Sedwick barks a sarcastic laugh. "Yes, let us ask. Then you will see how preposterous the idea is."

"'Tis not!" Oshun shouts, and when he sees me, he runs over with the nature of a happy dog.

I make myself comfortable on the top of one of the bistro tables.

"Good idea or bad idea?" Oshun starts. "For our show next day: you walk in. On the stage, you see eight tigers. You have to guess which four are real tigers and which four are us. If you get it right, we hint at where one of the eight secret doors is located. If you pick wrong…"

He trails off and dramatically turns to Krael who finishes, "You get chased away by the tiger you selected."

I allow myself to look as if I am pondering the request, then ask, "Where will you acquire said tigers?"

"I already asked Lylee if we could borrow some from her and Shylow's room. She said she could spare four—hence the eight tigers."

"And how will you get the tigers to chase the patrons?"

"Lylee said she could give us a eutsi for the day to control them," Lukan answers.

"Does it not take time to learn how to do this?" I ask. "Even with the eutsi?"

"She said it was easy," Oshun answers excitedly. "So, what do you think?"

I pretend to muse. "One more question: what if one of the tigers catches the guests?"

The three Chameleons look at each other, and Krael offers, "You could stick around our tent for the morning?"

Nodding my head, I say, "So, to be clear, you suggest that giant felines hunt our visitors, and if they happen to catch the patron—which they will unless the guest is Gifted with speed—I am to be close at hand to renew any wounds incurred by the wild animals?"

Sedwick smirks. "I told you."

"It could be so much fun, though!" Oshun pushes. "This would be for the circus-goers looking for a thrill!"

"Find a way to create the thrill with no chance our guests will be mauled, and we can talk about it again," I answer firmly.

Suddenly, Krael turns himself into a tiger and pounces on Sedwick. Lukan and Oshun follow suit, and as all of the bistro tables and chairs fly around the courtyard, I shout at them to take it out of the tent.

Hoping she did not get lost, I decide to meet Merayal outside. I am surprised when I see her standing across the meadow staring at the tent—and now me—in disgust.

Aggravated that I have to do anything on her terms, but knowing I should, I cross the grass to where she stands glowering.

"Greet the shine," I make myself say.

"This is the *great* Unopened Gifts?"

I look back across the pasture at our circus. The black and gold tent stands at a measly three and a half meters. Its girth is about the same, making it a non-obtrusive, tall and thin shape. Some patches of the fabric are faded by the sun, making the black look more like grey. The top of the black and gold striped canopy is crooked, and some stray fabric strands sway in the wind.

It takes me a moment to understand why Merayal has not seen the circus before, and then I remember that she had used the QuickEntrance door in our office for her interview and our first practice. This will be her first time seeing the inside, as well as the outside, of the circus.

Not deigning her doubt a response—for I know the circus will speak for itself—I walk back towards it, and she follows. Once inside, Merayal's whole body jolts and freezes. Beholding all of our work, her face glows with awe. She is enraptured.

"'Tis nice to see a look besides contempt on your beautiful features."

At my words, she replaces her expression of wonder with disdain. As she throws her silver hair up in a bun, she bites, "Keep your filthy eyes to yourself, *gari.*"

I wonder if it is painful to be so unpleasant all the time. I contemplate asking her, but I best not provoke her derision any further.

But if *she* wishes to be so derisive, then I will not give her any time to soak in the circus and all its splendor. I will not tell her how the golden paths on which we walk were designed like tree root systems; with multiple paths shooting out of the main walkway, sprouting from one another in various directions towards all the ground-level doors. The stones on the pathways are various shades of gold as well, but the ground surrounding it is so black it almost looks as if one would fall into a bottomless abyss were they to stray from the path. At least, that is what we want the patrons to feel.

A number of golden paths traverse through the kiosks. But I will not tell Merayal that there are over sixty kiosks on the floor of the circus, all shaped like mini circus tents. Or that the ones with persimmon orange stripes are filled with an array of savory and sweet treats, while the blush-pink striped tents contain local vendors selling their merchandise. And the daffodil-yellow striped domes carry trinkets, oddities, and keepsakes. Some of the locations within the tent can only be accessed by circus-goers answering a question or giving up a memory. At the end of each visitor's time in the circus, they will seek out the moody, mauve-striped tents. Here, they will receive a playing-card-size duplicate of each of the doors they entered during that visit. Some circus enthusiasts have a goal to collect all two hundred and six doors in order to complete a deck—though none have accomplished this yet.

And I *definitely* will not tell her that there are seven hidden doors which, if found, give the patrons one year's free admission to the circus. If all were to be found in one visit—which hasn't happened yet—the attendee would receive a lifetime free admission card.

No, I will tell her none of this. Instead, I barrel ahead. Several times Merayal falls behind as she gawks at what we have created, but I do not wait for her, so she has to run to catch up. We walk down the center path—the widest one—which leads us straight to the largest door in the circus. At the center of the tent, the thickest titanium pole stands tall, splicing the wide path into two. Around the pole, the paths converge again on the other side.

After walking around the pole and to the other side of the tent, we approach our destination. This last door is enormous—as round and as tall as the perimeter poles. It is made from rich mahogany wood and painted red. Although it is cumbersome, we have made it easy to open for our own sake. Without any effort, I pull it open and beckon her inside. As Merayal slips past, she does not acknowledge me. Intent on ignoring her in return, I jog past her down the fifty-seven steps to the center stage. The panoramic seats lie eerily empty. This is just an open, echoic room during practice—but during performances, this room is alive with magic.

Allerish, our choreographer, hurries towards the stage with the grace and ease of a cat. Her toned, muscular body shimmers in the stage light, and her curly red hair flies behind her as she barks, "Dancers! You weren't hired to talk, were you? Not hired to socialize, you weren't! Get to the stage right now to practice Act One."

The dancers will use the stage for the first hour whilst Merayal and I practice on the side, but we will need to use it for the rest of the day. Merayal not only needs to memorize the entire show but she must also get used to performing in this mighty space. I still cannot believe she has agreed to this. Just then, Scout calls out to Merayal and me.

"Begin by practicing your two dances. Allerish will walk you through the flower sequence in an hour. After that, I will call Sedwick, and we will begin practicing Morbus' scene."

Merayal nods, trying to appear confident. Her body is taut like a predator about to pounce, but her eyes are wide like prey sensing a trap.

"You can do this," Scout affirms.

Placing a look of practiced disinterest on her features, she says, "Yep."

"I would not ask this of you if I did not think you and your fellow performers could pull it off," he assures her warmly.

Her smile is condescending. "Yep."

"That is my girl."

Her eyes flash ice. "I'm not your girl. I'm nobody's girl."

Scout's brows pull together as a frown creases his lips. Then, he grins suddenly. "That is my highly paid performer."

What seems a genuine smile replaces her contemptuous one. "Yep."

As she walks onto the stage, Scout turns to me. "I have an errand to run. Can you handle this?" he nods towards my new partner. "Can you handle *her*?" he asks meaningfully.

"Honestly?" I muse, "You had better keep your errand short. When you return, there is a significant chance I may have killed her."

Captus

Flister

83 years ago

THE FOURTH AEVUM HURRIES the Sixth Aevum along the transponder station subway. "Hurry now, Flisty, darling," she coos. "You do not want to fall behind."

Marvella Pinyin's cool sand-colored skin radiates in the sunlight. Her almond eyes are sharp either side of her long nose. Their dark depths burn as her gaze meets his. "You will love it," she adds.

The grand opening of Marvella's Quarantine was last month, but Flister could not attend. He had promised he would make it up to her, and he had set aside this time not only to fulfill that promise but also to complete a dare.

Flister had been eagerly awaiting this visit to Captus—the barbaric territory off-limits to the average Elusian—as this was to be his first time. Now, as they leave the station behind, the hot, Captusian air greets him, and he feels only ill will towards the city and its stench. The town—if that is what one could call it—consists of three buildings, one streetlamp, and a dirt road. Flister gawks at the crudeness of it.

"Is this it?" he asks incredulously. "Your Quarantine?"

"Do not be ridiculous, my sweet," Marvella titters as she gets into a waiting car.

Flister is shocked when he sees the driver's head is covered in blonde hair. Never has he seen a Captusian with his own eyes, and the prospect of being so close to such a barbaric man enlivens him.

Touching Marvella's hand, he asks, "Mar, is he a Cap?"

"Yes, but fear not. This one has been trained," Marvella answers, seemingly pleased at his touch. "They undergo a sophisticated and extensive domestication process before we allow them to be around us."

Flister suddenly shouts at the top of his lungs, scaring Marvella into a scream. The driver, however, does not flinch in the slightest.

"Is he still human?" Flister asks.

"Somewhat."

"Is it dear, sweet Oaken's work?"

Marvella bristles visibly at the mention of the Fifth Aevum. Marvella Pinyin and Oaken Bleu were the only Aevii born in the same year. Instead of making them close like sisters, it created a competitive, petty tension between the two women. The fact that Marvella hailed from Ortus and Oaken from Pexus had started a rivalry between the two territories that lasts to this day.

"*Oaken*," Marvella begins, saying her name as if it has a bitter taste, "was permitted by Mal to do some work in *my* facility. It was minimal. Mal said the peace we will experience as Elusians throughout the future is in large part due to *my* work," she goes on, pride dripping from her words. "Mal said that this is futuristic crime management." When Flister does not respond, Marvella shoves his arm. "Am I interrupting your thoughts, beloved? I thought today was about us spending time together?"

"And that is all I desire from this day," he responds huskily.

Marvella eyes him as though she is trying to decide how to respond. She settles on a smile. "You will not be disappointed. I know it. You will enjoy my work."

"I am brimming with anticipation," Flister says lightly as, lifting her hand to his mouth, he kisses it gently, allowing his warm breath to bathe her skin. Lowering her hand to his lap, he holds it there.

She cannot hold his gaze as her cheeks redden, and she quickly looks out the window.

Chuckling to himself, Flister looks down at his other hand. Even though he is merely twenty-five, he can already see small wrinkles that had not been there a couple of years ago. He need only wait five more years, and then he will be able to alter his features to look as young or old as he wants.

As they journey, Flister notes that the barbaric territory is a giant desert. And yet, it seems hotter, uglier, and emptier than any other desert he has ever seen.

Finally, in the distance, he makes out a tiny green dot.

Marvella leans forward as well. "There it is."

The green dot grows until Flister realizes it is an oasis. At first, all he can see are the tall giant sequoia, baobab, and coast redwood trees. Some landscape designers choose to use only flora that is native to the given soil, but others like to mix and match the plant life, drawing inspiration from all over Elusis. Flister would have taken Marvella to be the former type.

Suddenly the buildings come into view. There are five giant ones. Two are at least thirty stories high, while one is about half the height. The other two buildings are each only one story, but stretch to the sides farther than Flister can see. The buildings are pristine, beautiful works of art.

The closer they get, the more the greenery appears.

"We could have picked only trees that naturally grow in this area, but I wanted to pick the most majestic whether they were native or not," Marvella explains, seeing Flister eyeing them with interest. "I did that for you, you know. I could have kept it all bare, but I knew you would like the trees and plants."

"Thank you," Flister replies, honestly surprised.

Where Oaken is cute and endearing, and Mal is enchanting and pure, Marvella is striking and powerful. Over the past couple of years, she has made her growing affection for Flister more and more apparent. At first, it was in the little things: voting in his favor on decisions that mattered to him, elaborate presents, wearing more revealing dresses.

But lately, with his encouragement, she had started showing her cards. They had spent several evenings together enjoying lavish suppers and extravagant entertainment. He had invited her to a private showing of his Venture: Mal's Gardens—a flora sanctuary showing not only plants from all over Elusis but also plants from throughout all of the earth's history. He had used his Gift, along with several other horticulturists, to bring many extinct plants back to life. As the night had come to an end, she had kissed him on the cheek and lingered long enough for him to have kissed her on the lips, had he been so inclined.

 Now, the Captusian driver parks the car in front of the largest building. As they exit the vehicle, Flister finds himself even more impressed with the structure before him. The rocks that make up the construction of the building are, in fact, individually carved statues. The six Aevii are varied in their shapes, sizes, postures, expressions, and activities—the Fifth Aevum being noticeably least significant.

If someone had described the scene to him before he had seen it, Flister would have expected something gaudy, hideous even. But here, looking at it with his own eyes, it is mesmerizing… captivating.

"Is it not breathtaking?" Marvella whispers.

Flister smiles back. "Indeed."

"Each of your carved stones has a flower species within them. I made sure of it."

Flister kisses Marvella's cheek then places his hand on the small of her back as he follows her inside. He had not known what to expect—perhaps a vast, empty foyer—and he is surprised to be met with a flutter of activity. People are rushing around, and elevators are whirring past him both vertically and horizontally. Although most of the people are Ortusans, he notices a few red, black, and (to his disgust) light brown heads of hair among the dark brown heads.

As far as he can see—and he takes his time looking as Marvella leads him on a tour throughout the facility—there is not one grey head. Flister smiles to himself; Marvella is just as prejudiced towards Pexuns, due to Oaken, as he is towards Sanusians, due to Qualcum. It seems their Aevii family has more profound, divisive enmities than he realized.

Dakarai, Marvella, and himself are all Ortusans, meaning half of the Aevii representatives are of one territory. Although he *never* felt a connection with Dakarai, Marvella has been someone with whom he has felt a kinship due to their shared heritage. They could marinate in the same pride of having so many Ortusans within the Aevii.

"Captus has always held such a wealth of natural resources," Marvella explains as they begin the tour.

"Why do we need their resources?" Flister asks, genuinely curious. "We can just duplicate ours."

"Indeed, darling," Marvella answers with a smile, "but duplications are always inferior to the true element. It has been this way since the beginning of Gifts. We have only recently seen the true weaknesses in fourth, fifth, and sixth-generation duplications. We need the resources within Captus in order to continue to thrive as we do."

Flister frowns. He does not like hearing that the Hexum was dependent on Captus in any way.

"At first, the Caps tried to fight us," Marvella comments with a slight laugh. "But we have come to an agreement of sorts with their... well, one cannot call it a government... Nonetheless, we have come to an agreement with their authority figures."

Although she had explained much of her work during the day Flister had spent with her as a thirteen-year-old figuring out his own Venture, he had not given her or her work much attention at that time.

"How long have you been working with Caps, Mar?" Flister asks.

"I started my work after the Formosian Invasion of 216. I spearheaded the efforts to deport the Captusians out of Formosus and back to their territory. Since then, my work has led down many avenues." Her head rises high as her brows arc with pride. "And, here we are," she says, leading them out of an elevator.

They exit onto a brightly lit, welcoming entryway. People in lab coats walk hurriedly around several large workstations. As they emerge from underneath the threshold, Flister sees they have stepped into an open atrium with several floors overlooking them. Each level is filled with more workstations, more people. There is a lot of noise, but it is not overwhelming. It almost makes him want to join in on their work.

"These are Giftists working on Captusian resources. They tackle extraction, mobilization, utilization, reproduction, etcetera."

Flister looks around with interest. He can tell the Giftists are using the newest technology, glamulets, and eutsees—each throbbing with power. He also notes the highly sophisticated platimiculars, scrinners, and krimpins.

"You spared no expense, Sweetheart," he says, not trying to keep his voice down.

Marvella smiles. "My tithes funded most of this."

Flister did not have access to his tithings until he was eighteen; Mal was his conservator until such time. However, on his sixteenth birthday, Mal had taken him to the bank and allowed him to make a one-time withdrawal for his Venture. Within Mal's Gardens, his Venture, Flister had fulfilled every one of his desires—nothing had been out of his budget. Even so, it had barely put a dent in the ledger.

"Come, come, Beloved," Marvella beckons, leading him right across the atrium to two doors on the far side of the room. As they walk through the doors, the juxtaposed atmosphere on this side is jarring. Although the setup of the two vast rooms is almost identical, these workstations seem cold and hostile. The levels feel uninviting and foreboding. The Giftists themselves seem unfavorable.

"What are they doing?" he asks, whispering.

"These Giftists are working on Cap management."

"Meaning?"

"It means," Marvella says nonchalantly, walking past the workstations, "that they are finding ways to make Caps more pliable. They are attempting to banish their barbarianism."

"Would it not be simpler to exterminate them?" Flister asks, hurrying to keep up with her.

Marvella's almond eyes look around critically. "It would save time; but would, in the end, be a mistake, I believe."

"How so?"

She smiles back at him, and he is surprised at how vicious her expression is. "It is easier to allow the Caps to live and do as we wish than to pay for hundreds of thousands of simulans to come and do the same work."

At the end of this room is an elevator door on which the Aevum symbol is etched—three circles within each other, cut in two by a line running through their middles.

Flister almost laughs. "A private elevator? The whole building is not enough for you?"

"Never enough, Love," she answers, and their smiles mirror one another.

Marvella Pinyin quickly shows Flister through the rest of the buildings: the laboratories, testing facilities, housing cages, infirmary, and kitchen. They end the tour in her office.

Similar to her throne in the Aevum throne room in Silenda, the Fourth Aevum's personal space is clean, neat, and well-organized. Although there are bursts of muted color throughout the room, most of the features are white.

"Our world is perfect—Mal has made it so, Qualcum keeps it so," Marvella says as she pours herself and Flister a glass of aged blood-red eupee. "And yet, with all light, there is darkness; with all good, there is evil. It is as if these evil weeds keep growing in our perfect garden. We can continue weeding them out, but what if we found a way to exterminate them? And until then, what if we found a way to contain them? My Venture is to keep all evil on this one cursed territory. When I lobbied to have Hexum criminals sent here instead of sending them to eternal sleep, it was so that I could better study what makes them so. If we could eliminate evil forever... Oh, Darling, what an eternity it would be."

Facing her, Flister toasts her ambition. "You are extraordinary, Marvella, my Love." As they grin at one another, Flister watches the embers behind her eyes burn warmer. Slowly, she reaches up and touches his cheek with her hand.

His heart begins to pound, and he knows not if Marvella has employed her Gift to manipulate it thus, or whether it beats so frantically on its own accord.

Pulling his eyebrows together, he covers his features with a quizzical look. "Marvella?" he asks, feigning ignorance to the moment they have just shared.

"I am not asking for eternity," she whispers sensually. "Just this night."

Flister takes a moment to delight in the adrenaline flooding through his veins. He relishes the feeling of the thrill, the mystery, the opportunity to enjoy an hour or so with this gorgeous woman. As a young man, he had always been attracted to Marvella, even over Oaken—although he would never tell Oaken such, petty as she is.

As he inclines his head downward, Marvella rushes up to meet him, draping her arms around his shoulders. They stare at one another for a long moment, then Marvella leans toward his mouth. He allows her to advance until the last possible moment before their lips meet.

Ducking away suddenly, he brushes her neck with his lips. "Do you love me?" he asks.

"Yes," she answers, so quietly he almost misses it.

Ever so gently, he kisses the pulsing vein in her neck. As he pulls away from her nape to meet her eyes once more, he smiles. But his expression is not welcoming; it is not kind or inviting. It is cold and harsh. At Marvella's confused expression, his grin deepens, widens, sharpens.

"Oh, Darling," he says slowly. "I could never join bodies with one who has mated with a Cap."

For the first time since Flister Dubach has known her, Marvella Pinyin seems at a loss for words.

"Oaken told us about the Caps you mate with," he continues, enjoying the color fading from her face. "She told us you have several stowed away for your pleasure."

Her jaw moves, but no words come out.

Dramatically, he looks about as though trying to find her personal captives. "Are they hidden in this room? Are they somewhere in this building waiting for your command?"

Enjoying himself more than he had expected, the Sixth Aevum leans into Marvella and says slowly, "Your body has been lowered to that of a subhuman. No—lower. One of Oaken's spliced creatures. You have joined bodies with an animal, and I would not mate with you if it cost me my eternity. You have fouled yourself, my sweet Love. Mating with an animal… tsk tsk."

As if slapped, Marvella releases him, staggering backward.

Not wanting her to come to her senses and use her Gift against him, Flister Dubach quickly steps towards the door, eager to take his leave. As he hurries for the door, he turns back to look at Marvella one last time. She has not moved. She does not look at him when he speaks.

"Darling, you are a mongrel, and you disgust me."

With that, the Sixth Aevum leaves Captus, never to return.

The trek to Pexus is short, and the drive to the Data and Discovery Center even faster. The guards in front of the building recognize Flister Dubach, and he them. He tosses a couple of Vorbies in their direction, giving easy greetings like, "Greet the shine, Uoyk. How is your new son?" and "Ekam, how did the move go?"

As he maneuvers around the building's hallways with ease, he finds Oaken Bleu exactly where he thought he would. Plopping down in a hover chair next to the Fifth Aevum, he wipes the smiling skull tattoo off his chest and places it on Oaken's forearm.

She jumps at his touch, and when she looks down at the tattoo, she gasps and looks up at him. "You didn't!"

"Is my skin disintegrating?" he asks sardonically. "Are my bones protruding? No, I am as handsome as always—therefore, I have fulfilled the dare."

"But it's only been three months! How did you get her to fall in love with you so quickly?"

At his carnal grin, she rolls her eyes. "And the second part of the dare?" she asks.

"Her blood will be rotting for the next decade."

Oaken beams wickedly. "Oh, I wish I could have seen it."

Flister stands and gives his best animation of Marvella's devastation.

Oaken squeals giddily.

"Now," Flister draws her attention to the tattoo. "You dared me to make Marvella fall in love with me and then to deny her love." He allows a grin to twitch on the sides of his lips as she stares at him, waiting to hear what he will say. He has been thinking about it for the past month, and he cannot wait to watch her reaction. "In juxtaposition," he goes on, "I dare *you* to fall in love with someone."

Her reaction is not what he expected. Over the past fifteen years, the dares have been grotesque at times, humiliating, even demeaning, depending on the challenge. They were always uncomfortable and sometimes a little evil. No matter how they had pushed each other, Oaken had always taken the provocation with a sneer, a snicker, or a groan.

But this… this… *sadness*… was not something he had seen before.

"What is it?" he asks, suddenly sober.

"Nothing," Oaken snaps, and her lips harden in irritation. "I have to go, Flister." Standing abruptly, she adds, "I'll see you next week at Mal's party."

"But we were supposed to celebrate," Flister replies. "I know you have the time—I know your life too well."

"Well, you're an ignorant cow, and I'm busy." Without a backward glance, the Fifth Aevum storms out of the room, leaving the Sixth puzzled and vexed.

OAKEN DOES NOT SHOW up for Mal's birthday party, stating a work emergency has come up at the Discovery Center. It makes things most awkward for Flister because, without Oaken, he has no one with whom he can spend his time. Marvella spends the whole night pretending he does not exist. Dakarai drinks enough eupee to have killed him had he not been an Aevum. And to Flister's deepest dismay, Mal spends most of the night talking quietly with Qualcum.

Every time he tries to leave, Mal insists he stays longer, and he cannot say no to her. When he is finally able to depart, he calls Oaken, but she does not answer. For days, she declines all of Flister's calls and manages to disappear anytime he shows up unannounced for a visit at her house or work.

After six weeks, Flister is beginning to feel worried. Oaken has become engrossed in projects in the past, but she has never avoided him like this.

Finally, after two and a half months, Flister walks into the Discovery Center, lights a match, and drops it in the Fifth Aevum's office. It takes longer than he thought for the fire to grow—covering her desk, lapping at her chair, hesitantly falling on the floor. Using his Gift, he creates a can of oil and leads the flame outside the office and into the laboratories. Within minutes, the whole fifth floor is ablaze.

As the Element Regulators show up to put out the fire and fix the damage, Flister waits across the street. Employees flood out of the building like spilled milk, and it is not hard to spot Oaken Bleu when she emerges, coughing and covered in smoke.

Stealthily, without running but with purpose, Flister walks across the street and grabs Oaken by the arm, intending to lead her away from the building.

But at his touch, she winces and then cries out. At the sound of her pain, he releases her immediately. Shock hits her features as she looks to see who has grabbed her, but fury quickly replaces it.

"Was that *you*?" she screams.

"Well, when one is avoided like Captus, extreme measures have to be taken!" he shouts back.

"Oh, you—" As she rages on, calling him every outdated derogatory name from the early 200s, she pulls her left arm close to her as if it is wounded.

People in lab coats run around them, some burnt from the fire, many calling out names, trying to find one another. It is a chaotic scene, but Flister ignores what is happening in the periphery.

He waits until Oaken is done cursing him, then asks, "Do you need a healer?"

"No."

"You look hurt."

"I'm fine."

"You do not appear to be fine." Looking around the scene, he easily spots a pop-up healer facility. "Let me take you over there," he points.

Growling, Oaken looks up at him, wide-eyed and crazed. "I'm fine!" She shouts. "Leave me alone!"

"Are you burned?" he pushes.

She laughs then. It is the high-pitched throaty laugh that usually accompanies a particularly heinous dare.

The dare…

It clicks then, and Flister pulls Oaken's arm away from her chest. She gasps in agony, but before she can stop him, he has pulled up the sleeve of her shirt.

The smiling skull tattoo is right where he left it, but that is the only part of her arm that looks normal. The rest of the appendage is an unnatural grey color, the skin covered in lesions with a gaping wound right below the tattoo. Puss seeps from the corner of the gash while skin curls around it as though burnt.

"You *patka!*" he whispers angrily. "If you do not wish to fulfill the dare, just quit!"

Pulling her arm away, she gently tugs her sleeve back down. She looks around to see if any of the people milling around them have seen. "I won't quit," she responds tightly. "I am just trying to figure it out."

"Figure what out?" he asks with a harsh laugh. "Is it really that hard to fall in love?"

At his question, a new gash slices its way from her wrist to her thumb. Oaken grimaces and tries to cover her hand with her shirt as well.

"Quit," Flister commands, unbelievably angry at her for allowing herself to suffer this pain.

"No."

"Do it, Kenny!"

"No."

"You brainless *wee-un*! This is just your arm—for now! If you keep breaking the dare, your whole body will soon look like this!"

"I said *no.*"

"Fine. If you want to let your whole body rot because you cannot find it in yourself to fall in love or quit, that is on you."

Her eyes meet his, and he is surprised to see the sadness is back. She looks as if she might say something, but then she turns to look at the burning Discovery Center. Quietly, as if to herself, she asks, "Are you really that naive?"

It is then, amid the throng of scared employees, the sound of sirens in his ear, and the smell of smoke in his nostrils, that Flister finally understands. His temper cools like an Icer touching a flame. He stares down at the woman before him and cannot find words to speak.

Oaken winces, looking down at her hand. Tentatively, gently, Flister holds her arm and watches as the fresh wound begins to heal—as if her body is putting itself back together. The rest of her arm follows suit, and within half a minute, her arm looks normal again. All that remains is the black-inked skull smiling at him—taunting him.

They stand quietly for a long time, and Flister mulls over this new information. So Oaken was in love with him... the news is a shock with an unfortunate aftertaste. His feelings did not run adjacent to hers—what will this mean for their friendship?

She must have known he did not share her feelings. Rather than ever telling him, she would have let her whole body disintegrate until she was nothing but a walking skeleton. In that regard, she must value their relationship as highly as he did.

But why had the dare been broken? She was in love with someone—him. Should she not have just been able to take off the tattoo, having fulfilled the dare?

"I do not understand how you were breaking the dare," he states gently.

Ripping her arm out of his hand, she turns away from him and stares again at the chaos of the fire.

"Kenny," he pushes quietly. "If I am assuming correctly, was not the dare fulfilled the moment I spoke it?"

She forces herself to respond through clenched teeth, "Yes."

"So why did the tattoo act as if you had broken the dare?"

In a whirlwind, she turns to him, eyes ablaze with fury. "Because I was never going to tell you!" she screams. "And because *you* would never know the dare had been fulfilled, the cursed tattoo judged it as breaking the contract."

He wants to comfort her but has no idea what to say. She is so angry—and he would be too if *he* had been forced to relinquish information unwillingly. Should he leave? Perhaps she needs space.

When he was a child, he and Oaken had been physically affectionate with each other. They would hold hands, snuggle on a couch, and hug whenever they met or departed. But as he got older, they had stopped their easy affection. It has been years since he held her hand.

Now, not knowing what else to do, Flister pulls Oaken to himself. She is slightly shorter than he is, so he wraps one hand around her waist and uses the other to pull her face close to his. Warm tears fall down his cheeks, but they are not his own.

The cacophony of noise fades around them as he stands in the street, holding his best friend in the entire world, his blood aching because he cannot give her what she wants. Without a thought, he begins humming the Ninth Grade Song for her.

When Oaken finally pulls away, she keeps her gaze down. Slowly, Flister draws her chin up so she has to look at him.

"We could stop," he whispers.

Chuckling quietly, Oaken pulls Flister close and kisses his cheek. Then, placing her lips so close to his ear it sends a chill down his spine, she breathes, "But then I couldn't get you back."

Pexus

Kansis

SCOUT SHUTS THE DOOR on his way out, leaving me, Aker, and Amelia standing awkwardly in the lavish hotel room. As the two of them cannot communicate with each other, I know it's my job to say something—anything—but years of not conversing have dulled my social interactions. To my relief, Amelia makes it her business to inspect the room, so I follow her.

I slip the pocket watch from Scout inside my pocket. I still can't believe he gave it to me. I haven't received *any* type of present for over two and a half years, and even then, I think the last present was a plain old EverWarm cup from my parents for my eighteenth birthday.

Our hotel suite is more extensive than my house, probably covering over seven hundred square meters. It has three bedrooms, two bathrooms, two living rooms, a foyer, a dining room, a bar, and an entertainment room. Everything is white with trimmings in a luxurious creamy orange—the whole place has the air of an exclusive boutique, with impressive stone pillars and soaring ceilings. We open the oversized double doors at the back of the suite and walk out onto a terraced rooftop balcony with a HugMe jacuzzi and a cantilevered pool.

Amelia whistles. "Nice accommodations, Freckles. You're really hooking me up here."

"Don't thank me," I say. "Thank our Protector. He's paying for us to stay here."

"These people must be flow," she says as she runs over to the edge of the balcony and, leaning over the railing, stares down at the people below.

I join her. Although I am from this world, I've never been to Initium before and can also enjoy the scenic view.

"Who are those weirdos?" Amelia asks, pointing down.

I follow her motion and can't believe it when I see that she is talking about two Guardians. They are unmistakable in their majestic uniforms. The tough, armor-like, plate-like folds of the vest and shoulder protection are grainy, covered in a layer of keratin, and grey—they look as if they are wearing rhinoceros skin.

Their imposing horned helmets gleam in the sunlight, their belts filled with eutsees seem to exude a faint glow of powerful energy.

"Weirdos?" I ask, not really understanding what the word means, but knowing it's an insult.

"Yeah," she says and snorts, "they look too old to be walking around in costumes like that. I mean, they're pretty legit looking, but still."

"Costumes?" Flustered, I try to explain, "Those are our Guardians. They are respected and revered in our culture."

"Wearing that?" When her mirthful eyes meet mine, she hesitates. Clicking her tongue, she looks back out to them. "All right. If you say so."

"Those two Guardians in *costumes* have on their person enough tech to destroy an entire army from Mundus Senex."

At this, her critical eyes turn on me. Half-lidded, her eyes seem to mock me as she asks pessimistically, "Oh yeah? How so?"

"In addition to their specific Gift which is always hand-picked to aid their team, each Guardian has a comprehensive array of advanced technology designed to manage and contain individuals with superpowers. This includes power-neutralizing devices, adaptive armor, specialized restraints, non-lethal weapons, secure communication tools, and advanced medical kits, all aimed at ensuring safety and an effective response to any superhuman situation—" On one end of the patio, I notice a teleskep, and let my sentence trail off. I run over to the advanced technology and gingerly touch its copper plating.

"Is that a telescope?" Amelia asks as she eyes the tripod it's sitting on.

"It's a teleskep," I correct. "You can see miles away with this thing. And if you focus on a moving object, like a bird, the teleskep will keep up with its movements for you. You can even see if it goes behind a building."

"Whoa. Creeper central," Amelia says in disgust. "Wouldn't stalkers just use this to track their victims?"

I sigh. "It's sad that that's your first thought. The laws in Novus are much more extreme than in your world. If someone were to use a teleskep or other items of its nature to harm another metahuman, it turns off automatically. And if they were to be found out, they could have their Gift stripped, years taken off their lives, or even face a death sentence. Crime is taken very seriously here, and it's dealt with justly and immediately."

"Creepers don't care about the cost. It doesn't matter whether you're meta or not."

"I disagree," I counter. "People stand to lose far more in this world than the costs criminals face in your world."

"How would your police even know if this tele-whatever was being used for creeper purposes or not?"

"Teleskeps, and most other Novian tech, are paired with a Fluerant—an object that ensures the user is using the tech morally."

"Morally?" she laughs. "According to whose standard of morality?"

There's a loud knock at the door, and as Amelia and I step back inside the hotel room, Aker opens it. A simulan follows, pushing a cart full of food. Aker takes the massive leaf coverings off the top of the plates to reveal some of my favorite dishes: raspberry creme pudding, willow cake with greengage jam, wedges of speckled nut cheese, egg hoppers, wheat and oat bread, brik, blackberry flan, graveyard eggs, and even half a dozen small, mint creme cakes.

I start laughing at the horrified look on Amelia's face.

"What's wrong?" I ask her.

"What… the heck… is that?" she asks, pointing to the graveyard egg. The cooks have quartered them and set them out in wedges. The egg whites are stained a deep plum purple, while the yokes are greenish-blue.

"Those are eggs preserved in salt, quicklime, clay, rice hulls, and ash," I answer.

"Dude," Amelia says, grimacing in disgust. She swallows queasily and adds, "I miss Senex food."

"This *is* Senex food," I say. "You will enjoy these. Come sit down." We sit at the table, and I serve myself and Amelia.

Aker remains standing as he slaps food on his plate and grumbles, "We'll eat, and then we're leaving." He then takes his plate of food, stalks into one of the living rooms, and sits down on the peach fuzz-colored couch.

"What's his deal?" Amelia asks as she pokes at the speckled nut cheese. "Is he still mad because I punched him in the face?"

"He and I have not yet eaten a meal together," I explain quietly as I get started on my food.

"What does that mean?" she asks, perplexed.

"A couple's first meal together is incredibly special," I nervously explain. I know Aker doesn't speak any of the old world languages, but for some reason, I'm terrified he has learned English without me knowing and can understand everything I'm saying. "We don't eat with each other until our wedding day."

Amelia guffaws. "Why not?"

"It's a tradition. Sharing bread is an intimate thing."

"You're sharing with me."

"Yes, but we aren't building a life together," I explain. "Eating and sleeping, waking up and going to bed, sitting down and standing up—these are all the most common things you do every day. Yet in doing them, you are living your life. Starting these things with a mate is special because, day by day, moment by moment, one mundane activity after another, you're building a family and a life together."

"That's..." Amelia pauses then smiles. "That is surprisingly beautiful." She eyes Aker. "So he won't eat with you at all?"

"It wouldn't be proper."

"But he didn't marry you, and that's not proper," she retorts.

Suddenly, Aker stands and marches back to us. "I want to talk to you," he tells me, "without her," he motions his head towards Amelia.

"But she can't understand you," I reply.

"I don't care."

Considering that Aker has only told me three times that he wants to talk to me, I guiltily look at Amelia. "Would you mind hanging out on the patio for a minute?"

She rolls her eyes. "He knows I can't understand him, right?"

I smile pleadingly and nod.

"Whatever." She picks up her food and walks outside.

The door closes, leaving us in silence. I steal a glance at Aker.

He stands with his feet shoulder-width apart. Like always, he's dressed in the latest fashions, his style mostly business casual. He has always been an incredibly confident person and that's evident in the strong yet relaxed way he holds himself. As he regards me, he crosses his arms causing his black shirt to pull taut over his arms. I can't *not* look at how nice this makes his biceps look, so I avert my gaze.

Ontzi.

He's so beautiful.

I remember the night before my sister, Clista, attended her Announcement of Mates. I must have been seven or eight at the time. It was a hot summer evening, and Clista was sitting in the window nook with her friend Jessip. They were talking about who their mates might be, and I was eavesdropping from behind the door. Jessip hoped her mate was a boy named Nubis. "I'm drawn to him," she giggled.

"What do you mean?" I asked, peeping out from behind the door. I couldn't help myself.

Clista was upset I had been spying, but Jessip liked me and beckoned me over.

"Watch the moths, Kansy," she said, pointing to the flying, furry creatures outside the window. For a few moments, I watched the swarming, wooly insects. Some of them slowly glided towards the light, while others dive-bombed it. But whatever their means, whatever their ways, they all followed an invisible path toward its brightness.

When I looked back at Jessip, her eyes were filled with sparkles. "See them? They can't help themselves. They need the light. They're drawn to it." She giggled again.

"I'm drawn to Aker Vonbough," I told her confidently.

"Well, he's a looker, isn't he?" she replied.

"He's my mate; I know he is."

Clista scoffed at me. "You don't know who your mate is, Kansis. You're too young to know. Now leave." I knew better than to argue with her, but Jessip stopped me before I turned.

"I believe you," she whispered in my hair.

And even now, as I steal another glance at him, I know I will always be drawn to Aker Vonbough. The druzy quartz pendant hangs heavy on my chest. Without meaning to, I find myself holding it.

When Aker finally speaks, his frown is audible. "What are you doing, Kansis?" he asks quietly. "Why are we so far from home? Why are you helping this subhuman and Ortusan criminals?"

"I... I don't know." It's the truth. I have no idea what I'm doing. "I just know I need to help her."

"Why? Her life doesn't affect you."

"It does now."

"Why?" The word is like a bite.

"She's... my friend."

He laughs. It's a pitying, sarcastic laugh, and it makes me want to cry. "No, Kansis. She's not your *friend*," Aker responds. "She's using you to find her dad. You know, her *dad*. Arkarian Story."

"She is too my friend," is my pathetic reply.

The crack in my voice causes him to look at me again. He huffs loudly and says, "Look, I'm sorry. I know it's my fault you're alone. I know it's because of me that we're in this mess. I get that you feel you needed to help her because you didn't have any friends or family or… well, anyone, but—but you have to understand…"

Blood pounds throughout my veins, boomeranging painfully to and from my heart. I can't even hear him talking anymore the heartbeats are so loud.

I have to ask him. Now is the perfect opportunity.

Ask him!

I take a deep breath, interrupting whatever he's saying, and ask, "Why weren't you there that night, Aker? Why didn't you m-marry me?" I've practiced the words so many times, but hearing them come out of my mouth, they sound foreign and out of place.

"But just because you don't have any friends doesn't mean you have to stoop so low," Aker continues, pretending not to hear me. "Arkarian Story's daughter is not your friend. She is a Pod. She is subhuman." He takes a deep breath. "It's time to go home."

I ignore his rant and ask again, "Why did you run away with—with Mirindiss?"

Voice sharp and final, he states, "I'm not going to answer that."

For the first time, I entertain the thought that maybe he is as cruel as my subconscious has always told me. Tears roll down my face.

He sighs again. "Look, I'm sorry." For a moment, he's quiet, and I threaten my tears to stop their incessant flow, but they mock me by gushing faster until I can't see clearly or breathe through my nose anymore. Why does crying have to make you so unattractive?

"I'm staying," I finally state.

"No, you're not," he retorts, his face, neck, and even his eyes a slight shade of red. "We're going home."

"The papers didn't mention you being gone, so I'm sure you can get back undetected. You can go back to your life like nothing happened."

"I'm not leaving without you," he responds.

"Why?" I ask. "Yesterday was the first time you've spoken to me in two years. What does it matter now?" I wish I could talk to my subconscious. I always have such good advice for myself. And without me, I don't know what to do. But the wait to fall asleep is too far away.

"It matters *now*," Aker answers, "Because I need you in order to go back to my life. We need to…" he shifts his weight uncomfortably, "get married and… and once we're married, I can get a better job. There's a lot of traveling with it, so we don't have to see each other much. We need to… we just gotta pretend that we're in love so we can get our lives started."

My hands feel clammy and cold. My throat feels tight and hot. "Did you... Did you say we can *pretend* we're in love?" I whisper.

"I'm never going to love you. If these two years taught us nothing else, it was that. But that can't be our motivator anymore. Now we need to create something... I don't know. Something new. Something other couples don't have."

"And what's that?" I ask, my throat barely letting the words out of my mouth.

"We need to be like... like live-in acquaintances." His voice takes on an excited tone. "We'll put on a show when necessary, but other than that, we'll live our own lives. Have our own rooms—stuff like that. I've put a lot of thought into it, and I think this is best... getting married. We'll do it quickly, not a big ceremony. Just—"

"I'm staying," I repeat stubbornly.

Throwing his hands up in the air, Aker shouts, "Kansis, wake up! You can't just kidnap a Pod and run off with a freak circus act! You aren't an Arkahunter. You aren't a savior. You're just... You're just Kansis, and you belong in Depalo with... with," he swallows hard and looks away, "me."

"Do I disgust you so much that you can't even talk about being with me without gagging?" I ask quietly. When he doesn't answer, I step in front of him. He won't look me in the eye. "You go back to Depalo. I may not be a savior, but I will help Amelia, even if it means being imprisoned or killed."

"Why?" he shouts at me. "Who is she to you? She's nobody. She's just a subhuman Pod. *I'm* your mate!" He bellows these last three words in my face. "You told me once that all you ever wanted in your life was to marry me," Aker continues. "Are you a liar now?"

"A liar?" I ask, surprised at the accusation. "No, I..."

"And what if you are imprisoned or die? You'll probably be happy, seeing as you're so eager for that," he says mockingly.

"Then you'd be free to marry another," I answer honestly. I didn't mean to say it aloud, but the words slip out of my mouth.

Shocking me, Aker kneels in front of me. "What do I have to do?" I've never seen him so desperate in my whole life. "What do I have to do to get you to come home with me? I'll do anything. Isn't this what you want? I'm begging to be with you. Isn't this what you've always wanted?"

As I stare down at him, acid fills my blood. I cover my face with my hands. I can't look at his fierce eyes. "Yes, I want that... but not... not like this."

"Dean!" Amelia suddenly shrieks from the balcony. "Dean!" she screams again. I look outside to see her glued to the teleskep. Then, before I can say or do anything, she races back into our suite, swings open the door, and takes off down the hall.

It takes me a moment to realize what has happened, and it's not until Aker says, "Thank the Aevii; she left on her own," that reality catches up with my mind.

I start towards the door, but Aker stands up, grabbing my arm and wrenching me back. I jolt to a sudden stop. Other than when he tried to kidnap me the other night, the last time he touched me was the night of my graduation from Ward Training, three years ago.

"No, Kansis," he yells. "Let her go. For the last time, you and I are going *home.*"

I stare at him, not understanding the fight in my blood. Aker is *touching* me, making my whole arm buzz with electricity. He's staring me in the eye, *begging* me to go home with him and marry him. How am I not running towards the nearest transponder station?

As if outside of my own body, I see myself ripping my arm out of his grasp. I hear myself say, "I'd rather chase after a friend than go home with a live-in acquaintance." And I watch myself turn away without another word, running instead to chase after Amelia.

As I race down the hallway, I'm afraid I've lost her. But then, faintly, I hear her shout again, "Dean!" Her voice is silenced as the elevator door pings shut, and I pace back and forth impatiently, waiting for the next one. As soon as I reach the lobby her voice picks up again, this time echoing outside. I chase her through the streets of downtown Initium, and I can't believe how fast this girl can run!

We fly past stores, vendors, and houses. If I wasn't madly dashing after the daughter of Arkarian Story, I think I would have enjoyed the scenery. I hurtle past a community garden, a farmer's market, and a small art showing, but everything is a blur. As I gallop into a park, still following Amelia's frantic shouts, my lungs burn... I can't keep this up.

It's not until I bolt through an open courtyard that I see Amelia instead of just hearing her. I can also see the Sanusian man she's chasing. He keeps turning around to see where Amelia is, then bolting in another direction. As I sprint towards a busy intersection, I watch the Sanusian run into a cafe. I barely glimpse Amelia's red hair whipping around parked track cars. But just as I lurch forward to cross the street, someone pulls me back. A line of track cars flies by. When I look to see who has saved me, I'm surprised to see that it's one of the Formosians from Scout's bus. He's the one who told me that Amelia is indeed the true daughter of Arkarian Story. I just can't remember his name.

Knowing that's not what matters right now, I quickly gasp, "Thank you," and when the line of track cars passes, I race across the street and up to the cafe.

Before I even walk inside, I hear Amelia shouting, completely out of breath, "Where... is... he? I know... he's... in here!"

"Amelia!" I cry as I hurry inside. I try to pull her to one side of the cafe, but she's so much taller and stronger than me that I can't move her. Still winded, I whisper urgently, "You can't... go around... talking in English. People will call the Guardians on you."

"But I know him," she whispers back determinedly, trying to catch her breath. "That man was from Senex."

"Well, no wonder he ran," I respond, exasperated. "He's programmed to run at his Senexian name."

In an instant, Amelia's expression modifies. Her whole face fills with suspicion, distrust, and even bewilderment. Her brows furrow, her mouth thins to a line, and her eyes look ready to pierce me. She asks slowly. "What do you mean *programmed*?"

I don't know if it's the venom in her eyes or in her words, but I take a step backward. This dangerously angry person before me is an Amelia I haven't seen before. From the moment she woke up, she's been apathetic, prideful, willing, kind, intimidating, or happy. I had thought she was unlike any Pod I've worked with... but maybe she's not. Maybe under the lighthearted persona, she's just as angry, scared, and distrusting as every other Senexian I've met.

I keep thinking Amelia is my friend... but now I can't help but wonder if it's truly reciprocal, or if she's just using me to find her father.

"You best keep her quiet," someone urges from behind me.

I turn to the barista of the cafe, laughing as if self-conscious. That sounded real, right? Thinking furiously on the spot, I respond quickly, "Oh, um... Don't worry about her... She's uh... she's practicing for her language test for Ward school. I'm sorry she shouted at you; she's taking the role-playing a bit too seriously."

"She is foolish to be speaking so freely," the barista responds. Her bold statement is accompanied by a look of concern that momentarily flashes across her otherwise cheerful features.

Amelia easily pushes me aside and approaches the barista. "Where is that man?" she asks again.

The barista takes a step back, wary of this flushed, angry person speaking gibberish. Few Novies have ever heard another language.

"She can't understand you," I whisper to Amelia.

"Then *translate*, Kansis!" Amelia shouts, rounding on me. Her breathing is still labored, and her eyes wide with rage. Her whole body is tense as if she is going to tackle me to the ground and choke me again.

I don't answer right away, wondering whether it would be best to have this conversation elsewhere, and she grabs my forearms, pulling them upwards so they are practically in front of my face. "Ask her!" She growls through clenched teeth.

I have never let any Pod treat me as Amelia has, and I'm not going to start now. Friend or not, this is a Pod under my care. She is my responsibility, and I feel my Ward training kicking in as I purposefully look at her hands and then move my gaze to her eyes. I stare at her, my brows raised. She doesn't let go right away. Her anger is more heightened than my calm.

Knowing the barista and patrons are listening, I whisper sharply, "You *will* let go of my arms."

After a few more seconds of staring at each other, she finally releases me.

Even though my arms are stinging, I don't rub at them. Instead, I stare her down. "It's not my fault you don't speak the language," I say quietly but firmly. "You will not nip at my heels like an annoying dog while I'm talking on your behalf. You will wait patiently and respectfully, or I will not speak for you or share what is being said around you. If you want the honor of knowing what is happening, you will respect yourself and me by acting like an adult."

She is still seething as I speak, but by the time I reach the end of my monologue, it's as if the switch has been flipped again. Amelia closes her eyes, takes a deep breath, and intertwines her fingers at her belly. When she opens her eyes, she is as calm and in control as she has been since her Awakening.

As if suddenly aware of her surroundings, she looks around at the people in the cafe. Taking another deep breath, she whispers, "I'm sorry for shouting at you, Freckles. I didn't mean to lose control like that. It's just..." Her gaze flicks from the barista back to me. "I'm so out of my element, and even though I'm on Earth, this isn't my world at all. I have no home. But *that* man... he's as close as I can get. Thinking I might not see him again unless I caught up to him... it made me—" She stops and smiles sadly. "That's an excuse, I guess. No one and no circumstance can make me do anything. I chose to be out of control. I'm sorry."

I don't know if she's being genuine or if she's manipulating me. This girl is either an amazing actress or an incredibly self-aware individual. Which is it?

In the end, I choose to believe her.

For now.

Does that make me ridiculously gullible? I guess it doesn't matter. I nod to Amelia and turn to the barista. "Where is the Sanusian man who ran in here?"

"There are no Sanusians here," the barista responds guardedly.

The kitchen door opens, and an Ortusan man emerges. "What does she want with the man?" he asks. The Ortusan is of slight build. He has a long nose and large, round eyes. Although his cheekbones and eyebrows are very pronounced, the rest of his features are smooth. He has a look of true kindness about him.

"My friend knows the Sanusian," I answer in my best casual voice.

"From Senex?" he asks.

My heart beats frantically. How can I answer that? If I lie, he probably won't bring the Sanusian out. If I say yes, he will know I have a wild Pod with me. I lose either way. When I look at Amelia and see the anxiety tightening her face, I throw caution out of my veins.

"Yes," I answer.

"What's going on? What did he say?" Amelia asks me.

"He just asked if you were from Senex," I tell her.

The Ortusan man turns around, opens the door, and says something quietly in the kitchen. Then, to my surprise, the Sanusian man Amelia had yelled at and chased so frantically, tentatively steps out.

"Don't say my name," he declares quickly in English to Amelia. "I will involuntarily run away. Call me Tal."

Without saying a word, Amelia vaults over the counter and gathers the Sanusian man in a tight hug. I watch her unravel in their mutual embrace. She is overcome with deep, heart-wrenching sobs, and I look on silently, allowing Amelia her moment, being sensitive to how traumatic it must have been to be removed from everything familiar and thrust into an alien world.

Finally, Amelia pulls away. "Where is she?" she asks, her words muffled.

"I don't know, Milly," Tal answers. He looks bothered and upset. He won't look Amelia in the eyes as he goes on, "I… I haven't found anyone. I haven't looked."

"What do you mean you haven't looked? That was our mission," she replies, obviously agitated.

Tal finally meets her eye. "I couldn't, Amelia. There is so much you do not understand."

"What else is there to understand?" she asks, stepping away from him.

As he shakes his head, the three feather earrings in his right ear dance wildly. "The situation has changed—"

Amelia holds up a hand for him to stop talking, like a higher-ranking officer not willing to hear a subordinate's excuses for a failed mission. "Can I have your code?" she asks.

Tal clicks his tongue and shakes his head. "It's not that simple—"

"Can I have your code, *please*?" she interrupts forcefully.

"Amelia, I'm trying to tell you—"

"As was originally agreed, I only have half of what I need. Give me the other code, Commander," she demands, her voice now steely.

The Ortusan man touches Tal's arm. "Is everything all right?" he asks.

"She t'inks t'is is still about..." Tal starts in Elusian and then, eyeing me, whispers something so only the Ortusan can hear. The man watches us for a moment.

I sneak a glance at Amelia as she patiently waits for their side conversation to end. I've lived in this world my entire life, too afraid to speak or advocate for myself. And this girl, day three in my world, walks around with the confidence of an Aevum. She will not be bullied, pushed around, or kept in the dark. She is on a mission, and nothing—not even a world filled with magic and elements she is not strong enough to overcome—will stop her. I don't think I've ever met a metahuman I respect as much as this Pod.

The Ortusan man looks us over, his eyebrows arched sympathetically, mouth curved genially. "My name is Knimble Knox, and I think it might be best if we were to speak somewhere privately."

"I agree," someone behind me suddenly says brightly. I turn back to see the Formosian man from the circus. "I was on my way to introduce myself to you, I was," the man says to me. "I am Emerly Tosh, a member of the Unopened Gifts."

I have never been introduced to a Formosian before, and I almost forget their greeting, but I manage to say, "Healthy blood in your veins..."

"...and power to your Gift," Emerly recites, finishing the customary salutation. After placing his hand on his heart towards Knimble and Dean, he offers his hand to me. I put mine up against his, and our thumbs wrap around. Lowering his hand, he continues, "Scout had sent me to check on you two beautiful ladies when I saw you barreling past me with uncanny speed. Anyhoo, this brilliant fellow," he makes a grand gesture towards Knimble Knox, "has just worked out we're Arkahunters, he has." Emerly speaks clearly for all to hear. "He wishes to join our crew, as it were, because he too has stock in finding the villain, Arkarian Story, he does."

Knimble looks up at Emerly and smiles knowingly. "You are correct, Mind Reader. I think it would be best to find a more secure location for this conversation."

Before she can ask, I hurriedly whisper to Amelia, "They want to talk privately about this. Being out in the open isn't safe."

"Do you know of the Unopened Gifts?" Emerly asks Knimble.

Knimble Knox nods. "Who does not?"

"Come to our tent tonight at ten. Tell the simulan at the gate that we are expecting you." As he speaks, Emerly's expression changes to one of confusion. His eyes quickly divert to the right and left as if he is listening to something. After lifting his hand to his neck, he rubs it down toward his chest, pondering something deeply. Then he takes a step towards Knimble. "Who are you speaking to?"

"A Superior," Knimble answers, seemingly unfazed by Emerly's intrusion in his mind.

"Which one?" Emerly inquires, a sense of urgency in his tone. "The name you use… it is not numbered among the thirty-one, it's not."

"He is not," Knimble Knox answers and then asks, "You are a Seeker, then?"

"Yes," Emerly replies eagerly.

"I know whom you seek," Knimble states. "But we must not speak here. Until this evening. Greet the shine."

"Greet the shine," Emerly replies, and stares after the Ortusan as he walks back behind the counter and through the kitchen door.

I explain the latest development to Amelia. "They've just made plans for your friend and the Ortusan man to meet us at the circus later."

"I wish our first encounter had gone better," Emerly remarks to me. "But we must get back to the circus before any Guardians find you. That would be quite awful for us, it would." Turning to Amelia, he announces in English, "Welcoom. Meet you is cupcake for me. True Formosian be to are you. Acquaintance name Emerly to you."

Amelia grins at his attempted English pleasantries.

In Elusian, Emerly says to me, "Now, let us return to our hotel."

As we head for the door, Amelia leans over and whispers, "You pretend to be all weak, but you're not, Freckles. You're tough." She punches my arm and walks past me out of the cafe.

But as I step onto the threshold outside, my body freezes.

We're standing before four Guardians. Their rhinoceros armor gleams in the sun, their belts of eutsees practically hum with power.

One steps forward, wearing a self-satisfied look. Her stance is loose, as if we had previously arranged to meet her here. Most people go to Feature Manipulators to keep themselves looking relatively young, but this woman has allowed herself wrinkles and imperfections. But even with visible age, she is solid and confident. She has pulled her smoke-colored, Pexun hair high above her head in a tight braid. Her high cheekbones and long nose crinkle as she smiles at us.

"You'll be coming with us, Criminals," she states almost cheerily.

"Criminals?" Emerly responds congenially. "What are you accusing us of, Guardians?"

The Guardian smiles, then opens her mouth. She pushes her tongue to the top of her palate and juts her jaw upward. A substance squirts out from beneath her tongue, landing on Emerly. Quicker than I would have believed possible, she repeats the same motion at Amelia and me. As soon as the spittle lands on my cheek, excruciating pain seizes my whole body. As I fall to the ground, the Guardian turns in the other direction, away from us.

I scream.

At least, I think I'm screaming. It could be the screams of the others. I don't know.

As I lose consciousness, all I see is the Guardian's dull grey braid swishing behind her as she walks away.

Pexus

Pypen

"WE'VE BEEN PRACTICING FOR hours and getting nowhere!" Merayal yells at me. "I can't do this! Even if I had the three months we originally agreed on, I couldn't pull this off. I'm done!" Throwing a chair across the center stage, she stomps toward the stairs leading off the platform. For a Pexun, she is quite passionate.

Before I can shout at her *again*, Scout commands, "You will try again," from the front row. His tone is even and quiet. His expression is still and kind. His eyes are sharp and understanding. His words are final.

"You don't get it—" she starts.

"You *will* try again," he repeats, and she yells in frustration.

"I don't know if you think you're some kind of Gift-whisperer, but I know the extent of my Progift, and I know that I literally can't do what you are asking. I've never extracted something like this before. It is out of my realm of ability. I'm sorry, Ortusan, but you're not going to get what you want." Her words are drenched in contempt.

I would agree with her, were it not for the surety in Scout's eyes. From the two practices we had in Vultus, and the four-hour run-through we have had this day, she physically *cannot* do what he is asking. But then again, he is Scout, and he is never wrong about people.

As we work, I keep remembering Fabella's words concerning Merayal. Every time her face contorts in anger, I hear Fabella's ethereal voice: *You may choose to let the Pexun girl rot and rust in her blood, or you could tame her. You could earn her trust and affection as you did all of us.*

Until Fabella had put it that way, I had never thought of the circus casts' emotional stability as my responsibility. Bringing in compensation, following Arkahunter leads, helping their families—these are things I knew were on my shoulders. But their well-being? As I ponder her words, I vacillate between the strength such an honor brings and the threat of being crushed by it.

This feeling is only amplified with Merayal. It is preposterous that my burden is to keep her from her own darkness. Fabella said she might find a home here at the circus, but how could she make herself at home amongst people she views with such loathing?

"Close your eyes," Scout orders Merayal.

She looks as if to argue, then she slowly obeys. Her appearance is utterly stubborn yet completely serene.

"Now, ponder a time when you used your Gift at its greatest strength," Scout says.

Her eyes flash open with anger. "Like I can take inventory of my whole life and think of the *one* time—"

"I *said*," Scout barks loudly, and immediately she stops talking, "close your eyes," he ends his sentence calmly.

Reluctantly, she closes her eyes once more.

"Think of a time you used your Gift with the most power."

Although she does as he says, I can tell by her raised eyebrows and tight lips that Merayal's obedience is patronizing. But after a few moments, her brows lower and her lips soften. Memories must be arising. After another few minutes, she murmurs, "I remember."

Glancing around the room, I see Fabella's focus. She must be assisting Merayal in the sifting of her memories.

"What were the circumstances?" Scout asks.

"I was extracting… something… from someone's leg."

"Were you afraid?"

"Yes."

"Because you were afraid of hurting this person as you worked?" Scout asks.

Eyes still closed, her head shakes. "Not hurting them… Just not being able to get it out."

Scout's eyebrows furrow. "What was it?"

"A bullet."

"What is a bullet?" Scout asks and glances at me.

I shrug my shoulders. I have never heard of the word either.

"I was so surprised I was able to do it," Merayal continues, not answering Scout's question. "I still don't know how I did. And as I look back at that, I can still say with all certainty and with complete confidence," her eyes open slowly and connect with Scout's, "I can't do what you're asking." Her expression hardens as she adds, "Don't ever draw memories out of me again without my consent. Nobody in this room has the right to know that about me."

Eyes narrowing for a second, Scout looks to me and asks, "Can I borrow your fluerant?"

"Like he just has a pocket fluerant," Merayal mutters, rolling her eyes.

It takes me a moment to oblige. It is not well-known that I carry around a fluerant—it is not something I want others to know. As eyes on the room turn to me, wondering if I have one and if I will indulge this request, I feel exposed. It is not often—if ever anymore—that I feel this way, and I do not relish the recollection of the sensation.

Scout's expression changes for a heartbeat as he realizes my discomfort, and he quickly adds, "Or did you already return it to Cherise? I know she was itching to get it back."

An easy lie to protect my fragile ego.

Fluerants have three purposes. Most often, they are paired with other objects so the user has to wield the tech it is attached to in a moral fashion. There are many items that require it, for example, a teleskep, a kokatu, or a mowic. Secondly, some vocations require it—Guardians, healers, and therapists being some of them. This keeps the professionals accountable in their given fields. The third and least common reason is because one was mandated to possess it as a legal consequence of a crime.

My fluerant was given to me the day after Irenia and Cazney died. Citizens get two warnings before their Gifts are stripped, so I only have one warning remaining. Although I previously had no intention of revealing the fact that I possess one to the group, nor the reason why, I am a picture of casualness as I take the white object out of my pocket.

My fluerant has a thin, soft, fur-like covering. The length and width of a playing card, it is two millimeters thick. As it is in my pocket at all times, I often hold it in my hand as a means of comfort. Passing it to Scout, I respond, "I was supposed to give it to Cherise last day, but it must have slipped my mind."

"I am certain she would not mind us borrowing it," he replies.

Scout and I have known each other long enough to have created a non-verbal means of communication. Judging by his slight eyebrow crease, I know he is remorseful for exposing my secret. I blink a *worry not about it*, and we move on.

Turning back to Merayal, Scout says, "This is a particularly intricate fluerant. Each layer of the tech is infused with energy, and at the center of the fluerant are two thin coverslips encasing a drop of vacuous. I want you to extract the vacuous from the fluerant."

Merayal's mouth twists confidently. "Easy." Closing her eyes, her right hand extends towards the fluerant. Instantly, the tech rises from Scout's hand. When it hovers in front of her, she brings her left hand up next to it. As her palms separate, the fluerant begins to twitch. Tiny screws twist themselves out and hover in the air. Slowly, the different mechanical parts separate as the fluerant is held in the air. As far as her hands will stretch is the length of separated pieces. Then, her pointer finger moves up and away from her other phalanges. A tiny part of the fluerant flies high above the other components. It looks like a small glass square of bright green.

"Is this it?" she asks, still smiling.

"That is it," Scout responds. "Now put it back in and reassemble the fluerant."

With little effort, Merayal draws her finger down and, with it, the vacuous. As her hands come back together, the pieces of the fluerant simultaneously fly back into their original design. She opens her eyes, satisfied with her work.

"Now, if *that's* what you need me to do, I can do it."

Scout walks to the snack table beside the stage, grabs a banana, and returns. He tosses the banana to Merayal and commands, "Extract the fruit from its skin."

"I don't think—"

"Just do whatever feels natural to you."

Closing her eyes, she lets the banana float out of her hands and hover in front of her. Her eyebrows furrow as she thinks about her next move. Her hands come up together in front of the fruit. Lifting her pointer finger, she slowly draws it back down, and as she does so, the banana begins to tear from top to bottom. Merayal opens her hands slowly, and the banana responds by peeling itself, revealing the fruit within. After a few more cuts with her finger, the peel falls to the floor, leaving only the edible fruit.

Merayal opens her eyes. "Is that what you wanted?"

"Brilliant," Scout answers quietly. "Now, put it back together."

Shrugging her shoulders, Merayal closes her eyes and mentally lifts the peel from the earth. Clumsily, she tries to put the peel back on, but she manages only to squish the banana in the process.

"I can't." She opens her eyes and allows the fruit to splatter onto the floor.

A small smile plays upon Scout's lips. His eyes continue to pierce Merayal, but I can tell he is mentally scanning the room. Voices echo around the expansive area as people and simulans prepare for the circus' opening. Finally, Scout hears the person he is after. "Vielfrah," he shouts, causing Merayal and the other performers on the stage to jump.

"Aye, Scout?" Vielfrah, the shortest of the Controls, yells from the back of the stadium.

"Bring me your blade."

Vielfrah's long, pale brown hair falls into his eyes, and he pushes it behind his ears. "Me blade, me ol' sam?"

"Yes, please bring it to me."

I think I know where this is going, and I sincerely hope it will work. Quickly I scan the room to see Twigg is here. Good, we will need her.

Vielfrah hands Scout a bone blade. It is Gifted to be sharp when and where the wielder wants, and otherwise to be dull. Scout glances at Twigg and then down at Vielfrah with a knowing look.

"At least, I hope I know," I mutter.

When Scout's eyes land on me, I know what he is asking of me. Scout takes the bone blade in his hand and studies it for a moment.

"Merayal." Twirling the blade in his hand, Scout eyes the young Pexun. "I believe in you, even if you do not. I know you can do what I am asking. Your mind is stuck, not believing what I say is possible. So, we will start small."

Then, without another word, Scout takes the bone blade and stabs himself in the chest, pushing the knife so deep into his body that not even the end is visible.

Merayal gasps, frozen to the spot.

Breathing hard, Scout looks up at me and commands, "Seal it."

I close my eyes and see his chest as it should be: whole with no wound. I must work around the aspect of my Gift that desires to push the blade out of Scout's body. Circumventing these instincts used to be challenging, but now I effortlessly hold it at bay. I seal the lesion, blade between his ribs.

Scout's entire tunic is soaked in blood as he moves his gaze to Merayal. With a pained expression, he unbuttons his shirt so we can all see his chest. Then he commands, "Extract it from me."

"Are you insane?" Merayal asks, voice quivering, eyes dark with rage.

"Take a deep breath," Scout instructs slowly, his words slurred with effort. "Concentrate."

"No! I can't believe you just—you are—what is this? What game is this?" She searches the room as if gauging our group response. Her eyes meet mine.

"He trusts you," I say as calmly as I can. "*I* trust you." Slowly, I walk towards her. Her eyes dart back to Scout, whose internal bleeding is evident from his rapidly purpling skin. Knowing now is the moment to put aside anything and everything I feel for the Pexun woman, I do exactly as Scout would have me do. When I reach her, I gingerly place my hand on her shoulder. To my surprise, she allows my touch. "You can do this," I say calmly. "Extract the blade from his body."

Wide-eyed, she responds, "Even if I do that, I can't stop the bleeding—I can't heal him."

"Worry not," I state. "Just extract it."

"But the wound is sealed! I can't take it out the way it came…"

Scout's knees hit the floor, making her jump. "There is not much time," he whispers.

I turn her face back towards mine. "Exactly. No wound. You must open Scout's chest. Just as you opened the banana, open his muscles."

"But I've never done that before. And it will hurt him! What if I…" her voice trails off. Scout is deathly pale.

"Try," I beg. I can see that Scout is going to wait for her. "Please."

Looking into my eyes, I think she sees my fear. But instead of causing more panic, this calms her. Closing her eyes, she extends her shaking hands toward Scout's body. As if an invisible person is lifting him, Scout stands up, chest forward, head bobbing to the side.

She had better hurry.

Like the banana, a small cut appears at the center of Scout's chest. As her pointer finger falls, the lesion expands, revealing his inward parts. Blood gushes out of his body as she feels around for the blade, her Gift extending the reach of her fingers across the distance to manipulate his wound. Finally, she locates the blade and removes it. Incredible amounts of crimson liquid fall onto the stage as her brows furrow in concentration. I want to begin my part, but I know what Scout requires of me, so I wait for her to finish.

The instant the bone blade is fully withdrawn, I activate my Progift and envision his body whole; his blood inside his body, not out. Reaching down into the recesses of my Gift, I will my most substantial portion—I urge myself to swiftness. I know not how fatal Scout's wound is, but he will need all my strength.

All. My. Strength.

…All…

I clawed through the darkness and grime,

As death whispered softly, "'Tis time,"

Light-headed, I allow myself to sit, resting my face in my hands. Strength depleted, I close my eyes. A strong hand grips on my shoulder. "Thank you, Friend." If I could smile, I would. Someone forces an object into my hand, and I know it to be a Vorbi. With the tiniest amount of energy I have left, I rub it. Concentrating, I open up my mind and allow the Vorbi's power to fill my Gifted genes. Energy slowly fills my cells. Sitting up, I rub the Vorbi faster. I desire not too much energy at once because sometimes—

WHAM!

A jolt surges through my body, and I drop the Vorbi. Suddenly I am standing, adrenaline pumping. I feel like I could run ten kilometers. My wide eyes meet Merayal's. I almost forgot this was all for her. Next, my eyes find Scout's. He is standing but hunched, grabbing his knees. His head turns towards me, and he smiles. I cannot help but grin back. Picking up the Vorbi, I put it in my pocket.

Standing straight, Scout smiles warmly at Merayal. "Well done. I knew you could do it."

"You are insane." Her words are unsteady, her voice still shaking.

His laugh reverberates throughout the room. "Yes, I am. But you, our wily squid, are incredible."

Screwing up her face, Merayal snarls, "I'm not a squid!"

Scout inclines his head, "I meant no offense, Merayal. 'Tis an Ortusan expression."

"It means you are unexpectedly clever and talented," I explain.

"Just call me by my name," she growls.

Ignoring her rudeness, Scout goes on, "In the show, that is what I need you to do, but to yourself. Sedwick will change form and look like a strand of a black virus. He will insert himself into your body and wrap himself around your heart. Twigg, as she did for me, will handle pain management. You will not feel a thing. You will—"

"*As she did for you*?" Merayal angrily interjects. "You mean you didn't feel any of that?"

"I felt my blood becoming weaker. But no... I did not truly feel the blade inside me. Twigg is very talented."

"T'anks, Scouty me sam!" Twigg shouts from the back of the room. She jumps, clicks her feet together in the air, and bows, her eyepatch bouncing.

"This is ridiculous!" Merayal exclaims. "I can't do this *and* memorize the choreography for all the dances as well!"

"About that, you need not worry. Allerish, our choreographer, has a Puppet Gift and can guide your steps until you know it fully." Calling on his Suus, Scout brings up our act to appear before Merayal as a translucent replica. I see her, myself, and Sedwick. As Scout speaks, the holograms act out his words.

"Now, as I was saying, you will open yourself up, exposing first your lungs, and then you will bring forth your heart. To the audience, however, it will look like Pypen is the one doing the work."

"You think I'm going to stand naked in front of all those people?" Merayal snorts.

"Just watch," Scout assures her.

My lucent figure is dramatic as he pretends to extract the see-through Merayal's heart. Her dress tears from her collar down her chest until it gets to her waist, where it stops. Then, just her heart pulls through the exposed skin, but her clothes otherwise stay perfectly in place to keep all private areas covered.

"He will then 'extract' the virus from you," Scout goes on. "Once Sedwick is completely out, Pypen will put you back together. Your performance will be the main event. Never before has a live, beating heart been part of an act on a stage. We are calling this tour 'The Virus of the Soul.'" Scout finishes his speech with a triumphant smile as the limpid figures disappear.

He takes in Merayal's pale face. Walking towards her, he places his hands on top of her shoulders. "Will you do it? Or have we misplaced our assurance?"

I steal a glance at the prancing lion tattoo on my wrist, and I smile at its blue color. Scout is happy with his work. I look back across to Merayal.

Chin jutting, she pushes Scout's hands away. Determined eyes narrowing, she steps towards him, putting her face only centimeters from his. "I can do it."

Lightly tapping her cheek, Scout smiles mischievously. "Let us see it, then."

Scout and I jump off the stage, and I whisper to him, "She might be able to do the extracting, but how can she pull off Caedis?"

"She can do it; it will just take practice."

He is ever full of confidence.

"There is so much... softness and vulnerability to Caedis' character, though. How will Merayal pull it off with a face like *that*?"

Scout chuckles as he watches Merayal scowling at Sedwick.

"At this point, we have no other options." Addressing the room, he declares,

"Let us start with Act Two, Scene One. It is one of the most pivotal scenes. I need Pypen and Merayal on stage; Scotsky and Dommy on deck." To Merayal, he reiterates, "Allerish will help you with your moves until you're more comfortable."

She nods.

A recording of Gigi, Ryder, and Veeter's voices echoes throughout the room. When my cue hits, I walk on stage and quite literally stop in my tracks at the look on Merayal's face.

She loves me.

I have never truly seen any woman look at me like that, but I have seen the expression enough to know that only lovers gaze at one another in this fashion. Why is she looking at me like that?

"Pypen? Levels balanced?" Scout asks from the front row.

The expression leaves Merayal's face as quickly as paint being washed from an easel. Her countenance of total dislike jolts me back to reality.

I realize I am frozen, and I stretch my shoulders back. "Let us start from the top," I mutter and walk back to my starting position.

The music queues, and I turn to Merayal once more. This time I am marginally more prepared for how she will look at me.

She loves me.

No, she does *not*. This is Act Two, Scene One. This is her character, Caedis, looking at my character, Retter. In this scene, Caedis is possessed by the virus and needs healing love. Retter is the one who loves her.

"What freezes your cells so, Pypen?" Scout asks.

I did not realize I had stopped once more. "I am well," I tell Scout. "Once more. I am ready."

As we practice, we have to restart scenes twice more because Merayal's acting is so real I cannot move. Thankfully, she fumbles several times, and we must also start again on her account. I am increasingly astonished at how she can go from having nothing but loathing for me before each scene begins, to exuding total infatuation and rapture as we rehearse.

There was zero exaggeration when she guaranteed we would not be disappointed with her acting skills.

After Scout is satisfied with our practice, he has me rest and calls up Sedwick to practice Act One, Scene Three with Merayal.

"She is brilliant," I murmur softly.

I watch from the front row as her face portrays such genuine sadness, I have to grip the sides of my chair so as not to walk on stage and wrap my arms around her.

I would call myself a good actor, but I am in awe of how Merayal can so thoroughly transform her emotions, facial expressions, and even mannerisms to take on the character she is playing. I know not how she can completely turn herself off and immerse herself into another's psyche. At the least, I know I can accomplish a feat during a performance—but this is just *practice*. "She is brilliant," I say again.

"You are not too bad yourself," Scout says beside me.

I had not noticed him join me. "Yes, but this is a talent like we have never seen before." I cannot take my eyes off her.

"What was wrong with you at the beginning of rehearsal?" he asks.

"Merayal. I was quite shocked by her performance."

He laughs lightly. "I was more shocked by your reaction, but yes—she seems to be a completely different person when performing."

I laugh and shake my head. "*Matza*, Scout, even Cazney never looked at me like that."

We rarely talk about our deceased mates, and an honored silence lingers between us.

As the scene comes to an end, Scout stands. "Well done," he comments to Sedwick and Merayal. "You both did an astounding job on that take." He commands his Suus to show him a document. "Up next," he yells so everyone in the tent can hear him, "we will be practicing Act Two, Scene Four. We need Pypen, Merayal, and Sedwick on stage; Twigg, Scotsky, and Dommy on deck."

"Forget not the engagement," I say as I jump up onto the stage.

"The engagement?"

I scoff affectionately at him. "Yes, Scout Eekan. The engagement where we are being honored this night."

"Oh yes, yes. I did not forget... I temporarily misplaced the information." I laugh. "Indeed."

When we are all where we should be, Scout clears his throat. "I know this has been a long day, but let us just practice this scene, and then we can be done."

The first half of the practice goes perfectly, but our performances spiral as we move into the second half. After a half-hour of mistakes, miscommunications, and Merayal throwing a vase across the stage, we are all upset.

"Pypen," Scout shouts from the front row, "I want more emotion as you extract—Sedwick, take a break—you keep breaking form. How are you feeling, Merayal, any pain?—Twigg! Please, pay attention, Pet! Scotsky, keep them level;

Pypen is hovering slightly lower than Merayal... no, *Pypen* is lower... No! Ugh, everyone take five, yes?"

Scotsky lowers us to the ground. His slender frame shakes from his efforts, and sweat pours down his freckled forehead onto his shirt. I quickly renew him, and he throws me a genuine thanks. I make my way to Scout. He rubs his hands through his hair.

"It is going to work," I voice.

"I know. I just wish we had more time. This is cutting too close to the artery, it is," he speaks in a Formosian accent, a small smile reaching his face.

"What do you think a 'bullet' is?" I ask Scout the question that has been lurking at the back of my mind all day.

"Maybe some tree or bush? Merayal said she had to extract it from someone's leg."

Twigg approaches us and asks, "Are we all goin' ter ta Initium House of Worship teright? Or are we visiting t'ose from our hometowns?"

"Whatever you wish," I answer. "We have no preference this night, correct?"

When I turn to look at Scout, his whole body is frozen tight. His eyes dart back and forth like he is intensely listening to something.

"What is wrong?" I ask.

"Oh," he mutters and meets my gaze for a moment. "I am—'tis nothing."

When I look at the prancing lion tattoo and see it pulsating orange, I look back at him warily. "Why are you lying?"

Distracted, he answers, "I am headed to our office for my nap. I will be back in forty-five minutes." Suddenly, his eyes widen, and he starts running for the circular door that leads out of the main room. "Keep up rehearsals!" he shouts over his shoulder.

Although I know Scout will eventually tell me what is going on, it does irk me greatly when he keeps me in the dark like this. Turning back to the group, I start organizing Act Two, Scene Three. Just as everyone I need is finally assembled on stage, the circus door bangs open.

I look up to see Scout barreling back inside, shouting my name.

Jumping off the stage, I run to meet him. "What is it?" I ask.

When he reaches me, he is out of breath. "They have been arrested," he gasps.

"Who?"

His eyes meet mine, and I am surprised at the fear in them. "Kansis and the daughter," he whispers. "The Guardians have taken them."

Mundus Senex

Amelia

633 years ago; 2088

NEVER IN THE HISTORY of the Mountain School has anyone ever exceeded negative one thousand points or had to write more than one thousand lines.

But standing at minus three thousand, four hundred and fifty points, and two thousand, two hundred and fifty-five lines, Amelia is always one to break records.

The last two months have gone precisely as Amelia intended. She set a tone of disrespect, rebellion, and drama, easily gaining a following among the other girls. Very quickly, they became willing to cater to her, assist in her pranks, and even break the rules for her. Within two months, she has almost the entire school following her lead.

A few girls, namely Estephania—Amelia's *buddy*—and a couple of her friends, do not follow Amelia's new regime. Estephania hates Amelia and does everything she can to make her life harder at the Mountain. Thankfully, the Latin girl and her friends are in higher levels, so they are not around the group as much.

Amelia is therefore left with plenty of time to woo the junior girls to her side. She overhears several staff talking about how her presence has changed the school's culture, and she smiles to herself. Strategically, she lets herself cry in front of two of the female staff. They are so easy to break. Everyone except Miss Brimer, that is. There is something all-knowing in her brown eyes, and whenever Amelia is manipulating staff or students around her, the teacher always seems a step ahead of her.

The staff have a bet waging on who will win the battles of wills between Miss Brimer and Amelia. Never before has a student been so clever in rebellion, so manipulative in disrespect, nor has any staff member stood so uncompromised in patience, so determined in discipline.

Amelia has walked the perfect line between participating just enough not to get expelled and being disobedient enough to show that she is not completing the program, even though she is *in* the program. She refuses to do schoolwork, and the only chore she takes part in is farm duty once a week from ten to eleven, cleaning out the farm animals' pens and feeding them their breakfast.

As May approaches, Amelia has to decide for whom she will perform her "final breakdown". If Miss Brimer were not so annoyingly intuitive, Amelia would pick her as the obvious choice. She is the leader of leaders with the most power and say in the program—she would have been perfect. However, Miss Brimer seems to be the only one who doesn't want to warm up to Amelia, so she's off the list.

There are a few other contenders—staff who are well-liked and admired—but none stand out.

It isn't until after the first of spring that Amelia makes up her mind.

Across the campus—off-limits to the girls—is the boys' side of the program. From what Amelia can gather, it operates just like the girls' side of the Mountain. Several staff work at both programs, so there are male and female leaders in each. The head of the boy's program is an Australian man, Mr. Ari.

The tall, kind-faced man wears his dark brown hair in military-type fashion, and his clothes are always semi-formal. His laugh is easy, and everyone—other staff included—respects him. From the bits and pieces of conversation she's eavesdropped on, he is a pretty big deal at the military academy, although she doesn't know why.

It takes her a couple of weeks to track his schedule and whereabouts and to ascertain his responsibilities whenever he visits the girls' side of the mountain. After another six days of careful planning, Amelia is ready.

On the day of her proposed meltdown, she spends the morning as she usually does, causing disturbances in math class. Quickly, Amelia finds herself standing in an abandoned classroom (abandoned because Amelia wouldn't stop throwing pens at the other students), rolling her eyes at Miss Brimer who sits calmly at one of the desks. Miss Brimer has just finished another lecture on respect.

"Yeah, you said the same thing yesterday," Amelia yawns as Miss Brimer finishes.

The woman studies Amelia for a moment. Her expression is not exasperated as it should have been, but calculating. "Let me ask you something, Amelia:

if a student were to get zero percent on a multiple-choice test, what does that tell you?"

"That they're an idiot."

"Humor me. What does it reveal about the person?"

As if she can't help but take on the challenge, Amelia thinks for a moment and then answers, "They wanted to fail."

"Why?"

"Because even guessing at all the answers, statistically they should have gotten at least some of them right."

Miss Brimer nods her head in approval. "Exactly. That person went into the test with a plan. A bad plan, but a plan nonetheless. Which brings me to my next question: is failing seventh grade a part of *your* plan?"

Leaning casually back against the dry-erase board, Amelia asks with a sarcastic smile, "My plan? Whatever are you talking about, Miss Brimer?"

Not goaded by her disrespect, Miss Brimer explains coolly, "You are a girl on a mission. Every step you've taken has been strategic, from the moment you arrived here. So, I wonder: Is failing middle school a part of your grand plan? Or is it just a necessary byproduct of your calculated rebellion?"

Even though it's only for the space of a blink, Amelia's surprised face betrays her. Trying to cover it up, she answers rudely, "Failing seventh grade is just a perk of this amazing facility you have here."

Unfazed, Miss Brimer asks, "Did your master plan include getting out of here anytime soon? Because, as of now, there's no way for you to graduate the program until March of 2090."

Again, Amelia only just catches her expression in time. "But that's two years away."

Miss Brimer's brows rise, and she clicks her tongue. "So, you know a little math, at least."

That can't be right. Amelia doesn't want to give in to Miss Brimer's words, but is it true? "That's impossible," Amelia bites. "I'm getting out of here in six months."

"You *could have* gotten out of here in six months," Miss Brimer argues. "But your disrespectful and disobedient antics will cost you a year and a half of extra time spent here."

Amelia stops trying to hide her expression. "That's not happening," she says darkly.

"So, you didn't have all the facts before you got here?" Miss Brimer mocks her. "Then let me give them to you now. When we give you lines and take away points, that adds extra days to your time. When you don't do schoolwork and chores, that adds extra days to your time. When you disrespect or are disobedient to your leaders or the girls in levels above you, that adds extra days to your time."

Amelia is too shocked to respond.

"I don't know where you're at in your plan to escape, but next time make sure you calculate all the risks. Especially when a timeframe is involved."

"I'm not staying here for two years," Amelia shouts. "I want to call my dad, *now*!"

"Your father can't come to save you," Miss Brimer responds calmly. "You made choices, and there are consequences."

"I want to speak to him!" Amelia yells.

"Your temper tantrum isn't going to get you what you want. But do you know what *can* get you out of here? Completing the program."

Tears fall down Amelia's face as she screams, "You can't make me do anything!"

"I don't plan on it," Miss Brimer answers evenly. "You're the only one that can make yourself work through the program and get yourself out of here. Only *you*. You are completely responsible for yourself."

A knocking sound draws both females to look toward the door.

It's Mr. Ari.

"Hi, Ari," Miss Brimer states, her tone changing completely. "Sorry I missed our meeting."

"I figured something important had come up," he responds, and Amelia enjoys his Australian accent, despite her burning anger. "It's no bother; I just wanted to pop in and say a quick farewell."

Seeing this as a potential golden opportunity, Amelia shouts, "Miss Brimer is making me stay for eighteen more months!"

If she pushes, maybe Mr. Ari will try to console her. Then she can finally have her breakdown moment.

Mr. Ari laughs lightly. "Miss Brimer is doing it, eh? You didn't have anything to do with it of course, did you?"

"She doesn't understand me at all!" Amelia moans dramatically. "She's just trying to make this harder for me!"

Ari looks around the classroom. He takes a deep breath as if he's enjoying the taste of the air. "Did you know this school lies on a one-hundred-acre piece of property?" he asks. "Yup, we were gifted the land by a patron who, when he was a younger man, had a daughter in this very program. He believes in the school, the staff, and especially in Miss Brimer who has been caring for girls who have come here for the last twenty years."

"Ari, please—" Miss Brimer starts as Amelia responds, "You're old, Miss Brimer."

Mr. Ari laughs. "Forty-five probably seems ancient to you, but Miss Brimer is still very young, in the grand scheme of things. Did you know she was in the program at the same time as our patron's daughter?"

"Miss Brimer was in this program?" Amelia asks incredulously, staring at the unamused woman.

Seating himself on one of the desks, Mr. Ari continues cheerfully, "Indeed. She and Brittany—the patron's daughter—were rebellious for about six months, racking up for themselves another two and a half years here. Then, one day, they decided to unite and do the program right. They had planned to finish school and then return to their lives of juvenile delinquency, but the program changed them. They learned integrity, empathy, hard work ethic, and loyalty. They went to the military together once they graduated."

Amelia's teacher leans against one of the desks, seemingly surprised at Mr. Ari's knowledge of her history.

"Miss Brimer and Brittany fought together in the Dark War, the Europe and India War, and for a short stint they served in the Australian Wars," Mr. Ari goes on. "But Brittany died in Australia during their eighth year of service."

Miss Brimer's head bows silently, but Amelia keeps her eyes on Mr. Ari.

"Miss Brimer never really got over Brittany's death," he says softly.

Amelia sneaks a peek at her teacher, but the woman doesn't meet her gaze.

"She was honorably discharged and returned to Oregon to start the Casey Military Academy, for girls and boys who graduate from this program. Miss Brimer cares about kids like you because she *was* a kid like you."

Jackpot. With such little guidance, Mr. Ari has fallen perfectly into her plan.

The man crosses his arms and studies her for a moment. "Amelia, we want to empower you to—"

Putting on her best angry voice, she declares, "I don't need you to empower me. I have all the empowerment I need!"

"Do you?" Ari asks simply. He's not arguing; he's not even challenging. Amelia knows he's really asking her the question.

"From the time I can remember, I've always gotten what I've wanted," Amelia recites. "I almost always win. I'm strong enough, smart enough, and patient enough. And what I still need, I'm on a path right now to get. Once I have it, I'll be invincible."

"But right now, you're not invincible?"

Amelia rolls her eyes theatrically. "Whatever, Mr. Ari."

"I'm being serious," he pushes. "I want to grasp what you're saying." His kind eyes meet Amelia's, and he asks with genuine curiosity and care. "What will you gain that will make you invincible?"

Amelia almost smiles. This was too easy. Turning her face away, she shakes her head. "Never mind."

"Help me understand, Amelia."

Amelia cracks her neck and clenches her jaw.

Mr. Ari waits until her eyes find his. "Please," he says simply.

Taking a deep breath, she answers through her exhale, "I will get the strength I need to win every time."

"From physical threats, do you mean? Or are you talking mental, emotional, and spiritual as well?"

"All of them." She makes her face screw up with wrath and causes her eyes to grow distant. "I will keep everyone beneath me."

"So strength is the ability to dominate others?" Ari asks.

Amelia scoffs as her gaze snaps back into focus. "Is there another kind?"

"I think so."

Amelia rolls her eyes. "Ah, yes, the strength of *Jesus*. Let yourself be walked on and spit on, and all that turn-the-other-cheek crap. Look, Jesus had the strength to rise from the dead, so we're not really in the same league." As if the thought has just struck her, she adds, "And, he did have the strength to dominate others. He just didn't do it."

Ari raises his brows and smiles. "Now, isn't that interesting?"

"No, it's not," she pouts. "I'm not like the other girls; you're not going to trap me in some religious conversation where I suddenly realize I need to be saved. I don't need Jesus, you, Miss Brimer, or anyone else. I'm going to win."

Just a few more leading statements, and she would let him break her—he was so close.

"And what will you be winning?" Mr. Ari asks.

"Everything!" she shouts passionately. "I'll finally be in charge of my own destiny, I'll do whatever I want, and I'll be able to protect myself!" She grabs her chest and whispers, "I'll keep me safe."

Giving in to the moment, she finally allows tears to form. The silence rings heavily, and she waits patiently. She could fill the space, she could overshare, but she stays still. Leaning into the adrenaline of the act, she allows herself to start shaking. He's going to take the bait—he has to. Any minute…

And then, just as she had predicted, Mr. Ari asks, "Safe from what?"

If she could, Amelia would laugh out loud. She would take a moment to enjoy this sweet victory. Instead, she covers her face. Hunching her shoulders, she surrenders to a desperate sob. She lets it rock through her, and as she expected, both Mr. Ari and Miss Brimer keep their distance. Through her tears, she stutters, "S-s-safe from *her*."

Amelia waits for Ari to ask who *her* is, but he surprises her by inquiring, "Is that why you don't participate in the program? Because you know that once you graduate, you'll have to go back?"

Feeling this is an odd way to steer the conversation, but knowing she can use it, Amelia answers, "Yeah, ex-exactly."

"In that case, mission accomplished. You will be here for a very long time." And he laughs.

Genuinely confused, Amelia looks up at the man. "What?"

"At the rate you're going, you'll be here until you graduate high school. So, you're right—you win. You'll be nice and safe in the Mountain for the next six years."

Shocked at the turn of events, she blurts out, "I'm not staying for the next six years."

"Of course you are," Mr. Ari responds with a smile.

"No, I'm leaving in the next couple of months," she pushes back, forgetting to weep.

"I don't think so. Didn't you already try running away?"

Embarrassment washes through her. This is not going the way she thought it would. Trying to salvage what she can from the conversation, she plays her final card: "Well, if I do stay, at least I won't be abused anymore!"

"That's the spirit!" Mr. Ari smiles triumphantly, and Amelia can't stop the shocked expression that floods her features. "No, graduating would be too scary," Mr. Ari goes on. "Becoming a functioning adult is much too difficult." Leaning in conspiratorially, he adds, "I think you've figured this place out. If you were to do the program, you would have to write lines all day long and pick up every extra chore possible. And you would have to keep it up for five or more months. You would have to be respectful, keep your mouth shut, and do everything the staff tell you to do. And even if you did finish this program—which would take at least two years now—you would still have to attend military school. May as well give up and keep doing whatever you want, right?"

Standing, Mr. Ari shakes his head. "Giving in to this," he gestures to the whole Mountain, "would mean that we won. And you just said that *you* were going to win. What you're currently doing is definitely winning. When I find a medal, I'll make sure I get it to you."

Amelia clenches her jaw and fists; every muscle in her whole body pulls taut with rage and humiliation. She stares at the two adults furiously. She knows this is reverse psychology, knows her show has not been successful, and she knows they have won this round. But she has no idea what to say or do next.

She's never been bested like this before.

As if reading her thoughts, Mr. Ari finishes, "We all have weapons, Amelia. Don't use your trauma as one. We want you to be free from your past, not enslaved to it. And if you are brave enough, we'd like to help."

THAT NIGHT, AMELIA LIES in bed staring up at the dust-covered spider web that sways in the fan's soft breeze. Having rarely lost, Amelia finds the taste particularly bitter. How had Mr. Ari known she was being manipulative? Had she given something away? Over and over she replays the interaction in her head, but she keeps coming to the same conclusion: No. She had done everything right—perfectly, even.

Turning onto her side, she forces her eyes closed. It doesn't matter. Mr. Ari was the victor today, but she will win in the end. And that's all that matters.

THE FOLLOWING DAY, AMELIA surprises everyone by showing up for kitchen duty. She's told by Adoette, a plump Native American woman, that all she needs to do is stand behind the counter and help serve breakfast.

As Amelia pours gravy onto plates of biscuits, she gathers tidbits of conversations around her. When she hears, "Go to the back of the line right now," she isn't surprised to see it's Estephania, her *buddy*, talking.

Then Amelia looks to see who Estephania is commanding. Lily, a girl in Level B, stands with her head down, pretending she hasn't heard the intimidation.

"I said, *get to the back of the line*," Estephania seethes. "You're going to regret it if you disobey me."

Amelia looks around to see if Adoette, the kitchen staff member, has heard Estephania's threats, but Adoette is saying hello to a group of girls at the beginning of the line.

Amelia skips Estephania, places three biscuits on Lily's plate, and quickly pours gravy over the lot. "Looks like she can't go to the back," Amelia states.

Estephania glowers at her. "You're going to regret—"

Before she can finish, Amelia flicks a ladle full of gravy in Estephania's face.

Estephania's screams echo throughout the dining hall as Miss Brimer shouts at Amelia, "Go to the offices, now!"

"Sorry," Amelia mouths to her buddy, who immediately tries to punch her in the face. One of the staff grabs Estephania and restrains her, as Amelia puts down her utensils and obeys Miss Brimer's order. As she passes Lily, she winks.

Lily tentatively smiles back.

AMELIA AND LILY CAN'T actually talk to each other as they're both in lower levels, so they resort to other means of communication. When Amelia opened her feelings journal, she found a note from Lily that said, "Thank you for the biscuits." That afternoon, Amelia left an extra apple in Lily's desk.

After her disastrous showdown with Miss Brimer and Mr. Ari, Amelia begins to obey the rules of the Mountain. Although it wasn't the breakdown she had planned, she uses it nonetheless as the catalyst for her reform.

She decides to get on with her lines and spends every spare moment she has writing. To help her along, three or four pages of lines show up under her pillow every couple of days, written in a script much like her own.

Lily.

After the gravy debacle, it becomes Estephania's goal in life to make Amelia miserable. Half the girls want to be on Estephania's good side, and they gladly join in on the heckling, the pranks, and the attacks. Estephania even has three of the girls jump Amelia while she is in bed to beat her up. The scant followers Amelia has amassed in her time at the Mountain abandon her, too scared of Estephania to go against her. Lily is the only one on her side.

At the second three-week mark, Miss Brimer tells Amelia that she is still negative in points, but if she proves herself in the coming three weeks, she will forgive the girl a portion of her points debt.

Amelia doesn't mess up even once. Even when she stands up for the other girls who are being bullied by Estephania and her crew, Amelia does so in a way that breaks no rules.

After three weeks, she's back in the positive. In another twenty-one days, she has crawled up to Level B. With Lily helping with lines, almost half are now written. Amelia's silence and respect gain her further points, and after another three weeks, she's in Level C.

Then one Wednesday, just days before Amelia is due to level up to D, Miss Brimer addresses the school.

"This afternoon, we will have a game of Capture the Flag. I've never done this with you before, but we're doing it today. Estephania and Amelia will be the team captains. We will meet on the field at three o'clock, and they will pick their teams. This will be the only time everyone can speak to each other, no matter your level. The winning team gets dessert."

Lily and Amelia exchange excited looks across the table. Their notes to each other have become full-page letters that they've strategically hidden about the campus. After breakfast, Amelia finds Lily's abnormally short note on the archaic DVD shelves between the classic *Never Been Kissed* and the newer *Toy Story 9*.

Hey Biscuit,
You don't have to pick me for the game, just so you know. I know
I'm not the fastest, and I hear the dessert is angel food cake. I
don't want you to think there will be any hard feelings.
–Pad

That afternoon, the whole school gathers on the field. Miss Brimer has lined up all the girls, with Amelia and Estephania facing them. Estephania goes first and chooses her closest sidekick, Renee. Amelia chooses Lily. Estephania chooses another best friend, Christine. Amelia chooses Gardenia, a small, ten-year-old girl. Estephania chooses all the athletic, tall, strong girls; Amelia strategically chooses all the outcasts.

Once all the girls have been picked, Amelia's team walks to the northern part of the field while Estephania takes the south.

Amelia huddles her group around her. "Okay, Everyone. I chose all of you for a reason, and it has little to do with Capture the Flag—this is my one opportunity to talk." She takes a deep breath. "How many of you have been bullied by Estephania, Renee, or their trolls?"

Nobody raises their hand until Lily slowly does. Then most of the girls follow suit.

"This doesn't have anything to do with the game," a girl named Ellyn comments. "I'm going to tell Miss Brimer."

"You do that," Amelia snaps and gives her attention back to the rest of the girls. "Listen, none of you have to put up with how they treat you. If we all silently stand up against them, they'll have no one to pick on. We have to have each other's backs, and I want each of you to know that I have yours."

She looks down the field at Estephania's team who have already lined up, ready to start.

"Now, we're definitely not going to win if we take the offensive. Instead, every single one of us will stay on defense. Once all of their fastest girls are in our jail, then a few of us can attempt contact. We're probably not going to beat them, but that's not the point of this. Who cares about dessert? Yes, we'll lose, but we're going to lose together. This is about us being a team; it's about showing those girls that we're not going to let them bully us anymore." She smiles at the group. "You ready to have some fun?"

The girls cheer and hurry to line up.

At first, Estephania's team jeers at Amelia's for not making any bold advancements. They holler and shout insults, but Amelia's team stays steady, protecting their flag. After a few minutes, four girls from the southern team cross the line. Each one is tagged before they can get into the safety of the flag zone.

Estephania frowns. Then she walks up to the boundary line and shouts at Amelia's team of underdogs, "Run across the line. All of you. Now." She smiles grossly. "Or I'll make sure you regret it."

Four girls, led by Ellyn, run across and get tagged, but Amelia is proud to see the rest of them stay put. They look across to her, and she looks past Estephania as if she isn't there, staying strong. The game drags on, and more girls from Estephania's team trickle across, trying to get into the flag zone, but one by one they get tagged. Only once half of the other team is in jail, do Amelia, Lily, and five other girls run for the safe flag zone on the other side. Only Amelia and Lily make it.

"I'm going to distract them and run as fast as I can," Amelia whispers to Lily. "By the time they realize I don't have the flag, hopefully you'll have made it back to base." She grips Lily's shoulder. "I believe in you."

A smile fills Lily's small features, and she nods. Without looking back, Amelia pretends to take the flag from Lily. Then she takes off down the far side of the field, running as fast as she can and yelling—for reasons she cannot explain there or later— "For blood!"

The remaining members of Estephania's team hurtle after Amelia. So eager are they to take her down, they don't realize she is empty-handed, and eventually, they tackle her to the ground. As they start looking about frantically for the flag, Amelia shoves all the bodies off of her and looks expectantly towards the northern side. Lily is jumping up and down victoriously, both flags waving in the air. Amelia whoops and runs over to Miss Brimer, leaving Estephania's team in shock behind her.

"Can we play just one more game?" she asks Miss Brimer. "Please?"

"Why?" Miss Brimer asks curiously.

For the first time since arriving, Amelia says something honest. "It's for the girls."

As if she senses her sincerity, Miss Brimer slowly answers, "All right. One more game."

Amelia returns to her team. This time she tells them they will all walk across the boundary line together.

"But we'll all get tagged," Lily says, voicing the groups' collective thoughts.

"Trust me," Amelia says with a smile.

The game starts, and Amelia's team does exactly as she says. Predictably, each one is tagged and sent to jail. Estephania half-heartedly walks across the field to collect their flag and drags it back.

Loud enough so that all can hear, Amelia calls out, "Miss Brimer, you said the winning team would get dessert. Technically, it was a tie. So… could we all have dessert tonight? Everyone played really well."

For the first time since meeting her, Amelia watches Miss Brimer's lips twitch into a small smile. "That sounds fair."

Pexus

Kansis

*K*ANSIS*! K*ANSIS*! W*AKE UP*, talk to me... are you there? Kansis? Hello? KANSIS!*

Ontzi... stop yelling... where am I? Am I sleeping?

You were knocked out.

I was?

Yes.

By whom?

I was hoping you'd tell me.

I don't know what happened... I was with Amelia and Aker and... and this other man...

Emerly.

Yes... Emerly... How did you know that?

I'm trying to search your memories for what happened, and it is all jumbled. But I found that name.

Oh... okay...

...

...

Stay with me! Kansis! Kansis, talk to me!

I'm here... My head hurts really bad...

Who took you? Can you remember anything?

Stop being so loud! *Onzi...* Okay... Um... Amelia found a Senny she knew... she chased him... I chased her... we found an Ortusan... They're coming to the circus, which is nice, I guess. And then... Oh, wait... Oh, I remember! There were Guardians.

Guardians?

Yes.

What did they want?

I don't know. She called us criminals, and then everything hurt, and now I'm here.

Do you have any idea where they took you?

None. What am I supposed to do? Can you contact Scout, my Protector?

I don't know how this all works, but I'll try. It would be so much easier if you knew where you were...

How can you not know how this works? *You're* the one who's contacting people! Which reminds me, I know this is not the time, but are you aware that you've been talking to the Sixth Aevum? Like *the* Sixth Aevum?

The Sixth Aevum? That's news to me too.

Okay, I'm not sure I believe you, but more on that later. For now, what should I do when I wake up? How can I protect Amelia? Any Guardian with even a hint of a Mind Reading Gift will immediately know she's subhuman.

Create a distraction for as long as you can.

What kind of distraction?

A big one.

...

...What?

What if I die?

You're not going to.

Yeah, but what if I do?

You won't.

It won't matter either way, I suppose.

Really? You know, this might be bad timing for a pity party. Could we reschedule it for another occasion?

You know it's true. Nobody will care if I die.

I would care.

That's because you would die too.

So the party of pity has no end, I see. Either way, I'll find your Protector and send him. I will save you, Kansis.

I believe that.

And now sarcasm?

No, I'm serious. I trust you. You're the only person in the entire world that I know I can rely on. You know, using the word "person" loosely over here.

I love you too. Now, it is time to wake up. Wake up, Kansis...

"That was unexpectedly quick," a voice says nearby.

With effort, I make my heavy eyelids slowly rise. The Guardian with the dull grey braid sits on a wooden chair below me. We're in a dark room—at least, I think it's a room, but I see no walls— and my feet feel wet and cold. When I try to look down, I realize my whole body is frozen, suspended in the air. I can't move or speak. As much as I can, I look around using my peripherals, but all I see are dark shadows. Finally, I let my eyes return to the woman watching me.

"It usually takes another half hour or so for the poison to subside," the Guardian comments. "You must have a strong mind." The woman purses her lips as if trying to keep herself from smiling. She even coughs, covering her mouth with her hand. But I can see past it; she has a genuinely happy grin plastered across her wrinkled face. Meeting my eyes, she laughs. "I'm so sorry. This is completely unprofessional. I should be eliciting information from you—completing my job efficiently. But can I tell you something?"

The woman leans in and smiles again. The joy on her features makes her look young. "This is the last time I ever have to do this menial job. This is my very last field operation, and it was one of my fastest missions. I must thank you for being so easy to find and apprehend. All I need is your story, and I'm done. Getting promoted, you see.

"As you know, Chiefs get twenty-five extra years of life. Well, Dewdrop, after this little conversation, I will be the Chief Guardian of Demerkin." The woman beams, then puts her hand over her mouth again as if to wipe the smile away. "Listen to me ranting on and on about my good fortune like a young girl. I'm here to hear your story. So *speak*."

My mouth opens, and words come rushing out without my consent. "My name is Kansis Willow from Depalo, Pexus. I work at the Ward, and I found—"

With all my effort, I force my mouth closed and systematically shut down my conscious mind. If I'm going to keep her out, I need to get to my Mind Castle before she does. Must... be... first...

I KNOW MY CONSCIOUS mind is completely shut down when I find myself standing in the middle of a thick, overgrown forest. And I don't say 'overgrown' lightly. I'm surrounded by trees so tall I can't see the tops, with felled trees and slash littering the ground so thickly I can't see the earth. I don't take many opportunities to visit my psyche, and I see now that maybe I should do so more often. It could do with some maintenance. I waste only a second to take this all in before I start running.

As I climb over a fallen tree almost as tall as me, the ground shakes, causing the tree to throw me off like a bull bucking a rider.

She's here.

Her laughter seems to ride the wind as it whistles through the trees' leaves.

All I have to do is get to my Mind Castle. Once I'm there, it will be almost impossible for her to come in. I could never have afforded a Mind Castle on my own, but the Ward paid for me to have one installed during my training. We don't need that kind of safety precaution for our job, given we are working with subhuman Pods; it's just a well-being assurance benefit. Given I've never had a real-life experience where I needed to use the Castle, I have only ever used it for practice simulations. It has been so long since I've sought shelter there, I can't quite remember the way.

"Now, now. Let's not waste time," the Guardian coos. Her voice is muffled as if through water—as if it's coming with a storm. Lightning strikes a molting log near my leg, inciting a fire. Her voice thunders, "I have a party to get to."

I know the fire isn't real, but the pain licking up my leg feels real enough.

Quickly, I grab moss and leaves to put out the flames, and my skin smokes black where the heat has burned through my leggings.

I can feel her getting closer like the electrical field of an approaching lightning storm. Faster than I thought possible, I flee through the woods.

Pain shoots through my legs and up through my heart. More lightning strikes and the heat of it burns the skin on my side, arm, and face. It's so painful my eyes blur with tears and I cannot see where I'm running. Sobbing, I fall to the ground.

How do I fight back? I remember being taught mind self-defense classes, but I always assumed I was not important enough to have anyone try and attack me in my mind, so I didn't listen. Well, joke's on me!

After clearing my one good eye of smoke, I haul myself up and force my legs to run again. There's a chance I could procure a wall, but it's been so long since I've practiced, and I'm sure she'd know how to get over it. What about a barricade? I was always better—

Wait! There it is!

The trees have thinned, and I can see my Mind Castle across a meadow at the end of the woods. Although it's more of an A-frame cabin, its technical name is Mind Castle. No one can penetrate it. Well, except for someone with a Red Gift, I suppose. But it's not like people with Red Gifts are just walking around Elusis. I push my psyche's body towards the meadow.

The pain in my face and leg is excruciating. I don't know if I can go on, even as close as I am. What's the worst that could happen if they catch me?

They would find out about Amelia, take her to a PTS, and force her dad's location from her.

I have to go on. I have to do this.

For Amelia.

I gulp in deep breaths and will my body to run faster. As I crest the last mound of felled trees, emerging into the meadow, I almost cry with relief. I had forgotten about my sentinels! Three giant boulders stand erect in the field. Over thirty meters tall and made of razor-sharp stones, these rock guards should keep me safe. Their password flies from my lips like a trumpet shout: "Protect and defend your home!"

The guards come alive, their rocky joints cracking into shape. As their legs and feet gain form, they begin lumbering towards the forest, a deep, rumbling cry emerging from their beings. Each step they take is like a mini-earthquake beneath my feet.

Lightning strikes. Thunder booms. The wind chimes loudly, "You brought toys? What fun."

Suddenly the earthquakes stop, and I give myself just one glance back. My sentinels have stopped at the tree line. Their boulder heads swivel back towards me. My one glance turns into a horrified stare as their rock bodies turn and begin chasing after me.

"Your toys like me now," the trees laugh.

I stumble and catch myself, returning my focus to my goal. I'm so close. So, so close. If I could just run faster... a little faster...

The clouds above me darken as if it is almost night. The thunder is so loud I have to cover my ears. But what's this? What is this... fog? Even though I'm only thirty meters away, my Mind Castle is suddenly covered with fog so thick I can't see it.

Well, I don't care if I run face-first into the door. I'm not stopping.

When my feet hit the front steps, I fly forward and smack my nose into the wall of the A-frame.

I know I said I was willing to do it, but I hadn't considered the actual pain of breaking my face.

Weeping at the combined agony of the burns and now the smashing of my nose and cheek bones, I scour the wall until I find the door. Still unable to see, I grope around clumsily, desperate to find the handle. If I can find the handle, I can get inside—where is it?

"Foolish girl," the wind roars, whipping around my face. The fog becomes

smoke, filling my lungs with noxious gas. It's consuming me. I can't breathe. The Guardian's laughter fills my eyes, my nose, my ears, my mouth. "Looks like I won't be missing my party after all."

I OPEN MY EYES to see the Guardian looking nonplussed, still sitting in her wooden chair.

It takes me a moment to realize that I'm not burnt, my nose isn't broken, and I can, in fact, breathe. I take huge gulps of air and slowly hiss it out as she comments, "You're not very good at this, you know. That was one of the most pathetic escape attempts I've ever seen." The Guardian rises and walks towards me. She stands before me, staring as if studying a fascinating piece of art. Finally, she says, "Speak."

To my horror, I blurt out, "I found Arkarian Story's daughter."

One of her brows rises. "Did you really? Where is she now?"

"She's the Formosian girl you picked up."

The Guardian claps, delighted. "What a way to go out, don't you think? On my last mission, I find Arkarian Story's daughter. I could not be more blessed. I really couldn't. Thank you, Dewdrop."

At that moment, a humming noise begins. At first it seems distant, but then it starts throbbing in my ears.

Before the Guardian can say or do anything more, the wall behind her explodes.

At least, I think it explodes. Instead of a deafening boom, however, this sounds more like a loud crack. Pieces of the wall break apart, but instead of falling everywhere, the parts fly up to hang suspended in the air in organized patterns against the walls.

I don't remember falling, but I realize I'm on the floor. I pick myself up, but before I can step in any direction, my legs are kicked out from under me. The Guardian is suddenly on top of me, crushing my breath out of me. Her eyes are closed in deep concentration.

Through the haze of the debris, I make out two figures climbing through the hole the explosion has left in the wall.

My heart leaps when I see Scout's face. My subconscious got through to him! He searches the room, and when he sees me, rage fills his features. He is almost unrecognizable. When his average-sized frame comes barreling toward us, I almost feel bad for the Guardian.

Almost.

Above me, the Guardian's mouth is gaping open towards Scout. Her tongue is on the roof of her mouth and her jaw is tense, ready to shoot her poison. Her eyes are closed in focus. As she cocks her neck, ready to spit on Scout, I shove my hand as hard as I can up into her jaw. She bites her tongue so sharply that blood explodes from both sides of her mouth.

Her howl fills the echoing room as Scout hits her at a full-paced run. Her whole body seems to fly through the air in slow motion. When she lands, the facade breaks, and I see we're just in a cement cell, one wall half-exploded.

Scout looks down at me, relief flooding his face. He says nothing as he helps me up and takes my hand, leading me toward the hole in the wall.

Warm flames lick up my arm at his touch. I should let go… but I don't.

When we reach the other side, a female voice whispers, "We have thirty-seven seconds, Scouty." I turn around, and even though I know we're in a life-threatening position, I can't help but notice the Ortusan woman's purple eyelashes. They're like flashing feathers waving at me in the dim light.

She shuts her eyes, and I can feel her Gift ignite. It makes the hairs on my arms stand high. It vibrates throughout my whole being down to my bones. Using her Gift, Purple Eyelashes closes the hole. We're surrounded by darkness, in between the building's support beams. "Sing us out of here, Gigi," Scout commands.

"Where is Amelia?" I ask desperately.

"She is with the other rescue team," he whispers reassuringly as another high-pitched sound rings in my ears. A new hole opens in the wall behind us, and we run through it. The light hits my eyes painfully, but I can't stop as Scout pulls me along, our hands still intertwined. Gigi sings two more walls open, and the last one takes us outside. A Formosian woman stands waiting, anxiously rubbing her hands.

"Gigi! Scout! You're okay!" she exclaims, her face flooding with relief.

"Perfect placement, Winzer," Scout praises.

Several Guardians crash through the wall behind us, and I almost scream. But to my astonishment, they move straight past us.

The Guardian with the dull, grey braid races out of the front doors. Blood still oozes from her mouth. She closes her eyes and takes a deep breath like she's smelling something. Scout squeezes my hand gently, and I look back at him. His smirk is amused.

"Winzer is a Cloak," he explains, looking toward the Formosian woman. "A real one. The Guardians can neither smell, feel, taste, hear, nor see us. No Gifts can overpower hers as long as we are within two hundred and fifty meters of her."

Another Guardian walks up behind the one who interrogated me and clears her throat. "Deputy Chief Femme," the young Guardian starts, "We have lost all connection with them. Something has happened."

"I am aware," Femme says, wiping blood from her chin. "They have powerful friends, I see. Foolish creatures. Don't they know that nothing can stand against us?"

"So you're not upset?" the young Guardian asks. "Will you cancel your party tonight?"

I expect Femme to turn around and snap at the young Guardian, but instead she answers, "I suppose I'll have to, won't I, Sergeant Maxx? Now, let's go speak with Detective Mei. She loves a challenge."

As if sensing I'm still on high alert, Scout reassures me, "We are safe as long as we are next to Winzer."

"Nonetheless, we should get out of here, yes?" Winzer agrees. "I don't like risking it, do I?"

"You lead," Scout commands and points away from the Guardian Station.

As we start walking, I ask again, "Where is Amelia?"

"They are on their way back to the hotel," he answers. "We should arrive at the same time, I believe. Now, I must ask you. Why did you and Amelia leave your suite? I mind not this little saving escapade, but still, I must know, why?"

He doesn't seem upset, just curious, so I answer, "Amelia saw a man she knew from Senex through the teleskep in our room. She chased after him, and I chased after her. We wound up at a cafe where she talked to him for a minute. There was another Ortusan man, Knimble Knox, with the Senny, and he spoke with... I don't remember his name. But he's with your group, the mind reader..."

"Oh, Emerly?" Scout asks.

"Yes, him. Emerly and Knimble Knox talked about Arkahunters, and Emerly told Knimble Knox to come to the circus tonight."

"That is good news then," he says.

"Is Emerly okay?" I inquire. "Did he get rescued too?"

"He did," Scout answers. "We put together three teams to rescue you simultaneously." He scratches the back of his neck and looks at me from his peripherals. "You were courageous in there, Scoop."

It's not until he says this that I realize he's still holding my hand. I wriggle it free and wrap my arms around my waist.

"You have been through a lot today," Scout comments after a few blocks. "Do you need extra clothes? We can purchase you and Amelia new pieces."

Buy me new clothes? The pocket watch he gave me suddenly hangs heavy in my pocket. Who is this guy? "No, no," I answer quickly. "That's so nice of you even to offer that... But no, I brought clothes."

"If you need anything, please let me know. We can provide anything you require."

When I look up at him, he doesn't meet my eyes. "Why are you so kind to me?" I ask. "I don't... I don't understand. You don't know me. I'm a stranger to you, and you treat me... You act like..."

At this, he gazes down at me, but before our eyes meet, I glance away. "Like what?" he prompts.

"Like you *know* me."

He shrugs. "I know enough."

"How? How do you know anything about me?"

"The Sixth Aevum has shared..." he pauses. "He has shared some of your life with me. Information that you told him."

My feet move slower. Scout turns around and asks me something, but I don't hear him.

I'm sorry but—what? The Sixth Aevum told Scout stuff about me that my subconscious told him? Who am I that the Sixth Aevum would talk to my subconscious, let alone listen to facts about my life? And now Scout knows those things? What things? Does he know about Aker? But how could he know and not reject me?

"Levels balanced?" I finally hear Scout ask.

"Yeah, yeah, I'm fine."

Scout starts talking again, but I'm not listening. How can my subconscious not know she's talking to the Sixth Aevum? How can she not be aware of what she does when she's not with me? *What* is she? Scout comes back into my vision. What does he know?

"Are you sure you are well?" Scout asks.

"What has he told you?" I ask, ignoring his question. "What does she tell the Sixth Aevum? How do they talk?"

"Who is *she*?"

"My subconscious. How does she speak to the Sixth Aevum?"

"She?" he asks again, seeming very confused.

"Yes," I say a little rudely. "A voice in my head who only talks to me once

I've fallen asleep. She may be a Gift… probably is… but I've never had her checked out. Please, tell me: do you know how they talk?"

"I know not," he answers. "The Sixth Aevum has never given details."

"But she doesn't remember them talking. She knows nothing of their connection."

"Perhaps she has a subconscious as well," Scout muses, but I don't know if he's serious.

Impatient now, I ask, "Well, what has she told him?"

"Levels balanced, Scouty?" the redheaded woman named Winzer asks a few shop windows ahead of us.

"Indeed," he answers and starts walking again. I hurry to keep up. "Listen to me," he says. "I do not know as much about you as I would like, Kansis Willow, but what I do know is that you are special."

Blood rushes to my face until I'm burning with embarrassment. What is he even saying? "No, I'm not," I respond before I can stop myself.

"You are," he replies easily. "You are special to me."

This statement is so shocking that I stop walking again. He laughs and halts as well. Scout turns to face me. "You found Arkarian Story's daughter, Scoop. You were courageous enough to follow her and try to keep her safe. Those acts are exceptional."

"Stop," I say, unjustifiably upset at his words. "Stop it. You don't know me, Ortusan. I'm not any of those things that you're saying, and I don't appreciate you making out that I am. We're strangers. Please don't talk to me like we're friends. We're not."

"I can say whatever I want," he snaps, his eyes flashing with the same fire as is in mine. "You are special and brave, and I will say so if I wish."

He turns and walks away, not waiting for me to follow.

Pexus

Pypen

"**B**UT TO CLARIFY, YOU have not ever done this before?" I ask Thykas once more. "I just want to make certain you and I are entirely in the same vein."

Thykas winks at me. "We're ridin' ta same blood wave, me ol' sam."

"Worst-case scenarios," I muse. "One: We are imprisoned and sent to high-security blood reclamation dens. Two: Our Gifts are stripped. Three: We are somehow killed in your experiment."

"Ta Sixth Aevum will get us out of any tight spotsnsuch," Thykas responds easily. "Oi manipulate matter, right? So, it makes sense t'at Oi should be able ter move our matter from one place ter anot'er."

"And you have never once tried this previously?"

He shrugs his shoulders. "Oi have wit' non-human matter."

"And it was successful?"

Thykas clicks his tongue and moves his shoulders side to side as he answers, "Mostly. Most of ta time, aye."

"Well, that is better than most of the time *no*, I suppose." This is probably not the wisest decision I have ever made, but Scout said to hurry.

"If Oi may be so bold, Pip, t'at is very Scout of ye ter say. Normally ye aren't a risk-taker."

"Are you rescinding the offer now that I am confident in you?" I ask, amused.

"Not at all!" he answers, offended. "Oi'm just sayin' t'at Scout is wearin' off on ye."

"This situation is quite the tourniquet, therefore risks need to be taken. Remember, once we are in the interrogation room, we have less than a minute to recover the Formosian woman. After that, we will be unable to ward off the quantity of Guardians present."

I look at my wrist, which displays the time—one minute to go.

Thykas scratches his beard (which now looks like an octopus crawling up his face) and asks warily, "And yer contact made sure ta interrogation room's security system has been turned off, aye? Because if it hasn't, we'll be disintegrated on ta spot. T'at's how ta Guardian Stations work."

"My contact is certain. Now, Thykas, I give you my trust and my permission. When I say so, draw us a door."

Thykas whoops loudly and then sets his body in a deep squat as he closes his eyes. "Ye grabbed yer Precautionary Bag, aye?"

Patting my red Jackette pocket, I answer, "Always."

He waits until I give him the go-ahead.

"Now," I say at exactly five minutes past two. Thykas opens his fingers wide like sun rays and then slowly draws them all together like duck's beaks. Slowly, he lowers in his squat until his fingers touch the ground. He draws a square around himself with each set of fingers still pressed together.

"Come now," he whispers, and I jump into the square.

I can feel him muster up the reserves of his Gift, and with the strain of lifting a two-hundred-kilogram weight, he rises out of his squat. He shouts in exertion as he raises his pinched hands toward the ceiling. Then in an instant, in a breath, he slams his hands on the wood panels beneath our feet, and my body is pulled into the wood.

Floating in the void

Where thoughts and dreams intertwine

An eternal dance

Without dimension

Just between the particles

Flying in the nothing

Substance calls to me

The free fall is at an end

Recall existence

It takes seven of our precious sixty seconds for me to regain consciousness. Before I open my eyes, I renew all the broken bones in our bodies. I rewind time, back to when our blood vessels were not burst and Thykas' brain had not been severely damaged. I landed on my behind, whereas he landed on his head. He is fortunate he did not die. It is not until I have wholly renewed us that I hear the blaring alert sounding around us.

I look around the room to gather my bearings. The room itself is plain, with three of the walls made of concrete. However, the ceiling and the fourth wall are reflective mirrors. In the center of the room is a very disfigured Formosian woman—I do not have time to fully comprehend how badly they have maimed her—suspended in the air. Two Guardians stand in front of her, hands ready to defend.

"Forty-two seconds left," Thykas whispers next to me as he stands.

"Do it," I command.

Pinching his fingers together once more, Thykas draws something in the air.

One of the Guardians screams, the sound an offensive Gift, making our eardrums blow. I renew them immediately. The other Guardian punches the air, but I feel it as though he were standing right in front of me and has made contact. Although I renew all of the places his punches and kicks injure me, it still hurts.

Badly.

Thykas endures it in a praiseworthy fashion—never once allowing his concentration to waver no matter the pain the Guardian inflicts upon him.

When Thykas pulls his hands above his head, the Guardians suddenly fly up into the air, trapped in a mess of ropes, twine, vines, and even paper mâché.

I run over and grasp the woman, pulling her from midair. With her clutched tightly in my arms, I race back to Thykas who has already drawn a new square around himself. I jump in with Amelia bundled over my shoulder. Six Guardians materialize into the room just as Thykas slams his hands on the floor.

We are gone.

AMELIA WAKES UP BEFORE Thykas or me. I only know this because it is her screams that rouse me. We are back in Thykas' room at the circus, having landed right where Thykas had initially drawn our door.

I am taken aback to see that the lips gaping open in a terrified scream are not on her face but on her foot—one of her eight feet.

Amelia's whole face has no features; rather, it is a canvas of pearlesque skin. Her eyes—wide in terror—are on the inside of her arms. Her nose is nowhere to be seen, and one ear rests on top of her head, while the other lies on her neck. Her hands have no fingers but have been replaced with fin-like extensions. Instead of two legs, she has eight, all kicking as they recalcitrate their own existence. Her waist is bloated and disjointed like... Ah. I see it now. Like the thorax of an insect. The cruelty of the Guardians, it seems, knows no end.

I know I should speak words of encouragement to her, but that is Scout's department, not mine. "And what could even be said?" I mumble to myself as I check my prancing lion tattoo. It pulsates black and greenish brown. My adrenaline spikes. Knowing I need to handle my present predicament first, I check Thykas for any critical injuries, and when I find none, I concentrate all my effort on renewing Amelia's body to its original design.

As I work, I notice the extensive pain Amelia's body must have gone through during the disfiguration. Her pain receptors were never impaired. However, when I focus my attention on her brain, I see that there had been some pain deduction—but only enough to keep her from passing out. And from the looks of her temporal lobe, her body tried to send her into a seizure or coma, but the Guardians had stopped this natural reaction.

When I have finished with Amelia, I renew Thykas' wounds. This time, thankfully, his injuries are much more minor than those inflicted by his headstand as we entered the Guardian Station.

Work complete, I open my eyes to see Amelia sitting on the floor, staring at her hands, her restored face a mask of horror. Silent tears fall down her cheeks. She stopped screaming when I commenced work on her, and she has not made a sound since. After moving each of her fingers, she places the palms of her hands beside her on the floor and takes two deep, shuddery breaths. Then she is back in control. She opens her eyes and calmly looks around the room, assessing her surroundings.

"You are a very brave person," I say to her, even though I know she cannot understand.

"Who is she?" Thykas whispers. "Why did ta Guardians take her? And why did we save her?"

Although Scout and I had discussed not sharing with the crew Amelia's identity quite yet, Thykas and Emerly always seem to find out our secrets (and Emerly already knows), so I might as well share it now. "She is the daughter," I answer. "Arkarian Story's daughter."

"Is she now?" Thykas asks, eyeing her. "Genuine? Verified by Emerly?"

"Indeed."

My eyes flick to my forearm. The colors have not changed.

Amelia looks up at us and asks, "Kansis?" Tears well up around her eyes, but she is no longer crying.

Thykas and I look at each other for a moment. How do I tell her that Kansis is also being rescued, but we have no idea where she is or if she is unharmed?

"Kansis?" Amelia asks again. Putting a frown on her face, she takes her finger and slices it across her throat. "Kansis?" she inquires a third time, and, putting her thumbs up, she throws an exaggerated smile on her features.

Thykas laughs. "She's pretty fair at communicatin' wit' no words."

"Kansis," I say similarly and then put my hands palm up and shake my head. I hope it communicates, *I do not know,* as I had intended.

Amelia nods as if she understands.

When I check my tattoo again, this time the black has mostly receded, the brownish green taking over the lion's frame. Relief floods my system.

"Is me ol' sam Scout safensuch?" Thykas asks.

"Not injured and ostensibly safe," I answer, "But still in danger, it seems."

"As is his way," Thykas comments with a snort.

I smile. "As is his way."

AFTER RECEIVING A CALL from Scout that his rescue company is heading back to the hotel, Thykas and I lead Amelia back as well. When we enter the lobby, Kansis and Amelia cry out and run to each other, embracing tightly. They hurriedly whisper in that ancient language, inspecting one another to make sure the other fairs well.

"Thykas drew a door?" Scout asks me with brows raised. "That was risky of you, Pip." He throws Thykas an impish smile. "I thought you were going to try the door with me first?"

"Oi was just as shocked t'at Pip agreed," Thykas comments and tightens his waterfall ponytail.

"Well," I say, "I cannot have Scout making all the senseless and shortsighted decisions around here. I needed to even the score a bit."

Scout eyes me dubiously. "Is that a challenge, Pypen?"

"No, no, old friend," I respond and pat his arm. "I have now had my fill of it. I will leave the rest of the stupidity to you. You are just too good at it."

"T'ere's enough stupidity for bot' of ye ter share," Thykas says with a wide grin, making his octopus-styled beard extend so it appears more like a squid.

Emerly joins us. His emancipation party was also successful. Dommy, our light illusionist, Lylee, our invisibility specialist, and Veeter, one of our singers who focuses in vibrations, used their combined skill to orchestrate the rescue.

At the overly excited look on Emerly's face (which is saying something for him), I ask, "What is the good news, Em? Or are you merely excited not to be in jail anymore?"

Ignoring my words, Emerly, attention entirely on Scout, proclaims, "Scout Mnason Eekan… the Superior we've been looking for, yes? I met someone who speaks with him."

Scout's jaw drops.

Anger ignites my veins. Why is Emerly feeding this curiosity in him? Why does he not just leave it alone?

"Who?" Scout asks. "Where were you?"

"It's an Ortusan man named Knimble Knox," he answers and does a little jig before continuing. "He's coming tonight to the circus, he is. His pursuits include Arkahunting, which is the primary reason for his coming, but he said this Superior is the one I've been looking for, he did!"

Matza. This is exactly what Scout needs—another distraction. Another quest.

"Why is he coming to the circus?" I ask, trying to change the subject.

"He has a Pod with him—the one Amelia was chasing when we got arrested, he does. This Ortusan let his mind defenses down so I could see that—"

"How do you mean Amelia chased him?" I ask, purposefully interrupting.

Emerly smiles boyishly. "She saw him, shouted his name, he ran, she pursued. Pretty basic chasing procedure."

Rolling my eyes, I clarify, "*Why* was she chasing him?"

"I assumed she knew him, I did," Emerly answers.

"Kansis told me the story," Scout says. "I can fill you in on the details later."

"As I was saying," Emerly continues, "The Ortusan's mental defenses were down, and I saw that he had Arkahunter information. Then, he began speaking to someone in his head. At first, I thought he must have a mental communication Gift, but the response was not in his mind; it was… it was everywhere. It was all over him. And it wasn't words, it wasn't even feelings… it was something more… It was something *other*, something not human. I knew it was a Superior; it had to be, didn't it?"

At Scout's rapt expression, I slap his arm and announce, "I must speak with you for a moment."

I walk to the other side of the lobby, and before he can say a word, I round on him angrily. "I understand, I truly do," I begin, trying to stay calm. "This is what *you* have been awaiting. But that *girl*," I motion to Amelia, "is what *we*," I vigorously point between him and myself, "have been awaiting. The circus. This family. We are more important than your Superior hunt."

Scout's gaze meets mine. He does not disagree, but he also does not concede either.

"We *are* more important, correct?" I ask, fighting to keep the indignation out of my voice.

Our eyes search one another's for a moment, then Scout lowers his gaze to the ground. "I am plagued by unwilling ignorance, Pip. Haunted by questions that I know have answers." His eyes return to mine. "My soul is not at rest; it is seeking, ever waiting for even a wisp of truth. I would be lying if I said that the circus is more important than that."

Hurt and jealousy stab through my veins like shards of ice.

Kansis approaches us tentatively, and Scout turns to her warmly. "You will join us for supper," he pronounces.

She seems shocked at his forwardness. "Oh... well... I was going to ask when we can leave to find Charles Wrightly?"

"Next day," Scout answers.

Her brows rise in surprise. "Okay, so not tonight?"

"No, not this night."

Nodding, she remarks, "That's... I'm sure that's fine. Okay. Well, greet the shine."

"Until supper," Scout replies.

She moves her weight from one foot to another. "Okay, it's just that I wanted to go find Aker... well, I think he'll want to know we're okay."

"He may join as well," Scout says, but I can hear the change in his voice. He does not wish for the Pexun male to join.

"I don't think we should be out of our room with the Guardians looking for us," Kansis counters. "We probably should not risk being out in the open." Suddenly paranoid, she glances around the lobby as if Guardians are going to jump out from behind the couches.

"Winzer will not leave the hotel, and as long as she is here, you cannot be detected," Scout replies reassuringly. "And if it makes you feel better, I will keep you hidden while in the restaurant. My Duogift allows me to do this well."

Kansis opens her mouth as if to make a rebuttal but then closes it and nods. "Sounds good."

"See you at seven at the restaurant," he says and points to the other side of the massive lobby. "One more thing: would you and Amelia like to come to the circus with us later to meet Knimble Knox and the Senexian man? Emerly said that you were there when the introductions were made."

"Uh, sure, yes. Thank you, I'm sure Amelia would like that."

"Brilliant. Until then."

Kansis offers an obligatory smile and returns to Amelia's side.

"Escort them," Scout commands Emerly, who obeys without question.

As they walk away, I say, "You could have made it sound more like a request to Emerly, you know."

"It was not one," he responds and runs his hand over his braid.

I roll my eyes. I do so despise it when he is in this frame of mind. Whenever I push too hard against his Superior obsession, it places him in a foul mood for the remaining day. "I will be at the circus if you need me," I say and add under my breath, "Oh Aevum."

"Mutter not, Pypen. If you have something to say, say it loud enough for us to hear," Scout responds.

Ignoring him, I stalk out of the hotel lobby and down the street, towards the circus.

Scout follows after me and shouts again, "What do you have to say, Pypen? Hold not back on my account."

When I turn back to him, his face is a mixture of anger and amusement. *Matza.* I *hate* that look. "I said I would be at the circus, oh high and eternal *Aevum.*"

"Oh, I am one of the Aevii now," he says and laughs derisively. "If I am an Aevum, that would make you…"

Walking backward a few steps, I say with mock meekness, "Your humble simulan. My sole purpose on this earth is to fulfill your every wish."

"Indeed?" Scout's voice is high with delight. "If that be the case, I need my shoe tied, simulan."

I disregard him and resume my march to the circus. In downtown Initium, Pexus is quaint and well-kept. With the beautiful scenery and the light evening breeze, I could have calmed down. I could have let it go. But Scout follows behind, repeating the phrase, "My shoe is untied, simulan."

So I do not calm down.

I do not let it go.

The moment we pass through the gates and enter the circus, Scout shoots his body forward, preparing to shove me.

But I am ready for him.

I dodge his thrust, and he stumbles.

"Leave me be," I declare, and when I pass him, I shove him with my elbow.

He is not done, however, and thrusts my arm behind my back. As he forces me down to the earth, rage surges in my veins again, and I twist out of his grasp.

But before I can get away, he lunges at my legs. Flattening me, he tries to clasp my hands together behind my back.

"Get off!" I grunt.

Quickly, I jolt my body to the left, and his grip loosens. I shove him away as hard as I can. He tumbles and collapses onto his back. Taking advantage of his fall, I stand to walk away, but somehow, he manages to get up in time to jump me again, pinning me to the earth.

"Get off, Scout, I mean it!" I roar as he shoves my face into the ground.

"You said you were my simulan," he replies, slightly out of breath. "I need my shoes tied."

I jam my elbow into his arm. He winces and releases his grip on my face. Wriggling as hard as I can left and right, I manage to get Scout to tumble off me. But once we are both back in standing positions, Scout rams into me, bringing me to the floor yet again. Lying on top of me, he growls in my ear, "If you are my simulan, tie my shoe!"

"Enough!" I bellow.

"Indeed!" he yells, elbowing me in my kidney. Shoving me hard to the floor, he suddenly stands, panting.

Groaning, I slowly turn onto my back and look up at Scout's hardened expression. "What was that for?" I ask as I push myself up into a sitting position.

"You want me to treat you like a simulan? I will."

Rubbing my back, I stand. I am not precisely certain what to say. I know I was in the wrong, but so was he. "You were a *patka* first."

"No, I was honest about my desire for the Superiors. My honesty birthed fear in you, and you chose to see me as a *patka*."

"Fear?" I scoff.

"Fear that I care more about the Superiors than you."

It infuriates me that Scout can see through me like a glass of water. I am not ready to settle this argument yet. When he looks down, I rush him, driving my forehead into his solar plexus and pulling on the back of his legs. I take him fully airborne, and we crash to the earth, forcing the breath out of his lungs. I quickly mount on top of his chest and pull his arms over his head. "I only fear that you are growing weak."

Grinning, he tries to gulp down air. After allowing myself a moment to enjoy my victory, I release him and stand.

Once he catches his breath, Scout's eyes meet mine, and he smiles. With all my facial strength, I keep myself from returning it. With as even a voice as

I can manage, I say, "Tie your own *eend* shoes."

As I walk past him, he jumps to his feet and places a hand on my shoulder. "I am truly proud of all you are doing, Pip."

I know this should make me feel better, but it makes me feel worse. My temporary joy at besting him is scattered like the popcorn that litters the circus floor. Guilt and shame leak into my veins. I rub the prancing lion tattoo on my wrist. It is shifting between red, yellow, orange, and green.

"Cannot decide how to feel?" I ask, jesting to cover my own discomfort.

He turns to me, eyes very serious, and says, "Pypen, I know it is hard for you because you do not understand my fascination with the Superiors; but you must know of my loyalty to you. You are my brother, Pypen. You are the most significant relationship in my life, and I do not think I could go on if I lost you as well."

At this, I meet his gaze. Why does he speak this way?

"We may no longer have mates, but we have each other," he continues. "And I need you on my side more than ever."

"How do you mean—"

Before I can finish, he continues, "Your word, Pypen. Your word that you will protect my blood over any other."

From where is this coming? "But of course. Why do you say this?"

Scout rubs his hands over his braid again. "Our world is stirring. Events outside our control are unraveling, and it scares me. No matter how I seem or how I may act, I need you." His earnestness is both blood-warming and concerning.

"You have my word," I respond. Suddenly, adrenaline shoots through my veins, as my Suus reminds me of the time. "Our engagement! Scout, we need to be at the Humani House in fifteen minutes—we will be late!"

He puts a hand on my shoulder and gives me an impish half-smile. "Let us find Thykas, my friend. We cannot be late for our engagement."

Pexus

Kansis

As soon as I see Amelia entering the hotel lobby, I run to her as fast as possible. She sees me as well, and I'm both shocked and pleased when she rushes to throw her arms around me, forcing me into a hug. My whole being warms at her embrace.

"Are you okay?" I ask her. "Were you hurt?"

"Freckles, we have to get out of here," she whispers into my hair.

Panic floods my veins. "What do you mean?" I ask as I pull away. "What happened at the Guardian Station?"

Her hazel eyes are clear. She's not frantic or fearful, but there is a steel in her gaze that makes me both scared and confident. She looks around the room like she's expecting someone to leap out at us. I can't stop crying as she tells me how the Guardians were trying to get her to take her sciath off by distorting her body. Pypen and a Sanusian man named Thykas had saved her, and Pypen had renewed her limbs and features back to normal. "We don't need these people," she finally whispers when her tale ends. "We just need each other."

I wipe my eyes. "This is all my fault. If you had put the sciath on yourself, then you could have taken it off and—"

"You decided to protect me, and I'm thankful for that," she interrupts, genuine appreciation in her eyes. "No one knows the future, so—well, I mean, I guess some people *here* might know the future—but *you* don't. And you made the best decision you could with the facts you had. I'm not upset with you."

My blood warms again at her words. "Well, I'm sorry you had to go through that."

"It doesn't matter," she snaps and waves my words away. "We just need to go."

"What about Charles Wrightly?" I ask, confused. "I thought you wanted to find him."

At this, her brows crease, and she clenches her jaw. Her conflicted eyes meet mine. This is probably the first time she's ever looked her age.

It's strange, but I would do whatever this girl wanted. Even after everything in the cafe, even if a part of her genuinely didn't trust me, I would do whatever she asked. If she wanted to leave the safety of my protector and these people, I'd do it. If she wanted to stay with them, I'd do it. Even if she wanted to leave Aker... well... I mean...

"Do you *need* him?" I whisper to Amelia. "Do you absolutely need Charles Wrightly?"

After looking at the ceiling, the ground, her shirt, and my hair, she finally meets my gaze. "Yes."

"Look, we need these people. I can't get into the PTS—I mean, the Pod Tracking System—without them. I could never have gotten us out of the Guardian Station... they saved us. I'll go where you go, but I don't know how we'll manage without their resources."

Grunting, she moves away from me. I intend to give her a minute, but she turns back to me within mere seconds. "Okay, go tell your protector that it's time to go. *Now.* We need to get Charles Wrightly."

I nod. "I will; I'll do that." However, when I turn to find Scout, I see him talking to Pypen, the Formosian named Emerly, and a Sanusian man with a bizarre beard that looks like an octopus. I hesitate.

I can't just walk over to them. They'd all... *see* me.

"What's wrong?" Amelia asks.

I turn my head towards her but keep my eyes on the group. "It's just... People have been shunning me for years, and now all the normal attention is messing with me a bit." Cold sweat drips down my stomach and back.

Amelia briefly places a hand on my arm, and electricity shoots through my veins. "Kansis, I trust that you are trying to help me. I believe you. And the fact is, I *need* you. I wanted to wake up and complete my mission alone, but I need an Elusian. I need an Elusian who knows this world: the language, traditions, history, and how to get me through. It pains me to say it, but I can't complete my mission without you."

"What is your mission?" I ask.

She clenches her jaw and studies me. Once she's clearly made a decision, she answers slowly, "I've been tasked to keep something safe. To keep someone safe. And I can only do that if I find Charles Wrightly."

"What do you need him for?" I whisper.

Again, she analyzes me, and I try to look as trustworthy as possible. Finally, she answers, "I need him to find Arkarian Story."

This throws me. "What? Don't you know where he is? The Book of Instructions says—"

"It doesn't matter what it says. I need Charles Wrightly to find Arkarian Story." She looks past me to Scout and Pypen. "Okay, they look like they're close to being done. Go and ask. You're strong—you can do this."

I look at the group of men again, and adrenaline shoots through my veins. But then I remember how brave Amelia has been today—every day I've known her, in fact—and I shove fear and anxiety out of my bloodstream and make myself walk toward Scout and the others.

MY CONVERSATION WITH SCOUT did not go how I thought it would. Particularly the part where he insisted we join him for supper. When I'm done telling Amelia what Scout had said, she asks, "Did he give you his word that we would leave as soon as physically possible?"

"His word?" I ask, lightly laughing. "Well, I didn't make him sign in blood if that's what you mean."

"We've thrown away a whole day, and I don't want to waste any more time. Isn't there anything that we can do to prepare?"

"Well, I think if he needed something from us, he would have asked."

"You don't wait for others to ask the right questions, Kansis; *you* ask them."

I chuckle. "I'll keep that in mind next time."

"Very good," she responds. The elevator arrives at our floor. As we get out, Amelia asks, "Hey, I have a question for you."

"Go ahead."

"What did you mean the other night when you said you've got bad blood?"

Cortisol shoots through my veins and I look around to see if anyone has heard her, forgetting I'm the only English speaker around. "What?" I ask.

"When we were still at the Ward—that night you were freeing me—you said you've got bad blood. So, what's up?" She leans her shoulders and one of her feet back onto the alabaster hall wall.

If it weren't for the fact no one could understand her, I would be freaking out right now. Even uttering the words *bad blood* can make people feel edgy and unsafe. "In our society," I begin, "our blood means everything to us. If you have good blood, you are honored."

"What makes someone have good blood?" she asks.

"Good blood would be evidenced by exceptional Gifts. Or if you have more than one Gift—"

Amelia interrupts, "One Gift is a Progift. A second is a Duogift, and a third is called a Trigift."

"Correct. More than one Gift indicates good blood, and if your Gift is powerful, potent, or you possess exceptional stamina, you are honorable too. Another example is a person's blood being traced back to someone famous in our history or someone who used their Gifts to help society.

"Adversely, bad blood includes people who have weak Gifts, those who do not have enough power to wield their Gifts, or people who use their Gifts for evil. And... lastly... people whose mates are not drawn to them. For example— the only example, really—me."

Shame swarms my veins at the admission. I focus my gaze on the gaudy painting on the wall behind Amelia's head. Having Aker physically near to me—even if he's down the hall—makes my body hot with embarrassment. "My blood should draw Aker, but he doesn't want me. I've been shunned for the last two years because my blood was declared insufficient. It has been rumored that bad blood can be contagious. Those who have it, and even extended family members, are shunned by others so it won't spread. If my bad blood is contagious, I am glad my family and friends have stayed away from me. I wouldn't want anyone else to ever feel the way I feel every day of my life."

The words come out of my mouth, and I realize how much I believe them. I hate the shunning, despise it, loathe it... But if it keeps everyone safe, then I choose that.

When I steal a glance at Amelia, she's smirking. Quickly, she covers her mouth when she sees I'm looking. "What could you possibly be laughing at?" I inquire incredulously.

She looks down. "I'm sorry, Freckles... It's just all so... so stupid."

I'm speechless.

Seeing my face, she laughs and goes on. "Just because your mate doesn't want you, you think you have a bad blood germ that could spread to other people? It just sounds so..." At the look on my face, she tries to wipe away the smile. "It's very silly."

Her perspective, although a relief, is alarming. Clearly they had no respect for blood in Senex.

"Listen, I'm sorry I insulted you," she says. "And I'm sorry about your blood. It just doesn't seem to matter to me. Why should your mate not loving you mean there's something wrong with you?"

I try once more. "Our blood is the most important thing about us," I explain slowly. "Life is in the blood. Our Gifts come from our blood. Our love comes from our blood. Death comes from the lack of blood." I take a deep breath as the muscles in my throat constrict. "Don't you see? My blood was planted into Aker and vice versa when we were both in utero. He was supposed to be my natural mate, but my blood wasn't enough. It was empty. Dirty. *Worthless*." I feel so defeated. I've never actually had to *say* it before. Hearing it spoken out loud makes it all the more painful.

Sighing, Amelia pulls herself off from the wall. "Hey." She reaches out and places her hand on my arm.

A warm breeze seems to travel up to my shoulder.

She rubs my arm, almost aggressively, and says soberly, "Your blood doesn't matter to me."

A small smile finds my lips. Ignorance is bliss, as they say. Well, *her* ignorance is *my* bliss, that is.

Amelia looks at me apologetically and asks, "I still don't understand something."

"What's that?"

"Was Aker shunned too?"

"No."

Uncharacteristically nervous, Amelia pulls on her earlobe as she asks, "I'm sure you don't want to talk about it… but I don't get why you're shunned and Aker isn't. Wouldn't both of you have bad blood?"

I'm touched that she cares whether I'm sensitive about this subject or not. I *am* sensitive about it, but I don't mind answering her question. "Every cell in my body wants to be with him," I answer, even though it's embarrassing to hear myself. "There's nothing in the world I want more than him… so his blood is strong in me. His blood was not defective at all. But *my* blood…" I swallow. "… it was so weak, it's as if it's not even in him. It's had no power over him. My blood is frail and powerless."

She doesn't respond right away, but when she does, she asks quietly, sadly, "And you really believe that, don't you?"

"What is there not to believe?"

Amelia shakes her head. "We are what we believe we are, Freckles."

I scoff, not even meaning to. "Me *believing* that I'm something else wouldn't change anything."

"I disagree."

Not knowing how to respond, I lead us back to our hotel room. I know I shouldn't just walk away, leaving the subject hanging between us, but she's wrong... And I don't know how to properly communicate that. When we get to our door, I use my wrist to open it.

"You know," Amelia says as the door clicks open, "I don't like Aker. And I'm not just saying that because he can't understand me—I'd be willing to say it to his face."

This makes me smirk. As we walk in, a sudden movement catches my eye, and I turn to see Aker in an awkward standing position, as if he has jumped up with a fright.

His brows furrow in confusion. "They let you go?" he asks.

"Who let us go?"

"The Guardians," Aker answers, crossing the room to shut the door behind us.

How did Aker know the Guardians arrested us? Unless... "Did *you* call us in?" I ask incredulously.

At this, he meets my gaze. "Of course I did. I figured once you were in custody, everything would get straightened out, and we could go back home." He walks past me and throws himself onto one of the peach-colored sofas.

"Well, for your information," I state angrily, "Amelia was *tortured* at the Guardian Station." I've never talked to Aker like this, but Amelia was agonizingly disfigured because of his actions.

Aker shakes his head. "I don't care."

I can't believe the words coming out of my future husband's mouth. I can't believe this person—the love of my life—is acting so heartlessly. This can't truly be how he feels.

"So will you call the Guardians on us again?" I ask. When he doesn't answer, I turn away from him. "If you're this mad about being here, maybe you should go," I declare, and I can't believe how much I mean it. After the way he acted earlier and now this... I guess I don't know anything about Aker Vonbough. I turn to Amelia, who is stuffing her face with the food we hadn't finished earlier, and command her in English, "Come on. Let's go to the other room."

As I forcefully shut the door behind me, the adrenaline in my blood evaporates, immediately replaced by a flood of regret and guilt. I can't believe I spoke to Aker like that... Did I really tell him to go home? What if he actually leaves? What's wrong with me? If he does go, any chance I'd ever have to get married and live a normal life would be completely gone.

I decide to go back out there and apologize, but Amelia asks, "Can we keep going with my Elusian lessons? I want to learn it as quickly as possible."

As I stare at the door, I'm torn in two. Half of me desperately needs to make things right with Aker. No matter how upset I am, I shouldn't have told him to leave.

But the other half of me feels somewhat justified in what I said—for Amelia's sake—and I don't want to apologize. He should be the one to say sorry for the pain he caused her, for the pain he caused me.

Filled with nausea, I agree to stay and work with Amelia. I can always apologize later.

Amelia and I work on basic verb conjugations for a while; I have her memorize all the nouns in the room, and we practice her Formosian accent. I share more of the history that lies between her world and mine. Most of the time is filled by my explanation of our Gifts' origin, potential, and protections. Near the end, we discuss the Aevii.

"So there's nine of them," she says, verbally processing my last lecture. "Mal Fey... Daiquiri Elbowson—"

"Dakarai Ebelson."

"Oker Green."

"Oaken Bleu, and she is the Fifth Aevum. You missed a few. You forgot Qual—"

Closing her ears, she interrupts, "Okay, okay, let me try... It was Qualcomm Oldest—"

"Qualcum Elder."

"Marvella Pinball—"

"Marvella Pinyin."

"Oaken Bleu... Something with an *R*..."

"That's Root Besendere, but she's the Seventh Aevum—"

Covering her ears again, she continues loudly, "The one we're working with that you talk to even though you don't remember..."

"Flister Dubach." Even just the mention of his name makes me queasy. How can my subconscious be talking to him and telling him things about me? It's itching my veins that I don't know what he knows!

Exasperated, Amelia shouts, "Kansis! Let me try!" Closing her eyes in concentration, she mutters, "Okay, after Flister Dubach is Roots Besonden."

"Root Besendere."

"Gersons Librisso—"

"Gerisson Librisso."

"And Vakson Something…"

"Vakker Schon."

"Yes. Okay, well," she smiles triumphantly. "I was really close, though. Come on, that was after only hearing their names twice. Give me something here."

Clicking my tongue, I respond, "Well, you really only got one right—"

Silencing me with a hand, she goes on, "Each one has a Venture which they use to enrich the world. They run the government but work with five chancellors from each territory."

Clapping, I respond, "Yes! Very good. See, that was all correct."

Rolling her eyes, she continues, "The Aevii care for Elusians, and it's their job to consistently keep the world in a state of harmony. Forces—whatever that means—keep trying to bring the world back to the way it was when the Sennies—"

"Senexians," I correct.

She arches one of her brows. "I've heard you say *Senny*."

"*I* am allowed to. But you will use the formal name."

Huffing, she recites, "When the barbaric *Senexians* ruled the earth, it was chaos and darkness and death, but the Aevii waged a bloody war against this."

"I don't know that I said it that graphically, but yes."

"They're like your celebrities, and you… you worship them."

I smile. "As is their due."

Noticing the time displayed on the room's mainframe, I pull out the bag of clothes I brought along with us. Both our current outfits are pretty much destroyed. We rifle through the pack, looking for something classier to wear, but I don't have anything. I want to make the excuse that I didn't think about bringing anything nicer, but honestly, even at home I don't have anything suitable for a night out. All that hangs in my closet are work clothes for the day and loose-fitting relaxing clothes for the night. We pick out anything that could pass for somewhat suitable supper attire and start getting undressed.

Now that I've had time to think—given that I know the lessons about Elusis inside-out and can teach them and think about Aker at the same time—I wonder if Aker may not be the person I always thought he was. I know he has his harsher side—that is, I've seen it in every interaction I've ever had with him—but I've always believed there was something deeper to him. Something kinder. And I know it's there because I've seen it whenever he's been with Mirindiss. I know he's capable of such sweetness… just not with me. I think there was always a part of me that truly believed that if I could be alone with him, something would spark, and my blood would draw him. But now, after just one day, I don't think so.

As I take off my leggings, I draw out the pocket watch Scout gave me. Whoever etched it used a cross-hatching style to draw a dark raven on its lid. The bird's profile shows one glistening eye, intently staring at something—probably its prey. Its feathers are bustled, and it appears agitated. At one point, there had clearly been more etching around the edges of the watch, but those must have worn away a long time ago.

I still can't believe Scout gave this to me. It's beautiful. As I pull on a fresh pair of pants, I place the watch inside my new pocket.

"You're very quiet," Amelia comments as she holds up my red wool sweater for inspection.

"Just thinking," I reply, scanning the pile of clothes to settle on a top.

She slips on the red sweater and asks, "Thinking about what?" Before I can answer, she adds, "That's a pretty necklace."

Looking down at the crescent moon druzy quartz pendant, I nod my thanks. The teacher part of me wants to explain that it is a piffy—a portable fantasy simulator—but every other part of me cringes, so I will definitely *not* be explaining that to her.

Turning away, I pull off my shirt to swap it with an oversized crochet sweater.

"What's *that*?" she asks, her voice sharp and concerned.

I whirl around, expecting to see some crazy-looking hybrid insect, but she's staring at *me*. "What's what?" I ask.

"On your back."

I whirl around, trying to see what she's talking about, but immediately feel foolish as I cannot see. "What?" I ask, frantic. "What's on me?"

She walks over and grabs my shoulders, touching the back of my left one. "What are these?" she asks again.

I squint towards where she's touching and when I realize what she has found, I smile, relieved that nothing nasty is on my back. "Oh, you mean my Memory Scars?"

"What's a Memory Scar?" she asks as she lightly touches the thick linen thread sewn into my back.

There are three of them, each one five centimeters long and one and a half centimeters thick. One is sage green with a long-armed cross-stitch, the second is bright gold with a wheat-ear stitch, and the last is a dirty beige with a vandyke stitch. They remain tucked against my shoulder, almost wholly forgotten by me.

"They are memories I have had taken away," I tell Amelia.

"I'm sorry, what now?"

I lightly laugh. "I had three memories taken away from me. I'm not sure what they are—obviously. The green one is a memory I can never recover. The gold means there is a way for me to recover the memory, but I would have to go to the Memory Guild where they would start me on the journey. And the tan one I can remember at any moment if prompted correctly."

"Why would you do that?" she asks, incredulous.

Snorting, I ask, "How would I know? I've forgotten. But, whatever they are, they must be pretty bad to have had them professionally removed. That's an expensive procedure."

"And you're not curious about what they are?" she asks.

"Of course I'm curious," I respond, pulling on my sweater and covering the scars again. "But I had them removed for a reason, so I'm sure it's better that I don't remember what happened. If people get memories removed, they usually only do one… but to have three? I already have enough rot in my blood without stepping into knowing whatever secrets I wanted to forget."

Amelia shakes her head. "You're crazy, Freckles. There's no way I'd keep myself in the dark like that."

I shrug. "Sometimes, the darkness is better left in the dark, I think."

"And sometimes hiding *from* the darkness just means you're hiding *in* it."

Not knowing how to respond, I turn away to put on my shoes. As I do so, something seeps into my blood.

I've known people with Memory Scars and never thought much of it. I got mine right before my wedding day—well, my non-wedding day—and when Sheerly, my closest friend at the time, saw them, she didn't react. It isn't as if everyone has them, but they aren't uncommon, either.

But seeing Amelia's reaction stirs something in me. For the first time ever, I feel *embarrassed* by them. I *am* hiding. I didn't want to face something unpleasant, so instead of dealing with it, I chose to forget it. My life isn't exciting, so it probably wasn't anything horrific or intensely traumatizing—it was just something I didn't want to handle.

And here I thought I couldn't get any more pathetic.

I sure showed me.

Lost in my thoughts and Amelia in hers, we finish getting dressed in silence. I take out the few cosmetics I have and show Amelia how to put them on. She brushes through her straight hair, and I'm jealous when after just a minute of brushing, her hair looks amazing. I can never control my curls, and tonight the ones that frame my face want to stick straight up.

"Are you excited to see Dean again?" I ask as we fold the rest of the clothes and put them back in my bag.

Her eyebrows flicker up. "Well, there's not much to say, so no, not really."

"Did he betray you?" I ask.

Shrugging her shoulders, she answers, "I don't know. He said he didn't have a chance to find the person I'm looking for. I don't know why he'd lie about it, but he didn't seem to be telling the truth."

"Maybe he's realized Novus has more to offer than his old mission did." I know I've said the wrong thing by the look on Amelia's face. "Or—or maybe it was more complicated than he realized," I quickly amend.

She looks away from me. "Maybe." Then, quietly, almost to herself, she adds, "Or maybe he's been brainwashed into becoming a traitor."

"A traitor? To your mission?" I ask.

When she turns back, her eyes are both sharp and vulnerable. "Tell me straight. Is that what you do to the Pods, Kansis?"

"Do what?"

"Do you brainwash Pods?"

This causes me to pause. I guess it depends on your definition of brainwashing—but I don't think that will be a helpful answer. *Brainwash* has such a negative connotation, and the K-Pax is only positive. But she won't see it that way. Knowing I have only one second to hesitate before she thinks I'm being dishonest, I do something I have never done in my entire career.

I look at my Pod, and I lie.

"No, we don't do that."

For a moment, she stares and me and then nods. She believes me. I lied, and she accepted it as the truth. I know this is wrong, and I know I'll regret it, but I don't know that I could endure any more rejection. Even from a Pod.

When did I get to be so pitiful?

As we leave our room and emerge into the lounge, Aker stands up. "Where are you going?"

"To supper," I answer and continue towards the door.

"With whom? With those Ortusans?"

"With those Ortusans," I respond.

"Hey," he says, and I stop with my hand on the doorknob. He hesitates for a moment. "I... I am sorry about your Pod. I said I didn't care, but I do. I didn't mean to get her hurt. Were you... were you hurt?"

I should walk away. I should make a defiant, angry statement that he doesn't get to suddenly start caring now that he sees the consequences of his actions. But... I can't.

He's staring at me—looking *me* in the eye—feeling bad about what he did. How could he have known that Amelia was going to get hurt? He thought he was doing the right thing. It *wasn't* the right thing, but he didn't know.

Sighing, I answer, "No, I'm all right."

He takes a step closer. "I really am sorry. I'm sure it was scary."

I can feel my cheeks redden. "No, it's fine. I'm okay."

His brows knit together for a heartbeat, then he states, "You could stay here, you know. You could eat in one of the living rooms, and I could eat in the other... we could shout at each other from across the room."

I laugh, and I almost say I'll stay. The words are on my lips, but I can't speak them. I did tell Scout that we would come to supper, and I have a sneaking suspicion he would come to get me if we don't show up.

"Let's go," Amelia prompts and gently grabs my arm, pulling me out the door.

"She's a bossy one, isn't she," Aker comments looking at Amelia. Before I can respond, he asks, "So, what's the plan? That Ortusan said you were the one with the plan."

Pulling myself free of Amelia, I turn to face him, half my body inside the hotel room, half in the hallway. "We need to find a Pod for Amelia. And once we find him, we can locate Arkarian Story."

As I slip more of myself out of the room, he asks, "Is it the Pod she was chasing earlier?"

"No, she needs to find a different one." Just my head remains. "You know, you're welcome to come to supper too," I add.

He grimaces. "No, I'll stay here."

"We'll be at the restaurant downstairs if the Guardians need to know where we are," I remark, surprising myself.

He looks up at me and laughs. But, like, a real laugh. Not the kind where I'm the joke, but the kind where he thought something I said was funny. That's good, right?

As I prepare to shut the door, he blurts out, "Kansis, I'm sorry. For... everything." I peek back in as he goes on. "This is all very..." he winds his finger around his head, "hard to circulate. This isn't really how I thought my weekend was going to go."

He smiles then and it makes my insides shiver. His eyes are soft and warm, his expression open and kind. In this moment, I could melt into my own shoes.

I'm not sure what my face is doing, but it must reveal something because Aker's smile sharpens. With a voice much softer and deeper than his normal intonation, he simpers, "You know, you're welcome to stay with me, Kansis."

Before I have a chance to concede, Amelia pulls me into the hallway, firmly shutting the door behind us.

Pexus

Pypen

THYKAS DRAWS A DOOR several blocks away from the Demirkan House of Worship. This time, the travel is much less jarring, and we break far fewer bones.

Once I am done renewing our bodies, we dust ourselves off and head into the busy city street. As is the case with all the territories and capitals, Pexus has a different feel to Ortus. Everything about the Ortusan capital, Cisse, is warm, inviting, captivating, and eclectic. Although we are formal in how we speak, our cities and towns are relational and family-oriented.

Pexus is the coldest territory. Not a frosty chill or a frigid wasteland, but gloriously hard, rigid, and powerful in their manner. Albeit their casual way of speaking, everything about the capital city speaks of strength, fortitude, and respect. A circus patron once told me that in order to set up a shop in Demirkan, everything must be approved by the municipality—down to what color one paints the bathroom. Pexuns value continuity and want the entire city to feel cohesive.

Even from where we have stepped out, we can see the flared roof of the Demirkan's House of Worship. We traipse along in its direction. Most of the Pexuns who hurriedly pass by us wear black coats and do not speak, even when they accidentally bump into one another. The streets are immaculately clean, the walkways crisp, and the buildings are all in the same color palette.

As we approach their House of Worship, I cannot help but feel overcome by the glory. The building is truly a piece of art. Everything about it boasts architectural symmetry—even the ornate boulders lining its exterior. An arcade of arches besets the House on either side, and several elaborate balconies elegantly jettison off the main building. The open-sided gallery is a bit much, but this *is* the capital's House of Worship. No expense was too great, I am certain.

As we get closer, I can see that the balusters appear to be genuine mother-of-pearl, while the balustrades are pure onyx, both etched with gold-filled flitting. As we walk into the House's elegant and towering doors, we are met by a deep bay constructed into a eupee tasting bar. Within the foyer is the most enormous rhinoceros I have ever seen.

The rhinoceros—Pexus' emblem—is fifteen meters high and carved with incredibly accurate detail. The rhino itself is in an aggressive position, with its horn poised to strike. Even though I know it is just a statue, my heart pounds with fear. I am certain it has been Gifted to make me feel this way, but at this moment, the feeling is authentic.

And with that fear, I find I am suddenly very nervous. Scout and I have been worshipped at many Houses, but never in a capitol—and never with this much pomp and circumstance. My blood pounds, my head sweats, my hands shake. As fast as I renew my jitters, they return.

"Oi t'ink ye should have told ta performers about ye bein' worshipped ternight. T'ey would have enjoyed watchin' ye," Thykas whispers as he stares in awe around us.

"We wished not for it to be a well-known affair," I reply, licking my parched lips with a dry tongue.

"Ye bosses want eupeeinsuch?"

"I will take a glass," Scout answers, but I decline.

As Thykas walks away, I feel my gaze drawn to the rhinoceros again. I do not often experience this sense of anxiety and dread, but feeling it now brings me back to another time in my life. Without meaning to, I quietly say to Scout, "My mother used to tell me that the only thing in this life I would ever earn was an acceptance letter to the Den of the Insane."

I cannot meet his gaze, but I know Scout looks at me with compassion. He knew my mother, and was often present for her outbursts. It was he who used to sneak me out of my house and let me stay at his. Some people need explanations, but it is a relief to be known by another in such a way that no commentary is required. More than any other, he knows exactly what I mean and how hopeless my life used to be.

"Well, here you are, my Friend," Scout says, slapping my arm, "being honored in the Demirkan's House of Worship. You deserve this, Pip. You have worked so hard these past eight years, and I want you to marinate in this moment. Your mother was no prophet—she knew nothing of your future. You earned your way to this through hard work, tenacity, calculated risks, loyalty, and of course, your striking good looks."

I smile, longing to record his words and play them on repeat come the nights when the only sound I can hear is my mother crying in disappointment.

A flute sings out into the atrium, the sweet melody telling us that the service is due to begin. When Thykas returns with the aged eupee, he also hands me one too. Each goblet has been crafted to look like the head of a ferocious rhinoceros. "Oi took it on meself ter bring ye a glass anyway. Ye'll not want ter miss out on t'is."

I take it as Scout remarks, "We are supposed to meet someone at the outer sanctuary doors. They will tell us where we are to sit."

When we arrive at the outer and inner sanctuary threshold, a young priestess approaches us and bows low to the ground. She is dressed in a simple, tight black tunic. Her whole back is revealed through the thin fabric.

When she stands, she speaks ethereally: "Blessed are you to be honored here today. Praise waits for you within the walls of the holy place. Come, Consecrated Ones. Let us cover you with our affirmation and affection." She kisses us one by one on both cheeks, then leads us into the hallowed place.

The whole room—or stadium, more like—appears to seat even more than our main tent at the circus—at least sixty thousand or more. The priestess shows us to our seats in a booth situated to the right of the stage. I take a sip of the aged eupee, and my whole body warms. "This is probably the best eupee I have ever drunk in my life."

"Pypen," Scout groans. "The mumbling."

"I was just thinking this eupee is phenomenal," I explain more loudly.

"So say it," Scout snaps. "Just say that."

"Why do ye get so flustered at his mumblin'?" Thykas asks Scout. "Ye learn so much more about dear old Pip when ye listen ter his murmerin.'"

"That is not true," I remark, sincerely hoping it is not the case.

The stage, which has been black and quiet until this moment, abruptly explodes in sound and color. A voice rings out through the stadium, and people start screaming in excitement. I, too, know the voice; Thykas, Scout, and I exchange thrilled looks.

It is the June Bugs!

For the past year, they have been promoted as the upcoming Saturday night entertainment at the Quintrall. They are the most well-known band in all of Elusis, as they use every genre in their work. I love all their music, as does everyone—precisely why they are performing at the Quintrall.

The show is not as long as I—or anyone else in the crowd—would have wished. Although there is a unanimous cry from the people for them to play longer, the High Begirale soon comes to the front of the stage to start the service. I have never attended a ceremony with an actual High Begirale present.

Reigning over all the Houses throughout Elusis is the Ruffe. The current Ruffe is a Silentar woman named Wesfeather Reichmuth. Underneath her are the five High Begirales who oversee each territory. Within a territory, the generic Begirales supervise the districts. Each individual House of Worship is led by a Gotzain and at least five priests.

Over the past four years, we've met numerous Gotzains and Begirales, but this is our first time at a capital House.

"I could have listened to them forever, couldn't you?" the High Begirale booms, and his voice fills the whole space in such a way it feels like his words are in my chest.

The crowds scream in agreement.

"But there is much more for you to enjoy and worship tonight. And don't you worry, they'll be back at the end. Simmer down, simmer down. I hear you all; the June Bugs will be back. Now, let us sober ourselves and remember why we are here tonight."

Another musical group walks onto the stage. As they do so, the June Bugs and their instruments shimmer away as if they were scorched by the heat of the sun. In their place, the new group's instruments materialize. There is a cry of delight from the crowd, although less so than for the June Bugs. This group plays a well-known hymn about the first Gifters. It is inspiring, and their unique take on the melody is entertaining.

We sing several more songs about our Gifts, the Aevii, and our blood. I know most of them, but a few are new to me. The High Begirale returns to the stage, his diamond communion beads glittering in the dappled stage lights. He shares a captivating and engaging dissertation on the balance needed between worshipping others and worshipping self. He further gives practical examples on determining when one loves community excessively over self and vice versa, how to discern between what one's blood needs in various seasons of life, and how to communicate such needs to one's friends and family. Although this teaching is not necessary for me, I can see that it is helpful for those who do not have a *Scout* around them, keeping the perfect balance of self and communal worship.

As his message comes to a close, he shouts to the gathering, "In the name of the Aevii, I welcome you here!"

"We welcome power and intellect," the congregation recites back.

"This is it," Scout whispers to me. "We are about to go on."

"From the highest to the lowest, power and energy can dwell in any veins," the High Begirale shouts.

"May it dwell in our veins," we recite back.

"In our own streets dwell those worthy of our worship," the High Begirale goes on.

"May we bless our homes with our Gifts," we say.

Nervous energy floods my veins. Over and over, I push the adrenaline out of my blood, but it continues like a waterfall.

In this service, there will be three people brought up on stage (although Scout and I will be together), starting with the least and ending with the greatest. We assumed we would be the first to go up and are surprised when the first to be worshipped is a Pexun Medisacerdos who is working on a cure for Gift blockage—a common sickness in those who have overused their Gift. Apparently, she is very close to discovery. A well-known choir sings a song in her honor, and the High Begirale gives her the bronze rhinoceros—a tribute only given out once a year. Offerings are taken for her.

Surprising us again, we are not the second to be worshipped. Instead, it is a Formosian author, Solys Aadrif. This woman has written several novels and trilogies. She is the most-read author in all of Formosus and is very popular throughout the Hexum. She has just released *My Cell, Your Cell*, the final installment of her series *The Tastemaker's Tales*. For her honor, fifty fans come trooping out from stage left dressed as their favorite characters from her series. One at a time, they kiss her hands and feet and contribute an offering. She receives Vorbies of all shapes and sizes, precious artifacts prohibited from duplicating, and several offer her packages from Abaed-Don Interterritorial (surely filled with the latest technological gadgets). Tithes are taken for her.

To our glory, we are the last of the three. The High Begirale gives a gusto-filled introduction. "Now, a few words about the third and final honorees today." He pauses dramatically. "When you want to take your mate to an entertaining night out, maybe you'll take them to supper, maybe a show, maybe a cinematic experience, or the theatre… But have you ever taken your mate to the circus?"

The crowd starts murmuring excitedly.

"Circuses were an archaic mode of entertainment, in which a group of Senexians would travel around showcasing various performances by acrobats, clowns, and trained animals. Even at their best, the subhuman's attempts at pleasure were woeful. And yet, two brilliant Ortusan men took the idea and molded it into something truly glorious. Definitively breathtaking.

"Their circus tent has over two hundred doors leading to unique and amusing attractions. Be they exciting, intelligently stimulating, frightening, or artistic—each room could be a stand-alone show. Yet they are all together Gifted into something truly magical.

"But that's not all, oh no. A giant, round door at the end of the tent leads to a seasonally performed show. This main event makes the other doors look like Senny work. Of all the shows I have ever attended, this was the most moved I've ever been. Their storytellers are truly praiseworthy."

The High Begirale gears up for his finale: "Tonight," he continues, rubbing his pudgy hands together, "we have present in our very midst, the manager and main performer for the circus of which I speak. Please, join me in worshipping Scout Eekan and Pypen Tross of the Unopened Gifts!"

The applause is so loud it hurts my ears. As sixty thousand people stand to praise us, the ground beneath us shakes. We walk up onto the stage, and the buzzing energy and beaming lights bake me like the sun on a scorching, windless day. Sweat beads all over my body, making my clothes feel tight and sticky. Endorphins flood my veins, and I permit myself to savor it all.

We offer the High Begirale the traditional Pexun greeting, slapping our hands onto his and then wrapping our thumbs around his palm.

Caught up in the moment, the lights, the sounds, the cheering, I find myself giving a deep bow. This causes further screaming. One might say 'tis the thespian within me revealing itself.

When I look at Scout, I expect to see a grin mirroring mine; and although it is technically there, it does not reach his blood.

"When we considered your worship," the High Begirale divulges, "we found ourselves at a loss. Our very best singers, dancers, and actors all fall short compared to your show, so that would not be honoring. To recite a poem of your praise felt weak, and to make a show of your fanbase would take all night. Even to have every congregation member dress in honor of Ortus wouldn't be impactful, as your show boasts members from every territory.

"What to do!" the High Begirale shouts, shaking his head dramatically as if asking the crowd for their insight.

"There is always energy," I answer cheekily, and my voice carries throughout the stadium. Laughter erupts at my suggestion.

"Yes, yes, but could there not be something more than a mere monetary value? We wanted to give you a part of our hearts." As he says this, with incredible showmanship, he broadly puffs his chest and points to the side of the stage.

A Pexun girl, no older than nine years old, walks out to us. The *oo*'s and *ah*'s are almost as loud as the applause and laughter.

"This young worshipper has written her very own hymn," the High Begirale says, inciting yet more *ooing*. "She visited your circus last week in Eoutab, and after we read the words she has composed, we knew this was how we were to honor you. Now, come, come, dear Child. What's your name?"

"Vanery," she answers, her voice so sweet it fills my blood with wonder.

"Can you sing to us your hymn?"

She clears her throat and moments later, Vanery's light, melodic voice fills the vast room.

I know I'm just a child
The world I have not seen
My experiences mild
My lifetime short and lean
But after today, all has been remade
I'll never be the same, this feeling will not fade

I know I can bear it all
All the pain my life gives
As long as I can recall
Your creativity lives
And now nothing could steal this joy from me
I was sightless before today but now I see

I know I'm just a child
Of pain what could I know?
Yet on me it has smiled
Declared me as its foe
For Mom and Dad aren't with me anymore
The accident removed them both forevermore

You gave me hope when all
Was lost and there was none
Who were able to trawl
Me out of the season
Of sadness in which I lived my days
So now I must utter nothing besides your praise

It takes a moment for the audience, and for me, to digest her words. When no applause meets her hymn, Vanery shuffles her feet slightly and nervously looks up at the High Begirale.

Then, in the pump of an aorta, the expanse explodes with applause.

It is not until I lean down to thank her that I realize I am crying. Hurriedly, I wipe away my tears. "Thank you for your wonderful words," I yell to her over the deafening applause.

She smiles with so much affection it makes my veins ache. "You were magnificent," she shouts back to me.

"Well, we have a new show coming out in a few days," I tell her. "You will have to come to visit again, and when you do, just tell the simulans you are Vanery, and I will give you a personal tour of the circus."

Her eyes are wide, and her smile spreads across her whole face as she replies, "Yes, oh yes, please!"

Scout kneels next to her as well, but he puts his back on the crowd. This, of course, breaks an unwritten performer's law. You never turn your back on the audience.

"Thank you for that," he says to the girl, his voice soft. This, more than anything, causes the crowds to be quiet. They want to hear what he is saying.

I know not if Scout realizes the crowd is listening to him or if he merely cares not, but he continues, "However, there is so much more hope out there than our humble circus can offer."

Embarrassed by his words, I hurriedly say, "Scout—" but he does not listen.

"You need something more than us," Scout goes on. "Because even in the circus, I find myself in that season of sadness that you spoke of—"

Before he can say anything else, I haul him up by his arm, spin him around, and pull him down into a bow with me. The applause is still loud but much less so than before.

As I stand upright, I shout out, "We could not have been honored in a more heartfelt, blood-warming way. Thank you." And then I turn to Vanery and add, "And thank you once more, Little One."

Tithes are then taken in our honor. By the time we leave, we have amassed over eleven cheio—about half what Scout and I made in the entirety of last year.

The territorial liturgy and praise of the Aevii go by in a blur as I sit dazed in my booth. Vanery's words dance around in my veins. Her thoughts seem to echo those of Fabella's. It seems that I am responsible for more of the world's well-being than I ever would have imagined… 'tis both an honor and a nightmare.

But for now, remembering little Vanery's sweet face and words, I find the honor to weigh heavier in my veins.

When the service finally ends, I barely notice that we are standing for the final pronouncement of the High Begirale.

He shouts, "And they said to themselves, 'Nothing we propose will be impossible for us!' Praise be the Aevii, praise be our Gifts, praise be our blood!"

We shout our reply: "Nothing we propose will be impossible for us!"

"And now," he says slowly, with mastered showmanship, "who wants to hear more of the June Bugs?"

As WE MINGLE WITH the worshippers, I am overwhelmed by their support and passion for the circus. I know our show is good, and I know the sacrifices Scout and I have made to accomplish what we have, but seeing these people appreciate our hard work makes everything feel worth it.

One of the last worshippers, a tall man with curly grey hair, places his hand on his heart to greet me in the Ortusan way. "I've been to your circus dozens of times," he states excitedly. "And every time I go, it's as if it's my first time."

I beam at him and have to renew my cheek muscles as they are getting tired from so much smiling. "That is wonderful to hear."

"I always leave entertained, inspired, and honestly encouraged to try my best in my work," the Pexun goes on. "You hit me like a bullet every time."

The word catches my ear. "Like a what?" I ask.

The man seems flustered by my question. "Oh, sorry, my mate always tells me to leave the jargon at work, but sometimes it slips."

"Worry not," I remark hurriedly. "I just want to know what that is. What is a *bullet*?"

"It was what they used as ammunition in Senex," he answers distantly. He tries to turn to leave, but I ask him to explain more. Tentatively, he goes on, "See, I'm a historian, and my particular interest of study was the Senny means of war. A bullet was usually made of metal, formed into the shape of a tapered cylinder or a ball, and then it was expelled or shot out of a firearm—usually a gun. I don't know if you've ever heard of those."

"One of our performers is very interested in Senexian memorabilia, so we have an entire room filled with ancient weaponry," I reply. "I have been told that guns are like finitums."

Finitums are Gift-stripping weapons held by only elite Guardians. If a person is hit anywhere on the body with the finitum's ammunition, their Gift is immediately stripped. But if they are hit in the heart, the person will perish.

"Quite similar," the man says, now eager over my curiosity around the subject. "The gun is the finitum, and the ammunition is the bullet. But, instead of stripping one's Gift, the bullet tears through the victim's body. If something vital like an organ is hit, the person would die.

"Do Novians ever use bullets?"

The Pexun man laughs loudly, "No, no. They are illegal to make or own. The only people who would know what bullets are would be historians, enthusiasts, or Sennies—you know, Pods."

Automatically, I bid the man farewell and give him a free ticket to our next show. As far as I know, Merayal is not a historian. And even if she was, Merayal did not say she was studying bullets. She said she *extracted* a bullet. Perhaps she knew an enthusiast with an illegal gun that still held a bullet. But how would she know what the bullet was? Unless she was an enthusiast as well.

Perhaps.

Fabella had said that Merayal is not from this world. Fabella had also said that Merayal came from a wicked place populated with evil people. If she is not of this world, what world *is* she from? And who are these wicked people?

Perhaps... perhaps she *is* from this world *and* another world... from another timeframe. And who was more evil than the Senexians?

Perhaps...

Could Merayal be a Pod?

Sanus

Flister

78 years ago

T HE SIXTH AEVUM CANNOT feel his face. He is not even sure he has appendages anymore. Every thought is gone, every feeling suspended. He is nothing and everything and here and there and nowhere, and it is all delicious.

The pounding bass keeps his body rooted to the moment, or he would float away forever, lost in a kaleidoscope of sound and color. Bodies push up against him, and he is uncertain as to when he last took a full breath into his lungs.

Suddenly, he is hurrying off the dance floor. In his intoxicated state, he thinks maybe his feet are moving of their own accord. But why is he leaving? Where is he going?

The irritation and anger in his blood cause him to focus, if only for a moment—if only to take him back to the dance floor.

Someone has his arm, although he cannot perceive who it is. Who would dare touch him? Let alone lead him anywhere? The body beside him is not Mal's—not that she would ever enter a place like the Vermilion Fang. No, the only other Aevii who would ever be inside a club like this would be Dakarai Ebelson—but thank the universe that he never frequents this one.

Still, maybe it is Dakarai, Flister reasons, and he tries to make his eyes pivot. But the person pulling him along is still too blurry to identify, although they look to be male.

Flister now finds himself tripping up the stairs toward the VIP lounge.

After being moved again and taking a few more steadying blinks, he realizes he has been set down on a couch. In fact, it is one of the HugMe black velvet couches he had been on but a couple of hours ago, filling his body with the toxic tonic that now courses through his veins.

A figure sits down across from him, and although he tries to perceive who it is, a wave of nausea hits him so strongly that the next thing he knows, he is staring at a pile of vomit splattered across the silk-feathered carpet of the VIP lounge. Oh, the Pexun who gave him this unbalanced concoction will pay.

To his great displeasure, when Flister leans back up and focuses his eyes—although they are still blurry—he sees that Qualcum Elder is sitting across from him.

After a string of curses, the Sixth Aevum spits loudly, "Was that your man who pulled me up here? You had *no* right!"

Even in his inebriated state, Flister can see the Third Aevum eyeing him with disgust.

Flister guffaws. "Do you not like what you see, Eldermydearest?" he asks, his words slurring together so much he is not sure Qualcum can understand him. "Now you know how I feel *every* time I look at *you*. You are vile and revolting. I throw up in my mouth every time I see you."

In one sudden moment, Flister realizes he is shouting and standing and shaking uncontrollably. Before he can succumb to the very real threat of passing out, he sits back heavily on the black velvet couch.

Qualcum responds, but the music from the club is so loud Flister cannot hear him.

"Wuther!" Flister roars and his assistant appears at his side. The portly shapeshifter's Pexun hair falls into his face. The man pulls the strands behind his ears and asks, "Yes, Aevum? How can I serve you?"

"I cannot hear a cursed word with all this noise!"

Wuther nods, bows, and pulls a veil infused with sound-canceling tech around the two Aevii. Immediately, silence descends as if he had switched off the club's clamor. The silence rings in Flister's ears louder than the music had.

"What do you want?" Flister asks Qualcum sharply, his voice booming.

After clearing his throat of an abhorrent amount of phlegm, Qualcum answers, "Oi know ye've been seeking Arkarian Story against Mal's wishes."

Heat rushes to Flister's face. For the last three years, he has been flexing his power, testing his limits, and finding his allies. Searching for and attempting to murder Arkarian Story without Mal's knowledge has proven difficult. She has already confronted him twice and reminded him of his promise to leave the prophecy business alone. That conversation was the angriest he has ever seen her.

His love and affection for her had almost stayed his search. Displeasing Mal went against every cell in his body. But he knew he had to keep going—he has to find the old warlord. If not, he will die—and not even Mal is worth that.

Since then, he has been so careful, so mindful when conducting his searches—so how could Qualcum have known? Unless…

"Have you been spying on me, Elder?" he asks, trying to keep his voice even.

Qualcum grimaces. "Of course Oi've been spying on ye, Flister. What an ignorant and unintelligent question."

The anger that wells in Flister is so overwhelming that his vision blurs entirely for a moment, and again he almost loses consciousness.

"Before ye wet yer diaper," Qualcum says with a twisted smile, "Oi am here ter give ye some assistance."

"Assistance?" Flister snaps. "I need nothing from you, Elder."

The Third Aevum eyes him, and there is something cold and dark in the assessment. A notion worms its way into Flister's veins that he has somehow made a terrible mistake, and this is his one chance to amend it.

Licking his dry lips, Flister mutters, "I apologize… I—What can I do for you?" His head pounds, and it takes everything in him not to close his eyes and lie down on the silky floor.

"Oi have been waiting fer ye ter become a man ter have t'is conversation," Qualcum begins, "but Oi see t'at won't be happenin' anytime soon. Here ye are, t'irty years old, and ye're bent on actin' ta part of a boy. Oi'll wait no longer."

The words wash over Flister, but he does not know how to respond, so he merely nods.

"Accordin' ter yer back, what is ta only t'ing t'at can kill ye?" Qualcum asks.

The world darkens around Flister's peripherals. He tries to answer, but he cannot move his lips. Qualcum keeps talking, but he cannot hear him—the Third Aevum is much too far away.

A sudden pain in his face makes his eyes flash open. Qualcum gathers a whip back into his lap, and Flister touches his cheek. When he pulls away, blood covers his fingertips.

"Ye will listen, or ye will die," Qualcum declares, and when Flister's gaze focuses on the older Aevum, he sees a fit of anger there that before he has never seen. "Answer me question," Qualcum commands.

Flister licks the insides of his cheeks; they are woefully dry. "The—the Reader. And Scion… To—" he takes a deep breath and licks his lips. "Together with me. We can wake up Arkarian Story together, and I will die."

"Incorrect," Qualcum responds. "Ta Scion and Reader don't need ye. T'ey can find him all on t'eir own."

Flister knows this statement should worry him, but he is so focused on staying awake and present, it does not penetrate his anxieties. But when Qualcum adds, "And so t'ey have," adrenaline shoots through his veins.

"They have *what*?"

Qualcum takes out a black handkerchief from his sleeve and blows into it. With everything in him, Flister keeps his face from grimacing, keeps himself from yelling at Qualcum to answer.

Turning away from Flister, Qualcum shouts, "Happenstance!"

The veil behind the Third Aevum's head moves like an invisible person is flailing in the fabric. But then, Qualcum's assistant appears, flustered and breathing heavily.

"Yes, Lord?" Happenstance asks, flattening his greasy, disheveled hair. Since he was a boy, Flister has always thought the assistant's frazzled locks had the color and appearance of a pile of wet hay.

"Ye know, Oi *will* take me drink." As he says this, his eyes never leave Flister's.

"Yes, Lord. Oi will get it right now." Happenstance turns and runs into the veil again but disentangles himself more quickly this time.

The Third Aevum's gaze does not waver.

Even under the influence, Flister understands this is a power move—understands that Qualcum is declaring his authority over him. He also understands that, if he says the wrong thing, he will never find out the truth.

Wishing he did not know such things, Flister predicts the exact drink Happenstance will bring his Aevum. From the time Flister was little, the only drink Qualcum would ever take was a cocktail called a Sick Day. The concoction combines ginger, vodka, lemon juice, dry vermouth, and a pain-relieving agent.

It is not until Happenstance's return, and after Qualcum has taken a long draught of the Sick Day, that he finally divulges, "Five years ago, ta Scion and ta Reader found each ot'er. And just last week, t'ey found Arkarian Story."

Flister's heart pounds so violently he becomes lightheaded once more. "They—they found him? Are they going to wake him up? We must act now—" He tries to stand, but his legs refuse obedience. Overwhelmed and terrified, he asks, "Well, where is he? Where is Arkarian Story hidden?"

"Oi don't know," Qualcum answers.

"What do you mean *you do not know*?" Flister snaps before he can stop himself. "Why not use your Gift to watch them?"

"Arkarian Story's location is hidden wit' ta aid of powerful Gifts," Qualcum answers in a voice void of inflection. "Anytime t'ey spoke of it, t'eir words would become muffled, and Oi was unable ter hear t'em."

How can that be? A nauseating concoction of frustration and fear fills his body and causes his voice to crack as if he were a boy undergoing puberty. "How—how can Arkarian Story have Gifts protecting him? He is a Senexian!"

"'Tis a mystery, ain't it."

Flister shouts a curse. "Elder, this is not a joke!"

"Oi have found it ter be quite amusing."

Dawning hits Flister like a hurricane wind. "You… you want me to die?"

Ignoring Flister's question, Qualcum states, "Ta Scion and Reader are in t'eir graves."

This information makes Flister's head spin. "Did… did you—"

"Oi dispensed of t'em fer ye."

"*For* me?"

"Is it yer intention ter die?"

"No."

"T'en Oi would say gratitude is required."

Qualcum's sneer makes Flister want to hit his putrid face, but instead, Flister steels himself and states, "Thank you."

Even though he is still upset, sudden and sweet relief floods his veins. They are dead. The Scion and the Reader are dead—the prophecy is void. Without lifting a finger, the only threat to his immortality had been eliminated. The fact that it was at the hand of the man he hates most in the world is immeasurably infuriating, but he'll take the win.

Sighing, the Sixth Aevum repeats, "Thank you," and adds a sincere, "truly."

"Ta next one will be yer responsibility."

Confused, Flister asks, "The *next* one?"

"Ta next Scion and Reader."

The peace he has enjoyed for a mere twenty seconds evaporates. "The next—" Cortisol spikes the venomous elixir brewing in his veins. "How do you mean?" he cries.

"Yer prophecy meant *any* Scion—any descendant of Arkarian Story—and *any* Reader. T'ere are hundreds of t'ousands of Elusians who have varying amounts of Scion blood in t'em, and t'ere are hundreds of Readers. And any of t'em—*any* variation—could find Arkarian Story and wake up ta warlord."

Flister's head spins, both from the concoctions and from the grim reality of his newly explained situation.

After taking another deep draught of his cocktail, Qualcum goes on. "Now, Oi must explain ta rules before ye begin ta game. Yer not allowed ter look fer

Arkarian Story—Mal has written it, ye know it. Fer now, until Oi can find a way around t'at, ye will keep watch on ta Scions and Readers. As much as ye can, ye must keep t'em apart. Ye can't just kill all of t'em because Mal will find out yer purposes and punish ye. Killin' needs ter be a last resort, see. Also, *if* ye have to kill, take ta Scion, not ta Reader. If too many Readers start dyin' off, an investigation from ta Guardians will be enforced, and t'at is attention ye don't want. A Gift bein' killed off is more suspicious t'an a bloodline.

"Oi have current lists of all Scions and Readers throughout Elusis, and Oi will send it ter yer house in ta mornin'. Yer job, Flister, is ter keep t'em from findin' each ot'er. Aye? Do ye understand?"

"If there are really as many as you say, how could I possibly keep them all apart?"

"Ye'll play ta game by ta strategy of yer choosin'. But t'ere be fewer Readers."

"How have *you* been keeping them apart?"

Qualcum laughs then and, with apparent pain, stands up from his chair. Clicking his tongue, he drawls, "Oi'll not do all ta work fer ye. Ye must be a man at some point in yer eternity."

"You have to tell me what to do!" Flister shouts, standing also. But he does so too quickly, and lightheadedness has him back in his chair within seconds. His vision blackens around the edges, a dark blur slowly closing in toward the center.

"Oi've helped ye more t'an ye'll ever know, little boy. Enjoy yer hunting."

"You cannot—" Flister tries, but all has gone black. "You cannot—" Head too heavy, Flister lets himself slip into the nothingness of restless sleep.

THE SIXTH AEVUM SHOOS away the bulbous fly that keeps landing on his car window, impeding his sight. It takes a moment for the fly to settle again, and then he tries to smash it. When he misses, it flies to the back of his car. Only once the buzzing has stopped does he turn his attention back out his window to the small Formosian boy playing across the street with a neighbor.

Flister would have preferred to wait until the boy was older, allowing him a few of the pleasures life offers... but that was not meant to be.

The Aevum sighs again. He blames the little boy's parents. It was their fault for moving across the territory to Ryuin. If they had just stayed on the east side, remained in Yupre, Flister would not be in this position. He had used much power and influence in an attempt to trick the young boy's parents into staying back. He had arranged a pay raise for the mother. He had moved some residents out of the family's dream home so that it came up for sale. He had even given the boy entrance to a highly sought-after school. But the parents had been *insistent* on moving to Ryuin. They were bent on ignoring the signs and taking their family across the territory.

He knows that this little boy, the Reader, and the Scion will not fulfill the prophecy, being as young as they are—the boy six years old and the girl eleven. Perhaps they would not even fulfill it during the next five or ten years. But the prophecy did not give ages, just Gift descriptions. And thus, the Sixth Aevum finds himself in this conundrum.

He has tried to keep them away, but some unspoken magic has drawn them together.

The Aevum knows what the magic is, of course. He knows what has allured them. It is the cursed prophecy—but he will win. He always does.

He could wait of course, but what if he waited too long? The boy's life is certainly not worth his. He will make the arrangements this very night. It will be better to get it over with quickly. The couple will be allowed to have another child. The Scion will move on to new friends. All will be well, and he won't have to worry for another fifty years.

The peace of mind that this thought brings puts a smile on his face. This Reader killing suits him much better than the many Scion killings of the last four years. So much easier, so much more efficient. Qualcum had told him to use killing as a final measure, but he found trying to keep the Scions and Readers apart too exhausting. Killing the Scions *before* they met the Readers took away much of his growing anxiety.

An hour later, as his car emerges from the Silentar transponder station, the Aevum makes the call. Once he is quite sure the little Formosian boy will die within the day, he lets out a deep sigh of relief. When he walks into his house on Wintour—the ground level of a three-tiered designer building in downtown Jukantytär—the Silentar guards worship him. He does not acknowledge them. Instead, he walks towards the elevator that will take him to his home as if they do not exist.

Flister does not watch downtown Jukantytär fall away around him as he ascends in the sky towards O'Brien—the sky level—nor does he hear the charming chime ring as he arrives at his abode. He does not notice the exquisite and rare art lining the hallway walls, nor does he take in the colors or the imported smells. The door recognizes him and allows him entrance, and he steps into his home.

His house is bright, filled with sunlight. Half of the front area is a living room, while the other half organically shifts into his coveted outdoor garden. Brick-colored slate hangs off the edge of the roof to be met by a great glass dome covering the rest of the space. The whole room seems as if it has one foot outside and one foot inside, for the Aevum has filled the interior with plants, and various pieces of furniture are dispersed throughout the exterior garden. Even his study is situated on the edge of the small garden.

However, Flister does not look upon any of this as he makes his way through the expansive dwelling towards the kitchen.

As he moves through the rooms, the texture of the house subtly changes from bright and open to dark and moody. The walls are made of rich brick and stone, making the hallways, the second and third living rooms, the library, the entertaining room, and the kitchen feel warm, intoxicating, mysterious.

The Aevum walks straight to the refrigerator and says, "It is I, open hence," and the refrigerator swings open. It is not a door to access a food compartment, but rather the whole refrigerator opens to access a secret room. Flister walks through the door, turns on the light, and closes the fridge behind him.

As he walks across the small but heavily decorated room, Flister takes off his outer and suit jackets. Behind his private bar, boasting some of the rarest wines, scotches, vodkas, and eupees, Flister pours himself a three-fingered glass of his favorite one-hundred-year-aged eupee. Today is cause for celebration. Fingering his books, he picks one that had been sold to him on his sixteenth birthday by a prophet in Pexus.

He takes a moment to look at the vials of blood he has displayed on two of his shelves. The larger one has purple silk draped underneath dozens of vials, and a smaller one next to it only has four vials decoratively laid on ancient pieces of paper. Each small glass container is a reminder that one life is not more important than the whole. Each life he took was a trade: his life for theirs. But where their lives just served themselves, the Sixth Aevum's life serves all. He deserves life more than they did, for the good of all metahumans. A fair trade, he would argue.

At first, there had merely been the one shelf. However, it was not proper for the Scions and Readers to share the same space, so after the first Reader died, he crafted a special rack specifically for their blood. Soon, his newest vial would arrive, and he would place it right in the middle of the other four.

The Sixth Aevum loves collections.

A hologram of his simulan appears on his desk as it states, "The Fifth Aevum is here."

Flister sighs. It has been four years since he chose not to continue the game with Oaken Bleu. He rubs the skull tattoo on his wrist. She had been so angry and hurt—so upset that he had kept a secret from her. If only she would have given him a Blood Assurance that she would not dare him to divulge what he had been up to, he would have continued their game. But she would not.

It became her sole goal in life to find out what he was doing, and it took all of his genius, wit, security, and pride to keep her in the dark. Had she not made it such a big deal, he may have given in years before. But her persistence kept him strong. It was their new game.

In the last six months, she has distanced herself from him. Although they often see each other due to their Aevii responsibilities, they have not spent time together. Had he not been so consumed with the Scions and Readers, he would have tried to make amends.

When he walks out to meet her, just seeing his old friend standing rigidly in his living room makes him very sorry he has not done so.

"Oaken, darling," he drawls, kissing both of her cheeks. "I am so sorry I have not reached out lately. You must forgive me."

She neither smiles nor responds to the comment as she declares, "I'm here to threaten you."

This takes him off guard. "Oh, really?"

"Yes."

"How so?"

"I'm not too prideful to admit it: I miss you. I miss our game. And if you will not resume it, I will tell Mal that you are up to something."

Immediate anger rises in his chest. "You will do no such thing."

"I will," she counters, just as upset. "Whatever is consuming your mind is making you distant and boring, Flister. You will dare me to do something, and you will tell me what you've been doing, or you will regret it."

"Now, now," Flister coos with forced calm. Adding venom and spite to his tone, he adds, "You must not say such things."

"Call my bluff then," she bites back. "See how serious I am."

"I am not going to be forced—"

"Dare me."

"—by *you* or by anyone for that matter—"

"Dare me."

"—to share anything I do not wish to divulge. And—"

"Dare me!" Oaken screams, her fists tight by her sides. "Stop being a coward and dare me!"

He laughs derisively. "Ah yes, cowardice keeps me from playing with you."

"Whatever you're doing, you don't want Mal to know. So there are one of two things going on. One, you're breaking one of her rules—doing something you've been forbidden to do. Or two, for four years, you've been searching for even a gram of courage to finally tell her you're in love with her, and you've come up short."

Her words sting like a slap, but she does not stop there.

"Or maybe you're coming to terms with the fact that she will never return your affections. You're mourning that a three-hundred-and-forty-two-year-old woman isn't interested in a thirty-four-year-old baby."

"Desist." Rage fills Flister as she speaks, and if she does not stop, he will make her.

But Oaken carries on. "You're immature and self-focused, and you only care about yourself—"

"Desist!" he shouts.

Face twisted with rage, she screams, "Then dare me to! Because that's the only way I'll stop describing just how laughable your love for her is. In what world would she look at you and *want* you? She sees you as a son—what kind of sick love would she have if she desired you? How could you—"

As if something inside him has snapped, Flister wipes the tattoo off his forearm and, grabbing her arm, pulls the Fifth Aevum closer to him. As he swipes the tattoo onto her cheek, the green flecks in her hazel eyes sparkle with the thrill of the game.

"I dare you to kiss me," he seethes.

Oaken's brows leap in surprise.

Flister continues, "I dare you to kiss me with all of your restrained passion. Use your lips to tell me all you have chosen never to say. I want you to hold nothing back—let me completely in. And as you do so, I want you to taste my rejection."

The Fifth Aevum strains against his grip, but Flister squeezes her arms, pulling her closer. His breath is like wind in her hair as he goes on. "I want you to feel the warmth of my lips, knowing that I do *not* return your affections. I want you to truly, deeply understand just how much I hate you in this moment—how I despise you."

The small Aevum's body trembles with anger, her brows buried deep, her mouth a hard line.

Loosening his grip, Flister finishes huskily in her ear, "And I want you to hope, Kenny. I dare you to kiss me, dare you to dream that doing so will change it all, and perhaps—just maybe—this one kiss will cause me to love you in the same way."

The Sixth Aevum's heart pounds as he releases her.

The two Aevii stare at each other, poison swirling in their eyes. When she doesn't move, Flister roars, "I dare you, Oaken Bleu!"

So she does.

Oaken closes the gap between the two eternal beings and, throwing her arms around his neck, she kisses him. It is tentative at first, and he can taste her anger—her shame. But then it softens as her passion grows.

As much as he had wanted to feel nothing, Flister is moved. He can feel her wrath and fear, sense her vulnerability and yearning, and it touches his very marrow.

Of all the lovers he has ever had, no one has ever kissed him like this. Not the most ardent worshipper nor the most well-paid L'oubli.

"Give me a chance," Oaken whispers when she finally pulls away. When their eyes meet, hers are filled with open fear. "I dare you."

The words send a shiver down his spine. Suddenly, he realizes that he wants this. He wants her. It is as if the feelings have been locked away, and now they are finally free. Not knowing if he will regret it, Flister pulls Oaken's arms down from around his neck and, taking a step backward, offers her his wrist.

Her lips twitch in a smile, but she still looks so afraid—like she cannot believe he has agreed.

Gently, he places her hand on her cheek so she can swipe off the tattoo.

As she places it on his wrist, he pulls her against himself and kisses her again.

Pexus

Kansis

SUPPER GOES SURPRISINGLY WELL. I expected it to be awkward or that I would embarrass myself. But Pypen, Scout, Emerly, and Thykas are so easy to talk with. Even before my town-wide shame, this type of effortless conversing was still rare for me. I had friends... but nothing like this... camaraderie.

While we ate, I was presented with a lot of opportunities to teach Amelia, so I tried to focus on that instead. We started with Novian eating habits, mostly focusing on how we eat for nourishment versus the Senexian way of eating for pleasure. Not that we do not indulge in the delicious—but the intention of such a meal *is* to eat for pleasure. Breakfast, lunch, and supper, however, are for nourishment. This conversation led to our health practices, and I explained how each Novie can be perfectly healthy at all points in time. Lastly, I ended by explaining our mealtime blessings and how one is given before eating communally.

Throughout the meal, Thykas played small tricks for us, and Emerly kept trying to speak in English, which made Amelia and me giggle; Amelia laughed so hard a rice noodle shot out of her nose when he tried to tell her she was strong but instead called her "the heaviest niece" he'd ever seen. Pypen and Scout's playful banter throughout also added to the hilarity. The four men interacted in a way that made me jealous. I realized it's because they live life together almost every second of the day... and because of this, they're so open with each other.

I tried not to dwell on it, but I couldn't help but think that this couldn't be farther from my reality. Yes, I lived with my family growing up, but they were all so busy we rarely saw each other. Where some households had family suppers every night, my parent's motto was *'The simulan put supper on the stove. Eat it whenever you want.'* It was only on special occasions that we all sat down to share a meal, let alone spend the day together.

Even before I was shunned, I don't remember ever feeling at home anywhere or with anyone. It's always been me—just me. I've spent years wishing there was someone else—*ahem*, Aker, *ahem*. But really, anyone would have filled the void. A friend or a sister or a parent… but there was never another person. I've always felt alone—minus my subconscious, of course, but she doesn't count.

Supper ends, and Scout motions for me to come across to him. Anxiety pumps through my blood. We are sitting on opposite sides of the table, and everyone will be looking at me when I stand up. *Can I get over to where he sits without them all seeing me?* Knowing there is no way around it, I stand stiffly and walk as fast as possible to stand beside his seat.

"Yes?" I practically squeak.

"Are you enjoying yourself?" he asks quietly.

Not expecting this to be his reason for calling me over, I answer, "Oh, um, yeah. It's fine."

"Just fine?"

"No, I'm—it's good. This is fun."

He lightly laughs then asks, "What was your favorite part of the supper?"

What's with the small talk? "All of it," I answer honestly.

"I got ahold of a friend, and she will make a eutsi for your Pod. I am not certain it will work, but we will try."

"Oh, th-thank you," I state, not knowing why he would be so considerate towards Amelia, she being subhuman and all.

But then, I realize it must be because she's Arkarian Story's daughter, and it would be easier to communicate with her directly… And then… Well, then, once she has the eutsi, they won't need me anymore…

Oh, I get it.

Once she has the eutsi, I'll be sent home. Although this makes my blood slushy, I logically understand that having Amelia independent of me will be easier for everyone.

Bringing me back to the present, Scout asks, "Before we go to the circus, would you mind if we do a little errand on the way?"

Again, I'm confused about this conversation. Why is he asking my opinion? "Sure, whatever you need," I answer.

He smiles. "Good. 'Tis just around the corner."

"Fellow Seekers!" A male voice fills the room. "Greet the moon, and welcome to all of you!" The Buscador raises the insignia—a flame surrounded by smoke—and pins it behind him on the wall. "There are not many of us out there, but we have one goal, and that goal we seek as one. Stand, and may we share our intentions."

Everyone within the restaurant rises to their feet. "We are the Buscadors. On the world's behalf, we seek the Superiors to find answers to life's most complex questions. We will exchange information, share findings, give testimonies, and support each other in our individual journeys to the truth. Superiors, may we find you." The seekers shout a hurrah and return to their seats. Amelia and I sit as well.

"To those of you who are new Seekers, you are most welcome," the man continues. "Over the past three hundred years, the Buscadors have been seeking out the Superiors. Thirty-one of them have been communicated with or spoken of throughout Elusis. They have revealed themselves by different names. Tonight, we will have testimonies of Tajamnica, the Parent Superior; Huyền Bí, the self-existent Superior; and Skrivnost, the wise Superior. Such a unique lineup. So first up, we have a testimony from a Tajamnica follower." As a woman walks up, the man finishes, "Seeker, share your findings."

"Is this a cult?" Amelia asks me.

"To a degree," I answer quietly. "These are the Buscadors I was telling you about. They believe there is something outside of humanity, which is silly, of course."

"Why is that silly?"

"Because of our Gifts. We no longer need to believe in anything higher than us. You did back in Senex. People needed religion and gods to feel a sense of purpose, to understand their existence and comprehend the world around them. We don't need those handicaps or easy explanations anymore."

One eyebrow arched, Amelia laughs, "Can you hear yourself? I mean, are you listening to the words coming out of your mouth right now?"

"I am. And they're true. In your defense, I would say that we revere our Aevii in the same way your world revered your gods. The Aevii watch over us and protect us. Mal Fey, our First Aevum, is four hundred and sixteen years old this year. She has established worldwide harmony during her lifetime, and her continued study of the Gifts constantly enriches our lives. She is kind, and our happiness is the most important thing to her. Once a year, she visits each of the territories to bless her people."

Of all the Aevii, Mal Fey is my favorite. I doubt I'll ever get to meet her, but if I did, I would kiss her hand and tell her how thankful I am that she has been such a great steward of Elusis.

Amelia shakes her head and yawns. "Could you just translate all of this at the end?" she asks and motions toward the rest of the room. "Or just let me know if something interesting happens." She crosses her forearms on the table and rests her head on the little nook she's made.

I smile understandingly. "Yes, I'll do that. Sorry about all this."

I, however, am both overwhelmed and intrigued to be here. I've never been to a Buscador meeting before, and it's not really what I expected. As the testimonies come to an end, I find myself people-watching. Throughout the restaurant, patrons—or seekers—converse. Their countenances vary between happy, longing, sad, and aloof. Where some speak with passion, others keep their voices to a whisper. Why are they so ardently seeking what is already known?

When Scout said he had an errand, this was the farthest thing from my mind.

To my surprise, Pypen was angry with Scout for coming here, yelling at him, "Your obsession is blinding you! You would put the asset in danger because of this? Your foolishness knows no bounds, Scout!"

Scout had assured him that Winzer had promised to stay at the circus and that the restaurant where the Buscador meeting was to be held was within proximity of her Cloak Gift. But Pypen wouldn't hear him. He had told Thykas to go with him, and they had stalked across the street to a bar. Now it's just Scout, Emerly, Amelia, and I sitting at a round table near the back of the restaurant. After another long look around the room, I turn back to our table and am startled to see Scout staring at me.

He leans over and whispers, "What are you thinking?"

I hesitate, thrown by his interest in my thoughts "I... I think these people are crazy."

In the candlelight, his eyes seem darker than their usual light green. "How so?" he asks.

I've never understood the Buscador sect, yet I've never actually talked to one in real life, either. I guess now would be a chance to have an educated conversation. "You call yourselves seekers," I begin, "but what exactly do you seek?"

His eyes fill with passion as he answers. "We seek truth. I know Auctus and Effio left Mensonge and found Elusis, the perfect planet... but how did Elusis get here? Where did Mensonge come from? How did any planet or star in the universe come to be?"

"The universe has always been and will always be," I recite.

"Yes, but how? I believe someone created it. A long, long time ago… I think there was a beginning."

"That is not what is taught," I retort. As a historian, knowing truth and history has always been of the utmost importance to me. The brightest minds in the history of Elusis are alive right now, and they all conclude the same thing: the planets and stars have always been.

Scout continues, "Imagine, Scoop—"

"That's not my name—"

"Imagine if you could know the truth and speak with a being who was there. Imagine asking any question and knowing the answer is absolute fact."

"This Superior creates and knows all? That's a lot of power for a single being."

"All the Superiors embody a different truth. Asiri teaches us compassion. Rahasya shows us light. Tayna possesses all knowledge. Alghumud personifies perfect love. We need them all to understand all. And one day, they will reveal themselves, and we can finally know the truth."

I am not convinced, but his conviction is endearing.

Applause fills the room as the Buscador woman sits back down. Another woman stands; this one is tall, wiry, and very nervous. After making it to the front of the stage, she says, "Tajamnica came to me in a d-dream the other night. A-a-at least, I think it was Tajamnica, as he talked about his children. His appearance w-was like no human I've ever known. His clothing was… it was sparkling. He had on this… this," she makes a movement around her waist with her hands, "this gold belt. His skin… was glowing, and his face was shining, and his eyes were… they were fiery. And the sound of his voice was like the roar of a crowd. It was t-terrifying, and yet… so beautiful.

"When he spoke, he told me not to be afraid. And, and then he said that he *sees* me. He said he is gathering his children, and I am to be ready when he reveals himself. The Superior told me to wait for him."

A hand raises in the back, and the woman points to the man waving it.

"I heard the same message at another meeting, but it was from Tayna. That Seeker explained Tayna in the same way you just did. Did Tajamnica say anything about Tayna?"

The woman shakes her head. "Just that he, Tajamnica, is coming."

An Ortusan man shouts from the back of the room, "How do you know it was Tajamnica if he did not give his name?"

The woman looks so nervous she might faint. "He… w-w-well, he spoke of gathering his children... I assumed... but I..."

The man from the back of the room speaks up again, but this time he directs his words to the man who had raised his hand. "You said that Tayna gave the same message. At that meeting, did the Seeker say that it was specifically Tayna?"

The Pexun man who had asked about Tayna shakes his head. "No, not necessarily. But it was easily assumed by what was communicated."

"What if the message was not from Tayna?" the Ortusan man asks, now standing and walking towards the front of the room. "What if this message was not from Tajamnica?" As he comes into the light, I realize that this Ortusan is the same one we met earlier in the cafe, Knimble Knox.

"That's him," Emerly says excitedly, suddenly slapping Scout's shoulder. He points in delight, like a small child, at the man.

"Who?" Scout asks.

"The one who speaks to the Superiors! He's speaking to one *right now*, isn't he?"

"What is he saying?" Scout asks.

Instead of answering, however, Emerly continues listening to Knimble Knox.

"I believe that a Superior is speaking to you," Knimble says to the shaking woman, "but it is not the one whom you have guessed."

"Who then?" someone from the crowd shouts.

"There have been many manifestations over the years from the thirty-one Superiors. They have made predictions that do not come true, given assurances that have turned out to be false, and given untrustworthy council." At the groans and loud whisperings, Knimble speaks louder. "As Seekers, we do not wish to acknowledge such things as it discredits our beliefs. However," he shouts over the din, "I have something to offer each one of you this night... Truth."

I can feel Scout straining against the table. It's as if he's trying to get as close to the man as possible.

"There is one Superior who is not false, whose words are always true, who sees and loves in a way none of the supposed Superiors can—a Superior who wields all Gifts."

"No *one* being can possess such power," a woman shouts out angrily. "That is why the powers are dispersed among the thirty-one."

"Yes, no physical or even supernatural being could. It would have to be a being above all beings. This one being, this one Superior would have to be the culmination of all of the Superiors. This being would have to be all, and all the time."

Silence meets these words. Then, a stern voice from the crowd states, "This is not what is taught in the Buscador doctrine."

"Buscador doctrine states that there are questions that even metahumans cannot answer," Knimble goes on, unfazed. "This is why the original Buscadors sought beings besides humans to find out if these questions had answers. The first Buscadors wrote down their findings, as we all know. There are beings superior to even the metahumans, as they dwell in an intangible plane. These beings are either benevolent or malevolent. The evil ones are called the etsaia, and the good ones are called the Superiors.

"I believe," Knimble goes on, "that the original Buscadors were mistaken. They had encounters with messengers from the one true Superior and wrongly thought that they themselves were Superiors—"

The room erupts in shouts and derision.

"What's going on?" Amelia asks loudly in my ear.

"Knimble, the Ortusan man we met earlier, is speaking against the doctrine of the Buscadors," I answer.

Amelia opens her mouth to ask another question, then smiles bemusedly at the din filling the room. "Okay, I guess you'll have to explain all of it later."

The shouting escalates until Scout stands and bellows, "Let him speak!"

The room falls quiet.

"Buscadors have put the thirty-one Superiors in boxes," Knimble continues, "limiting but one trait to each Superior. All acts of compassion are attributed to Asiri, all acts of deliverance are attributed to Mea Huna, and so on—but there is one Superior who encompasses all of these and more. He is all and in all. He wields all Gifts and possesses all power. He does not dwell in your boxes; he does not play by the rules of the metahumans, the Buscadors, or even the Aevii—he is above all. He is the Rogue Superior."

This time the room erupts so loudly that even Scout's shouts are drowned out. The jab at the Aevii has lit the listeners' blood on fire.

"How dare you question the Aevii!" someone shouts.

"They are the preservers of peace and our way of life!" another cries.

"We couldn't survive without them, Ortusan scum!"

The Pexun man overseeing the meeting rushes across to Knimble and speaks urgently in his ear. It's too loud for anyone else to hear what he's saying, but Knimble nods and abruptly leaves.

"What's going on?" Amelia asks again. Her body is upright, ready for action.

As the master of ceremonies tries to quiet the room, Scout stands and gestures to us to follow him in pursuit of Knimble Knox. We rush out of the restaurant, and Scout looks around desperately.

I feel bad for him. He's consumed with passion for something he won't ever grasp. "I don't understand," I say aloud, "Why are you so determined to listen to these lies?"

Scout stares out into the night, still searching for the Ortusan man. "His words… it is as if I have always known them. They are true, Kansis; I know it. They draw me…"

"How can his words draw you? It sounds like he pretty much believes the same things you do. That instead of there being many Superiors, it's just one."

"Yes, but if that is true it changes everything," Scout responds. "If all power was in one Gift wielder—"

"There he is!" Emerly shouts, pointing across the street to where Knimble Knox is casually leaning on a brick wall, lighting a cigar.

Scout grabs my hand to pull me across the street, but Amelia slaps his wrist. He releases me as she shakes her head at him, then he laughs, bows, and dramatically points the way across the street.

"You don't want him holding your hand, right?" Amelia asks me as we cross.

"Of course not," I answer.

Of course I don't want a complete stranger holding my hand. I don't want this handsome Ortusan I just met *yesterday* touching me and making me feel warm and seen.

No, that's ridiculous.

Knimble looks at us as we approach and immediately recognizes Amelia, Emerly, and me. "Hello, again," he says and takes a puff. "I was just on my way to the circus."

"I am Scout Eekan, manager of the Unopened Gifts," Scout begins, placing his hand over his heart in the customary Ortusan greeting. "I am very interested in what you were sharing in there. My friend and I have heard whispers about the Rogue Superior in Ortus and Formosus over the past six months. Do you… Have you… Can you speak with this Superior? Emerly, my friend,"—Emerly waves as if Knimble can't see him standing right in front of him— "said he heard you conversing with the Superior in your mind. How do you do that? I have purchased an expensive array of communication agents, and never have I ever… I just—"

"Why don't you let him answer you," Emerly remarks to Scout, interrupting his monologue.

Knimble smiles so warmly, so kindly at Scout that it makes me grin too.

"Oh, yes, please, forgive me," Scout says. "I have possessed so many questions for so long—" he stops, then curses suddenly. "Will you excuse me? I have a call."

As Scout answers his Suus, Knimble eyes Emerly. "What do you want from the Rogue Superior?"

Emerly's face turns serious. "I want to know…" he stops, grimaces, and starts again. "Someone told me that he could cleanse bad blood, they did. That he can… he can take the darkness away. He can take the pain from the things you've done away from you forever."

"He can do all of those things," Knimble affirms.

"How?" Emerly asks.

Knimble takes a puff of his cigar and asks, "Do you not think that the better question is *why*? *Why* would this great being even care about your blood or your darkness?"

Emerly's brows furrow in thought.

Knimble goes on, "Is not the better question to ask why this eternal being— truly eternal with no beginning and no end—with all of the power in the world, would concern himself with such petty, fleeting creatures?"

"Why, then? Why does he want to?" Emerly asks.

Before Knimble can answer, Scout swears again loudly. "We must finish this conversation post hence," he says, raking his hands over his braid. "We must head back right away. Emerly, gather Pypen and Thykas; Knimble, you are more than welcome to join us."

"I must collect my friend, and then I will meet you there," Knimble answers. He nods farewell and walks away from us.

Emerly turns towards the bar Pypen and Thykas have vanished into, asking hurriedly, "What is wrong?"

Scout smiles non-humorously. "The circus is on fire." He looks down at me. "Again."

Pexus

Pypen

Smoke billows from the top of the circus like molten lava escaping a volcano. Chestin, one of the circus' storytellers, is pacing in front of the black and gold tent. I run towards him. When he sees me, his whole body trembles with relief.

"Where is Scout?" he asks.

Although I am accustomed to others preferring Scout over myself, I do not understand it now. Clearly, it is my Gift that will renew the fire damage, not Scout's. "He is just behind me. What happened?" I ask, staring at the smoke, now seeing the yellow flames dancing out of the circus flaps.

"I don't know, do I?" he answers, eyeing the circus with worry. His red hair blazes as brightly as the fire. "I was in my room, and suddenly my door burst into flames."

"Well, thank the universe you were here to alert us."

"Where is Ruelle?" Scout asks, suddenly beside me. He is trailed by Kansis, Amelia, Emerly, and Thykas.

Chestin looks around. "She should be here any minute."

Kansis stares wide-eyed at the circus, her hand covering her mouth.

"Worry not," I tell her. "When our comrade gets here, all will be well."

While we wait for Ruelle to arrive, Kansis, Amelia, Scout, Chestin, and I silently stare as the circus slowly burns from the inside out. Although its exterior is small and homely, the sounds of its innards sizzling hurts my ears.

After twenty minutes, the Chameleon crew arrives.

"I am sorry we took so long!" Sedwick shouts as they run up to us.

Without a word, Ruelle closes her eyes and reaches her hands out toward the circus. The billowing red and orange flames diminish as she turns the oxygen molecules into carbon dioxide. Although she attempts to limit her Gift to the circus, I can feel the oxygen around me being affected as well. Many of us step back so that we can breathe easier.

As the last flame is extinguished, Ruelle starts the real work of changing the smoke molecules back into oxygen. Several times in the past, I have sat down with her and had her explain how complex a feat like this is—and every time I walk away feeling a little less intelligent.

If Lukan's mate were merely working with the area around the tent, I would be impressed, but the fact that she is also working inside all the rooms affected has me amazed.

Ruelle falls to the ground, her energy spent. I renew her with a little of my own power, knowing I only have a small amount to spare. Putting the circus back together will take as much energy as I can muster.

Reaching down into the depths of my Gift, I summon a great force. I reverse the damage, renewing the circus and its rooms as if the fire had never been. It takes me over a quarter of a Vorbi to restore the whole circus.

As my work comes to an end, Scout helps me lower myself to the ground so I can rest.

An Ortusan and Sanusian come out from behind the trees. "That was amazing," the Ortusan man says. "Beautiful Gifting." The Ortusan is not particularly tall or large, and he reminds me of Scout: not physically intimidating, yet exuding strength.

"Thank you," I reply wearily.

"Pypen," Scout waves his hand, "This is Knimble Knox. He is interested in our archery display."

Code: he is an Arkahunter.

"It is a pleasure to meet you," I respond, turning to the man, my hand on my heart as is the Ortusan way. "I am Pypen Tross."

The man mimics my gesture and says, "This is my friend, Tal." He points to the Sanusian who is wearing dark leathers and a feather earring dangling from one ear.

Chestin takes a step forward. "I am Chestin Enigme."

"Healthy blood in your veins…" Knimble starts.

"…and power to your Gift," Chestin recites, finishing the customary Formosian salutation. "I am honored," he adds, placing his hand on his heart.

After Scout introduces Knimble to Thykas and the Chameleon crew, Chestin turns back to the restored circus. Shaking his head, he smiles and says, "What would we do without you, Pypen?"

"Burn."

Kansis snorts, which causes the rest of us to laugh as well.

"Why, thank you, my dear," I say, still chuckling. "It is so nice when someone can appreciate my extensive wit and humor."

"And following that lack of humility, shall we head in?" Scout motions toward the circus.

As we lead the group towards the tent flaps, I whisper to Scout, "How, pray tell, do we know Knimble Knox?"

"Kansis met him earlier when Amelia chased the Senexian into a cafe," he answers. As he speaks, the details come back to me. Scout had filled me in on the entire story earlier, but this part is still fuzzy.

"So why is he here?"

"He has information about Arkarian Story, I believe," Scout answers.

"And the Sanusian?"

"He is his Senexian."

"His Senexian? How do you mean—" And then it hits me. I remember. This is the Senexian that Amelia chased through the city; he is the reason she and Kansis were caught by the Guardians in the first place. And Knimble Knox—oh, this is the man who speaks with the Rogue Superior. My whole attitude towards him sours. As we step into the freshly remade circus, the newcomers openly gawk in wonder.

In the courtyard, a light, cool breeze swishes through my dreadlocks, and I breathe in the scent of summer nights. Above us, tiny lights twinkle as if we are looking up into the evening sky. Warm orbs of brightness hover throughout the courtyard like tiny moons. Every other stripe of the tent is a magnificent hue of gold, bright enough to light the high roof, yet looking around, the room is so dark, it is as if they are not connected. The courtyard's ground is gold, matching the stripes in the tent. Booths line the perimeter, empty and waiting. When we open the next show, these booths will be packed with souvenirs, trinkets, treats, and meals, filling the air with a sweet and salty scent.

"May I join?" Chestin asks from behind me.

"Of course," I say, surprised. Chestin normally keeps to himself. Although he is a solitary character, he has been an asset on many missions. In fact, when we line up our Arkahunter teams, he is usually one of the top three on whom we rely. I cannot think of a single reason not to allow him to join us.

Scout leads us to the invisible staircase and we make our way up to Thykas' room on the second level—our favorite room in which to hold meetings, much to his chagrin.

The Sanusian man pulls Amelia to the side, and when Kansis tries to follow,

Amelia says something to her in English. Although I do not understand the words, it is evident she is dismissing Kansis.

"Join us," Scout tells the Pexun woman. He must have been watching the exchange as well.

Quickly, I update Chestin on Amelia. We do not discuss all matters with every member of the group, but somehow Chestin always seems a step ahead of everyone—including Scout and me at times.

As we settle into the various HugMe-infused cushions, I do not even try to soften my words as I ask Knimble, "Why do you have a Senexian traveling with you?"

"I could ask you the same thing," he responds pleasantly.

"You could," Scout remarks, "but I do believe you have already worked out the answer."

Knimble nods.

"Why do you have yours?" I ask again.

"We rescued him from a Ward unit."

"Rescued him?" Kansis asks, brows furrowed, mouth in a line. She quickly looks at the two Pods huddled in the corner of the room and goes on, "I think you mean you stole him. Pods are meant to go through the reintegration program."

"We rescued him from being forced to the back of his own mind, imprisoned, forever trapped to watch an autopilot version of himself run his life," Knimble expounds.

Kansis seems offended. "It is for their good."

"I am certain you believe this," Knimble replies with profound kindness, as if he genuinely pities Kansis for being taken in by a lie.

"So you, as well, are after the treasured reward of Arkarian Story, yes?" Scout asks, refocusing the conversation.

"Quite incorrect, actually," Knimble responds. "That is not the nature of our pursuit. Some of us believe the Senexians buried Arkarian Story with a book of unspeakable power—for that only do we seek him."

"I think if that were true, the Sennies would have put it in the Book of Instructions," Kansis argues, clearly unable to help herself. I am surprised at her boldness as, thus far, she has seemed quite timid.

"There are other writings, other prophecies and legends that say so," Knimble explains without hesitation as if he was expecting our disbelief. Before anyone can respond, he continues, "You have the daughter of Arkarian Story, who allegedly knows his location. However, I know she has not shared the full truth with you."

"And what is that?" Chestin asks.

"She only possesses half of the coordinates."

"How do you mean?" both Scout and I inquire.

"Amelia is looking for the Code Breakers," Knimble says. "They are an elite group of people from Senex who will help her identify the other half of the coordinates to her father's Hull."

"But the Book of Instructions says the daughter will know his location," I push back, glancing at Kansis, "Is that not correct?"

"Honestly, it's mostly seen as legend as it's only off-handedly mentioned within the Book of Instructions itself; but, there are outside resources that confirm it," she affirms, and her attention flickers to the Pods again.

"Did you know about this?" Scout asks her.

Kansis shakes her head. "Very little. She only just told me she needs someone else to find him."

"Charles Wrightly?" Scout asks.

Kansis nods.

"Like all the Code Breakers, Amelia was instructed not to share this information with any Novians, so that does not surprise me," Knimble comments.

"How do the Code Breakers help her find the other half of the coordinates?" Scout inquires.

"Imagine with me a pyramid with four names at the bottom, two in the middle and one on the top," Knimble begins. "The four names on the bottom are the Base Breakers. Each Base Breaker possesses half of a Pod Identification Number—their PIN. When correctly paired, they reveal the PINs of the two Center Breakers—the two names in the middle of the pyramid. The two Centers also possess half of a PIN each; combining these would lead you to the Peak Breaker—the name at the top. The Peak Breaker possesses half of the coordinates to Arkarian Story's location.

"Due to this, we have two pyramids. In all, there are eight Base Breakers, four Center Breakers, and two Peak Breakers. Your little Amelia is the Peak Breaker for her Code, and she possesses the latitude coordinates for Arkarian Story. Dean, my Senexian, is one of the Base Breakers for the longitude coordinates. We need to find the other Code Breakers with Amelia's help and Dean's code, and thereby we will find Arkarian Story."

He takes out his cigar and starts prepping it for another lighting. "Now, there is this one small matter to consider," he says slowly. "The PINs of the other Base Breakers are hidden within the pages of the Book of Instructions."

I laugh without intention.

Scout smirks as well and clicks his tongue. "Yes, that is a minuscule snag."

"Now, now," Knimble leans back in his chair, puffing at his cigar. "I know the Book of Instructions has been hidden from the public eye and is under extreme protection somewhere undetectable and unfindable. But I was under the impression you were backed by someone powerful and with connections. I did not think this would be much of a feat for such great and Gifted individuals."

"You well know how to stroke a man's pride, Knimble Knox," Scout laughs, "but this may be outside even our spectrum of influence. As you say, I will have to take it up with our powerful backer. I will reach out to you once I have more information. Is Initium your dwelling place?"

"For the next month, it will be. I am staying with a friend in a suburb a few miles from town. I do not wear a Suus, so contact me via this if you need me for anything."

Knimble hands Scout a kaixo—a communication gadget that the government does not track. This one is several versions old, back when kaixos were still thimble-shaped. Scout need only say Knimble's name into the kaixo, and the two men can hold a ninety-second conversation.

Scout puts the kaixo in his pocket.

"Let me know a day or so before you relocate your circus," Knimble says.

"Of course," Scout answers.

I stand, knowing the meeting has come to an end, but the others stay seated. For a moment, I alone stand awkwardly before slowly sitting down. "Are there other matters to discuss?"

"Yes," Scout answers, and by his tone, I know this has something to do with the Superiors.

"Scout…" I warn.

"Can you speak with the Rogue Superior?" Scout asks Knimble, ignoring me.

"I can indeed," Knimble answers.

"What communication gadget do you use?"

Knimble smiles. "I do not need one."

"Then how do you commune?"

"You seek false Superiors, Scout, but the Rogue Superior seeks you," Knimble responds.

"Me?" Scout says, obviously thrown by this statement. "I do not understand."

Knimble leans forward, business-like again. "Can I share something with you?" He looks between Emerly and Scout as if he is just speaking with the two men.

"Of course," Scout says eagerly.

Knimble eyes Emerly for another moment then divulges, "I am on a secret mission for the Rogue Superior. Hidden among Elusians and Pods are many children of the Rogue Superior. Those children do not yet know who they are, and it is my mission to find and awaken them."

"To awaken the Pods, is it?" Chestin asks for clarification.

Knimble turns to welcome Chestin into the conversation. "Pods and Elusians alike."

"Where are these children sleeping?" I inquire sardonically.

"Everywhere," Knimble answers. "They walk around with physical, mental, and emotional operations completely functional. Meta or subhuman, they are all like Pods—their bodies are alive, but their minds are on autopilot. Their blood is dirty, their souls are dead, and only the Rogue Superior can cleanse and give them life."

I laugh. I do not mean to, but I do it. It is loud and it is raucous, and I know it hurts Scout, but I cannot help it. "So these children are sleepwalking," I say between chortles, "carrying within their veins dirty blood, and you... wake them up? Clean them?"

"I do not do that work," Knimble says patiently. "The Rogue Superior does."

"Where are these children?" Scout asks with genuine interest.

"I do not know who his children are. I merely speak of him, and his children are lured to my words like moths to a flame. They may not know their identity as his children, but they hear of the Rogue Superior, and a child knows their father's voice."

Kansis looks at Scout disbelievingly, while his mouth smirks in one corner.

"So anyone could be one of these children?" Kansis asks, tearing her gaze away from Scout and back to Knimble. I am pleased that both the question and her words are laced with skepticism.

"Yes. You could be one, Scout could be one—even our doubter here," Knimble says, gesturing to me, although he winks playfully.

"How do you know if you are a child?" Scout asks.

"His words will awaken you."

Scout's look is disgustingly desperate as he asks, "What are his words?"

"And you never answered my question from earlier," Emerly adds, equally invested. "Why would he even care about our blood?"

Knimble smiles, seemingly amused by something. "You ask the perfect questions, my dear fellows. Normally, this conversation takes hours, days, months to get to, and here you are asking questions that lead straight to the marrow of the matter."

He laces his fingers and leans forward again. "The Rogue Superior is called such because he does not play by the rules of the other Superiors. He is not contained, he is wild, he is raw power, he is the Wielder of all Gifts; and yet, this Superior is also love in its most basic and complex forms. You have heard that Auctus and Effio came from a distant world and made ours perfectly, hiding the Gifts within the folds of the earth—this is not so. There was a beginning, and it was the Rogue Superior who created."

"Blasphemy," Kansis whispers, and again, I am appreciative of her presence.

"Blasphemous of what, exactly?" Knimble asks.

"Your words dishonor and attempt to discredit that which is," I answer, and Kansis nods her agreement. "You come here spouting nonsense about sleeping children, dirty blood, and a creator. You have no right. We do not have the ears nor the patience to listen to any more of your lies."

"Pypen—" Scout starts.

"No," I stand abruptly. "This will not go on, Scout. I will not allow this man to water the seeds of doubt already plaguing your mind."

"Perhaps those seeds are ones of truth," Knimble pushes. "Perhaps my words are the water for the first real growth he has ever known."

"You do not know him," I say slowly and quietly. "You will not be permitted to speak so."

"I permit him," Scout contends. "Leave if you must, Pypen, but I will listen to his words, blasphemous or not."

I curse, using the most colorful array I can muster on such short notice. I move away from Scout and slump down next to Kansis.

The space is quiet for a moment until Chestin prompts Knimble, "You were saying?"

"When the Rogue Superior created the earth, he did all the work himself. He spoke, and the matter listened. It obeyed explicitly and with joy. The last of the Rogue Superior's many creations were a man and a woman—humans with perfect blood, pure hearts, and minds free of evil intent. They were an image of the Rogue Superior himself. Once the humans were created, the Rogue Superior, who had once accomplished his work alone, now passed his work on to the humans. Imagine with me, the creator himself trusted the work of his perfect world to mere humans—"

"Were they metahumans or subhumans?" Kansis asks.

Knimble considers her question for a second then answers, "They were the antehumans. Forehumans, if you will. The forehumans were what all humanity was meant to be. They were given such responsibility. What humility and love the creator displayed, giving them such! And from then on, the Rogue Superior has partnered with his human creations to continue his work on Earth. Still, to this day, he is seeking out human partners to speak, heal, touch, love, and help on his behalf."

Knimble takes another puff on his cigar before continuing, his tone now becoming less light-hearted.

"The world the Rogue Superior created was perfect, just as he was, and there was perfect unity between the humans and himself. He held the definition of good and evil, right and wrong, and he asked the forehumans to trust him. And the man and the woman did. One day, however, a creature came and offered another definition of right and wrong. This creature offered Superior-like powers. Metahuman powers. The creature accused the Rogue Superior of keeping something from the forehumans."

"Did the man believe the creature?" Scout asks.

"Of course not," I answer, annoyed that I have been pulled into the tale. "Why would the man believe a mere creature over the creator himself?"

"Very intuitive," Knimble says, and I am irked at the compliment. "Indeed, why would the man believe the creature over the creator?"

"The man wanted power, didn't he?" Kansis asks.

Kimble's eyes twinkle in the dim light. "Indeed."

"The man didn't want to listen to the Superior?" she goes on.

Knimble nods his head appreciatively. "Brilliant minds surround me. Indeed, Kansis. The man and his mate decided to listen to the creature, and they disobeyed the Superior. Instantaneously, their blood was fouled, their hearts were hardened, their minds were darkened, and their souls died. Since then, all humans have been born with dirty blood and dead souls. However, the Rogue Superior did not want to be separated from his creation, for he loved them. He put into place a rescue plan to bring humans back to himself, blood cleansed and souls alive. And we are living out that plan even now."

"But none of this matters," Kansis says, shoving her frizzy curls behind her ears. "We are not forehumans or subhumans anymore; we are metahumans. We do not need any Superior's help. Our Gifts give life to our blood and our souls. We are perfect, just like the first man and woman you described. And we did it all on our own. 'Nothing we propose will be impossible for us.' We don't need your Superior."

Knimble's gaze falls on Kansis, and it is filled with so much understanding, it is as if her soul is written on her face to be read at his leisure. "You require nothing, Kansis?"

The Pexun's face, naturally a light brown, pales several shades, and her dark freckles seem to pop. "That's not… My circumstances are…" She shakes her head, and her silver curls bob with the motion. "I don't need a Superior."

"You, of all people, should find hope in what the Rogue Superior has to offer," Scout comments to Kansis.

To my disbelief, she pales even more. Their eyes meet for a moment, and where there is confusion and hurt in Kansis' eyes, there is understanding and warmth in Scout's. "I don't need a Superior to fix my problems," she finally states.

"What would fix your problems, may I ask?" Knimble inquires.

"No, you may not," I say, intercepting his penetrating gaze. "Her business is her own. I also do not need this Superior, and neither does Scout."

"What is the Superior's rescue plan?" Scout asks as if there has not even been an interruption.

"What are you willing to give up, in order to know his rescue plan, Scout?" Knimble asks.

Scout's features harden with conviction. "Everything," he answers.

Bile floods my veins. "Does that *everything* include the circus, Scout?" I ask, barely able to control the rage in my voice.

Scout's face falls apologetically as he remembers I am in the room.

I continue before he can speak. "Does that *everything* include Emerly? Gigi? Fabella? The Chameleons?" I cannot even manage the word *me*.

"Pypen—" he starts.

"You are willing to give up *everything*, yes?"

"Pypen, I did not mean it like that."

My veins burn with indignation. "You said it as easily and involuntarily as an aortic pump."

"If someone could rescue you from your evil, would you not give up everything?" Knimble asks me.

"I am not evil! I need not saving!" I shout, and Kansis nods her head beside me. "We do not need you or your Superior. We can—we *have* saved ourselves. You capitalize on the weaknesses in others. Surely there is no more degenerate type of person on Elusis! You disgust me, Knimble Knox—your work is vile, evil, and deserving of destruction," I am sputtering now. I cannot think of anything else to say, but I want to go on. I want to express in no uncertain terms just how corrupt his thinking is, but I am too riled to say anything more.

"You seem like a genuine person," Kansis speaks much more softly than me. "But you are misguiding people, making them weak, as Pypen said. We metahumans are strong; we don't need what you're offering."

"I do," Scout whispers. He looks at Kansis and then at me. Then, louder, he expounds, "*I* need it."

"You are a metahuman, Scout—a strong, powerful metahuman," I insist, my anger flaring to new heights. "You are worshipped by many and adored by all. You need not be saved from any evil as there is none in you." Focusing all my rage on Knimble Knox, I finish, "Your invitation to join our Arkahunter efforts has been rescinded."

"It has not," Scout argues, and for the first time, his voice matches my anger. "He will join us. Above all things, this circus' mission is to find Arkarian Story."

"How convenient for you to remember your mission now," I respond sarcastically.

"Knimble, let me walk you out," Scout says, standing, and Chestin follows suit.

Although he rises, Knimble does not follow Scout to the door. He stares at the floor for a moment as if collecting his thoughts, then he turns his eyes on Kansis and me.

"If you have everything, why do you fear? If you need nothing, to whom does your soul cry?" Although he directs the questions to both of us, it is clear one is meant for the Pexun woman and one is meant for me.

Neither of us answers, and Knimble follows Scout and Chestin out of the room.

"I'm worried about Scout," Kansis comments as the door closes behind them.

"Ah yes, I know the feeling well. 'Tis one of my life's most consuming hobbies," I respond and offer a small smile.

"Would he?" she asks. "Would Scout give up everything for Knimble's Superior?"

I do not reply. Not because I do not know the answer, but because I do not want to say it out loud.

I WAKE UP TO someone shaking my shoulders. "Pypen," Emerly whispers. "Wake up, Friend." He leaves my side, and I can hear him whispering to Scout.

My Suus tells me it is just after one in the morning; I must have fallen asleep in the last thirty minutes.

"What is it?" I ask Emerly.

"The Play Back is here."

This awakens my senses. "Now?" I ask.

"She said this was the only time she could fit us in, she did," Emerly answers.

"Have you awoken Gigi and Ryder?" Scout asks.

"They are next. I left the Play Back in Thykas' room."

"We will meet her there," Scout states, and Emerly leaves our office quietly.

It does not take long for us to get dressed, but we both do so groggily. Once I am slightly more awake, I use my Progift to renew our energy.

Scout stretches and sighs contentedly. "Thank you, Pip."

Refreshed, we make our way to Thykas' room. The Play Back—a Silentar who worked at the circus briefly a couple of years ago—is waiting for us, lounging on one of the couches.

I had almost forgotten that Merayal only joined our group based on our promise to help her find the man who assassinated her mother. The Play Back will hopefully give us the answers we need for her.

"Hello, Anoushka," Scout speaks and extends his arm towards her.

In the traditional Silentar way, Anoushka grabs his forearm with her hand whilst Scout wraps his hand around her arm. "Scout, Pypen," she says with a sharp smile. "Anoushka is profoundly pleased to be present once more, returning like a familiar breeze flitting through town; though she must apologize for her poor timing, a dark cloud that shadows our reunion."

"You are performing an enormous favor for us," Scout replies. "Your timing is perfect."

Anoushka's black hair is cut short with longer bangs clipped to the side by a flashy pearl clip. She is dressed in a formal work suit. Although we enjoyed our time with her as our employee, she was always meant for the professional arena over a performing one.

I listen as Scout and Anoushka share small talk, primarily focusing on her new job at Cupido Interterritorial. When Ryder and Gigi arrive with Emerly, they share greetings, although Ryder is visibly upset at having been awoken.

"Anoushka must be brief, for time is a thief, and in three short hours, Silenda calls my name," the Play Back says.

"No need to apologize," Scout responds. Motioning to Ryder, Gigi, and myself, he explains, "It was the four of us who were on the beach. It was Dixember third, just before noon, when we encountered the assassin. We are hoping you will be able to find any means of identifying him."

Nodding, Anoushka hands each of us a small silver disc. "Position this precisely betwixt your right forefinger and thumb," she commands, her voice soft but sure. "It will prevent your mind from meandering into a maze of memories. Now, like actors on a stage, Anoushka requires you to return to your places, exactly as you stood when the curtain rose on the event."

Scout and I swap places to stand as we were on the Sanusian beach. Anoushka closes her eyes and extends her hands in our direction. After muttering to herself, she grunts, and within two heartbeats, I am suddenly standing back on the sand the day Xoana Kapu was killed.

There is no sound of the ocean nor touch of the wind, as Anoushka's illusion only affects our sight. Suddenly, the assassin walks in front of me. My head had been frozen that day, so I had not seen from whence he came. As Anoushka's Gift depends on what all of us had seen, we cannot know how he arrived on the beach, given none of us saw it happen.

When he stops in front of the blank space where Xoana stood, Anoushka freezes the scene. Using our collective sight, Anoushka analyzes every slight movement he makes. Using her Gift, she captures visible moments whenever light penetrates the assassin's hood.

The first moment shows a partial viewing of his left eye. She throws this image above the man's head. As she walks through the scene capturing more moments, the face comes together. First it is just the eye, then a partial jaw, then a forehead, then some of his mouth. By the time the assassin taps Scout's cheek with the infoship and leaves, there is almost a fully formed face hovering above his head. Anoushka also gets a complete picture of the hand he used to kill Xoana.

Anoushka releases the vision, and Thykas' room is visible to me once more. The Silentar takes a picture of the man's face and hand and sends it directly to Scout's and my Suuses. "You should be able to put these through the Sixth Aevum's database and get something back."

"We could not thank you enough," Scout nods to her.

"Anything at all for Anoushka's circus folk, always," she replies kindly, offering the Ortusan greeting—her hand over her heart—to each one of us. "Whenever the winds of want whisper your name, simply say the word, and

Anoushka will be there in a heartbeat."

"We will do," Scout responds with a smile.

Emerly leads her out of the room.

"Can we go now?" Ryder asks grumpily.

"Yes, go back to bed now, honey," I answer, and Ryder throws me a rude hand gesture as he and Gigi leave.

Sighing, I sit down on one of Thykas' couches.

"Once we learn the assassin's name, we cannot divulge it to Merayal immediately," Scout says.

"Why not?" I ask, genuinely confused.

"She is still getting her feet settled at the circus. I worry that if we tell her, she will leave."

I have no qualms about this plan, but it surprises me. Scout has such strong moral ideals. Everything is black or white with him. It is odd to see him dabble in a grey area like this.

"That does not sound like you," I comment.

"We need Merayal right now. We cannot risk losing her."

"You need not justify the deception to me—I am in agreement with you."

"'Tis not deception," Scout remarks.

Laughing, I slap my thighs and stand. "Oh, Scout, there is no reason for disillusionment—we told her that we would give her information about the assassin as soon as we received it. Now, because it is in our best interests to do so, we are keeping said details from her. 'Tis deceitful."

Shaking his head, Scout leaves Thykas' room to return to our office, and I follow behind.

As we quietly get back into our pajamas and clamber into our beds, I know Scout is feeling uneasy over my words. After the lights have been off for a few minutes, I speak into the silence, "You cannot be perfect all the time, Scout. Sometimes you have to be false to protect the other."

"Who am I protecting?" he asks.

"The circus. You are protecting all of our interests. Your first instinct is to put our collective wellbeing above our promise to Merayal, and you have to do that as our leader."

Fabella had said that the circus' well-being was on my shoulders—how much more so for Scout?

After a few more minutes, Scout asks, "Is it worth it?"

"'Tis."

He sighs and does not push the subject further. "Greet the shadows."

"Greet the shadows."

I have always appreciated Scout's conscience. His goodness is what has kept this circus going. But with that, he has needed me to help him follow through with any less-than-above-the-table choices. And as I have never been as black and white as Scout, I mind not leading him through the grey. I do not give it even a second thought.

Mundus Senex

Amelia

632 years ago; 2089

WHEN, ON ONE PARTICULARLY rainy spring, Estephania and Renee graduate from the program, Amelia becomes the girls' leader. Without any formal announcement or changing of the guard, they follow her, being respectful when Amelia is respectful, sassy when she is sassy, and ready to work hard whenever she does.

Amelia can tell the staff recognizes the power shift, and she goes to great lengths to ensure the girls listen to and respect the leadership.

When her father comes to visit at Christmas, he is proud of her progress. As they walk through the school grounds, snow crunching under their feet, Amelia notices that a light snowfall has covered the dirty snow from the last storm, making the campus look magical instead of grungy. Rubbing his hands together for warmth, her dad asks, "So how did you do it, Milly? How did you hoodwink every person here?"

Smiling to herself, Amelia kicks a small pound of snow and answers, "Spells, of course."

Although he doesn't laugh or even smile, she can feel his approval. "You have done everything I've asked," he states. "And now, seeing your loyalty and obedience, I have another charge for you."

"What is it?" she asks, careful to be interested but not overly excited.

"The lady of the Mountain—Miss Brimer—has requested that you attend Casey Military Academy when you've finished here."

Knowing she will be doing no such thing, Amelia asks innocently, "And is that what you want me to do?"

"Yes."

The response takes her by surprise. She doesn't catch her reaction in time, and her dad notices.

"I know this was not the original plan, but it is better for us."

Tentatively, aware she must tread lightly, she states, "I miss my friends. My life… I was hoping to be able to come home."

"Indeed, indeed. And you have earned such a ticket, I assure you. However, I am not going to allow that."

She stays silent, seething, yet keeping her features calm.

"If you were to come home now, you would continue on the path you set out for yourself—achieving nothing. But if you were to stay, you could be a part of *my* plans." Suddenly changing the subject, her dad gestures towards Cedar House. "Do you like these people?" he asks.

"Not really," she answers. Immediately Lily's face wisps into her mind, and she feels guilty. And following the pleasure of having a friend, is the soft smile of Mr. Ari. Every time he visits the girls' side of the campus, he makes sure to check on Amelia and see how she is doing. Without wanting to, she has found herself growing fond of him.

"Good, good," her father approves. "So, if I were to ask you to spy on them, would that bother you? Would you feel conflicted?"

It is a test, not a question.

Feeling as if there's mostly truth in her answer, she says, "Conflicted about what? I don't care about them."

His smile is not warm and inviting but sharp and commanding. "When you enter the military academy, you will get yourself into their council and then report to me about their dealings."

"Why does a youth military school in Oregon matter?"

"You have earned this charge, but not my trust. Prove to me that you can do this, and I will give you answers."

Determined, Amelia answers softly, "I will."

AFTER A YEAR OF being in the program, Amelia levels up to E. A staff member, Miss Tiffany, comes to her classroom and explains, "In this level, you get access to a Behavioural Insight Staff Member. If you don't care who it is, we'll assign someone for you. If you have a preference, you can request them. If they approve, you'll meet once a week to talk to them about your past and what brought you here in the first place."

"I don't need to talk to anyone," Amelia responds, making sure she sounds respectful yet determined.

"In your case, a staff member has requested to meet with you," Miss Tiffany continues as if Amelia hasn't spoken.

"I don't want to talk to anyone."

"You'll meet Miss Brimer today at four in the Cedar House," Miss Tiffany ends and walks away.

Lily leveled up to E a month earlier, and today is the first day the pair have been able to talk openly since. "What's up?" Lily asks as Amelia turns back to her schoolwork.

"Miss Brimer wants to be my Bissim." Former students of the school had taken the original title of Behavioral Insight Staff Member, turned it into an acronym, and somewhere along the way, over many years, it had morphed into something new—Bissim.

"Miss Brimer? She isn't anyone's Bissim. A lot of girls have requested her, and she's said no to everyone."

"How do you know?"

"I asked," Lily says sheepishly. "Miss Tiffany said Miss Brimer never does issues."

Amelia snorts. "Why would you want her to be your Bissim? She's awful."

"I thought that if she were my Bissim, maybe she'd be a little easier on me. But I don't care. I love Miss Tiffany; she's my favorite."

Amelia huffs. "I don't want a Bissim. I don't have any issues."

"Oh, sure. You love authority, family, and rules. There's nothing to talk about," Lily responds, smirking.

Amelia playfully punches her arm. "Exactly."

Later that afternoon, Amelia walks into the Cedar House to find Miss Brimer sitting at one of the tables. Amelia sits down and waits for her leader to talk, but the woman merely stares at Amelia silently. Finally, Amelia says, "I don't want to talk about anything."

"Perfect," Miss Brimer retorts and continues to stare at her.

Amelia meets her gaze but looks away after a few moments. They sit silently for a painful hour, then Miss Brimer slams her hands down on the table and smiles. "See you next week."

Amelia watches her as she leaves the room.

In times past, she would have liked to have someone pour their presence into her life and care about her and her issues… but not now. Not when attaining the power she needs is within her grasp. Everything is going according to plan, and she doesn't need anyone rooting around and messing that up. She has a new assignment from her dad, and she has no plan to let him down.

The following week, Amelia and Miss Brimer again sit in silence for the entire hour. This goes on every week for the next four months. The day she levels up to F, Amelia sits down at the table, still smiling.

"Happy today?" Miss Brimer asks.

"Only six more levels," Amelia answers, removing the joy from her face. She settles into her chair, ready for another silent hour.

One of the girls in Level B walks up to their table and leaves a peach on the desk for Amelia. The young Asian girl gives a quick smirk as she walks away.

"You've sure got a lot of friends," her Bissim muses.

"They're not my friends," Amelia retorts quickly. "They want me to help them with points and the chore chart." She looks up and then shakes her head. "Not that I mind. I like them all, and I like helping them. But... They're not... I've just never had friends. And I'm okay with that."

They don't speak for a long time until Miss Brimer suddenly states, in a faraway voice, "I had a stepmom."

Amelia takes an involuntary breath and looks at her, but the woman is looking out the window.

Her issues staff doesn't say anything else for the rest of the hour.

The following week, Miss Brimer sits silently with Amelia for thirty minutes before she says, "My mom left my sister and me with our dad when I was six years old."

Amelia stares at the table without moving.

The following week, Miss Brimer doesn't say anything until right before the hour ends. As she slaps her hands on the table to signal that their time is over, she expands, "My dad met my stepmom, Gloria, at a bar."

Amelia nods but says nothing. She leaves and finds Lily doing homework in Pine House.

"What did she tell you this week?" Lily whispers as she sits down.

"That her dad met her stepmom at a bar. And her name was Gloria." Amelia shakes her head. "I don't get why she's telling me any of this."

"Maybe she thinks telling you stuff will help you open up."

Amelia scoffs. "She's got another thing coming then. I don't care what she says; I'm not talking to her."

Last year, it had been her intention to share her past with Mr. Ari or someone similar, in order to gain favor and pity. But now, doing so well in the program, Amelia knows she doesn't need this strategy anymore. As she has gotten to know the staff over the months, she's realized that she doesn't want anyone to know what happened within the walls of her childhood home. It *had* been an important part of the plan, but she has achieved all she has needed to without it… So now her past will stay hidden in her soul, never to be talked of again.

"Would you share with me?" Lily asks in a quiet voice.

Amelia looks up at her friend and studies her face for a moment. Blue eyes, dirty blonde hair, medium color skin, sun freckles under her eyes, long nose, small lips.

Slowly, Amelia looks down at her own hands. "Not now," she answers.

The following week Miss Brimer sits down at the table with a sigh. She rubs her neck for the first half of their time together. Finally, she states, "Even though I was only ten, I didn't let Gloria push me around. But I couldn't stop the things she did to my younger sister. When I told my dad, he didn't do anything about it."

There is no response from Amelia; instead, she closes her eyes for several seconds before looking out the window. Something about Miss Brimer's easy way of sharing this story, the hollow inflection and her matter-of-factness, makes Amelia start thinking about her own dad.

The dad who comes and visits her every other month is different to the one she has grown up with. Granted, he is still just as cold, just as mean… but since he had given her this new charge, he looks at her differently. She knows he is relying on her, and she likes the feeling.

But now… now she remembers things about him that she hasn't thought about in years. The gleam in his eye as he hit her brother, Carter, for the tenth or eleventh time. The way the leather of his office chair would creak as he readjusted his position. The twist of his smile as he eyed her from across the dinner table when Alex was visiting.

Within a few days, she finds herself lost in memories, her mind becoming hazy, her stomach constantly churning.

By the end of the week, Amelia has thrown up three times. She barely eats or drinks. Over the weekend, she goes to the nurse complaining of a fever, but the older woman checks her vitals and declares her healthy. All the girls in the program are worried about her.

Most nights, Amelia lies in bed with her eyes shut as tight as possible, tears spilling down the sides of her face and pooling in her ears. Although the memories of her dad stalk her by day, it is another face—a feminine one with green, snake-like eyes—that haunts these dark hours.

At their next session, Miss Brimer tells Amelia she has heard she was sick all week. Amelia nods wordlessly. "Are you all right?" her issue staff asks.

"I don't know," Amelia answers.

After forty minutes of silence, Miss Brimer breaks it, stating, "I hated my dad. I hated him because my mom was gone. I hated him because he married Gloria. And I hated him for not protecting my sister. In an attempt to save her, one day when I was twelve, I cut Gloria with a knife."

Although Miss Brimer is sharing her own story, it brings up flashes of Amelia's own. Things she has tried to forget for so long. "Please stop," she whispers, abruptly covering her mouth before she can say anything else.

She runs to the bathroom where she throws up everywhere, not even reaching a toilet. As she cleans her chin of what little lunch she has eaten, she stares at herself in the mirror. Her eyes are bloodshot from vomiting so hard.

As she walks back out, Miss Brimer remains at their table. Amelia takes up her seat again, and the woman says nothing.

By the end of the next week, Amelia has visibly lost weight. She hasn't been running or exercising at all. She does her chores, her schoolwork, and then spends all her free time lying in her bed.

Lily is very concerned.

The following week, Miss Brimer says, "I walked in on Gloria touching my sister one day. She had a camera in the room recording it."

The slight color that was in Amelia's cheeks fades. When a warm hand touches her own, she pulls away. Tears start to fall down Amelia's cheeks, and she covers her face in her sleeves. Within minutes, she is sobbing.

She feels so betrayed by her own body. Why these tears? Why this nausea? As the sobs roll over her like waves, her breath coming out short and winded, Amelia forgets about Miss Brimer altogether.

When Amelia's breathing is somewhat normalized, her teacher clears her throat. With no preamble, she states, "Gloria is in prison today for child exploitation." She takes a worn piece of paper out of her back pocket. "I wrote her this letter when I was eighteen." Rubbing her hand under her eye, Miss Brimer begins reading:

> Gloria, I hate you. I hate everything you've done to me, my dad,
> and Robin. You deserve to be in a place much hotter than prison,
> and when you die, Satan will meet you there. What I hate the
> most about what you did is that you enjoyed it. There was no

shame or regret. Your only regret is that I managed to steal enough evidence to get you convicted.

You disgust me. I can't listen to the Pink Albatrosses without wanting to scream and smash furniture. Whenever I hear their music, I think of you dancing and singing in the kitchen while making dinner. You made the best pancakes, and I will never eat one for the rest of my life.

I hope the things you did to Robin will happen to you while you're in prison.

With all that said... I met a man a few months ago who told me that everyone deserves forgiveness. Even people like you. I've been filled with so much hatred for so many years. This man told me that Jesus' burden was light and that He could take my anger and give me peace. And you know what? He did. I've never been lighter or filled with more joy than I am today.

I know God is real because He's taken away my desire to kill you. And even though I know you're getting what you deserve, I just wanted you to know... I forgive you. My counselor told me I would have to keep forgiving you over and over again—every day. This morning, I hated you. But right now, at this moment, I forgive you.

Miss Brimer doesn't speak for a long time, and neither does Amelia, mostly because she can't stop weeping.

Clearing her throat, Miss Brimer says, "I never sent that letter to Gloria. I just wrote it for myself. This week, I want you to write a letter in your journal. I want you to write a letter to someone saying something you've never been able to say out loud." Without another word, Miss Brimer leaves the table.

For the next seven days, bile-tasting anger surges through Amelia every second of her waking and sleeping. Who does Miss Brimer think she is? Who is she to tell her to do something like this?

She won't do it.

They can't make her.

This is not a part of the plan, and it doesn't help her current assignment, so she will *not* be doing as she was asked.

Amelia cannot wait for their next meeting, and when it finally comes, she slams her hands on the table and shouts, "I didn't do it, and I'm never going to do it!"

Miss Brimer nods. "You graduate into K next month."

Amelia stares at the table.

"With all of your good behavior, extra chores, and extracurricular assignments, you'll be able to graduate from this program in three months—five months earlier than scheduled. After that, you'll go to Casey Military Academy."

Amelia nods.

Miss Brimer waits until Amelia meets her gaze. "I will not allow you to graduate from this program until you write that letter," she states slowly.

For the first time in almost sixteen months, Amelia loses it. She springs up, throws her chair across the room, and screams at the top of her lungs. "You can't make me!" she shouts in a deep voice, entirely unlike her own. She runs out of Cedar House and rushes to her room.

She throws herself on her bed and screams into her pillow until her throat is raw. *Get your act together!* she commands herself. If all she needs to do is write the stupid letter, she can fake one. She could write anything to anyone, and Miss Brimer would never know the difference. But something about that idea makes her stomach turn even more. Because, for the first time in her life, she doesn't think she can play-act her way out of her situation.

Too many sleepless nights... too many days without enough food... too many nightmares in the light and ghosts in the dark.

When she looks up again, Miss Brimer is standing in her dorm room.

"I don't want to forgive her," Amelia utters through clenched teeth. "You can't make me."

"You're right, I can't," Miss Brimer responds in a soft voice Amelia's never heard her use before.

"I'm sorry for your sister," Amelia hears herself sobbing aloud. "I'm really sorry, Miss Brimer. But your stepmom doesn't deserve to be forgiven. You should hate her for the rest of your life."

"My hate shriveled me up," Miss Brimer responds. "I was suffocating, and I couldn't go on living. Your hate will kill you, Amelia."

"I'm living just fine! Am I on suicide watch? No. Because I'm not going to let her take any more of my life." Suddenly she tears her sweatshirt off her body and throws all six mattresses in the room off the bedframes. "Who told you?" she screams at Miss Brimer. "Nobody knows! Nobody! My dad wouldn't have said anything."

"Nobody told me anything. Jesus told me to tell you my story," Miss Brimer says.

Amelia rolls her eyes and, through sobs, manages a scoff. "Jesus?"

"Yes. He told me to tell you my story and to read you my letter. I have no idea what your past is."

"Well, you're never going to hear it," Amelia seethes. "It doesn't matter. None of it matters." Amelia throws herself to the ground. Tears, snot, and drool drip from her chin onto the floor.

"You're the toughest girl I have ever met," Miss Brimer slices the silence. "And that's saying a lot, being the warden of a school like this. You're special, Amelia, and I'm not saying that to make you feel better. Do you know why the girls follow you? Because you lead with wisdom and compassion. You genuinely and passionately care about the girls in this program, even though you lie to yourself that you don't. You've convinced yourself it's an act, but it's not."

Miss Brimer takes a deep breath. "But there's also something very dark lurking in your heart, Amelia. Something unstable, unkind, and violent. That hatred that you carry is poisoning you. You will find more freedom than you ever thought possible in letting it go."

Amelia scoffs again. "I like the hatred." The hatred will help her get power.

"I love that courage," Miss Brimer replies with a kind smile. "But I want you to experience true peace."

"I don't want anything to do with Jesus."

Miss Brimer sighs. "Can you honestly say you have peace?"

Although she doesn't answer right away, she finally snaps, "No."

"Jesus offers peace, forgiveness, hope. A chance to move on and find true healing." Miss Brimer walks over to where Amelia kneels and places her hand on Amelia's head. "Write the letter. Just see how you feel."

Her Bissim leaves, and Amelia gets up and throws her journal away.

THE FOLLOWING WEEK, MISS Brimer and Amelia sit at the table at the same time as usual. Amelia's back is rigid, and her palms are shaking. "I wrote a letter," she growls through clenched teeth. "And I didn't do it because you wanted me to or because it's good for me—I did it so I'd stop feeling... Stop feeling so... so..." Steeling herself, she pushes the letter towards Miss Brimer, adding, "I'm not going to read it." Miss Brimer clears her throat and reads out loud:

I remember the first time I ever saw you. You were talking with my brother in the middle school parking lot, and when you turned to me, you looked like a snake. Your eyes seemed more yellow than green. They were so narrow, so piercing. If I close my eyes, I can still see them. You were talking to my brother, but you didn't take your eyes off me.

You came over that night and charmed my parents in a way that impressed even me, and that's saying something. You're beautiful. You have an intimidating type of beauty that attracts followers and keeps those below you in line. I respect that in any girl. So, I couldn't understand why I felt so cold around you, but every time your snake eyes turned on me, I couldn't breathe. My stomach was in knots, and my jaw seemed clenched shut.

Do you remember that night you stayed in the spare room? Do you know what I remember about that night? My door creaking open. The light from the hallway spilling into my room. You getting into my bed. You shushing me. Me, not understanding. Me crying. I was only seven.

When I told my mother what had happened, she frowned and said I'd start a scandal. When I told my father what had happened, he smiled and said it would build character. Neither of them did anything about it, and neither stopped you from coming to our house and spending the night, over and over and over, year after year.

Ironically, when Carter found out about it, he stopped inviting you around. He never talked to me about it. I think he didn't like that there was someone else hurting me more than he ever could. It was his job to hurt me, and you were doing it in a more effective, longer-lasting way than he could ever imagine. He jealously kept you away from me. But he still uses you. He uses you as a weapon.

You know that's why he invited you over two summers ago, right? He'd used you as a bargaining chip, and I'd called his bluff. But he wasn't bluffing. You came over, and my family treated you like a long-lost relative. You were given the royal treatment, weren't you?

I locked my door and placed my bed in front of it. How could I have known Carter would show you how to climb into my window? How could I have known he had unlocked the latches earlier that day?

I hate you for what you've done, and it's eating me alive. I can't eat, I can't sleep. I'm afraid that this is all my life will ever be. Hating you, hating Carter, hating my mom, hating my dad, hating me... What if this is all my life ever is? I'd do anything at this point to get out of this hell.

So I'm writing this letter hoping that Miss Brimer is right. Hoping that maybe I could find peace somehow, somewhere, someday. If forgiving you is the only way back to life... I may just have to try it.

Miss Brimer clears her throat. She'd had to stop several times during the letter to regain her composure. The pair sits quietly for a long time. Finally, Miss Brimer whispers, "I'm so sorry, Amelia. That should never have happened to you."

"Look," Amelia says, "I don't know about Jesus, but I would like to let go of my hatred. I do want peace."

"That's a start," her teacher responds, smiling kindly. "But there's more once you're ready."

This time, when Amelia rolls her eyes, it's done playfully. "You keep your religion; I'll keep the peace."

Miss Brimer chuckles as she replies, "Well, you did it, Amelia." Reaching across the table, she shakes the young red-headed girl's hand. "Congratulations. You have graduated from the Mountain School for Troubled Girls and have been accepted into the Casey Military Academy. You will start on Monday."

A strange excitement glows in Amelia's stomach—the first good feeling in a long time. She is finally going to the military academy where she can get started on her father's next assignment.

Miss Brimer's phone makes a strange alarm sound, and she takes it out of her pocket. As she reads the text message, she jumps to her feet, her face pale.

"What is it?" Amelia asks.

Miss Brimer's voice shakily answers, "Russia just launched a mole nuke, and it is headed for Washington, D.C."

11 DAYS UNTIL QUINTRALL

Pexus

Kansis

WOW. I KNOW.
What a day, Kansis Willow.
I know! I feel like I'm using my piffy, and this is some crazy fantasy world!
Yes, except, you probably wouldn't fantasize about being tortured.
True. Very true.
So, what did Amelia and Dean talk about?
He shared how Knimble saved him from a blood reclamation den. When they were away talking, I was so afraid that Dean was going to tell her about the K-Pax, but he didn't. At least, she didn't say that he had. She referred to the Pod Specialists as *doctors*, and when I corrected her, I accidentally let it slip that we call ourselves shepherds. She didn't like that. I kept trying to explain it correctly—it's not that we see them as stupid sheep—but I was creating a deeper wound. I thought she would keep pressing me to explain everything, but eventually she said, "I know you're different, Freckles. Just like you know, *I'm* different."

I like her.

Me too. Then she asked me what a blood reclamation den is, and I told her: "It's a facility for rehabilitation when someone's blood has become so weak or dirty that the person is hurting themselves or others."

She laughed at me and told me she could see I genuinely thought it to be true. She said, "I can't even be mad at you for not seeing everything around you, because you actually believe it all from a pure heart." Although her words sounded rude and sarcastic, I know she was being sincere... If only she knew all the things she can't see around her.

Anyway, Aker was sleeping when we got back—
I don't care about him. No update needed.
I thought... I don't know why... but I really thought Aker would be different after leaving Depalo for me.

He left Depalo because he had to, not because he wanted to be with you.

Wow, thanks for that.

I'm just stating a fact. Look, I don't want to fight with you. Let's change the subject.

Okay, here's a topic for you. I don't know what to do about Amelia… I feel like I owe her the truth. I should tell her about what really happens to Pods, but I'm afraid she'll lose trust in me.

She wouldn't see it as humane.

That's because she doesn't understand! She doesn't get that what we do is in the Pods' best interests. Before the K-Pax, Pods were constantly in a state of unrest and unease. Because they can't have mates or Gifts, they were miserable. But now, because of the K-Pax, they can enjoy their short lives. Free from the reality of who they were and what they are, they can live a somewhat normal, even happy, life. But Amelia won't see it that way, I'm sure. I mean, I don't know that any Pod has *enjoyed* the K-Pax. Or remembered it. But it's necessary.

Would she still be your friend if she went through the process?

I don't—I'm not sure. I—well, I never reached out to any of my Pods afterward, so… I don't know.

She would be different but better for it.

That's right. Yes, she would be. They all are. That's why we make them do it.

Why do you sound like that?

Like what?

You sound like you don't actually feel that way.

I… I've never… What if she is different?

She will be. But better.

Yes, yes, I know. I agree. Amelia is brilliant, you know. I still can't believe how much information she has retained in the few days I've spent with her. I had no idea she was even paying attention at first. But what I'm getting at is… I like her as she is. What if I don't want her to change?

If she did change, it would be for the best. Either way, I don't think you should tell her about the K-Pax, at least for now. You're doing the right thing. Your relationship is delicate and it doesn't need unnecessary conflict or tension. Maybe when you have fully gained her trust, you can share the whole story with her.

I agree. Explaining the K-Pax now won't help. But I don't know what else I can do to show her I'm trustworthy.

Maybe you just need an opportunity to prove your loyalty.

How do I do that?

Maybe there will be a chance tomorrow.

What does that mean?

Just keep your blood alert.

Okay, be honest with me. Do you have a Prophetic Gift? How do you know stuff like that? And we still need to talk about the Sixth Aevum and how you talk to him! Scout says he knows things about me because of what *you* told the Sixth Aevum! How can you not be aware that you're talking to him?

I don't know. As your *subconscious, it's not a part of* my *conscious mind.*

You have to know *something.* You can't just have a Gift and not know how to use it or when you're using it.

I didn't say I thought I had a Gift.

What if *you* are a Gift?

Bagoi *yeah, I am. The best gift you've ever received.*

Ugh, bleed me dry.

So, what do you think about the Rogue Superior?

Why are you changing subjects? I still don't believe you don't know anything about your own abilities.

Do you think I'm lying to you?

If you thought it was in my best interests, yes, you would.

…

So…?

…

 Ontzi! You do know something! Please, tell me, I can handle it—I give you the assurance of our blood. Please tell me.

I don't know the intricacies of how it all works… Do you trust me?

Of course. With every cell in our veins.

Then please let this go, just for now. I don't want to lie to you… But I can't tell you the truth right now either.

Why? Who's keeping you from telling me?

Please let it go? For me?

Ugh. Fine. But I'm only going to let it go for *now.* I'm going to ask tomorrow night and again the night after, and every night until you tell me.

Sounds good. So, what did you think about the Rogue Superior?

Well, I feel bad for Scout.

Why?

Knimble seems nice enough, and I bet he believes what he's suggesting, but it's not true. And Scout just… he just drank in all those words like he was dying of thirst.

Maybe he was.

Oh no, not you too? You believe all that stuff about a creator and dead children?

It is interesting.

I think it's a waste of time and emotions. We have all the answers we need—we are everything we need.

So you have all you need?

I have you, don't I?

…Get some sleep. And look for an opportunity tomorrow to earn Amelia's trust.

Will do. It's always better…

…When we're together.

"I DON'T WANT TO go to the circus, Kansis; I want to find Charles Wrightly," Amelia's words are calm, but her voice is laced with frustration.

"We can't go until Scout says it's time," I say, trying to soothe her impatience. "And we can't stay here because we need to be in the vicinity of the Cloak, Winzer, and she's going to be at the circus." Amelia tries to interrupt me, but I keep talking, "We can't do anything without the help of Scout and Pypen's contact, and as I told you already, Scout said we will plan the mission after the circus is closed for the day. They close at one this afternoon, so at least we don't have to wait the whole day."

"If we're at the circus, won't people recognize us there? What if the Guardians find us again?" Although she hides it well, I can hear the fear masked in the question.

"Winzer's Cloak keeps anyone looking for us from finding us."

"But what if someone isn't looking for us but then recognizes us? What if there's a loophole?"

"Then, if they try to find us again, they won't be able to."

Her brows raise as if she's accepting a verbal challenge.

To be clear, I didn't offer one.

She asks, "What if they keep us in their sights the entire time?"

"How would they be able to call the Guardians on us then?"

"Do you need to be able to see your Suus to make a call?"

I sigh. "Not necessarily."

She grins triumphantly. "Ha! Yes. I knew it: loophole."

"It's *not* a loophole, Amelia. If a person has ill will towards anyone the Cloak is protecting, the Cloak will hide them. So if someone sees us and wants to turn us in, we'll be protected."

"But ill will is relative. Maybe someone could call the Guardians on us and genuinely not wish anything bad to happen to us. What are the exact rules? Why are you not more worried about this?"

I laugh. "I'm not worried about this because I trust Winzer's Gift. A genuine Cloak is incredibly powerful. There's no besting that kind of Gift. A Cloak is a Cloak."

"You're that confident in it?" she asks. "You're that sure that we will be safe?"

"I am," I say. "There are some rules in this world that can't be bent, particularly when it comes to Gifts. There are five levels in the power hierarchy. Very few people possess Gifts from the top level—the Red Gifts."

Fetuses which are detected as having a Red Gift are actually eliminated because of the threat they pose to our society, but I don't want to share that with Amelia. Instead I say, "Red Gifts have to be monitored because they are so powerful. In fact, it was Auryn Novel's Red Gift that gave all of Elusis their hair color. A Cloak uniquely sits on the line between the first-level Red Gifts and the second-level Yellow. So although we don't classify it as a Red, it is the highest of all the Yellow. Those in this rank have Gifts of extreme power. Most Gifts are in the third level, the Green. And then below these Gifts are the Blue and Black."

Amelia stays annoyingly unimpressed during my spiel and doesn't even wait a second before saying, "So all I hear you saying is that people with Red Gifts can overcome the Cloak and find us."

I can't help but smile at her persistence. "I suppose you're right. But there won't be any people with a Red Gift at the circus."

"But you don't know that!" Amelia shouts, exasperated. "This is a logistical nightmare! We can't trot around the circus like deer hoping we're not found by a hunter. I don't know about you, but I don't want to go back to the Guardian Station."

"What would make you feel more comfortable?" I ask sincerely.

"Doesn't someone have a Gift where… well, what if… If there was…" She growls. "Everything I think of can be bested by something else."

"Except for an almost-Red Gift," I respond. "Look, this is hard to understand because it's all new, but Red Gifts are so highly monitored—" *Or eliminated,* I think, but continue, "And I trust our protector to keep us safe."

Although I know she's still upset, Amelia sighs in acceptance and starts folding her pajamas.

"The fact that they can even get into the PTS is pretty astounding. We should be thankful for them," I continue.

"I am thankful," she retorts. "I am. Had I known I was going to wake up in a world like this, I couldn't have wished for better allies."

"Speaking of allies..." Maybe this isn't the right time to bring it up, but I say it anyway, "Knimble told us last night that you're a Code Breaker."

Neither her body nor voice show any outward signs of shock at my words. She simply responds, "Did he now?"

"He did... is that why you need Charles Wrightly? Is he another Code Breaker?"

"Mhmm," she says as if discussing our breakfast. "That's exactly why I need him."

"Is he the other Peak Code Breaker?"

Shaking her head, she answers, "Nope. He's just the only one I knew for sure was a Base Breaker."

"Why did the Book of Instructions say you know where your dad is?"

She shrugs her shoulders. "Don't know."

"You're acting awfully casual about me finding out one of your secrets."

Amelia smiles mischievously. "Ah, yes. But that's just one of many." Then, she breaks into an evil laugh that makes me giggle. "So, listen," she says once the mirth has subsided. "I was thinking a lot about what you said..."

"Which part?" I ask. Is she going to share more about the Code Breakers? Did she catch me in a lie? Is she going to ask about the K-Pax? She won't listen to me when I start telling her about what happens to a Pod's consciousness... she'll only see it as a bad thing.

"Well..." she begins and then says very seriously, "if we're going to go to this circus thing, I guess we might as well enjoy ourselves."

I laugh, so, so relieved. "We might as well."

As we prepare to head out, I can't help wishing Aker would come with us. But of course, he won't.

Without thought, I grab my druzy quartz pendant. The half-moon sits heavily in my hand. The more I spend time with the real Aker, the more I wish Dream Aker was real. I thought it was worse back in Depalo when he simply didn't speak to me, but this reality is even more brutal.

Just this morning, he tried to convince me to leave again. He was begging—

something I never thought I'd see him do. And if Amelia hadn't been there, I would have given in.

I would have said yes to anything.

Ontzi, he was so handsome. At one point he was talking, but I wasn't listening because I was stuck staring at his jawline. He left quickly after that, storming out of the hotel room, not even looking at me.

Releasing my necklace, I pull out Scout's pocket watch. I look at it closely again, enjoying the raven etched onto its top. I smile over how irked the bird looks.

My thoughts return to Aker...

I haven't told Scout and Pypen that it had been Aker who turned us in to the Guardians, and I don't plan on telling them anytime soon. But seeing Aker leave so angry makes me worry. I don't think he would turn us in again...

But what if he does?

THE CIRCUS IS LIKE nothing I have ever seen before. My parents never took me to see traveling amusement groups. They never permitted me to go with friends to visit the Entertainment Wonders in Formosus, And they wouldn't fill up my Vorbi to see the Fantasy Pictures in Depalo. But here—seeing the circus live in action before me—I don't need to have seen anything else to know this event will make other experiences pale in comparison.

Before the main show begins, we explore four or five exhibition rooms. The first one is entered via a door on the second level, which we reach by climbing a giant spinal cord complete with ribs for ladder rungs. Inside the exhibition room, a Formosian man completely breaks and then heals every bone in his body. We make our way to the next door by climbing up a one-meter-thick braid of licorice. In that room, we spend a half-hour flying.

Yes. Flying.

Through another door, a short man and a tall woman entertain the crowd with baby animals performing silly tricks and sweet acts. I *ooh* and *aww* when a litter of black panther kittens are gently put to sleep by a lullaby sung by the performer.

We get our futures told in another room, and a large-eyed, pink-skinned Formosian woman tells me I will find the truth behind one of my Memory Scars sometime soon. This fact weighs heavy in my veins as we enter the next door—this one made of hundreds of beige buttons. In here, we're told we can have a significant memory recalled. We pick themes from a list, and, trying to keep anything else from overwhelming me, I choose *The Memory That Started Your Career Path.* I am delighted to watch my seven-year-old self visiting the Depalo Ward for the first time on a school trip.

Amelia didn't want to talk about what memory she picked, but after I read her all the options, I did see that she'd picked the theme *The Memory of Your Favorite Holy Day.*

Heading down the various ladders and stairs to the main floor, we visit the mini tents within the belly of the circus, learning that the pink-striped ones sell goods from local vendors while the yellow ones sell keepsakes and oddities. I don't have much left on my Vorbi, but I buy Amelia and myself shirts with the Unopened Gifts logo across the front. The orange-striped tents have food so delicious I spend the rest of my Vorbi getting us lunch.

After we finish eating, we wander to the mauve tents, where we're told to come back at the end of our visit to receive playing-card-sized duplicates of each of the doors we visited today.

Finally, the bells ring, signaling the main attraction is about to start. We quickly climb back to the ground, leaving our giggles behind in a room where you can change any feature of your face or body—I'd been able to see what I'd look like with blue skin. We follow the crowd, making our way towards the main sets of double doors at the far end of the tent.

When we finally get inside, we find we have entered *another* circus tent. The sound of the excited audience is almost deafening. Their cries for the show to start are so loud, I swear the whole city must hear them.

Someone behind us shoves his elbow into my back. "Keep it moving; we want to get to our seats before someone finds Arkarian Story!"

The seats line the entire perimeter of the circular tent, and the stage is set in the middle of the expanse. The center stage looks as big as my entire house, probably sixty meters across and thirty meters wide. It is blank, with only one bright purple spotlight at its center.

A chill comes over my body so suddenly and intensely it's like I've been doused in frigid water. As a whole, the audience silences in seconds.

The show is about to begin.

A pale light begins twinkling as, slowly and delicately, small flowers begin to grow on the floor of the stage. Each one is completely white—pure from stem to petal.

The purple spotlight flickers, and a Pexun woman adorned in a flowing red dress appears out of thin air. She begins to sway about the stage; it looks like she might fall when, as if blown by a gust of wind, her fragile body leans gracefully in another direction. Low, mournful notes ring out from a harmonica. The Pexun woman's head rolls back, and her hair begins flying about her face as though she is underwater. Gently, the red-dressed dancer reaches down and plucks one of the white blossoms. Pressing the petals to her bosom, the flower melts into her chest. A dull white light shines brightly and then fades.

Caedis.

The name echoes in my head, and I know it is the dancer's name. More performers enter from hidden doors on the outside of the room, dressed in the same red ensemble, and mimic Caedis' actions. They balletically weave through the crowd but never seem to bump into anyone as they make their way to the stage.

The harmonica's sad melody is echoed by a piano as an Ortusan dancer in a white, silky dress enters the scene, making her way to the stage. She circles the red dancers, touching their faces in a tender, motherly fashion, as if she is ensuring her children are safe. Then the Ortusan woman steps across to Caedis. A violin fills the soundscape with a deep, longing note. The two women dance in unison, like two shades of one form.

The white dancer pulls away, but Caedis tugs her back. She begs the Ortusan woman to stay, but lovingly caressing Caedis' face, the woman in the milky dress kisses her forehead and flits away.

The harmonica changes again—deepens—as if scared. The piano does not notice, however, and begins a sweet, blithe tune. Caedis, hearing the harmonica, knows that it's a warning. She floats to the other red dancers, waving her hands, but they seem only to listen to the piano. They do not heed her beckoning pleas.

The room grows cold. A chill rushes through my blood… Suddenly, a black swirl appears above the stage. It has the appearance of a cloak, flying through the air. The hood seems to be searching for something. It takes further shape and I see that it's not a cloak. It is a person; a man.

My painfully beating heart skips a beat. He sees her. He sees Caedis. Now he is behind her, and she does not see him! I want to scream out to her—to expose his presence. But my throat is closed tight, and I cannot speak.

Still hovering behind Caedis where she cannot see, the hooded figure pulls out his arm. The limb is dead. Filth falls from it as he reaches inside his cloak, drawing out a black flower. The petals are dried and lifeless. He blows on the floret, and, like a corpse rising from its grave, the blossom twists awake.

Obsidian.

The word echoes in my brain, and I realize the darkness just gave the flower a name. The man gently sets the floret down just to the right of Caedis as she beseeches another dancer on her left. When the other dancer departs, Caedis turns and sees the flower named Obsidian.

At first, she is repulsed and flies away, scared of its stark contrast to the white flowers around her. But slowly, she floats back. Twirling around the bloom, she wonders at its presence. Obsidian stays silent. Mysterious and sensual. Caedis bends down to touch the floret but flinches back. Then, ever so slowly, she reaches for it once more. Plucking it from the earth, she holds it up before her eyes for a better look.

Desire fills me, and I know without a doubt that I am feeling Caedis' desire for the flower. *Don't do it!* I want to scream. Caedis lifts Obsidian to her heart and gently presses it in.

A scream fills my ears, and I know it's mine.

I realize my eyes are closed, and I force them open to look back at the stage, but they are assaulted by a terrible sight. In the second I have had them closed, the scene on the dais has changed dramatically. The green grass is now withered. The red dancers are now dressed in black, their movements no longer fluid but broken, contorted, like marionettes. And the soft white flowers have become a loathsome black, like an evil force painted each one with dirty ink.

Children of Obsidian.

But Caedis! Caedis is what dries my blood. Her beautiful face has become scarred. Her red dress is now onyx. Her hair is matted, her feet dirty. She's been violated.

A hand on my shoulder makes me jump, and I whip my head around. For a moment, I don't know how to register the face that is looking down at me. I quickly look back towards the stage, but it seems distant and muffled. Caedis is still dancing, but the moment is lost. I am no longer a part of the story.

"Can I talk to you?" Aker asks.

"Now?" Wasn't he watching?

"This might be our only chance for a while," he whispers.

I glance at Amelia sitting next to me, still mesmerized by the story. "I can't leave her," I whisper back. This is crazy. Never in an Aevum's lifetime would I have guessed I would deny talking to Aker. Then again, I never would have imagined that he'd seek me out to have a conversation in the first place. He had been pretty adamant about not attending the circus this morning. He's probably just going to ask me to go home again.

As if reading my mind, he assures me, "I promise I'm not asking you to leave. Come on. We'll be right outside this door. We won't be far away."

How can I say no? "Amelia, I'll be right back," I whisper.

Without looking at me, she nods an acknowledgment. Aker leads me up the stairs and out of the big tent.

As I step outside the main event room and back into the primary circus tent, I gulp in a deep breath. My heart is still beating with the emotion of the show. It was all so real in the moment. They must have Storytellers somewhere on set. I have never experienced the Gift of a Storyteller, but I have heard they can make you feel things you have forgotten, imagined, or never experienced. The fear, the excitement, the pain... it was all too real. I desperately want to know what happens to Caedis.

As he leads me to the center of the main tent, Aker takes a deep breath. Caedis quickly fades from my mind. More than I could ever care about a show, I want to know what Aker has to say.

"Okay, listen," he starts. "I've been thinking a lot, and finding Arkarian Story is a good idea."

Not sure what brought on this change of heart, and automatically feeling anxious, I respond uneasily, "Oh... that's great."

"So, when we find him, do we share the reward with only the Ortusans?"

Thrown off by this question, I ask, "What reward? What do you mean?"

"The one hundred and fifteen cheio reward for finding Arkarian Story," he answers as if my question was idiotic. "Is it just split four ways? You, me, and the two Ortusans? Or is it split between all of the Unopened Gifts company?" Pointing back towards the sets of double doors, he goes on, "I asked this morning, and apparently, there are forty-four of them. That's a lot more directions to have to split the reward. But still, even if it were broken up between the forty-six of us, it would be enough compensation that I wouldn't have to work another day of my life. Obviously, I'd rather go for the four-way split. But I'd take either. Anyway, what did the Ortusan say?"

Thrown by his interest in this subject, I answer weakly, "Well, I didn't ask him."

Raking his hand over his face, he asks angrily, "What do you mean you didn't—" suddenly, he stops and forces a smile. Speaking in a much kinder voice, he continues, "No worries. I will ask him myself. I think it's best if I take over the financial conversations from now on."

His frustration and forced attempt at graciousness make me feel small, exposed, and inadequate. Of course I should have asked about the reward. That's a pretty important detail. Whenever I get a chance to talk to Aker, I always run thin in the vein. Why do I always look so pathetic? Not knowing how else to respond, I mutter, "Sure."

"We'll use the compensation to buy ourselves a home," Aker keeps on speaking, eyes wandering to the circus' doors. Although he's talking out loud, it doesn't feel like he's addressing me. "You can decorate it however you want. We can buy new vehicles. You could get a job at the Demirkan Ward and travel whenever you want, and I can open my own nursery in Depalo. We could allot certain Vorbies for both of us to spend as we want—but I'm getting ahead of myself." He finally looks at me. "What can I be doing right now? How can I help find Arkarian Story? I want to haul my share."

I click my tongue, and now it's my turn to look around at all the doors. "Um... I mean, there's nothing to be done right now. Join the impatient club with Amelia if you like. When the circus is over, we are meeting with Scout and Pypen, who will tell us how we're going to get into the PTS—"

"I think I should be there for that meeting," Aker interjects.

"Why?"

"Why not? I need to be more involved with what's happening."

"Why?"

His brows furrow. "Do you not want me involved, Kansis?"

"No, it's not that," I respond, flustered at his irritation. "I just don't know what you can do right now. I don't even know what the plan is."

"Exactly. So when the plan is being made, I would like to be there. You're the leader, right?" Then, with great purpose, like he has been practicing the motion, he reaches out and places a hand on my arm. "I would like to be a part of the planning team, if you'd permit it."

My whole arm buzzes at his touch, my mind whirling as I stare into his eyes. Never before has he looked at me for this long. It's enough to make me want to stay forever. I want to give in to his request and respond, *of course!* but my mind whirls with too many thoughts.

Okay, okay, okay... let me catch my pulse. I look away from him so I can gather my thoughts.

Aker is asking for something. Not that he's really *asking*—he knows and I know he could demand almost anything, and I'd go along with it—but it's still technically a request.

This may be my only chance at having any leverage… my one opportunity to have the stronger blood…

Say it! Say it now!

"I want to spend my Vorbies on a Blood Transfusion," I state abruptly. Aker removes his hand, and my arm grows cold. "If we find Arkarian Story, I want to do a Blood Transfusion with you. I'm not going to be your live-in acquaintance. Either… we try my blood again, or I'm not marrying you."

He scoffs. "You can't *not* marry me. It's illegal."

"It's what you've been doing for the past two years."

"Yeah, and why do you think I came to the Remembrance Ball the other night? Guardians came to my house earlier in the week and told me that if we didn't get married by Onzember first, they would send us both to blood reclamation dens." He smirks sardonically. "Why else would I have come to you?"

I pretend I didn't just see that expression and stare down at my feet. All I want to do is cry and beg him to do the Blood Transfusion, but I know that won't achieve anything.

"Counter deal," he states, and when I look up, his brows are raised roguishly. "I'll get the Blood Transfusion if you leave the circus. Right now."

"But how would we pay for it?" I ask. "It's too expensive."

"We could save up."

"That would take too long."

Smiling smugly, he argues, "Then we'll get married, and we can do the transfusion later."

Clenching my jaw, I take a deep breath. He's not going to win this. But how will I? I've never won anything with Aker.

Amelia flashes through my mind. What would she say? What would she do if she were me? Thinking of her spirit and fire, I retort, "Well, I'd rather go to a den than live the life you've described. So, what will it be? And this isn't like the other night; I'm not leaving until you answer." I look up at him and am surprised when he keeps my gaze.

After studying me for a moment, he glances at the doors again. "You know, our whole lives, you've seemed so weak. So annoying. Your obsession with me has been sickening."

My blood curdles at his words. Tears spring to my eyes, and I'm so shocked that I stay rooted to the spot.

"But," he goes on, his voice softening. "You're not weak. I don't think… I don't think I ever really got to know you until now. I think…" he clears his throat, "I just saw you as an obstacle and had this preconceived notion of who you were. But I was wrong. The way you take your job so seriously—trying to protect your Pod and all—is impressive. Very praiseworthy."

All I've ever wanted in every second of my existence is to hear him say these words. Or at least words like these. But now that he's speaking them, I have no idea how to respond.

"So what do you say?" he asks playfully. "Will you let me come to your meeting?"

"What meeting?" someone behind me asks.

I whirl around to see Scout casually leaning against one of the cuisine kiosks.

"A conversation between mates is none of your concern, Ortusan," Aker responds aggressively.

Between mates? Is he… did he publicly call me his mate?

"I concede," Scout replies. "A conversation between *mates* would be none of my concern."

"What's that supposed to mean?" Aker asks, his voice rising.

Scout shrugs. "I would muse that you know exactly to what I am referring. And to answer your question, no. You may not come to the meeting."

Aker laughs sardonically. "You can't keep me from my mate. She wants me there—so I'm going to be."

"You want him there?" Scout asks me.

His gaze is so piercing and raw; guilt seeps into my veins. Why do I feel like I'm betraying him when I answer "Of course"?

Scout's jaw clenches, but he says nothing else.

Aker, on the other hand, laughs and barks, "What did you expect her to say, *gari*?"

For a moment, the two men stare one another down—Aker grinning triumphantly and Scout studying him like a Medisacerdos examining a blood cell.

Then, with the ease of a showman, Scout plasters on a grin and says to me, "I was on my way over here to tell you that our meeting must be postponed. I am on my way to seek counsel from the Sixth Aevum to find out more about our options. Please wait in the circus courtyard with Amelia for my return."

"The Sixth Aevum?" Aker scoffs. "If you're going to blow us off, at least make it sound more realistic."

"You will have to lend me your notes," Scout replies pleasantly.

Immediately the self-satisfied expression falls from Aker's features.

Winking, Scout offers me another smile, but his green eyes look so sad. What does he have to be sorry about? Why does he care if I want Aker at the meeting?

As Scout turns to leave, he adds, "You have always been praiseworthy to me." And before Aker or I can respond, he disappears into the shadow of the kiosk.

"What's that supposed to mean?" Aker asks angrily.

"I don't know," I answer. And I really, really don't.

Pexus

Pypen

"SCOUT, WAIT, I BEG you!" I cry as he practically runs across the street. I call his name a second time, and he still offers no response. Finally, forcing authority into my voice, I shout, "Scout Mnason Eekan, stop now!"

He halts, whirls around, and says gruffly, "I do not wish to speak with you, Pypen."

"Why not?" I ask angrily.

"I just—I cannot—" Scout starts, but being so upset, he cannot finish.

I had been on my way to Thykas' room to celebrate the best show we have ever performed, when Scout shoved past me, his face screwed up in ire. I tried to engage him on the topic of his anger, but he divulged nothing. After grabbing something from our office, he told me to celebrate with the others and said he would return soon.

After so many years of knowing me, I cannot believe that he honestly thought I would listen to his instructions.

"What is wrong with you?" I shout at him. "You cannot be this upset and keep it from me. I am here to help you and to protect you. How can I do either of those things when you run away?" All of a sudden, a dawning lights my consciousness. "If this is about the Rogue Superior—"

"It is not," he snaps.

"Then what is it?"

"You once told me you would protect my flank no matter what. Does that not still hold sway?"

"Of course it does," I respond, offended. "But does that mean it is not permissible for me to inquire about your eccentric actions?"

"That is exactly what it means," he answers, and then turning around, strides away again.

"Where are you going?" I yell after him.

"You can come if you want," he barks without looking back.

He allows me to catch up, but his pace quickens as soon as I reach him. I want to ask him where we are going again but I wish not for him to dismiss me. We are walking, or jogging, more like, down the street of our hotel, and I am surprised when we pass it. "Where are we going?"

Passing by a pub, I can hear the voice of Tyge Aetas, the Pod Advocate, carrying through the air. He is giving a speech to the High Chancellors about why Pods should be allowed to marry. Recently, he seems to be on the news every day. The Quintrall is a half fortnight away, and the High Chancellors will decide on Pod marriage, along with other topics of debate. I believe someone wants to change the marriage age to sixteen.

When we enter a transponder station, Scout rents us a car and puts in coordinates to Silenda. *Why are we going there?*

In Silenda, we walk out of the transponder station and into the opening of the great city of Jukantytär. The capital of the world is designed like a three-layered labyrinth. There is the ground level called Wintour, the above-ground level called O'Brien, and the below-ground level called Puck. All of the buildings on Wintour—the ground level—are shaped in various-sized glass squares connected by crystal cylinders. Hovering above the glass buildings is O'Brien—the above-ground level. These structures are diamond-shaped and made of actual diamonds. These are also connected by crystal tubes so one could walk from any building to another—save for the homes and flats.

The whole city shines, playing with shades of light from the sunrise to the sunset, from dawn to dusk, coloring the streets with all of the shades of the rainbow. Every corner of the capital is painted with beauty.

Cordless elevators rise and descend from the glass squares to the diamonds and back, filled with passengers moving from one level to another.

Underneath Jukantytär is the final level, Puck. These below-ground buildings are made of light-infused concrete and are connected by human-sized metal pipes. The buildings are cozy and moody, filled with some of the best restaurants, the most unique drinks, and the most thrilling entertainment clubs in all of Elusis.

We trek through the city to the heart of the capital. The pristine streets are painted in the dusk's pinks and oranges. Scout heads towards one of the largest of the glass buildings on Wintour. Suspended above it in O'Brien is a diamond with greenish hues swirling through it. As he advances on the buildings, the simulan at the front of the door moves to bar our entrance.

"You will let me in," Scout commands simply, and the simulan obeys.

We walk into the grandest lobby I have ever been in, and that in itself, is significant. Silentar guards immediately charge towards us. Without knowing their Gifts, I can feel their power humming, ready to strike if necessary.

"How did you get in here?" one of them demands. I am surprised as it is rare to hear a Silentar ask a straightforward question. *Who are they guarding so heavily?*

Finally, it dawns on me. "The Sixth Aevum," I mumble.

"The Sixth Aevum welcomes me," Scout responds.

The men and women look alarmed. "You bleed an empty vein," one of the female guards retorts.

"I do know of what I speak," Scout counters. "Ask him," he demands. "He welcomed me here. Go, tell him we have arrived. I am Scout Eekan and this is Pypen Tross."

After hesitating for a second, one of them speaks into his Suus. His face is shocked at the reply he receives, but he indicates that his fellow guards must cool their Gifts. "To have the blood of fortune is to find fortune in your blood, Ortusans. The hallowed Sixth Aevum grants you a gracious gate into his glory."

The Silentars permit us to use the elevator. The ride is quiet as we ascend over the world's capital. The beauty of the city is breathtaking, and had my heart not been pounding so painfully wondering what Scout is up to, I may have been more moved by it. We rise higher and higher until we reach the top of the diamond. The elevator leaves us in a hallway, but it is far more than just a hallway. The building's designer has covered every wall in art—not framed, the walls themselves have become tapestries. They depict people walking, eating, and laughing—brimming with color and vibrance.

To myself, I mutter, "Things you would see in your everyday life."

Scout growls, "Pypen, keep your thoughts to yourself, or I will rip your vocal cords out."

Usually, I would take him up on this threat, but not here. Not in the doorway of an Aevum.

"He will see you inside," a simulan states. It leads us to a door at the end of the hallway gallery.

We enter a front parlor with a colorful design rivaling the one that has led us there. Light floods the room, yet the walls are a dark, rich olive green. Plants grow all along the shelves, which I am shocked are filled with actual books. The room is part inside, part outside, equal parts furniture and horticulture.

The simulan maneuvers around the heavy, eccentric decor into a beautiful garden. I have never seen anything like it. Plants, trees, shrubs, and flowers fill the expansive area. It is so well-manicured yet it has a raw, wild feel about it. As the simulan leads us around a particularly thorny bush, we see the Sixth Aevum standing with pruning shears in hand.

We bow before him as we approach. "We salute you, Sixth Aevum," Scout recites. "We praise your name and your life. May the legacy of your kindness live as long as—"

"Enough," the Sixth Aevum says. He continues snipping stray leaves from his hedges for several moments, and we do not stand from our prostrated position.

"Rise," he finally says, his voice tight. "You are very talented, Eekan," the Sixth Aevum continues without looking at us. "And yet..." he says slowly, turning his eyes toward us; rubbing his chin, he finishes coldly, "I told you never to use your Gift on me."

What is Scout keeping the Sixth Aevum from seeing?

When he holds out the pruning shears, the simulan takes them and lays them on a nearby stool. "Answer me, Eekan," the Sixth Aevum commands, sending a chill throughout my nervous system.

I am not scared of many people, but I am terrified of the Sixth Aevum. Without scruples, he does what needs to be done to achieve whatever he wants. I have seen what he does to people who get in his way.

"I hope never to be such a person," I mutter.

Thankfully the words are so low that the Sixth Aevum does not hear me. However, Scout's sharp elbow to my rib tells me he does.

Several times over the years, the Sixth Aevum has asked us to do things that were not particularly lawful. To some of the requests, Scout would object, and then the Aevum and Scout would *talk*. I am not certain what they shared, but the Sixth Aevum always got what he wanted. All the same, Scout is not necessarily afraid of him. He does not cower before him the way everyone else does.

For Scout, it seems to be akin to fearing lightning: although one dreads the damage it renders, there is no need to hide under the covers, shaking about it. One can stand at the window and respectfully watch it. I steal a glance at Scout now, and he seems undaunted.

"I wanted to have this conversation in person," Scout responds.

"Did it occur to you," the Sixth Aevum's words are sharp and purposeful, "that it was not *my* preference to have this conversation in person?"

"Yes, it did occur to me."

"And yet, you still chose to come here to my home, to my private sanctuary, and then disrespect me further by bringing your little friend?" He points his well-manicured finger in my direction.

Little friend?

"I brought him along because I trust him. My judgment is sure."

"You are cocky, Eekan. You may be Gifted, but you are not as Gifted as you think."

Scout does not respond.

Squinting his eyes, the Sixth Aevum states with feigned sadness, "You force me to punish you."

"Punish?" I cannot help but say it out loud. I know what a punishment from the Sixth Aevum would look like. The last time the Aevum punished one of our performers, Harper, he disappeared at the end of our show and never again showed up for practice. To this day, I have not seen him, and it has been almost a year.

"Yes," the Sixth Aevum's eyes turn on me. "To the end that no miscommunications will be had about who is in charge. I cannot allow my worshippers to use their Gifts on me, giving others a false impression of my expectations."

"But you cannot—" I start.

"I cannot what, Tross?" the Sixth Aevum shouts, his eyes now ablaze. "Do you not see the obvious problem just in your interruption? By your addressing me as an equal? By your looking me in the eyes as if you have the right?" His voice booms throughout the garden. I quickly cast my eyes down, and Scout shoves me back into a bow.

"Obviously," the Sixth Aevum goes on more calmly, "I cannot allow my worshipper to disrespect me by speaking out of turn. Am I correct, Tross?" he says my name with such intensity that when I try to speak, I stutter.

"Before you find that necessary," Scout states boldly, "May I share my reason for breaking these rules of yours?"

I sneak a glance upward. The Sixth Aevum's look is that of a child deciding whether or not to squish an ant. Doing so would bring the child no pleasure as the ant is so tiny, but at least its presence would be exterminated. "If you must," the Aevum finally says slowly.

"As you know, we tried to read the daughter's mind, but a Gift of some variety has kept the location of Arkarian Story hidden. Kansis has tried to get information out of her, and that has been unsuccessful as well. The daughter told us she needs to find a Pod named Charles Wrightly in order to give us his location. However, we spoke to a man last night who told us that the daughter is part of an elite group of Senexians called the Code Breakers. There were fourteen of them in all. The daughter possesses the latitude coordinates to Arkarian Story's location, and she's trying to find those who possess the longitude coordinates—I believe Charles Wrightly is key here. With that being said, we need to break into the PTS in Silenda. Do you still have your contact?"

The Sixth Aevum points at his shears lying on the stool. Scout leans down to retrieve them for the Aevum and when he hands them back, the Sixth Aevum rips them out of Scout's hands. For several long moments, he continues pruning his bushes as if we are not there. Finally, after an uncomfortably long time, he asks, "Are you planning without me?"

Scout bows. "I have been thinking of options, but, of course, your plans reign supreme."

The Sixth Aevum doesn't respond but stares at Scout who meets his gaze steadily. After turning his eyes away, the Sixth Aevum begins picking out yellowed leaves from the bush by hand. When he speaks, his words send chills down my veins. "Why are you not eliciting the latitude coordinates from the daughter?"

"She says she will not tell us her half of Arkarian Story's location until we help her find this Pod."

"And you are indulging this request... Why? You know I have contacts who could easily retrieve this information from her."

"Your own mind reader could not—"

When the veins in the Sixth Aevum's neck visibly expand with rage, Scout quiets himself immediately.

"I am not talking about *mind readers*, Eekan," he states, resuming calm. "I am talking about *making* the Pod tell you."

"You want me to... torture it out of her?" Scout asks slowly.

"Torture? Must you make it sound so barbaric? This Pod has no training in defending herself against any Gift. It would not take much for her to sing the coordinates to you." He turns back to face us.

"I do not wish to hurt this girl at all," Scout responds.

Lips pressed into a thin smile, the Sixth Aevum argues, "You would rather waste time, energy, manpower, resources, and the risk of your staff's lives, just to maintain the well-being of one Pod?"

"Yes," Scout says. I am surprised at his confidence.

"Since when have you cared about Pods? Has someone changed your mind?" the Sixth Aevum asks, faking curiosity, but fire burns in his eyes. When

Scout does not answer after a moment, he blinks and looks away. The Sixth Aevum is quiet as he continues to prune his hedges. A minute passes before he says, "Leave now."

"You will call your contact?" Scout asks sharply.

The Sixth Aevum's brows raise in surprise as he smiles dangerously, "Are you telling an Aevum what to do?"

"Time is important," Scout replies. "I wanted to start these plans immediately so I can book the next performances in the cities we will need to frequent. Is this not our goal? Finding Arkarian Story?"

The Sixth Aevum's face hardens into something menacing. "You dare question me?"

"I dare *ask* a question. I mean not to question your intentions, oh most praiseworthy Aevum."

The Sixth Aevum's brows rise to the middle of his forehead. I suspect this is not because he is impressed with Scout's diplomatic response, but rather it is in pure disbelief at his insubordination. As his brows lower, he eyes Scout shrewdly. "Why do you always put me in this position?"

"I am ready!" Scout suddenly shouts. "I am ready to have that cursed prophecy fulfilled, and I want to wash my hands of this. I apologize for rushing you, but I desire to see the end!"

What does he mean by *prophecy*? I look back to the Sixth Aevum.

Unfazed, the Aevum eyeballs him. "You said you were prepared for this mission."

"I am. I am prepared to *complete* it. I am prepared for it to be done." Scout lowers his head and says quietly, "I need to be done."

"Are you saying you will not continue the course?" the Sixth Aevum asks, and he seems genuinely inquisitive.

Scout's head whips up. "Of course not. I am saying that I want to be purposeful, watchful, and vigilant. As soon as we find this other Pod for the daughter, we will find Arkarian Story. I want to make swift, deliberate decisions to that end."

"Am I not working hastily enough for you?" the Aevum responds. "Now, now, Eekan. You are the one who wants to break into the PTS to procure the location of a Pod. And not only that, you have to *find* the Pod. What if he is still asleep? Will you need to awaken him? What if he is lost? What if he does not have the information the daughter needs? I gave you the quickest route to end this mission by suggesting you take the information by force, but you denied the proposition. You are the one elongating the plans, not I."

Looking the Sixth Aevum square in the eye, Scout pleads gruffly, "Please."

The Sixth Aevum laughs at Scout's entreaty. Turning to me, he asks, "Do you know why I chose your friend, Tross?" It takes me a moment to register what he is asking me, and I need to answer.

"Er, I know not."

"Sixth Aevum, bless your name, I do not think—" Scout starts. When I look at him, his face is anxious.

"Did you know," the Sixth Aevum interrupts, "that there is a prophecy about the finding of Arkarian Story? It was made in the year 311. Your friend, Eekan, is a part of that prophecy."

Scout slowly lets out the breath he must have been holding. I glance at him, but he has fixed his gaze on the ground.

How could he have kept this from me?

As if reading my mind, the Sixth Aevum continues. "I instructed Eekan to tell no one when I assigned him to his post. He has done this part well. But it would seem," his words sharpen, "he needs help with his resolve. If we are to fulfill this prophecy, we need Eekan. Tross, will you help him stay on course?"

Again, it takes me a moment to comprehend that he requires a response from me. "C-certainly," I stutter.

The Sixth Aevum assesses Scout for a moment. "I warned you about your affections." Although his words are sympathetic, his eyes are amused. It is a blood-chilling sight. "I warned you, Eekan."

To whom is the Aevum referring?

Jerking his head towards the door, the Sixth Aevum dismisses us. "I will call my contact this day and let you know what the next step is," he says, then adds, "in my good timing."

"Praise be your name and your long days," Scout responds and lightly hits my arm to let me know it is time for me to stand. We bow together and follow the simulan as it leads us out of the garden.

We move as quickly as possible out of the parlor, down the elevator, and out of the diamond skyscraper. We walk in silence for a few minutes, Scout allowing me to digest what I have just heard.

Finally, he speaks. "Do you remember when I started working for the Sixth Aevum?"

Thinking back, the first thing I remember is that our mates were still alive then. It was soon after Scout and Irenia were married. We were all so honored on his behalf that the Sixth Aevum had personally hired Scout to use his Progift to watch people for him. He was most blessed, most worshipped that year.

"I remember," I say.

"When we met, he told me about the prophecy. He said he needed me to use my Progift to fulfill it." He speaks so nonchalantly of the Progift that has been stripped because of me. "After our mates passed, he offered me a job working with the Unopened Gifts; this is where I was to be until the Reader was ready."

"How do you mean the Reader?"

"The Reader is one of the other roles in the prophecy."

"What does the entirety of the prophecy state?"

Scout takes a deep breath and pulls a well-worn fabric piece out of his chest pocket. The material is thick yet soft, almost like leather. Handing it to me, he recites it as I read:

In a new world, looking for a leader of an old

Three will unite to awaken him

The Reader will know the intentions of his book

The Scion will bear the mark and help the Reader know the way

The Prophecy is the lifeblood of the Child whose birth wrought these words

And Their death will be one.

"You are...?" I ask.

"I am the Scion—the descendant. Arkarian Story had a daughter, as we know, but he also had a son. I am the descendant of that son."

"How can that be? That means the son would have had to survive the Great Destruction."

"The son did not survive, but his own daughter did. The granddaughter of Arkarian Story survived. And I am one of the last remaining of her descendants."

"How could you possibly know that?"

"I bear his mark like the prophecy says."

"And what is his mark?" I ask.

"Do you remember the Five Families Civil War?"

"You know I hate history."

"Well, one of the five families was the Story family. When Gifts were incorporated into society, the Storys received the Gift of Sight. But instead of the normal Gift where they could make people see things, they could—"

"Keep people from seeing things, like you," I finish.

"Exactly."

"But what are the odds that only that family kept that Gift? I bet there are loads of families—"

"That is exactly what I asked the Aevum," Scout interrupts. "But record keepers track family trees through their Gifts. And if you follow the line, I am one of the last remaining members of the original Story family and one of the few with the family Gift. The Aevum showed me."

Part of this is starting to make sense. "There are three of you in the prophecy?"

"Yes. So, I am the Scion, the Sixth Aevum is—"

"Wait, the Aevum? Who is he?"

"Oh yes!" Scout smiles, getting excited. As I am the first person he has been able to talk to about this, I am certain it is a relief to get it out of his veins. I cannot help but smirk at his exuberance. "I forgot to tell you one of the most important parts. This prophecy is one with which the Sixth Aevum was born. It is inscribed on his back."

"That is not an image I needed in my mind."

Scout continues without a beat, "It is as if he *is* the prophecy." He points to the line that reads, "The prophecy is the lifeblood of the Child whose birth wrought these words."

"The Aevum is the Child, you are the Scion... Who is the Reader?"

Scout looks up at the sky and sighs. Rubbing his hand through his hair, he swallows loudly.

"Who is the Reader?" I ask again. Sometimes, Scout takes much too long to answer a simple question. Being impatient, I keep asking over and over until he answers. He so loves it when I do this.

A small grin takes over his lips. "No presumptions come to mind?"

"*Matza*, man, just tell me!"

"Perhaps I will share after I take my nap."

"Scout Mnason Eekan!"

He laughs, but it almost sounds like a sigh. "I thought it was obvious. The Reader is Kansis."

Pexus

Kansis

"*You've always been praiseworthy to me,*" Aker recites Scout's words, voice mockingly high. Turning his angry eyes on me, he asks, "What was he talking about, Kansis? Didn't you only meet him a couple of days ago?"

"Yes," I answer quickly, wanting to reassure him.

"Doesn't seem like it," Aker argues.

"I swear, I just met him."

I *could* tell Aker that Scout knows much more about me than I do him because, by means and for reasons I literally can't explain, the *Sixth Aevum* talks to my subconscious and then tells Scout parts of the conversations—possibly including the fact that Aker and I aren't married... But I think I'll keep that to myself.

Aker goes on, "Well, I don't like it."

"Don't like what?"

"Him!" he shouts petulantly. "I don't like how he is with you, how he looks at you, how he talks to you or praises you. None of it should be happening."

Because you'd prefer everyone to still shun me, I want to respond. Instead, I sigh. I don't know why this is making Aker so mad, but honestly, I'd like to go through just *one* interaction without him being upset. "I don't know what he was talking about, I promise."

"From the moment we met him, he's acted like he knows you—like you are friends."

"He's just being nice," I retort.

"Why? Why be nice to you when you're a Pexun stranger?"

"Some people are simply kind, whether to strangers or friends, people of their own territory or others. Scout is—"

"*Scout?*" Aker demands. "You're on a first-name basis with him, huh?"

"What else would I call him? That's his name." Sighing again, I say, "I'm just saying he's a nice guy."

Rolling his eyes, he sneers, "And you obviously love it."

"Love what?"

"His attention, his affirmation. His *praise*."

So what if I do? I think, but don't dare say it out loud. To Aker, I reply, "I don't know him. Why should I care what he thinks?" Although I phrase it as a question, I don't want to hear his answer, so before he responds, hoping to make light of the situation—hoping to defer his anger—I joke, "Are you jealous?"

A quiet falls between us as he stares at one of the doors. A heartbeat passes, and then another, and then another. It's only when his eyes turn on me that I realize I've made a mistake.

He takes me in then, like a buyer assessing a painting. From the top of my frizzy head to the bottom of my mud-crusted shoes, he looks me over. Crossing his arms, he smiles sardonically and scoffs, "*Jealous*?"

My cheeks burn at his evaluation, and I reply quickly, "I was kidding. Obviously, you're not jealous—there's nothing to be jealous about. It was only a joke."

Aker keeps staring at me, the buyer unconvinced of the art's value. He steps closer, and although part of me wishes I knew what he was thinking, most of me is too terrified to know.

After taking a deep breath, he responds, "I *am* jealous."

I blink.

When he smiles, it's not warm or kind, but at least it's not a grimace... right?

He continues, "I am jealous that the Ortusan acts like he knows you better than I do, and you believe it. I'm jealous that you chose to leave Depalo with him over staying home with me. And I'm jealous that you stood there, emotionless when I praised you, yet when *he* says you're praiseworthy, you blush and can barely hold his gaze."

Cheeks burning once again, I stammer, "Th-that's not true! I did not—I don't—"

"I *am* jealous," he interrupts, "that no matter what I say or do to get you to come home with me, you choose to stay here with him."

"I'm not here for *him*," I make myself say, and it comes out very loudly. "I am here for Amelia—that's it. He's just helping us do what she needs to do."

"I don't believe you."

A loud gong echoes throughout the tent and the double doors to the main stage open. People begin pouring out, flowing around Aker and me as we stand like rocks amid a flowing creek.

I try to catch his eye, hoping to tell him again that he's wrong, but he keeps his gaze focused on the ground.

Giving up on him, I scan the crowd for Amelia and don't see her anywhere. As the people fizzle out, I decide to go back in to find her.

When I turn back to him, Aker has moved closer and his eyes are on me. "You should be ashamed of your disloyalty."

"Dis—" The word is so shocking, I can't even finish it. Leaning towards him so no one else can hear, I respond angrily, "*You* were the one who tried to run away and marry someone else! You can't call *me* disloyal!"

Stepping even nearer, he seethes, "I didn't want you—I don't want you; I'll never want you. So, I tried to make the best of this tortured existence, and I'll never *ever* feel bad about that. But it didn't work, and now the only way we can move on with our lives is if we do something about it. And instead of doing the hard thing—the honorable thing—you'll run away with your Ortusan playing Arkahunter to make yourself feel better."

Completely out of nowhere, Amelia strikes Aker across the face, knocking him to his knees.

I shriek in surprise and then accidentally laugh. I don't mean to—I'm not even sure I think it's funny. But be it nerves or humor, I can't stop laughing.

Aker, recovering his feet, turns to face his attacker, his eyes alight with shock and rage. Amelia stands undaunted and unperturbed, watching the blood drip from his nose. He takes a breath and turns to me, "Why did you sic your dog on me?"

"I didn't even know she was here," I answer, trying to stop the giggles unsuccessfully. I ask Amelia between chuckles, "Where did you come from? And what did you do that for?"

She smirks at me and answers, "I just came out of the show, and it sounded like he was insulting you."

Finally regaining control, I answer Aker without looking at him, "She thought you were offending me."

When I sneak a peek at him, I'm surprised he's wearing a rueful grin. "I suppose I was," he responds.

His emotional pendulum swing is so disorienting!

He sighs and wipes the blood off his nose. "Look, I'm sorry. I know this is hard for you, but it's hard for me too. I don't want us cutting each other's wrists, okay? I just…" He shakes his head. "We don't really know each other. So let's start there."

"Start where?"

"Getting to know each other."

"Okay," I say, and before I can stop myself, I add, "That's all I've ever wanted." Immediately, my face feels as if it's on fire, and I look away.

"So… you guys good?" Amelia asks.

"I think so."

Although I don't look at him, I grin when Aker comments, "You've trained her well."

"I didn't train her to do that," I reply. "She was just defending me."

"Exactly, so well done." Before I can respond, he adds, "Don't argue; come eat with me."

I look up at him. "Eat *with* you?" We have still never shared a meal together, as we're not married.

"Well, eat *near* me."

"Both of us?" I ask, not willing to leave Amelia behind.

Smirking, he answers, "Yeah, you and your rottweiler. Let's get some food."

AMELIA INSISTS I CONTINUE teaching her about Elusis. We take our food to the circus courtyard, sitting at a far table where others can't hear our foreign words. Although he doesn't sit with us, Aker takes a bistro table nearby, where I can see him. As we eat, Amelia soaks up my stories, anecdotes, and facts. By the end of the hour, she can give the Elusian name for almost everything within the circus tent. Aker doesn't interrupt me or ask if we can leave, but he gives me a half-smile when I catch his eye.

After lunch, Amelia and I decide to take Aker to some of the entertainment rooms we have already tried. It's fun to watch him because he so desperately doesn't want to enjoy himself, but he can't help it.

The circus is too alluring.

And… well, it's just fun to watch him in general. He's so handsome, and his laughter fills my veins with vanilla and bergamot. It's heady and refreshing, and I can't get enough. But then, just when I'm so filled up with his scent I could leave for Depalo with him right then and there, his words come back to haunt me.

I didn't want you—I don't want you, I'll never want you, he'd said. *Instead of doing the hard thing—the honorable thing—you'll run away with your Ortusan playing Arkahunter to make yourself feel better.*

His words echo through my mind, and it feels as though I've been punched in the gut. The vanilla and bergamot burns, and all that remains in my veins is blood and ash.

A chime fills the air, and somehow I know within myself that the circus has ended. I wonder what kind of Gift they're employing to cause this knowledge to land in their guests' psyche. We rush to visit one more room, but when we try to get in, we find the door is locked.

People are walking through the mauve-striped tents, retrieving their collectible cards representing the circus rooms they visited. Amelia and I each collect our own circular door with raised shells surrounding it and alabaster throughout its center, a tall rectangular door made of thousands of small pieces of streamers, a misshapen door made of glass but framed with animal pelts, a standard-sized door made of beige colored buttons, and the final card, representing the main event, features the faces of Caedis and Pypen.

The lights within the tent slowly dim, making it feel as though the sun is setting. Aker strolls along next to me, and although we're nowhere within touching reach, I feel close to him.

After most of the patrons have milled out, simulans appear and begin to clean up.

As we walk back to the courtyard where Scout told us to meet him, Amelia asks me, "Do they work for the circus?"

"Who?"

"Them," she says, motioning to the simulans. "Those guys who are cleaning up. And why do they have white hair? You never said which territory has white hair."

I look over at the simulans working. "Oh..." I say and think about how I should answer. Yesterday Amelia had asked about Suuses and touched on AI, and I hadn't told her the whole truth. But she was also very sensitive about the way I approached my explanation. So I have to approach this more gently...

"Those are simulans. Remember the one from back at my apartment? Well... they are not human."

"What do you mean by that?" she asks hesitantly.

"They are... um... mechanical devices that... well... resemble humans and are capable of performing... a... a variety of complex human tasks on command or by... being... um... programmed in advance."

Fear and accusation fill her eyes. "You *do* have AI!"

Trying to calm her, I say soothingly, "They are not the AI that you know.

When you asked me if we have Artificial Intelligence, you were asking about the kind that existed in your world. Our simulans are *not* like that."

"Oh yeah?" she responds angrily. "How are they so different?"

"They do not have self-rule or hive-mind," I answer. "There is no hierarchy within their system—they are all on independent servers. They cannot attain information that they're not directly given, and they can't connect and unite against us."

She eyes them warily, unwilling to rest with my words.

"They were designed to look like humans—and not just on the outside. Instead of mechanics underneath, they have internal systems much like our own, so they can truly understand the human condition and assist in the best possible way—" Before she can interrupt, I state, "But they all have white hair, so we know they're simulans. They can't impersonate a human because they can't change their hair color any more than I can. They are meant to understand our ways but are not programmed to understand how to take over. They are completely and entirely subservient."

"That you know of," Amelia mutters.

"Oi!" a voice rings throughout the now-empty circus tent. "Those are the girls we picked up in Depalo." I turn to see four young men strolling toward us.

"And the man," one adds, seeing Aker.

One of them runs ahead of the others. His brown hair seems uncommonly dark for an Ortusan. As he reaches us, he places his hand over his heart—the traditional greeting of his people. "What mischief are you up to, eh?" His words sound welcoming, not accusing.

"Hello," I say in return. I have been ostracized for so long, I'm still struggling to adjust to ordinary conversations and superficial small talk. "How are you guys doing?" I add.

"Splendid," the young man responds.

"What are you doing in here?" the beefiest one of the group asks. His features are hard and chiseled, his creased brows and hard-set lips stern and intimidating.

"Well, where else would we be?" I retort with a playful, albeit nervous, smile. This is how ordinary people interact, right?

As he folds his arms across his chest, Aker asks, "What does it matter to you?"

Had we been a different type of couple, I would have slapped his arm for being rude.

"We meant no harm," one of them responds, a broad smile spreading warmly across his friendly face. It makes his whole muscular frame shine. His shaggy Ortusan hair covers his eyes, and he swipes it away with one of his large hands. "I'm Lukan."

"My name is Sedwick," the tall, slender one states. He towers over the other young men, who are all of average height. His athletic body is tense, like he's about to be pounced upon. "This here is Oshun," he explains, pointing to the first guy who spoke with us, "and you have met Krael." He motions towards the aggressive one. "We make up the Chameleons."

"You do an act together?" I ask.

"Yes, our act is the best in the circus, I will have you know," Oshun declares. "But Sedwick is actually in the main event," he elbows the tall Chameleon.

Sedwick nods and looks down at the floor with an embarrassed smile.

"You are going to love it," Lukan exclaims. "The whole show; it is amazing."

"I saw part of it, but I can't wait to see the ending," I respond. "And your act, of course," I add.

"What is your name?" Krael asks Amelia.

Amelia's eyebrows raise, and she nods her head yes. Cool as can be, she looks at me.

"This is Amelia," I answer. "I'm Kansis, and this is Aker."

"I have not heard her say one word since you got on our bus," Krael observes, eyeing her.

To her credit, Amelia gazes back at him contentedly.

"Lay off, Krael," Sedwick responds.

"Why?" Krael asks. He steps toward Amelia and looks her up and down as if her physical appearance will solve the mystery of her muteness. Amelia, although a head shorter than him, is utterly undaunted. "What do you like about the circus?" he asks her.

Although "she's not fond of talking" is on the tip of my tongue, I don't say it. My throat tenses up in nervousness and then all words leave my mind. It's my job to help her, and I don't know what to say! I remain unmoving, unspeaking, allowing the young men to stare at Amelia.

Aker steps in front of her and barks, "Back off, Ortusan. If she doesn't want to share in the same conversation with a *gari*, she doesn't have to."

"A *gari*?" Krael gripes, puffing out his chest. "Who are you calling *gari*?"

"She just doesn't like to talk," I answer hastily, wishing Aker would stop using that word.

"Why not?" Krael asks.

"Krael," Lukan reprimands, voice firm. But when Krael looks in his direction, Lukan lowers his gaze and says more quietly, "She need not explain herself."

Still looking at Lukan, Krael says, "Oshun, do you think she is mute? Or is it that she thinks she is too good to converse with lowly circus performers? Perhaps she believes her Formosian blood is better than ours?"

Laughter emerges from Oshun's mouth, but it doesn't touch his eyes. "Perhaps she hates the smell of eupee—that's the fragrance of your breath."

Lukan joins the laughter, and Sedwick rolls his eyes.

"We better get going," Sedwick hedges.

Aker clears his throat. "Please do."

"No, not until I know why this girl will not talk," Krael refuses, the last two words slurring together.

Drawing back his shoulders, Sedwick states, "Step down."

"Are you commanding me, Sed?" Krael asks with a sardonic smile. "Because I would *love* to see the follow-through."

Sedwick's face remains solid, as does his unmoving body.

"Come on!" Krael challenges, motioning towards himself with both hands. "Silence me, Sed."

After several moments of quiet, Lukan laughs nervously and explains, "Sorry about these two. They are always—"

Suddenly, with exploding speed, Krael rushes to tackle Sedwick to the ground. Responding with uncanny quickness, Sedwick transforms into a marble statue, and Krael's body slams into it, bounces off, and crashes into Aker and Amelia.

Aker growls, "Get off me!" at the same time Amelia cries, "Watch it!" in English.

"Sorry about that!" Lukan shouts as Oshun moves towards her, saying, "Are you well?"

Aker and Amelia regain their balance, but it takes a moment for Krael to struggle into an upright position. Sedwick turns back into his human self and, with a grin, helps Krael to his feet.

Krael's eyes are wide, staring at Amelia again. "What was that?" he asks her. "What did you say? It sounded like another language."

"It did," Oshun affirms. "What did you say?"

"The only people who can speak other languages are the..." Krael eyes light up like a cat who's trapped its prey. "You are a Pod!"

"*Vous êtes un imbécile et vous devez arrêter,*" I declare loudly, taking their eyes off Amelia. "That is French, and it's not the only other Senny language I know. And I'm not a Pod."

"Yes, but she cannot speak Elusian. Your logic does not hold sway." His smile is confident. "Tell me I am correct."

"I think you're just as right as you are sober," Aker scoffs.

"She is a Pod?" Oshun asks, now staring at her like a specimen under a microscope.

"Why would Scouty pick up a Pod from Depalo?" Lukan asks.

"Because Scout and Pypen are on a mission to gather all of the outcasts in the world into one place and call it a circus," Oshun answers happily.

"A Ward member and a Pod went missing from Depalo the day we left," Sedwick states, joining the conversation. He eyes us curiously.

"How do you know that?" Krael asks.

"I read," Sedwick answers, and I almost laugh—but I don't because they're getting too close to the truth.

"So, she *is* a Pod!" Oshun exclaims excitedly.

"And what are you? Her translator?" Krael asks.

"I heard Pypen say we've found a lead on Arkarian Story's location. This Pod must know where he is!" Oshun shouts.

"No, *patka*," Lukan responds, "Only Arkarian Story's daughter knows where he is."

I hate the dawning silence. Then their faces light up, and their mouths drop.

"*She is Arkarian Story's daughter!*" they all yell at once.

And just when it seems things can't get any worse, several performers are passing on the far side of the food kiosks as the Chameleons shout. As the bellowed revelation sinks in, some of them stop dead in their tracks while many gasp. Then they run over to join us, and ten or more voices clamor at once. Their interterritorial accents echo throughout the courtyard.

"What? It can't be!"

"How did Scouty, our ol' sam, find 'em?"

"We're going to find Arkarian Story, aren't we?"

"Going to be rich we are!"

"Ol' sam, which be the good ol' daughter, eh?"

"I think it's the Formosian!"

"Everybody, quiet!" Krael finally yells. Eyeing me, he smiles contemptuously. "Tell me, Kansis," he turns to Aker, "and you, angry Pexun man. Just try and tell me this is not Arkarian Story's daughter."

"She's not," Aker says, but they all turn to me.

Normally, I can throw out a good lie when needed. But staring at all these expectant faces—seeing all these people *not* ignoring me... A nervous grin breaks out on my face, and Krael whoops triumphantly.

"I knew it!" he yells.

"*Ontzi*, you're bad at that," Aker comments, but when I look at him, he's smirking.

The performers start asking us a million questions a minute. Amid the hum of voices, I repeatedly hear, "Arkarian Story's daughter." They jostle for a turn to take Amelia's hand, placing it over their hearts as a sign of affection.

She smiles at each one and says something in English, like, "It's nice to meet you too." "Yeah, I'm famous; it's cool, right?" "Wow, you have some big hair, girl!" "Oh, friend, you could use a mint." The performers gasp and whisper. Few alive have ever heard English spoken out loud.

"Let her breathe!" Sedwick finally yells above the clamor.

The performers back up, but one handsome man comes forward. "We are so honored to meet you," he says, Ortusan accent thick as he bows to her.

Amelia smiles and responds, "I like your circus."

"He says he's honored to meet you," I tell her. "She doesn't understand Elusian," I explain.

"To speak another tongue is to know worlds unknown," a Silentar dancer in a red dress retorts.

"Uh, yeah, for sure," I reply awkwardly.

"Do you speak any more of the ancient languages?" the attractive Ortusan man asks me, clearly interested. I wonder where he's from as his accent is different than Scout and Pypen's. His has a bit of a twangy warble to it.

"I speak Chinese, Spanish, English, Hindi, Arabic, Portuguese, Bengali, Russian, Japanese and French," I answer.

The crowd quiets. "Incredible, it is," a short, Sanusian man remarks.

"Extraordinary!" someone exclaims.

"Speak! Show us!" several yell.

Blushing, I look around. "I don't know what to say," I confess to no one in particular. I've never been with so many people from different areas of the Hexum.

"Say 'hello, how are you?' in all the languages!" Oshun yells out.

"Yes!" more agree.

I laugh. "Okay. There's '*Bonjour, comment allez-vous*?' that's French." I suddenly feel how close Aker is, and embarrassment washes over me. He's never cared about any of this and he must think I sound so stupid right now. "'*Hyālō, āpani kēmana?*'" I go on. "That's Bengali. '*Hello, how are you?*' that one is English..." I go through all the ten languages I know, and applause follows my last words.

"Be that yer Progift, sam?" Thykas asks me.

I smile at him. It's nice to see a familiar face, even if I just met him yesterday. "No," I laugh nervously. "I've just always been fascinated with languages. I had learned English, Portuguese, and Chinese by the time I was ten. A prerequisite for working as a Pod Ward member is knowing at least five languages, so I decided to pursue that. It was an easy way to study what I loved and find a job where I could use them."

I know this monologue over-answers his question, but I've always wanted to talk to Aker about this, and as he'd never asked, it feels like an opportunity to tell him without telling him.

"Pod Protector and mate, and the daughter of Arkarian, you are most welcome to our after-performance party, aren't you? We were on our way now, if you would like to join?" a Formosian woman with green eyelashes and skin asks.

"Is Winzer here?" I ask no one in particular. "We have to be wherever she is."

"Yes," Lukan answers. "I just saw her in Emerly's office."

When I ask Amelia what she wants to do, more *ah*ing follows our English exchange. Agreeing to join the group, we nod to the crowd and follow the performers towards one of the many doors.

Finally, the attention turns away from us, and Amelia and I share a sigh. "I didn't realize how cute I was," she remarks sarcastically, comically rolling her eyes at me.

The group ascends a staircase made of feathers, and we follow behind. Screams of welcome meet our ears as we enter a door built from sticks. The performers are all so happy and loud. We are introduced to everyone, and I'm repeatedly asked to say things in ancient languages. By their slurred words and excessive touching, I can tell several of the performers have already had too much to drink. One Ortusan woman stands to ask me something and sways so much she falls over. Some of the performers laugh as they help her back into her chair.

"Where's Pypen when you need him?" Krael loudly asks the group, and his words are met with laughter.

Aker, to his credit, stays beside me. He's tense and can't bring himself to be friendly when the performers try to talk to him, but he remains. Our hips aren't touching on the couch but we're close enough that if I stood to get food, I could sit a little closer when I came back…

Both Amelia and I are offered drinks, but we decline. I, for one, want to make sure I have a clear mind while I am with Amelia. If I were to lose myself to drink, she would have no one to speak to or for her. When I encourage Amelia to try some eupee she declines, saying, "Like I'd drink in a place like this. I'd try to go to the bathroom and get lost in a circus room for the next week!"

If I *had* taken them up on their offer, I would have ordered my favorite drink, a Sit With Me. It has grapefruit juice, raw sugar pieces, rum, and an honesty agent that helps you think and communicate more clearly.

Not that there was anyone to ever communicate with, as I always drank them alone… but the combination is delicious.

Aker drinks, but only one stein filled with local beer. I was hoping it would loosen him up, but it doesn't.

People ask Amelia questions via my translations. Since all other Pods are hidden in society, and it is illegal to find them, everyone present wants to know about Senex. Amelia tells them stories of technology, businesses, politics, and families. When she talks about Senex relationships—divorce in particular—the crowd gets heated. It's a blasphemous way of living, discarding one's mate for another, and many performers boo while I'm translating.

A few hours into our jovial time with the performers, someone places something in my hand. When I look to see who it is, a short Ortusan man in a gaudy green overcoat is swiftly walking away. I glance down at my hand and am surprised to see I'm holding an actual piece of paper. Written on the miniature sheet are the hand-scripted words *Hello, Darling*. Immediately my Gift ignites, and my vision blurs. And suddenly I am looking out through a different set of eyes…

The Ortusan man, sweaty and shaking, comes out of his reverie. It has happened–finally happened. As with every circus, he scans the patrons. But this day, unlike any other day, he spots her–a young Pexun woman who actually has it–the last piece of evidence for which he has been searching. With this, his claim is verifiable. He can finally take his case to the Chancellors.

She will make it complete, he thinks as he wipes sweat off his forehead and onto his lurid emerald blazer. Urgency fills his blood. I need it. How can I get it?

　　With his Gift, he follows the young woman as she laughs with a Formosian girl. The Ortusan scans the Pexun's Gift. **A Reader, is she? I can use that.** Once his consciousness is back in his own circus room, the Ortusan races to his bed. Frantically, he digs underneath until he finds the box for which he is looking. Tentatively he opens it, revealing a small stack of real paper and an ink pen. He takes one paper sheet out and carefully writes on it, "Hello, Darling." **I cannot wait to meet you, Kansis Willow.**

Amelia's elbow digging into my ribs draws me out of the trance. I blink my eyes as hard and quickly as possible to see the world around me clearly. Amelia grabs my face and looks into my eyes. She seems genuinely concerned. "What's wrong with you, Freckles? You went all… rigid and… empty."

I try to spot the Ortusan in the gaudy jacket, but I don't see him. Where has he gone? When I look at the space next to me, Aker has departed as well.

"Kansis," Amelia says and makes me look at her, "I'm serious. Are you all right?"

"I… I don't know," I say honestly. "There's someone who wants something from me."

"Who? Who wants something from you?" she asks, clearly worried. "What do they want?"

I'd sensed it in the vision. It was hidden behind his thoughts, lurking in the shadows. The green-coated Ortusan thought I couldn't see it; he didn't know that the desire was as noticeable to me as if a sunbeam was resting on it. "He…" I take a deep breath, "He wants a memory."

"Wait, what? What memory? Who wants a memory?" Amelia asks.

Again, I look around, searching for that gaudy green coat, but I don't see him anywhere.

Without warning, Amelia lightly slaps me across the face. "Talk to me," she demands.

I know it was to shock me into answering, but it's not appropriate Pod behavior. "Amelia, you are not allowed to hit me," I reprimand. Then I sigh and explain, "There—there was an Ortusan man who gave me this paper," I hand it to her, "and in my Gift, I could see that he wants a memory."

"What does that mean?" Amelia asks, clearly frustrated, as she can't read the words.

"My Gift is Word Interpretation," I say. "Whenever I read something, I enter the author's mind. I see what they saw and hear what they thought as they were writing. I mostly hear their thoughts when they *are* writing, but I can also hear their subconscious thoughts."

"Explain more," Amelia commands.

"Say you wrote a note that said, 'I'll be back soon,' and while you were writing it, you were thinking about how we would meet at a cafe later. Well, I would read it and be able to see through your eyes as you wrote the note and hear you thinking, 'I'll meet her at a cafe later.'"

Impressively, Amelia nods as if this makes total sense to her. She looks down at the Elusian words she cannot read: *Hello, Darling.* She asks, "So what was the dude thinking when he wrote this letter?"

"His actual thoughts were, 'She will make it complete' and 'I need it. How can I get it?' He found out I was a Reader, and then, his final conscious thought was, 'I cannot wait to meet you, Kansis Willow.'"

"You said you could see through his eyes? Where was he? What was he doing?"

I close my eyes to think. "He was in a bedroom, I guess. I mean, there was definitely a bed, but the rest of the room was so dirty. Clothes and food and mismatched furniture. He was looking for his paper and pen when the vision started. They were under his bed. He took them out, wrote the words, and then the vision stopped."

"So how do you know he wants a memory?" Amelia asks.

"I don't practice my Gift that much—it's not been all that useful. Honestly, it's more annoying than anything because I can't read anything without getting sucked into some person's thoughts. With that said, there was a short time in my early vocational studies when a professor encouraged me to work on my Gift. She told me I should focus on the peripherals while reading thoughts. She said that although people use their conscious brains while doing activities such as writing, their subconscious minds are always awake, always working.

"It was under her guidance that I learned how to do this. Hearing someone's thoughts while reading comes naturally to me—it's not hard at all. Reading their subconscious thoughts is much more difficult. You see, they aren't words, understandable and hearable. They're feelings and moments and memories and colors. It's more confusing. This professor taught me how to look into and decipher the subconscious. Anyway, while I was in the Ortusan's thoughts, that's where I looked—and he wants a memory."

"What memory?" Amelia asks.

"Something about how I have the piece of evidence he's been looking for, and with it, his case will be complete—or something like that."

Amelia seems deep in thought, and I can't tell if she's saying it to herself or me when she asks, "What if it's one of your scar memories?"

I find myself biting my lip and twirling my druzy quartz pendant. What if it is? This must be what the Formosian prophet had been talking about. She had said I was going to learn the truth about my Memory Scars... but do I want to know now?

I hid it from myself once... maybe it's better if it stays in the dark.

Pexus

Pypen

THE TRANSPONDER TRIP FROM Jukantytär back to Initium is quiet. It seems outlandish that Scout, Kansis, and the Sixth Aevum are all part of a prophecy to find Arkarian Story. I cannot wrap my veins around it. I am unsure whether or not to be upset with Scout for keeping the secret, given the Sixth Aevum had commanded him to do so. My only comfort is that he has never lied about it—he has not deceived me. Instead, he has just been keeping something secret. Although betrayal wars within my veins, I rest in this knowledge.

"Are you going to tell her?" I ask Scout as we leave our rental car at the Initium station and walk back towards the circus. Scout has cheated Kansis of this information for too long, and she has a right to know.

I watch as Scout's face turns from sorrow to anger or perhaps anxiety. Glancing down at the prancing lion tattoo on my wrist, I see its grey color confirms my thoughts.

"She is so young, Pypen. I desire not to put that kind of responsibility on her shoulders," he finally answers, genuine sadness lacing his words.

"I understand not. Perhaps she is young in years, but she is old enough to know her life has a destiny. It is better to know younger than older, I would think. She has a job and a place in society. She is an adult; she has a mate."

"She does not—" he stops himself.

"She does not what?" He looks like he wants to say something, but he keeps it in. "What is it, Scout? Is there something else you are keeping from me?" I despise the words even as they come out. "He has been keeping so much from me as of late..."

"Pypen, for the love of Vorbies, speak up!"

"Why so many secrets?" I try to push patience in my voice, but it does not shine through. "You need to tell her this night. No excuses."

"Who is in charge, you or me?" he snarls.

"Who is acting deceptively, you or me?" I counter. And before he can answer, I add, "*You*, Scout. *You* are the one acting unreasonably towards that oblivious Pexun! What if the roles were reversed, and she was keeping this information from you?"

"I would be infinitely grateful."

"That is not true," I respond. "You will tell her."

Running his hand over his braid, Scout takes a deep breath. As he releases, I watch as the anger drains from his arteries. Calmly, he says, "You are right, of course."

"Of course." I take a deep breath in so as to push my point, but I let it go. I believe he will tell Kansis. However... I cannot help but snarkily add, "And to clarify, *I am* in charge. Just in case there was a miscommunication."

Scout's lips twitch as he tries to suppress a smile. "I appreciate the clarity." He pats my shoulder and squeezes it. "You did amazingly this day. I could not be prouder." When I look at his face, he gives me an honest smile.

As we walk through the downtown shops toward the circus, I notice Merayal standing in front of a clothing store, staring at the moving mannequins. Throughout our performance this morning, I kept thinking about my revelation. What if she truly is a Pod? Does that matter? What does it mean concerning my responsibility for her?

"You go ahead," I tell Scout. "I want to make sure she is doing well."

"I wanted to check in with Knimble Knox anyway. I should update him on—"

"Do not think I am a *patka*," I hiss. "I know why you wish to speak with him, and we possess not time for it. I will be quick with Merayal."

Scout throws me a viciously mischievous grin and walks away from me, a cursed skip in his step.

I halt at her side, and Merayal's body visibly tenses at my presence. As I look at the mannequin modeling the newest Pexun fashions, I see flashes of our performance dancing in my mind's eyes. Merayal was phenomenal. Truly a sensation.

Right after the show—before I had run into Scout, noticed his fiery mood, and decided to accompany him—I had been on my way to congratulate Merayal on her performance. At the time, she was talking to Vielfrah, one of the Controls, wearing a genuine smile. She still had beads of sweat resting on her forehead, and her costume clung to her skin. Although her silver hair had fallen out of its bun and her make-up was smeared, I knew that I had never seen anything so beautiful. It was the first time I had truly noticed her features: long, athletic arms, powerful fingers, narrow nose and muscular legs, lengthy grey hair. Like a gazelle—lean and lithe, high-spirited and wild, and simultaneously vulnerable, enthralling and elusive.

As I stand beside her now, she keeps her gaze focused on the mannequins. "You did well today," she comments without moving.

"Was that a compliment?" I ask. She does not answer, nor does she smile, but she also does not leave. "You were amazing," I respond. "I have never flowed so well with another performer."

I know little about Pods, but I do know that they go through a reintegration program. Kansis had mentioned it the previous evening. Had Merayal gone through it? Or had she escaped like Knimble Knox's Pod?

I wonder if I should tell her that I know she is from Senex, but before I can decide, she asks abruptly, "Is one of the dancers your mate?"

"My mate died several years ago," I respond, a little taken aback.

"How did she die?" she asks, still looking at the moving fashion in front of her.

No tact, this woman. But maybe it is easier than skirting around the issue. "She killed herself," I answer.

This gets her to look at me. "Suicide?"

I know of no person other than Cazney to have taken their life. It is incredibly rare. "Yes."

Pulling her hair out of its lopsided bun, Merayal gathers the long strands and wraps them in a ponytail. "Why?" she asks, looking me in the eye. No shame. As if reading my mind, she turns back to the store.

In light of the way this conversation is going, perhaps I can get her to entrust the truth of her own past with me. Off-handedly, I ask, "How about I tell you the story, and then you tell me something about yourself?"

Shaking her head, she responds, "Nah, I'm good. Thanks, though."

"No, it will be great," I tease. "We will share our traumatic experiences and become just the chummiest of friends."

"I'm not telling you anything," she responds, not picking up on my humor.

Starting to enjoy myself, I wheedle, "No, Merayal, this is good. I can tell you all about how my wife took her own life, and you can tell me how you killed your mate."

Much to my surprise, she grins. "That could be fun," she remarks, "but I'm still going to go with *no*."

"Come on," I propel onward. "We have family, tragedy, loyalty, sacrifice—all the elements of a good story." Reaching over, I place my hand on her shoulder. "Let us be friends, and I will tell you my tale."

Serious once more, Merayal shoves my hand away with unnecessary force and shouts, "Don't touch me, *gari*! I don't need you or your story!"

Savoring her rising anger even though I know I should not, I push harder. "Oh, little darling, are you just afraid to share the truth about your murderous blood? Are you ashamed to admit that you enjoyed his death? Your sad tale will be safe with me."

The venom that taints her eyes roots me to the spot. "Oh, shut up, Pypen! I can sympathize with your wife not wanting to spend even another second with you!"

All the humor drains from me, as quick temper licks up my veins like a forest fire. "I can show you the cliff from which she jumped," I state. "If you desire her fate, let us send you off with sparkling showmanship."

Dawning a spectacularly sardonic grin, she asks, "Are you threatening me?"

I laugh and do not attempt to curb its crazed edges. "If I were to threaten you, Merayal Kapu, you would need not question my intention; you would know."

She opens her mouth to respond—her lips already dripping with poison—but then she closes it. Her brows furrow as if she is suddenly upset with herself, and she shakes her head. Surprising me, she flicks her attention back to the mannequins, allowing my intimidation to hang in the air betwixt us.

After a minute, the flames in my blood cool, and I take a deep breath. Putting me in a position of responsibility for anybody besides Scout was a heinous mistake.

Readying to leave, I mutter, "I will see you at the circus."

As I turn away, she says quickly, "You can tell me your story."

Scoffing, I look back at her. No longer in a silly mood, I ask angrily, "Why?"

After licking her lips, she turns her frame to face me, her flowing beige dress twirling around her. Smiling toothily, she states, "I've got nothing better to do."

"Well, *I* do."

Her sage green eyes sparkle as she mocks, "Oh, don't be a baby. Just tell me your story; I know you want to."

"And you suddenly want to hear it?" I ask.

"Desperately," she says in a Silentar accent. "It's all I've ever wanted. Now, I'll walk you back to the circus, and you can tell me all about it."

We stand for a moment, our eyes locked. Why the outburst and then the sudden backtracking? I do not understand this woman. Before, it was funny thinking about telling Merayal about Cazney, but now that it has come to it, I realize she is the last person with whom I wish to share this story. So I state, "I will only share my story if you tell me what happened to your mate."

"How about you go first. You're desperate and pathetic, and it sounds like you need to unload."

I could hit her. "I am done—" I begin but she bursts out, "*Ontzi*, Pypen, you're so sensitive! Look, I don't care about what happened, but we're going to be around each other for a while. So I should probably know a bit more about you. We'll never be friends, but we don't have to be enemies."

"It will be a trade or nothing. I share about my mate and you yours."

"Fine."

"And you are going first or no deal."

"Fine!"

I take a deep breath.

If I am not mistaken, that was a victory—a hard-won step in the right direction. When I start walking, she follows. As we pass the stores and cafes, I wait for her to start speaking.

After we have covered a block, she crosses her arms and says quickly, "There's really no story. My mate drowned when he was only two years old. My parents couldn't afford a new Blood Transfusion procedure, so here I am, thirty-three years old and no mate." Grinning obnoxiously, she finishes, "That's all I've got."

I marinate on her story for a few moments. If she were genuinely a Novian, this would be quite a tragic tale. But if she is a Pod, this is the perfect cover story.

"Your turn," she prompts.

Suddenly, I realize my palms are sweaty. I have never told anyone the entire story of my mate's suicide. Once I shared minimal details with Gigi, but I have never had to put the story into words. I could tell it in quick succession like Merayal's own story. However, I feel that doing so would dishonor the memory. Instead, I crack my neck and commence my tale.

"Scout's mate and my mate were twins, and they meant the world to each other." I begin. "Despite having my blood in her veins, my mate Cazney's undying loyalty and love was for her twin, Irenia. The draw for one's mate is supposed to be the strongest desire in a person, yet for Cazney… devotion to her sister was the deepest."

Thinking back to that time makes me physically wince. Suddenly, the biting tenor of Cazney's voice reverberates through my memory. At least once a week, she would wait right up until I was falling asleep to wake me, telling me how much she hated me. How much she wished she could have just stayed in her childhood home with Irenia. How I was such a disappointment. She would keep me up for hours, spouting vile sentiments until I was screaming as well.

I realize I have stopped talking, and I force myself to tune into something other than my thoughts. 'Tis the sound of the leaves being crushed beneath our feet as Merayal and I walk that eventually soothes me. Slowly, I resume. "Irenia and Cazney had always wanted to see the big cities on the mainland. We all managed to get the time off work, and when we got to Apsess... it was phenomenal. Irenia finally got to see the Tagore Mountains, something she had dreamed about since we were kids. And Cazney loved the city..."

A smile finds its way to my lips as I think about her being on her best behavior that weekend. She had not wanted her sister to know how bad things were between us, so she had been the perfect loving, supportive, and flirtatious wife. Those few days, we pretended everything was great... and the time together was a dream. A hazy image of Cazney's face floats across my mind's eye. I can hardly remember how she looked. It has been too long since I have allowed myself to think about her. I clear my throat.

"It was late afternoon, and the girls wanted to go shopping to find dresses for that evening's supper. Scout and I meandered around the town, trying to find a pub in which to relax. As we were walking, we happened upon a circus. We had never heard of one, but we were intrigued by the giant tent, so we bought tickets. At the door, attendants asked us to be vacuoused—to have our Gifts turned off—so we could better enjoy the show. Scout and I chose not to participate since we were not invested enough in the experience to limit our abilities.

"It was the most enormous tent I had ever seen. The colors were magnificent, the sounds thrilling, the smells intoxicating... The acrobats, the speakers, the singers... They were incredible. Unlike the Unopened Gifts, this circus replicated the exact shows of the Senexians, but it was thrilling, nonetheless. We called our wives and told them they had to see it. They were intrigued and joined us quickly.

I glance over at Merayal to see if she is still engaged, or if her interest was purely false. When I see that she is listening intently, I continue.

"At one point during the show, two volunteers were asked to come to the stage. Irenia, who sought adventure like one side of a magnet seeking another, leaped onto her chair in delight and excitement, with Scout stirring the storm in her blood. She moved so quickly that her chair leg slipped off the wooden amphitheater ledge. I reached up to steady her, and in doing so, I also rose to my feet. Much to Scout and Cazney's delight, Irenia and I found ourselves on our feet with a giant spotlight shining on the two of us. The ring father took us for mates. He asked us if we had been vacuoused, and I shouted 'Yes!' not wanting to miss out on the opportunity."

I pause here and let myself turn introspective. "'Tis uncanny that the slightest decisions in our lives may wield the greatest influence." For a moment, I focus on the sound of my leather shoes smashing the fragile foliage under my feet. Merayal does not interrupt and waits for me to continue.

"The moment I said, *Yes*," I resume, "my intuition said, *No*. I knew that we should not go up on that stage, but I was caught up in the excitement. I assumed that Irenia had been vacuoused, as she was such a rule follower, and I knew that if anything happened to me, my Gift could renew it. It felt as though the lie did not matter." I sigh. "And so, a moment of fun turned into the gravest decision of our lives. Had I known that Irenia had also not taken the vacuous—had I understood what was to come—I never would have let us go up there."

I look up at the well-manicured trees lining the walkway. Light dapples through them, making me squint. Focusing back on the cobblestone street, I continue, "We were hoisted onto two trapezes on opposite sides of the tent. Two Gift Givers walked up and touched us. Had we taken the vacuous, we would have temporarily received the Gift of flight. But as we had not, and as our Gifts were still in control, we did not receive this Gift.

"A performer helped me up on the trapeze and then told me that when we swung across the open space to reach each other, I must stretch out and grab Irenia—and our bodies would do the rest. It was all so exciting, the thrill of it pounding in my ears, that what he said did not truly register. I did not think about it—I just did it.

"So there we were, dangling by our feet and swinging our bodies back and forth. We were facing away from each other, and the blood was rushing painfully into my head. All I could hear was the roar of the crowd's anticipation and the pounding of my adrenaline-fueled heart. When we arced higher, we could lift our heads and see each other, and our outstretched hands drew closer and closer."

My blood goes cold as I continue my story in a softer voice. "I can still remember the look on Irenia's face from across the tent as we drew close to each other... The moment had enraptured her. Both our arms were outstretched, and our fingers touched, but we separated for another return arc. Then, as we came together again, we were high enough and close enough to grasp each other's wrists in a tight grip. I felt my weight shift forward, and our legs lose their purchase on the trapezes. And then... well, our body's weight immediately pulled us down. We were over one hundred meters up in the air, and our bodies just plummeted toward the ground. At first, I thought it was part of the show, but I knew something was wrong as we approached the circus floor. Irenia's face went from joy to fear in milliseconds. As she tried to look toward Scout, her body twisted to the side.

"When I landed, I felt my rib cage collapse, crushing my lungs. My elbows and wrists shattered, along with my kneecaps. On impact, I passed out, but my Progift ignited automatically and renewed my body. But Irenia... I am certain they had healers nearby, but she died on impact. Where I landed on my chest, she landed on her neck, breaking it and killing her on the spot."

Sighing, I crack my knuckles and back. Now I remember why I have not thought about this in so long. "I woke up in a Healing Clinic, completely healthy. Scout was in my room, bone-faced, staring at the wall. I asked him what had happened; he said that Irenia was dead, and that Cazney—unable to live in a world without her sister—had killed herself an hour before I awoke."

I know I can stop my story here. I need not tell Merayal anymore, for what I have said can be enough. But now that I have started, I am compelled to see it through. I need to free my veins of this weight, and if nothing else, saying this will remind me why I am where I am now.

"A Guardian walked in and told me that my actions would have substantial consequences. Because of my lie, the circus was suing me. The punishment would be a Gift-stripping." I stop and wait for Merayal to react, but she says nothing. I understand not her reaction—to have one's Gift stripped is the worst thing that could happen to a person. It is the ultimate punishment. Faced with her silence, I can only continue.

"Scout asked the Guardian if he could speak with him in the hallway. I knew not of what they spoke, and cared not as I was so shocked at the deaths and my new fate. When Scout returned, he told me the charges had been dropped and I was not to worry about it. I had spent all my emotional energy and mind power, and I did not even think on it further or ask questions. I just received what he said and fell asleep.

"When I woke up again, a nurse was cleaning my room. I asked where Scout was, and she told me that Guardians had taken him to the Gift Protecting Agency to have his Progift stripped."

"He had his Gift stripped in your place?" Merayal asks, her voice dull.

"Yes. He had convinced the Guardians that he had encouraged us to lie to the Ring Father when asked if we had been vacuoused. They agreed to give him the punishment instead."

She opens her mouth to say something but then closes it.

"What?" I ask. When she shakes her head as if she is not going to answer, I state harshly, "Tell me. Whatever it is, I can handle it."

Throwing her hands up, she fumes, "Why in Elusis are you two working at a *circus* if that's what killed your mates? And why are you two still friends if his Gift was stripped because of you?"

Insensitive and poignant questions, to be sure, but I did tell her I could handle it. After thinking for a moment, I answer carefully, "We went back to our hometown for about six months, and everyone," and by *everyone*, I mean my family, "blamed me for our wives' deaths—which, of course, I was at fault on both accounts. Directly for Irenia and indirectly for Cazney. I was not enough for her, and that was on me."

This admission cuts too close to the marrow, and my whole body burns with humiliation. Hurriedly I continue, "I wanted more than anything else to leave and never see them again, but I had nowhere to go. Then, one night, Scout came to my house and said we were leaving." I smile sadly as I remember his confidence, strutting into my parlor, telling me I had no choice—that we were going together.

"At that point, he had been working for the Sixth Aevum for some time, and the Aevum had offered Scout a job in Vultus, leading an undercover Arkahunter group. And Scout, for motives I still understand not, wanted me to go with him.

"I never had any interest in finding Arkarian Story, but I did not care about anything at that point. Getting out of Sleepy Hollow was my main priority. Scout took my punishment even though it was my fault his mate had passed. Then he provided me a way out of my shame and gave me a job doing something I love more than anything else. I owe him everything." Scout is the most supreme comrade anyone could have. I am thankful that out of everyone, he still chooses me to be his closest confidant.

"Do you even enjoy being in the circus, or are you just here for him?" she asks.

"Does it matter? I owe him my life, and my life he will have." After a moment, I add, "And honestly, the circus has become my passion. Finding new talent and creating more exciting attractions is my new life. Scout and I took this little performing arts group and turned it into a successful and, in my biased opinion, Hexum-worthy circus. I found a way to use my Gift that truly brings me joy and contentment."

"So you're content? Here? Working with the circus for the rest of your life?"

"For the rest of my life? I know not. But I am happy right now." I know not exactly if that is the truth, but I desire not to be anywhere else. We are now a mere block from the circus.

"I would never be content here," she mutters.

"Are we that poor of company?" I ask, and we both hear the dejection in my voice.

"Look, we all have pain, okay? And what happened to your mate is awful. It really is—but I can't help you with that. I can't be here for you or support you in any way. We're not friends."

Quite uncharacteristically, my blood stays cool despite her words. Normally I would have interrupted her with a malicious laugh, a biting comment, and an insult to match. Instead, I permit the words to slap my veins without reciprocation. Knowing Merayal may be a Pod changes the situation for me. If she is from Senex, she must feel utterly alone. Xoana—a mother figure, even if not her blood mother—her one ally, has died. She has no one else.

As if she has read my thoughts, as our homely circus tent comes into view, Merayal asks, "Have you found out anything else about my mom's assassin?"

The desire to divulge what I know of her true situation has been oozing from my blood all day, but Scout told me not to, and I trust his judgment.

"Not yet," I lie to the Pexun. "I will let you know once we have."

She stops and turns to face me. "If I was a nicer person," she asks, "would you try harder?"

At this, I cannot help but laugh. "Well, that is the question, is it not? The easy answer—one that would make my life more comfortable—is certainly. It would give me more of an incentive, I suppose." I pause a moment and then finish, "However, the honest answer is 'no'. Scout and I made a promise to you. Whether it be bile or benevolence that you throw our way, we are trying to help you." Although this is entirely untrue, earlier this morning I *did* half-heartedly look into which Guardians were on shift the day of her mother's murder.

She smiles unpleasantly. "I know your kind, Ortusan. You can't sweet talk me into your affections."

"My kind?" I ask, smiling again. "And what kind would that be?"

"Men."

Honestly, I am shocked at the word. "*Men*? You have contention with all men?"

Rolling her eyes, she walks away towards the circus.

I fall into step beside her and press further. "No, no. Come now, you chose the vein. What is your grievance with all of mankind."

"Forget it, okay?

"I will not. So, men in your life hurt you? A friend? A brother? Your father?"

"Shut up; it doesn't matter."

I cannot help but push the button. 'Tis not my fault she showed it to me. "Merayal," I argue, "if I based my feeling towards all women on how I find you, I would despise them all as well."

Her eyes flash, and she whirls toward me, intent on hitting me. Used to this kind of interaction with the Controls, I catch her wrist before she can strike me. "I know not who these men were, but half of humanity is male, and you cannot project your feelings for the few on the majority."

She moves her face towards mine, closer than I thought she ever would. If I was to but twitch forward, I could kiss her. "The few I've met have showed me the true nature of the many. So I'm only here for two reasons. One, because of the incredible compensation this job is giving me. Two, because I want to avenge my mom's death. I don't need you. I don't want anything from you."

"Then why listen to my story?" I ask caustically.

I see my mistake only after the words have left my mouth. I have opened myself up for the fatal blow—like an ancient soldier blocking a sword strike up high, only to expose the heart via unprotected ribs.

Merayal sees the opening and strikes.

"Because now I know where you bleed the darkest," she whispers. "Now I know you are so worthless that even your mate couldn't stand living in a world with just you. Now," she says, her voice deep and melodic, "I know who you are, Pypen. An empty shell pretending to be a full house." Venom as I have never seen fills her eyes, and I miss a breath.

Blowing a kiss at me, Merayal Kapu retreats, the victor.

Fabella is wrong—I cannot tame her.

Silenda

Flister

73 years ago

THE SIXTH AEVUM HOLDS the handmade paper invitation to Mal Fey's three hundred and forty-third birthday celebration. The thick, burnt orange card feels soft at the touch, yet keeps its rigid, rectangular shape. Ruby red flecks hem the exterior, and the words are written with iridescent squid ink.

It took weeks for Flister to pick out Mal's birthday present. For the woman with everything she wants, access to anything she desires, and unlimited funds to acquire anything she fancies, choosing the perfect present was quite the challenge. But when he finally decided, he knew that Mal would love it.

The Sixth Aevum takes the handmade invitation and places it inside the glass case he had made to display every card Mal had ever made him. Half of them are notes she sent him on his birthdays throughout the years, and the other half are invitations to Mal's birthday celebrations. Although he is running out of space, it is an exciting feeling rather than an annoying one. It is the classic collector's conundrum: does one create more space by reducing the collection, or by expanding the display area?

More display space it is, for the Sixth Aevum.

The evening of the party, Flister dresses in his very best suit. It is a blend of five textiles—royal qivuik, ambassador, HugMe, silk, and fifteen-point-eff— and has four hundred and eighty 0.5-carat diamonds scattered throughout the fabric. The suit took six hundred hours to create, and there are only three of its kind in the world. The Sixth Aevum owns all three.

Earlier in the day, he had his hair cut, his age advanced so he looks to be in his forties (the age Mal Fey has looked since he was born), and had his eyes changed to brown to match Mal's. Then he spends the rest of the day at a spa where he receives a manicure, pedicure, massage, and rejuvenation. He will look his best for her.

As usual, Mal Fey only invites the Aevii to celebrate her birthday. On other holy days, she asks additional people to join, but for her birthday, she wants only family.

Before Flister was even born, Mal Fey made it a requirement for the other Aevii to live in Jukantytär. They could have homes elsewhere and stay within the Hexum for any period, but they had to have their primary residence within the bounds of the world's capital. Never one to make a rule and not follow it, Mal Fey's house rests on the southern coastline overlooking the Zabal Ocean.

Flister drives up her private driveway, and his wheels crunch the warm-colored precious stones that cover the road like gravel. To his left runs the Plo River, and to his right the Zabal spans out to the horizon. As he pulls up to the main grounds, he can see by the cars that all the other Aevii have already arrived. Mal designed her house—or cottage—to be small, cozy, and intimate. With stone walls, well-worn wooden floors, minimalistic decor, and soft, yellow light for illumination, the house feels like the home of the average citizen rather than the First Aevum.

But that has always been the way of Mal Fey. As the First Aevum, she has been able to accumulate wealth without any constraint, but she has never flaunted it. She has nothing to prove and is self-possessed enough to be confidently austere. The First Aevum has always been *one of* the people *for all* the people.

Surrounding Mal Fey's home are five miniature replica cottages—one for each of the other Aevii so they can spend the night if they desire. Everything about the estate promotes community and fellowship—particularly the games laid out around the grounds.

The Sixth Aevum gets out of his luxury car, and seeing Mal's property causes him to pause. A cacophony of memories invade his mind. Mornings watching the sunrise with turmeric tea in hand, afternoons playing in the ocean, evenings with ukuleles and singing, and late nights sitting in front of blazing campfires.

Flister looks over to the open-concept barn that houses Mal's sporting equipment. From the time he was a child, he came to her property for summer break and played all kinds of games like hover ball, witty darts, archery, capture the precious gem, strict and loose red rover, and tree jumping.

He smiles as the rope swing catches his eye. He had put it up himself. Mal had wanted the facility helpers to assemble the swing, but he had been insistent that he could do it. All in a moment, Flister has a visceral need to run, launch himself off the rope swing, and freefall into the ocean below. He resists.

Inside her home, Mal has an entire wall-sized closet dedicated to board games and cards. As a centerpiece for her rennix table, the First Aevum has a hand-carved special edition—the only edition—Gedankenspiel board made by the world-renowned sculptor Borr Nery.

The other Aevii had visited throughout Flister's summers at Mal's and, much to his chagrin, he had many good memories of them too: Dakarai teaching him how to take a eupee shot effectively, Oaken changing him into a bird and teaching him to fly, Marvella snuggling with him after he had fallen and hurt his ankle. However, even in all those memorable moments, Flister had always preferred when it was just Mal and himself.

When he was younger, she would come into his cabin at night and read him stories until he fell asleep. As he got older, they played cards or Gedankenspiel in her living room until she fell asleep. One of his most precious memories was the night before he came of age. Mal had fallen asleep on his shoulder as they watched a moving picture. He had scooped her up in his arms and taken her to her bed. It was the one time he had ever been inside her bedroom.

As he laid her down, she kissed him on the cheek.

Now, as Flister looks toward Mal's cottage, he can almost feel her lips on his face. He makes his way toward the house, allowing the nostalgic feeling to fill his veins. It is quite gratifying.

Although it was not his intention to be the last to arrive, he had wanted to be late, albeit not disrespectfully so. Light chatter carries through the stained-glass window overlooking a meager but well-loved oasis.

Dakarai Ebeleson's voice hits Flister's ears first as he walks inside the cottage.

"Yes, but why not let the people possess moral freedom?" Dakarai is asking. "Why not let them pursue their passions?"

"Of course, sweet one," Marvella Pinyin responds. "Why not invite everyone, everywhere, to your levels of corruption? Would it enable you to sleep better at night if you were not alone in your debauchery? Or, what do you call it? Pleasure?"

Flister takes a deep breath and walks out of the entryway and into the cozy living room. The other six Aevii lounge on the various eclectically matched couches, HugMe sacks, and rugs.

Oaken Bleu catches his eye. Her expression is both amused and sensual. She had twirled her long grey hair into a bun on top of her head and applied diamond sparkles to her cheeks.

Marvella, as she had done for the past decade, pretends Flister does not exist, unwilling to acknowledge him at all.

Flicking his attention from the Fourth to the Second Aevum, Flister watches as Dakarai eyes him with malicious interest. "Flister agrees with me, do you not, Darling?"

Ignoring him, Flister walks over to Mal Fey and kisses her on the cheek. Her muted brown dress is only a few shades lighter than her cinnamon skin. The chiffon and crepe fabrics flow over her legs to her bare feet. She has pulled her red hair back into a clip made of fall leaves from her favorite tree in the front yard.

"Happy birthday, my Love," he whispers and hands her his small present.

"Come now, Flisty! Will you deign to share your lofty thoughts with the rest of us mere, humble Aevii?" Dakarai presses. "Whether you give it voice or not, we all know you have an opinion, and naturally, anyone in disagreement with you is undoubtedly wrong."

Still disregarding him, Flister sits beside Mal and watches as she unwraps the package. The others continue their conversation as Mal looks inside and sees a small flower.

"It is a mussaenda erythrophylla," Flister explains quietly. The flower has five beautiful red and yellow petals; words have been etched onto each one. When Mal picks it up, the flower grows from the size of her finger to the size of her palm. It is only once it is large that the inscriptions are clear. On each petal is the name and date of birth of each of the younger five Aevii.

Tenderly, Mal touches the petal that says Flister's name, and the words turn into an etched painting of his face. When she releases her finger, the picture turns back to letters. When she touches the other names, the same transformation occurs. After a moment of no interaction with it, the flower recedes to its smaller size.

Flister takes the flower gingerly from her, pulls it slightly on the back, and draws a gold chain out of the stem. Mal turns away from him, revealing that her dress has an exposed back, so he can put the jewelry on her. As he clips the chain, Flister fleetingly wonders if everyone in the room can hear his rapidly beating heart. When Mal turns back to him, he can see that the necklace rests perfectly in the middle of her chest, so when she looks down, she can see it. As she touches it, the chain automatically extends so she can hold the pendant in her hand and look at the petals again.

Mal smiles tenderly at the necklace for a long time and finally up at Flister. "It was a sacrifice for you, wasn't it? To put the others on the flower as well."

Flister chuckles as he stares at the necklace. When he looks up at her, he drinks in her beauty as he admits, "I wanted you always to feel like you had the person who loves you the most, the closest to your heart, and for a long time, I was just going to do my face. But I wanted you to love it. And I wanted you to know just how much you are loved. So, yes, I sacrificed to add the others; I did it for you, my Love."

Mal reaches over and kisses Flister's cheek, making every nerve in his body buzz. "Thank you," she whispers, and one of her tears splashes onto his arm as she sits back in her chair. As she pulls his hand into hers, he stares into Mal's eyes for a moment, and his blood pounds longingly throughout his vascular system. He could get lost in her twin amber orbs forever. After a moment, Mal returns her attention to the lively debate going on around them. Reluctantly, Flister does the same.

When he eyes Oaken, he sees that the Fifth Aevum is staring at Mal and Flister's intertwined fingers. For just a moment, her hurt is exposed, but then she hides it like a talented hunter covering tracks. He tries to catch her eye, but she pointedly looks away and continues with her conversation.

"We can't just let people do whatever they want," Oaken says to Dakarai. "It would be anarchy."

"Letting people enjoy extra-marital exchanges is not anarchy," Dakarai responds. "Allowing them to drink past the legal blood limit is not anarchy. *Matza*, letting them gamble and enjoy narcotics is not anarchy."

"It *leads* to anarchy," Oaken retorts.

"How?"

Oaken crosses her legs in front of her as she responds, "If Elusis abided by the laws of nature, then it would be every person for themselves. There would be a constant fear of death. Nobody would have a sense of responsibility or any desire to help one another; there would be rivalry and the same war-like mentality as those in Senex. If two people wanted the same thing, there would be no collaboration to reach the goal; instead, they would become enemies. Rules, and more so the rules of morality—"

"Stop trying to sound smart, honey," Marvella interrupts. "We get it."

"I would like to hear the rest," Mal remarks serenely.

Regret at having opposed anything Mal wants fills Marvella's face.

With a self-satisfied smile, Oaken continues. "Rules, particularly the rules of morality, are essential for safety. The rules and regulations we set up may impose upon some of the people's freedoms, but only to an extent, and only so people will have a more profound sense of freedom and well-being. A society cannot sustain peace without any moral regulations. We need morality to keep our society from falling apart and to resolve conflicts in an orderly fashion. In each of us, there is a darkness that unleashes whenever there is a conflict of interest or a moral lassitude. If we do not keep a pulse on our internal conscious morality, we will quickly lose ground from under our feet, and we will lose all sense of reality—we will become animals living in a world under nature's bitter reign."

"I am not saying we should not have rules or laws," Dakarai responds, hands raised in protest. "I am merely stating that the people should be able to pursue their passions if they so desire."

"But what if those passions lead to destructive behavior?" Oaken asks.

"So only allow the behaviors that are not destructive," Dakarai expounds.

"But who decides what is destructive?" Oaken asks. "Destruction is relative."

"Destruction is not relative," Marvella states, rolling her eyes. "Everyone knows right and wrong."

"Whose definition of right and wrong?" Flister asks. "Yours?"

Dakarai stands and applauses raucously. "Kel and Kelis, let us take in this moment! Flister Dubach has deemed us worthy of conversation!" No one pays him any heed.

"We are the Aevii," Marvella answers Flister's question, although she keeps her body facing the Second Aevum and not the Sixth. "We would be a reliable source."

Flister barks a laugh. "*Reliable source*? Darling, despite your pride, you must see that even our definition of right and wrong varies. It changes with the season and with our age. An act you may commit could be completely foul to me."

Marvella's eyes flash as she understands his innuendo. "Who is more qualified than we?" she asks, her voice high pitched. "Of all the metahumans, we are most capable to conceive the highest of moral laws."

"If all humans walked around calling what you did right, the world would be filled with bastard children," Flister snaps.

"No thank you, Flister," Mal reprimands, her fingers squeezing his own.

"I apologize, Mal," he responds quickly, regretting offending her. Turning to the Fourth Aevum, and only because he knows Mal wants him to, he adds, "I apologize, Marvella, my Sweet. Nonetheless, we do not live as models every citizen should emulate."

"Mal has given us laws that are good," Marvella goes on, her body language rigid, clearly rejecting Flister's apology. "Thus far, our society is orderly, conscious, communal, and moral because of what she has set up."

"And yet there is still evil," Oaken points out to Marvella. "And how do we know that her law is good? How do we know that it is perfect?"

"She could use her Gift to write the perfect definition of right and wrong, and then it would be," Marvella answers.

"Mal is not inerrant," Oaken states. "No offense, Love," she adds quickly to the First Aevum. Mal smiles graciously and motions for her to continue. "She's made mistakes—she's said so herself. Even she doesn't know all. We could run scenarios by Dakarai, and he could tell us if we're telling the truth. For example," turning to Dakarai, Oaken declares, "Dakarai, it's okay to murder someone." Turning back to the group, she explains, "Since he clearly knows I was lying, we know that's morally wrong."

Dakarai smiles. "Interestingly, Oaken Love, you were not lying when you said that."

"What's that supposed to mean?" Oaken asks, her heart-shaped face screwed in frustration. "Of course, I know murder is wrong."

"Believing that murder is wrong is dependent on a person's values," Flister counters, uncharacteristically joining Dakarai's side. "You kill Captusians with no objection from your moral code."

"But they are sub-human," Oaken responds defensively.

"'Tis still murder," Flister repeats blandly. He knows he is crossing a line with her, but he continues. "And thank you, Oaken, for that example. Because in it, truth is relative. And if the truth is relative, then there is no ultimate definition of right and wrong."

Glaring at him, Oaken huffs, "We could find someone with a Gift to discern perfect morality."

"How could they?" Flister asks. "If there is no absolute truth free of variation, prejudice, and relativity, how could anyone declare that something is good or evil?"

"The human would have to be perfect to know right and wrong perfectly," Oaken expounds.

"Exactly!" Flister exclaims, clapping his hands. "And there are none. There are no humans who are without some level of evil. Therefore, there is no absolute definition of right and wrong. There is no inerrant truth. And if there were some higher truth, it would need to be a definition above the fallacies of the human race."

"There is nothing above the human race," Marvella snaps.

"And what if t'ere was?" Qualcum Elder asks, speaking for the first time.

The five other Aevii turn to the Third, astonished at his voice. While Flister is, on rare occasions, goaded into conversations, Qualcum *never* is. Unless Mal asks him a direct question, Qualcum never shares his opinion.

"How do you mean?" Dakarai asks.

"What if t'ere was a being outside of humanity who had no evil in him?"

"If there were a being like that, it would be female, not male," Oaken interjects.

Ignoring her, Qualcum continues. "What if t'is being created ta world and spoke what was good and what was evil? Oi agree wit' Oaken; Mal is not an adequate definition maker; she is a creation as much as ye or me. But if ta being who created t'is world declared an entity to be good, it would be; and if he declared an entity to be evil, it would be. And what if t'is being left a book fer ta human race and explicitly shared what was right and wrong?"

"Clearly, you believe in this being," Dakarai comments.

"I had no idea you were secretly a Buscador," Oaken jabs.

"Are you meaning Auctus and Effio?" Marvella asks.

To the shock of all in the room save Qualcum, Mal states calmly, "Auctus and Effio aren't real." The declaration permeates the room like a noxious gas. "They never existed," she goes on. "They were pawns that Qualcum and I created to give the people a reverence and heightened sense of their humanity."

This announcement is met with a moment of silence, then the other Aevii all break out, speaking simultaneously.

"What are you talking about?"

"How do you mean?"

"What is this?"

"The stars have aligned that this conversation would come up," Mal says serenely. "I have wanted to discuss this with you all, but there hasn't been a good time up until now." Before continuing, she looks each of the Aevii in the eyes. "On each of your coronation days, I told you that I had not shared everything with you, and I would spend eternity revealing to each of you the secrets of Elusis." Turning to Dakarai, she adds, "Even you. I told you I was keeping information from you until you had gained my trust."

"And it has taken over three hundred years?" the man asks desperately, his face etched with hurt.

"Of course not," Mal responds. "You have proven yourself decade after decade. This is a… sensitive matter. And I had hoped to share it with you when you were all together, but Flister wasn't ready until now."

Flister feels a flick of pain at her lack of trust in him, but the kind look she offers him soothes the ache. The Sixth Aevum believes Mal Fey when she says she loves him. He trusts that she cares for him. If Mal had kept this from him until this night, he believes it must have been in his best interests.

"I'm sure that you three," Mal motions to Dakarai, Marvella, and Oaken, "remember that we made many changes when Qualcum joined our family."

Dakarai and Oaken scowl, and Marvella nods her head.

Mal smooths her flowing dress and pushes stray locks of her red hair behind her ears. "Qualcum brought so much wisdom into our council." She says it persuasively as if she is trying to convince the other people in the room of its truth. "Together we penned this history of Elusis, and he helped me rewrite many of our laws. During that time, Qualcum brought many disturbing facts to my attention. Qualcum, do you want to share?"

Flister eyes the Third Aevum with contempt. He is just a disgusting, sick old man who deserves no dignity, and it erodes Flister's blood that Mal leans on him for anything.

"T'is world was made by a creator who had a purpose. One cannot look at creation and intelligently say it has no design or t'at ta design was a universal accident."

"Who was this creator?" Oaken asks. "Was it someone else from Mensonge?"

"Mensonge doesn't exist," Qualcum announces, and the other Aevii balk again. "T'ere is no ot'er planet filled wit' even more evolved metahumans. T'ere is just t'is world."

"Of course Mensonge exists!" Oaken sputters. "Studies have been done—"

"Studies we fabricated," Mal inputs.

Oaken turns to Mal as if she has been slapped. After a moment of silence, she whispers, "Why?" Her eyes fill with tears. "Why lie about our origin?"

"T'at is a great question," Qualcum inserts.

"If we were to tell the people about the creator, they would worship him," Mal answers.

"Well, would he not be worthy of worship?" Flister asks.

"Who is it?" Oaken asks. "Who is this being? What is he?"

"He is an enemy, a trickster, a fiend—Oi call him Jeog," Qualcum answers. "He isn't human—he's something other. He is insanely complex as he is t'ree persons, but one being."

Oaken slaps her hands on her knees, "How can you be three persons but one—"

"Oaken, Darling," Mal says gently. "Let Qualcum share."

Flister can see that wanting to please Mal wars with her desire to ask more questions. Finally, Oaken tightens her lips and leans back in her chair.

After looking at each person quickly, Qualcum announces, "Since our evolution ter metahumans, we are now like ta creator. And as such, we are declaring our independence from him."

"Independence? How does he have dominion over us?" Marvella asks angrily.

"And why would we not worship him?" Dakarai pushes. "If he truly possessed the power to create our world, should he not garner our loyalty and praise?" Turning his gaze to Mal alone, he adds, "What have you done?"

Ignoring Dakarai, Qualcum goes on, "Jeog created ta world upwards of ten t'ousand years ago—"

"Ten thousand?" Oaken interjects. "This planet is much older and—"

"My loves," Mal utters. Although she doesn't raise her voice, the rebuke is clear. "Let us tell you the story, and then we will answer your questions." She motions to Qualcum to begin.

Clearing his throat, the Third Aevum starts again. "Jeog created ta world upwards of ten t'ousand years ago and accomplished t'is feat in just six days. His purpose in creation was so t'at ta humans could share in his work—tending ter ta earth and takin' care of ta creatures. At its beginning, our planet was truly wit'out evil—"

"If he is really that good," Dakarai interjects, "why are we rebelling against him?"

Qualcum makes a sound as if he is about to shout at the Aevii, but the inhale of breath sends him into a coughing spasm. After wiping drool from his chin, he looks to Mal, utterly furious, and states, "Oi will speak no further."

Sighing, Mal picks up the tale. "Jeog started the world with just two humans—a male and a female. They also were without any evil in them. The creator made a perfect oasis for them to live in, and there was only goodness, light, and love.

"But Jeog played a dirty trick on the humans. Instead of merely allowing them to enjoy this peace and prosperity forever, he created a test of loyalty. He had formed the man and woman not so they could enjoy his presents or presence but to create an experiment of sorts. Now, it's important to remember that there was no evil in the world. The humans had nothing to compare their solely good existence to.

"And this fact played heavily into the test. The creator offered the humans two options. The first was to believe everything Jeog said was perfectly true. Blindly, they would have to accept everything the creator had set up was excellent and perfect—there would be no questioning it.

"In the other option, they could find out what evil was for themselves. They would be able to discern what was wrong and right just as Jeog could—but they would be able to arrive at their own conclusion. Now, this is very important in order to understand our enemy, so listen carefully. He wanted the humans' uninhibited allegiance, their total faith, without ever having to prove himself or show another side. He hoped they would live endlessly in that oasis, never understanding anything outside their limited perspective.

"Well, these wise humans 'failed' his test. When offered the chance to know the difference between what was right and what was wrong—to be like Jeog himself—they took it. And what was the creator's reaction? He punished them. He cursed the man and woman and cast them out of the oasis he had made. Like a toddler, Jeog threw away his new toy because it didn't give him what he wanted.

"At that time, he should have just left the humans alone. But he was so consumed with his own power and need for the humans' affection and obedience, he continuously intervened in their lives."

"So where is he now?" Dakarai asks. "What territory does he dwell in?"

Qualcum speaks up, clearly unable to remain silent on a topic which evidently means so much to him. "He does not dwell in places made by humans. He is spirit and lives in t'at realm."

Aevii Two, Four, Five, and Six erupt with astonishment at the same time. "How can he live in a spiritual realm?" Dakarai demands above the din.

"He is spirit," Qualcum reiterates. "He is all-powerful, all-knowing, all-seeing. He possesses raw, boundless power. In him are no weaknesses," Qualcum's lips twitch into a sneer, "save one." He looks back to Mal who continues for him.

"About two thousand years after Jeog created the world, the population began to unite. They all spoke one language, and they came together to build something magnificent. See, they knew they were divine—they knew they deserved access to their god-like powers, but Jeog had taken it away when he kicked the man and the woman out of the oasis. They knew that Jeog dwelled in the spiritual realm, and they thought they could gain access to it by entering the sky. This, of course, is preposterous, but they didn't know better at the time.

"They hoped to build a bridge of sorts to break through the sky. They started with a tower. They were eager to claim what was theirs, but Jeog, ever greedy, ever egotistical, didn't want this."

Mal pauses and looks at Qualcum. When he speaks, his words, clearly a quotation of some sort, feel ancient, dark, and mysterious. "'Look!' said Jeog, 'Ta people are united, and t'ey all speak ta same language. After t'is, nothing t'ey set out ter do will be impossible fer t'em! Come, let's go down and confuse ta people wit different languages. T'en t'ey won't be able ter understand each ot'er.'"

Mal picks the tale back up. "Jeog scattered the people so they couldn't build the city or the tower any longer. But the creator exposed himself in his declaration. He showed that all humans had to do was unite, and then nothing would be impossible for them. We saw this in Senex."

Qualcum laughs. "T'ere is much ter criticize about ta Sennies, but of t'is t'ey truly deserve praise."

"They united themselves," Mal explains. "Although it was not a spoken language, it was one of knowledge. They used the archaic internet to connect the entire world. Once they did that, nothing was impossible for them: including the rediscovery of our divinity. Our powers.

"Since evolving into metahumans, we defeated Jeog at his own game. We are now equal to him. Granted, he possesses more power, more knowledge, more knowhow, and can wield all the Gifts—"

"He can wield *all* Gifts?" Oaken shouts.

Ignoring her, Qualcum picks up again, "But we are like him now. We have power, wisdom, and universal know-how, and we can wield Gifts as he can."

Dakarai emits a barking laugh. "How exactly do you plan on declaring independence from him?" he demands angrily. "If he is as powerful as you say, how do we stand a chance against him?"

"And why are we fighting against him anyway?" Oaken asks. "What rule does he have that you are so eager to cast off? I have never heard of him until now—his power seems quite ineffective in the people's daily lives."

Mal raises her hand to stop the questions pouring from the other Aevii. "One at a time," she states, "and I'll work backward. Jeog is relatively unknown because Qualcum and I have made it so. Using my Gift, we rid the world of his name, his story, and his book. And we did something..." she shares a smile with Qualcum, which is both amused and wicked. "We did something special to his followers."

"But Jeog works in ta shadows," Qualcum inserts. "He is dangerous, manipulative, and cunning. Even now, all t'ese years later, Jeog still hoodwinks

Novians inter following him. T'ese people are given persuasive power, and t'ey have ta ability ter manipulate and destroy even ta strongest among us. Jeog is relentless, but so are we."

"How does he destroy them?" Oaken asks.

"He turns them into spiritual simulans," Mal answers. "He makes them like that very first man and woman: stuck in a world where he holds the only options. He demands complete obedience and punishes when there is any variation. The thing is, Jeog set up the rules of right and wrong and put them in the very fabric of Elusis. As long as they are followed, one's existence on the planet is successful. For now, we must follow those rules. But once we emancipate ourselves, we can come up with our own definition. We'll probably keep true to most of what the creator decreed, but we have some variations in mind. Now," she turns to Dakarai, "to answer your question. How are we to defeat Jeog?"

She smiles at the group and says in a slow melodic voice, almost like a lullaby, "A prophecy is coming that will reveal to us the secret of success."

"What prophecy?" Marvella asks.

"We cannot speak of it yet," Qualcum interjects.

Imploringly, Mal looks out to the Aevii. "That is all we can say for now, but you must have faith. You must trust me now, for my love for you is always first."

This utterance is met with silence. Even Oaken, consumed with questions, is without words. There are no statements of mutiny, but there are no declarations of faith either.

Flister Dubach stands. Everyone looks at him—even Qualcum.

"This is a lot to mull over. I must be alone with my thoughts," he states monotonously. Before he leaves, he pecks a kiss on Mal's cheek.

Of all of the Aevii, he knows he is the least offended by this new information, due to his affection for Mal. However, it still bothers him greatly. If he is going to be around to wage war against this creator, he will have to find a way to survive the prophecy tattooed onto his back.

He is going to have to find a way to murder Arkarian Story.

As he opens the door to his home in Jukantytär, Flister starts. Oaken is sitting on his armchair, warming herself by the roaring fireplace. "You weren't going to say goodbye, huh?" she asks.

"I have much on my mind," he answers.

She does not respond, and as much as he had wished to numb his senses in a bottle of spiced eupee, he respects the woman in his living room enough to remain with her. With a groan, he falls into the chair opposite Oaken.

The atmosphere radiates warmth, and while it may not be benevolent, it certainly is not unwelcoming. Having known Oaken for decades and been romantically involved with her for years, Flister understands that while she seeks space to organize her thoughts within, her body longs to share physical closeness with another amidst this contemplation.

Finally, Oaken breeches the silence. "I've sought Auctus and Effio my whole life." Her words are enunciated and distant as if they left her lips without permission. "Since I was a child, I wanted to find Mensonge—to see the place where creators were created. To submerge myself in the creative and intellectual quality of that kind of world—it has been my lifelong dream." Just one side of her lips turns up, but the slight smile is for some faraway recollection and not for Flister. "At ten, I commissioned a rocket to search the universe on my behalf. Marvella loved that rocket."

"Marvella?" Flister asks, not meaning to speak.

Ignoring him, Oaken continues, "And for it all to be a lie—a ploy. The very thing my marrow longed for... just a gimmick of Mal and Qualcum. I..." Tears form in her eyes as her face contorts into a grotesque grin. "I feel so stupid. So childish for believing in a farce for so long." A noxious laugh fills his living room as she continues. "I... It's like... I'm like a man on his death day, realizing everything was pointless. Here, at the end of things, all was vapor after all."

Flister wants to push the Marvella-comment but understands it is not the time. Unsure what to say, however, Flister stands and gently lifts Oaken into his arms, cradling her. As he returns to his seat, the Fifth Aevum wrapped tightly around his chest, Flister hums the Ninth-Grade song. She had told him once that although his singing voice was not meant to be admired and applauded, it had the kind of mistaken quality that fills broken spaces with warmth. And so he hums what he hopes is comfort into all of her shattered dreams.

When the tune reaches its end, he sighs loudly. "I wish the truth was not as it is, Kenny. I wish, for your sake, that all was as you had hoped."

She lifts her head from his chest and looks up into his eyes. The longing that swirls there has both the comfort of familiarity and the intoxication of the unknown. More unshed tears swirl within her eyes and as she blinks, they fall down her cheeks. "Why did Mal have to lie?"

As Flister wipes her tears, he answers, "I am sure she had her reasons."

Oaken flinches at his words as if he had swatted at her. "You're not defending her, are you?"

"No," he answers, not quite understanding the anger in her expression.

"You're not *furious* with her for lying to you?"

Shaking his head, he responds honestly, "I trust her."

Oaken scrambles out of his arms as if he were hurting her. When she whirls at him, she shouts, "Mal can do nothing wrong in your eyes, Flister! Oh, to be so revered by you!"

Grimacing, Flister says, "This is not about Mal; this is about *you*. Let us keep on topic."

"On topic?" she asks, incredulously. An uncharacteristic sneer paints itself across her mouth. "All right, *on topic*, Flister, can you explain to me why you spent the whole evening holding Mal's hand, drooling over her affection."

Annoyed at her jealousy, he bites, "That is what has you so upset? You have but one tear to shed for Auctus and Effio being a farce. An impending war or a seemingly undefeatable enemy elicits no response. No, no. What riles Oaken Bleu, the blessed Fifth Aevum, into a child-esque tantrum is the fact that I gave Mal a present."

"Don't minimize your actions, Flister. I have *every* right to be envious of your attention!" Slamming her fist on a side table, she shouts, "You don't get to just look at her like that and touch her and give her that present and then—"

"And then what, Kenny?" Flister counters. "Will you punish me?"

"You may not treat me like this."

"Like what?"

"What *is* Mal to you?"

Unbidden anger surges through his veins. "That is not your concern."

Her expression turns unreadable as Oaken wipes the skull tattoo off her collarbone and places it on his palm. For but a moment, she holds his hand. She places it to her cheek. She kisses it. It feels as if she is saying goodbye as she whispers, "I dare you... Flister, I dare you to tell me who you love most."

He pulls away from her, horrified at the request. Holding his hand by his chest, he mutters, "Do not do this."

"I dare you," she breathes as she wraps her arms around her waist.

Flister turns away, intent on ignoring her question, but he knows he will have to answer it sometime. He will not quit the game, and he has no desire to let his flesh rot away, so why not now?

Reluctantly and unwilling to look at her, he states with all the sorrow he truly feels, "Mal... It will always be Mal."

He does not watch her as she runs from the house. He does not call her name. He does not chase after her. Instead, the Sixth Aevum finds the spiced eupee that had consumed his thoughts but an hour before and drinks until it does once more.

Pexus

Kansis

ICAN'T REMEMBER WHEN I last experienced as much physical human contact as I have this evening, celebrating post-show with the circus performers. Little gestures explode my senses. Someone patting my hand. Another touching my hair. A dancer brushing my arm. I received eight hugs in less than sixty minutes—yes, I was counting! I can't wait to tell my subconscious!

I feel so warm. So wanted. So... can I say loved? No. No, not loved. But warm and wanted are good enough for right now. I never thought I'd be this comfortable around people again.

I keep wondering why Scout wants to search for his Superiors so badly. His job is creative and fulfilling, he's successful, and he has fantastic friendships. I would trade everything I've ever owned or could own for friends like these. If he had a terrible job, no sense of purpose, and no friends, I could see him trying to find something outside himself. But with all of this, how could he want more? What does he think the Rogue Superior could offer him?

After we finish an early supper of sausages, cheeses, and a delicious soup made of vegetables and herbs, Fabella, the masked Formosian woman, uses her storytelling Gift to share a tale with Amelia and me. Amelia can feel the story even though she can't understand Fabella's words.

As the story winds its way around my mind, I get sucked in. It's only five or so minutes after Fabella has started narrating that the hairs on my neck suddenly rise, and I realize it has nothing to do with the Formosian's tale.

Someone is watching me.

I'm not sure how I know, but I begin looking around the room. All the faces are turned towards conversations, plates, drinks, and such. None are looking in my direction. I look up and down toward the far end of the room. Left side, right side. No one is looking at me.

Taking one last glance behind me, I see him—it's the Ortusan man with the gaudy green coat. His eyes meet mine, and instantly everything around me freezes, and I'm standing centimeters from him. His eyes are abnormally large, his smile irregularly charming, his demeanor strangely intimidating. The Ortusan's lips don't move, but his unexpectedly high-pitched voice coos in my head, *Do you want to know?*

I try to use my lips, but instead, my mind asks, *Do I want to know what?*

His eyes narrow, and his lips upturn seductively. *You know, Shamed One. You know, Ignored One. I will only ask once more: do you want to know?*

My blood has turned to slush. The half-frozen shards poke my skin as it travels through my body. I know that I shouldn't answer him. I know that I should turn around. I know that I should...

"I want to know," I answer slowly.

I'm back in my seat, back in my body, and I have use of my mouth. "I'll be right back," I whisper to Amelia. She's so enthralled with Fabella's story that she barely acknowledges me.

The Ortusan is already walking out of the room. When I reach him, he's standing between a cobalt blue door and one with gold studs hammered into it. He picks at his fingernails, and although his eyes are not on me, I feel him staring. Feel him probing. Feel him touching me.

"I have a price," he whispers.

When I reach for my Vorbi, he laughs. "No, no, Shunned One. Your energy will do nothing for me."

"What do you want?" I ask.

"Your memories."

A sense of danger fills my veins, replacing my curiosity. I knew it! I knew he wanted a memory. But it's not arbitrary; he's looking for one in particular. "My memories?" I ask innocently.

"Yes, Shunned One. I want to sift through your life recollections and... record them, if you will."

"Which ones?"

"Whichever ones I want," he responds, his voice rich with allurement.

I know I should leave. I don't know exactly what he wants, but all of my mental training is screaming that I should run away, that I should not allow anyone into my head to listen, let alone record.

I take a step back. "No."

He shrugs indifferently. "Then you will never know, Shunned One. It is no blood from my veins."

I waver. "How will you record my memories?"

"I will take what I want," he answers, avoiding the question, "and you will get what you want. You will get to find out *why*."

"Why? Why what?"

"Why your love is poison to your mate."

His words ring in my ears, and I have to remind myself to breathe. Giving someone this type of access to my brain is foolish. Reckless. Idiotic. And dare I say it, pathetic. Because the truth is, no matter the cost, I would pay anything to find out why Aker doesn't love me.

Finally, I take a deep breath and answer, "I want to know."

"Then you both agree," the Ortusan speaks in a sing-song voice.

"Both?"

And as an answer, from behind a kiosk, Aker walks up to join me. "Avenir," he addresses the Ortusan man, "You said the price was a Blood Confession from one of our parents."

Aker's sudden appearance has adrenaline and self-consciousness pounding through my veins. Had he heard all of that?

"The Blood Confession is *your* price, Disregarded One," Avenir answers Aker. "*Her* price," he points to me with seductive grace, "is her memories." I feel the words more than I hear them.

Aker looks uneasily at Avenir. "So you… You know for sure what happened to us?" As if casting all pretenses aside, he adds, "You know why Mirindiss and I love each other?"

Avenir looks at me as if he can sense the sudden nausea that sweeps through my blood. He winks at me and then answers Aker, "I do indeed."

I've known since grade six that Mirindiss and Aker liked each other like mates. I had never heard either of them admit this out loud, but I always knew. And now I know from his own admission.

Aker refuses to look me in the eye as he continues talking to Avenir. "You said this had something to do with a social experiment?"

Shaking his head, Avenir says, "Tsk, tsk, tsk, Pexun. I will give no information unless a deal is struck." He eyes me for a moment then returns his piercing gaze to Aker.

Aker seems to struggle within himself for a moment and finally, cursing, growls, "Fine, I'll do it."

"Do what?" Avenir says, his high-pitched voice sing-song.

"I will make my parents give you a Blood Confession."

"Brilliant!" Avenir declares and rubs his hands together. "Now, now, my miserable duo, I want to show you something first." A giggling fills the air as if thirty different Avenirs were laughing at the same time. With a sound more like a breath than words, Avenir states, "The Shunned One will choose a door."

Barely keeping the vomit that fills my esophagus out of my mouth, I look out into the vast tent, and a bright orange door halfway up the tent's height catches my eyes. I don't point because it is clear that somehow, Avenir will know which door I mean.

"That one."

Within a blink, Aker and I are standing in front of the orange door on the platform. Avenir is still leaning against the tent. His eyes aren't on me, yet they are.

"Go in, my pitiful pair," he coos.

I know I should go back. I should tell Aker that we're making a mistake… I know—

Saying nothing to me, Aker opens the door and steps inside. I take a deep breath and follow him. The room is such a bright red that I close my eyes to the pain of it. It takes a few seconds for my vision to adjust, and then I see an empty crimson room that goes on forever in every direction. Then, the red seems to gather itself into some type of shape. It continues to grow and take form as if I were watching someone sculpt clay right in front of me.

When it is done, I see clearly that it is a man. Around us, blurry images begin to materialize but stay unfocused. I think we're in an alleyway of some kind.

As the man turns around, other colors seep into the space. His hair turns grey, his shirt mustard yellow, his shoes black. As I take in the colors, I realize I know this man…Daisei Fransen?

"Kel Fransen, what are you doing here?" Aker asks him.

Ignoring Aker, Daisei looks up and down the alleyway, clearly expecting someone.

I have only officially met Daisei, Kaileb's dad, once—at Kaileb and Mirindiss' engagement party. We had not spoken as we had no reason to, but I knew who he was. When Kaileb and I were younger, we would sneak into each other's houses to talk about Aker and Mirindiss' relationship. I often saw Daisei as I crept in and out of the house, but he had never seen me.

"Kel Fransen?" Aker asks again. Daisei doesn't turn around. Instead, he fidgets with his pant pocket. Aker walks around Daisei and stands directly in front of his gaze, but there is no recognition. "Hello? Can you hear me?" Aker waves his hands in front of Daisei's face, but the man doesn't respond. He's clearly waiting for someone.

As we watch, Daisei asks his Suus several times what time it is, eyes searching the distance. Suddenly, I realize how young he looks. From all my memories of him, he has kept himself looking in his forties, but he looks to be in his twenties now. What is this place?

"Daisei?" a voice behind us asks.

We three turn to take in the newcomer. Thas Vonbough, Aker's dad, slinks over to Daisei with an annoyed expression on his face. I had forgotten how much Aker looks like his dad.

"Dad?" Aker asks, but Thas continues past his seemingly invisible son. Numerous times, Thas glances behind him as if he's making sure no one is following him.

"We said we wouldn't meet," Thas whispers angrily. "We are never to talk about this, Daisei. We signed the contract."

"I know it, Thas," Daisei snaps. "*Ontzi*, I know it. Nakshatra would kill me if she knew I was here—"

"Then why are you here?" Thas seethes.

Daisei looks around again and then, after a string of cursing, whispers, "I think we made a mistake."

Thas shakes his head. "It doesn't matter. We all made a choice."

"The kids are suffering," Daisei says in a harsh whisper. "All of them. I see it every time they're together. Or separate. Thas... We have to tell them."

I try to catch Aker's eye, but his gaze is set on his dad and Daisei.

"We can't," Thas states, voice sure.

More cursing from Daisei. "I can't even look Kaileb in the eyes anymore. I—I can't—I won't do this anymore. My blood turns to acid every time I see Chet's girl."

Chet's girl? That's me.

Thas' eyes narrow. "You been saving all the Vorbies you get every month? Can you give it all back? Because I know I can't. Beaut can't. We have used every single one to supplement our income. You have all those Vorbies stored at a bank somewhere?"

Daisei curses. When Thas asks him again, Daisei hollers, "No, I've been spending them every month!"

"We'll all go to blood reclamation dens if we tell them. We knew what we were getting ourselves into," Thas bites.

"*Ontzi*, I didn't know they'd be in such pain!"

Thas sneers, and the expression curdles my blood. "Don't play stupid just because your blood is rotting with guilt. What did you think was going to happen? That Cupido Interterritorial chick made it clear what we were signing the kids up for. They would be a part of a social experiment to show what love would be like without the Cupido. They explained the love triangle to us. I was sitting next to you when the lady told us one of the girls would be loved by both our boys, and neither boy would love the other girl. She told us one of the boys would get the right blood, and one would get the wrong blood. Of course, we all hoped our kids would get the better lot—but we knew the costs.

"Chet knew there was a chance his daughter would be the one with no love, and he signed her up anyway. I knew there was a chance my boy would be the one who didn't get love, but I did it anyway. We didn't do this to them so they'd have good lives, Daisei." Thas' expression darkens even deeper. "We did it to fill our Vorbies. Cupido Interterritorial is making a point, and we're getting compensated for showing that their method of pairing works. When we signed that contract, we signed the kids up for a life of pain."

"No, I didn't sign Kaileb up for that," Daisei moans, shaking his head.

Thas scoffs. "Oh, but you did."

Daisei throws his hands up in the air. "I didn't realize what the Cupido woman meant by all that! She said they'd only do the experiment until it had run its course—I didn't think that would mean past their fourteenth birthdays!"

"I don't know why you're trying to prove your innocence to me. You're just as blameworthy as I am."

"Do you enjoy watching Aker pine after Mirindiss knowing she loves my son? Knowing she will marry him?"

I chance a glance at Aker, but he has not moved. His face is frozen in shock.

Thas spits on the ground. "I'm not a monster," he hisses. "But I'm also man enough to drink the blood I spilled. I don't need your guilt, Daisei. I have enough of my own." With that, he turns and leaves Daisei staring after him.

A cold hand seizes my shoulder and pulls me backward.

I'm facing the orange door.

I can't think. I can't breathe. I can't… understand.

"Shunned One," the Ortusan's childlike voice whispers in my ear, "There is more pain in your veins than they can bear—with it, your blood belabors. I will feast on it." He giggles again, and it echoes throughout my body. "I know how you die. Do you want to know? Do you want to know, Shunned One?"

When I open my eyes, I'm standing in front of the main event's giant round door, and Avenir is once again leaning against the canopy's canvas fabric. Aker stands beside me, shaking.

Can it be true? All this time… There was nothing wrong with me… And my parents knew… all the parents knew and they just let the town shun me for two years. My mom and dad just sat there accepting compensation from Cupido Interterritorial while their daughter… while I…

Avenir starts talking as if he had been in the middle of sharing something with us and had been interrupted. "For centuries, many have been lobbying to end the Cupido. Just as it was in Senex, these people desire for their children to have the ability to choose whom they wish to marry. Cupido Interterritorial has been able to silence, blackmail, or bribe these lobbyists not to make any more efforts for hundreds of years. However, one politician, in particular, would not be silenced, blackmailed, or bribed. She was bent on showing the weaknesses and cracks within the Cupido system.

"To prove its validity and necessity, Cupido Interterritorial conducted five social experiments over the past seventy years—the four of you being the last set of couples experimented upon. Each experiment was to show the strength of the Cupido and exploit the weaknesses of human choice concerning romantic love. Each experiment varied in its players, the scenario, and the outcome. Your social experiment was to show the catastrophic events of what Senexians called a 'love triangle.'"

"A love triangle?" Aker asks.

"Yes. In Senex, it was a romantic relationship involving three people wherein two compete against each other for the undivided romantic attention of a single interest. Normally, in these scenarios, the single interest would have feelings for both the other people."

I'm so angry my body feels weak. "But there are four of us," I say, and my tongue feels too big in my mouth.

"Yes, well, they had to pick two couples to get to three of them. The two people competing would be the men, and the single interest—I am afraid—was not you." A grotesque smile spreads across his features. "There was no part for you to play in the scenario."

Hot tears spring to my eyes, but Avenir continues, "As you know, within three days of a mother finding out she is expecting, she checks herself into the local Cupido Agency. The parents then have three weeks to determine and choose the mate of their unborn child from a list of other mothers in the area who are also with child. Your parents all followed the same protocol.

"However, a few days before the mothers returned to Cupido Interterritorial for the Blood Transfusion, a Cupido agent visited your four families. They were under strict orders not to share the information or discuss the agreement with anyone else. You see, your parents—their unborn children rather—had been chosen to be a part of said experiment, and each family would be paid significantly for the duration of the child's life—that is, until the trial period was over.

"A Cupido employee told them that four times a year, a Cupido Interterritorial employee would meet with you four to keep updates on the research—"

"Whyab Walt!" Aker exclaims. "The four of us were issued to a student counselor four times a year. No one else in our grade had to see the counselor, but we did. The same man came every time. He was nice enough but always asked strange questions—" As if he realizes he is talking aloud, Aker stops and scratches his chin.

"Indeed," Avenir giggles at Aker's outburst. "Obvious as it is," he says slowly, "I can confirm that all four sets of parents agreed to allow their child to be a part of the experiment. When the mothers went to their respective appointments, although it seemed that all was well and routine, the vials of blood were not distributed as they should have been.

"Now, before I share another obvious fact, let me remind you: in Senex, people had to find their own mates. In doing so, they were permitted and even encouraged to betray one another. It was acceptable to have two mates and wicked things of the like. The director's board of Cupido Interterritorial wanted to prove that couples would not last without the Cupido, just like in Senex. If our people now had to live in a world without the Cupido, they would revert to the old ways: being unhappy, depressed, and unloved.

"With that said, in the case of you four, it was documented that Aker Vonbough was mated with Kansis Willow, while Kaileb Fransen was mated with Mirindiss Tekill. However, this was not the case. The assistants put Kaileb's blood in Mirindiss and Mirindiss' blood in Kaileb, but then put Aker's blood in Mirindiss and Mirindiss' blood in Aker and… and Aker's blood in Kansis. A love triangle plus a tag-along." He winks at me again.

"But I don't want to marry Kansis!" Aker suddenly shouts, unknowing or uncaring of my feelings. "I ran away with Mirindiss—we were going to get married in secret. We were going to be together! For two years I refused to marry Kansis and was only going to do so now because I didn't want to get sent to a blood reclamation den. Doesn't that prove it worked?"

Avenir smiles ruefully. "They wanted to make their point."

For a moment, I think I'm going to pass out... Wait... No, I'm okay. I mean, I'm not okay, but I'm also not unconscious. A cold gust of air drafts in from the bottom of one of the doors next to me. It plays with my curls and then flies into my open mouth, drying it out. I feel the cold stone floor before I realize I've sat down.

The pocket watch in my pants jingles, and I take it out. Staring at the agitated raven, my mind wanders. I find myself staring out at the circus again. It is a very different angle to observe from, down here on the ground level, surrounded by the mini-circus kiosks, sitting on the yellow precious stones. For the first time, I notice that all of the colors in the room are like a sunset, with the golden stones like the sun bidding its farewell.

I'm not sure how long I stare out into nothing, but I suddenly realize Aker is yelling, and it takes me a few seconds to hone back on his words.

"And why wouldn't they have told us? How could they do this to us?" he screams, and it sounds like a roar. "Why wouldn't my mom tell me? Do you know how many conversations we had about this? And she told me that even though it was blasphemous, she wanted me to be with Mirindiss! Why would she say that? Why would she go along with it? How could she—" He roars again, like a wounded animal. "My dad told me he was disappointed in me. That I was a curse for our family... How could he say that when he knew it wasn't my fault?" He turns on Avenir. "Does Mirindiss know?"

"I would assume not," Avenir answers pleasantly.

"I should call her and tell her. Maybe—"

I can barely breathe, but taking as deep a breath as I can, I ask, "Maybe what?" My voice is so tight I don't even sound like myself.

Moaning, Aker crumples to the ground as well. After a few moments of silence, he asks, voice monotone, "So this was supposed to prove that the Cupido works, right?"

"Correct," Avenir affirms.

"And the Cupido is supposed to pair mates that were always supposed to be?" he asks in the same voice. Without waiting for an answer, he goes on, "So maybe this was the way things are supposed to be. Maybe I am supposed to be with Mirindiss... I mean, how could I feel this way if it was just a mistake? Even if Kansis' blood was in me, I have to believe I would have still loved Mirindiss."

"Why do you *have* to believe that?" I ask, trying to keep my voice steady.

"Because this can't all be a lie!" Aker shouts. "How can every emotion, every thought, every dream, every feeling be a lie? A product of someone's curiosity? I can't look back at our whole lives and think it was a mistake!"

"I want nothing more than that," I state, my own voice rising.

"That's because your existence is a joke!" Aker bellows.

Avenir erupts in girlish giggles.

As the high-pitched notes die away, Aker's words settle in the spacious tent like a sound-dampening fog. Avenir's eyes meet mine, and his smile does not waver—he seems to enjoy my anguish. I pull my knees close to my chest but sneak a peek at Aker.

As if all the fight drains out of his body, Aker clicks his tongue and looks around the room. "I'm—I'm sorry," he apologizes quietly. "I didn't mean that."

"There is no need for the charade," Avenir laughs lightly. "You have been relentless in your phlebotomy, my dear man. 'Tis no need for pretense now."

Aker shakes his head. "No, I didn't mean that. Kansis, I—"

"No, you meant just that," I reply. "Although my existence has been tragic, you are quick to judge it a good joke." I let out the poison I've been bearing all these years. "You are in love with someone who rejected you and married someone else. Your pretty lover has yours and Kaileb's blood equally within her veins, yet she chose him over you. Your life is a more tragic comedy than mine."

To my utmost surprise, a soft laugh escapes Aker's lips. He scratches the back of his neck and laughs again. "You're right... Spot on discernment. My life is the worst out of all of us." His lip twitches, and his eyes redden. "I never thought of it that way. She did choose him, didn't she?"

It's a statement, not a question.

Silence descends. I try not to, but I keep looking at Aker as he stares down at his feet with a hurt yet bemused smile. It is as if all the parts are finally clicking into place for him.

"So when is the experiment over?" Aker finally inquires of Avenir.

"In the case of your social experiment... When one of you kills yourself."

Shock slaps me in the face. "Why go so far?" I question.

Avenir smiles broadly. "Cupido wanted to make their point."

"How do you know this?" Aker asks. "How do you know *any* of this?"

Avenir opens his arms wide as if about to introduce a cast. "Because I, Avenir Yym, was also in a social experiment."

This statement is met with silence. If he was also part of a social experiment, how could he treat us so callously? Laughing at us and mocking what's happened? When I voice this, Avenir merely shrugs his shoulders.

"I am unsure. It makes my pain more palpable, I presume," he answers.

Before I can push back, Aker inquires, "What was your experiment?"

"Mine was to play out betrayal. I walked in on my mate, making love to our neighbor. I found out later that the Cupido had set up the whole scenario, and neither of them were in their right mind, but my neighbor's wife and I were each forced to deal with the betrayal of a mate."

"What happened?" Aker asks.

"Before I had a chance to decide what I wanted to do, my neighbor's wife turned them into a blood reclamation den. I never saw my mate again. She..." For the first time, Avenir's smile wavers. "She was murdered for a crime she did not commit." Before either of us can say anything, he goes on quickly—his smile glittering brightly once more—"But I was unable to collect the proper evidence at the time. So it has become my mission to collect pieces of evidence proving that the experiments have taken place."

Avenir claps his hands together and then rubs them as if warming them by fire. "Before you rot in the spoilage that is your existence," Avenir says, his teeth flashing white, "you owe me something."

"My memories," I answer as if he had asked a question.

He waves a hand at me. "Oh no, Shunned One. I took those already. And may I comment that they were particularly difficult to extract. You have hidden much from yourself." He stares at me then, and I don't understand the intensity in his gaze. Was he trying to get memories that I had bound up in my Memory Scars?

Blinking, Avenir looks away. Speaking quickly, he continues on, "No, no, I need the Blood Confession from your parents now," he tells Aker.

"We didn't talk about a timeframe," Aker hedges.

"It will be *now*," Avenir responds slowly, "or I will take my information back, and when you seek it once more, the price will be higher than you can pay."

"The Guardians are looking for us," I tell Avenir. "If he leaves now, he will get arrested, and then you'll never get your confession. Give us a month, or you can take the information back."

Avenir studies me for a moment, and it feels so invasive. Finally, he gives another of his malicious grins and says, "I will accept a Blood Assurance and nothing else."

"I don't have an Assurance Blade," I say, hoping he doesn't either.

His expression reveals the opposite. He reaches into his coat pocket and takes out a small black rhodium-plating knife. Like all Assurance Blades, on the side is a small inscription that says, *One drop is needed, one promise given. To break the one is to dry up the other.*

Aker doesn't reach for it, so reluctantly, I do.

Avenir pulls it away from my grasp. "Your payment is settled," he tells me. Turning to Aker, he drawls, "This is for *you*."

Jaw tight, hands shaking, eyes furious, Aker walks to the Ortusan and opens his hand. After taking a deep breath, he places the blade on his thumb.

After a few moments of Aker standing motionless, Avenir mocks, "If you are truly too cowardly to complete the Assurance, I will allow your should-be mate to perform it."

Aker looks to me and when our eyes meet, my blood pressure rises. Is he really going to make me do it?

With an expression between anger and fear, he says, "We'll both do it." When I don't move, he demands, "You'll do this with me, right?"

Before I really process my answer, I say, "Yeah."

He looks back down at his thumb and presses the knife inside. "I, Aker Vonbough, give my blood as assurance that I will give a Blood Confession from one of our parents to Avenir..."

"Yym," Avenir inserts.

Aker finishes, "To Avenir Yym within the next thirty days. I will do this."

Outreaching his arm, he offers the blade to me. "Take it," he commands.

Inhaling a deep breath, I cut my finger for the second time that week with an Assurance Blade. "I, Kansis Willow, give my blood as assurance that I will give a Blood Confession from one of our parents to Avenir Yym within the next thirty days. I will do this."

A sneer smears across Avenir's face as he states, "One month, Pexuns. You have one month."

In the pump of a ventricle, he's gone. Vanished as if he had never been there.

Aker and I sit in silence for some time. It might be for a minute; it might be for half an hour. All I know is that I'm drowning in memories of my parents shunning me, Aker's parents' long-held preference of Mirindiss over me, Kaileb and I never understanding the affection Aker and Mirindiss had for one another... My whole life has felt like these disjointed jigsaw pieces trying to shove together and never making sense. Now, I hold the piece of the puzzle that makes everything else fit into place. It all makes sense now. Everything... my whole life is finally clear.

I think about earlier today and how the pink-skinned Formosian had told me that the truth of one of my Memory Scars would be revealed soon. Was this it? In the past, had I found out about the love triangle, and wasn't able to handle it, so I had the memory taken? That *does* sound like me: too cowardly to face the truth.

Quickly, I reach behind me and feel my shoulder.

Nope.

The three scars are still there.

Looking at the circus ceiling, I fleetingly wonder if people with flying Gifts can soar up to the doors that line the canvas top or if their Gifts are inhibited from doing so.

"Kansis."

My breath hitches at his voice, and I slowly move my eyes from the ceiling to the man who never had the chance to be my mate.

He stares at me as if he's seeing me for the first time. He, too, now knows it was never my fault he didn't love me back. Aker stands, walks over to where I'm still cross-legged, and sits near me. Very close. Okay, not *that* close, but closer than he's ever voluntarily sat next to me.

"We were cheated the chance at a normal life," he begins. "A normal marriage... We were set up to fail, and we did. But we don't have to fail anymore. Since we know it's neither of us at fault for my not loving you, we can do something about it. We can get the Blood Transfusion." He takes a deep breath. "Kansis, I want a mate. I want someone who loves me and only me. I want to have a wife and a family... and we can have that. We can have that if we put your blood in me —for real this time."

I want to ask him something, but I know it's an unfair question. So before I have the chance to decide whether I should or not, I make myself blurt it out. "Because you need my blood in you... for you to love me?"

"Of course," he answers as if this is a stupid question. "And we can do that. I can finally see you as a mate, care about you, and love you with all my blood."

I nod, not knowing why his words make me so sad. Isn't this the best news I've heard? Aker wants to do the Blood Transfusion so he can love me. So he can care about me. So he can see me.

These are all things I want...

I grab the druzy quartz pendant around my neck. With it, I've been able to be with Aker. Even if it wasn't real, it's been a massive part of my life. But it could be real... We could really be together. And even though this should be the most exciting news of my life, another thought won't stop taking up residence in the forefront of my mind… Yes, I finally get Aker…

But why do I keep thinking about Scout and how—even though I'm not in his blood—he's seen me and cared for me from the moment I met him?

"So our little escapade with the circus is over, right?" Aker asks. "We can go home now?"

I shake my head before I know what I'm going to say. I find myself fingering the pocket watch again.

"Kansis, we only have a month to get the Blood Confession from our parents before Avenir takes our memories back. Who knows how long it will take to convince one of them to give it to us!"

"Why don't you go?" I ask hesitantly. "They'll want to talk to you, not me, anyway."

"We *both* took the Blood Assurance," he replies angrily. "This is something we have to do together."

"But the Guardians are still looking for me. If I leave, they'll arrest me."

"And when they do, you can leverage the location of your Pod—"

"I'm *not* doing that," I retort and barrel on before he can interrupt. "But I'll see if Scout can make a eutsi for us with Winzer's Gift. I can wear mine and go back to Depalo with you to get the Blood Confession."

"Okay, let's find him now—"

Interjecting, I say quickly, "I can't make any decisions before we go to the meeting with Scout and the other Arkahunters. I'm not just going to abandon Amelia without knowing if she's going to be able to find her dad."

That gives me at least a few more hours with Amelia and Scout.

Obviously upset but realizing I won't budge, Aker sighs and states, "Fine. We'll go to the meeting." Waiting until I meet his gaze, he finishes, "But the second it's done… we're leaving, Kansis."

"But what if—"

Huffing, Aker cuts me off. "As soon as you know Amelia doesn't need you, we're leaving."

"Okay."

I know that I should care more about keeping this new memory—I should care more that I finally understand that my blood isn't bad and that it's not my fault that Aker doesn't love me.

But… if I'm honest… I would choose to forget it all and stay here where, bad blood and all, I'm liked by someone. By *someones*. A place where I'm wanted just as I am.

Pexus

Pypen

IT TAKES ME A moment to recover from Merayal's words—and the expression that overtook her features as she spoke them. Had she truly feigned interest in my tale so she could ascertain my weakness? I wonder if she is really that clever and if I am that blind. Or perhaps, as Fabella said, Merayal knows no other way. Perhaps I got too close, and this was her way of pushing me back.

It does not take long to reach the circus tent, and when I enter the courtyard I stop, not knowing exactly what to do. Although the circus would be a great source of distraction, I do not feel much like revelries. I am certain that all the performers will be in Memory and Fiddy's room enjoying a job-well-done celebration for our show. A couple of hours ago, I would have preferred to be there over anywhere else. However, after conversations with Scout and Merayal (not to mention the Sixth Aevum), I want to be alone. Turning around, I mosey through downtown Initium while I think.

As I walk, I realize I have never much thought of myself as a kind man, nor a soft man, nor even a good man; but I *am* a loyal man. I would forsake all on account of Scout—no questions or doubts. And to my surprise, affection for many members of our crew has snuck into my blood. I find there are now many lives I would seek to protect and for whom I would sacrifice. But this Pexun—this cruel, angry, pernicious girl—is not among that number.

For Scout to have thrust the responsibility of her upon me was a mistake. I am not certain whose mistake it was, but it was made nonetheless. She will fall into darkness, and I will stand watching without a drop of regret in my blood.

I try to purge these feelings from my arteries. They do not bode well.

I find myself wondering about Merayal's history. Did she elude the K-Pax? Had she been tortured as Amelia had been? What nightmares did she endure that metamorphosed her into the cantankerous and vile creature she has become?

I wish Fabella had not spoken over me that night. I wish I could dismiss the girl instead of wondering about her story. I slap my face to get away from my dark musings—I need to think about something else. Anything else.

Perhaps I will do as Scout does and take a nap. Thinking this sounds pleasant, I change directions and make my way toward the hotel.

It takes a half hour to get to our accommodation, and as I walk into the hotel lobby, I hear the loud, Sanusian voices of the Controls. I do not feel that tired. Instead of a nap, perhaps an afternoon with their company will serve as the distraction I need, so I make my way toward the sitting area where they lounge. However, right before I reach them, I hear Merayal's voice.

Matza! Can I go nowhere without her noxious presence polluting my interactions? And for what purpose is she spending time with the Controls?

I have a mind to go over and expose her in front of everyone as being a Pod. Perhaps I will…

Quickly, I take in the scene and then hide in the shadows of a colonnade on the other side of the company. Without meaning to, my mind lingers on the casual way she is leaning against the armrest, the familiar way she is laughing at Manny's joke, the easy way she drinks her beverage.

When did she start associating with the Controls?

Well, 'tis a good matter. She has found people who can belay her venom. That is what I wanted for her.

"Play with us, Mer," Vielfrah begs in a pouty voice, his prominent blue eyes twinkling with mischief. "Ye just got here, and yer already leavin'? Oi'll be easy on ye t'is time, Oi swears it."

This time? Merayal has only been with us a couple of days, and most of her time has been spent practicing or pouting. When did she play Gedankenspiel with the Controls?

"Oh, please," Merayal responds, and I can hear her smile. "I almost had you last game."

"*Almost* is relative, dear," Thykas remarks. "And eit'er way, ye still didna win. Only Sanusians win Gedankenspiel; yer hair is just a few shades ta wrong color."

"Merayal doesna want her hair darker," Vielfrah says with fake innocence. "Ye wants it lighter, right, Mer?"

The group laughs.

"Ye know, Oi may need to report ye ter Pip and Scouty," Vielfrah goes on. "T'ey probably want ter know we have a Cap lover in ta group."

"That's right," Twigg says, her voice high and sweet. Adjusting her eyepatch, she adds, "Who would be guessin' ta shinin' star of ta Unopened Gifts wants ter be a dirty Cap."

Merayal's laugh circles around my head, mocking me. I wonder if I have ever heard her laugh previously. Irrational anger percolates in my blood, although I know it to be unnecessary. 'Tis good she has found friends.

"If being a Cap means I never had to meet you *vogns*, then a Cap I'll be," Merayal responds playfully.

Vielfrah utters a colorful series of Sanusian curses, making the group laugh louder.

"You've never even met a Captusian," Merayal shouts, trying to reign in the group.

"As ye continue ter remind us, me ol' caploverinsuch," Thykas responds. "We don't need ter meet t'em ter know how putrid t'ey are."

"Eh, Oi just saw a Captusian last day," Vielfrah begins. Then he feigns a gasp of realization and adds, "Wait, no, sorry, t'at was just a dog's backside."

"Have ye ever met a Cap?" Twigg asks Merayal.

Licking her lips, Merayal answers, "No, but that doesn't mean they're who you say they are either."

"Well," Veilfrah spits, "Come toe ter toe wit one—stare 'em in t'eir cruel eyes, and t'en ye can tell me how much ye love t'em."

"Let's just play the stupid game," Merayal snaps.

"We had just decided ter play ta next game at ta circus," Thykas remarks. "Let's cleanupinsuch, and ye'll join us."

The sound of the group putting away the board and cards drowns out their voices, and I almost leave. But as I take a step, I hear Vielfrah say, "Ye know, ta first time Oi play t'is game was wit Pip and Wigs. Ye remember t'at?"

Twigg giggles. Her laugh has always made others join in the mirth—her joy infectious. "Oi remember," she answers. "Ye was a mess when t'ey found ye, wot wot."

"Ye was a mess when t'ey found ye too, Wigs," Dommy chimes in, her voice an octave lower than Twigg's. "We all was, righty-o."

"What do you mean?" Merayal asks. "Who found you?"

"Pip and Scouty-sams. T'ey find all of us," Vielfrah answers.

"*Kachna*," Thykas swears and chuckles, "t'ey should call us ta Fugitive Gifts instead."

The Controls roar with laughter at this.

Manny, the only non-Sanusian Control, adds, "A lot of us were on our way to blood reclamation dens when they picked us up. Right before I joined the group, I was on my way to Fort Clipso." There is an awkward silence, and

Manny repeats, "You know—Fort Clipso?"

"What's that?" Merayal asks.

"You don't know what Fort Clipso is? *Ontzi*, Merayal, how can you not know? What part of Pexus are you from?"

Merayal clears her throat. "Barns. It's northeast of Demirkan. I told you, my town was very sheltered."

"Apparently," Manny responds, exasperated. "Well, Fort Clipso is the den where they send people who have leaky blood."

A moment passes and then Merayal asks, "Crazy people?"

"Yes," Manny answers. "We're not all that welcomed into society—"

"Well, just look at him, sam," Thykas whispers loudly to Merayal, who snickers.

Manny continues, "My mate was born with a… dysfunction. No healers could fix her brain. When we were fourteen, they took her to a den. I didn't understand what that meant, but I knew I would be assigned a new mate. Because of her bad blood, they would make the Blood Transfusion more affordable for my parents. But I didn't want anyone else. So I ran away to the den they had taken her to, and I broke in. When I discovered what they were doing to the people there, they decided I needed to stay there too."

"Scouty and Pip saved me from Fort Nyata in Sanus," Dommy adds.

"Oi questioned me professors," Twigg opens up. "Questioned ta government, Arkarian Story, Gifts, Aevii, history, all of it. Well, Oi asked one too many questions and was told if Oi didna stop, Oi was going ter be sent ter a den. Well…"

"Wigs is too curious," Dommy inserts.

Twigg guffaws and continues. "Yeah, well, Oi got arrested by Guardians. Oi was declared insane and forced ter go ter Fort Nyata. Ta night Oi was being transferred, we stopped in ta same town as t'ese *vogns*. T'ey were performin'. Oi was in a car bound and guarded one minute, and ta next t'ing Oi knew, Oi'm lookin' at Scouty's face t'rough ta car door, askin' me if Oi wanted ter run away ter ta circus."

"How did they know to free you?" Merayal questions.

"Whenever we travel, Emerly seeks minds calling out fer help," Thykas answers. "If he hears anyone, we find t'em and help any way we can. We ask t'em ter join if t'ey have ta disposition and Gift-set ter enhance our group. We usually find *kaczkas* like Vielfrah and Manny."

The sounds of them cleaning up the game have ceased, but the group stays seated, caught up in their conversation.

"Oi was on my way to Fort Nyata," Veilfrah states.

"But t'at is because ye *are* crazy," Twigg expounds confidentially. "He refused ter do his appointed job."

"No one is goin' ter tell me what ter do," Vielfrah huffs.

"My mate had just passed," Dommy goes back to her story, and the group hushes. "Oi t'ought t'ere was nothin' left fer me. But Pip found me and offered ta circus."

"Well, *Emerly* found you, right?" Merayal asks.

"Emerly did his job well, just as we all do. But it's Pip and Scouty who saved us."

"Why Pypen?" Merayal pushes. "You said it was Emerly and Scout."

"What's up yer nose concerning our Pypen?" Thykas asks her. "Ye've been quite ta gnat ter him since ye arrived."

Merayal rolls her eyes. "I just know his kind."

My blood bristles at her words.

"And what kind be t'at?" Thykas asks.

"The kind that lords power over you," she answers. "He's in charge, so he thinks he's in charge of you."

Thykas chuckles. "Is t'at so?"

Merayal stiffens as she answers, "Yeah, it is. He's a narcissistic *vaunut*."

Several voices rise at the same time.

Veilfrah spats, "Ye don't know our Pip, girl."

Dommy states, "T'ats not ta way of t'ings."

Twigg laughs as she asks, "Who've ye been hanging out wit, Mer? Not *our* Pip."

A swell of pride rises in my veins listening to the Controls defend me. I have worked closely with each of them individually over the years and gained quite a respect for them all. I was there when they respectively were brought back to the circus for the first time—and I hand-picked each one to join the Control team. Scout and Emerly aside, Thykas is my only true friend.

Merayal stands as if to leave, "I've been dealing with men like him my whole life. I know what I know."

"And what is t'at?" Veilfrah asks, standing as well. "What kind of man is Pypen?"

"I'm done," Merayal growls, but when she tries to walk past him, Veilfrah stands in her way. With uncanny speed, Merayal punches Veilfrah in the face and pulls his body into her knee, forcing a loud *oofga* to leave his lips. As she tries to get past again, he kicks her legs out from underneath her, and before I can blink, the two are wrestling on the floor.

The other Controls whoop and holler their encouragement for both fighters.

Quickly, two hotel simulans approach and physically separate the two. I expect rage to be flaming behind their eyes, but when they rise, Merayal and Veilfrah are smiling at each other.

"Please take this behavior outside," one of the simulan states.

"We're done," Veilfrah tells it. "We'll be good, Oi promise."

The simulans nod and walk away. Veilfrah laughs again and asks Merayal, "So, come out wit it. What's yer t'orn with Pypen," while rubbing his chin.

Merayal does not answer right away.

Twigg fills the silence asking, "Do ye like Scout?"

"He's okay."

"Why dunna ye hate him?"

After thinking about it, she answers, "I know he's trying to help me."

Twigg takes one of her short curls and twirls her finger in it as she asks, "And ye like us?"

Merayal smiles sardonically. "Well, I don't hate you."

"And why's t'at?"

Her smile slowly fades. She stares down at her hands for a moment as if she can read the answer off of them. Sighing, Merayal answers, "I don't know. You remind me of my family, I guess."

"Where is yer family?" Thykas asks.

"Dead."

The group hushes at the word.

Obviously regretting the admission, Merayal snorts and says, "I'm fine. It's fine. *Ontzi*, you guys are a bunch of *ahirus*."

Twigg clears her throat and continues, "Okay, so ye don't mind ta Scout-sam and ye don't mind us-in-such… so what is it about Pypen t'at has yer veins all knotted?"

"I don't know how to explain it."

"Try," Thykas prompts. Merayal looks up at him. He softens his handsome features and adds, "If we're goin' ter be ta only companions ye have in all ta circus—"

"You're not my companions," Merayal interrupts.

Chuckling, Thykas continues, "Well, if we're going to be ta only people in ta circus ye don't hate, then ye might as well trust us a smidgin. Maybe not

Vielfrah, but ta rest of us, t'en."

Veilfrah races over and jumps on Thykas, and the two grapple on the small couch. Before the simulans return, Veilfrah shushes Thykas loudly and says, "Go ahead, Mer. Why do ye despise Pip so?"

Merayal grunts, "I don't know, okay? I don't know how to explain it. He just... I know... he... he wants to be more than just friends, you know?"

"More t'an friends?" Thykas asks.

"Yeah."

"Merayal, Pypen's friendship is not somet'ing easily gained," Thykas responds. "T'ere are many people in t'is circus and ta people Pypen considers his friends Oi could count on one hand. Oi don't t'ink he wants yer friendship, let alone anyt'ing more t'an t'at. Oi t'ink he just wants a performance partner who isn't going ter suck his blood dry every time ye interact."

"That's... that's not what I meant," Merayal responds, agitated.

"Well what's more t'an friendship?" Veilfrah asks. "Do ye mean like family?"

"Because he isn't lookin' fer family in ye eit'er," Thykas goes on. "Scout's ta only one he sees as family."

Flustered, Merayal groans loudly. "I don't know how to explain it to you. I just know what I know, and I'll be as mean to him as I have to be in order to keep him from trying to walk down that path with me." Before anyone can respond, she throws up her hands and states, "Listen, do you want to play your stupid game or not? I'm done talking about this. Either let's go back to the circus and play, or I'm leaving."

"Ter ta circus, t'en," Veilfrah states, and the group stands. As they noisily walk towards the door, I move around the colonnade so they will not see me. Once they have left the hotel lobby, I walk out from behind the shadows and move toward the elevators.

What did Merayal mean? What is more than friendship? Thykas is correct—I am not looking to be Merayal's friend. Perhaps Merayal also knows about taming... I do not see her being keen on the idea—particularly being tamed by me. Fabella said that creating ties means preserving proximity. That is the last thing Merayal wants from me.

"Pypen Tross?"

Surprised at my name being said by a voice I do not recognize, I turn around to see who it is, and my heart beats twice instead of once. Three Pexun Guardians walk toward me with casual expressions on their faces.

Having just entered the hotel, I know there is nowhere to go, no excuse to be had. "Indeed," I answer hesitantly. "Can I help you?"

One of the Guardians steps forward. She has allowed herself to age, looking somewhere in her fifties, and has braided her long, grey hair into a plait down her back. "We are looking for this Pexun woman," she says, displaying a holographic picture of Kansis. "Have you seen her?"

My gaze barely flickers to the Guardian next to her, and I can feel the hum of her power. She is checking to see if I will lie.

Thankfully I am wearing my sciath, which will keep me safe from her Gift. "I have not," I answer.

The Guardian looks me over and then, as if answering a question, remarks, "Government-issued sciath."

The Guardian with the braid nods appreciatively. "Government-issued?" she repeats. "That is very fancy for a performer."

"I possess superb taste," I remark dryly.

"I am Deputy Chief Femme," the woman declares and points to the tall Pexun with short-cropped hair. "This is Sergeant Maxx." Motioning towards a Pexun covered in floral tattoos, she explains, "And this is Detective Mei."

"'Tis a pleasure to make your acquaintance." I put my hand over my heart in the Ortusan fashion. It is not necessarily disrespectful, but the honorable thing would be to offer these Pexuns their own territorial greeting—our hands coming together while our thumbs wrap around the back of each other's palms.

I am not in a decent mood.

The Guardians return the Ortusan greeting.

Deputy Chief Femme shows me the picture of Kansis again. "We're looking for this woman because she kidnapped a Pod from Depalo three days ago."

I laugh and ask, "What gain is there in kidnapping a Pod?"

"We'd like to ask Kansis Willow that," Femme responds.

"As I said, I have not seen her," I repeat. "As you knew my name and knew to look for me here, however, I must ask how you think I am connected to the Pexun?"

"A potent Gift is concealing Kansis Willow, so we can't track her exact location. We lose her if we get closer than a quarter-kilometer to her. However, we have powerful Gifts up our sleeves as well, and Detective Mei has sensed that she's been only two places the last few days. This hotel—where your crew is staying—and your circus."

Blood pounds through my veins. I flush the adrenaline out of my body. "Ah. So, this Kansis has great taste as well," I respond jokingly. "Our circus is without rival!" None of the Guardians laugh with me.

Femme smiles patiently. "Yesterday, Kansis Willow and the Pod were apprehended, along with one Emerly Tosh. However, in the middle of their interrogation, unknown Gifters stole them away from us. And fortune was on their side as our recording devices were miraculously hindered, so we have no evidence of their escape. Would you know anything about that?"

I shake my head. "Must have been a rough day at the Guardian Station."

Femme's eyes narrow. "Indeed. It was beneficial in two ways, however. It allowed us to see our weaknesses, so the criminals won't have the same luck the next time. And secondly, we were able to cross-reference this breakout with several other jailbreaks that have been executed in a remarkably similar fashion over the years. We believe this same group is responsible for extracting up to twelve prisoners from Guardian Stations and dens Hexum-wide."

Fourteen, actually, I think to myself. We have helped fourteen people escape prisons and dens.

She waits for me to respond, and when I do not, Femme continues, "Your story is fascinating, Pypen Tross. You and Scout Eekan both had tragic and accidental deaths in the family. You've had close calls with Guardians but have never been formally accused of anything. But you know what I found most interesting?" Her wrinkles turn up as she smiles.

"Tell me."

"What I find most interesting is that your circus happened to be performing in all of the cities where the jailbreaks took place."

"Happenstance strikes again," I remark, trying to look innocent and witty.

Femme studies me, her eyes alight with amusement. "Do you know the legal ramifications for breaking someone out of jail or a den?"

"A slap on the wrist?"

"Ten years off of life for each instance. For these criminals, their punishment would be close to one hundred and twenty years from life. And, as you know, a life sentence of over fifty years also means a Gift stripping. With a sentence like one hundred and twenty years, that would also mean a Duogift stripping."

I swallow and calm my frantically beating heart. "That would be quite unfortunate," I remark.

"However, if these criminals were to confess and present their fugitives, that life sentence could be cut in half."

I bow. "If I see these criminals, I will alert them to you and your magnanimity."

Femme's eyes gleam: she is getting close to her denouement. "I checked your bus manifest, Pypen Tross. What were you doing in Depalo three nights ago?”

“Sightseeing,” I answer.

“In the evening?”

“’Tis the best time.”

“Pypen,” Femme says slowly. “We are not after you. We want Kansis Willow and her Pod. We’re willing to let your circus pass with a warning if you hand them over.”

“Deputy Chief, I already told you I know nothing of the Pexun and her Pod. How about you give me your Suus number, and I will call you if I see them?”

Femme’s nose flares as her mouth twists into an irritable grin. “This will be your only chance. When we find Kansis Willow and her Pod, we will prosecute all who have helped them. In fact, anyone in possession of either woman will be prosecuted immediately. We have a Gift Stripper at our station and plan on completing the sentence within the hour of the arrest. There will be no mercy then. There will be no escape. Wouldn’t it be bloodsucking to know that an entire crew of entertainers were, in one fell swoop, stripped of their Gifts and their lives cut in half? Do you speak on behalf of all of them?”

“Ask whoever you want,” I declare confidently, although my blood falters with each word. Fabella’s words echo through my veins once more: *“You’ve made yourself responsible for every person in this circus, Pypen.”* Could I bear the weight of knowing I had allowed this punishment for them?

Still lost in my thoughts, I barely hear Femme when she says, “I was hoping to place some Guardians at your circus for the next couple of days.”

“We are leaving next day,” I reply. “And we will be in Formosus for the rest of the week.”

“We don’t mind the travel,” Femme remarks. “We will be undercover, so we won’t bother your patrons.”

Not seeing any quick way to dismiss them, I nod. “Of course. We are at your disposal.”

“I was hoping you’d say that,” Femme responds. “We are already searching this hotel, but we would like access to your tent.”

Kansis and Amelia are at the circus, are they not? There is nowhere else for them to have gone. If the Guardians are already searching the hotel, Winzer will keep them hidden at the circus as long as she is close to them. But what if Winzer has walked away for a moment?

Conscious that I have hesitated in giving my answer, I smile graciously and place my hand on my chest. “It will be a pleasure to help local law enforcement.”

Femme's expression resumes formality. "We will go now then, and—"

Suddenly, Detective Mei snaps her fingers and sniffs the air. "She's moving, Deputy Chief."

"Which one?" Femme asks eagerly.

"Kansis Willow. It's hazy, but she's moving away from her source of protection. Within minutes I'll be able to track her."

Adrenaline floods my veins. "Should we head to the circus?" I ask the Deputy Chief, hoping this will temporarily distract her.

"No, thank you, Pypen Tross." Offering a sickly smile, she drawls, "I'm sure I'll see you soon." Turning to Mei, she commands, "Lead on, detective."

The three Guardians rush out of the hotel. I wait until the door shuts before casually walking towards it, slipping out in the opposite direction, and sprinting towards the circus. I call Scout on my Suus. When he answers not, I call again. By the fifth try, I am hailing a taxi to get there as fast as meta-humanly possible. I quickly give the driver directions to the field housing our tent and overpay him, requesting that he speed.

Before the car even comes to a stop, I open the door and run towards the circus. Through the tent flap, on the paths, up the staircase, into Memory and Fiddy's room.

Searching for Scout, I realize, is pointless because the room is too dark to see anyone. Racing to the front of the room, I scream at the top of my lungs, "Quiet!"

It takes three or four more screams for someone to turn down the music and switch on the lights. "Where is Winzer?" I ask.

"Here, aren't I!" A little Formosian hand raises high, as Winzer skips to the front of the room so I can see her.

"Where is the Formosian woman we picked up in Depalo?" I ask.

"Arkarian Story's daughter?" Sedwick asks.

"How did you—when—" Growling, I dismiss my concern. It seems there are no secrets in the circus. "Yes, is the daughter here?"

"Scout wanted to talk to them, didn't he," Emerly answers. "The daughter and Kansis."

"Where did he take them?" I ask.

Emerly shakes his head, my fear mirrored in his eyes. "I don't know, do I? He didn't say."

"Well, we need to find him now!" my voice echoes throughout the room. "Ruse! Where is Ruse?"

"She went back to the hotel," someone answers. "She was tired after the show."

"Oi could go fetch her?" Thykas volunteers.

I swear. "No, there is not enough time. Guardians have tracked Kansis and the daughter here. They are on their way to apprehend them and will probably arrest Scout too."

"I just called him, and he's not answering, he isn't," Emerly shouts.

"He must have disabled incoming calls," Thykas speculates.

"Can you draw a door to him?" I ask Thykas.

Thykas shakes his head. "T'at is most definitely outside ta scope of me Gift. Oi don't know where he is, and drawing a door ter an unknown place is too dangerous. Oi'm sorry, me sam." Moving closer to me, he whispers, "Perhaps ye Precautionary Bag?"

I feel it heavy against my chest, knowing this day may be the one I finally need to use it.

Before I do, however, I close my eyes, indexing the Gifts of our team to see if anyone can help: Molecular Manipulation, Puppeteering, Material Manipulation, Multiplication, Prophet, Animal Communication, Emotion Manipulation, Harnesser, Light and Hue Manipulation—

"Pypen, what are we going to do?" Emerly asks. "We could always rescue them from the Guardian Station if—"

"No," I interrupt. "They are aware of our ways now. We have one trick, and we have already used it. The Guardian said they would be looking for us to interfere."

"Couldn't the Sixth Aevum—"

"No," I interrupt again. Heart pounding, I continue, "The Sixth Aevum made it clear we can never allow ourselves to be arrested, and if we are, he will not be there that day to save us. We have to find Scout." Not knowing what else to do, I command, "Emerly, you stay here and keep calling him. I am going out to look for him."

"Look where?"

"Anywhere," I groan. "Scout cannot be detained."

"Oi'll come too," Thykas says.

"Do you want our help, Pip?" Krael asks.

I stare out at a room filled with at least thirty expectant people ready to do anything for Scout and me. All of these people's futures and their well-being are my responsibility. All that Femme said concerning the legal ramifications for them washes through my veins, and I feel so lightheaded I almost pass out.

Quickly, I renew myself. Everyone here needs me.

Above all of these people, however, I have loyalties to Scout. He is the priority. After we find him, Scout and I will find a way to protect the others; but we need Scout.

My eyes fall on Merayal. Her expression vacillates between apathy and concern as she looks out at all of the other performers. She settles on the former when she sees I am looking at her. Averting my gaze, I shout, "Listen to me now; we must all look for Scout. Use any means of your Gifts to help him. Find him before the Guardians do!" To Thykas, I order, "Call Ruse and get her onto this as well." To Winzer, I demand, "Stay here until we find them."

"I will, won't I!" Winzer shouts.

Quickly, I look up local Buscador meetings on my Suus. There is one only a kilometer from here, and I flee from the room as fast as my body will take me.

BETWEEN FOLLOWING DIRECTIONS TO the various Buscador meetings around Initium, checking local news to see if the Guardians have apprehended Kansis, Amelia, or Scout, and crew members calling me to check in, half of my mind is glued to my Suus. I keep looking at my prancing lion tattoo and do not understand its relaxed green color. Scout must be under the influence of a suppressing Gift.

Every Buscador meeting I barge into, I hope with all of my blood that he is there. *Matza*, I would prostrate myself before and worship the Rogue Superior if I could just find Scout. After leaving the final Buscador meeting with no success, I start running into any restaurant or cafe I pass, looking desperately inside. After the first block or two, I start shouting Scout's name in the various eateries.

My Suus rings for the tenth time, and I answer Emerly's call as I have all the others: "Did you find him?"

"Who?" he asks.

"Who do you think? Scout? Have you found him?"

"I thought he was back at the circus with Kansis and the Pod?"

"Emerly, have you been drowned in eupee? He went missing! Unless you know where he is, I need to go."

Emerly pauses and then says, "I was just told that the Guardians have found him."

Adrenaline and serotonin flood my veins in equal amounts. As they contend for superiority, their opposing effects make me nauseous.

"Where?" I ask.

"I just sent you the address."

I like not his inflection. Why does it sound so hopeless? I change course immediately as my Suus guides me to the location. "Is he safe?" I ask through gasps as I run.

Emerly doesn't respond right away. He takes so long, I have to ask again. Finally he replies, "It's bad, Pypen. It's really bad, it is."

Turning the last corner, I see Scout emerging from a bar flanked by the three Guardians. Although I want to rush toward him, I know I cannot save him now.

They force Scout into the back of a Guardian van, as Femme struts triumphantly around to the passenger side.

She has arrested Scout and now she is going to strip his Progift. He already lost one Gift due to me, and I fear I cannot save his other one.

"What are we going to do?"

I turn around to see Kansis and Amelia holding each other. A tear trickles down Kansis' cheek. "Pypen, what are we going to do?"

Mundus Senex

Amelia

631 years ago; 2090

A MELIA HAS BEEN AT Casey Military Academy for six months already. In the wake of the nuclear attack on the United States, most of the students were convinced that the academy should be shut down. However, many of the parents believed that—more than ever before—it was important that their children were trained in combat.

After Russia's molenuke took out America's eastern seaboard—the fourteen states bordering the Atlantic Ocean—Amelia had thought that life would never return to how it had been. And yet, almost two hundred days later, the remaining states seem to have found a new normal—albeit one where the original flag of the thirteen colonies is flown everywhere.

Unlike the current flag with thirteen stripes and fifty stars to represent the fifty states, the original flag of the United States wore thirteen stripes and thirteen stars for the thirteen colonies at the time of its independence. This tribute to the eastern seaboard seemed to sweep the remainder of the nation and was represented through television commercials, online ads and social media campaigns, branded merchandise and fashion, sponsorships of events and sports teams, and digital billboards.

Amelia's fourteenth birthday comes and goes, but she looks and acts much older than fourteen. Unlike other girls at her age—obsessed with grades, crushes, and friends—Amelia is preoccupied with shooting automatic rifles accurately, fighting to survive, and memorizing facts about world cultures and geography. And how geography has changed.

Even after losing fourteen states, their president said they would not return fire as it would cause a worldwide nuclear war that could kill them all. Already, one hundred and twelve million people had died.

From the moment Amelia entered Casey Academy, it felt like boot camp.

The recruits were sure they would not survive the training it was so intense, but they endured. *She* endured. Spurred on by news of the horrific attack and the vital need for trained soldiers to defend a country under dire threat, the boot-campers got stronger, faster, and more agile every day. They all lived with a nagging fear at the back of their minds—when would the next nuke strike, blowing them all to oblivion?

Amelia's training regimens have become harder every week. In school, she doesn't do math or English anymore. Science consists of weapons training. Physical Education entails driving and flying.

They bring in a helicopter and planes for the students to practice aviation. A lot of their schooling focuses on history, culture, geography, and the study of human emotions and interactions.

Some of the staff from the Mountain School for Troubled Girls also work at Casey. Amelia had been thrilled to learn that Mr. Ari teaches history, archeology, and an exciting course on preserving historical artifacts. The last week of every month, Mr. Ari facilitates small, *mostly* safe missions to extract relics and antiques from compromised museums worldwide. Many museums in various countries had been attacked—most of the history it protected forever lost. Sometimes they went to such places. Sometimes, however, they chased rumors, extracting pieces from exhibits that were alleged to be attacked. No matter the kind, for each task, Mr. Ari selects those who have the best scores in their classes.

Amelia has gone on every mission.

With each assignment, Amelia realizes that Mr. Ari is the first man she's ever felt safe around. He's kind and compassionate, understanding and funny. He pushes her, trusts her, and allows her to make mistakes so she will learn in her own way. By far, Mr. Ari is her favorite teacher.

When Miss Brimer—now referred to as Sergeant Major Brimer—tells her that her father is coming to visit her the coming weekend, a nervous energy floods Amelia's body. Her dad had instructed that, once she was a student in the military academy, she must get into the council of the adults, but she has yet to break that barricade. Mr. Ari was easy enough to pry open—sensitive and kind as he is—but he has, so far, steered clear of all things Casey-related. And... for reasons she can't explain... Amelia doesn't want to use him for information. Using her charm and wit, she has kept him close, but she has also forced herself to do no probing.

Instead, she has focused her efforts on the other teachers and professors. The issue isn't that it is impossible to get them to divulge information; Amelia just hasn't had an opportunity to prove herself to them. Will her father be disappointed that she has no information for him yet?

"How can you have nothing?" her father demands as he stares at her across the table of the local restaurant, his handsome features somehow more glorious as they sharpen in anger.

"It's military," she recites the excuse she has been memorizing and perfecting over the past week. "Hierarchy is a religion to them. Allowing a cadet into their inner sanctum isn't something that's done or even allowed. I just need more time."

"You've grown fond of them."

"I haven't," she lies. "Whatever I do, I will do it to the best of my abilities. Trying to force the timing on a discussion will make them suspicious, and then I will never get any information for you."

His eyes seem to zoom into hers like lenses. "For me?"

"Yes, you. Everything I do is for you."

Although he doesn't say he approves, he doesn't push it.

"How much time do you need?" he asks.

Putting on an expression as if she's thinking, Amelia makes herself hesitate before she answers, "Six months." Even though she had decided on the timeline the night before, she knew that if she had answered immediately, her dad would have thought she was being hasty. The six months has been decided on not because she necessarily needs it—in fact, she knows that an opportunity to prove her merit is approaching sooner than that—but because she wants to give herself extra time.

Finally, her father grunts in acquiescence. "Six months, Milly. That's it."

"That's all I need."

"If you don't have anything for me by then, I'm taking you home."

Heart suddenly pounding, she repeats, "Home?"

"Yes. If you cannot complete a simple task in a year's time, you will come home a failure. And let me tell you, Amelia, it will take a *long time* to regain my trust."

Not knowing what else to say, she simply responds, "Yes, Daddy."

Christmas rolls around, and many of the students leave for home—

including Lily, her only friend. Having planned on spending the holidays alone, she is surprised when Miss Brimer invites her to spend the time with herself and Mr. Ari. It is more fun than Amelia ever would have imagined. They spend the three days playing board games, range practicing, eating microwave meals, resting, and at night Mr. Ari reads them *The Lord of the Rings.*

Amelia watches the two adults with growing curiosity. Although they act familiarly with each other, they aren't a couple. They sit close together on the couch, joke around with each other, and once she even sees them holding hands. But they are not... *together.* Not dating... not romantic with each other. And yet, there are these moments—a stolen glance, a prolonged touch, a whispered affection—that makes her wonder otherwise. She wants to ask Miss Brimer about it, but she is certain the consequences would include many, *many* push-ups.

The holiday ends, and life resumes normalcy. Mr. Ari continues to take top students on missions. Their latest one was a flight to San Diego, California, on a mercy mission, feeding the hungry and housing the homeless, trying to make roads passable. On the flight back, Amelia sits in the co-pilot seat next to Mr. Ari. He starts speaking, and his voice sounds squashed, blaring in her ears. "You know, if I had a daughter, I hope she'd be like you."

His words take her by surprise. They're so heartwarming, sudden tears itch the corners of her eyes. Quickly, Amelia shoves the feeling aside and blinks away the emotional response. She has a mission—her father's—and she can't let anyone, even Mr. Ari, compromise that. Looking in his direction, she smirks and responds, "You know, if I had a cat, I hope he'd be like you."

As Mr. Ari howls his deep laugh, she smiles and looks back out the jet window at a world destined for destruction.

It is just another exercise, another sparring partner. But this partner is different. He doesn't go easy on Amelia, he doesn't flirt with her before the match, he doesn't show off. He just beats her fair and square. He bows slightly and walks away as if she is just another sparring partner, and this is just another exercise.

The boy has light brown hair, a hawk-like nose, and one of his ears looks like it's had a bite taken out of the top. He is medium in build but incredibly muscular. She learns that the boy's name is Russell Wrightly.

Around the same time, Amelia also finds out she has three friends. She hadn't recognized it at first, thinking Chad and Jessie just wanted to be chummy with Lily who has also advanced from the Mountain to Casey, but sure enough, they have ended up being her friends too. They eat at her table, play games with her during her free time, fetch her items before she realizes she needs them, and they make her laugh.

It is when Jessie lets a black widow spider crawl into her hands to save it from other students killing it, that Amelia realized she likes her. It is when she is laughing at Chad telling her they'd have to get on a poop schedule if they ever went out on a mission together, that she realizes she likes him. Her three friends are strong, intelligent, caring, and dependent on each other in a way that makes her want to be a part of it.

For years she had had "friends" back home, but not like these ones. Friends like Marley and their group were only there because of what Amelia's wealth and vicious wit could provide them. They were there based only on her performance—not that she could blame them. That is all she had looked for in friends as well.

But now, it surprises Amelia to find that having companions like these is actually really fun. The more they do for her, the more she wants to help them. She wants them to be happy, have special privileges, and go on the best missions. She finds herself giving Jessie her extra cookies, Lily her free time passes, and she even takes a few of Chad's breakfast shifts so he can sleep in. And if any of them ever got into tiffs with other students, she would find herself intervening in a sort of over-my-dead-body-type of way.

As often as she can, Amelia partners with Russell for sparring. He beats her effortlessly and then moves on to someone else. She hates it, so she trains harder, runs faster, drills quicker. Each time she fights him, she gets stronger, more agile, and harder to beat.

One day in August, she beats Russell for the first time. He nods at her as usual, but this time he comments, "Well done," as he walks away.

She yells after him, "That's it?"

He turns and smiles for the first time. "Let's see you do that again tomorrow, Red."

Amelia smiles.

"Your family is coming to visit," Miss Brimer comments to Amelia one day as weapons training comes to an end.

Amelia is suddenly lightheaded, and Miss Brimer catches her arm to steady her. "Are you okay?" she asks.

"Yeah, sure," Amelia responds, her voice distant. "When is he—when are they coming?" Her stomach cramps and she grimaces at the uncomfortable sensation.

"Next week… Amelia, are you ill?"

She has known that the six months are coming to a close, and it is time for her to update her father. And what should be bringing her ease and joy is the fact that she actually has information for him.

After proving herself in every class she participated in, Amelia and a select few others—Russell included—had been allowed to sit in on a meeting of the military board of directors. Having been to two sessions, she has plenty to share with her dad.

But now… now she finds herself not wanting to tell him anything. She doesn't want to betray Lily and Chad and Jessie and Mr. Ari… and Miss Brimer even. She stretches her neck and rolls her shoulders, seeking to shrug off her worries.

"I'll be fine," she answers her teacher.

Miss Brimer studies Amelia for a moment before she answers. "Your dad said he wanted to see your progress and meet the staff." She pauses then adds, "He made it sound like there is a chance you could be going home with him."

Bile climbs up Amelia's esophagus.

"Do you know why he wants to take you out of the academy?"

Amelia can only shake her head.

"Do you want to go with him?"

Taking a deep breath, she answers, "I don't know… I don't think so."

A silence clings to the air for a moment before Miss Brimer shatters it asking, "Did your father send you here for something other than behavior modification?"

She feels her pulse quicken as she asks coolly, "Why? Did he say something?"

Miss Brimer is quiet for a long time. Amelia stands unmoving, only able to guess at what her teacher is thinking about.

All in a moment, she wants to tell Miss Brimer everything. To tell her about her father and the mission he has given her. She wants to say that she's loyal to the school and her friends and not her dad anymore… but she can't. This would be a perfect moment, but her mouth stands sentry, unwilling to allow the words a way out.

"Amelia," Miss Brimer takes a breath and continues, "I care about you, you know. And I know I'm hard on you... But it's because I believe in you. You mean a great deal to me, and I would do anything in my power to help you if you ever needed it."

Purposefully looking her teacher in the eye, with a sincere blend of joy and sadness, Amelia responds, "I knew you liked me."

The older woman playfully punches Amelia's arm and smirks at her. "Is there anything I can do to make your father's visit easier for you?"

Amelia walks to the door of the classroom. With one foot out the door and a hand already on the outside wall, she turns back to her teacher and says in a strangled voice, "Don't let him take me."

Then she is gone.

AMELIA'S DAD HAS COME alone to see her today. Her mother has not accompanied him, claiming she is too busy with her campaign to visit. Carter has also declined the invitation to meet his now fully combat-trained sister.

Coward.

Miss Brimer stands on one side of Amelia, and Mr. Ari on the other, as the luxury vehicle carrying Amelia's father pulls up to the entrance of Casey Military Academy.

"I'll stay with you the whole time," Miss Brimer remarks without looking at her.

"He won't let you," Amelia responds, focusing all her strength on keeping her voice steady.

"We're not going anywhere," Mr. Ari says with such force Amelia looks up at him. His face is set in an uncharacteristically hard expression.

Knowing her father, Amelia places her hand on Mr. Ari's arm and says, "Please let me speak with him when he asks. It'll be much worse if you fight him."

Mr. Ari turns away without affirming or denying her request.

When the car pulls up, Amelia, dressed in her best uniform, dutifully walks and welcomes him to the academy. Having not eaten or slept much in the last week and a half, Amelia struggles to keep her breath even when he steps out of the car. His shoulders are broad as he stands, and his head is held high, as if he is the highest-ranking officer at Casey. With casual grace, he strides toward her and buttons up his overcoat. His handsome, piercing gaze fixates on her face.

"Amelia," he says and opens his arms for a hug. The last time she hugged her dad was before she started kindergarten. Not wishing to bring out any negative emotions in him, she quickly embraces him. His cologne fills her nose, and images of her childhood flash through her mind.

The crunchy, red carpet in his office.

The mauve, velvet chair in his bedroom.

His special grey ink pen with the eagle etched into the side.

As she pulls away, she squeezes her hands repeatedly to force some of the adrenaline to leave her body.

"We're glad you could make it," Miss Brimer welcomes Amelia's dad. "We have set up lunch in the cafeteria."

"I would like to speak with my daughter before our time together," her dad states crisply.

Miss Brimer smiles pleasantly, "I think it would be better if…"

Amelia's dad gives Miss Brimer a calculating look. Although it is not intrinsically threatening, Amelia knows otherwise and finds her mouth opening and saying, "It's okay, Sergeant Major," to Miss Brimer. "We won't be long, and then we will join you in the cafeteria."

As a cadet, interrupting a superior officer is a punishable offense; but Miss Brimer gives no reprimand. Instead, she smiles—less pleasantly—and responds, "Of course."

As Amelia steps towards her dad, Mr. Ari places a hand on her shoulder. "We will be close by if you need anything," he says to Amelia but keeps his eyes locked with her dad's.

"We won't need anything," her dad responds.

"Still," Mr. Ari states. "We'll be *very* close by, just in case."

Amelia wriggles free of Mr. Ari's hand and points to the school's grounds. "Let's walk," she suggests.

When they are out of earshot, her dad chuckles softly to himself. "Impressive. You know, I had some worries about you, that their weak beliefs had brainwashed you. But I see now you are still the witch you've always been, casting your spells where you wish, on whom you wish. Well done, Milly."

Before, when her father gave her these compliments, it would make her feel special. Now, it makes her feel dirty.

As they walk the grounds, her dad talks about America's resistance effort defense plan. With part of the country gone, their resources, manpower, and morale have also been cut. Consequently, there is a focus on defense instead of offense.

"Have you heard of the Pod program?" her dad asks.

"It's a technology which freezes people to keep them alive during the nuclear war. We were trained in the encapsulating and awakening process last week," she answers quickly, thankful to know the answer. Her father doesn't deal well with ignorance or incompetence.

"Indeed. It's a brilliant ruse. There are few wealthy enough to afford the procedure. Among those who can are the leaders of many countries," he expounds with a laugh. "The more they Pod themselves, the more dictators take over. Do they let you watch the news here?"

"Three times a day," Amelia replies. "And we get real-time updates every hour."

"So you've heard about Dayie Tueur?"

"Yes," she nods. "He is the most powerful of the warlords trying to take over the Middle East."

"What do you think of him?" her dad inquires. Although he does so casually, Amelia knows this is a test.

"He is clever but more of a maverick than a statesman," she answers. "Even though he's a world leader, he hardly seems officer material, taking huge risks and using guerrilla tactics like the berserkers in our history lessons. It might be more dumb luck than anything else that he has been so successful. I'm not convinced he can keep it up."

Amelia's dad chuckles. "Excellent, Milly. Very good. Yes, Dayie Tueur is reckless, but he has something that the other leaders don't possess: purpose and rage. His father was killed in a nuclear power plant accident, and no one was held accountable. Since then, he has been vocally anti-nuke and an ardent enemy of societies supporting nuclear proliferation." Her father smiles again. "They call him a warlord, but many of the countries he has conquered came to him on bended knee. In combination, he is leveraging existing power structures based on their fear of another holocaust and their ideals of nuclear disarmament. He is giving them what they want while making promises to protect them from what they don't."

After taking a moment to look at the surrounding mountains, her dad states, "But you know why I'm here."

"Yes."

"And?"

Amelia keeps herself from touching her ear—she'd noticed in her last body language training class that this was a nervous tic of hers.

For weeks she has agonized over whether she is going to share with her dad the information she holds. Some nights, she fell asleep with a strong sense of peace, knowing that she would choose bravery; she would choose her friends and school and keep her findings secret. Other nights however, she would weep, knowing she was not that brave.

"And…" she starts, still having not made a decision. But when she looks up into her father's elegant and suave face, the words tumble from her. "The cadets are undergoing training for various missions aimed at obstructing, undermining, confusing, or dismantling Dayie Tueur's and the other warlords' attempts at domination. Depending on each cadet's unique strengths and skills, the training prepares them to counter and combat the ongoing takeover efforts."

"In what ways?" he asks.

For the next thirty minutes, Amelia explains every detail she has acquired in the last year. Some cadets will join mercy missions to help territories taken over by Dayie Tueur, while others will do reconnaissance. A select few will be inserted into various child armies around the world, their goal to help the children escape, while others will join an organization called the Preservers, whose mission is to conserve as much of this world as possible before it's all destroyed.

When Amelia finishes talking, her father gives her the closest thing she has ever seen to a genuine smile. It isn't quite all there, but she can feel that he is pleased. Part of her is proud of her hard work but the other half is ashamed.

"Well done," he purrs. After twice patting her shoulder, he goes on, "Plans are going perfectly. As you have played your part so well, and these people are deep under your spell, I will reward you with both a secret and a task."

She knows he wants her to be intrigued to hear the secret—eager even. But he also wants her to control her emotions, never allowing herself to become too excitable. Having practiced long in the mirror, Amelia puts on an expression perfectly portraying subdued interest. "What's the secret?" she asks.

"The world's order will be changing soon," he answers, also trying to suppress his ardor but not accomplishing it quite as well as Amelia. "Things will change and never be the same. And this will be to our benefit."

"How so?" she questions, walking the line between cool and interested.

"I cannot tell you now, but our need for secrecy will be gone soon."

"And the task?"

"There are several concentration camps around the world containing Christian pastors and missionaries."

The turn of topic surprises Amelia. Why do pastors and missionaries matter to her dad?

"Many of them have escaped recently," her dad goes on, "and I would like to know how this is happening."

"How would I find that out?" Amelia asks, not understanding.

"The person responsible is your Sergeant Major Brimer."

At the mention of her teacher's name on her father's lips, Amelia feels faint. Controlling herself, she asks innocently, "Is there evidence it's her?"

"Not yet," he responds slowly. "Do you like the woman?"

"Of course not," she answers quickly, and the lie tastes like soap.

"Good. Don't trust anyone, Amelia. Remember, there's only you to look after. You remember my offer, yes?"

"Yes."

For the first time, he stops and looks down at her. "I'm offering you the world," he states. "I'll be handing the heads of people like Carter to you on silver platters. You'll be unstoppable. Untouchable. No one will hurt you."

"I know," she responds. "That's still what I want."

Her father straightens, and a frown creases his brow. "Is it?"

"It is," she answers eagerly but wonders why she's saying so. It hasn't been her desire for the past six months. But looking up into her father's cold, stern gaze, she repeats, "It is, Dad."

He continues walking, and she doesn't know if she's convinced him. As they return to the cafeteria, he commands, "Complete your task in the next few months. Get into Brimer's counsel and find out all you can about their operation. I will reach out with the required intel and collect you when the time is right."

"Collect me?" she asks, keeping her voice calm.

"Yes, your banishment is coming to a close," he says as if this should bring her great joy.

Not missing a beat, Amelia places a beaming smile on her features. "It is?" she asks excitedly.

"Yes. You can come home very soon now, Milly."

As Amelia claps like this is the best news she has ever heard, she dies a little on the inside.

"What did he want?" Miss Brimer asks as they watch her dad drive away, his sleek car glistening in the sunlight.

"Nothing," Amelia answers. "Just checking in."

A twang of guilt slithers through her stomach.

AT THREE IN THE morning on December 9th, the whole of Casey Academy is awakened from their beds. They are packed into the auditorium where the news is broadcasting.

With so many of the world's leaders encapsulated in Hulls as part of the Pod Program, Dayie Tueur has now taken control of most of the planet's governments. With a team of highly talented hijackers and some very impressive bribes, Dayie Tueur has now acquired the location and codes for every single nuclear bomb active on Earth. Diplomats, politicians, and law enforcement throughout each country of the world have sworn loyalty to him. In the first hours of his world domination, he has murdered all who encapsulated themselves in Pods, calling them a generation of pro-nuke, gutless worms unworthy of life.

Following this news is a long dissertation by Dayie Tueur, which outlines that there are particular people groups throughout the world who are pro-nuke. He makes it clear that he will be identifying and executing them swiftly.

Against a previous promise, Dayie Tueur does not disarm every nuke on the planet but instead says he will keep them to use only if a significant enough threat arises, worthy of such mass destruction.

He announces that he would, like a father with arguing children, allow the world to continue its squabble. Then, in the end, when only the strong remained, he would support and heal those countries. This, of course, is not widely interpreted as paternal behavior, but Dayie Tueur insists it is.

A hand finds Amelia's, but she barely reacts. It's not until Miss Brimer tells the cadets to return to their rooms that she sees it is Russell's hand. He doesn't say anything. He looks down at her with eyes filled with fear and determination and then releases her fingers.

AS IS THE CASE with all nations that are agreeable to him, the United States, already in submission to Dayie Tueur, is given aid, weapons, and food. Two weeks into his reign, he announces that he will extend more favor to the countries that hand over all pro-nuke societies—those still searching for Hull technology.

Miss Brimer starts turning off their devices at six o'clock every night as, from six to eight, Dayie Tueur publicly burns those who are being turned in as pro-nuke. Instead, the staff and any students who want to are invited to gather together and pray throughout the two hours. Many nights Amelia and her friends remain to pray.

Amelia doesn't believe there is a god listening, but it makes her feel better knowing that the others find so much hope during these nights.

Amelia spends many of her days half-heartedly fulfilling her father's task. She knows he will want results when he returns, but every time she tries to root around for information, she can't bring herself to try too hard. Guilt takes up a home in her gut, an unwelcome squatter that won't leave no matter what she does.

Even though she may or may not suspect what Amelia is up to, Miss Brimer continues to invite Amelia, along with a few other cadets, to their board meetings.

After one particularly illuminating meeting—one she is sure her father would want all the details of—Miss Brimer stops her before she leaves the room.

After clearing her throat, Miss Brimer says, "You know I trust you, right?"

"Right."

"I care about you, you know."

"I know."

Amelia puts on her most sincere smile and then leaves the meeting room. Within a minute, her head is in a toilet, her body emptied of her dinner.

ONE MORNING IN LATE May, Amelia sits with Chad, Lily, and Jessie during breakfast. The news is on as it always is during their meals. Dayie Tueur is publicly honoring diplomats, politicians, warlords, law enforcement officers, and many others from each continent who were instrumental in his rise to power. He offers them a position in his world government and honors them with land, slaves, and treasure. By now, he has renamed each continent by the number in which he conquered them.

Finally, he honors those who have given up their country's nuke codes and best aided him towards his new position, by declaring them their continents' new Supreme Rulers.

Dayie Tueur honors a man named Xi Yandum from Asia—or as it's now called Ek (the Hindi word for 'One'). Xi Yandum thanks Dayie Tueur and honors him with a portion of his gifts. As Dayie Tueur moves on to Jennifer Simpson, the diplomat from what was previously Europe but is now called Do (the Hindi word for 'two'), Amelia focuses on her breakfast.

Dayie Tueur honors men from Teen, Chaar, and Panj, but the cafeteria quiets as he calls on the diplomat from Chhah (North America). Everyone wants to know who has given up their nuke codes to the warlord. Then Dayie Tueur says the traitor's name, and Amelia freezes. A half-chewed egg turns to gravel in her mouth as she looks up from her breakfast to the screen and sees her father standing next to Dayie Tueur. The warlord shakes her dad's hand and places his insignia pin on his chest. Her dad kisses Dayie Tueur's ring as all the others have done. He is named the Ambassador of Chhah. And before she knows it, Dayie Tueur moves on to honor the Ambassador of Saat.

Before she even knows what's happening, Amelia runs. She sprints until her lungs feel as if they are bleeding, and then she hides.

A year ago, this is exactly what she would have wanted. Her father is now one of the most powerful men in the entire world. But seeing him up there—betraying the entire country, betraying her—she can't pretend anymore. She hates him.

It's not until that night that Miss Brimer finds Amelia in her dorm. The young woman's pale face stares up at the ceiling. Miss Brimer lowers herself slowly onto Amelia's bed.

"I don't need a lecture about forgiveness, Miss Brimer," Amelia states, her voice limp. "I don't want any advice about moving on, any consolations about being my own person..." Her voice grows passionate until by the end of her speech she's yelling. "I don't need you to tell me that there's forgiveness for everyone, I don't need to hear that one day things will get better, I don't want any hope about Jesus—I don't want any of it!"

She sits up in her bed and, for the first time, allows the emotions in her chest to release. "I don't need you to tell me—I don't need—I can't—"

When Miss Brimer opens her arms, Amelia clings to her sergeant's uniform and weeps.

Amelia doesn't appear for her duties the following day.

Her friends try to cheer her up, but Amelia does not seem any better. She gets angrier every day, especially after leaving the gym.

"Where's Russell?" Jessie asks one afternoon. "He's always in the gym when we're here. I haven't seen him much the past week."

Amelia doesn't respond.

Chad claps his hands. "That's it! That's what's pissing off Amelia. See, we were wondering if there was something else, but she just misses Russell—"

Amelia growls and throws her book at Chad's head.

In their human interaction class, Sergeant Sweeney brings in twenty civilians. As a test, it is the students' assignment to read the people's facial expressions, body language, tone of voice, and eye movements to determine which five persons of the group are trustworthy and which three persons intend harm to the class. The remaining twelve are decoys.

The students spend three hours with the civilians. At the end of the time, they are told to write on a piece of paper which five people are trustworthy and which three persons have planned to harm them. Amelia is one of two in the class who accurately spots the antagonists in the group. Although most of them get three out of five correct, Amelia is the only one who determines all five trustworthy civilians.

Never before has a student been able to identify each person accurately. Amelia is honored before the class and then the whole of Casey Academy, but she doesn't care. She is asked to attend a secret board meeting that night, to which she replies dully, "Anything for my country."

Today when Amelia spars with Russell, she punches him in the jaw. By the time the instructor shouts that she's docked twenty points, Amelia is already storming out of the gym. Chad jumps up to follow her.

She makes her way to the dining hall, and when she reaches their regular table, Amelia sits down, slamming all her weight onto the cold, metal bench.

"Feel better?" Chad asks, sitting down next to her.

"Better?"

"Yeah," Chad smiles sardonically, "do you feel better now that you've made him bleed?"

Amelia smiles. It's small and sad, but it's a smile. "Yeah, I do."

The next day, Russell asks Amelia to spar, and he looks angry. They fight for over thirty minutes, but neither is able to take down the other. Students gather around to root for one of them. Amelia's body is drenched in sweat, but there is a fierce determination in her eyes that has students betting their desserts on the results. Finally, Amelia's footing slips, and Russell takes advantage with uncanny speed. He drops her and places all of his weight on her chest. Amelia doesn't tap out, and finally the referee has to intervene.

It is a sore loser move, but Amelia readily admits she *is* a sore loser.

Russell watches her struggle to her feet, not lending a hand. Amelia turns to walk away, but Russell shouts out after her, "You're mad at me." It's a statement, not a question.

"I'm not mad at you. I don't even know you," she bites back.

"I didn't do anything," Russell claims, exasperated.

She rolls her eyes. "I'm not mad at you."

"I didn't know if you wanted to talk about it or not," Russell yells loudly enough for everyone in the auditorium to hear.

Amelia looks around and, seeing the whole school watching and listening, her already sweaty face burns brighter. "I—I didn't... I don't know you. It's fine."

She turns to walk away, but when Russell says, "I'm sorry," she stops. "I'm sorry about your dad," he adds slowly, more gently.

Amelia turns back to face him.

"I don't know what to say. I wish there were something I could do to make it better," he says.

She barely meets his gaze. "You don't owe me anything."

The only sound in the auditorium is the buzzing of the old lights. Finally, Russell asks, "Can I sit with you and your friends at dinner tonight?"

Amelia's jaw clenches. When she looks up at him, her hazel eyes are soft. "Yeah—yeah, sure."

Russell sits with Amelia's group of friends at every meal. He gets along well with Chad and Lily. Jessie keeps accidentally making comments about him not being a part of their group. She's embarrassed, but it makes everyone laugh.

More holidays pass, and Amelia spends each one with Miss Brimer and Mr. Ari. Before she realizes it, she finds herself spending parent weekends with them as well. A couple of times a week, she is welcomed to Miss Brimer's office after curfew so Mr. Ari can continue reading his favorite books out loud to them. Amelia had thoroughly enjoyed the *Adventures of Hawk and George* with its offbeat quirkiness and John Rose Archer's short stories with their exciting exploits and creative intellect. The *Harry Potter* series had engrossed her for months, Zarah Sandall's works were page-turners, to say the least, Skye

Graham's books were gruesome and hilarious, and although the *Regalian Stone Chronicles* were clearly for young readers, she loved each of the adventures. Her favorite, however, had to be the classic *Wingfeather Saga,* which both broke and warmed her heart.

Christmas comes again, and the time with the two adults is so sweet, Amelia cherishes every second in her heart.

The night that Mr. Ari finishes the final installment of the Wingfeather Saga series, *The Warden and the Wolf King,* Amelia lies in bed, unable to fall asleep. For the past couple of months, more so than ever before, thoughts of her father have haunted her throughout the days. Constantly, she thinks about him, his mission for her, her promise to him, and his claim that he will come to collect her.

As she stares up at the ceiling, she knows with all her heart that this isn't what she wants anymore. The change has been subtle, almost imperceptible, but she can clearly see that she has changed sides. Mr. Ari and Miss Brimer are more like parents to her than either of her true parents have ever been.

Drifting off to sleep, she realizes that, for the first time in her life, amidst the greatest war the earth had ever seen, she has found a place, or rather people, to call home.

Even though he has done nothing but claim to be anti-nuke, because of their impeccable loyalty, Dayie Tueur returns control to Russia of their mole nuke. Russia immediately sends it through the Pacific Ocean towards the new eastern coast of the United States. Everything from Michigan to Mississippi is destroyed in minutes—the country once boasting of fifty states now only consists of thirty.

Miss Brimer orders the whole school to the auditorium for an announcement. Everyone on the staff is there as well.

"In addition to my duties here, I am a member of a society known as the Preservers," she announces from the podium. "Last night, I was made the president of the Preservers as our previous president was murdered in the most recent mole nuke attack. We, the Preservers, have made it our duty to preserve the many cultures of our world before they are destroyed.

"The lead scientist behind the Pod Program, Klaus Klingemann, is the one who founded the Preservers. Without Dayie Tueur's knowledge, he has been encapsulating people from every country worldwide. I lead those with military backgrounds to go into the more hostile countries and extract people for preservation.

"It is now my duty to leave Casey Military Academy and serve and support this cause with the remainder of my time. I will depart this evening. Any of you—staff or students—who want to come with me are welcome. Otherwise, continue training until a time or a cause comes to claim your service. Good day to all of you. It has been an honor serving with you," she declares, looking across at the other staff. "And it has been an honor serving you," she states as she looks out over the students.

Miss Brimer's gaze hovers on Amelia for a moment, then she steps off the podium and walks out of the auditorium.

Pexus

Kansis

WHEN AKER AND I return to Memory and Fiddy's room, Amelia asks me if my digestion has been off, as my "bathroom trip" has taken so long. Instead of acknowledging the question, I do my best to paraphrase what Avenir revealed to us.

"So you don't have bad blood then?" Amelia asks excitedly.

It takes everything in me not to begin sobbing right here on this couch. Reliving what I have just learned by telling Amelia, makes it even more real somehow. How can I feel so relieved and yet so burdened in the same heartbeat? I can feel Aker slumped down next to me, lost in his dark brooding. Amelia is talking to me, but I can't even hear what she's saying, I'm trying so hard not to cry. When she punches me in the arm, I open my eyes.

"Are you okay?" she asks. "Isn't this good news?"

"Kind of," I answer, taking a steadying breath. "It's both the best and worst news of my life."

"How did the jerk take it?" she asks, avoiding Aker's name. Quickly—as she'd been doing all night—she looks to the door to see if Scout has returned. She has been waiting—not patiently, mind you—for him to get back so we can have our meeting and discuss our next steps in finding Charles Wrightly.

I shrug. "How did he take it? I'm not sure. He said he wants to get the Blood Transfusion so we can get married."

"Yuck. Was that his way of proposing?"

I can't help but smile. "I guess."

Amelia glances at the door again, and this time her face alights with excitement instead of continued disappointment. "Scout's back," she crows, completely forgetting our conversation and leaping to her feet. But then, she forces herself to sit back down, to focus on what we were talking about. "So are you going to get the Blood Transfusion?" she asks.

Something about this little kindness almost sends me over the edge. The contrast between my parents' betrayal and this Pod's care leaves me with a confused muddle of weary grief and perky gladness. I breathe in deeply and forbid my tears from leaving their ducts.

Standing, Aker announces, "The Ortusan is back," and points to Scout.

"I'll tell you another time," I answer Amelia, rising too. "We need to have this meeting. You've been waiting for days."

I know it's a generosity and not an actual offer when she asks, "Are you sure?"

Chuckling, I respond, "I'm sure."

She races towards Scout while Aker and I follow behind. As we approach them Amelia says to me, "Ask Scout where he wants to have the meeting."

When Scout's and my eyes meet, I can feel all the tension leave my veins. After all I've learned about Aker and me, my heart has not stopped pounding, my stomach has not stopped churching. But seeing Scout... I feel like I'm finally breathing again.

I know I only feel this way because he told me I was special after he rescued me from the Guardian Station.

Ugh.

Yet another layer of my patheticism to unravel and wallow in later.

Clearing my throat and my thoughts, I ask him, "So, where should we have the meeting?"

SCOUT TAKES US TO one of the rooms that he calls Aneece's Transparency Room. The door itself looks to be made of bones. The only way to open it is to find a bone on the door—for instance a femur—and put your own matching bone beside it. Once she understands, Amelia wants to unlock it and finds an ulna bone oddly fast. She places her forearm against it, and the door swings open.

The dark, warm room is set up like a cafe. There are small tables suitable for intimate conversations, couches for lounging, and a bar to drink at and enjoy company. Yellow candles litter the room, creating a cozy atmosphere. As we walk in, Amelia asks, "What are we doing in a bar?"

"It is not a bar," Scout answers, and both Amelia and I stare at him in amazement.

"Did you—do you speak English?" Amelia responds in shock.

"I do not," Scout answers with a smile. "It is a pleasure to speak to you for the first time, Amelia." He places his hand over his heart in an Ortusan welcome.

"Yeah, but how?" she asks, returning the hand over heart gesture.

"I knew not if it would work, but I was hoping," Scout begins. "This room allows all communication barriers to fall. 'Tis one of the Chameleon's rooms. They designed it so miscommunications, misunderstandings, and deceit could never be a part of the conversation when people are talking here. In our situation," he points between Amelia and himself, "we literally speak not the same language. That, of course, is a great means of miscommunication, but nothing can be lost in translation here. This will be how we make your eutsi."

"Am I speaking Elusian?" Amelia asks.

"I am not certain if we speak each other's languages or our own, but we can understand one another perfectly in this room."

"What would the point of this room be for people who spoke the same language?" I ask, amazed at the creativity the Chameleons have exhibited.

"As I say, you can understand another person flawlessly. Intended meanings can never be misconstrued. We often have meetings here so we can completely understand one another as we make decisions. Did you enjoy your afternoon at the show?" he asks, striding across the room to a couch.

I planned on saying, "I did," but the words that come out of my mouth are: "I've never enjoyed myself so much in my whole life." I put a hand over my mouth.

"I appreciate your honesty," he teases. "And you?" he asks Amelia.

Amelia closes her lips tightly, catching on to the ruse more quickly than I did. "Do you *have* to speak the truth in here?" she asks.

"In a way," he says and then smiles mischievously. "I am your favorite Novian, am I not?"

Sensing a game is afoot, Amelia grins and asks Scout, "What do you want more than anything else?"

Without the slightest hesitation, Scout answers, "To meet the creator of this world."

Really? More than anything else? What is it about the Rogue Superior that draws Scout so? I have never once been interested in the Superiors, but Scout's dedicated search has me contemplating it all for the first time. Who *is* the Rogue Superior?

Amelia, however, is not intrigued by his answer. She squints at him and says, "Not as fun of an answer as I had thought you might give." Turning to address Aker for the first time, she asks, "So, what's your deal? You've been rude since the moment I met you, and I haven't even met you yet."

Aker sneers but tries to keep his mouth shut. Then, as if he physically cannot hold the words back, words rush from his lips like a spicket. "What is there to be joyful about, Pod? The woman I love is married to another man, and my mate left me to run away with some circus because she cares more about helping her protector and you than coming home to marry me."

Silence fills the small space. *I* know this information… Amelia knows some of this information. But I don't know how much Scout knows.

Finally, after too long an awkward silence (although Scout looks amused rather than uncomfortable), Aker clears his throat. "I wish I hadn't shared that." He turns and looks at Scout. "Are you going to report us?"

"Report you?" Scout looks genuinely confused. "For what?"

Aker scowls. "You know why. It's blasphemous that we're not married."

Calmly, as if we were discussing the weather, Scout responds, "Many of us in the circus are here because we have committed blasphemous acts. You can feel right at home."

"I've never felt so out of place in my whole life!" Aker shouts. "I've always been on the 'in' with the people I'm around, and to feel so excluded, so misunderstood—" he places his fist in his mouth so no more words can come out. As the outpour of mumbled words stops, he tentatively takes his hand out and whispers, "Let's go to another room."

"No, no, my good man," Scout responds pleasantly. And then he launches into the plan before Aker can say anything else.

"Our goal is to acquire access to the Book of Instructions. As Knimble Knox has explained, in order to find Arkarian Story, we need the latitude coordinates of his location. In the Book of Instructions, we hope to discover the digit codes to the Base Breakers of the latitude coordinates. There are several immediate problems. Primarily, the Book of Instructions has been hidden in a secret chamber in the Museum of Senex in Silenda so that no one can tamper with it. Our solution is to have the Sixth Aevum locate its position.

"How we get into the museum is the second problem. Even with Winzer as our Cloak, we cannot simply walk inside, stroll into the chamber, grab the book, and leave. Security measures are in place to keep out those employing their Gifts. We could have Gigi sing the walls open for us, but that kind of disturbance to the building may trigger their defenses.

"So, drum roll please…" he waits dramatically until we make a small beating sound on the counter, "our solution is to create a disturbance in the city—a distraction—to throw off all Gift detection mechanisms and the Guardians.

That way, if they do notice us, they will dismiss our activity as simply being part of the distraction.

"When we do manage to get inside the building, we encounter problem number three. If we take the Book of Instructions, the Guardians can easily deduce we are searching for Arkarian Story. However, we will not have the time to stay inside the museum trying to decipher the book's meaning as the distraction may be an interference for us as well."

Scout suddenly looks at me and pouts. "Oh," he says in a mock-whiney voice, "if only we knew of someone with a Gift who could just *read* the book and find the answers without having to know for what she is looking?"

"Me?" I ask, completely surprised to be a part of the plan. I had assumed Amelia and I would stay back at the circus. "But I—"

"Possess the perfect Gift for this mission," Scout finishes and then, feigning amazement, adds, "What are the chances you would have the exact Gift needed for this?" He goes on, "The solution is easy, see? Kansis will read the book, meaning our time there need not be prolonged. Once she has the answer we need, we can simply sing our way out and be on our way."

"Kansis is not doing that," Aker states angrily at the same time as Amelia asks, "What if the walls are made of something Gigi cannot sing through?"

Ignoring Aker, Scout answers Amelia, "Unless the walls are made of humans, Gigi can sing through it." At Amelia's confused expression, he explains, "Gigi's Gift extends to all matter and creatures on Elusis. Human beings are her only exception."

"Exception?"

"It's a Gift term," I explain to her. "Remember, most Gifts have exceptions, limitations, and boundaries."

"So, what do you think?" Scout turns to Amelia.

Amelia steeples her hands and rests her chin on them. "You think it will work?" she queries.

Scout's lips twitch in the corners. "I used to make plans that I thought would not work, but it was so very exhausting," he says seriously. "'Twas an abundance of added toil, if you could imagine that. Consequently, it is now a habit of mine to create plans I deduce will find success."

Amelia looks at me and asks, "Is he always this snarky, and you just edit it out for me?"

I chuckle. "Pretty much." But at Aker's stern expression, I try to cough it off as if I hadn't been laughing.

Amelia asks, "What is the distraction?"

Scout lowers his brows, opens his hands wide like he is about to say something grand, and whispers deeply, "The Goi Armiarma."

"The what?"

"The queen of spiders."

"What will she do?" Amelia questions, eyes wide and brows raised in incredulity.

"She will call all other arachnids within a kilometer radius to her side," Scout announces, very sure of himself. "Hundreds of thousands of spiders will flood the museum."

"Where did you find her?" I ask, amazed.

"The Sixth Aevum has a contact. Said person will drop off the arachnid queen at the circus in the morning in a soundproof box—meaning the queen will not call the other spiders before the time is right. Then we will go to the Museum of Senex next evening."

Amelia dramatically sighs. "Finally, we're doing something! Okay, give me my orders. How can I prepare for the mission?"

Scout's features turn grave. "In other circumstances, I would not permit you to join our group, as your presence is unnecessary and endangers our mission. However, neither you nor Kansis can leave Winzer's side. Therefore, if Kansis goes, you must attend as well. It is preferred," Scout continues slowly, "for you to be in a form other than human. This allows you to remain near Winzer but keeps you from endangering the group."

"I understand that I bring nothing to the actual mission," Amelia states, "but my military background could be helpful in an unexpected circumstance. And I'll protect Kansis."

I want to say that I can protect myself, but even I can see I have no skills to add in this situation. My Gift will do nothing to save me.

Scout nods but says thoughtfully, "Your military background will not prepare you for what we are going to do, and *I* can protect Kansis."

Ontzi, I'm not completely defenseless... I mean, I *am*, but still. Aker stiffens beside me, and I can tell this statement bothers him.

"I want to stay human." Her voice hardens. "That is, if I have a choice."

"You do, but may I persuade you..."

As he and Amelia begin debating the details of her attendance, Aker whispers, "I don't like the plan."

"What don't you like about it?" I whisper back.

"Why do *you* have to go?"

"Well, I am the only Reader in the group."

He shakes his head. "I'm sure they could find another way to get the information."

"Like what?"

"I don't know. We were going to leave after the meeting, remember? We need to get that Blood Confession."

"Yes, I know, I know. I will do this mission and then go home with you."

Growling, he whispers, "And now there's *another* thing for you to do. Why can't you—"

"Now, before we go," Scout says, and I can tell by the volume he has added to this statement that he means for Aker and me to hear as well. "I need to discuss a matter with Kansis." His gaze flickers to Aker. "Alone," he adds.

"There is nothing you need to say to her that needs to be private," Aker snaps.

"Sorry, boys," Amelia interrupts. "It's *my* turn." She moves my stool so our knees are touching one another, straightening her back so I am forced to look up to meet her gaze. "Since we're in this room where you have to be honest: Kansis," she says slowly, "do you brainwash Pods?"

With all my might, I keep my lips shut. I know I have to think quickly of a clever response—something to outmaneuver her question—but I can't think of one. I mean, technically, *I* don't put Pods in the K-Pax, but the room won't let me skirt around what she's really asking. I can't think of anything to say.

It doesn't matter. Because it seems, by my silence, I have given Amelia an answer.

Her jaw tightens, and her brow furrows in betrayal. "I knew it," she bites.

"If I told you, you wouldn't trust me," I start desperately. "Even if you stayed here with the circus and me, you wouldn't be my friend anymore. And in a life that's known nothing but fleeting moments of friendship, I couldn't have you hate me."

"First of all, I just want you to know I knew you were lying," she seethes. "You're not very good at it." Grabbing one of her earlobes, clearly trying to smooth the resentment out of her expression, she adds, "Just tell me the truth, Kansis. Lying is what breaks trust, not facts I can't accept."

I don't see a way out. I know my subconscious told me not to say anything to her, but if I don't, this will end worse.

At least, I'm pretty sure it will.

Conceding, I bow my head in defeat. "We put the Pods through something called the K-Pax. It's a way to expedite reintegration. We create a new personality for the Pod—one that truly believes they are Elusian—and allow that identity to rule the conscious mind."

Now to justify the process, I add quickly, "Before the K-Pax, Pods were miserable because they knew they were subhuman. They couldn't have Gifts or mates, and everything about their short lifespan was hopeless. Without a family or a purpose, their existence was tragic. But with the K-Pax, Pods are content. They can live out their lives in relative happiness and peace."

"Does their real self know what's going on?" Amelia asks carefully.

"I don't know," I answer, and, for the first time, I'm thankful for this room so she knows I'm telling the truth.

Her eyes meet mine, but there's no kindness there. "Were you going to let them do that to me?" she asks, and then, as if the question can't stay in her any longer, she yells angrily, "And how can you think that's what's *best* for them?"

"The majority of Pods killed themselves before they ever reached full integration," I answer desperately. "This keeps them alive. It keeps them happy."

"But they're *not* happy, Kansis! They're not even themselves!" she continues in a loud volume. "Do you even feel bad about it? Are you sorry that you're stuffing Pods to the back of their own minds?"

I try to meet her furious gaze, but I can't hold it. Looking at the wooden bar at the side of the room, I answer, "Not until you."

Her anger deflates as suddenly as if pricked with a pin. Her enraged expression subsides, but before it can transform into anything kind—if it *was* going to turn in that direction—she looks away from me. The room grows silent.

It's only then I remember Aker and Scout's presence. Aker is staring at his hands, but Scout gives me an encouraging smile and nods.

Finally, Amelia sighs and turns back to me. "I'm mad at you, Kansis. I get why you lied, and I know this is the world you grew up in and… and I believe you thought you were doing what's best for the Pods. But you're wrong. You're wrong to be a part of something like that. And as long as you believe that's what's best for a human being—sub or meta—I can't trust you."

Her words are like a knife to my veins.

"But with that said," she continues, "I need you. I can't do this without you. I'm not going to walk around angry at you because that's a stupid waste of emotions. But I can't trust you."

"Amelia—"

She waves her hand at me. "I don't want you saying you've all of a sudden had a change of heart because I'm sure you haven't."

"Alas," Scout interjects, "hearing what she has to say would best be accomplished in this room. Not that it is any of my business," he adds at Amelia's glare.

"I will speak," I state, trying to stand strong like her. "Amelia, I believe in what we do because of our history, and I don't like to see people suffer. My people struggled to even wake yours up because of the destruction the Sennies caused. Many believed that the Pods should just be euthanized. However, more people began to feel the Pods were humans, even if sub, and should be given the dignity of life. The fight for humanity won when the Aevii decided to allow their awakening. And then those people who fought so hard to be allowed to wake the Pods had to watch as hundreds killed themselves because they didn't want to be in this new world.

"The K-Pax was created to give a semblance of comfort to the Pod. I don't know if the Pod is aware of themselves, but I hope not. And if they're not, I think their short lives are better lived in ignorance."

"And what if they are aware?" Amelia asks. "What if they're completely conscious and have to watch their lives played out by an imposter."

"That would be tragic," I answer. "There is much that you don't understand, and I've never really had to share this side of our society with a Pod. Please forgive me for lying to you. I won't do it again. Even if I think you can't handle it, I'll tell you the truth. I give you my blood's assurance."

"You don't need to *assurance* anything," she responds. I give her a moment to process my words. Finally, she states, "I'm still mad at you, and your words won't earn my trust. But I believe that you mean well. I guess we'll have to start there."

"That's fine with me."

"You cannot leave her in a public place!" Scout suddenly shouts. I didn't realize he'd begun a call on his Suus. I don't mean to eavesdrop, but he's yelling pretty loudly. "The deal was that you were to bring her here to the circus. What if someone were to find her?" There's a pause. "Calm down, calm down," Scout soothes in quieter tones. "You are spooked, is all. The Guardians will not suspect you. Just walk past them… I know not why they are here—do not—You cannot—No!"

The call clearly ends and Scout turns to us. "Our contact left the Goi in front of a shoe shop three blocks away. Apparently, there are Guardians posted outside the circus. I must go before anyone finds her."

"What happens if they do? If she's let loose?" Amelia asks.

Scout's face visibly pales. "I will return shortly."

"What if the Guardians are waiting for you to come out?" I ask. "Shouldn't you send someone else?"

"I will get by undetected," he answers easily.

"But what if the Guardians have a Gift that can detect you?" Amelia protests. "Maybe you should bring that Cloak girl with you."

"There is no time," Scout retorts, hurrying to the door.

"But—" I start.

"He says he's fine," Aker says to me. "Let him go."

Amelia calls after Scout, "If you get stopped by the Guardian's questions, should I go and get the Goi?"

"You will stay here no matter the circumstances!" Scout shouts as he runs out of the Transparency room. Amelia bolts after him, so I do as well.

We jump down the platform, descend a ladder made of coagulating water, and jog through the golden paths. Scout doesn't take us to the front tent flap but to a hidden one at the back. It doesn't even look like there's a flap until Scout pulls it aside and fading sunlight spills in. Before he goes out, he turns on us and commands, "You may not follow. I forbid it."

Not realizing he had come with us, I'm surprised when I hear Aker's breathless voice respond, "You can't forbid us from doing anything."

Ignoring him, I reassure Scout, "We don't want to go back to the Guardian Station. There's no way in Senex I would follow you."

He hesitates for a moment as if to say something, then winks at me and slips out the door.

"Let's find the Cloaky Girl and tell her Scout told us to follow him," Amelia says.

"No!" I hiss. "Scout said to stay here. Do *you* want to go back to the Guardian Station?"

At this, she cools. Carefully, she looks out of the tent and grunts. "The Guardians stopped him," she states. Suddenly her eyes alight with an idea.

I'm starting to not like this look.

"Scout said the Cloaky Girl could keep us safe up to a couple hundred meters," she starts. "There's no way this circus is anywhere close to being that size. I bet we could go out there and listen to their conversation without them seeing us."

"Do you have hypoxemia of the mind? No, we're not doing that!"

"I don't get the insult, but yes, we are."

Aker moves as if to nudge me but doesn't actually touch me. "What's she getting all excited about?"

Amelia, not understanding Aker, asks, "You said we could trust the Cloak, right?" She eyes me, testing me.

Hesitantly, I say, "Yeah, we can. But is it worth it? Is it worth getting caught?"

"We won't be caught," she responds. "You have to be willing to take risks, Freckles. You told me that the Cloak was foolproof. I trust that you were telling the truth about that. Now, trust me."

"What are you doing?" a voice says behind us.

The three of us whirl around to see one of the Pexun performers. She's the one who plays Caedis. I had tried to catch her eye several times—we're both Pexuns and could connect on that front—but she'd always looked away.

"Everyone is searching for you two," the girl points to Amelia and me. "Are you with Scout?"

"Scout is outside talking to Guardians," I tell her. "Why is everyone looking for us?"

The girl seems flustered. Like she wants to answer but doesn't want to be involved at the same time. "Pypen said the Guardians were closing in on finding you both," she finally answers. "He sent everyone out of the circus, hoping they can get to you first."

"Can you call Pypen?" I ask her.

The glare she gives me is as if I had just insulted her entire family line. "Of course not," she snarls.

Without even asking "What's going on?" Amelia pushes open the flap and marches outside.

I'm not much of a curser, minus the occasional "*ontzi*" here or there, but I allow myself a colorful profanity or two before I follow her outside. Aker grabs my wrist, but I twist out of his grip.

Thank you, Ward training.

Scout is speaking to three Guardians, and I immediately recognize the middle one as Deputy Chief Femme. They're facing us and staring right at us—or past us. We're entirely invisible to them.

We are at Scout's back, so he doesn't know we're there.

Yet.

I hope he doesn't jump when he sees us.

As we walk toward them, I freeze on hearing my name. "A potent Gift is concealing Kansis Willow," Femme is saying. "So it's difficult for us to track her exact location. When we get within a few hundred meters of her, we lose her. We have powerful Gifts up our sleeves as well, and my associate, Detective Mei, has sensed that Kansis Willow and the missing Pod have only been in two places the last few days. Your circus here," she points at the black and gold tent, "and at the hotel where your crew is staying."

"What is your question, Deputy Chief Femme?" Scout asks directly.

"Yesterday, Kansis Willow and the Pod were apprehended. However, in the middle of their interrogation, unknown Gifters came in and stole them from us—"

"That is very unfortunate," Scout interrupts. "As I said, I am in a hurry. Can we not skip to the question portion of this exchange?"

Femme's brows raise and then steepen into her eyes. "All right, Kel Eekan. Where are Kansis Willow and the Pod?"

"I know not."

"When we find Kansis Willow and her Pod, we will prosecute all peoples involved in their escape. And if we discover that it is anyone in your circus, we will also prosecute the jailbreaks you've facilitated over the past eight years. That's about one hundred and twenty years from a two-hundred-year life for each of your crew—"

"Marvelous," Scout interrupts. "Can I go now?"

One of the other Guardians, a woman covered in flower tattoos, snaps her fingers and sniffs the air. She says, "She's moving, Deputy Chief."

"Which one?" Femme asks eagerly.

"Kansis Willow. It's a little hazy, but she's moving away from her source of protection. Within minutes I'll be able to track her."

Although Scout's body tightens, I'm impressed he doesn't turn around.

Femme looks coldly at Scout. "I'm sure I'll see you soon." Turning to Mai, she commands, "Lead on, Detective."

As they walk away, Scout turns around and freezes when he sees us. Slowly, he twists and watches the Guardians until they are out of sight then whirls back to us.

"What happened?" Amelia whispers to me.

"What was that about?" I ask Scout.

"Levels balanced, Merayal?" Scout asks the Pexun woman behind us. I didn't even realize she'd followed us out. Aker is next to her as well. He comes out from behind her and stands next to me, so close our arms are touching.

I don't move.

Merayal, once more, seems torn between wanting to help and wanting to run away. "Pypen thinks Guardians are tracking you."

"Please, elucidate," Scout commands calmly, but I can tell he's worried.

Merayal quickly explains Pypen's announcement to the group and his command for the performers to scour the city, trying to find Scout, Amelia, and myself. Once she's finished, I translate for Amelia, and Scout rubs his hands over his braid while he thinks.

After a few moments, Scout observes, "Either they are tracking the wrong women, or they are bluffing to see how we would react to you being found."

"And Pypen fell for it," Merayal voices.

Scout looks back towards where the Guardians disappeared. "It would appear so. Twice now, I have tried to call him but it does not go through to him. The Guardians must be blocking our calls somehow. I must find him."

"If the whole point of this is to see if you might lead them to Amelia and me, you going to look for Pypen will seem suspicious," I comment.

"What about the Goi?" Amelia asks.

"And there is still the Goi," I add to Scout.

Scout paces while he thinks. Merayal seems increasingly uneasy and takes a few steps backward as if to leave. But before she can disappear, Scout turns to Merayal and states, "I need you to meet Pypen for me."

Anger flashes in her eyes. "I'm not going to—"

Scout steps forward and drops to one knee. "I am begging you, Merayal Kapu, will you please help my brother? Undoubtedly, the Guardians will not allow anyone from the circus to interfere and warn him. I hope he can detect the trap on his own. If he does indeed see through it, he will go to our meeting place. You must meet him there and bring him back. I need you—I am on my knees begging you to help me. I will repay you in any way you see fit."

"Information on my mom's assassin," she answers without hesitation.

"I will provide you the name by next night."

Merayal takes a deep breath and then growls, "Fine."

Scout stands, elated. "You must go to Lufys, Sanus. Right next to the transponder station is a little fishery with an attached diner in the back. Pypen will meet you there."

"How do you know he will?" she scowls.

"If you get there before him, wait until midnight and then return."

Rolling her eyes, she jogs away from us, without a goodbye of any kind.

"I will go and retrieve the Goi," Scout pronounces, staring after Merayal.

"Can they monitor your Suus?" I ask. As a good citizen, I wouldn't have ever asked or minded. But now, it matters. A lot.

"Perhaps," Scout muses, then adds, "Farewell for now. I will see you in a heartbeat."

As he walks away, I call out, "May the stars have their way!" I don't know why I said the idiom—maybe because I really want him to stay safe—but I wish I hadn't. Mostly because he stops running, revolves, and smiles at me as if I'm the only person in the entire world.

"Good fortune to you as well, Scoop," he calls back.

As he spins around once more, Aker growls, "I hate it here," and stalks back into the circus.

"Come on," Amelia says, oblivious to Aker's words. "We need to find Cloaky Girl."

Pexus

Pypen

KANSIS AND AMELIA ARE both crying. This development—particularly the tough Pod weeping—would be more shocking if I had not just watched my best friend getting hauled away by the Guardians. However, there are only two things I can think about at this moment. On the one hand, I know that Scout would prefer that I forsake him and take the two girls to safety. On the other hand, I know they are not my priority.

Scout is my first concern, as he always will be.

If I forsake the girls, Scout will be furious with me. The last time I expressly saved him before someone else, he refused to speak to me for over a week. But I care not for these girls. That is, I care for their well-being, but they are not worth the loss of Scout. Without him... without him, *I* would be lost. "I am not going to leave him," I mumble.

"Are you going to break him out of the Guardian Station as you did us?" Kansis asks.

Barely looking at them, I simply state, "Follow if you wish." Not checking to see if they are trailing behind, I run after the Guardian's van. The Guardian's vehicles are the only ones not stuck on the tracks throughout the cities. This has both pros and cons when chasing after or running from them. In this instance, it works in my favor, as they have to take so many side streets that I can keep up with their faster vehicle.

The girls chase after me, calling for me to slow down. As heartless as it is, I do not. We traverse blocks in this fashion: them screaming out at me, me ignoring said pleas and keeping my eyes on the van.

The girls finally catch up to me just as the van pulls into the Guardian station.

"How are we going to get him out?" Kansis asks, entirely out of breath.

"We are not," I answer. For the fourth time, I try calling Emerly, but the call does not go through to him. I try others. By Thykas and Vielfrah, I am wondering if something is wrong; but by Krael, Fiddy, and Allerish, I know someone or something is keeping my calls from reaching their intended recipients. It must be the Guardians.

"The Pod is scared," Kansis presses. "We can't be out in the open like this. Are you going to take us back to the circus? You have to keep us from being caught by the Guardians!"

I know what Scout would wish me to do. And if I do not honor his wishes, Kansis is right; the Guardians will capture the two girls, just as they did him.

"Wait…" I mumble.

Thoughts collide in my head. Why *did* they arrest Scout? Why would the Guardians capture him and not Kansis and Amelia? If Winzer is not protecting the young women, we have no other Gifts to keep them undetected. Certainly, my Gift is doing nothing to aid them. Without Winzer's Gift, the Guardians would have captured them by now.

It is then that I finally see the two girls with fresh eyes. They look exactly like the Pexun and her Pod, but their facial expressions are wrong. Kansis appears confident, albeit a little shaken. Amelia is timid and scared, like a Pod who understands not this world or our ways.

This is not as it should be.

Even after being tortured at the Guardians' hands, Amelia never lost her strength. In addition, I have not once seen Kansis leading. It has been clear from the beginning that Amelia is the one in charge.

So why swap identities now? Why the fear and the tears and the timidity? Unless… unless this is *not* Amelia and Kansis.

Unless I am being played.

Twisting my wrist, I rip up my sleeve. The colors of my tattoo vacillate between black and orange and silver. 'Tis our code for danger.

Oh—that devious Deputy Chief. She must be behind this. Perhaps the whole story about her finding Kansis was a ruse. If that is the case, then she must have impersonated the call from Emerly. With all my blocked calls, I wonder how many incoming ones have been blocked as well. If all I have speculated concerning Deputy Chief Femme is accurate, she would not in all actuality have Scout. Perhaps he is at our meeting spot even now.

Scout and I have long agreed that if we were ever to be separated or find ourselves in a situation where the circus has been compromised, there is one place where we would meet. It was the location where our first circus performed: Lufys, Sanus. But how to get there without being followed by these Kansis and Amelia clones?

That I am aware of, I have said nothing incriminating thus far. I cannot let the clones know that I have realized they are not the genuine article. But I cannot cordially dismiss them as if I know them either.

Either way, they will track me.

I have to lose them first.

There is an interesting fact that few members of society besides the Guardians know, and it concerns a safe space they created for themselves. Had the Sixth Aevum not given us the tip, I do not believe Scout and I would have found it ourselves, but now that we know about it, it is self-evident.

Years ago, if ever a Guardian was being tracked, all they needed to do was walk into any government building. Immediately, they would be vacuoused, and although their own Gift would be hindered, any Gift clinging to them would also reset. This was meant to be a secret reserved only for the Guardians, but many people avoiding the law found out about this and began using it against them.

"It became so well known that the Guardians had to stop the resets. However, they still needed a safe spot, so they just kept the bathrooms—"

"What are you mumbling about?" the Kansis-replica asks me. "We need to get out of here."

Correct, Clone. I do need to get out of here. Gathering my dreads behind me, I tie them in a ponytail. "Do you trust me?" I whisper to the Kansis-clone without looking at her.

"What do you mean?" she asks.

Trying to put on a friendly expression, I ignore the question. "You are fans of the circus, right?"

"Right, I mean. That's not how we met, but—"

"So, you know me?"

"But—"

"So, as far as strangers go, do you trust me?"

The Kansis-clone seems flustered. "I mean, we're not strangers, but yeah I—"

"Great, yes. All right, I need you to take the Pod and go inside."

Looking from me to the Guardian station and back at me, the Kansis-clone asks, "Into the Guardian Station?"

"Yes. Inside."

"Why?"

"You said you trusted me," I say and playfully pat her arm. "Now, go inside."

"What's your plan?" she asks. "Are you going to break me out again?"

I allow my voice a tinge of testiness as I state, "When I asked if you trusted me, your reply was yes; however, your actions scream otherwise. Now, for the final time, take your Pod and go inside."

The clone seems torn but eventually mumbles something to the Amelia-clone. No doubt the speech is supposed to sound like English, but now that I'm paying attention, it does not. They tentatively walk towards the station. As soon as they cross the threshold of the entrance, I bolt toward the transponder station. I know now that Guardians are following me, but all I need to do is get to a government building's bathroom.

However, it is almost nine in the evening here in Pexus, and all the buildings closed at five. I must go at least five hours east to where the government buildings are still open. The travel time for a five-hour time change is at least half an hour. That would put me in... Montera.

When I reach the Initium transponder station, I rent a car as fast as possible and set my coordinates to Montera. The ride is more bumpy than usual, and I feel Pila sick when I exit the vehicle. In Montera, Pexus' largest island, the inhabitants all mill around with grey hair, yet it has often been said that Montera is more Ortus than Pexus. Their mannerisms, values, family culture, and even the way they speak are a medley of the two territories.

Commanding my Suus to give me directions, I race through the crowds of Pexuns as they happily return home, their workday coming to an end. I quicken my pace even more when I see their city hall. As I reach the steps, I notice the air around my ears cracking. Guardians are close by and seeking to enter my mind. Erecting my defenses, I race up the steps, zigzag through the colonnades, dodge around the people in my way, and duck down on my knees when I reach a crowd huddling in front of an elevator.

I wait for the buzzing to stop and bolt toward the bathroom. Whenever I enter such a room, I expect the vacuous to have a tactile feeling—a whoosh of cold air, a sting or a chill, but I feel nothing. I know the Guardians have stopped following me, but they are close. Reaching into my inner vest pocket, I pull out a small leather pouch: my Precaution Bag. Inside are five primary-colored gumballs. Picking up the purple one, I examine it closely.

Inscribed, barely visible, is the face of a rat. No, too suspicious. Placing it back in the pouch, I take out the green one. Inscribed on this one is a small box with a bow on top. No, no. Not reliable enough. I place this one down and seize the yellow one. It takes me a moment to find the inscription—it is a gust of wind.

Scout and I had both bet the other we would be the one to try this first. I suppose I am winning a bet this day.

As the door to the bathroom opens, I stuff the gumball in my mouth and my Precaution Bag back into my jacket. As the sour taste hits the back of my throat, I suddenly remember the instructions from the woman who sold us these illegal chewable eutsees. She had told Scout and me to make sure we got a running start with this one. The Guardian detective, Mai, stands before me. Before she can say anything, I run towards her at full speed. Just before our bodies collide, I feel my whole being burst into moonlight and then explode into a gust of wind.

Swirling, twirling, upward I push
Churning, turning, onward I rush
Freedom I seek, and thralldom defy
As a wild streaming vapor, I now dwell up high
To lose and loose myself in weightless abandon
Too thin to know my name, no home to land in
Spellbound by the outcome of this wheel roulette
Slowing, then flowing into a final pirouette
Until unwelcome heaviness lays hold to draw me back
Into a substantive world of white and black

My limbs slowly regain shape as I drift through the dark backstreets of Montera. My feet have not yet fully formed when my knees smack down on the concrete ground. My skull hits the pavement before the skin has been recreated completely, and I quickly renew the gaping crack in the bone.

I have never been the wind before, and although I could not use the sense of sight whilst in the form, I could *feel*. Feel the space of the rooms, the pull towards the sky, the power of being intangible. I think I could enjoy that experience more often. If the wind could laugh, I know I exuded the sound as I blew past Deputy Chief Femme. I must have flown fifteen kilometers by now.

Once I am fully human again, I regroup my thoughts. Guardians will be protecting all the transponder stations, so I cannot risk them. I am still six hours west of where I need to be with only a few remaining tricks up my veins.

But I require only one trick, and possess it, I do.

Quickly, I check the prancing lion tattoo on my arm. At least Scout is well. Not happy or safe, but also not in danger. Knowing he is fairing favorably for the moment, I ponder on my next move. Before I reach into my pockets again, I look up and down the alleyway to see if any locals are watching me, but all

I see are doors and lock boxes. I listen, but all I hear is a faint wind rustling through the buildings.

When I am certain no one is about, I reach into the inner pocket of my vest again. This time, I pull out a small, orange vial from my Precaution Bag. When this item was given to me, I had wondered what kind of circumstance would lead me to use it.

I have only ever heard rumors of the tolláns—the monsters who dwell in the earth's crust. For a royal Vorbi, they will transfer a person anywhere in the world in less than fifteen minutes. The fee is high, the transportation is unpleasant, and the transporters themselves, foul. Not seeing any other options for myself, I pour the acrid-smelling contents of the vial onto the concrete.

The ground begins to sizzle and burn. The inner part of the puddle turns bright orange and then dips into the earth. Slowly, the surrounding area begins to melt away until there is a human-sized hole in the road. An eerie voice whispers up from the small chasm, causing gooseflesh to emerge all over my body. It almost seems to laugh as it asks, "Where do you desire to go, Man Child?"

I rid the adrenaline coursing through my veins and reply calmly, "Lufys, Sanus."

"Does the child have the compensation?" the voice asks, warbling like dice rolling down an abandoned street.

With feigned ease, I throw my royal blue Vorbi into the hole.

A ferocious giggle sprays up in my face. "Is the child's blood blue as well?" it asks. "Maybe we should look."

"Lufys, Sanus," I say again, renewing my adrenaline levels once more. I will not be bullied by this faceless monster.

"Well, well. We're in a hurry, we see. Jump in, Man Child, jump in. The only one stopping your little trip is you."

Closing my eyes, I remind myself I can renew any wounds they inflict upon me. Holding this thought firm in my mind, I leap into the hole.

Scaggle Tooth, are we to be keeping his fingers? Let me be having one! I is being able to add them to my collection!

Or his toes—I is being able to add them to mine.

You two is having no imagination. I is declaring we put his eyes farther apart than they should be and raising his ears like those wretched animals they call dogs.

Poison Breath, if we is having imagination, let us being truly clever. We is more wickeder. We emasculating him.

Oh, you is being wicked, Death Claw! Deliciously wicked. Can we be doing it, Scaggle Tooth?

His payment was not lacking, unlike so many we take from.

Wait... Scaggle Tooth... Is we only taking from the humans who don't pay the blue?

Of course.

I wasn't being aware of that.

Ha! Me either, Poison Breath!

Coming to thinking of it, I is guessing I be owing some humans their fingers back. Ha!

Ha! And toes, Fake Face! And toes!

His payment was not lacking, you fools. We will not harm him.

Can't we take something, Scaggle Tooth? Anything? I won't hurt him, I swear it.

Hmm... Death Claw, you is deciding. What will you being taking?

The ground spits me out, and I land on my hands and knees. Potential wounds are the least of my worries as I hurriedly check all my body parts to ensure they are present and in place. It is only when I reach a hand up to my head that a whimper escapes my lips without consent.

They took my dreadlocks.

It took me eight years to grow those out. I refused to employ beauticians as I wanted them to grow naturally... And now they are gone. My scalp feels painfully light and cold. How could they take them? Scout will laugh at me, to be sure.

I know that every Sanusian who passes me sees an average dark-skinned Ortusan with unremarkable hair only two millimeters high, but I feel quite naked with my head as it is. As I break into a run, I pull up my hood, rushing through the small town towards the dock on the far west side where a fishery lies. In the back of the fishery is a little diner which serves freshly caught seafood. With hope, Scout is waiting for me. If he is not there, I made the wrong call, and he is back in Pexus in danger. I will wait to punish myself until I know for certain if I am right or wrong.

Even though it was almost nine in the evening when I left Pexus, it is eleven in the morning here in Sanus, and the lunch patrons are just milling in the diner. Trying not to be outright rude, I dash past them, calling out apologies, and burst into the restaurant. I search the room for his braided head but see no Ortusan hair—only Sanusians... and one lone Pexun. A debilitating shock wracks through my bones.

Merayal is sitting in the cozy, dusty room alone.

With her chin resting in her hand, Merayal watches the few customers indifferently. As she takes a deep breath, she reaches up, brings her hair out of the ponytail, and then throws it back up into a bun. I cannot tell if she does this because her hair needs to be redone or if this is an involuntary action when she is bored. I have seen her do it several times during practice. When she finally notices me, she stands and then sits back down. Then, presumedly after deliberating her next move, she stands again and walks towards me.

"What in the universe are you doing here?" I whisper when she reaches me.

"Scout told me to come," she answers angrily.

"What has happened?" I ask, sudden anxiety flooding my veins. "Was he caught by the Guardians?"

"Not since last I saw him," she answers, crossing her arms.

"Why did Scout not come himself?" I ask more harshly than I mean to.

With a tone matching mine, she answers, "The Guardians were tracking him."

"Why did Scout ask you to come?"

"Because I was the only one there."

"And why, after our last conversation, would you ever agree?"

"Because he's going to give me the name of my mom's murderer."

"So he's safe?"

"That I know of."

There is a palpable tension between us. If I were to reach out, I feel sure an invisible barrier would shock me backward.

The conversation between Merayal and the Controls comes to my mind. She had told them I want to be more than friends with her. What is more than a friend? And why would she think I want that from her. I want *nothing* from her.

Utterly unbidden, Fabella's words echo through my mind again. *You may choose to let the Pexun girl rot and rust in her blood, or you can tame her. You can earn her trust and affection as you did all of us.*

I do not wish to feel angry—even though her last words to me were a threat. In fact, I do not desire to feel anything toward her at all. Complete apathy would be delightful at this moment.

For now, I will choose to feel nothing. I will not care for her, but I will not be cross either.

Making my blood cool, I take a deep breath, attempting to release the tension from my body. In doing so, I finally smell the delectable scents from the diner. My stomach grumbles.

Not knowing what else to say to Merayal, I ask, "Well, are you hungry?" Her confused expression makes a wry chuckle escape my lips. As my body finally begins to relax after the adrenaline dumping of the last few hours, I sigh. To Merayal, I state, "Come now, Pexun. Let us grab some food before we rush back to your territory. You know," I begin, walking towards the line of customers, "Sanus is the only territory where people still fish for their meals by boat, just as they did in Senex. All others either duplicate their fish and crustaceans or call them up from under the sea."

Merayal follows not, but I continue my dissertation, walking backward. "Of course, the laws keep them from overhunting, but no skill is needed to get the meat. Here, at the Divin' Diner, the fishermen get up every morning and go out to collect the fish and crustaceans for the day. Whatever they catch, they sell, and once it is all eaten, they close up shop."

As I wait in line, I loudly monologue everything I know about Lufys, Sanus. The other patrons laugh at the random trivia I share—half-remembered anecdotes from when Scout and I stayed the evening with a local some years back. Cheers arise from the dining room and the kitchen when I say only the hardest-working Elusians hail from Lufys, Sanus. When I finally reach the front counter, the cashier gives me our lunches for free and hands me a shirt. I admire the soft wool and hold it up so Merayal can read the front: "We went divin' fer yer supper!"

It almost looks like she might smile, but she firmly shuts down the expression.

When I sit at a table, Merayal does not. I do not have the energy for her intense aversion of me. Sighing, I look up at her. "I will make you a deal. You sit here, eat lunch with me, and answer one question of mine, and I will give you something you desire."

"You have nothing I want," she retorts spitefully.

"Scout said he would give you the name of your mother's assassin. I offer my services in the dispensing of the creature."

This makes her sit down. "You will kill the assassin?"

"*Matza*, no, of course not. But I will help you accomplish this quest."

She eyes me warily. "Have you ever killed before?"

"Spilling someone's lifeblood is not something I am eager to do."

This makes her snort, and she opens my brown paper bag instead of her own and grabs a fry. "How noble of you." She looks at my head and remarks, "You look stupid without your dreads."

The comment bites as I already feel self-conscious without them. Rearranging my hood down over my forehead, I ignore the statement and ask, "And you? Have *you* ever killed someone?"

By the casual nod she offers as she grabs another one of my fries, I am genuinely unsure if she is kidding or not. "Was that a yes?" I inquire.

Eyeing me over her half-eaten fry, she asks, "Is that your question?"

"It should be, but no, I did have another." For the time being, I will put this new mystery on a shelf in my mind and try to sort out the questions I have for her. I do not want her to know that I think she is a Pod, so the question cannot be overtly obvious.

Merayal grabs her own bag now and takes out her food.

After much deliberation, I ask, "What was your childhood like?"

Licking the fish juice off her fingers, she laughs and repeats, "*What was your childhood like?* That's your question?"

"Indeed," I answer, unfazed. "But you must be honest and give a full answer. If it does not satisfy, I recede my offer to help."

"Is this because I let you tell me about your dead wife?"

Looking up at her, I see she is toying with me. Having practiced much with Scout, I know not to take the bait. "Just answer the question."

Merayal rolls her eyes by way of consent. After stuffing the other half of her taco in her mouth and wiping the avocado salsa off her chin, she takes her time chewing her food and thinking. While she does so, I take out the other fish taco and start eating.

"I don't remember my real parents," Merayal says after a few minutes. "For most of my life, I lived with a man who claimed to be my father," her eyes darken, and a look of utter loathing—filled with more hatred than she has ever bestowed upon me—crosses her features. "I had a lot of… well, you could call them brothers. I mean, we weren't really a family, but the man wanted us to feel like we were.

"That was always so important to him. No matter how sick or twisted or foul he was—he tried to convince all of us we were family. For a long time, I believed it. I didn't know anything better, so I thought the way we lived was what family members do… how family treats each other. We all had jobs. Even as a kid, I had to bring in money for the 'family'. I worked with one of my brothers to scam local kids into giving us their money—"

"What is money?" I ask.

"You know… like…" Suddenly, she licks her lips and juts her jaw to the left. Fixing her hair, she explains, "I meant compensation. We scammed them into giving us Vorbies."

"Oh," I say, understanding. "Go on."

"And the man was so proud of us." Her gaze glazes over like she is pondering something very far away. "What's so sick is, even after everything he did to me, I wanted to make him happy. And what made him happy was outrightly hurting those not in the family, while slyly hurting those within. He was proud when I manipulated my brothers to get what I wanted."

An angry smile spews on her lips. "And then, one day, I *didn't* make him happy. One day I made him really, *really* mad." The smile turns bemused and then bitter. "So he sent me away as a punishment. He let me know what the darker desires of men look like."

Gooseflesh erupts all over my body. I am a man and I was married, but the way she talks about it makes me wonder what she means.

Merayal's expression clouds over, and I can tell that, although she is physically here, her mind is far away. It takes a couple of minutes for her to mentally come back to Lufys, Sanus, and finish her tale.

"I never saw my father the same way after that, and I wanted to escape. So… well, I found a way to get away from him forever. I tried to take one of my brothers with me, but he betrayed me. When the choice came to stay in our living hell or to take a chance at a whole new life—he chose hell. He…" Suddenly, she closes her eyes tight and clenches her jaw. When she opens her eyes, her expression is apathetic. "It doesn't matter," she voices. "I got away, and I never have to see either of them again for the rest of my life. They're dead to me." Finally meeting my gaze, she says, "So. Was that a satisfactory answer?"

"What is *hell*?" I ask. "Why did your brother want to stay there?"

"Hell?" She laughs at my question, and then studies her hands for a moment. When she looks at me, it is as if all life has left her irises. "Hell is the place where every hope is lie, every choice is a trap, and every fortune is a trick. My brother stayed because he knew of nothing else."

I nod, sensing that she speaks in metaphor, but knowing she will say no more. Looking away from me, she takes another fry. I push my food away from me. Appetite utterly gone, I ponder her story. It was just as Fabella said. She did come from a wicked place populated with evil people. But now that I truly understand her story, I know not how to move forward.

Even if I wanted to build a friendship with Merayal—which I am not certain I do—there is not even a droplet of openness toward me in her blood. As she finishes her meal and her disinterested gaze meets mine, I can *feel* her walls. I believe she spoke no truer words than when she said she wanted nothing from me.

How can I possibly tame her when all she has in her blood is hate?

Pexus

Kansis

WITH AKER IN TOW, Amelia and I search for Winzer—aka Cloaky Girl—and when we find her, Amelia insists I must convince her that Scout wanted us to follow him. It doesn't end up working, because Aker immediately tells her we are lying.

Winzer moves to use her Suus to tell everyone that the search for Scout, Amelia, and me is off, but I quickly tell her not to. If the Guardians are tracking Scout and Pypen's Suuses, they might be monitoring all of the performers. A few other dancers have remained at the circus, and Winzer sends them out to pass on the message that everyone can return. The process is long, but after an hour, performers start trickling in.

They all have questions, and Winzer repeats the same thing to each one: "We don't know what's going on, do we? We don't know where Scout and Pypen are, and no, we can't reach them. We all should stay at the circus until they return, we should."

As she will not leave our sides now, Winzer suggest we wait for Scout by the hidden flap at the back of the circus. The tension and expectancy are so thick she finally declares we need a distraction and asks us if we've played Gedankenspiel before. Others join, and for the next few hours, the group teaches Amelia and me the cult-classic game.

I've known people over the years who have become obsessed with Gedankenspiel, but I've never actually played myself. It's an insanely clever and strategic card and board game hybrid that can be played in many ways. Some mini-adventures can take as little as twenty minutes, while some quests take at least three hours to play, and I've heard that the long campaigns can last months. You can build your own deck and board or buy the standard game, but either way, both beginners and experts can enjoy the game simultaneously.

The game is interactive and features collaborative storytelling, where players assume roles and contribute to a shared narrative. Although there is a winner for each round, how and what you win affects an overall score that you can bring into your next game. Those who play well have become celebrities, and it is common for their fans to watch their games live.

Aker is very excited to play. I'm surprised he knows so much about Gedankenspiel. It turns out he has his own deck and board at home. "I'll show you when we get back to Depalo," he comments meaningfully.

Even though I'm enjoying myself, I cannot stop worrying about Scout and Pypen. I'm afraid that the Guardians have found them and that *right now* they're being tortured, and we're all just sitting around playing a silly game. In my mind's eye, I keep seeing Scout's smile as he turned away to fetch the Goi.

Ontzi, he'd better be all right.

When Scout himself walks through the back entrance, he is met with such a loud reception I'm sure he doesn't hear Aker shout, "Way to keep us waiting, *gari!*"

"Has Pypen returned?" Scout calls out over the din.

Several people answer, but the overall response is just a resounding "No" followed by "What's going on?"

Scout quiets everyone and explains that the Guardians had played a ruse on Scout and Pypen to get to Amelia and me. Scout had stayed away from the circus as long as he had in order to show his innocence, and he is certain Pypen will be returning soon. "If you are worried, feel free to stay up with me. We will rest in Thykas' room. But, for those of you who wish to go to bed, please do so. It is very late, and we have another wonderful workday next day."

Some performers head towards Thykas' room, but many trudge back towards the front of the circus to return to the hotel. Although Scout seems like he is looking for us, Amelia approaches him first.

Before she can ask me to translate anything, Scout tosses something to her.

Amelia catches it easily, and we both inspect the small item. It's the size and shape of a kidney bean and the color of ivy. "What is it?" Amelia asks me.

"Tell her to put this on her sciath," Scout commands.

"Is it the eutsi?" I ask him. Will Amelia be able to speak Elusian now?

"Trust me," Scout says. "Just have her clip it on her sciath."

Surprised that I really do trust this man who was so recently a stranger, I pull the sciath from underneath her shirt and clip the small eutsi onto the chain.

"Are you going to tell me what it is, are you?" Amelia asks me.

"I can tell you if you prefer," Scout answers, grinning.

Amelia looks up at him, shocked. "So you *do* speak English!"

My Protector smiles and answers, "Not quite. That tiny item is the translation eutsi I promised you. When you speak, your words will be in English, but we will hear it in Elusian. I had a friend change the translation dialect to Formosian, given your hair is naturally red."

"Thank you so much!" Amelia says. "This will be very useful indeed. Being misunderstood is a great irritation of mine, it is."

I know this is the perfect moment to ask Scout if he can make a eutsi of Winzer's Gift, but I can't bring myself to ask.

"Is that what took you so long?" Amelia asks him.

"I wanted not for the Guardians to think my grabbing the box was suspicious, so I ran a few errands. But," he pauses and pulls something palm-sized from his coat pocket, "I did get it." The box holding the Queen of Spiders is an ornate, dark ebony container adorned with silver spider etchings on its side. The lid has a sparkly web patterned on its face and is held secure by a claw-shaped latch.

"She's in there?" I ask. "The Goi?"

"Indeed she is." Turning around, he shouts, "Thykas!"

The Sanusian man runs over. He's changed his beard again, and this time it's in the shape of a giant snake which appears to be slithering across his face. "Scout, me ol' sam? What can Oi do ye fer?"

"Take this to my office and put it in the safe underneath my desk; you know the one. Do you remember the password?"

"Of course, Sam." Gingerly, Thykas takes the box and starts toward the invisible walkway.

"Now," Scout looks at Amelia, Aker, and me. "It is too dangerous for you to return to the hotel, so you will stay here this night. Fret not. The room you will be staying in was designed so that patrons can have the best nap of their lives. We have set up mini bedrooms throughout the space, and you can choose any one you would like. They are cleaned after every use and are ready for your immediate enjoyment."

Scout leads us to the fourth level, and without having to open it, we pass through a door that looks like a billowy cloud. The room itself has a dim, warm light bathing its contents. Like Scout has said, there are twenty or more little bedroom set-ups, complete with bed, nightstand, lamp, fan, nightlight—anything one would need.

"I'll pick this one, I will!" Amelia exclaims, then immediately, all of the enjoyment on her face is replaced with annoyance. "Why do I keep repeating myself?" she asks me. "I keep saying something then affirming it, I do." Her eyes flash. "Like that! Why am I doing that?"

Scout and I laugh. "It's the way the Formosians speak," I answer.

"Well, it's annoying, it is," Amelia states and immediately growls. "This will be irritating," she says slowly and then physically closes her mouth so she can't say more. Without another word, she jumps into a mini bedroom set up like an Ortusan palace. Once her body hits the bed, an amber-colored film covers the room like digital curtains.

"For privacy," Scout explains. When Amelia walks back through the amber film, it disappears so that we can see the mini-bedroom again.

"At the far end are bathrooms; you will find everything you need, including pajamas."

Amelia immediately leaves to go check it out.

Extending his arms wide, Scout bows his farewell. But, as he passes me, he puts up his hand as if to offer me the standard Pexun greeting. When our hands touch, I feel a slight spark, and he winks at me.

I look down at my hand. On my palm is a simple one-word message written in black ink: "Scoop." In an instant, my vision fogs over, and I am no longer seeing with my own eyes…

How am I going to get her away from him?

Pypen is talking, discussing one of the few mistakes made in their act with Allerish. Their voices wash over Scout, heard but not understood. He knows he must talk to Kansis, but how to do it without igniting jealousy from Aker?

An idea quickly forms in his mind. Slowly, Scout takes the black ballpoint pen he has recently acquired in a bet out of his pocket. He examines its heavy, regal frame.

Yes… I believe that would work.

With excellent penmanship, he writes the word "Scoop" on the palm of his hand.

Hello, Kansis. Meet me outside in an hour.

I'm squinting my eyes while Aker is speaking, but I can't quite understand him yet. Finally, at his touch—at his *touch*!—I come to.

"Are you okay?" he asks, hand gingerly on my shoulder. "What is going on?" Turning on Scout, he demands, "What did you do to her?"

"It was nothing, sorry," I answer. "Just had a headache come on." I don't like the lie, but he would *hate* the truth.

"Are you all right?" Scout asks, but his eyes twinkle impishly.

"I'm fine," I answer, trying not to smile.

"Greet the shadows," he says, bidding us farewell. Scout leaves the room looking back at me only once before he disappears through the cloud door.

Grabbing my wrist, Aker twists my hand to see the word, *Scoop*, written on my palm. "What does that mean? Why does he keep calling you that?"

"I don't know," I answer truthfully.

Tossing my hand back, he states, "You know he doesn't like you, right?"

The words hit me like splattered mud water. They don't hurt, but they're uncomfortable and I feel cold. "What do you mean?"

"He's just using you to get to the reward. The way he treats you… it's all a facade. I know you haven't interacted with people outside of Depalo, and I don't want you to be… you know… hoodwinked or whatever into thinking he cares for you. He doesn't. He's not your friend; he's a businessman. It's cruel how he's tricking you, and I can see you falling for it. Anyway, I don't want to see you get hurt."

"Oh, thank you," my mouth responds. I have no idea what to do with this information.

"Okay, see you in the morning." He turns around but then quickly reverses back with a quirky smile. "Look, I'm not happy about this mission, but I'll allow it. This *one* last thing, and then we're out of here."

I think I nod.

Aker goes on, "So… what if we picked a day for the wedding? I don't know if you had any time of the year you wanted specifically… but let's set the date tomorrow."

I don't put any thought into the word "Okay" before it falls out of my mouth.

"Great!" he responds and claps his hands. "I'll see you in the morning, Kans."

"See you in the morning."

"Greet the moon."

"Greet the moon."

Seemingly happy, he makes his way toward the men's room.

I see Amelia leaning against a wall outside the women's bathroom. She must have heard—and now understood—our conversation. Not wanting to hear if she has any remarks about it, I hurry past her into the bathroom. However, once I'm in, I stop mid-step.

Scout wasn't joking.

The whole bathroom has everything I could possibly want, cosmetic and pampering-wise. Amelia and I spend a good half hour checking out all of the cleansers, anti-aging mowics, moisturizers, and lotions. We each take a blissfully toasty shower, and I find a hair cream that makes my curls actually look good. Like… *really* good. For once in my life, they have definition without the crunch, and they seem to shine and bounce in the bathroom mirror.

At one point, as we soak in the blissful hot water of the showers, Amelia calls across to ask me for a razor. "What do you need a razor for?" I ask, almost horrified.

"For my legs, duh?"

"Why do you need a razor for your legs?"

"To shave, duh."

"To shave what?"

"My hair, I say!" she laughs. "Geesh, Freckles, it's like you—" She gasps. "Do you just not shave, or do you have no hair on your legs?"

"At puberty, both young men and women can decide where they want hair to grow, and then the healer formulates their hormone shot to accommodate," I respond.

"What do you mean?" she asks, her voice echoing around her shower.

"Novian puberty is very different to what you experienced. We receive a hormone shot at the beginning of adolescence that regulates the negative hormone effects. No acne, voice breaking, unwanted hair, menstrual cycles—"

"No periods?" Amelia exclaims.

"Women only menstruate if and when a couple decides to have kids. Then, the healers give them another shot that allows their bodies to get pregnant."

"You can only get pregnant if you get the shot?"

"Yep."

"So you've never had a period?"

"Oh, *ontzi*, no."

Amelia whistles. "Okay, I could get on board with that, I could." Loudly, she moans. "Why is this accent so annoying? If I repeat myself one more time, I'll going to scream, I will!"

She screams.

"You'll get used to it," I assure her.

She resumes her questions. "When can I get my shot? I'd like never having to shave again."

We find the pajama closet, and I'm blown away. This sleepwear is more stylish than anything I've worn during the day! I end up picking a sleep hoodie made of silky soft bamboo sherpa. The matching bamboo and hemp leggings are butter on my legs. While putting the hoodie on, I catch Amelia looking at my Memory Scars again.

When she shakes her head, I ask, "What?"

"It's just…"

"What?"

"Don't you wonder about them?"

I laugh lightly. "Not as much as you do."

"Seems like…"

When she doesn't finish, I prompt, "Mhmm?"

"Well…" she looks away from me and back to her own reflection. After brushing her hair, she still doesn't finish.

"Yes?" I ask.

"I just…"

"What? *Ontzi*, Amelia, it's not usually this hard to get something out of you. Spit it out."

"I know if I forgot all the painful things in my life, I wouldn't be who I am today, would I? It all… it made me who I am. If I forgot my experiences, I'd forget me, I would."

I don't know how to respond, so I don't. I'll add that to the ever-growing list of things to talk to my subconscious about.

When we finally emerge from the bathroom and head back towards the bedrooms, steam spills out around us. We slip through the doorway and make our way toward the beds. I chose one next to Amelia's that looks like a Formosian safari hut.

Quickly, I look at the time on the alarm clock beside the bed. It says it's eleven twenty, which means I still have a few more minutes before I'm supposed to meet Scout. As we enter our individual rooms, the digital curtains rise so we cannot see each other. Soft ambient music plays around me, so I cannot even hear Amelia. Three minutes later, I stand up as quietly as I possibly can. As I tiptoe to the cloud door (can you even call something without matter a door?), Amelia clears her throat.

She's standing just outside her little room, her digital curtain down. "Just so you know," she whispers, "Aker is wrong. Scout *does* like you. Up until a few hours ago, I couldn't understand anything he said, but I could tell."

I don't know how to respond to this, and I also don't know how to explain what I'm doing. I start talking hoping I'll think of something mid-sentence,

"Oh, um, I'm just going—"

"You don't have to explain yourself to me, you don't. Go have fun with Scout."

It's too dark to see her face, but I nod my appreciation for her words. Without responding, I slip through the misty veil.

"WHAT IS THIS PLACE?" I ask Scout.

"This," he answers, spreading his arms wide, "is *my* room."

As I see no bed or anything bedroom-like, I open my mouth to question him, but then it hits me. This is his *circus* room.

He has created it.

The whole room—from ceiling to floor—is white, not stark and sterile, but a warm, pleasant white. At the room's far end, there's an ivory podium with an alabaster, open-faced book statue fixed on top. There's nothing else.

"What is it?" I ask hesitantly.

Scout beckons me over to the book statue and tells me to put my hands on it.

"What will happen if I do?"

"'Tis a surprise," he states.

"A hint?" I ask, feeling somewhat nervous.

"Would you trust me if I said I know you will really enjoy it?"

I want to say no. I barely know the man—how does he know what I will or won't enjoy?

But the truth is, I do trust him. This whole week I've trusted this Ortusan with my life. And, for some crazy reason, I honestly believe that he does know what I would enjoy.

In answer to his question, I put my hands on the open-faced book and close my eyes. When I open them, I can't stop the gasp that leaves my mouth.

The whole room has drastically changed!

Now, it is filled with the things I love. The walls are my favorite color: olive green. The furniture is my favorite style: Igak Contemporary. There's an adorable Sanusian mid-era-inspired desk covered in all my favorite foods, and along the walls are pieces from my favorite artists. On one of the walls are simplistic drawings of each Senny flag that correlate with the languages I know. There are books—real books!—over in the corner. Although I want to know what they are, I also don't want to be pulled into anything by my Gift. I want to enjoy what the room has become. The walls are lined with beautiful shelves that hold little knickknacks of objects that hold some significance for me, including an exquisite red fox that almost looks real.

"This… it's beautiful."

"I think so too," Scout responds, and I notice he's investigating all the knickknacks. He looks at me inquisitively when he picks up a Vorbi holder in the shape of an octopus.

Sheepishly, I explain, "I'm fascinated by creatures that scare me."

"Why do octopuses scare you?"

"Their mouths are beaks." When he doesn't respond, I say again, slower, "Like bird beaks. It's horrifying."

He laughs and places the octopus back on the shelf.

"What does it look like when you're in here?" I ask him.

"I would enjoy showing you another time," he responds, and I can tell from the way he says it that there's a purpose in our meeting. He's not just showing me this room for fun.

"What's up?" I ask him. When he rubs his hand over his braid, I know I'm right that something is on his mind. "Is it bad?" I ask. "Is Amelia in trouble?"

"No, no. Nothing like that," he responds but turns away from me to study a piece of art. It's a mid-century, Rodruegez oil painting of various mushrooms. Each mushroom has female legs, and their caps are depicted to be their skirts. I don't know why, but I've always loved mushroom art.

It takes him a long time to say anything, but I wait. I'm used to being silent and don't mind looking around at my favorite things.

Finally, he clears his throat and begins. "Kansis, I have been trying to figure out how to tell you this for a long time. So… Well, I've decided to start this way: I was not fabricating false feelings when I told you that you were special."

Just like Amelia's comment about my memory scars, I don't know how to respond, so I don't even try. I just let him continue.

"Your Gift is incredibly rare; only one person every fifty years is born with it. And even though that makes you unique all on its own, that is not the source of your specialness. Avenir told me you discovered earlier this day that you are part of an ongoing social experiment."

My pulse spikes and I feel faint for a second. Avenir told Scout? That wasn't his business to tell! Before I can freak out anymore, however, Scout goes on. "Of the four people involved, your life, in particular, has been made tragic to prove that the Cupido is good. You have suffered in a way few Elusians have. And even though that makes you extraordinary, that, as well, is not the source of what makes you unique."

My heartbeat calms, but only slightly. What is he even talking about?

"You found Arkarian Story's daughter. For hundreds of years, people have been searching for her—but *you* found her. This, in addition, is not what makes you truly distinctive." Scout pauses for a moment to let out a breath. "Lastly, you are part of a prophecy that includes me and the Sixth Aevum; one that foretold we would find Arkarian Story together. Yet even this—even this prophecy—is not what makes you one-of-a-kind."

Scout turns to me then. I think he is waiting for me to interrupt, to stop him, to ask questions, but I can't. What he is saying is so preposterous I am having difficulty swallowing any of it. I feel like a mainframe so overloaded that it's malfunctioning. His words swirl around my mind, unwilling to settle. Prophecy. Sixth Aevum. Arkarian Story. They coil and whirl—every time I try to focus on even one thing he's said, they churn once more. I can't get my mouth to move or drag my eyes away from Scout, who has locked his onto mine.

He continues, "You are not special because of the things over which you have had no control. You couldn't pick your Gift, stop your parents from signing you up for a social experiment, plan to find Arkarian Story's daughter, or cause yourself to be a part of a prophecy. These circumstances were thrust upon you. No." He pauses and walks towards me. He reaches out both of his hands and places them on my arms.

I want to move; I try to move. But I'm still out of working order.

"No," Scout repeats. "Scoop, what makes you the singular most interesting and wonderful person I have ever met, is the *choices* you have made despite those happenstances. You chose to pursue your Gift even when it felt useless to you. You stayed strong in the face of a town-wide shame; you continued going to work and surviving. Many people would have cracked under that burden, but you did not. And when you found Amelia, you could have turned her in and, perchance, won some favor in your town, not to mention with the rest of the Hexum. You could have used her for your advantage, but instead you protect her like a mother. Mothers, after all, are the fiercest of creatures."

I keep thinking he's gotten me mixed up with some other person, but all these examples are from my own life. It's me. He's talking about *me*. But how could he be so wrong?

Finally, I gain control of my lips again. "I... I am not that person you're describing—"

"But you are," he states passionately. "You cannot see it, but I do. Blinders have been forced over your eyes, and I will not acknowledge them. I will not give them place."

I find myself sitting heavily in one of the oversized corduroy chairs. With effort, I replay everything Scout has just said in my mind. There are several things I don't understand.

So.

Thing number one.

"Did you say I'm part of a prophecy?"

When he doesn't respond, I look up to see he's wearing a mischievous grin. "I did," he answers in a deep voice.

"Wh—what prophecy?"

He hands me a piece of paper from his pocket.

"No, please, you read it." I don't want to be sucked away from this moment as my Gift strains to ignite.

"I think you should."

Obediently I reach for the paper and take a deep breath before allowing my eyes to focus on the first word.

Okay. Here we go. My vision fogs over. I am looking out of a different set of eyes...

Two men sit in a cavern with a small fire burning between them. The chamber is vast and covered from floor to ceiling with fiberglass storage containers, two of which are separated from the rest. Beside it lies a Hull. With such little light, the scene appears almost to be in black and white.

"We need to think carefully about this," one of the men says. "We just need a little more time." His hair seems white in the darkened light. His accent is of Pexun descent, but his hair is too light to be grey. Is he a Captusian?

"You know we've run out of time," the other man—a Pexun—responds. "We have to do this now before the sun rises. You will go back to sleep when it does, and it will be as if I never existed."

The first man looks across the fire. "Six years... and we're simply done. Our work is over."

"We have finished the Book of Instructions, and once the prophecy is written... yes. All will be as it should once again."

"What if our interfering somehow affects—"

The Pexun puts up his hand to stop the other man. "Arkarian, stop. For two years, we have been over every scenario. You know, as well as I do, this is the only way to ensure your future. Without this, your mission will fail. It's the only way." With a wave of his hand, a digital parchment and pen appear in his hands. He writes...

"In a new world looking for a leader of an old..." **We are doing the right thing.**

"Three will unite to awaken him..." **This keeps Arkarian safe. He has to survive.**

"The Reader will know the intentions of his Book..." **The words must be protected.**

"The Scion will bear the mark and help the Reader know the way..." **The descendant is essential; his Gift is the key.**

"The prophesy is the lifeblood of the Child whose birth wrought these words..." **A necessary sacrifice.**

"And their death will be one." **Death comes to all.**

The Pexun looks at Arkarian Story once more. "Goodbye, old friend."

The mournful voice fades as I blink my eyes as hard as possible. Scout's face fills my vision once more. I take a minute to gather my thoughts and then state softly, "I'm the Reader."

"Yes."

"Who are you?"

"The Scion."

"And who is the child?"

"The Sixth Aevum."

"Ah." Why am I so calm? I must still be glitching. How does Scout know for sure the Reader is me? I'm sure there are many other people with my Gift. I voice my doubts to him.

"As I said, you are the only person in the past fifty years born with this Gift," he responds.

"How do you know you are the Scion?"

"I am the last of Arkarian Story's descendants to have his family Gift," he answers confidently. "Arkarian Story had an elder son who bore a child who survived the Great Destruction."

"But it says the Sixth Aevum will die when the prophecy is fulfilled, and

Aevii can't die."

"Apparently, this one can."

What? But that would completely defeat the point of the Aevii! Everything Scout is saying is wrong—from his first word to this one.

"Why would the Sixth Aevum want Arkarian Story found if doing so will kill him?" I ask.

"I believe he plans on murdering the subhuman before he has the chance to awaken."

"Okay, fine. And how will you help me stay on course?"

He shrugs his shoulders. "I am not certain."

"How can we trust this prophecy? The guy who wrote it only wanted Arkarian Story found so he could keep him safe."

For the first time, Scout seems uncertain. "How do you mean?"

I quickly explain to him everything I had seen in my vision. "It was obvious the man cared for Arkarian Story. He wanted to protect him, and he wrote the prophecy to do so."

"No, I do not believe that is the case."

"I saw it in the peripherals of his mind, Scout. He tampered with the Book of Instructions, which is his way of protecting Arkarian Story. If we find Arkarian, we're accomplishing the prophet's will."

"What are you proposing? That we leave Arkarian Story hidden?"

"If we're the only ones who can find him, doesn't that mean that if we don't find him, he'll stay hidden forever?"

Scout clicks his tongue. "Ah, but that is just it. We are not the only ones who can find him. We are just the ones who are meant to find him." I stare at him, and he adds, "And the Sixth Aevum has no intention of dying. He has been planning this for over a hundred and fifty years. Arkarian Story will not be awoken."

"You're wrong." The statement comes out as a whisper, and I drop my head into my hands. I feel so, so tired.

Scout walks across to the overstuffed chair and squats down at my feet. "I trust the Sixth Aevum," he says calmly.

"I'm not talking about that," I say, but the words feel heavy coming out of my mouth. "You're wrong about me. All of those things you said... I'm not strong like that. I can't do this."

"You have only seen weak versions of yourself, Scoop, because that is all you have been allowed to see. But here at the circus, you can be someone else—you can be yourself."

"You don't know me," I push, looking down at him. This kind Ortusan makes me feel safe and seen and understood, but he's wrong. "I'm a coward, and I have three Memory Scars on my back to prove it. Instead of working through my pain, I erased it. For years I have been so hurt that Aker wouldn't marry me. I have felt so sorry for myself, and never once did I consider his perspective. And then today, I find out it wasn't even his fault that we aren't married—"

"Oh, it is his fault indeed."

"No, it wasn't," I argue miserably. "Was it his fault that my blood wasn't in him? Was it his fault that Mirindiss' was? No."

"Your mate chose not to marry you," he states firmly. "Blood transfusion or not, he should have honored and protected you by marrying you. Love is the choice to put someone above yourself no matter what. Feelings be damned."

"But that's not how love works," I press. "Two people come together because the Cupido—"

"A person can love someone else without their blood being forced into their veins. People, believe it or not, loved each other for millennia without technology."

"Yes, but—"

"No, Kansis. You are wrong. Aker should love you, blood or not. He should marry you, blood or not. And the fact that he cannot see this makes my blood turn to rust. You deserve to be loved because of *you*, not because his blood tells him he *must* love you."

I smile sadly. This man's capacity for optimism is inspiring. It's… life-giving. But it's also incorrect. "That would be nice," I finally respond. "But that's just not how love works."

Scout's gaze is fierce as he argues, "But it is." He stands abruptly, and I feel obligated to get up too. "Aker does not love you because he *chooses* otherwise. It is that simple. The Blood Transfusion will be a placebo—it will only make him think he does. But mark my words; if he cannot love you—really love you—now, he will never love you. And post-transfusion, when he does say those words, they will be hollow, I assure you."

I don't know how to respond. Why is it that everyone in the world says one thing, but Amelia and Scout—perfect strangers—say the opposite, and all I want to do is believe them? I want them to be right. I want to be the version they see of me.

But I, and the rest of the world, know that it's fiction. And even though I know it, and I know that *they* know it… I'm going to choose to believe Amelia and Scout. I'm going to believe the lie. I'll be the strong person they think I am.

Ontzi. My piteousness knows no bounds.

"Okay," I say slowly. I know I should tell him that I'm leaving with Aker after the mission—I should ask him about getting a eutsi for Winzer's Gift—but I can't seem to form the words. If I do, they're real. If I say them, it means that I'm actually leaving Amelia and Scout very soon.

Too soon.

Instead, I ask, "So, what do we need to do?"

As I sink down into my bed, I close my eyes tight. After only sixty seconds or so, I take out my druzy quartz pendant—my fantasizing piffy. The small moon that encircles my little tech almost sparkles in the dim light. I hadn't realized until just now that I haven't used it in the last couple of days.

I think about the world I have created using my piffy pendent. A world where I have a husband and two daughters, and a successful life in Depalo. I think about everything that Dream Aker and I have experienced and finally, *fully* realize that it's not real. It will never be real. For the first time in two years, I take the pendant off and place it on the bedside table.

Grabbing the pocket watch, I stare into the predatory gaze of the raven. Wondering what it is hunting, I rub my thumb against the ridges of the etching.

What I have—these friends—is better than any life I could have made up on my own. This is a life worth fighting for.

I always knew there was nothing wrong with you and only ever something wrong with Aker.

Yeah, you and Scout would get along well. Look, there's so much I want to unpack from the day, but let's move on to the next portion of our time, where I ask you again how you talk to the Sixth Aevum, what your relationship is with him, and who you really are.

I am a part of you.

A part of me that I found on my twelfth birthday?

On your twelfth—You… Do you remember that?

Of course! There I was, crying myself to sleep because I'd had the worst birthday in the world, not knowing that my real worst birthday was, in fact, going to happen three years later. My dad had forgotten, and my mom was working. I had tried to do something fun with Clista, but she was too close to her Announcement Ceremony and couldn't care less about her kid sister. So I had just cried myself to sleep when I heard you say, *Stop crying.* It was such a sweet introduction to such an encouraging friendship.

Did I say that? I don't remember it happening that way.

Those were your first words.

How did you know it was me and not just you thinking to yourself?

I don't know… you just felt different.

I don't think so.

What do you mean? How else would I have known it was you?

I honestly have no idea.…Maybe I am the type of Duogift that only awakens once you come of age. There are Gifts like that.

That's true. …Okay.

Okay what?

Okay, I've waited long enough. How do you talk to the Sixth Aevum? I need to know.

Kansis—

No. Tell me. I've waited, and I need to know now.

…

…

…

Well?

I'm not allowed to tell you.

Who is keeping you from telling me?

The Sixth Aevum.

The Si—He personally… You talk to him personally?

No.

…

…

Okay, then what?

…

…

Tell me!

I've known about the prophecy.

…You have?

Yes. I've known for a while. Because of it, you're important to the Sixth Aevum. He hired someone who checks in on you to make sure you're safe. And that person... well, they talk to me.

Why? Why you?

So you wouldn't have to be burdened with the prophecy before it was necessary.

Who is it? Who do you talk to?

...I can't tell you.

Why?

I was told not to.

Who *are* you? What are you? How do you have these outside relationships? *Ontzi*, are you conscious when we're not talking? Do you have form, or are you just in my head? Are you me, or are you someone else? How—

Kansis.

WHAT? What is going on?!

My whole purpose is to keep you safe. I speak to this person and give them pertinent information concerning your safety and well-being. I need you to trust me.

Trust you?! I didn't realize I had a reason to distrust you until now!

Should I go then?

Go?

Yes.

You... you can leave?

I can if that's what you want.

Where would you go?

Nowhere. I'd just leave you alone.

...

Is that what you want?

...

Kansis?

You... Are you going to leave me?

I should.

...

...

...

Kansis, I will stay if you ask. I will leave if you ask.

...

...

You're threatening to leave me just because I'm asking questions?

I'm not threatening anything! Look, I'm not going anywhere unless you ask me to. But there are certain things I can't talk about, at least for now. You'll have to be okay with that.

You can't lie to me.

What do you mean?

There's no one in this world that I trust explicitly but you. You are my only stability. And what makes it so sad—what makes me needing you so utterly pathetic—is that I just love myself. It's disgusting—vanity to a nauseating degree. And even though I know that... I still need you. So I *have* to know I can trust you—that you're not lying to me.

...

...

It's not vanity.

Let's call a cell a cell. I both love and need myself—there's no other title to describe me better than vain.

I disagree.

Okay, fine. What would you call it?

I have my own mind and my own choices, and I chose on my own accord to like you. We are connected... but we are also separate. It is not the love of self... It... it's communal love.

Ha! That is a better-sounding description, for sure. Inaccurate, but it does feel better, doesn't it?

If you think I'm just going to stand here and let you talk about yourself like that—

See, and that's why I need you! I need you to lie to me—just as Amelia and Scout do—and I'll go on blindly believing it... as long as you don't lie to me about other things.

Okay. I won't. But you have to be okay with me not answering all of your questions.

Deal.

Deal.

...I love you.

I love you too. It's always better...

...When we're together.

10 DAYS UNTIL QUINTRALL

Pexus

Pypen

I AM NOT EXACTLY certain when it started, but it seems Scout's new favorite way to wake me up is by slapping me across the face. I cannot say I enjoy this way of meeting the new day, but there is nothing much I can do about it… except to forcibly seek my vengeance.

Instantly alert, I grab his arm, swing him over my shoulder and throw him on the bed. This is a feat, considering Scout usually bests me when we wrestle. Confidence surges through me. Bouncing off the bed, Scout kicks off the wall to spring at me. I am not as prepared as I had hoped, and we crash to the floor. Using the momentum, I shove him upward with my legs. He does not go far and jumps back onto my stomach. The breath is crushed out of me, and I am rendered defenseless. Taking advantage of my weakness, Scout leaps onto my chest and pins my arms down with his legs—humiliation at its finest as he begins poking my forehead with his forefinger.

I bellow for backup, but none appears. Finally, he relents and lets me up as his laughter fills the room.

"Someone is in a good mood?" I comment as I catch my breath.

"The sun is shining, you and Merayal made it back safely and undetected, we outsmarted Femme, and I told Kansis about the prophecy—what more could I want in a day?"

Honing in on his last statement, I ask, "You told Kansis?"

"Last night right before your return."

I had been wondering if he would confide in her. "What did she say?"

A smirk covers his features once more as he looks at my bare head. "Stop staring!" I grumble and throw on my hood.

"You look so different without your dreads," he responds, laughing. "Why not regrow them? No one can ever take away the fact that you put in the effort to grow them naturally the first time."

"I wish not to talk about it," I answer defensively. "Simply tell me what

Kansis said."

Still chortling to himself, he answers, "She did not say much but received it well. She just asked a few questions."

"Was she at peace with it all?"

"Yes, truly so." Suddenly Scout raises his hand to stop the conversation.

"Is that your Suus?" I ask quickly. "Do not answer it—the Guardians may have it tracked."

Scout shakes his head. "The Aevii are not tracked." Turning away from me, he answers, "Sixth Aevum, hallowed be your name." He nods his head a few times as his eyes grow wide. "What? How can—" he stops. "That is amazing... Do you want—" More nodding. "Wait, what happened to the Ju—" another interruption. "But what about the circus?" Pause. "Will we meet him there?" He begins to pace around the room. "We will leave immediately, then." He runs his hand over his braid. Pause. "Perfect. We will see you in Silenda."

"Silenda?" I question in the background, bewildered as to what their conversation might concern.

"That is unbelievable," he goes on. "Oh, yes, I am certain you are busy—my apologies. Thank you."

"Silenda? What? What is going on?" I ask the instant his call ends.

A huge smile takes over Scout's lips. "We just got asked to interview," he says slowly, "for the main entertainment on the Saturday night," dramatic pause, "of the Quintrall."

I am too shocked to say anything. The Quintrall meets every five years to discuss political matters and make decisions to better the future of our world. The event lasts an entire weekend; three days in which the whole world is permitted to take a holiday. Friday night is usually light entertainment and country-honoring ceremonies. Saturday day, political matters are discussed and decided. Saturday night is the main event. People from all over the world pay one to ten kra to attend the Saturday night entertainment. This year's Quintrall is in a mere ten days.

"H-how?" is all I can stutter.

"The Sixth Aevum heard of the auditions and put our name in the draw. We were allotted a spot for next night. We will perform our entire act for them, and they will decide within the next twenty-four hours. Imagine if we could land the audition and perform at the Quintrall..."

He need not finish the statement. It would be the most epic event of our career, if not our lives. "But what happened to the June Bugs?" I ask. For the past year, they have been promoted as the upcoming Saturday night entertainment at the Quintrall.

"The Sixth Aevum said they were in a terrible vehicle accident in Jukantytär—they were all killed." His excitement wanes as his eyes grow thoughtful. My prancing lion tattoo glows orange. He is anxious.

"What is it?" I ask.

"How could there be an accident when the DPPD runs the system?"

About a decade ago, the Railroad system was adopted in all the capitals and major cities throughout the Hexum. With the exception of Guardian vehicles, there are no longer independent cars being driven about the city. All non-Guardian vehicles drive themselves on tracks woven throughout the cities. The Data Processing and Programming Department (DPPD) does not make mistakes.

Scout takes a deep breath and looks at me. "Do you think the Sixth Aevum had them killed?"

That would be terrifying. "He could have."

We allow the silence to fill the room as we brood on our own dark thoughts.

Scout, always the one to emerge to the light first, asks slowly, "Well... should we tell the troops about the audition?"

The dancers' squealing is almost unbearable. "Calm yourselves!" I yell over the clamor. Sound in the conference room echoes off the walls, and I bet all the guests in this hotel can hear their excitement.

"We leave by the end of the day," Scout announces. The exhilaration in the room is tangible.

"What about the patrons who purchased tickets for the other three days we were meant to be here?" Allerish asks. "They are going to be very disappointed, they will."

"The financial team will make certain ticketholders are refunded their pre-purchased tickets," Scout answers.

"Is that where Pypen's dreads went?" Krael calls out. "He sent them out as sympathy presents?"

The group explodes with laughter. It was not a funny joke—everyone is just in a good mood. Grumpily, I put my hood back on.

Chuckling, Scout finishes, "We will perform next night in Perdidi, and then we are going to Silenda! Maybe we can find an octopus to be Pypen's new hair." More laughter. "On an important note," he begins seriously, calming the crowd, "after last night, we know the Guardians are tracking our Suuses and dispensing their Gift-power to keep us from communicating. Be careful of what you speak of via your Suus, and keep all Arkahunting conversations away from them.

"In addition, we have agreed to allow some undercover Guardians into the circus. Be on the lookout for them. I will buy drinks for whoever finds them first."

Whispering erupts. Our group loves a good competition.

"Whether you are here at the hotel or at the circus, make sure you are so very careful concerning what you discuss with one another. We are on high alert until we leave Initium. So, pack up your things. You are all dismissed."

As the company loudly begins clattering out of the room, Scout turns to me. "Did you get my joke about your hair? An octopus because it is Silenda's emblem? Do you see the humor?"

I roll my eyes. "No. It simply is not a laughing matter."

The Chameleons have turned into squirrels and are chasing each other around the room, clearly needing to burn off some excitement before they settle down to pack their things. I also find myself lingering, not quite ready to leave. I sink onto a chair, my mind still reeling over the possibility of performing at the Quintrall. And even if we do not perform, "To even audition!" I mumble. The groups that audition for the Quintrall become world-famous simply for being considered. Our popularity is going to explode over these next few days.

Suddenly, four squirrels run up and down my legs, and I yell in surprise. Brushing them away, I command, "Go and get ready, you hooligans!" As they scuttle out, chattering to one another, I try to let the reality of what is happening sink in: we are all about to become interterritorial stars.

"Thank the stars we found Merayal and her Gift," Scout says wistfully.

Merayal's Gift...

A sudden dawning hits me, and I feel like a *patka* that I have not seen it until now. Pods do not possess Gifts. How can Merayal have a Progift if she is from Senex? I must be mistaken... but how can I be? Is there any way a Pod *could* have a Gift?

I must ask Kansis.

"Forget not that you are busy this morning," Scout says pointedly, and I look up to see I am the last person remaining with him in the room. "You have plenty of time to finish before we leave."

Knowing to what he is referring, I curtly nod and heave myself off the chair.

But before I go back to the circus, I have one more errand to run…

"It will only be a minute," I tell Kansis' mate, the surly Aker. "I speak with complete honesty when I say I need just two minutes of her time."

When Aker does not respond right away, Amelia asks, "Oh, what does it matter if he talks to her really quick?"

It has been odd understanding Amelia for the first time, but I am certainly glad Scout retrieved the eutsi for her. She is quite witty in my opinion.

The Pod and the Pexun man scowl at each other for a moment, then Aker nods reluctantly, permitting me to have a private conversation with his mate.

I do not go far, taking only a few steps to be out of hearing range, and Kansis follows. When I turn to her, she has a quizzical look on her face. I am certain she is wondering why I need to talk to her specifically.

With no explanation, I ask, "Can a Pod have a Gift?"

She seems surprised at the question but readily answers, "No, they've not been allowed them."

"Are there any exceptions?"

Shaking her head, she answers again, "No."

"No special requests?"

Confused, she chuckles and answers, "No, no. Not at all."

"But has there been any testing or trials or anything like that?"

At this, Kansis suddenly looks abashed.

"Well?" I push.

Clearing her throat, she answers softly, "I'm still going to say no. Pods are not given Gifts. The archaic act of awakening the Gician Particle within humans hasn't happened for hundreds of years."

When she does not go on, I press. "But…?"

"But…" she pauses and then states hastily, "Now, this is just hearsay—Ward legend, really—"

"Kansis," I say kindly. "I will not share what you tell me."

Nodding, she goes on. "While in school, there was this story—told by students, not professors, you know—that some of the first patients to be tested with the gene therapy were Pods. None of them made it through the testing, so the Medisacerdos turned to the criminals in Novus for experimentation. But…" She looks at me guiltily—as if she has done something wrong herself.

"But?"

"But… it's said… that they… that some Medisacerdos *still* experiment on Pods… Gene and Gician Particle studies that they don't want to try on metahumans."

"Is it true?"

"I don't know." Looking back to where Amelia stands with Aker, watching us, she adds, "I sure hope not."

"Have any of those Pods ever escaped?"

Shrugging her shoulders, she answers, "The official answer is no… but one of my professors told me there had been many hidden escapes over the centuries."

"Escapes by Pods with Gifts?"

"Maybe. I don't know. The professor never specified. Anyway, why do you ask?"

Painting on an award-winning smile, I assure her, "Just curious, Pet."

"Was that all you wanted to know?"

"Indeed," I reply and walk her back to her antsy mate.

As I head for the circus, I ponder Kansis' answers. So Merayal *could be* a Pod. But if she is… she only escaped after being a product of experimentation—tortured even. Is that the dark world of which she spoke?

Who *is* Merayal Kapu?

Tent maintenance is one of my duties, but I get around to it less often than I should. It takes no more than an hour to go around all our tents and renew them back to a pristine state, yet I avoid the task like Captus.

But, my feelings aside, a spruce up is what the circus requires. Zjon and Penryn remind me every time we perform in a new city, but I have not found the time… Or, more accurately, I have not *made* the time.

I wish to think more on what Kansis has said, and to ponder what this might mean about Merayal, but as I work, it is the Pexun Guardian Femme's words that haunt me. In each room I renew, I hear her voice: *For these criminals, their punishment would be close to one hundred and twenty years from life. And, as you know, a life sentence of over fifty years also means a Gift stripping. With a sentence like one hundred and twenty years, that would also mean a Duogift stripping.*

My body grows hot and then cold as I recall her question: *Wouldn't it be bloodsucking to know that an entire crew of entertainers were, in one fell swoop, stripped of their Gifts with their lives cut in half? Do you speak on behalf of all of them?*

Do I speak on behalf of them? Who am I to do such a thing? The weight of my responsibility that Femme has brought to light is heavier than I can bear this day.

The circus is already opening for our next performance when I get caught up in a conversation with Thykas about redesigning the interior of his room. By the time I get back to renewing the rooms, the tent is swimming with patrons, and it warms my blood. I love being around circus-goers. Regulars and newcomers alike step inside our tent to be mystified, terrified, entertained, and whisked away to a new world. They remind me why I love my job so much.

When I am almost done with my rounds, a voice behind me calls, "Mister?"

Turning around, I am shocked to see a young Captusian girl. She must be only twelve or thirteen, and her blonde hair makes her look pale and sickly. I have never seen a Captusian before with my own eyes, and seeing her now seems surreal. I wonder how she even got inside the circus. She must have eluded payment somehow, breaking in without our front staff's knowledge—everyone knows Captusians are law-breaking barbarians.

"What are you doing here?" I ask angrily.

"Mister, I lose my parents. You able to tell me how to get to courtyard?" She shivers as she looks around. "I lost for over a hour in these rooms."

"A likely story," I snap. I did not even know Captusians could speak in complete sentences.

The girl takes a deep breath and asks again, "You able to tell me where courtyard located?" The Captusian accent is almost unbearable to listen to—squawky and disjointed. "You truly think I believe that you came here with a sweet, innocent Captusian family, and you just happened to get lost? What are you *actually* doing here?"

Tears well up in her eyes, and she turns to leave.

I move out of her way so she cannot touch me. "Where do you think you are going?" I demand.

She does not answer, and I feel obligated to follow as she walks away. I will not let this little Captusian out of my sight—she will not take advantage of my circus if I can help it.

As the girl makes another wrong left turn, she sees some patrons. She asks them the same question she posed to me, and they respond appropriately: one calls her a "dirty Cap", one spits at her, one laughs, and the rest walk by as if no one has spoken.

What I am certain are fake tears fall down her cheeks as she glances back at me. Seven more wrong turns and four more groups of patrons later, and still no one has told her how to get to the courtyard.

What *I* want to know is how she got inside our tent. As I have never encountered this type of situation in my life, I do not know what to do. Where are the undercover Guardians, and why have they done nothing?

After another several minutes of watching the Captusian's aimless wandering, I decide upon my course of action. Quickly, I call the local Guardians and inform them of the Captusian loose in the circus. They ask me if she has done anything, to which I reply, "She is *in* the circus, is she not? How am I supposed to know what she could have accomplished before I spotted her?"

The Guardian is understanding, assuring me they will send over a unit to collect her. Throughout this interaction, I speak loud enough for the Captusian girl to hear. She fake-cries even harder.

As we pass by Keleigh's door, Merayal walks out. Her face is covered with her usual disinterested sneer, but when she sees the young Captusian girl, she stops in her tracks.

"You… able to… tell me… where courtyard… located?" The Captusian can barely get the words out between her sobs.

Motherly tenderness fills Merayal's features. "Of course, Sweetheart."

Even crying, the Captusian eyes Merayal warily as if she does not trust her genuineness.

Merayal juts one of her hips out and places her hand on it. With her other hand, she waves around the corridor. "Haven't had much luck with the rest of the *wayas,* huh?" She wears a mischievous grin.

Even though the young Captusian's eyebrows are creased with suspicion, her mouth twitches into a small smile.

When the Captusian does not answer, Merayal goes on, "It's like they say, *wayas* live in the blind world. The fact that they can't see what a beautiful, brave young woman you are, is proof."

I huff from my watchful post several meters away, but all distrust leaves the Captusian girl's face as she gazes at Merayal in awe. "You is Pexun, and you speak this way?"

"My hair may be grey, but I am no Pexun," Merayal states, face stern for the first time. "Are you here with more Captusians?"

"No, I adopted four years ago by Sanusians."

Merayal seems taken aback. Her eyes glaze over as if she is somewhere else entirely. Finally, as if snapping out of a trance, she asks, "You were adopted? How did you get out?"

The Captusian rubs her hands together and takes a small step towards Merayal. "A Silentar come to my village and speak into minds of all kids fifteen and younger. He ask all kids if we want to go with him. He promise us we safe. I follow his instructions, and he help me to get out."

A sad smile covers Merayal's face. "You were fortunate."

"I love couple that adopts me. All of their family cut them off because they allow ugly Cap like me to join their family, but they no care. I never possess a real family before."

"If they love you so much, where are they?" Merayal asks, clearly upset. "They must know that something bad will happen to you if you're alone."

"They required to fulfill business here in Initium. They possess no one to leave at home with me because none of their friends lets me stay with them. They bring me here to have fun day."

"Where are your parents now?"

"That my problem. I lost them. I try to find the courtyard and wait for them to find me."

Merayal sighs. "Well, let me help you find them, Honey."

As they walk away, I surreptitiously follow. This is the kindest I have ever heard Merayal speak to anyone, so for her to speak so fondly and copiously with a Captusian is inconceivable!

Merayal leads the young girl through the maze of kiosks. As she emerges into the openness of the courtyard, I stop a few meters behind, still watching closely.

"I don't see any Sanusians..." Merayal says as they scan the crowd. "Oh! Look over there—is that them?" she asks, pointing at a couple with pale brown hair hovering anxiously by the front gate.

"That my parents!" the girl shouts. Turning to Merayal, she says, "Thank you so much for your help."

"Of course," Merayal responds with a smile.

The girl takes a few steps away, stops, then turns back to Merayal. "Why you help me?"

A look of undeserved affection for this little Cap fills Merayal's eyes as she smiles wider. "Because your life matters as much as any other person on Elusis. Your hair color does not define you. Go in health and prosperity." Closing the distance between them, Merayal takes one of the girl's hands and places it on her forehead.

Shocked, the girl rips her hand away. In a harsh whisper, she asks, "Notre Corpse?"

"No," Merayal answers solemnly. "But I have the utmost respect for you."

"Sala!" two voices scream over the hubbub of the circus. The two Sanusians must have spotted the Captusian child, for they are now running in our direction.

When they reach her, they throw their arms around the girl—an affectionate show that the Cap does not deserve. The woman is weeping. "We didna know where ye got ter, Sala," the man says, tears in his eyes.

"I lost," the little Captusian speaks from within the embrace of the Sanusian couple. "This Pexun help me find you," she explains as they release her, waving a hand towards Merayal.

"T'ank you so, so much, you are a mighty good sam," the woman says, bowing respectfully to the Pexun woman. Merayal returns the Sanusian greeting solemnly.

"It was my pleasure," Merayal states. "You have a beautiful daughter."

"T'ank yer again," the man repeats, and he turns the two women around to leave.

The Captusian stays rooted in place, staring at Merayal. "You strangest Pexun I ever meet," she observes.

"And you're the *bravest* girl I have ever met," Merayal responds.

Seemingly out of nowhere, three Pexun Guardians stride up to the Sanusians and their little Captusian. I have been so engrossed in the exchange before me that I have not even noticed their arrival.

"What's going on?" the Guardian asks the Sanusian man. "Is that Cap bothering you?"

"No sir," the Sanusian replies respectfully, "T'is here be me daughter. We adopted her a few years back."

"You adopted a *Captusian* girl?" the second Guardian asks with a sneer. "Good cover story, isn't it? Use the Cap to do your dirty work and then claim her as your daughter."

"I must ask," the first Guardian questions, "where did you buy her? I hear they're almost impossible to afford, aren't they?"

"You can't talk to them like that!" Merayal yells, her eyes alight with the anger I thought was only reserved for me.

The first Guardian glances at her. "Don't get involved, Sweetheart. You might not want to drink the blood you draw."

"We would simply like ter take our daughter and leave," the Sanusian woman states bravely.

"I'm sure you would," the second Guardian retorts. "We got a call saying this Cap was causing a disturbance among the staff and patrons. Let's head down to the station, shall we, and we can talk it over there."

"But we have done not'ing wrong," the Sanusian man replies.

The second Guardian laughs again. "We can sort it out at the station."

"They've done nothing worth investigation!" Merayal shouts. "You leave them alone!"

The first Guardian nods to the second, who looks in Merayal's direction. Within a heartbeat, Merayal falls to the floor, unconscious.

"Now, let's go. Don't make a scene," the second Guardian is saying to the Sanusian couple. "We can do this the easy or hard way. Up to you. Don't try to fight me, wise guy; you'll regret it."

The Sanusian man closes his eyes, seemingly ready to ignite a Gift. The Guardians take power stances, preparing to fight.

"No, please!" the Sanusian woman shouts. "We'll go wit ye." She whispers something to her mate and the Captusian girl. "We'll go wit'out a fight. We've done not'ing wrong."

"We'll see about that," the first Guardian growls and shoves the girl in front of him.

As the group heads out of the circus, I run over to where Merayal is lying. I pick her up gently and renew her consciousness. She comes to and rubs her eyes. When she opens them, it takes her a minute to register my face. But the moment she does, she is up and pushing me away from her.

"Did you see where they went?" she asks angrily.

"Where who went?" I ask, feigning ignorance. I am not entirely certain why I do this—of course I know of what she speaks. But, for some reason, I do not wish for her to know my part in all that transpired.

"Never mind," she murmurs and looks around the area frantically.

"Merayal, let me help you," I offer. "What has caused you to be so upset?"

Her agitated gaze finally lands on me. "Do you really want to help," she hesitates as if she cannot bring herself to say any more, then slowly adds, "*me*? Can you help me?"

"Yes. What is it?"

"There was a young Captusian girl innocently walking around the circus, doing nothing wrong, and then Guardians showed up out of nowhere saying that someone had reported that she was causing a disturbance, but she didn't—I swear—and then they took her into custody even though she did nothing wrong." She finally takes a breath. "Can you do something to help her?"

My blood cells feel as if they are being split in two. For some reason, I find I want to aid Merayal, but I do not want to help a Captusian. However, I see this for what it is: an olive branch. She is giving me this opportunity as a test.

"Yes. I will call the local station and tell them the Captusian caused no disturbance and should be released."

A relieved smile crosses her face. "You will? Oh, thank you. She was so sweet and did nothing wrong; I can attest to it if you need. Should I stay—no, just let me know how it goes. Yeah, okay. Thanks…" As if she hears herself, she stops. Looking at me from the corner of her eye, she says again, "Thank you, Pypen."

I try to think of what to say—I want to question her kindness toward the Captusian, but I just stare at her, unable to collect my thoughts.

Suddenly, her expression turns sour. "I told you not to look at me like that."

Snapping out of my reverie, hot blood pumps through my veins. Every time she shows even a hue of openness, she slams the door in my face when I have done nothing to deserve it. *Matza.* We are sorting this out here and now.

"What did you mean when you said I wanted to be more than friends with you?" I ask angrily.

Although she seems surprised by the question, the scowl stays predominant on her features. "Did Thykas tell you I said that?"

"Well?" I push, ignoring her question. "What did you mean? What is 'more than friendship'?"

Her voice is tinged with anger. "Don't pretend you don't know."

"I honestly do not," I respond.

As if she cannot tell if I am being serious or not, she answers hesitantly, "Love."

"Love? Merayal, how could I love you? I do not even know you. Love is garnered over years of dedicated friendship and—"

"No," she interrupts, frustrated. "As in… I know you want me to be *in love* with you." I still do not understand this distinction, and my face must express that because she rolls her eyes and adds, "Like mates. You want to mate with me."

"Mate with you?" I declare, exasperated. "*Matza*, Merayal, about what do you speak?"

"I see the way you look at me, Pypen. I see how you want me, how you lust after my body. I can see straight through you."

I laugh loudly. "Lust after—Merayal, if you understood Novian life at all, you would know that I have been antzuaized."

She barks a laugh. "What in the universe does that mean?"

I take a deep breath. This is it. This is the moment I should expose that I know she is a Pod. But is this the right time? Perhaps I need to gain more of her trust first.

At the fury in her eyes, however, I realize that there is no way I can gain her trust, so I might as well share my cards.

"*Antzuaized,*" I repeat. "It means made sterile. Any hormones that would make me want to..." I swallow uncomfortably, but make myself finish, "*mate with you have been made dormant.*"

Merayal scoffs. "Oh, sure they have."

"It is what is done to the widows and widowers of Novus..." I hesitate dramatically, "And you would know that if you were, indeed, a Novian widow."

Merayal's brows furrow, then she visibly winces back like I have just landed a blow.

"I know you are a Pod," I announce. "There is no need to deny it, I know for certain." Her eyes keep darting to the left and then back to me—she is pondering my words. As she sorts out her thoughts, I add, "And I have told no one. Not even Scout."

After studying me for a moment, she asks, "How do you know for certain?"

"You have made slips, and I am a clever man."

"But I have a Gift," she hedges.

"I have a theory about that as well," I answer, "and I would love to hear the story one day."

The tiniest of smiles play at her lips. "So you feel nothing for me?" she asks.

"Was that an admission? Am I correct?"

Smirking sardonically, she states, "I thought you said you were certain, clever as you are."

"Will you confirm or deny?"

"But that wouldn't be very fun," she states, and now there's a small twinkle in her eye.

"Listen... I know... I am aware that Xoana Kapu was not your real mother."

This causes her to sober.

"From your own admission, your family is dead," I go on, "and... if I am assuming correctly, you never had a mate. I say all of that to attest to this: No one in the world knows who you really are but me."

When she takes a step back, I take one forward. "Allow me to earn your trust," I implore her. "It may or may not seem like it, but I am for you. I can be a friend if you would but permit it."

Anger flashes in her eyes again, "Answer my question first: do you feel anything for me?"

"I cannot," I admit. "I can visibly see that you are a gorgeous human being with desirable attributes. I can appreciate your beauty, but I do not and cannot have physical reactions, hormone releases, or feelings towards you. Towards anyone."

"So you…" she falters, but then rushes on, "so you really just want to be my friend? Nothing else? You don't want my body?"

I step back, shocked at her words. "Merayal, there is no need to be so graphic. No, I do not want your…" Taking a deep breath, I assert, "I want nothing from you."

Then, something happens that I did not expect nor think I would ever behold. For the first time since I met her, Merayal Kapu smiles genuinely at me. It is charming and open and sweet, and I am surprised to find something stirring within me. Something I have just told her does not and *cannot* exist in me.

Shoving the feeling aside, I return the smile.

Sighing, she looks back to where the Captusian disappeared. "So… you'll call the Guardians?"

"Indeed. Now… to my question. Are you from Senex?"

Eyeing me, she slowly answers, "Yes."

Smiling at her, I say, "I cannot wait to hear your story."

"And I *may* share it… in time."

"The deal is struck."

She turns to walk away, but before she disappears around a pastry kiosk, she turns back. "Thank you…" she smirks at me and adds, "Friend."

The warm feeling stirs again. "You are welcome," I respond.

I watch her walk away, my blood belabored and hazy. I understand not how she thought I had wanted to… to mate with her. If that had been something I wanted from her, I would have actually had to enjoy her company. From the moment I met her, she has been nothing but a noxious nuisance. Why would I want to marry someone like that?

In addition, it would be illegal for me to marry her. She must not know that only those from the same territory are allowed to marry. Now, had she been an

Ortusan and I was interested in her being my mate, I would have shared my intentions with her. I would have started the courting process. Certainly, I have enough compensation that I could pay for a Blood Transfusion if I so desire.

How preposterous she thought those were my intentions! No, if I were ever to re-marry, it would be with someone whom I could make happy and who would seek to make me happy... Even laying her Pexun heritage aside, neither of those would come to fruition with Merayal.

With all that standing true, I do not understand these feelings coursing through my veins. The week after Cazney died, I went to the Widowing Association to discuss my options. At the time, I had no intention of re-marrying and was encouraged to get antzuaized. They said the injection would last a decade. It has only been eight years, but now I wonder if its effects are beginning to fade.

Because as I stand alone, here in the belly of the bustling circus, I find myself attracted to my new Pexun friend. I shiver. Knowing these feelings will do nothing but cause me unnecessary trouble, I bury them deeper and deeper until, as I walk away, I no longer even notice them.

WHEN I MAKE THE call to the Guardian Station to retract my statement, they care not. I am not certain whether my efforts have changed the Captusian's lot whatsoever, but at least I have done as Merayal asked.

When I enter the office, Scout looks up from his desk. "Have you finished?"

It takes me a moment to understand that he is referring to my duty of room restoration. I shake my head. I hate that I cannot feel my dreads hitting my temples as I do so. "The tent maintenance is not quite done," I answer Scout.

"What has happened to delay you?" Scout asks me.

"Scout!" Emerly shouts as he runs into our office, interrupting any answer I may have given.

Seeing his pale, drawn face, Scout hurriedly asks, "Levels balanced?"

"I would like to talk to you in private, wouldn't I?" he declares, glancing at me and then down at the ground.

Heat rushes up my neck. "Have I wronged you, Emerly?"

"No," he answers promptly. "Nothing like that, Pip. But I want to talk about the Rogue Superior, don't I? And I know how it upsets you."

I roll my eyes and sit down at my desk, commanding my Suus to bring up the schematics of Perdidi—our next performance location before we reach our audition. "Carry on; I will study something that *matters* whilst you discuss."

Not waiting for another second, Emerly's words tumble out of his mouth. "Scout, something happened to me this morning, didn't it? I went to Knimble to ask him more questions about the Rogue Superior, and what he told me… It's changed everything, it has. The Superior has this crazy plan to bring his children to a place where we will be like true Aevii—we will never die there—and there is only joy, peace, and love in that place. But the only way you can get there is if you die—" Emerly throws his hands up. "*Vaigín*," he swears, "I hear how this is all sounding, but it was amazing, Scouty, it was."

I try hard not to scoff and look pointedly at the schematics before me.

"Listen, it's like he opened up my eyes to see these things that I've always known," Emerly goes on. "And I know that the Rogue Superior is real and that he is who Knimble says he is. So… so I said that.

"And after I told Knimble that I believed in the Rogue Superior, something… changed… something *shifted* inside of me. I… Scout, I spoke with the Rogue Superior. I *heard* him, except it wasn't in my head, was it? It wasn't out loud, either. It was… it was *in* me. All of me. He… Scout, he forgave me for all the evil things I've done, didn't he?"

At this point, Emerly looks down and shifts his weight. "I… There's something I have to tell the pair of you." He looks in my direction, and I know I am being invited into the conversation. Closing my schematics, I lean back in my chair to hear what he has to say.

After chewing on the inside of his lip, swallowing loudly, and then looking up at us, he starts, "I should have told you a long time ago… I didn't know how to, though, did I? I never knew how to say it. Mostly because of the thought of it… it turns my stomach." As if steeling himself to speak, he takes a deep breath and begins. "There are places in the Hexum that are… evil. Places where darkness lives, schemes, and multiplies. They're hidden places, they are. Kept secret from the people because if they knew…" His voice cracks, and he stops.

I stare at him, barely breathing.

"Seventy years ago, I was in Rodruegez working for Maz Lerue as one of his bodyguards."

"Maz Lerue, the Formosian Chancellor?" Scout asks, surprised.

Emerly smiles weakly, "The one. As you know, I'm good at what I do, and I intercepted two attacks on his life in the same week. This brought me to his attention, and he made me his personal bodyguard. With the job came compensation I couldn't believe, and… and…" Emerly clears his throat, "*perks,*

Maz called them."

At his pause, I know this word has hidden meaning, but to what could he be referring? Scout must not know either because we both wait silently for him to continue.

After too long a pause, he goes on, "The first one was a woman… She came to my room, and I didn't know what she wanted, did I? But then… she made it pretty clear fairly quickly, she did. She had been sent in to… she'd… she was supposed to mate with me." Emerly looks down at Scout's desk and fidgets with one of the knickknacks on its surface. Clearly, he feels shame in sharing this.

"Mate?" Scout asks, astounded. "Why? How could she have done that with you? Where was her husband?"

"She didn't have one," Emerly answers quickly but then adds soberly, "or so I was told later. She was hired by Maz's team to… It was her job to reward those in Maz's good favor, it was."

"But why would she do it?" Scout asks.

"I didn't know until much later that she didn't have a choice," Emerly answers miserably. "They were forcing her to… She was like their simulan, and I honestly had no idea… at first. For years I worked for him and said no to these perks, I did. Because it wasn't just her, was it… There were so many vile things done in that mansion. So many horrible things that rot my blood to even think about, it does."

The same ominous chill races up my spine as when Merayal told me the story about her childhood. "The darker desires of men?" I ask very quietly.

"Yes… yes, exactly," Emerly answers sadly.

Is that what happened to Merayal when she was in Senex?

After a pregnant pause, Scout asks Emerly, "But… eventually you… participated in these perks?"

Emerly nods.

Scout asks, "Did Winzer know?"

Emerly's brows knit, and he swallows hard. "No. She didn't. Our kids were young at the time, and Winzer was busy with them, she was. All she knew was that I was changing and becoming someone I never wanted to be. I found myself saying and doing things that had appalled me only a decade before, but it was my whole life, wasn't it? It was everywhere. One day I found vital information on one of the other Formosian Chancellors. At the time, the Third Seat was open, and Maz had made it clear he planned on taking the seat, he did. However, this other Chancellor had plans to do so for herself. I had heard it from one of her assistants and had shared it with Maz. Within the hour, that Chancellor was dead, and Maz sent one of his 'perks' to my work apartment, didn't he."

At this, Emerly's eyes begin to water. "But it wasn't a woman... it wasn't even a man this time... it was a child. A little Sanusian girl." Tears pour down his cheeks. "And looking into her large brown eyes, it all hit me. It hit me what I was doing, what I had become, and where I was heading. The darkness that had been so vile before had become my normal, hadn't it."

Neither Scout nor I say anything as Emerly weeps in front of us. This man that I have trusted and loved for years... He deserves to be in a den.

"I picked up that little girl and went as fast as possible to a Guardian station, I did. And then... I left her. I just left her at the front of the building and ran." He begins cracking every knuckle in his hands as he goes on, almost breathless, "I didn't know where to run, so I raced all around Rodruegez, and while doing so, I saw the city for what it was: a kingdom of death. Everywhere I looked I saw despicable, evil intentions and exploitations. When I finally returned to my apartment, one of the other bodyguards was there, wasn't he? He told me I was done; I was to leave Formosus and never return. Maz had sent me a message: 'You're only alive because you've saved me so many times. But if you say anything to anyone, then you, Winzer, and your children will be dead within the hour, you will.'"

Emerly takes a steadying breath and clenches his fists together. I glance at Scout. His expression is indiscernible, and even my prancing lion tattoo cannot pick a color.

"I have felt dead for a long time, I have," Emerly finally says. "And the Rogue Superior... he forgave all that. He made me whole in places I didn't even realize were broken. In my soul, in my blood, in every corner of my being, the Rogue Superior healed me. A-And not because I deserve it, do I? No, because he is filled with this... this compassion and empathy. And he is anxious to heal. He wants to forgive because being clean... being clean like him makes us truly ourselves."

Silence rings throughout our office. Scout stares down at his hands while I keep my gaze focused on Emerly. I want to tell him to get out of the circus, but if he goes, so will Winzer, and we need her to stay as Kansis and Amelia's Cloak. I wait for Scout to respond, and when he does, I am annoyed with the direction of the conversation.

"You said you spoke with the Rogue Superior?" Scout prompts, voice emotionless. "What did he say?"

"Yes," Emerly's face alights with excitement. "I didn't need water or candles or gadgets. Knimble told me I could just talk, and this all-powerful being would hear me wherever I was. The Rogue Superior told me I was forgiven. He told me that I was meant for him and he for me, and he would do a mighty work in my life. He was going to change all the things I thought were ugly into things more beautiful than I could imagine. 'You are forgiven. Live not in the darkness, my son. Live in my light,' he said to me, he did."

"The Superior said that?" Scout whispers.

"It was like it was everywhere and nowhere. A voice in my blood, wasn't it. A voice that forgave me."

Enraged, I shout, "Could you be a more gullible idiot—"

"Pypen, *no*," Scout commands.

I bridle my mouth only so as not to offend Scout, but internally I scream, *There is no forgiveness for what you have done!* I want to beat Emerly over the head while yelling, *There are no Superiors, and you have been deceived into peace!* I want to ask, *Do I even know you?*

But I say no more.

And neither does Scout.

Finally, Emerly sighs. "I know I don't deserve your forgiveness, I don't. And I'm not asking for it. I just… I feel the Rogue Superior in my blood. He's with me now, and my veins are warm with his understanding, aren't they. I've never felt more fully… human. And I want you to feel that, Scout. After all we've been through, I want you to know this." Flicking his gaze in my direction, he adds, "You too, Pip."

As if sensing the conversation is over, and neither Scout nor I have anything to say, Emerly departs.

Formosus

Flister

71 years ago

THE SIXTH AEVUM WATCHES as Oaken Bleu absentmindedly rubs the skull tattoo on her thumb joint. Her flowing chartreuse dress stands out from all the dark brown, deep red, and onyx black dresses around her. Although there is no official dress code for this year's Remembrance Ball, it is traditional for both men and women to wear darker shades.

But Oaken was never one to care for tradition.

She is talking to Chancellor Itti's oldest son, Sekatsym, who is in line to take the Chancellor's seat when he turns one hundred. Sekatsym and Flister were born the same year and have attended many of the same parties, balls, and celebrations. The Chancellor's son had even been invited to a couple of holy days at Mal's cottage over the years.

Ire rushes through the Sixth Aevum's veins when he sees Sekatsym place his hand on Oaken's lower back as he leans in closer to whisper something to her.

Oaken, ever the tease, giggles and gently shoves him away. The skull tattoo catches Flister's eye again.

He had placed it there two years ago, following the night of Mal's birthday party. Oaken had once again showed up at his house unannounced and promised that after she had performed whatever dare he braved to inflict on her, she, in turn, would dare him to hurt Mal.

And so he had dared her not to talk to him for a year. He had regretted it the moment the words had left his mouth, but a dare is a dare. It had been the most uncomfortable twelve months of his life—especially around the other Aevii.

Three hundred and sixty-five days later, he had arrived at her doorstep with an arrangement of flowers that he had hand-picked that morning. It was filled with her favorites: sweet peas, stargazer lilies, begonias, and plumerias. In his other hand, he held a very rare kokatu. It had taken months to have one built just for her. Most kokatus are used for easy travel, but they cost a lot of energy for each use; they are clunky to travel with, and the actual transportation leaves one feeling lightheaded and nauseous for at least an hour afterward.

Not that any of those were necessarily deterrents for the Fifth Aevum—but they were inconveniences. And why have inconveniences when one is an Aevii?

So, the kokatu Flister had made for Oaken was exceptional. It was made of white crystal and crafted into a thick dagger. She would be able to keep it in her pocket or wear it around her neck, and there would be no travel sickness once she arrived.

But after repeatedly knocking on the door, one of Oaken's simulans had come out to inform him that the Fifth Aevum would not be taking his visit that day, or any visits for the foreseeable future.

It had taken months, but he had finally tracked her down while she was shopping for a Springolatry dress. He had confessed all that he had been up to with Arkarian Story, hoping it would warm her to him, but it had done no such thing. She had acted as if he did not exist. This avoidance had gone on for months, and he thought nothing could be worse than her frigid demeanor, but he was sorely mistaken.

That Quintrall, when Flister had greeted Oaken, he was beyond surprised to find her warm and kind once more. He was so entirely caught off guard and thrilled by her response that he had hugged and kissed her. But at her touch, he realized that his passion was not matched. She was merely being friendly.

Of all the Aevii, Oaken has always been the most tenderhearted and relational. Even in normal interactions with strangers, she is amicable. So, having her treat him like he was just another person—an acquaintance, even—was somehow more painful.

Even now, after two *more* years, she still treats him with genial apathy. Flister can barely stand to be around her. Were he in possession of the tattoo, he would dare her out of her indifferent behavior; but she still holds it, having successfully completed her dare.

As Flister watches Oaken and Sekatsym flirting, seeing the familiar way with which they touch each other's bodies, something percolates in his blood.

With no thought and all folly, he leaves the shadows. Flister strides across the ballroom, pushing past dancing couples. Emerging from the throng, he struts toward Oaken and the Chancellor's son.

It is Sekatsym who sees him first.

Bowing low, the Formosian man states, "Greet the moon, Hallowed Sixth Aevum. Bless your name and your Gifts."

Not acknowledging him, Flister says to Oaken, "You look mesmerizing this night."

"As I do every night," Oaken responds and shares a smile with Sekatsym.

"How goes your Venture?" Sekatsym asks Flister. "I hear your Observatory is a feast for the senses, isn't it? I, unfortunately, I have not made it out yet—I must prioritize it this winter."

"Oh, yes, you must," Oaken remarks. "It is like nothing you have ever experienced before. We are all so proud of our Flisty."

Her condescending tone and public use of his nickname do not go amiss. Flister's spine visibly stiffens, but he takes the slap without remark.

"What has kept you so busy?" Flister asks Sekatsym.

The Formosian man smirks and shares another sideways look with Oaken. "I have been busy with work," he hedges. And, either to brag or because he genuinely cannot keep it to himself, the handsome man admits, "and this little rascal has been keeping me distracted, she has."

Playfully, Oaken swats his arm, then, feigning embarrassment, she adds, "Sekatsym has been helping me at the Discovery Center—I've hired him to help me with some... defenses for the building."

"Have you really?" Flister asks, forcing himself to play the game. "Well, you must be particularly skilled at what you do, Sekatsym."

Looking Flister in the eye for the first time, Oaken responds, "He is."

As the two Aevii stare at one another, Sekatsym, clearly uncomfortable, takes a sip of his eupee.

"Would you care to dance?" the Sixth Aevum asks the Fifth.

"I would," she answers, and grabbing Sekatsym's hand, she pulls him to the dance floor.

Flister remains frozen as the pair glide away. He allows himself a moment to watch Oaken as she happily jumps into the Rae—a lively dance in an eight or six-count rhythm to the tune of cheery wind instruments, drums, and guitars. The dance is full of fast footwork—taps, kicks, and spins.

As Flister turns away from the pair, his thoughts occupied on finding a way to make her talk to him, he bumps into Marvella Pinyin, the Fourth Aevum. Offering a half-hearted apology, Flister hurries past her. Ever since he had humiliated Marvella at her Captusian Quarantine facility, she has kept her distance, and whenever they have to be in contact, she is irritable and noticeably short with him.

So it comes as a complete surprise when she calls his name. Filled with curiosity, Flister turns back to the woman. Her long features are hesitant—her eyes round with anxiety.

"Yes, Marvella, did you need something?" he asks, amused.

When she swallows, he can see her esophagus jump. "Oaken must be pretty upset with you," she comments, trying to put on an easy smile.

Flister gazes at the dancing form of the woman who used to be his best friend. Biting the inside of his lip until it hurts, he clicks his tongue and turns back to Marvella. "So it would seem. You must be thrilled."

The Fourth Aevum shrugs. "I would have been happier if you had jilted *her*, to be honest."

Not expecting this response, Flister studies Marvella for a moment. At his perusal, the Fourth Aevum looks out at the crowd of revelers.

"I must know why you hate her so much," Flister says to Marvella. He nods his head towards the dancing Aevum. "Is it purely jealousy?"

Marvella smiles, but it could turn the room to ice. "The only thing I have ever been jealous of concerning our Oaken is her monopoly of your attention."

And before Flister can respond, the Fourth Aevum strides away.

Back at his house, the Sixth Aevum makes his way toward his hidden room behind the refrigerator. This night's interactions with Oaken and Marvella have left his blood dehydrated.

He has no idea how to regain the affections of the Fifth Aevum. Perhaps, in the morning, he will seek guidance from a Prophet.

Closing the refrigerator door behind him as he steps into his secret room, Flister takes a moment to admire his collection of Scion and Reader blood. It is the only treasury of its kind, and just looking at it gives him a satisfying hit of dopamine.

But suddenly, the look on Marvella's face right before she walked away fills his mind once more, setting his heart pounding. Why had she let down her defenses? Is this a ploy to hurt him? To hurt Oaken? It has to be.

As he eases himself into his favorite armchair, Flister grabs the cigar Oaken had given him on his coronation night all those years ago, places it between his lips, and reaches for his lighter.

"Foul habit."

Flister yelps and jumps up out of his chair, his heart beating so vigorously it is painful.

There, lurking in the shadows across the room stands the Third Aevum.

"How dare—how did you—you cannot—" Flister's voice trails off and he waits until his heart's pounding is less painful. Finally, he takes a deep breath, wipes the broken cigar pieces off his shirt, and stares at the Sanusian man. "What are you doing in here, Elder?"

Qualcum Elder coughs. The fringe of his light brown hair covers one of his eyes. His sallow cheeks are prominent as he smiles unpleasantly. "Wanted ter have a chat wit ye, Flister."

"You should have called," Flister responds, trying to stay calm. "I would have welcomed you into my home. We should be talking in the drawing room." *Not here; not in my hidden sanctuary.*

Qualcum shrugs as if this is of no consequence. "Oi came here ternight ter give ye a present, Flister."

"I want *nothing* from you, Elder," Flister seethes. "Get out. *Now.*"

After coughing again, Qualcum asks quietly, "Ye didn't want ter know about ta Scions and ta Readers when I first told ye, did ye, me boy?"

Flister's rage hesitates. Does Qualcum know more about Arkarian Story?

Steeling himself, Flister turns away from the Third Aevum. More than anything else, he wants to kick the man out of his house. Literally. He wants to grab him by his frail neck and forcibly remove him. But Flister's obsession with staying alive is more significant than his overwhelming hatred for the Sanusian man standing in his sacred room.

"Let us speak elsewhere," he finally says resignedly.

"'Tis no need," Qualcum rebuts and motions for Flister to sit back in his armchair. Flister has no desire to obey the command, no wish to stay in this room where Qualcum's presence is making him feel so exposed, yet he sits.

"Oi have done some investigating into ta Book of Instructions," Qualcum begins evenly, "and I found a piece of information Oi t'ought ye'd like ter know." He coughs into his black coat again. "T'ere be sommat called ta Code Breakers."

"What is that?" Flister asks, hating how curious he is.

"*Who are t'ey*, ye mean. Ta Code Breakers are anot'er group of people who have ta ability ter locate Arkarian Story."

Flister can feel the blood draining from his face. *Another* means of finding Arkarian Story? How could there be *another* way?

"How can they locate him?" Flister asks.

Qualcum smiles again. "T'rough a code, i'nit."

"What code?"

Qualcum's folded hands open for a moment as if he is holding something invisible, then they knit back together as he answers, "A hidden code ter Arkarian Story's location found only in a book t'at has been long lost ter ta world."

For a moment, Flister's veins flood with relief. If the book is lost, no one can decipher the code. However, within one heartbeat, he jolts with adrenaline. Why would Qualcum tell him about the Code Breakers unless it was an actual threat?

"Can the book be found?"

"'Tis wit'in ta imagination."

"Is it an immediate threat?"

"Not necessarily."

"Are the Code Breakers looking for the book?"

"Not yet."

Flister takes a steadying breath. "Are the Code Breakers not alive yet, then? They will be born soon?"

"Sommat like t'at."

At the calm look on the Third Aevum's face, Flister loses his patience. "*Matza*, Elder, just tell me what you have come to say!"

Qualcum pushes his light brown hair back from over his forehead. He takes a deep breath which causes another coughing spasm.

Flister cannot even look at the man. Everything about him is repugnant. Only once the spasm subsides does Flister turn his gaze back to the Third Aevum.

The man's soulless eyes bear into Flister, daring him to say something, but Flister stays utterly silent and completely still.

Finally, Qualcum continues. "T'ere be t'ree fronts on which Arkarian Story can be found, aye? Ye have been fightin' one head wit enthusiasm, ye have been. One head ye been patiently waitin' fer as the daughter is still not found. And now we have head number t'ree. Ye can sit back and wait as yer doin' wit ta daughter, or ye can be proactive."

Flister thinks about these words. "How do you mean?"

"T'ere is a person meant ter initiate t'ese Code Breakers, aye? If ye want ter be in control of who wakes up Arkarian Story and when he wakes, ye need ter be in control of ta Code Breakers, ye see?"

Qualcum pauses, waiting for Flister to answer. Fury fills Flister's body. These subtle reminders of Qualcum's power over him make the Sixth Aevum feel infantile. Finally, when it is clear Qualcum will not go on until Flister acknowledges him, he shouts, "Yes, Elder, yes, do continue!"

Qualcum nods. "Oi can provide t'is infermation fer ye, Flister."

"What will it cost?"

At this, Qualcum Elder smiles. "T'at be an excellent question." Qualcum sits on one of the stools next to Flister's private bar. "Oi need ye ter start sommat."

"Start what?"

"A group."

When it seems no more information is coming, Flister snarls, "What kind of group?"

"A group t'at will help protect our interests."

"Why can *you* not start it?"

Qualcum smiles as if he is explaining something to a small child. "Ye will need ter be ta one, Flister."

"Fine. What will this group do? Who will be in it?"

"T'is group will help ye on yer search, and ye will fill it wit very Gifted, talented people. T'is group will take about fifteen years ter put terget'er. Oi already have one of yer first members. He will be of utmost help ter ye."

"I do not understand. Why do I need this group?"

"Flister, if ye would but use t'ose ears ye were born wit, ye would understand. Listen as Oi explain once more. Oi need ye ter put terget'er a group of Gifted people who are goin' ter help ye keep Arkarian Story hidden. T'is group will help ye find ta daughter, will help keep ta Scions at bay, and will keep ye in control of ta Code Breakers. Ye'll need t'is group to stay hidden in plain sight, so Oi was t'inking ta group could be a traveling entertainment group, see. Go where ye need wit'out being suspicious. Do ye understand now?"

The Sixth Aevum eyes the man in front of him. Even though Qualcum Elder stopped aging around his forties, the Sanusian-haired man looks old—ancient and sick. Something very dark and cold lies behind his eyes.

"Why are you doing this, Elder? Why are you helping me? What do you get out of it?"

At this, the Third Aevum stands. It seems to cause him pain. He looks at Flister with a rare expression of interest—as if he may share a secret only if he finds Flister worthy.

Flister tries his best to look so.

When Qualcum begins to speak, the Sixth Aevum listens intently.

"T'ere once was a very hungry fox. He had gone many days wit'out eatin'. He happened upon a burrow where a mot'er rabbit and her five newborns lived. Ta rabbits would be a good meal, and t'eir burrow would be a good home, t'ought ta fox. But when he tried ter rush inside ta burrow, ta rabbit bit and scratched his nose, and he came out wounded and bleedin'. He must get t'em out, but how ter do it?

"A blackberry bush grew on top of ta burrow, and ta next mornin', one particularly ripe berry fell right at ta mouth of ta burrow. Ta fox watched as a baby rabbit jumped on ta berry, grabbed it, and raced back inside. An idea grew in ta fox's mind.

"At dusk ta next day, he stood atop ta burrow and dropped anot'er particularly ripe blackberry at ta entrance. A baby rabbit came out of ta burrow, and ta fox pounced upon it. Had he not been so hungry, had he not been so desperate, he would have realized sooner t'at ta baby had not pounced on ta blackberry but had been tossed upon it. Had he not been in such great need, he would have noticed ta baby was dead. Nonet'eless, he ate it in just a couple of bites.

"He peered inside ta burrow, and there, protectively coverin' her ot'er babies, crouched ta mot'er rabbit.

"'Yer kind is doomed ter die lest t'ey have eyes,' she said to him. 'Ye gained one full stomach fer a forever empty one.'

"It was t'en t'at ta fox felt ta poison in his system. Wit'in a few moments, ta fox no longer felt his legs and fell ter ta ground.

"'Twas yer child,' ta fox gasped.

"Ta mot'er spat, 'One arrow isn't wort' ta whole quiver.'

"Out of ta corner of his eye, ta fox saw a raven land softly on ta autumn leaves next ter his head.

"'As agreed,' said ta mot'er rabbit. 'One fox fer yer protection.'

"'Agreed,' ta raven cawed, and an unkindness of twenty or more ravens descended upon ta fox.

"As ta red creature was eaten alive, he finally saw, finally understood, just as his eyes were plucked out."

As the fable comes to an end, Flister remains still, pondering the meaning of the tale.

"Am I the mother rabbit?" he finally asks. "And are you the raven?"

Smirking to himself, Qualcum treks to the door and states, "Oi have me reasons fer helping ye, Flister, and t'ey be not reasons ye need ter know. Oi will be back later t'is week ter start planning."

Still lost in the story, Flister replies offhandedly, "I would rather meet elsewhere."

"We'll meet here," Qualcum responds simply and opens the refrigerator door. "Anot'er Scion was born last night. Are ye still set on lettin' ta Scions live now? 'Tis not safe."

"This way is better," Flister states, glad to be in control of something. "It is easier to kill a Reader once every fifty years."

"Yer ways," Qualcum replies and raises his hand as if giving a toast. Then, quietly, the Third Aevum hobbles out the door and closes it gently behind him.

So, is he the rabbit?

As he returns to his armchair, the Sixth Aevum has a sinking feeling that he is the fox.

ANOTHER YEAR PASSES, AND Oaken's resolve has not waned.

Taking another shot of the concoction he was served at the bar, the Sixth Aevum roars, and the crowd around him howls in a deafening echo.

As Flister makes his way back towards the gambling table where he has already lost over a hundred cheio, he shakes his head to clear his mind of the Fifth Aevum.

But how can he when *she* is being so entirely unfair?

How is it his fault that he loves Mal most? Who can control such things?

He has loved Oaken—truly loved her with body, soul, and mind. But that is not enough for her. Why is he being punished when her rejection is so thoroughly undeserved?

Hours later, after losing another seventy-five cheio, the Sixth Aevum makes his way outside the club towards his waiting vehicle. To his utmost surprise, when he slides into the velvet back seat, Oaken Bleu is waiting for him.

Misunderstanding her presence as a ceasefire and maliciously deciding to make *her* beg *him* to come back, Flister asks angrily, "What the *itik* are you doing here?"

"It's our anniversary." Giggling, she observes, "I see you celebrated in an emblazoned fashion."

"And how did you celebrate?" Flister asks, wishing he was more sober so he could have this conversation properly.

"With this," she answers and reaches into her tiny black beaded purse. She pulls out a small vial containing a viscous, amber liquid.

"What is it?"

"It's a dare."

"But what is it?"

"I dare you to drink it."

Anger flashes through his veins like lightning, Flister shouts, "What is it, Oaken?"

With infuriating calm, she repeats, "I dare you to drink it."

"No, I refuse."

"Then you quit."

"I know not what that will do to me," Flister complains, his blood on fire. "And seeing the loathsome state you are in, I believe this goes against the dare code. You cannot willfully put me in danger."

Oaken guffaws. "Flister, you dared me to drown myself once."

The statement rings in the air.

Flister had forgotten about that.

"I dare you, Flister Dubach, to drink this," Oaken states slowly and offers him the vial.

As he reaches to take it from her, Oaken moves with lightning speed, slapping the tattoo onto his hand. Like always, it bites his skin, making him wince. Ripping the vial out of her hand, he studies it for a moment. Finally, he asks, "What will it do to me?"

"I don't have to tell you."

Humbling himself, setting down his pride, and willing himself to be vulnerable with her, Flister says slowly, "'Tis not a command, Kenny. I am merely asking; will you tell me what it will do to me?"

He is uncertain whether it is the pet name, his tone, or her inherent sweetness that does it, but Oaken's defiant expression capitulates. Sighing, she looks out the window and answers softly, "It will make you forget."

"Forget what?"

"Us."

The word is like lead in his veins, a knife to his radial artery, poison in his blood. Barely able to speak, he makes himself ask, "What about us?"

"All of it."

"As in… as in my whole life?"

"It will rewrite a version of me where I am in your life, just like the other Aevii, but our friendship will not exist in your memories."

Unable to comprehend her words, the Sixth Aevum closes his eyes and rakes his hands over his face. Knowing the emotions welling up inside of him are real yet enhanced by the alcoholic beverages he has been imbibing all night, he wills away the tears that suddenly want to fall.

"Kenny, how can you be so angry—"

"I'm not angry."

"OF COURSE YOU ARE ANGRY!" Flister roars. "Why else—" His voice cracks, but he makes himself finish, "why else would you do this to me?"

Oaken moves across to him and puts her legs over Flister's lap. She rests her head on his chest and wraps her arms around his waist.

They stay like that for a long while.

Flister lays his head atop hers and listens as their breathing falls into rhythm. He initiates no conversation, knowing he will stay like this as long as she permits. When she starts humming the Ninth Grade Song, he joins the tune with his own broken sounds.

After some time, but too soon for Flister, Oaken straightens. When their eyes meet, hers are as red as his, tears still falling down her cheeks.

"I can't do it, Flister."

"Do what?"

"I can't let you keep all of those memories of us, knowing that they'll always be a trophy for you."

"A troph—Kenny, is that what you think of me? That I seduced you for some prize? I did no such thing."

Pushing away from him, she shakes her head. "It doesn't matter. I can't have you, so you can't have me. *Any* of me. What we've experienced, what we've shared—those are parts of me you will hold forever. It's not fair."

"Not fair? What you are doing *right now* is not fair! Why can you not just allow our love to be what it is—"

"You don't get it!" Oaken screams and then gives a shrieking laugh tinged with hysteria. "If I can't have your whole heart—the loyalty of *all* your blood—I don't want any of it! I'm not going to spend my eternity coming in second-best to Mal Fey. Flister, we're done."

Grabbing her wrist, Flister growls, "We are done when I say we are done."

Using Gifted strength, Oaken pulls away from him and declares, "I dare you to drink this, Flister Dubach."

"I cannot believe—"

"I dare you."

"—you would treat me so unfairly—"

"I dare you."

"—after all we have been through together—"

"I dare you."

"—all our years of friendship—"

"So you give up?" Oaken cries. "You quit, just say it, and it's done!"

Flister knows this is the moment in which he could win her back. If he chooses now to lose the game, he will show her how much she means to him.

Sobering, he asks, "Will my memories be erased forever, or can they be recalled?"

Visibly annoyed at the question, Oaken answers, "Technically they can be recalled, but there would be no reason for me to do so."

The Sixth Aevum knows what he must do. The words hum in his blood. He need only quit, and he can have her back.

"Will you kiss me?" he asks.

"No."

"Not one last time?"

"Not one last time."

"I dare you."

Oaken laughs. "You haven't fulfilled your dare, Flister. It's not your turn yet."

Reaching over and cupping her face with one hand, he repeats, "I dare you."

Slowly, hesitantly, the Fifth Aevum leans in and allows Flister to kiss her. It is playful and gentle and sweet and everything Oaken Bleu has ever been to him.

As he pulls away and stares into her eyes, the words, *I quit*, are heavy on his lips. He opens his mouth, and a sudden surge of adrenaline floods his veins.

He wants Oaken... but why let her win?

Unscrewing the vial, he pours the contents into his mouth. It tastes like rotten honey. Not knowing how fast the serum will work, Flister grabs Oaken's hand and slaps the tattoo on top of her wrist. "I dare you to remind me..." As his vision becomes fuzzy, he pushes on. "When your pride has exhausted its pitiful self, remind me of us, Oaken Bleu... I... I dare you..."

The world around him grows black as his eyes close, and his heart returns to its steady rhythm.

Pexus

Kansis

THE DAY FLIES BY in a blur. We won't leave for our mission until six in the evening, so Amelia, Aker, and I spend the time exploring more of the circus. My mind is in turmoil. Whenever my thoughts turn to my role in the upcoming mission, it immediately makes me sick to my stomach. When I think about the Cupido experiment, I feel lightheaded. When I think about Aker wanting to get married, I get a headache. When I think about the prophecy, I need to sit down.

So. I try not to think at all.

Instead, I focus on Amelia.

I focus on how nice it is for her to speak with everyone on her own. She spends most of the morning incredibly annoyed at and trying to stop herself from using the Formosian dialect's affirming phrases, but by the afternoon she gives in to her Formosian lot in life.

I focus on how Amelia and Aker—to my utmost surprise—are getting along. Granted, *getting along* means they're fighting and insulting each other non-stop, but it's all in good spirits.

Early in the morning, Aker and I had talked about our plan. He is eager for the mission to be over so we can leave, but he has said he won't bring it up again so I can enjoy my last day at the circus.

I keep second-guessing my decision to go with him, but by early afternoon I stop. It's the right thing to do. For one, with her eutsi, Amelia doesn't need me anymore. She can talk to everyone now. And two, it's clear that my contribution to the prophecy will be reading the Book of Instructions. I have no other talent or Gift to help with the mission. I agree that they need me for this, but they won't require me for anything else. Scout and Amelia will find Arkarian Story without me.

One good thing about this choice is that Aker has finally started to relax. When he's not being a jerk... he's pretty great. It's like he is finally breathing enough to be himself, and I really like him.

Ontzi, I like him.

But as much as I am struck by this, Scout's words keep creeping into my mind, interrupting and ruining these moments. Every time Aker smiles at me, I hear Scout say, *Aker should love you, blood or not.* Every time Aker cracks a joke at Amelia and then catches my eye, I hear Scout say, *You deserve to be loved because of you, not because his blood tells him he has to love you.*

It's annoying, actually.

We spend much of the day with the Chameleons and their mates. They're interesting and funny, beautiful and interconnected. The relationships between the four men are equally entertaining and uncomfortable to watch.

Krael is the group's apparent leader, although Sedwick does not listen to him as the other two do. Krael is easily angered by Sedwick's independence and instigates a good number of arguments. Lukan and Oshun seem to sympathize with Sedwick on different matters, but when Krael calls them to take sides— which he does a lot—they choose the stronger brother. Surprisingly, this doesn't seem to bother Sedwick. He and Lukan often exchange secret glances, with Lukan looking very apologetic. Poor Oshun simply wants everyone to be happy and will do anything to keep the peace.

In the early afternoon, the Chameleons ask us if we want a guided tour of the circus' secrets. We end up skipping the main show to continue our circus exploration with them.

Between introspective closets, challenging mazes made from water, and future-telling crustaceans, Amelia and I (and Aker, too, even though he acted like he wasn't) are swept away in the wonder of it all.

I want to talk to Amelia about what had happened the day before—when the truth about the K-Pax had been forced out of me—but I also don't want to upset the ease of friendship that has settled between us. And there is no time anyway, between all the Chameleons and their mates showing us around.

At one point, following the circus closing, I lose track of Amelia. Thykas tells me that she and Aker have found a room where they can compete against one another to determine which is the better athlete. A group of the performers has followed them, wagering on who will win. While I wait to find out who is the victor, I enter into a conversation with Scout about Knimble's Superior—to the greatly displayed dismay of Pypen. After calling me a traitor, he and Thykas leave us to our discussion.

"Why do you want to meet the creator of this world?" I ask Scout. We sit

in the courtyard, lounging in the HugMe bistro chairs. "You said yesterday…
you said the thing you want most in this world is to meet its creator. Why?
Even if there is one, what would meeting him do for you?"

Before answering, Scout looks at me for a moment. His brows twitch
downward, and his lips frown slightly. When he opens his mouth to answer,
he shuts it. It's only then he looks away.

"You don't have to answer if—"

"'Tis not that," he explains quickly and then sighs. "If there's a creator, then
there was most likely purpose in what was created. For example, when Pypen
and I make a new door, what happens inside the room is always intentional.
The room itself reaches an objective, but it fits into the circus harmoniously
as well. Each part that we add has both micro and macro meanings. And if we
put that much thought and intention into mere entertainment… would not the
creator have had micro and macro meaning woven into their creation as well?
Why make the ocean blue and the land brown? Why make animals at all? Why
tall mountains and deep valleys? Why rain to water the earth?

"If there is one thing I can see, Scoop, it is that there is creative design
everywhere. From how we breathe to the weather, to how animals hunt, to the
tiny—seemingly pointless—insects, our world screams of order and structure.
Each animal and plant has a reason for existing—they play a part in their own
existence and the existence of the living things around them. From the moon
who pulls the tides to the squirrels who bury seeds to the plants who sustain
all things, their lives have a purpose."

Scout runs his hands over his braid. "I believe there was a being before
humans—one who made the earth… and that being created humans. So, if he
has a purpose for the squirrels… I think he has a purpose for humankind as
well. And not just as a whole… but individually. Why was *I* created? What is
my purpose? What am I doing here in 419 Mundus Novus?"

The silence that falls between us is kind. I don't know how I know, but
Scout doesn't want this conversation to be over… and honestly, neither do I.
His passion is inspiring.

"Is that why Knimble's Superior means so much to you? He offers purpose?"

Scout nods. "I want not to believe in something if it is false. If the Rogue
Superior is not the creator for whom I am looking, I will not hesitate to cast
aside such claims. I am not holding firm to what Knimble says. However, if
what Knimble says is true… then yes, he would offer me ultimate purpose.
That is why Knimble's Superior means so much to me. Because if he is correct,

then the creator of this world did not merely create humans in some existential and detached fashion—but he made them in order to be relational with them. Why? Why would he want to be relational towards his creation? How does he view us? Who are we to even be considered?

"And if he truly created us to be in relationship with him, why design the world so we cannot see and touch him? So we cannot talk to him? Why does he dwell in the spiritual realm when we are physical creatures? And if he is truly as good as Knimble says, why does his world not look good? Why is there evil? Why death? I have to believe there are answers, and I believe this Superior may have them."

When he looks at me again, I have to wipe the smile off my features. I can tell I didn't do it in time by the frown that crosses his face.

"You mock me?"

The hurt that shadows his eyes makes my blood weaken. "Not at all!" I reply much too loudly. Not knowing why, I reach out and grab his hand. "You… you have so much passion about this. You've put so much thought into it. I've just never once thought about who created me and why… I still don't understand why that would mean so much to you."

This seems to give him pause, and he stops to think. Placing his other hand over mine, he gently plays with my fingers, making my whole body radiate sunlight. He looks at me earnestly and answers, "Before we started the circus, I worked at a healing and therapy facility for people who had damaged their Gifts. I was able to use my Progift to help them find themselves and rediscover their Gift—if it had not been completely damaged, that is. I learned much about the psyche of a human, and although I enjoyed my work… it depressed me."

When he doesn't continue, I prompt, "Why did it depress you?"

Tracing the freckles on the back of my hand, he answers, "I have never been able to put into words how I felt." He pauses for a long while. Then finally he shares, "It just seemed that inside each person I helped heal… something was missing. No matter how deep I went into their minds, a void needed to be filled."

"What do you mean?"

"It is as if our blood needs more…"

"More what?" I ask, perplexed.

"I know not," he answers, gazing into the distance, face troubled. "I could never figure out if they needed something more of something they had or something completely outside of themselves… And it mattered not if they were wealthy or struggling, at the end of their days or at their beginnings, worship-worthy or not... They were all equally insufficient. And every day, it made me feel as if... as if I, too, needed more. Like... like something was missing in me as well." He looks back at me. "That is when I became a Buscador. I decided there must be answers."

I think about the hollowness in my veins before leaving Depalo. Everything was missing, but it's all different now. As I watch our fingers intertwine, I feel happy. Content. Being at the circus fills all those spaces... I still don't understand why that's not enough for him.

Scout continues, "I think I was created to be known and to know the one who created me. 'Tis this deep feeling... I am meant to know him. Pypen does not understand, and it bothers him greatly—but I know it in my marrow... I am meant to meet the creator... to know him."

"What do you want from him?"

Scout's brows flicker, and his lips twitch into a smile. "Nothing." He looks down at our hands. "I would say the question is, what does he want from me? If he is my origin, do I not owe him my life? Am I not in his debt?" His smile becomes wistful. "I pine to know."

I think back to Knimble's challenge the other night. "What if the Superior wanted you to leave the circus? Would you do so?" I remember the rejection painted on Pypen's face at Scout's hurried response.

As if reading my thoughts, he answers, "I would bring Pypen with me."

I laugh. "How did you know I was thinking about that?"

He chuckles as well, our joy mingling in the air between us. "I could just tell."

Suddenly, a shiver runs up my spine. I know someone is watching me, their eyes like fingers trailing down my back. Searching the area, my body jolts when I see Pypen sitting at one of the bistro tables across the courtyard, his eyes glued to mine and Scout's hands.

Quickly, I pull my hand out of Scout's. If it weren't for the fact that this is probably the last time I'll ever be alone with Scout, my embarrassment would have made me want to run away.

But it is.

These are the final moments I'll ever have to speak candidly with Scout Eekan, so instead of fleeing, I choose to stay.

Without mentioning my sudden withdrawal, Scout places his hands behind his head and stretches. As he does so, his prancing lion tattoo peeks out from beneath his khaki suede jacket. Right now, it is orange and olive-green.

"Why does your tattoo constantly change colors?" I ask.

Scout drops his hands and looks at his forearm. Smiling ruefully to himself, he begins, "When Pypen and I were fifteen, a Pied Piper came to town."

"A what?"

Scout stops and looks down at me. "You do not have Pied Pipers in Pexus?"

"No, I've never heard of them."

Scout whistles under his breath. "I know Ortus is superior, Pexus posterior, but now—"

Playfully, I hit his arm, and then embarrassment washes through me as I remember Pypen's penetrating gaze.

Not noticing—or at least not commenting—Scout laughs as he explains, "I jest. They are charlatans, really. Pied Pipers go from town to town, usually rural places, and disguise themselves in such a way that only children can see and hear them. They trick children into buying sketchy, off-brand eutsees, arnesses, sciaths, and the like.

"Our parents had warned us against listening to any Pied Pipers, and we knew it was wrong to entertain the one who visited Sleepy Hollow—our hometown. But he had this confident, powerful air about him, and Pypen and I decided we were going to see what he was selling. Long story short, we were conned and spent all our savings on these tattoos." He laughs at the memory.

"Why would you do that?" I ask incredulously.

"Because he told us that we could communicate with each other through them. What he did not tell us was that there is no real communication—just that we would always be aware of how the other one was feeling." He stops and pushes up his jacket so I can see the tattoo clearly. "The color of the tattoo changes with our moods. Mine reflects his emotions and vice versa. Presently, Pypen is both anxious," he touches the orange, "and worried," he points to the olive-green.

"That's amazing," I say. I want to touch the colorful ink, but I keep my hand where it is, knowing Pypen's attention is still on me… and now knowing that his attention is both anxious and worried.

"It is. It makes it hard when you want to hide your feelings, however," he states and smiles.

We move on to other subjects enjoying small talk about Scout's favorite rooms in the circus, and he hints at where the hidden doors might be located. Finally, Amelia and Aker return—Amelia, the victor.

Obviously.

We play one game of Gedankenspiel with Scout, Pypen, Thykas, Gigi,

Merayal (who was in the best mood I've seen since meeting her), the Chameleons, and their mates. It lasts three and a half hours, but as the rounds go by quickly and all the players are so involved, the time doesn't feel that long at all. I am shocked when someone announces it is almost five o'clock.

"I must depart," Pypen declares and stands. Nodding meaningfully at Amelia and me, he heads out the door. Scout leaves soon after. The plan is for Amelia and me to make our way out in another ten minutes to avoid attention. Scout had said he doesn't want everyone to know we were going out tonight. "They will be hurt I am not including them all on the mission," he'd explained.

Amelia and I sit casually on one of the couches drinking a glass of mineral and vitamin-infused water. We'll remain here for five minutes, drink our drink, and then make our departure. As we sit together quietly, I find myself listening to a conversation taking place on the couches beside us. Many of the female circus members are sitting around drinking, and Peu, one of the performers, is in the middle of a story. "So, I found myself behind Pypen, and I heard him talking to himself, as is his way, and he murmured something about a prophecy." She whispers the last words with raised brows as if she has just shared a treacherous secret.

"A prophecy about what?" Ruelle, Lukan's mate, whispers back. Her dark, Ortusan hair sweeps over her eyes as she leans in. Six foot four and dressed in a fuchsia-colored jumpsuit made of feathers and sequins, the woman has the appearance of a giant, sparkling bird.

"I know not. Someone called out to him, and he stopped mumbling. But what could he be talking about?" Peu gushes.

I hope my face isn't showing my guilt, as I'm sure the prophecy in question concerns a Scion and a Reader...

"Perhaps there was a prophecy about the finding of Arkarian Story's daughter?" Ruelle asks.

"Perhaps," Memory, Krael's mate, responds, but then quickly adds, "Krael thinks the Sixth Aevum has spies in all the Hull Facilities, and they inspected every young woman who was awakened for her true identity."

"I doubt that," Nova, Oshun's mate, says. It wasn't until today that I realized she plays the white dancer in the show. She is so beautiful. Pulling her gorgeous hair across her front, she rolls her eyes. "There are no spies in the Hull Facilities."

"Maybe it is a prophecy about finding Arkarian Story," Peu plows on.

"Or about the future of the Unopened Gifts!" Ruelle exclaims. "Maybe it says we are going to perform at the Quintrall," she giggles.

"That would be something, huh?" Gigi speaks up for the first time. "Can you even imagine what it would be like to perform in front of that many people?"

"Even if it did happen, you would not know, would you, Gi?" Nova responds with contrived sympathy. "As you will be under the stage in the Orchestra box, unable to see any of the people."

"Nova, honey—" Memory chides, but Gigi quickly replies, "Yes, Ryder *and* Veeter *and* I would be down there, together, hearing the crowd reactions clearest as we are at their level. An experience you will never know."

"An experience I do not envy," Nova retorts.

Re-routing the subject, Ruelle suggests, "Perhaps the prophecy is for Pypen himself. He may have been prophesied over by Avenir."

Avenir. The name sends chills throughout my bloodstream. Although I will always be infinitely thankful that he showed Aker and me the truth of our situation, he is still a very creepy man.

"Whatever it is, Pypen deserves good fortune," Fiddy, Sedwick's mate, remarks quietly. The woman has cut her hair as short as she can, leaving only two millimeters of growth on her head. Rows of hoop earrings curve from the tops of her ears down to her lobules. Fiddy is the quietest of the Chameleon's mates, yet she seems to be the 'mom' of their little family.

As if noticing her juicy bit of gossip has run its course, Peu pipes up with a new topic. "I want to ask Amelia and Kansis more about Senexian relationships—they are so intriguing!"

Both Amelia and I shrink back on the couch, not wanting to get caught in a conversation.

"No, that is so depressing," Gigi responds. "I want not to hear any more of it."

"It is depressing that people did not like their mates and left them?" Nova asks. Her look is almost feline, like a cat toying with her prey.

"You enjoy thinking about mates leaving each other?" Gigi asks, brows raised in disdain.

"I find it fascinating that there was a choice. Say one's mate—a male mate, for example—wasn't satisfied by his wife, he could simply find a female who did satisfy him," Nova purrs.

"I think I have had enough *enjoyment* for one evening," Gigi states firmly. Standing, she takes the last sip of her drink and sets the glass on the floor. "Greet the moon, Everyone." Yawning dramatically, a slight sound—almost like the first note of a songbird—emits from her mouth, and Nova's glass shatters.

She yelps as the drink cascades over her.

"Oh, sorry, Nova," Gigi remarks, feigning sympathy.

Cursing, Nova leaps to her feet and storms out of the room.

"It's time, it is," Amelia whispers to me.

As we stand, Aker calls my name. He meets us at the door and asks Amelia if he can have a minute.

"You can have five, and that's it," Amelia responds sternly. "Otherwise, we'll be late, we will."

Aker laughs as she climbs down the licorice ladder. "I never thought I'd hear myself say that I enjoyed her company today. I see why you like her so much." His smile fades as he looks at me. "I need you to be careful tonight."

"As careful as I can be," I reply with a fake smile.

Aker looks down at his right hand. Palm up, he begins twirling his fingers clockwise. A red hue appears. Slowly, the mist starts molding into something more solid. I watch as it takes its final shape.

He extends his hand, offering the Gifted strawberry to me. It's as big as an apple. I gently take the fruit without making eye contact. But when I take a bite, I smile sideways at him. It's incredibly delicious.

"Do you like it?" His voice is barely above a whisper.

I want to reply, *It's the most amazing thing that's ever touched my tongue,* but all that comes out is, "Mhmm."

"I've been thinking..." he says slowly, looking me straight in the eye. "Forget all this. Forget this mission. Why put your life in danger? Kansis, you'll probably be captured by Guardians, and you won't escape this time. I know you said you'd go back to Depalo after this mission, but why risk everything? Let's just leave now."

Although his words don't come as a shock, I still hate hearing them. Mostly because *I'm* afraid too. I'm not a warrior like Amelia; I'm not brave like Scout. Who do I think I am going on a mission like this?

But knowing I won't disappoint Scout or leave Amelia, I retort, "You said you wouldn't bring this up again."

"Yeah, well, this is *ente*, Kansis! Dirty, rotten *ente!*"

Shaking my head, I respond, "I can't leave them."

"You can," he says firmly and reaches out his hand as if to touch me. But he scratches his ear instead and puts his hand in his pocket.

At his closeness, my face burns, and I can't think straight. "I want to help them," I explain, closing my eyes tight.

Scout's voice enters my thoughts, *Aker does not love you because he chooses not to. It is that simple.*

"How much help are you, though? Really?" Aker asks. "Can't someone else do this for them?"

I think about the prophecy. "I'm… I'm…" How do I say it? I want to tell Aker, but I know he'll find a way to make fun of it. A hollowness seeps through my veins.

"You're what?" he prompts. When I don't say anything, he pushes, "Come on, Kansis. Spill the blood. You're what?"

"I'm in a prophecy with Scout. It's about Arkarian Story."

His brows knit together. "What are you talking about?"

With much stumbling and stuttering, I tell him about the prophecy, sharing all Scout has told me. When I finished, I chance a look at him but his face is unreadable.

"Time's up!" Amelia calls from the bottom of the stairs. "We've got to go, don't we!"

"So…" Aker begins, "they need you?"

"Kind of," I admit. Technically speaking, they could wait another fifty years.

"Kind of?"

"Yes, they need me." It may be a lie, but it also might not be.

"So… you're special here. To them."

His words sting. "That's hard to believe?"

He shakes his head and leans back against the door. "No, it all makes more sense now."

"What makes sense?"

"Why you'd prefer these strangers over your family and your home."

His observation leaves me without a response.

He continues as if to explain himself. "At first, I thought you needed an adventure of sorts—working at the Ward and all, you don't get out much. Then I thought it was because these people weren't shunning you, and I'm sure that was a nice feeling. Then I thought maybe you were becoming friends with Amelia and wanted to help her. But now, I see it's just that you like being needed. You enjoy being special to them."

His words knock the air out of me. "That is so unfair," I whisper.

"You've always been like that, though," he goes on. "I don't know why it should surprise me now."

"What are you even talking about?" I ask, my anger finally catching up with the injustice of his claim.

"Time to go, Freckles!" Amelia yells from below.

Ignoring her, Aker continues, anger burning in his eyes. "In Grade Six at the Vocation Ceremony. You completely sabotaged Mirindiss' and my display so that you could come out looking like the hero of the evening."

It takes me a moment to remember what he's talking about. The Announcement Ceremony had taken place the month before, and I knew that Aker Vonbough was to be my mate. Then Kaileb had come to me after classes one day and asked if I noticed how Mirindiss and Aker looked at and acted around one another. I told him I had and asked him if he'd seen how much time they spent working on their Vocation Project.

After discussing their actions, we came up with a plan. It had been my one stroke of insane genius, and Kaileb had helped me do it.

I can't help but laugh a little now, and I don't even look at Aker to see his response. "If you remember correctly, *Kaileb* was the hero of the night, as he put the fire out. And we just did it to get you and Mirindiss to stop spending time together."

"Yeah, well, it worked since we didn't end up getting the jobs we wanted. We could have worked together."

I laugh again. "Mission accomplished." At his look of shock, I open my hands in a gesture of surrender. "Look, I'm sorry, but I don't know what you want me to say. I didn't want you to work with her. I didn't want you to spend time with her. I didn't want her to be special to you because—breaking news—*I* am your mate. Not her. I'm the one who is supposed to be special in your life. *We* are supposed to be married, not you and her. I will be the mother of your children, not her. I'm not even sure why you're trying to make me feel bad about that—I don't."

What has gotten into me? Why am I speaking so freely to him? When I glance up, I'm surprised at his thoughtful expression. His eyes meet mine, and I capitulate. "I am sorry that I ruined that night for you."

He snorts. "No, you're not."

I dare to match his smirk. "Not even a little bit."

He laughs, and it's the hearty one that makes my veins feel full and my face feel hot.

When the laughter falls away, he says warmly, "Kansis, the longer I'm around you, the more I realize that…" He eyes me. "The more I realize that I like you." Then he does something he has never done before… he reaches for my hand. Right before he touches me, however, he hesitates.

"Weighing pros and cons?" I ask quietly. "Con: I have to touch her, pro: I might get what I want?"

"Now, that's not fair," he says and moves his hand away.

"Not fair? Your pendulum-swing emotions aren't fair. You go from being a huge jerk to really sweet in mere sentences. It's exhausting."

"I don't love you, Kansis," he growls. "I'm not attracted to you in even the slightest degree. I don't want to touch you because the only woman I want to touch is Mirindiss. I don't want to hold your hand or sit close to you because your blood is not in me, but *hers* is. Do you understand that? I can't love you right now. So forgive me if I'm having to try and be nice to you. There's a war going on in my blood!"

A silence falls between us, which is quickly filled with Amelia calling up to me again. "We're going to be late!"

"Up until yesterday," Aker says, ignoring her, "I thought I would be miserable every day for the rest of my life being married to you... But it's different now. We know the truth. And I believe that, once we do the Blood Transfusion, you and I... that we..." He reaches out and finally grabs ahold of one of my hands. I look at our fingers interlocked, barely able to breathe. With his other hand, he takes one of my newly-controlled silver curls and places it behind my ear.

"I don't want you to go on this mission; I don't want to be here at the circus. All I want to do is go home and marry you," Aker states, rubbing the wisp of hair between his fingers. "And I won't stop asking you when we can go. But for now... I'll stay and wait for you to get back." He moves closer to me, our fingers still interlocked. As he slowly moves his hand from my hair to my lips, he stares for a few seconds as he caresses them. Quietly, he remarks, "I don't think I ever realized you have freckles on your lips."

I don't move. I can't move.

He looks at my face, forehead, cheeks, chin, nose, and finally, my eyes. "You're... You're pretty."

I don't breathe. I can't breathe.

"I never noticed."

I don't speak. I can't speak.

He leans close to me, his face only a couple of centimeters from mine. "I'll kiss you if you come home with me right now," he whispers hoarsely. "Forget this mission; come home with me."

"I... I..."

"Say my name. You never do, and you don't think I've noticed, but I have.

Kansis... Say my name."

"I..."

"Will you come home with me? Will you marry me, Kansis Willow?"

I can't think, I can't remember why I'm here... Why am I even hesitating? I close my eyes tight, trying to remember why I don't want to go back to Depalo.

Suddenly the spell breaks. The moment is over. I don't know how or when it started, and I'm just as confused about how and when it ends. But he's pulling away. *My* Aker is pulling away from me because I am choosing Amelia and the circus over him.

When he opens the door to go back into Fiddy and Memory's room, I can tell he's shaking too. "Your loss," he states huskily and slips through the doorway.

As if he were next to me, Scout's words ring in my ear: *Love is a choice to put someone above yourself no matter what. Feelings be damned.*

I steel myself and try to relax my beating heart. What Scout says is lofty and beautiful and *preferable*... but it's not real. Aker only loves Mirindiss because her blood is within him. And as soon as *my* blood is in him, he will love me too.

He will.

He has to.

I look back at the doorway where my future husband has disappeared. Why am I choosing Amelia and the circus over him? I *should* go home with him like he's asking...

"Kansis! Don't make me come get you! I'll make it unnecessarily painful, I will!" Amelia shouts from below.

Wiping away the tears that have disobediently fallen, I clear my throat and make my way down to meet her. I gave my word that I would help, and so I will. But I will leave with Aker tomorrow. It's the right thing to do.

When I jump off the licorice ladder, I quickly pull a smile over my features. I don't want to talk about what happened yet.

"Took long enough," Amelia remarks playfully. As we walk towards Scout and Pypen's office, she goes on, "Well, today was fun, wasn't it?"

Trying to get Aker out of my head and blood, I respond, "It was. You were really good at Gedankenspiel."

"No, I'm just competitive," she replies, and I can hear the smile in her voice. "Hey, Freckles?"

"Hmm?"

"I don't know all that much about friendship, but what I do know looks like today, doesn't it." She pauses. "Those people enjoyed your company, they did. You didn't have to *make* them feel anything for you."

I smile but don't respond. Why do I finally feel at home in this clash of worlds?

And now the mission... The plan is easy enough... you know... except the part where the entire mission depends on my Gift and me.

When we walk into Scout and Pypen's office, Amelia strides in as if she is this group's leader. I hesitate by the door, still nauseous from my interaction with Aker.

But when I look around the room, I see two sea-foam green eyes already on me. Scout's brows crease, and he mouths, "Levels balanced?"

I nod quickly. Not because it's true but because I don't want to reveal anything else. When Pypen calls his name, Scout doesn't look away from me—face worried, he searches mine.

"Scout," Pypen repeats. "'Tis time."

Reluctantly, Scout turns away and addresses the group. "With the intelligence of the elephant, the determination of the rhinoceros, the cunning of the octopus, the strength of the jaguar, and the devotion of the wolf—let us complete this mission successfully and then return safely."

"Let it be!" everyone in the room, minus Amelia and me, shouts with one voice.

As I turn to follow the others out of the office, a hand grabs my elbow, and I turn to see Scout. Electricity seems to run from my arm through my heart and into the rest of my body.

"What has happened?" Scout asks.

"Nothing," I lie, hoping he doesn't let go of me. "I'm just nervous about the mission."

Taking the bait, he slowly grabs my hand and affirms, "You can do this. I know you can."

The hard edges of my anxiety wanes at his touch and words. For a second, I forget about Aker and just take in this moment of being seen and cared for by another human being. But then I remember that I'm leaving... tomorrow.

I should tell him. I should just say it... but I can't.

"Thank you," I finally respond.

Still holding my hand, he pulls me towards the door. "Come now, Reader," he says playfully. "Let us show the world of what Kansis Willow is capable."

Silenda

Pypen

SCOUT REHEARSES THE PLAN with our team one more time as we drive through an outlying town in Silenda. He ends his monologue with, "Any questions?"

"What if the Guardians show up?" Kansis asks.

"Thanks to Winzer, even if the whole building is covered in Guardians, we could still just walk past them," I answer confidently. "Our activity may be detectable, but our mere presence will not. Our attempts to get into the secret chamber may set off alarms, but that is why we have the distraction."

"So there is no way at all, no matter the circumstance, that the Guardians could detect us—I don't mean detecting what we are doing in there—but *us* as people?" Kansis presses.

Amelia nudges her. "I thought you were confident in the Cloak?"

"I'm just asking," Kansis remarks, but fear shines through her brown eyes.

"Technically, they could bring a Moth," Emerly answers. I turn away, repulsed by his mere presence as he continues, "There are only three Moths in all of the Hexum; if they employed one, he or she could find us, they could."

I cannot look at him without hearing his admissions regarding his past running through my thoughts.

"Moths are Red level," Chestin, one of our storytellers, argues. "It is not likely they would be let out of the precinct just so that they can find a Ward member and Pod, would they?"

"Maybe one was made an offer they couldn't refuse," Emerly replies. "Or maybe their handlers were made the offer, they were."

"Either way, the only person who could overcome Winzer's Cloak is a Moth, and the Guardians will have no reason to suspect our interference regarding the spider epidemic at the museum. That they would send a Moth there this night is highly improbable." Scout is convinced, and I see no evidence to go against him.

"It is more likely a squadron of Guardians will be armed with finitums, blindly shooting throughout the museum hoping to hit us," Winzer remarks and giggles nervously.

"What's a finitum?" Amelia asks.

"'Tis a Gift-stripping weapon," Scout answers. "If a shot lands anywhere on the body, one's Gift is immediately stripped; if a shot hits the heart, the person dies on the spot." He looks over at me. "Not even Pypen could do anything about that."

"How likely is it the Guardians will have finitums on them?" the Pod asks, eyebrows raised.

"Highly *unlikely*," I answer. "Guardians have plenty of weapons that they utilize without such an armament, because its effects are irreversible—even with a Red Gift."

"Wouldn't they wear them for that reason?" Amelia asks. "If they were walking around with finitums, people would be on their best behavior, they would."

"'Tis a dangerous weapon," Scout replies soberly. "Few are given the power to wield it—only the Deputy Chiefs and Chiefs are licensed."

There is an unusual tension in the group, and I wonder if it is because of Kansis and Amelia's presence. The rest of us—Chestin, Emerly, Winzer, Ryder, Gigi, Scout, and myself—have worked together multiple times, but never with people as inexperienced as these two young women. Furthermore, with so much depending on Kansis and her Gift alone, even I am uneasy.

However, if I were to be honest with myself, I can't help but wonder if I feel uneasy because of what I witnessed earlier. It had taken me by surprise seeing Scout holding Kansis' hand in the courtyard. The action seemed familiar and easy, like he has known her for a long time. When I looked down at my prancing lion tattoo at the time, I was even more disturbed by its pink and violet shades. It has not taken on those colors in almost eight years. Granted, there have been moments throughout the years when the two colors have swirled with the orange and yellow greens of anxiety and sadness, but never... never *just* pink and violet.

When Kansis saw me watching them, she had immediately taken her hand back from Scout, and within a heartbeat, oranges, yellows, and light greens swirled into the tattoo. But perhaps I had just seen things... Perhaps I am wrong. It has been an odd day, after all...

That morning, Scout and I had taken the Goi Armiarma to the Museum of

Senex. We walked around for a few minutes feigning interest in the Senexian artifacts and art, then we went into the bathroom. Once within, we locked the door, and he took the box out of his jacket. Inside, the queen of the spiders lay very still. He placed the box on the sink, and as carefully as he could, he unfastened the small claw clasp. Not knowing what to expect, we had both taken a huge step backward, away from the spider. Slowly, one hairy leg poked out of the onyx container. It was quickly followed by seven more.

The queen had four giant eyes perched on her head—two large ones flanked by a smaller pair. Her thorax was black, while her abdomen was blood red, onyx black, and bright, turquoise blue. Behind her eyes was a stripe of turquoise, and below was a matching red. However, the top of her head was a shimmering gold—like the crown of queens of old.

All four eyes seemed to be fixed on me. She seemed innocent enough, just like any other spider. But then she did something I have never seen an arachnid do. There was a slight cracking sound, like a shoe stepping on a piece of hard candy, as the queen lifted her head away from her thorax. A skinny, black neck pushed the head high above her so that she resembled a tiny, monstrous giraffe. She opened her mouth, and it seemed as if her jaw disconnected so it could open unnaturally wide. What looked like an Adam's apple bobbed rapidly as a sharp cry emitted from her mouth.

My blood turned to ice. Scout and I ran, getting out of there as fast as possible. Only an hour later, the news was everywhere that the Museum of Senex had been closed due to a spider infestation. In only sixty minutes more, the whole city of Hydranja had been overrun. Everyone within the town limits had been evacuated, and Arachnid specialists had been called, but no one could find the infestation's source. It mattered not how many spiders were killed; hundreds of thousands more converged on the city from neighboring districts. The queen had a vaster range of power than we had realized.

Now, as we drive towards our critical mission, I wonder again if this is a terrible idea. Kansis looks to be on the verge of vomiting.

"Would you like me to regulate your hormones?" I ask her.

With her permission, I flush out her adrenaline. Even still, her legs shake in nervousness.

The car we rented has three rows; the back two face forward, but the front row points backward, so the first and second rows are opposite each other. The driver is facing the proper direction, but this is just for show. As the vehicle is on the railroad system and drives itself, if Chestin wanted to, he could turn the driver's chair around to look at the second row as well.

Scout and Emerly sit in the back, their heads close as they have a private conversation. Let them talk. I have had no words for Emerly since his confession. He has tried to be friendly with me all day, and although I have not outright dismissed him, I have not been welcoming either. We knew Emerly had a life before coming to the circus, but I had no idea it was filled with such evil. Scout, in the other ventricle, spoke to him during the entire show. I have not asked what they discussed. I am not ready to hear it.

Although I know he is not the person he described any longer, Emerly *had been* that person. He had been capable of such things. It seems the only person in the entire world I can trust is Scout Eekan.

Our pila arrives in Hydranja, Silenda, and when we drive out onto the street, we are met with chaos. Almost every surface is covered with spiders running, climbing, and even swinging toward the museum. The car drives on, innumerable sickening crunches popping under the wheels.

Eager not to dwell on our gruesome surroundings, I let my thoughts wander to Merayal and our new venture together. This morning I had spent some time on the local databases attempting to track down the face of Xoana Kapu's assassin. Although my search was unsuccessful, I am not worried. The Sixth Aevum has given us access to more extensive mainframes, and I can sneak into the Formosian library next day and hopefully retrieve an image there.

I do not think Merayal will murder the assassin once I provide her the opportunity. Many people claim to be seeking deadly revenge, but no one commits the act. Once presented with closure, I believe Merayal will walk away and be able to move on from her mother's death. After all, I was able to move past my own tragedy—I believe Merayal can as well.

The picture of her smile replays over and over again in my mind. The warmth in her eyes, the sweetness of her mouth, the openness of her posture… it is like I met Merayal Kapu for the first time this day.

"What if the book is in a box we cannot open?" Kansis suddenly asks Scout, eyes fearful. "What if we can't get to it?"

Scout turns his attention to her. "We brought Ryder and Chestin for our journey's unexpected twists and turns. Something always strays from the course, so we brought them along for those unforeseen moments."

"And what if they can't help?" she asks, wringing her hands.

"We have all night. I believe, between us, we will overcome."

Staring at all the spiders outside, Kansis stammers, "A-Are you sure about this? What if—"

"There are no *what-ifs*," Ryder barks. "We have done this before, unlike you."

"Back off; this is her first mission, isn't it," Amelia growls, while Scout reprimands, "Unnecessary, Ryder."

Ryder throws the sack he has been holding down on the floor of the car. "No, *she* is unnecessary, Scout. The *daughter* is unnecessary. Why are you endangering us like this? They should not be here!"

"We cannot complete this mission without Kansis," Scout replies. "We need her Gift."

"We need not the daughter," Ryder protests.

Scout keeps his anger simmering low. "We cannot separate either of them from Winzer, or the Guardians would find them."

"We can take the Senexian in another form. I can make her into a piece of paper, and you can carry her next to your chest—"

"I told her she could stay in her human form. I am a man of my word."

Ryder broadens his shoulders. "And that flaw hurts all of us."

Scout's anger boils. "I apologize that my integrity inconveniences you—"

"It is not an inconvenience, it is—"

"Enough!" I shout. Rarely am I the one intervening on Scout's behalf, and it feels awkward to do so.

Thankfully, Scout does not reproach me. "I agree," he says. "We are very close now." And he returns his attention to Emerly so they can continue their whispered conversation. Looking away from them, I see we are near our destination.

I glance at Amelia, who openly glares at Ryder.

There is something about her that reminds me of Merayal. They are both confident and willful. They are both confrontational and aggressive. They're both beautiful, domineering, and strong. It must be the Senexian nature inside of them.

And yet, even in that, they are very different. Amelia immediately allowed Kansis into her confidence. She was willing to trust Kansis in order to get what she wanted. Merayal was the opposite. She knew that Scout and I were the ones who could help her find her mother's assassin, yet she had placed no trust in me up until a few hours ago.

Despite her propensity to violence, there is an openness and softness to Amelia. She is eager for friendship and adventure. Taming Amelia would have been much simpler.

"Prepare," I say, and all the chatting, quiet though it has been, falls into complete silence.

As we arrive at our drop-off point, Chestin stops the car. Spiders crawl all over the vehicle until Gigi emits a little noise, and they all scurry away. Gigi keeps up a slow tune as we leave the vehicle, creating a little spider-free path for us to walk down single file. It is not far to the museum. We move up the stairs and approach the main entrance. The six-meter-high oak door is so covered in spiders that one would not even recognize it is a door, save for the surrounding archway.

Gigi's tune changes, and not only do the spiders get out of our way, but the door itself splinters open with a loud *crack*! Once we're all inside, she sings the door back into place. Darkness surrounds us. All that can be heard is the disturbing scuttling and clicking of millions of spiders.

Just as planned, after he uses it on himself, Scout moves towards each member and drops a bead of liquid from a small vial into each of our eyes. With it, we will be able to see perfectly in the dark. Once he puts the liquid in my eyes, however, I almost wish he had not.

The statues, paintings, relics, and exhibits are all covered in arachnids. It is one thing to hear them, but seeing them roiling over the museum's interior like a spiky black wave makes me shudder.

"Let us do this quickly so we can get out of here," Ryder remarks gruffly.

Gigi, leading in the front, valiantly sings the spiders out of our way. We walk the length of the museum toward where the Book of Instructions is hidden.

Finally, we get to a wall that I know leads to the offices. Effortlessly, Gigi moves the spiders and bursts open the wall. We emerge into a large office. With all of the spiders, I cannot even see where the door is. Gigi sings a path to the westward wall and breaks it apart easily.

On the other side is a laboratory. The tech looks like it is moving itself across all of the workstations, but then I see the spiders are moving objects towards an open doorway. "Over here," Gigi instructs, taking us to the southward wall. This time, we walk into a large storage room.

Gigi keeps a path clear as Scout leads us to aisle nine, row one. The secret chamber is located directly below this spot. Once there, we all take a few steps back to make room so Gigi can sing a large hole into the concrete.

A high-pitched note leaves her mouth, but nothing happens. The sound lowers, but still nothing. She closes her eyes and lets out a sound like a flute. Still, nothing happens.

When she opens her eyes, she smiles ruefully. "Oh, it is clever."

"What is it?" Scout asks.

"The Sixth Aevum did not divulge that the entire chamber is made of ever-changing matter."

"Inconceivable," I hiss, while Amelia asks, "What's that?"

I wait for Kansis to answer, but she seems so on edge I am not certain she even heard the question. So, I answer, "It means we cannot enter the chamber."

"Not necessarily," Chestin remarks thoughtfully. "We merely need to deceive the matter into fixating on one element, and then we can slip through another, we can."

"It would be fighting us on three other fronts," Gigi counters. "It would be better if we were to cause disturbances in three of the elements, and then we could use the fourth as a door."

Chestin nods. "If you could focus on the solids, I will take the plasma and gases. Slipping through a liquid would be easiest, wouldn't it?"

"Unless said liquid is acid," Gigi retorts.

"I will try to counteract as many as possible, but liquid would be safest. Pypen," Chestin turns to me, "you will have your Gift at the ready in case we are poisoned."

"What will you have us do?" Scout asks.

"When I give the word, jump. Even if the floor still looks like concrete, everyone must jump," Chestin commands.

When we all agree, Chestin and Gigi close their eyes. Although there is no change in the ground—no trembling, no sound, no crackling—I can feel the power they are both emitting. After five minutes, they both stop, heaving for breath. Quickly, I hand them both Vorbies so they can recharge their energy.

"What is it?" Scout questions once they have recovered.

"It's tricky, isn't it," Chestin answers, scratching his red beard. "It senses we are excluding our disturbance from one, so it began focusing on the liquids and then barred our entrance."

Gigi snaps her fingers and looks at Ryder. "You could transform into water and enter into the ever-changing matter. Inside, feign manipulation so the matter will not sense that one of the elements is being excluded."

"You make it sound so easy," Ryder retorts, his mouth set in a jeer. "It is much more complicated than that."

"You can do it," Scout replies curtly. "At least, you could try."

"There are so many factors we have not considered," Ryder seethes. "I will not jump into ever-changing matter without knowing I can get back out."

"The matter is not looking to keep in—" Gigi starts, but Ryder interrupts her, snarling, "I was not asking you, *batata*!"

At the same time, Chestin seethes, "Wash out your mouth, shouldn't you!" Scout hoarsely whispers, "You may not speak to her that way!" and I yell, "Bridle your tongue!"

Ryder takes a step backward at our onslaught. Recovering quickly, he argues, "You do not get to tell me how to talk to my mate."

"You should not talk to *anyone* that way, let alone your mate," Scout counters.

Ryder snorts derisively. "If this was anything like Senex, you could bet every Vorbi in the world she would not be my mate, and I would choose another!"

Gigi pales instantly. Then, anger like I have never seen springs into her eyes, and she slaps Ryder across the face.

As Ryder raises his hand to slap her back, Scout grabs it and shoves it up behind his back while Emerly punches Ryder in the face.

I shove Emerly away from Ryder and then push Scout back. I quickly renew Ryder's bloody nose and cry again, "Enough! This is not the place for this conversation." Turning to Ryder, I state, "And we will have this conversation later." Softening my voice, I go on, "But for now, Ryder, we need you. You are very talented, and we need your Gift. Could you please try? The ever-changing matter is not offensive, only defensive. You will be safe."

Ryder rolls his eyes. "Fine." After taking a deep breath, he releases it, and as he exhales, his whole being liquifies, cascading onto the floor. Instead of dispersing across the concrete as ordinary water droplets would, Ryder seamlessly absorbs into the floor.

Gigi and Chestin close their eyes once more. After the first couple of minutes, they both begin to grunt and sweat with the effort.

Suddenly, with a strained voice, Chestin growls, "Now!"

From the corner of my eye, I see Amelia grab Kansis and jump with her into the hole the three Gifters have opened below us. I wait until Emerly and Winzer drop in before I motion for Scout to go next. He nods quickly, and then I follow after him.

When I land, several things happen at once. Blinding pain hits my eyes. Shrill screams fill my ears. Fear floods my veins.

When I try to renew whatever injury is causing the pain in my eyes, I cannot. Or, rather, the injury keeps reigniting. It is as if a knife is being plunged into my eyes, and every time I take it out, another one stabs.

Everyone is screaming my name, begging me to take their pain away. Reaching past my own agony, I try to renew theirs. But I cannot.

I cannot help anyone. I cannot even help Scout.

"The drops!" Emerly shouts above the din of screams. "Scout! The eye drops!"

I hear Scout yell, "On it," in a strained voice from somewhere nearby. He is quiet for a moment, and I do my best to bite my screams back as I wait for him. Within a half-minute, he grabs my face and tries to force my eyes open to let in the liquid, but the pain keeps them shut. Finally, he is able to claw them open enough to get some drops into the ducts of my eyes.

Slowly, I feel the agony start to subside. Scout moves on, and one by one, the wails cease. I can sense retina damage in each of our eyes, so I renew them all. Finally, the stinging stops and I can open mine.

We are in a sunroom filled with bright afternoon sunlight. There are floor-to-ceiling windows on three walls, looking out to a quaint and humble garden. The sunroom has rocking chairs, rennix tables, sitting poufs, and a kitchenette in the back. The windows are flanked with golden curtains that cast diamond-like sundrops on the white shag carpet.

"What was that?" Ryder shouts, shattering the moment of confused serenity.

"The night vision serum exposed our eyes to too much light, didn't it?" Emerly answers.

"It was meant to regulate if there was to be interior light, but not true sunlight," Scout adds. "I knew we would be going inside in the evening, so I did not anticipate natural sunlight being an issue."

"What is this place?" Amelia asks, gazing about her.

"It belongs to the president of the Pod Tracking System," Scout answers.

"How do you know that?" Ryder asks.

"Because he is the one who was tasked with hiding the Book of Instructions," I answer.

"Speaking of which," Emerly starts. "He did not make much effort in hiding it, did he."

"He did not," Winzer replies.

We all walk over to where they are standing. The Book of Instructions lays atop a tall lectern made of periwinkle blue stones underneath one of the windowed walls. There must be some type of preservation Gift on it, because the pages look fresh, almost like they were just penned in last day.

When her shaking hands reach for the book, Scout grabs them. "Do not touch it," he commands. "It may have a way of tracking or identifying you if you do so." Turning to Gigi, he asks, "Can you turn to page seventeen?"

Gigi closes her eyes and ushers in a slight wind to turn the pages to the correct location.

"Read as fast as you can," Scout commands the trembling Pexun. I reduce Kansis' adrenaline levels as she closes her eyes and takes the last step needed to read.

"You can do this, Freckles," Amelia encourages, squeezing her hand.

Kansis smiles at her, then turns to the Book of Instructions. Her eyes seem to glaze over as if she is in a whole new world.

Amelia stays right by Kansis, never taking her eyes off her. Scout takes a few steps back but keeps his attention on the girl as well. The rest of the group drifts around the room, eager to inspect the space. Ryder marches away to the farthest part of the room by the kitchenette and Gigi goes in the opposite direction.

"I need to show you something," Emerly whispers to Scout and me. I wish not to follow. I desire not to speak to him at all, but when Scout follows, I do as well. Emerly leads us to a glass cabinet. After snapping his fingers once, he points inside. At first, I do not know what he is bringing to our attention. All I see are shells, small plants, and other trinkets covered in a light film of dust. But then I see it. A small black box textured like a turtle's shell with not a speck of dust upon it. "Could be a detection object, couldn't it," Emerly says quietly. "Winzer's Gift keeps those under her protection from being detected by those who have ill intentions. An inanimate object doesn't have intentions, does it?"

"Formerly, Winzer has kept us hidden by employing sensor Gifts and gadgets," Scout replies.

"It's been set there recently," Emerly says, noticing the dust on the other objects as well. "Within the last few days."

"It matters not," I say. "No one knows we are here."

Kansis suddenly takes a deep breath as if she has just emerged from a body of water. Amelia turns Kansis to face her and asks, "Are you okay?"

Kansis blinks several times before her vision comes back into focus. Her eyes connect with Amelia's and at first she looks confused, but then her brows furrow and the corners of her mouth turn down. She takes a step back from Amelia. "You..." Her jaw shutters. "You lied to me. You're... you're not Arkarian Story's daughter."

Amelia does not get a chance to answer, as the windows of the three glass walls explode.

"Assume a submissive position!" a loud female voice blares throughout the sunroom. "We know you are in here!"

"Femme!" Scout and I shout at the same time.

"The Deputy Chief followed us here?" Emerly asks incredulously. "How?"

"Are you not doing your job?" Ryder growls at Winzer.

"I am unsure how they know we're here," Winzer whispers, "but they cannot pinpoint exactly where we are. They can't sense or see us. It is a bluff, it is."

"Maybe it is a Moth?" Amelia asks.

"You did call it, Em," Winzer comments with a wry grimace.

I shake my head. "We would know if the Guardians have a Moth. No, we need to follow our plan and leave. Chestin, Gigi, and Ryder, get us out of here."

However, at that exact moment, ten or so people suddenly appear in the backyard. Each is covered from head to toe in slim-fitting suits. One of the people walks forward faster than the others. The material around their eyes is transparent, and even from here I can see the hunger in Deputy Chief Femme's expression.

We are all exposed before her—none of us move.

Femme looks about and then closes her eyes.

What if there *is* a Moth? What if they are giving her information? Will she attack us? From where I am, I cannot protect Scout, and if there is one thing I am certain of, it is this: I will die before Scout does.

Slowly Femme opens her eyes and I can tell by the way she does not look at any of us directly that she cannot see us. She does not actually know for sure that we are in here.

Before I have time to relax, in an instant my blood pressure drops so low I almost pass out.

Two finitums materialize in her hands, and Deputy Chief Femme fires straight at us.

One impact hits Ryder right in his chest.

All around us, furniture begins exploding as the room takes the force of missed finitum shots.

I can feel the moment all the life leaves Ryder's blood.

Our members are screaming, scrambling to get behind the furniture.

Ryder collapses to the floor, instantly dead.

"Any ideas, Pypen?" Scout yells to me. I know not if anyone else saw Ryder fall. But he did fall... he died. Right in front of me. He was a *patka*, to be certain... but he was still our friend—a member of our family.

"Pypen!" Scout shouts, but I cannot think. Finitum shots shatter a lamp right by my face.

"Gigi!" Emerly yells. "See if the ever-changing matter is underneath the room as well or just around the top and sides!"

It takes her a moment, but she answers, "It is underneath, but they cut a corner, and there's one small hole over by the back wall! It might not even be big enough for us to get through."

"Try!" Scout shouts. "Tunnel us out, and if need be, we will remove limbs, and Pypen can renew them on the other side."

"Remove limbs?" Kansis shrieks.

"I thought you said Gigi's exception was humans?" Amelia asks, horrified.

A churning noise erupts from the back wall. "Go, go!" Scout shouts, and we all make a run for the small tunnel Gigi is singing into existence. Winzer, Chestin, and I grab furniture as we run and start making a bulwark to cover us when we enter the tunnel. Running backwards, I look behind me and see Amelia shove Kansis through first, but her hips get stuck.

Without thought, I look to Emerly and command, "Make her fit."

His shocked expression turns from me to Scout and back to me. "I told you when I joined, I would never use—"

"We are going to die if you refuse," I reply callously. "We will all die because you possessed not the guts to get us out of here."

"Pypen," Scout admonishes.

"No!" I shout. "We will all get shot if he does not use his sword."

Emerly swallows hard and looks over to Kansis' body, half inside, half outside the tunnel. Amelia is pushing her with all her might, and Kansis' cries are muffled in the tunnel.

With fear and determination shining in his green eyes, he walks over to Kansis' body. Emerly understands—this is the only way.

"No!" Scout shouts, but it is too late.

In an instant, Emerly's arm morphs into an ivory blade, its ending so sharp, I can see the gleam even amid the explosions.

Scout cries out again and runs towards Emerly, but I catch him. "It is the only way!" I groan, holding him with all my might.

"What are you doing?" Amelia screams.

Emerly slices one of Kansis' hips off in one fell swoop. Blood explodes from her side, her exposed hip bone bright like a light. With her head inside the tunnel, Kansis' agonized screeches are suppressed, but they still send chills racing through my veins.

"Renew her!" Scout hollers in my face. "*Now*, Pypen!"

"What have you done?" Amelia screams.

"Get in line!" I shout. "Emerly will make us all fit through! The pain is only for a moment—I will renew you on the other side."

Nobody moves, and Kansis' screams pierce the sound of the finitum shots.

From the corner of my eye, I see Gigi's head rise like a wolf for a howl, and she releases a sound filled with such strain and torment that my eyes fill with tears. To my amazement, the tunnel opens up another few centimeters. Before Scout can even ask again, I renew Kansis' hip. Amelia dives into the tunnel, pushing Kansis ahead of her, closely followed by Winzer and Chestin.

Shots fly all around us, and one barely misses my hand as the furniture behind us becomes less and less of a shield.

"Now, you," I order Gigi. "Go to the end and then close the tunnel in five minutes. Whether we are there or not. Do you understand me, Gigi?"

Too exhausted to argue, she nods and climbs through the gap.

"Go, my friend," Scout commands Emerly.

"We can't leave Ryder's body, can we?" Emerly asks.

I look past him to the kitchenette where Ryder fell. Explosions land all around us.

"We cannot get to him," Scout states desolately. "We will be hit."

"Ah, but I am quick. I am nimble," Emerly replies with a smirk.

"Emerly, it is not worth it," Scout says urgently. "We have to leave."

"But if we leave him, Femme will know we were here. If we take him with us, she will never know if she was right or wrong. Everything will be compromised if he remains, it will!"

Scout thinks for a moment, and I wait until he comes to the obvious *Scout* conclusion. Before he can even utter it, I command, "You are not going, Scout."

"I must," he retorts, strength and sadness in his voice.

"You will not," I argue. "I will not permit it."

"It will be me," Emerly states. He puts his hand on Scout's shoulder, "All will be well. To the praise of the Rogue Superior, huh?" He turns to me and smiles crookedly. "We'll get you soon enough, Pip."

With his stomach on the floor, Emerly crawls over to Ryder's prone body. A shot narrowly misses his head. Miraculously, he reaches Ryder. He grabs the body and uses it as a shield as he crawls back toward us. He has almost reached us when he suddenly screams out in pain as a finitum shot hits his hand. A wave of energy envelopes his whole body, making it contort in unnatural ways. His head, neck, and chest rise from the ground.

His Gift is being stripped.

He opens his eyes, and they meet Scout's for one painful moment. He smiles weakly. "I...I," he stutters, his body still contorting, "didn't need it anyway."

To my horror, another shot slams straight into his chest. His shocked, green eyes turn to me then. Their emerald hue swirls for a moment as his pupils try to connect with mine. But then, as if I am watching a light slowly dim, the life leaves his eyes. Emerly's dead body crumples to the ground in a lump of clothes and red hair.

A hand, forever frozen outstretched, extends toward us like a morbid invitation.

Scout kneels and reaches for the hand. Before I can pull him back, Scout crushes Emerly's body to himself.

Sobbing, Scout commands, "Y-You g-grab Ryder. I will pull Emerly through, and th-then you pull Ryder."

He enters the hole backward, holding Emerly's hands tightly as he pulls the lifeless body in after him.

I give him a moment, and then I go in the same way, dragging Ryder's body to the other side. The pitch dark is eerie and numbing. The work is hard, but it keeps me from believing what just happened. Every time I recall the sight of life draining from Emerly's eyes, I scream and pull Ryder's form as hard as I can. Then, out of nowhere, the tunnel begins to shake.

It is collapsing!

Forsaking Ryder's body, I focus all my efforts on climbing backward out of the hole. Someone grabs my legs and begins pulling.

I tumble out the other side and lie, deadened, by the hole's entrance. My eyes adjust, and I take in my surroundings. We are in a dark basement. The only sound is the chittering and scurrying of thousands of spiders. Once I have gathered my bearings, I state quietly to no one and everyone, "Ryder's body is still in the tunnel."

"We will come back for it another day," Chestin responds quickly. "We must get out of here before anything else happens, we must."

Gigi, her face slackened and limp, her eyes wide and empty, keeps up a quiet tune so the spiders stay away from us. Winzer... oh, Winzer. She lies over her mate's dead body, weeping into his red hair.

Sirens hit our ears.

"Now," Chestin commands. "We must go now."

Scout crawls over to Winzer. He speaks quietly to her. A wail leaves her lips, and she nuzzles into Emerly's chest. Scout places his arm over her heaving back. Tears stream down his face.

"We must leave," I state quietly. "We need only get out onto the street, and they will not be able to track us."

"So we think," Gigi replies without inflection.

"I can't talk to you right now!" Kansis shouts, and I look over to see Amelia backing away from her. Why did Kansis say that Amelia was not Arkarian Story's daughter? What did she read?

Scout gingerly lifts Winzer so her face meets his. He gently kisses her forehead and soothes quietly, "We have to go, Pet. I will carry him. We will not leave him here."

Amelia rushes over, helps Winzer to her feet, and holds her steady while Scout picks up Emerly's body and heaves him onto his back.

"Gigi," I prompt gently so she will sing us free of the basement.

Opening her sagged mouth, she emanates a sound I cannot hear but can feel. Within seconds, a new tunnel forms out of the earthen wall, and we follow her into it. Several times we bump into each other, but we all follow Gigi's voice. The tunnel rises gradually, and suddenly moonlight floods to greet us as she opens the tunnel into the ground outside the museum.

There is no need to run now. Unless the Guardians plan on attacking the Museum's entire perimeter, there is no way for them to find us.

We walk past Guardians and Arachnid Specialists who remain completely unaware of us, ignorant of the dead body Scout carries, oblivious of the emptiness in our veins. The sirens of the Guardians wax louder. They are just around the corner.

For a moment, I wonder if Winzer has let down her guard, and I call out, "Winzer, the Guardians are upon us!"

She says nothing, but the vehicles drive by without any hesitation or deviation.

As they pass, Winzer falls, and Amelia pulls her into her lap before her body hits the ground. The young Senexian hugs our Cloak tightly and whispers into her ear. Even when Amelia stops speaking, she caresses Winzer's hair and rocks her back and forth.

We stay like that for a long time.

Chestin moves his weight from his left foot to his right and then back, his hands in his pockets.

Gigi shivers, hugging herself, tearlessly eyeing the ground.

Kansis stares into the night, hands clasped by her chest, silver curls twinkling in the moonlight.

Scout stands unmoving, like a statue carrying a burden he cannot bear but cannot put down.

I eye each one of them, wondering what this night will mean. What will it mean for Winzer, for Scout, for me, for the circus...

And what will we do without Emerly Tosh?

Mundus Senex

Amelia

628 years ago; 2093

"**W**HY US?" THE MAN asks in a thick New Zealand accent. "We're just farmers out in the wop-wops. We're nobody special."

Clayton smiles. He is always the best when it comes to putting the families at ease. "You are representative of your culture, Mr. McKee. An average citizen living a normal life. The future needs you to remember New Zealand as it was for regular citizens."

"Will you freeze all of us?" the woman asks, voice shaking. "We've got five kids."

"Yes, you will all come," Clayton answers.

"My brother and his family live right down the road," the man states. "Could they come as well?"

Clayton's brows crease. "Your family was chosen at random, and provisions were made for the seven of you. We do not have the space on the plane or extra Hulls for others."

"I can't leave my brother and his family to die," Mr. McKee declares, voice hard.

"We offer this to you; you can turn it down," Clayton responds. "And if you choose to do so, we will go to the next family on our list. But if you choose to come, it is your family alone who will be encapsulated."

Amelia feels terrible for the man. What the Preservers are asking is a heavy burden to bear. But now, with the threat of nuclear war hanging over all countries, including tiny ones at the bottom of the world like New Zealand, people have been more willing to go.

Clayton continues, "We offer this not only for you but for future generations. You will most likely awaken to a world where there is no New Zealand, and this country is worth preserving if only in your memories."

The man stands silent as his wife weeps. Lily and Amerlia exchange looks—should one of us comfort her?

Mr. McKee asks, "Dayie Tueur said he'd burn any Hulls he finds?"

Clayton clears his throat. "Sir, the world is burning. With America bombing Europe, another nuke mole is bound to strike any day. It could hit anyone. It's our mission to keep the Pods safe from Dayie Tueur."

The man nods and pulls his wife into a hug. "This sounds like the kids' best shot, Anya."

"I'll pack our stuff," the woman responds through tears.

"You won't be able to bring anything with you," Chad says gently.

"But we'll need clothes," Anya argues as she rubs her eyes.

"You will be flown out to Norway and encapsulated this evening," Clayton replies calmly. "You don't need to bring anything."

The New Zealand woman is overcome with emotion and collapses to the floor in tears. Amelia and Chad help Mr. McKee gather their kids while Lily holds Anya and rubs her back consolingly. The family stares out the Jeep's windows as they are driven back to the Preservers' base. Most of the children cry along with their mother, but the oldest daughter stays tearless like her father.

As they pull up to the base camp, Amelia watches as Miss Brimer leaves the airplane hanger and marches towards them. As they approach, she holds up her hand, signaling for Clayton to stop. Clayton rolls down the window as the truck meets her. "All of you, meet me in my office in ten minutes," she commands, looking at Clayton.

"Yes, ma'am," Clayton replies and then drives the Jeep across to the plane that will fly the New Zealanders to Norway. The family piles out to meet the other Kiwis who have been chosen for encapsulating. "Jeff! Thank God!" one of those waiting shouts to the newcomers. The family hurries over to join the small group. Only three hundred and thirty-two people—point zero, zero, seven percent of their population—will survive to preserve New Zealand's culture and way of life.

As the cadets make their way to Miss Brimer's office, other Jeeps are pulling into the complex, ready to drop people off in the holding zone. The group has to run to make it to their meeting with Miss Brimer, and they arrive with one minute to spare.

As they approach Miss Brimer's door, Amelia sees Russell waiting outside. He salutes Clayton then falls in behind the group. He fleetingly smiles at Amelia, who returns the greeting.

"How'd it go, Red?" he whispers to her.

"Flawless. Like me, of course," she whispers back.

Inside, the group stands at ease in front of Miss Brimer's desk. "I have a mission for the six of you," Miss Brimer states without preamble. "There is a group of teenage revolutionists in Egypt who stole most of the Dead Sea Scrolls before Dayie Tueur burned the museums. They call themselves the Hama. We need you to gain their trust and convince them to allow us to place the artifacts in the chest."

Over the past few months, in addition to rescuing people worldwide to be encapsulated, the Preservers have been tracking down historical artifacts to preserve and protect. They have three different storage locations in various parts of the world, referred to as *chests*.

"Ma'am, how do we know they speak English?" Jessie asks.

The door opens, and Mr. Ari walks in. He winks at Amelia as he makes his way toward a seat beside Miss Brimer's desk.

Miss Brimer answers Jessie's question. "Most of them speak English, but those who do not, speak Aramaic." She looks to Clayton, who nods. At only twenty, Clayton already speaks four languages and is currently learning two more. "You will leave for Cairo in one week," Miss Brimer continues. "You have that time to prepare." As she hands them each a folder, she commands, "Memorize their faces, learn their history, know their lives. The success of this mission is imperative."

As she dismisses them, she asks Amelia to stay for a minute. When the door shuts behind the others, Amelia looks at Mr. Ari. The man stands up and leans on Miss Brimer's desk as he says, "There's something we need to talk to you about."

"What is it?" Amelia asks, heart suddenly pounding.

"Your father's contacts are honing in on us," Miss Brimer states. "I'm not sure how much longer we will be able to run from him."

A few months ago, Amelia had finally confided in Miss Brimer and Mr. Ari—she had told them everything. Starting with her real reason for attending the Mountain School for Troubled Girls, she confessed everything, right up to the tasks her father had set before her while she attended Casey Academy. She wept as she told them of how she had betrayed them, not leaving out a single detail of what she had disclosed to her father.

But instead of banishing her, her former teachers had embraced her. They had cried with her. They had held her.

They had forgiven her.

Amelia had never felt love like that before.

For days afterwards, she felt light and free. The guilt had vacated, replaced by peace.

But all too soon, the guilt took up its residence once more.

Every time Amelia was with Miss Brimer and Mr. Ari, she was keenly aware that she had *made them* like her. Painstakingly, she had tricked them—hoodwinked their affections. Then, within the span of a week, she realized the same with Lily and Chad and Jessie and Clayton and Russell… all of them were closer to her—trusted her—because she was good at manipulating people.

For the last few months, she had been trying her best not to manipulate—to turn off her magnetic charm, but she didn't know how. One thought haunted her every night: *Nobody really loves you because nobody knows the real you. They only think they love you because you tricked them into doing so.*

As much as she could, she tried to push the sentiment away, but it terrorized her, nonetheless.

Now that Miss Brimer and Mr. Ari were aware of her father's intention to take her back, they had made it their greatest mission to keep her hidden. It had proven difficult, and they had only barely managed their goal. It was getting more arduous with each passing day.

"I'm not joining him," Amelia declares to the people who have come to mean the world to her.

"We don't doubt that," Miss Brimer replies. "But…"

She looks to Mr. Ari, who continues, "But the fact is, he may not let you refuse. We've been focused on keeping you hidden… but we need a plan for the day he finds us."

"What do you propose?" she asks them.

Miss Brimer stands and comes around to the other side of her desk. "Amelia," she begins slowly, "I would rather die than let him take you." Amelia is surprised by the emotion in her superior commander's voice. "I think we need to consider leaving the Preservers."

Mr. Ari nods and adds, "Our work here is too exposed. But the three of us could leave, and we could elude his grasp."

Amelia takes a step backward. "I'm not leaving. *You're* not leaving. I mean," she looks to Miss Brimer, "this is *your* thing, You're the president—they need you." Turning on Mr. Ari, she exclaims, "The work you're doing for the Preservers is too important! How can you talk about leaving when the world needs you both."

"We care more about your safety than we do about this work," Mr. Ari speaks gently.

Amelia is so taken aback by the statement that she involuntarily sits down in one of the office chairs. Miss Brimer kneels before her. "We can keep you safe."

Rubbing her eyes, Amelia groans. She takes a deep breath and looks up at Miss Brimer. "You can't leave. Neither of you can."

"We don't know when your dad will locate us—and when he does, we'll just be reacting. If we leave right now, we would be proactive. Positionally, it's wiser to make the first move."

Mr. Ari comes to sit in front of Amelia. "We're a family now," he says, and it's the first time he's used that word. Although Amelia has thought it a hundred times to herself, none of them has ever said it out loud. As if he understands the weight of the title as well, he repeats, "We're a family."

Amelia closes her eyes. Although she would do anything they asked of her, she can't let them throw away their passion just for her. She isn't worth that.

Opening her eyes, she moves from one face to the other. Finally, she stops on Mr. Ari. "Let me do this one mission, and then… then we'll make a plan when I get back." That would give her time to figure out how to stay with the Preservers *and* keep away from her dad's clutches.

Miss Brimer stands and nods. "Agreed. You are dismissed."

When Amelia heads for the door, Mr. Ari calls her name. Amelia turns back to her teacher, whose eyes are ablaze. "I want you to know that if no other solution is found, we *are* taking you."

Miss Brimer half-grins and adds, "Even if we have to drug you—we're keeping you from him."

Amelia, heart happy, smiles. "Well, if that's the case, you better get me the good stuff."

In March, Dayie Tueur declares that all Judeo-Christian religions are pro-nuke and, therefore, practitioners should be turned into local authorities. His reasoning is that if a person is loyal to anyone besides his new reign, they are his enemies. And his enemies are pro-nuke.

Tens of thousands of Christians are executed on the third Saturday of March as the sun makes its way across the world, setting in hues of crimson. The day is forever to be mourned as the Day of the Red Sun.

Most of New Zealand has been unaffected by the war, aside from the tsunami floodings which came after the mole nuke hit Australia. The New Zealanders have decided to live life as normally as possible for as long as they can, so most businesses have stayed open.

Mr Ari's birthday lands three days before Amelia leaves the island country, and she wants to find the perfect present. Chad, Jessie, Russell, and Lily have agreed to help her find a gift. They walk through downtown Wellington perusing the various shops with interest. After three hours, they enter a cozy store called As You Wish. A tiny bell rings as they file in through the doorway. The eclectic shop has antiques, rare finds, books, collectibles, and oddities. Amelia picks up a beer-scented soap and asks her friends, "Does this say, 'I wish you were my dad'?"

The other three laugh, but Chad grabs a pair of red, white, and blue boxers and remarks, "No, but this says, 'I wish you had more style.'"

They meander through the store laughing and relaxed, enjoying each other's company. Amelia smiles to herself as Jessie and Russell break out into yet another debate over who would win a fight between Thor, the Norse god of thunder, and Obi-Wan Kenobi from the old cult-classic movie series, Star Wars. Real friends were something Amelia never dared to believe she'd find. But here they are. And they are as real as they get.

As real as they can be when you've manipulated them into liking you, she thinks bitterly to herself.

"You could get him a gun," Russell suggests, pointing to a giant display of antique guns.

"Mr. Ari doesn't use guns," Lily says. "He told me he's never even held one before."

"What does he need guns for when he has Miss Brimer?" Jessie asks with a mischievous grin.

"I swear they were flirting the other day," Chad comments.

"They flirt every day," Amelia retorts. "But they're never going to be together."

"Why?" Lily and Chad ask at the same time.

"If the end of the world doesn't give them enough incentive to get married, nothing will," she answers.

Jessie skips past the guns and comments, "Maybe they're together, and they're just not public."

"What would be the point of that?" Lily asks.

An employee of the store walks up to their small group and hands a note to Amelia. "Miss? A gentleman asked me to give this to you." To herself, she adds, "Gave me fifty dollars."

As she reaches for the note, Amelia does a quick scan of the room. She sees nothing among the shelves, furniture, clothing. Then she looks out the front window, and her heart beats so hard she has to physically stop her hand from reaching up to her chest.

It's her dad.

He smirks at her through the window and nods his head to the side, indicating she should follow him. Once he is out of sight, she quickly opens the note. It reads in her father's tight cursive, "Come."

"Who is that from?" Jessie asks, reading it over Amelia's shoulder.

If her father is here, he must be aware of their operations. With all his resources, he probably has the store and the entire town being watched. There is no escape for her.

Well, there will be an escape for her friends.

"Listen to me," she orders in a low voice. "My dad is here to take me with him. No, stop, don't interrupt. Listen, I need you to calmly return to base—enough! Stop and listen!" Their clamoring voices quieten as Amelia looks each of them in the eye with all the intensity of the adrenaline pumping through her body. "Get back to base and tell Miss Brimer that he's here. I am going to slip out the back to meet him. He doesn't want to take me by force; he wants me to go with him willingly. I will talk to him and see if I can get any information. I will convince him to let me stay. But Miss Brimer must know what's going on, and you all must be safe."

"Amelia," Lily begins with tears in her eyes. "What if he takes you?"

"What if he finds out you're on our side and kills you?" Jessie adds.

Chad nods. "We're not letting you go without us."

"If you think I'm leaving, you don't know me at all," Russell says with fierce determination.

"*Enough*," Amelia declares. "You will all go now," she commands. "I'm not going to let my dad take me, but I have to get him to leave. So you will trust me and do as I say."

It could be how she holds herself, like their superior officer. It could be the inflection in her voice, like she is utterly confident that things will go as she said. It could simply be the hard look in her eye, like she knows something they don't.

Whatever it is, her four friends hesitantly turn away and leave the store. As the bell on the door rings out its last note, Amelia makes her way to the rear of the store, where she'd spotted a back door.

A large man with spiked blonde hair and Japanese-lettered tattoos is waiting on the other side. "Follow me," he orders and leads her across the street, past Te Papa—the National Museum of New Zealand—and towards a lone black Aston Martin One-77 parked at the end of the lot overlooking Lambton Quay.

Amelia wipes her sweaty palms on her pants and pretends to cough into her hands but takes the extra moment to blow cold air onto them. She breathes deeply using her diaphragm and releases her breath slowly through her mouth. She does this until her heartbeat is relatively normal.

She is certain of two things.

One, her father has to believe she is on his side.

Two, her father isn't going to take her.

The man with the tattoos opens the passenger door of the luxury sports car, and she meekly slides in. The first thing that hits her is the smell of her father's cologne: bergamot, cinnamon, and cedarwood. Memories flood her mind's eye.

The crunchy, red carpet in his office.

The hard, cedar desk in his bedroom.

The soft, wool jacket he wore to her first ballet recital.

You can do this, she reassures herself. *You can beat him at his game.*

The car door shuts Amelia inside. Knowing her father wants this, she looks across at him and smiles. It's not an excited smile, but it is also not forced. She allows it to rest somewhere between pleasant and curious. "Hello, Dad. What are you doing in New Zealand?"

His smile is pure venom. "Why hello, Milly."

Use humor to soften him up.

"You missed my graduation," she says casually. "I cried myself to sleep, you know."

He snorts, but it's so elegant it couldn't really be classified as a *snort*. From the time she was a little girl, she knew her father was handsome. Everywhere they went, women flirted with him. When she was young, she enjoyed the attention he received and enjoyed being next to him when it came. She was proud of how powerful, rich, and attractive he was. Now, in his forties, he is still just as good-looking. His jaw clenches once, and then he says, "So, did they get you?"

"Get me?"

"Did they turn you?"

Amelia looks confused. "What do you mean?" She points back towards the shop. "The kids? Oh no, no. I just find them entertaining."

"Your act is very convincing," he remarks, his eyes searching hers as if he could read her thoughts. "I almost fell for it myself. The way you *enjoy* the company of those youths. The way you pray with your commanders. The way you excel in every mission you go on. Others told me you had been turned, but I told them that's just how good you are."

Amelia breathes in deeply through her nose and soundlessly out her mouth. She will remain calm. She will keep her heart rate steady. She will stay in control of her body and mind.

"I knew that, for the charade," her dad goes on, "you would have to hate me. You would have to run from me when I tried to take you. And you, being the actress you are, would play it well. Very well. So did you fall into the lie too deep, Amelia Brie Hazel? Or did you forget your name?"

Amelia knows this is the moment. She has just this one chance to prove her loyalty, or her father will never trust her again. She knows what she must do, but she still hates herself for doing it. If she is going to convince him, she will have to stick to the truth and then hide in its shadows.

Amelia gives her dad a toothy grin. "Au contraire, my dear old dad. I have been gathering intelligence for you." Leaning in, she starts quietly, "They have something huge planned. They are sending me to recover something significant to the Christians. Once we return, we will take this item to the place where they are hiding all of the relics, artifacts, and Bibles. They're putting all their eggs in this one basket. Before they seal it, they will encapsulate a man who will be able to protect all of their treasures from the inside."

"Arkarian Story."

Amelia's stomach lurches inwardly, while outwardly she breaks into a sweat. How does her father know Mr. Ari's name? "Yes, exactly," she replies earnestly to cover up the adrenaline rush. "He will be encapsulated hours after the mission is complete."

Watson Hazel gazes across the harbor. "I should just kill him now."

Amelia is thankful her dad is looking out the window so she can clasp her shaking hands in her lap. "If you kill him now," she remarks as casually as possible, "they'll call off the mission. And then neither of us will know where their precious cache is located. If it remains intact, they'll always have hope because they know it's out there somewhere. But if we bomb it, there will be no hope for them to keep holding." She pauses. "Let me complete this."

Watson's eyes bore into his daughter's. After an uncomfortably long silence held by extended eye contact, he says slowly, "Are you lying to me?"

Amelia had known for some time this moment was coming. She had fantasized about looking into her father's face and hollering that her loyalties lay elsewhere. She would scream that she hated him and couldn't stand the thought of him. She would punch him as hard as she could.

But every time, this fantasy ends in the reality that Amelia is terrified of her father. More than her loyalty to Miss Brimer, Mr. Ari, Lily, and all of her friends, the fear of her father has kept her up at night. She had once seen him get so angry at her mother, Gwen, that he had locked her in one of the many bedrooms in their mansion and set the door on fire. Gwen screamed and begged from inside the blazing room for him to let her out, and her father had merely stood on the other side laughing. The look on his face—twisted with crazed pleasure—was forever burned into Amelia's mind.

"Should I let her out?" Watson had asked six-year-old Amelia when he had finally noticed her standing there.

Amelia hadn't dared to move, too afraid to say the wrong thing and be thrown into the room as well.

When Watson finally let his wife out, Gwen had to be taken to the hospital. She had first and second-degree burns on her arms and legs, but she recovered well. One week later, the family sat at the dinner table, Gwen covered in bandages, pretending nothing had happened.

But Amelia had never forgotten. She had never forgotten her father's wrath or his delight as punishment was dispensed.

Now, when she has to prove her loyalty to him yet again, Amelia's fear rings so loud in her ears she can almost hear it. She can taste it. But this isn't time for fear—it is time for battle.

He has no attachments to anyone. Since he wants to see himself in you, be like him.

Looking at her dad with smooth apathy, Amelia snorts. "Why would I lie? What do any of them have to offer me?"

Still studying her, he asks, "Do you remember what *I* have to offer?"

Amelia breathes in deeply, as one would smelling a delicious pie, and allows greed to fill her voice as she answers, "Power."

Watson's intense expression hesitates. He wants to believe her. She can see it. *Play the card. Now is the time.*

She sets her face into a slight pout, searching for the right tone. It has to be perfect. "Isn't that what you said?" she demands. "You promised me I would have more power than Carter!" She raises the volume as her rant progresses. "You promised I would be able to stand by your side as you take over the world or whatever it is you're planning. I went to a freaking bad girls' school for *two years* and then to a military academy for another three. I did everything you asked because we had a deal. Are you taking it back now?"

With perfect precision, one glistening tear wells in her eye and slips down her cheek.

Watson's expression softens. Leaning back in his seat, he releases a loud breath. He closes his eyes, rubs them with his fingers, and then rests his head against the headrest. Amelia uses the moment to subtly wipe the sweat off her hands and stomach.

"You're good," Watson finally states. "You're really, *really* good."

As this statement could go either way—trusting her or not—Amelia stays strong in her act, bowing dramatically and replying, "Thank you, thank you."

When her father opens his eyes, his expression is one she has never seen on his face. It is an expression she had dreamed of her entire childhood. His brows are relaxed, his forehead smooth, his eyes warm, his smile kind. It's a look one typically sees fathers giving their daughters; a look filled with acceptance and love and affection.

Pain aches in her chest. This is all she has ever wanted, but she can't have it. She is going to betray him. But now... looking at him like this... he seems like a different person.

His eyes twinkle as he abruptly changes the subject. "I bought you a palace."

Amelia's eyes widen in genuine surprise. "A palace?"

"I've filled it with servants and clothes and weapons and technology so advanced you would think it is science fiction." Watson leans toward her as excitement fills his voice. "It has the highest security offered in the world. I filled it with paintings from Rembrandt, Frida Kahlo, Mary Cassatt, Ali Armstrong—"

"Ali Armstrong?" Amelia interjects without meaning to. How had he known that she was Amelia's favorite wildlife artist?

"Indeed," he says smiling. "I remember you loving her work even as a little girl. I was able to secure three paintings for you."

When she beams at him, nothing about it is contrived.

Watson continues, "I have also arranged a family gathering once you take up residence, so you will be able to have a private conversation with both your mother and your brother."

Pretending for a moment that this is real, she closes her eyes and lets a menacing smile play on her lips. "I think I will enjoy this reunion."

Watson gives a genuine laugh. Again, something she hasn't witnessed before. Granted, she'd listened to her father laugh previously, but it almost always had notes of derangement, anger, sardonicism, or crazed pleasure. But this... this is different. This is happy and sweet. "I hope you do," Watson replies.

"What will I do there?" Amelia asks, honestly curious about his plan. "What will my job be?"

"You will be my liaison and ambassador," he answers as if they were having a normal conversation. "Dayie Tueur will not hold his power for long; he is too reckless, as you once said. We will prepare the way for Chhah—the new North America—to become the leader in this recently developed world order."

"What is our timeline?" Amelia asks, and immediately hates that there is something lovely about saying *our*.

"Next week, Dayie will announce that any continents who wish to live will execute all their self-proclaimed Christians."

"Why does Dayie hate Christians?"

"Religion, politics, prejudices—take your pick. He will give the continents six months to complete the task—this arbitrary timeline is critical to him. Then on Christmas Day—now to be celebrated as Dayie Tueur Day—he will gather the highest officials of each continent at his palace where we will watch the extermination of the Judeo-Christian religion. He has something special planned, or so he says."

At this, Watson allows a cruel smile upon his lips. "Your precious teacher is among those named to be executed that night."

"Mr. Ari?"

"The very one."

The spell breaks. Amelia's hopeful peek into her father's heart slams shut, and the gravity of the situation rests on her shoulders once again. It takes everything within her to remain aloof. It takes every ounce of energy to stay calm. "Why? Who is he to Dayie Tueur?"

Amelia's dad laughs again, but it is not the warm one from before. This laugh is cynical. "So they haven't let you into their deepest councils."

"Not yet," she responds hurriedly.

"Your teacher, like David to Goliath, told Dayie Tueur via a social media video that he would be held accountable to God. Arkarian Story mocked Dayie, saying that he is nothing more than a small creature who will, in the end, bow before Jesus Christ. Oh, Amelia, it was pathetic. His passion was so self-righteous and egotistical. However, Dayie didn't appreciate the *small* reference. With poetic irony, he will crucify Arkarian Story along with several other well-known Christian leaders."

With every word, she is losing her cool, losing her grip on the act.

But Watson goes on relentlessly. "At that time, Dayie will be so drunk with power, he will not see the mutiny until it is upon him." His attractive face twists with greed. Turning to Amelia, he explains, "Most of the pieces are in place, and you are the only one missing. I know what you are doing here is important, but I need you with me. I need you by my side, ready for the moment."

Amelia nods, pretending to be thoughtful. "But this could put you in the optimal position for mutiny. If we were to deliver Mr. Ari and the cache to Dayie Tueur, he would honor you above the others. It would be a kingly gift."

Watson's eyes narrow. "Why are you pressing this?"

Amelia knows she is treading in deadly waters. Setting her jaw and putting on her best teenage angst face, she replies, "You know your situation best, and I know mine. I know what I've been working on for these past five years, and I know what I still have to offer. Leaving it behind now feels as if everything I've worked for and achieved has been for nothing. You sent me here with a purpose—so let me complete my task, Dad. I gave up everything for the moment when I can spit it all back in their faces, and you're taking that moment from me. Let me have it."

Watson laughs, and it's the warm one again. She hates how it weakens her defenses against him. For a brief second, she allows herself to remember that this is her father. Her only real dad. Amelia watches as his determination dissolves. Watson smirks and then nods. "All right, all right," he replies, putting his hands up in the air in surrender. His eyes are filled with such care, his smile so safe as he goes on, "You are right. You deserve this. When will you return?"

"We have one month until the mission, and then it will take another month to complete. I will be ready to join you by the end of August."

Watson studies her for a moment, and she tries not to feel self-conscious. She knows she's beautiful, intelligent, and now powerful, and she wants her dad to think those things about her too. Despite the rollercoaster feelings and the wild swinging between fear and hope that she's endured in the last ten minutes, right now, in this minute, all she wants is for her dad to think she is something. Something special.

"You remind me so much of myself at your age," he comments, and she wills him to go on. "We know what we want; we'll do anything to get it." He looks out over the harbor again. "I married your mother for social reasons, and when your brother was born, I thought he would be the person I shared my plans with. But they were both so weak. You, my daughter," turning his gaze back to her, "were unexpected."

Amelia's heart aches at the word.

"From the moment you were born, you were destined to be great. The way you manipulated and lied and hoodwinked everyone—even me—at times. I watched you, waiting, hoping. Hoping you would be the one."

Watson reaches for her hand and holds it gently, and she has to focus on her breathing to keep from tearing up again. "You're more than I ever could have wanted. And I'm going to give you everything, Amelia. Anything you want, you will have. I'm going to give you the world."

Amelia's emotions are mixed, warring within her. But for just this one second, she wants to believe it. She longs for it to be true.

Watson points back towards the shops and adds, "And if you've grown fond of any of those people, I will let you keep them."

Amelia shudders but plays it off by saying, "How could I have grown fond of any of those people?"

Watson laughs heartily again. "Yes, that's my daughter! That's my kid."

When his laughter settles, she asks with feigned concern, "So, what will I tell everyone?"

"Tell them you are still deep within my council and are using me to get more information."

She thinks for a moment and responds, "You'll have to tell me something worthwhile to make it believable."

Watson eyes her amusedly. Clicking his tongue, he answers, "You are right again. Yes, all right. As it will matter to them, tell your teachers that I told you about a prison in Nevada that is secretly using Christians for gene-related experiments."

The idea of anyone being experimented on turns her stomach, but Amelia keeps an even expression as she asks nonchalantly, "Is it true?"

"It is. And when it's confirmed, they will trust you again."

Amelia nods. "How will I contact you?"

"I'll come for you on the first of September. Be ready."

She feigns hesitation.

"What is it?" Watson asks.

"The team," she says, "...they're pretty efficient. Will you be angry if they free the Christians in Nevada?"

Watson laughs. "They won't be able to."

"But if they do?"

He bows his head graciously. "Then, I will applaud their triumph."

"I'd better go before they suspect anything." She sighs reluctantly for his benefit, but she knows her friends have probably just made it back to their base, and Miss Brimer will be stampeding her way soon.

"Amelia..." he pauses. "I just want you to know..." He seems uncomfortable as he finishes, "...I trust you. That's not easy for me to say... but I do. I trust you."

His admission incites actual tears to gather in her eyes. She blinks them away and says through a tight throat, "Is that the end of your sentence?" She is determined to hear his happy laugh one more time.

Watson looks genuinely confused. "What do you mean?"

"No threat at the end? No, 'I will trust you, but if you betray me, I'm going to gouge your eyes out and feed them to my dogs?' You know, every admission of trust has to end with a good threat."

Watson does laugh just as she wished, and she records it in her mind. "No, Amelia. No threat. I really do trust you."

Her father reaches over and takes hold of her hand again. He kisses it and then places his other hand over hers. "I never thought this was possible for a man with my ambitions. I always knew I would be on top in the end, but I thought I would be alone. Now, I realize that I want this dream *with* you. I want to do this with you by my side."

Amelia shuts her heart towards his words and glibly replies, "Pop the bubbly."

Watson smiles again. "Indeed. Now, get back out there to enemy lines. I will come for you in September."

"Can't wait," she says and, knowing he wants it, she leans over and kisses his cheek. "See you soon, Daddy."

He grabs her hand before she leaves. "I love you, Amelia."

Another first. With all the strength she has left, she whispers, "I love you too."

Amelia opens the car door, forcing her legs not to shake as she climbs out and starts walking back towards the shops. At the end of the museum, she makes herself stop, turn around, and wave at the black sports car.

Then she runs across the street towards As You Wish. Before she can make it into the store, she stoops into a clump of bush lilies and throws up so hard the capillaries in her face burst.

It isn't until she leaves for Cairo one week later that the last spot heals.

Silenda

Kansis

*D*EAN *PAT, CHARLES WRIGHTLY, Isley Slant, Liam Thomas.* I close my eyes tight and repeat the names: *Dean Pat, Charles Wrightly, Isley Slant, Liam Thomas.*

Scout climbs into the car first, taking Emerly's body to the back row, and then everyone else piles in silently.

I avoid sitting next to Amelia and maneuver to the back of the vehicle where Scout is. He has placed Emerly's body across the seat's length and seated himself on the floor against the paneling of the car. When he sees me, he scoots over so I can join him. As I sit beside him, my face is eye level with Emerly's body.

I've read—well, it's been read to me—that dead people just look like they're sleeping. But that's not how Emerly looks. Instead, he resembles a shell. An empty body. An imposter. A clone lying in wait for consciousness. A wax doll.

Without meaning to, I shudder.

Tenderly, Scout turns Emerly's face so he's looking away from us.

Dean Pat, Charles Wrightly, Isley Slant, Liam Thomas.

Emerly and Ryder are dead. Where are they now? We've been taught they will be in forever nothingness. I'm not ready for that. Even after my two hundred years are spent, I don't know that I'll ever be ready for forever nothingness.

As we enter the transponder station, no one says anything. The AP fills the room with the familiar shrinking sensation. The ride is seamless, silent, and empty.

The heaviness and the haziness seem right. It comes over me outwardly, matching how I am feeling inwardly.

Ontzi... I can't stop replaying what happened with Ryder and Gigi over and over in my head. How he called her that foul word in front of everyone. How he was completely okay with talking to her like that—like he hated her. How he wasn't apologetic when the others called him out; he was defensive... he believed it was okay to talk to her like that. And then... and then...

My throat closes, and I try to blink back the tears, but I can't.

Ryder said that if they lived in Senex he wouldn't be Gigi's mate. If he could have—if there were a way—he would have chosen *not* to be with her.

But she is in his blood—how could he not want her? He has to want her… he has to…

Because otherwise that means… *ontzi*, that means that even if Aker gets my blood in him, there's a chance he still won't want me. He could still treat me the way he does and talk to me the way he does—he could completely despise me every day for the rest of our one hundred and eighty years as mates.

Dean Pat, Charles Wrightly, Isley Slant, Liam Thomas.

As we emerge from the transponder station in Pexus, I look out the window at the passing street lights. I watch them fly by like one stream of light.

How am I going to spend almost two centuries being with a man who can't even stand to touch me? Who wants nothing to do with me or my blood? Who doesn't like my personality, my passions, or my blood?

Scout was right, after all.

Desperate to think about something else, my eyes drift to Scout who is leaning with his head back against the second-row seat. The passing evening lights paint his features yellow. Tears leak out of his closed eyes, running down his cheeks into his beard.

Putting aside my sadness, I enter into his. I think about the few interactions I saw between him and Emerly. They were obviously very close. "I'm so sorry," I whisper to him.

Dean Pat, Charles Wrightly, Isley Slant, Liam Thomas.

Scout's jaw quivers as he opens his eyes. He doesn't look at me right away, but his gaze pierces me to my marrow when he does. I've never known sorrow like his. Scout takes a deep breath in, like he's trying to stabilize his voice and emotions, but the breath catches in his throat, and he coughs loudly.

Not knowing why, I grab his hand and squeeze it. He pulls our interlocked fingers to his chest and closes his eyes once more.

My whole arm feels like it's bathing in the summer sun. Warm droplets fall onto my fingers. His tears slip through my knuckles and drip down my palm.

"I'm sorry," I whisper again, not knowing what else I can say to comfort him.

"I did not forgive him," Scout whispers back as if I had asked him a question. "I knew he wanted my forgiveness, but I had not offered it. I intended to do so… I had planned on talking to him on our return… But he is gone." His voice hitches again, and he sucks in a quick breath. "I will never… I can never…" His sobs keep him from finishing the statement.

Although I don't know the exact details of what he's talking about, I do have a lot of first-hand knowledge when it comes to regret. Quietly, I say, "I'm sure he knew you'd forgiven him."

"But I should have said so," he says between heaving breaths.

I squeeze his hand again, having no idea what I can possibly say to bring him solace. Silence falls between us once more.

After a few minutes, Scout clears his throat and asks, "And how are you?"

Taken aback that he would even ask me amid his own bloodache, I answer quickly, "Fine, I'm fine."

"You do not sound fine."

"You just experienced something… horrific. What I'm going through doesn't matter."

"Tell me," he presses. "It will give me something else to think about. Please, Scoop."

The conversation between Ryder and Gigi springs to mind again, causing my eyes to water and my throat to ache. "You were right," I finally manage to say.

Reaching over, Scout gently hooks my chin with his finger and moves my face so I have to look at him. My whole body buzzes at his touch. "How do you mean?" he asks gently.

"You said that Aker wouldn't love me even with the Blood Transfusion," I answer. "And I just couldn't accept that—I wouldn't. He has to love me… but after watching—after watching—" A sob threatens to wrack my whole body, and I physically swallow it down.

Scout waits patiently for me to finish.

Finally, I say, "Ryder didn't love Gigi. He made it clear enough. Even with her blood in him, he didn't want her. That's—that'll be Aker and me. You were right. Love is a choice, and Aker clearly wants nothing to do with me. We're going to get married, and I'll spend the rest of my life with someone who doesn't want me."

Scout lets go of my hand and wraps his arm around me. I know I shouldn't let him—I shouldn't snuggle closer—but I do. I let my head rest on his chest and I listen to his heartbeat until my own matches his steady rhythm.

Tomorrow I'm going back to Depalo with Aker, and I'll never know this closeness with him. He'll never hold me this way or care about my thoughts the way Scout does. Knowing this is probably the last time I'll be this close to any human being—let alone Scout Eekan—I squeeze him tighter. The Ortusan, who was once a stranger and is now a friend, rests his head on mine.

Dean Pat, Charles Wrightly, Isley Slant, Liam Thomas.

From the front of the vehicle, Pypen, voice thick, asks, "What will we tell the others?"

"The truth," Scout answers; his voice cracking sounds loud in my ear.

He rests his head on mine again, and another torrent of tears races down my face. How will I say goodbye to Scout? He won't want me to leave... but I have to go. And I've run out of time.

"Scout?" I begin hesitantly.

"Yes?"

"I need to tell you something."

"What is it?" his voice rumbles against my cheek.

The vehicle jolts as we pull into the field where the circus rests. Knowing we're back makes me lose my nerve. "Never mind," I say quickly. "I'll tell you later."

Chestin parks, but no one moves. I don't think anyone is ready to face what's next. Scout doesn't let go of me but squeezes me tighter to him instead. Finally, after a few long minutes of frozen silence, Pypen clears his throat.

"We must... It is time." The door opens, and I hear the rest of the group shuffling out of the vehicle. I wait for Scout to let me go, but it's not until Pypen says his name that he finally does.

I turn my back to Scout as I clamber out of the car, and I hear a sob sneak up his throat as he leans down to pick up Emerly's body. Chestin is waiting outside the car to help Scout bear his load.

Amelia comes to stand beside me. She doesn't speak, but I can feel the tension reverberating from her body.

As Scout and Chestin carry Emerly toward the circus, the rest of us follow behind.

Scout suddenly clears his throat and says, "Yes, Sixth Aevum?" A momentary silence, and then he answers thickly, "It was a success, but we lost two of our company." Pause. "Emerly and Ryder." We slip through the main circus flap as he listens to whatever the Sixth Aevum is saying. "Yes," Scout says. As we make our way through the courtyard, there is a long pause. When he answers this time, Scout sounds angry, "Yes, Sixth Aevum. Blessed be your grace."

Pypen leads us to a room I've never been in before, located on the first floor. The door is made of thick, white and dark brown fur. Pypen pushes it open with his hand and says, "On," as he walks inside. Warm light floods the room revealing a fourteen-meter table made of a rich golden wood slab. Twenty metal chairs surround the table. Thick, fur rugs cover the wooden floor. Beautifully carved statues of woodland creatures line the cozy room, while dark green corduroy couches face a blazing fire. A marble hearth holds elaborate candelabras.

Quickly, Pypen moves several of the chairs aside so Scout and Chestin can lay Emerly on the table. A loud whimper erupts from Winzer, and she throws herself upon her mate. Chestin stays beside her, gently placing his hand on the small of her back as she weeps.

Gigi sits on one of the couches and stares blankly into the fire. Before I think about where I want to sit, Scout touches my shoulder, sending electricity down my arm. "We need to debrief," he states sadly.

"Yes," I respond quickly. "Of course."

Dean Pat, Charles Wrightly, Isley Slant, Liam Thomas.

"Pypen," Scout calls, and the man looks over to us. "Debrief in our office."

"I'm coming too," Amelia says from behind me.

Scout looks to me as if it is my decision to include her or not, and I, feeling more tired than I ever have, reply wearily, "Of course you are."

I can't be mad at Amelia. After all, I did lie to her about the K-Pax. We both lied to defend our wellbeing, and I can't hold that against her any more than I'd want her to hold it against me.

We follow Scout and Pypen out of the room and up toward their office. Scout leads me to one of the oversized chairs in his office and beckons me to sit, and Amelia plops down beside me. Pypen and Scout collapse sluggishly into their desk chairs.

Tears stream down Scout's face as he looks down at his hands.

"Do you..." Pypen begins, but he looks uneasy. "Scout, do you want me to keep your emotions at bay whilst we do this?"

Without looking at him, Scout shakes his head. "The Sixth Aevum wants the names," Scout says to me, his voice stuffy with tears.

"Dean Pat, Charles Wrightly, Isley Slant, Liam Thomas," I say quickly. "Those are the Base Breakers for the longitude coordinates."

Scout has me repeat myself, including the spelling of the names, and records my words to send to the Sixth Aevum.

"Now," Scout begins and looks at Amelia. "Kansis said that you weren't the daughter of Arkarian Story. Please explain."

Clearing her throat, Amelia answers, "The man whose crimes you all attribute to Arkarian Story, the evil dictator who destroyed the world... well, he's my biological father, Watson Hazel. He was the one who betrayed his country, killed Dayie Tueur, and brought on the end of the world. Arkarian Story—the real Arkarian—is the one who is hidden, he is. He's the one that the Code Breakers lead to. The Book of Instructions was right: he is hidden with very precious things. And I bet, if he were here, he would say that what was buried with him will bring about the earth's salvation or destruction, he would.

"I never really knew him as Arkarian Story; to me, he was always Mr. Ari. He was like a father figure to me—a genuine, caring presence. No one informed me he would mention it in the Book of Instructions—that I was his daughter—but that's how he addressed me. His daughter. So, even though it's not literally true, I am the one he was referring to."

She smiles, but it is fleeting. "So I didn't lie, I didn't. Not really." She looks at me, and for the first time since we left the museum, her expression is open. She's reading my face, trying to see if I'm mad at her.

"Not really," I confirm, offering what semblance of a smile my facial muscles can muster. "So what is your true goal? I'm guessing it's not to kill him."

Snorting softly, she shakes her head. "No, that's not my goal, it's not. But you thought the infamous Arkarian Story was evil, so I couldn't have you thinking that I wanted to find him for good purposes. *Vaigín*, it's good to finally be honest with you..." Then, she pulls on her earlobe. When our eyes meet, she looks as if she's studying me. It's the same look she gave me the night we left Depalo—like she's trying to decide if I'm trustworthy or not.

"I'm glad we can be honest with one another," I say.

She looks away and bites her lip. Finally, she begins, "I spent most of my previous life manipulating people. Getting what I want from them. And—if we're being transparent here—I'm really good at it, I am. All I wanted was to get enough power to keep people from hurting me, and my real dad, Watson, showed me how. He was happy when I did it, and he loved me for it. That part of me was wrong... but with him, it was right. And it was good.

"But... Mr. Ari showed me another way. He and... this Senexian woman... they became my family, and things were different with them. And after..." Amelia clears her throat, "...after one of my best friends died, I realized I didn't want to be like Watson anymore. But it's hard not to be yourself."

Hot tears prick at my eyes. Oh, how true. If I could just stop being so pathetic, I would in a heartbeat. If I could just be strong... but how do you stop being yourself?

"I promised myself when I awoke from my Hull that I would be different. But the *world* was so much more different than I had thought it would be. And I met you," she says, glancing at me again. "And...*vaigín*, Freckles, you were such an easy mark."

I blush, knowing she's not meaning to chill my blood with her words, but they hurt nonetheless.

"You were so desperate for a friend, all I had to do was give you the tiniest amount of attention, a fleeting compliment, look you in the eye, and you melted."

Now my face burns with shame.

"Amelia—" Scout begins, but Amelia puts up her hand to stop him.

"Let me finish. This is important, it is," she says passionately. To me, she continues, "I was resolved not to manipulate anyone to achieve my ends, but I barely did anything, and you still did whatever I wanted. You left your whole life for me, you put yourself in danger's way for me, you taught me, and any question I had you answered... and even when you lied, you were so sincere in your apology. And I believe you when you say you won't lie to me again. Even if I wanted to trick something out of you, your sincerity would beat me to it. So a plan I hadn't even concocted was being perfectly executed because of your hopelessness."

I don't understand this exposing of me... why share all this? I can't even look at Scout, let alone Pypen. Instead, I stare down at my hands, fighting my tears away.

Fighting but losing.

My eyes blur as Amelia reaches over and grabs my hands. "Freckles, my specialty—my greatest strength—is manipulation. And in every relationship I've ever had, I've questioned whether they liked me or wanted me in their life just because I tricked them into it, I have. But with you, my specialty wasn't needed. And you are honestly the first friend I've ever had that chose me before I could hoodwink them into it. You're embarrassed that you were desperate for a friend—but you're my perfect fit. If you had been any different, I wouldn't trust you, I couldn't. But... because of your openness, your kindness, your selflessness... I feel free. I don't have to wonder if I tricked you... you picked me first and... well..."

She waits until I look up at her and says, "It turns out I'm an easy mark too." Wiping away my tears, she finishes gently, "What you see as weaknesses in yourself are strengths, they are."

A sweet silence fills the room as Amelia stretches across to rub my back in an affectionate gesture.

"So, now what?" Pypen asks with a heavy sigh.

"We have the names of the other Code Breakers," Scout sniffs, his eyes still red. "We will seek them out, awaken them, and get their codes. And then we will find Amelia's Mr. Ari."

"What of Ryder's body?" Amelia asks.

"Thykas and I can attempt to retrieve it—" Pypen begins, but Scout interrupts him.

"No. The Guardians will be patrolling the area. They may not even know it is there, and our presence may expose it. We must leave him there."

Sighing, Pypen rubs his face and states mournfully, "Emerly's sacrifice was for nothing."

We all muse silently, lost in our own dark thoughts until Amelia, all business, asks, "Will you have a funeral for him? People will notice there's not a body, won't they?"

Scout buries his face in his hands. When he raises his head, he answers, "We will have to fake it." He clears his throat, sniffs again, and goes on, "We will hold funerals for both Ryder and Emerly." Just saying his dear friend's name seems to cause him physical pain. Swallowing hard, he ends with, "We will bury them, and then we will find Arkarian Story."

"And you will go back to Depalo, will you?" Amelia asks me.

I'm surprised to have this question thrown at me. "Oh, um—"

"Why would she go back to Depalo?" Scout asks, brows furrowed.

"Wasn't that your plan?" Amelia asks. "I heard you speaking with Aker before we left, I did." Although she is definitely calling me out in front of everyone, this time it doesn't feel cruel. It feels as if she wants me to have this conversation with them instead of sneaking out in the middle of the night. I'm cowardly enough to do it too, except I need the eutsi…

I can almost feel Scout's gaze on me, he's staring so intently waiting for my answer. "Well, I—I have to go."

"Why?" Scout asks.

"Aker and I need the Blood Confession from my parents," I answer. "If we don't get it to Avenir in the next twenty-nine days, he'll take our memories back."

"What memories?" Pypen asks.

To Pypen, Scout answers, "I will explain later," to me, he responds firmly, "I will speak with Avenir."

"But we already gave him a Blood Assurance," I reply. "We *have* to go."

Repeating my own secret sentiment, he declares, "Aker can go alone."

"We *both* gave a Blood Assurance. I have to go too."

Scout growls, stands abruptly, and begins pacing.

"'Tis not a large matter," Pypen responds, seemingly confused by Scout's response. "Kansis and Aker can retrieve this Blood Confession and then can come back."

"The Guardians are after them," Scout snaps. "They cannot leave without Winzer."

"Winzer will not want to stay with the circus," Pypen states gently. "I have already been thinking that we will need to harness her Gift—"

"The eutsees would only be temporary," Scout counters. "It would be better if they stay, and we send someone else to retrieve the Blood Confession."

"Scout," I say, and when his eyes meet mine, my blood belabors with sadness for him. "You know how Blood Assurances work—it has to be Aker and me." Before he can argue, I add, "The prophecy said that you and I are going to find Arkarian Story. That I would know the intentions of his book—whatever they are—and that you would help me find the way. I want to remember why I've been shunned the past two years; I want to remember what our parents did to us. And once those memories are secure, I'm coming back." Trying to make him smile, I add, "Nothing will stop me from coming back to the circus, okay?"

And I mean it.

A few days ago, Aker said that we could get married and just pretend we are in love. He had said we needed to create something other couples don't have, like live-in acquaintances. It had been such a horrifying thought then… but now I see it as my only option. Aker and I will get married… but he will never love me… and I will always long for something else. He will live his life, and I will live mine.

And mine will be spent at the circus.

"Don't worry," Amelia states, "I'll keep her safe."

"You're coming?" I ask, relief flooding my whole body.

She smiles. "Of course!"

When I look to Scout, however, he's sharing a significant look with Pypen.

"What? What is it?" I ask.

Pypen clears his throat, "We cannot have both of you gone; since Kansis must go, you have to stay here. You are too important to this mission."

My blood chills. Even though it had only been for mere seconds, the thought of having Amelia had soothed all of my fears. And now… now it's even harder knowing I will be going alone.

"I can't leave Kansis," Amelia says firmly, and I sigh with relief. "I'll help her get the Blood Confession, and we'll all come back together, we will."

"We'll be fast," I promise.

"If finding Arkarian Story is really something you desire, you will stay," Pypen tells Amelia. Turning to me, he says, "You have no idea how long it will take you to get the Blood Confession, let alone if it is possible. Even if it takes you only one month, that is precious time lost on our mission to locate"—he looks back to Amelia—"*your* father. We need you here."

"Why do you think it will take her so long?" Amelia asks.

"I only met Kansis' father for a moment," he answers, "but he did not seem like a man looking to make things right."

My whole body feels heavy. Like I might just fall asleep in this oversized chair. "We have to try," I whisper.

Placing her arm around me, Amelia states, "If Avenir takes away your memory, I'll remind you, I will."

I smile sadly but answer, "That's not how it works. Because I have told you all this, your memories of it will be taken away as well. None of us will know what happened."

Amelia reaches over and grabs my hand. At her touch, my whole body calms. But, too quickly, tension rises again as I wonder how I'm going to go all the way back to Depalo with just Aker at my side. How will I be okay without Amelia who makes me feel strong, and Scout who believes I can be brave?

We all sit silently for a few moments. All I can hear is the breathing of four people lost in their own thoughts and mourning. I take out my pocket watch and stare at the irked predatory raven. A deep sadness fills my blood as I contemplate leaving the circus.

But I will be back.

I have to come back.

Pypen breaks the silence. "Kansis and Aker will go to Depalo in the morning, Amelia and I will start on the new list of Code Breakers, and Scout, you will handle Ryder and Emerly's funerals." When no one responds, he adds, "Agreed?"

"Agreed," Amelia says.

Slowly, I respond with a soft, "Yes."

But Scout doesn't answer. He's staring at his hands as if they hold an answer he cannot find. Finally, he stands and says, "All right." Turning to me, he adds, "I am coming to get you in twenty-nine days, whether you have the Blood

Confession or not."

Every cell in my body warms.

"I'll be waiting," I answer.

Acknowledgments

Jesus. It was December 2020. I laid in bed and prayed, "Either You give me the missing pieces of this book or I'm done. If this is what You want for me... If this is Your book... Tell me what to write. Tell me Your story or I'm finished." And then, as if downloaded from some mainframe, You imputed Your story into my brain. That was one of the craziest weeks of my life. You took all the pieces and laid them out so I could see what You'd been doing all along. Thank You for entrusting me with Your story—use it as You will.

Courtney Kuhnmuench. Can you believe we're here? It seems like a decade ago we were sitting on my couch reading one of my first drafts together... oh wait... it was a decade ago. Crazy! Other than myself, you have read more versions of my book than anyone else, and I can't thank you enough for being the best first fan a writer could have ever asked for. You gasp at the perfect moments, ask such amazing questions, and always freak out just the way I was hoping you would. Our time reading together will always be something I treasure—truly. FOR BLOOD!

Alli Richardson. I distinctly remember we were standing at the island in your Glenshire house and you were reading a section of my book from a three-ring binder out loud to me. When you finished, you threw your hands dramatically in the air with each emphasis and shouted, "LOVE, LOVE, LOVE!" My whole life your words have had such an impact on me, and that includes what you've spoken over me as a writer. With you, I am heard, understood, challenged, cherished, sharpened, and treasured—in your friendship I have found a beautiful thing.

Caleb and Missy Deiro. An Acknowledgements Page couldn't possibly cover how thankful I am for you both. You guys have truly been the hands and feet of Jesus to my family. Besides that, you've been such huge supporters of my writing. You've babysat my kids so I could write, read earlier versions and given great feedback, been available for me to call and ask super random questions to, helped me with the additional information, spoken truth over me in times where fear and lies were particularly loud, and just, overall, made everything feel so exciting. Thank you for walking with me through all of this. I love you both so much.

Linda Harris. Wow—what an adventure that was! Welcoming you into my world was so scary because of who you have always been to me: a mentor, friend, and literary expert. Having you be a Beta Reader was unimaginably fun, and then having you go through that last draft with me was honestly a treat. All of my conversations with you were so life-giving and exciting. Thank you for being such a support, a voice of reason, and a source of laughter and enjoyment. Love you, Linny—I'm hurrying.

Carolyn Hitchcock. My sweet friend. Between the times of just sitting with me while writing, letting me call you at all hours to just ask your opinion on a scene or character, helping me write the additional pages, and simply caring, you have truly been such a huge part of this accomplishment. Thank you, thank you for being so invested and encouraging in all of this. I love you.

Abbey Casey. I know it may have felt like a small thing when you donated to my Kickstarter, but at that moment, I was so discouraged and honestly wanted to give up. Your generosity and support then and over all of these years have literally pushed me to continue. From you reading one of my drafts in 2016 to you asking me about it whenever we hang out, I have always felt so seen and held up by you. Thank you for inspiring my passion and always speaking into that space of my life.

Sara Petersen. For so many years, I felt alone as a writer. Although your feedback on my book was invaluable as it took its final shape, more than that, I found my first writing friend in you! Thank you for your honesty, encouragement, and insight. I'll never ever think of Kansis and Scout on the bus without cringing at your reaction and laughing at our conversation—ha! Thank you for everything.

Russ Dyer. Hey, Hottie. Thank you for watching the kids so I can write, putting up with me when I'm in project mode, always being willing to cook and clean when I have deadlines, allowing me to spend a lot of our money on getting this thing published, and just overall being my best friend. I wouldn't be here without your support—thank you for believing in me. I love you more.

Mom, Dad, Danielle, Kelli, and Shannon. Thank you for all the times you each watched my kids so I could get some writing in. Shanny, you can finally read it now that I'm not going to change anything—ha! Kel, thanks for almost reading the monster, but I'm glad you didn't have to carry that weapon around. Dan, I know this is no Battlestar Galactica, but I hope you love it anyway. Dad, just have Mom read it to you—you can get through it, I promise. Mom, I can already see you with your notebook keeping track of everything—call me if you need to. Love you all!

Mandy and Brittany. You guys have been such a support system to me this entire process. Whether it was finances or Instagram posts, I have always felt that you are for me and for my dreams. For the past thirteen years, you both have been such cheerleaders to me, and I could never express how much that has meant to me. Thank you both, I love you sincerely. I hope you find your cameos—I enjoyed writing them!

Lydia Tolley, Jamie Howard, Clayton and Laura Lind, Jen Simpson, and Marley Palmer, thank you all so much for reading earlier versions of my book! Having people enter my world was scary, but you all made it so so fun. Thank you for the texts, conversations, and support.

Beta Readers: Linda Harris, Sara Petersen, Josh Wagner, Amy Kraft, Bethany Cornett, Matt Mansell, Ashley Barnes, Jessica Rademacher, Dr. Sam Illing, and Johann Du Toit. Thank each of you for being such an intrinsic part of the publishing process. Even though I don't know who said what, your input put the finishing touches on my story, and I'm so very grateful.

Torn Curtain Publishing: Anya and Jeff McKee, Eric McKee, Nina Peck, and Emma McGeorge. "They're the editors I never knew I always needed." I can't even tell you how many times I said this to people whenever they asked about you all. Having had so many bad experiences, I came to your team beat down and discouraged. But you believed in my ideas, loved how long my book was (ha!), and fought for my story. Thank you for your encouragement, your recommendations (even when they were hard to hear), your unbelievable support, and your belief in me. My story found its true form in you all.

Elusis Personality Quiz

Which Elusian Territory Are You From?

Connect with the Author

bonivondyer (Instagram)

@bonivondyer (Tik Tok)

www.bonivondyer.com